I0824970

# PRAISE FOR RONALD MALFI

"Ronald Malfi is one of horror's modern masters, full stop. The expansive tapestry that he has created over the course of so many books displays a bruised and bleeding Americana, cut from Staub's cloth and stitched together in King's yarns, but wholly his own. His writing is so good, it's a crime. In fact, it should be considered . . . Malfiasance."

Clay McLeod Chapman, author of *Wake Up and Open Your Eyes*

"From small-town nightmares to the fragility of memory, Malfi's work is as unsettling as it is unforgettable. One of horror's modern masters."

Lindy Ryan, author of *Bless Your Heart* and *Dollface*

"I say this as the greatest compliment: Ronald Malfi can turn any setting into a character—a dark, haunting, gothic, gritty character with a secret underbelly of hidden horror."

Delilah S. Dawson, author of *Bloom* and *Guillotine*

"Ronald Malfi is the rock star novelist . . . or the novelist rock star . . . and he's superb at both. His writing is profound and beguiling, and he's one of those writers that makes it all look so damn easy. He's an accomplished stylist and storyteller, and he's rapidly become one of our best. Rock on, Malfi!"

Tim Lebbon, author of *Secret Lives of the Dead*

"Writing of a rotted, haunted landscape where lovers become diseased and unknown to each other, where friendships eventually spoil and sour, where darkness curls toward every possible inch of remaining light, Ronald Malfi exists in a superior class of authors—a true visionary with unmatched literary powers, capable of possessing and infecting even the most assured of readers."

Eric LaRocca, author of *Things Have Gotten Worse Since We Last Spoke*

## Also by Ronald Malfi and available from Titan Books

*Come with Me*
*Black Mouth*
*Ghostwritten*
*They Lurk*
*Small Town Horror*
*The Narrows*
*Senseless*
*Little Girls*
*We Should Have Left Well*
*Enough Alone: Short Stories*

## Also by Ronald Malfi

*Bone White*
*The Night Parade*
*December Park*
*Floating Staircase*
*Cradle Lake*
*The Ascent*
*Snow*
*Shamrock Alley*
*Passenger*
*Via Dolorosa*
*The Nature of Monsters*
*The Fall of Never*
*The Space Between*

## Novellas

*Borealis*
*The Stranger*
*The Separation*
*Skullbelly*
*After the Fade*
*The Mourning House*
*A Shrill Keening*
*Mr. Cables*

# THE HIVE

RONALD
MALFI

**TITAN** BOOKS

The Hive
Hardback edition ISBN: 9781803365671
E-book edition ISBN: 9781803367620

Published by Titan Books
A division of Titan Publishing Group Ltd
144 Southwark Street, London SE1 0UP
www.titanbooks.com

First edition: April 2026
10 9 8 7 6 5 4 3 2 1



A CIP catalogue record for this title is available from the British Library.

EU RP (for authorities only)
eucomply OÜ, Pärnu mnt. 139b-14, 11317 Tallinn, Estonia
hello@eucompliancepartner.com, +3375690241

Designed and typeset in Agmena Pro by Richard Mason.

Printed and bound by CPI (UK) Ltd, Croydon, CR0 4YY

*For Ty Lewis, who made me do it*

*come join us!*

## PART ONE

# THE UNCANNY METAMORPHOSIS OF MARINER'S COVE

When it comes, the Landscape listens—
Shadows—hold their breath—

EMILY DICKINSON
"There's a certain Slant of light"

*And the Dragon opens its eyes . . .*

# CHAPTER ONE
# THE DRAGON

## 1

*Wake up.*

Not so much a voice in her head as a needling urgency prodding the base of her spine.

*Wake—*

Ellen McBride came reeling from the depths of some black, angry dream that roared like a dragon, only to find that the dragon was real. It shook the house, stressing the foundation and rattling picture frames on her bedroom wall in the dark. By the sound, it was carving trenches in the roof with its terrible claws, too. Pitch blackness all around her . . . but then a flash of lightning pulsed at the window above the headboard, momentarily projecting a blazing rectangle upon the opposite wall, blinding as a mortar explosion, and Ellen thought, with a finger of rising concern, *Storm. A big one.*

She lay in the dark for a moment listening to the storm rival the labored sound of her own respiration. Her heart was slamming in her chest, funneling a rush of blood through her ears. The nightmare she'd been having just a moment ago still floated close to the surface, some amorphous and sinister shape gliding beneath the murky sheen of a dreamscape sea, but she could not recall a single detail about it—only the sensation of acute apprehension that continued to tighten like piano wire around her throat. Her entire body felt coated in a slick of sweat.

Then, between a lull in the thunder, Cory's voice called out to her from somewhere deep in the house—

*"Mom?"*

She climbed out of bed just as the wind outside whipped debris against the corner of the house and at the windowpane above her bed. The thundering dragon exhaled what sounded like buckshot against the glass—*chattle chattle chattle.* She banged a hip against the nightstand—

"Ouch, damn it!"

—then staggered forward, blind, hands pawing at the darkness ahead of her.

It wasn't just the storm.

Something felt *wrong.*

Not so much a notion or a thought, but that same needling urgency that had followed her out of sleep.

The hallway was as dark as a mineshaft. She ran one hand along the wall, felt the nub of the light switch poke her sweaty palm, and thrust the switch upward. But the hallway remained dark. The storm must have knocked out the—

*"Mom? Are you there? Something's happening."*

She hurried to his bedroom and threw open the door.

Her son was sitting bolt upright in bed, his frail, shaggy-headed silhouette a shadow puppet against the intermittent flashes of lightning that kept illuminating the world outside his bedroom window. Cory's bed sheet lay in a tangled heap around his waist, and when she went to him, feeling for him in the dark, she found that the sheet was damp from night sweat.

"Mom . . ." His voice was a hollow drum, veined with a pulse of dread.

"I'm right here, Cory. It's all right. Everything is all right."

"It found me. It's trying to get me." Panic rising in his voice now.

"It's just a storm."

She slid beside him in the bed, pulled him close. She could smell him in that moment—the clean, sleepy, familiar scent of her ten-year-old son. He was small for his age, his shoulders knobby, his ribcage a delicate assemblage of quaint and tidy things bound together within that baby-bird torso. She held him against her now, and could feel his heartbeat, hummingbird-quick, frantic against her breast. For a moment, Ellen's mind summoned an image of him as an infant, a pair of wide, sleepless eyes gazing up at her from the darkness as she paced for hours and hours around the house in the middle of the night, desperate to get him to sleep.

"No," he said, the word partially muffled against the fabric of her nightshirt. She ran a hand down the nape of his neck and found his flesh hot and blistering with perspiration. At the feel of her touch, he drew away from her, glanced at the window beside his bed, then said, "It's something else. Something's happening. It's so loud—"

Outside, the dragon—

*(not a dragon)*

—roared again. Cory's fingers dug into her.

The sound of something cracking above her head caused her to look up at the ceiling. She saw nothing in the dark, but felt a dusting of drywall powder her face and sting her eyes.

Cory was right—it *was* so loud. Maybe not just a normal thunderstorm after all. Those dragon's roars didn't sound like ordinary thunder, and those flashes of light outside Cory's bedroom radiated with a sickly electric-white hue unlike any lightning she had ever seen: not just a flash, but a vast tapestry of light that seemed to linger. Ellen McBride had never experienced a hurricane, except for on television and in the movies, but that was the thing that launched itself into her mind in that moment.

Something heavy thunked against the bedroom window, startling them both. The glass didn't shatter, didn't even crack, but it was loud and abrupt enough to make them both cry out in unison.

"Get up, Cory. Quick."

"It's *here*," he said. There was an eerie sense of finality to his voice that sounded very much unlike him. "It's *here*, Mom. It *came*."

She didn't have time to process what it was he'd just said, nor to decode what it might mean. Instead, she was climbing back out of his bed, a bit more urgently now, one arm still wrapped around her son's narrow shoulders, tugging him toward her, urging him to follow.

"I think we should go to the basement," she said, her face suddenly next to his. Cory's breath came at her in warm, panicked jabs. "Everything is going to be okay. I promise. But we need to go downstairs where it's safer. Do you hear me?"

"I'm scared."

"Don't be."

They hurried together down the hall, and she knew she was squeezing his hand too tightly while pulling on his arm, their bare feet slapping hollowly on the hardwood floor, *pat pat pat*-ing along the dark train-tunnel of the small ranch house on Cloister Road. It was darker than it should have been, even at this hour. The power outage must have extended to the whole block, because when they scurried by the front windows, she could see that none of the streetlights along their stretch of road appeared to be on. Even that strange white light she'd seen simmering through Cory's bedroom window was no longer visible. It was as if a thick black cloak had draped itself down around the entire house.

Another roar directly above them—a deep rumbling sound, steadily gathering momentum, like a tractor trailer barreling down on them. Wind galloped across the rooftop, audibly stressing the ceiling joists. Cory paused, his bare feet skidding to a halt on the floor, and Ellen could feel her son's heartbeat throbbing in the palm of his sweat-slickened hand.

He seemed to be staring at something in the darkness ahead of them.

"We need to *go*, Cory."

She dragged him toward the basement door, which was nestled in a nook in the hallway between the dining room and the galley kitchen. She wrenched the door open, revealing a yawning rectangle of even greater blackness. A fragment of her nightmare rushed back to her then: running from some faceless, shapeless *thing* as it pursued her through a series of honeycombed corridors. That piano wire constricted more tightly about her throat.

*Just a nightmare.*

*Just a storm.*

But then something in the atmosphere shifted, causing the hairs along her arms to stiffen into quills. She turned to face the window above the kitchen sink, and saw that the world beyond was once again aglow with that same eerie, listless light. Beyond that light, she glimpsed the swirling, soupy miasma that was the world around them. In a moment of rising terror, she wondered if the goddamn hurricane had descended *directly onto their house*, and if they were currently in the eye of it, watching the rest of Mariner's Cove swim by in a rotating torrent of horror. Or worse: that the house *itself* was the thing twirling through the air, just like in *The Wizard of Oz*.

Cory was staring at the scene beyond the window, too.

Hypnotized.

She once again tugged at his hand, urging him toward the open basement door. "Cory, we need to—"

The window over the sink exploded.

Arrowheads of shattered glass fired across the kitchen, borne on a blast of furious wind and cool summer rain. Ellen shrieked, and wrapped protective arms around her son, whose body had gone rigid. She shielded him as best she could, her own eyes squeezed shut, face pressed against his, and braced herself for those countless shards of glass to drive themselves mercilessly into her flesh.

But that did not happen.

Trembling, holding her breath, she raised her head and opened her eyes. She still had her arms wrapped protectively around her son, his sweat-dampened hair now blown back from his forehead, his body as unyielding as the bole of a tree.

She saw that his eyes were impossibly wide.

She saw he was holding both his hands straight out in front of him, elbows locked, his palms out in a halting gesture.

She turned her head and followed his wide-eyed gaze.

The arrowheads of broken windowpane hung suspended in the air before them. Countless glittering glass teeth, shimmering in the eerie static-white glow issuing through the shattered kitchen window.

Dead leaves swirled about the kitchen counter, whisked along the tile floor, and stirred all through the air, a cacophonic whirlwind of leaves, but those sharp daggers of glass remained motionless in midair mere inches from them. Even the storm seemed to be holding its breath.

*This is not real,* she thought. *I am still in bed and dreaming.*

Crazily, she thought she might be able to reach out and *touch* one of those shards of glass floating inches from her face, just pluck it right out of the air or perhaps flick it with her finger, and maybe it would even make a pleasant chiming sound, *tink*, like flicking the rim of a wineglass. But she found herself powerless to move.

*This is not real.*

Cory's body shuddered in her arms. He swept both his hands toward the floor and the collection of glass shards obeyed the command, plummeting to the kitchen tiles with a tinkling, almost musical clatter.

Ellen felt her son's exhalation exit his lungs and a second shudder travel down the entire length of his body as she clutched him more tightly to her chest. It seemed as if his whole body had deflated. Rain rushed in through the busted window over the sink and danced along her face, and his skin felt so hot, she imagined those raindrops sizzling to steam. She stood there, staring at the arrangement of shattered glass among the slick black blanket of dead leaves that were slowly gathering along the kitchen floor.

Cory's voice, traversing across some distant plane of existence: "Mom . . . ?"

She couldn't move. A part of her was still staring at those jewels of broken glass hovering there in midair, staring at them in her mind, where they had only been—impossibly—just a moment before. And yet another part of her—

*(run chase run something's coming something)*

—was certain she was still snared in the nightmare, confident that she *must* be there, and that all the things that didn't make sense didn't *have* to make sense, because this was nothing more than a bad dream, a bad dream, a bad dream . . .

"Mom."

He was facing her now; somehow, he'd worked his way out of her arms without her knowing. She could feel the warmth of his breath against her rain-speckled face. It took a moment before her eyes could focus on him.

"You're right, Mom. We need to go in the basement where it's safe," he said. Her words in his mouth now.

A reversal of roles.

A tripping of a wire.

Something—

—*she knew*—

—had transpired between them.

"*Yesssss*," she said, and the word, snakelike, hissed out of her.

His hand in hers, gripping tightly. His palm no longer sweaty, but cold—nearly ice. That sudden reversal of roles, continuing, protracted and stretching in her mind like taffy: her son leading her down that yawning black throat that descended into the basement, step after blind step, closing the door behind them and letting the darkness swallow them whole. Yet a part of her mind still lingered in the kitchen, still gaped at those bright, shimmering teeth of glass, hanging there, suspended, all of them, impossibly so, frozen in time, and in her mind's eye a finger extended, a flick on the glass—

*Tink.*

It resonated in the echo chamber of her skull.

## 2

They huddled together on a pile of old clothes and bed sheets covered in dried splotches of paint in one darkened corner of the basement. Above them, the house creaked and moaned while the storm raged on. There was only a single narrow hopper window above the washer and dryer at the opposite end of the basement, but the fierce winds had dammed it with muck, preventing even the most stringent flashes of lightning—that odd, lingering, spectral lightning—from penetrating.

With her back against the cold cinderblock wall, Ellen pulled her son close to her. He went without protest, but his body remained stiff. She slipped an arm around his shoulders then waited to feel the soft presence of his head against hers. But he kept at a distance from her, even in such proximity; his head very close to hers, but their minds not touching. They did not speak, and she could not see his face in the dark.

*Tink.*

She was thinking about those arrowheads of broken glass.

*How long are you going to play dumb, Ellen McBride?*

Her son stirred beside her.

"Cory? Baby?"

No answer.

She listened and could hear him breathing. Deep and drawn out. He'd fallen asleep sitting up against the basement wall, supported by her arm around his shoulders. Gently, she pulled him toward her until he laid his head in her lap. She ran her fingers through the damp, matted curls of his hair while he slept.

*Tink.*

She was his mother, and she loved him dearly . . . yet she couldn't deny the sense that something between them—something that had forever existed heretofore within the shared universe of their blood—had just been terribly, irrevocably altered.

## 3

And then she was there again, pursued through a series of dark, narrow chambers by some unseen thing that shook the world with its dragon's roar and tore apart the atmosphere with its horrible claws, its sulfur breath filling the air, and with each corner she turned, another corridor stretched out before her: never ending.

# 4

When Ellen awoke, it was to an eerie stillness. Thin shafts of daylight poked through the meshwork of leaves, twigs, and mud that lay pressed against the hopper window above the washer and dryer.

Cory was not here.

She crept up the basement stairs to find that the kitchen had been cleaned while she'd slept: a trash bag sat by the side door, full of dead leaves, yard muck, and other garbage that had blown in through the broken kitchen window during the night. As she peered inside the bag, she could see those shards of broken glass, revelatory in their thereness, causing a shiver to trace down Ellen's spine. She tied the bag closed, then ran a pair of shaky hands through her hair. There was a dustpan and broom leaning against the wall in one corner of the kitchen, and a bottle of Clorox and some old towels on the countertop. The broken window was now covered with the corkboard from Cory's bedroom. Pinned to the board were some of Cory's drawings (he was a good artist) along with ticket stubs from movies she had taken him to see, coupons for the bowling alley off the highway, his last report card (straight A's, what a kid), and a few photographs. Her eyes lingered on one photo in particular—of Cory propped up on Ellen's brother's shoulders, impossibly wide grins on both their faces. Her brother was wearing a ratty Testament concert T-shirt and Cory had a baseball hat tugged down too far over his eyes so that his ears were flattened like airplane wings. The photo had been taken about two years ago. Just looking at it caused a pang of grief to well up inside her.

She drifted into the dining room and stared out the bay window and onto Cloister Road. There were tree limbs and random garbage in the street and the gutters were swollen with rain. The sky above the houses on the opposite end of the street was nothing but a bank of receding gray storm clouds; what daylight managed to penetrate them was an eerie, listless yellow. For a moment, she stared at a paper Dunkin Donuts cup as it bobbed along in the torrent before vanishing down a sewer grate. Next door, a tree had come down, and poor Mr. Zachs was out there on his front lawn in a blindingly white terrycloth bathrobe and rubber boots staring down at it with a look of utter defeat on his round, jowly face. As if sensing her eyes on him, he glanced up and seemed to catch Ellen standing in the bay window. But when she raised her hand in a languid salutation, Mr. Zachs just turned away and trudged back into his house.

Ellen continued down the hall, hesitating for a moment before Cory's bedroom door, which stood partway open.

*How long were you planning to deny this?* spoke up a voice at the back of Ellen's head. For a moment, it sounded like the voice of her estranged brother. *How long were you going to force yourself to remain willfully ignorant of everything that has been happening around here lately?*

The lights that would sometimes flicker when Cory walked into a room.

The drinking glasses that would spontaneously launch themselves off the kitchen counter and shatter on the floor when he was upset or angry.

The way the television in the living room would sometimes turn itself on and flip indiscriminately through the channels.

She eased the bedroom door open and found him lying asleep on his bed, the bed sheets bunched about his bare feet. His back was toward her, and he was curled in a fetal position, snoring gently.

*Can we pretend last night never happened?*

*Can we keep playing dumb?*

The room looked stressed: she followed a hairline crack in the drywall, all the way up to the ceiling, where it wove in and out of the plastic glow-in-the-dark stars that were glued there. A crack that hadn't been there before the storm.

It wasn't from the storm, she knew.

*Can we keep playing dumb?*

She went to him, carefully untangling the sheet from his feet, then pulling it up and over his slumbering body. He did not stir.

She felt a charge ripple through the air then—something akin to static electricity, but like the guitar amps in that *Spinal Tap* movie, dialed to eleven. The charge collected about her body, causing the hair on her arms and along the nape of her neck to stand at attention. She felt, too, a sudden and disagreeable buzzing sensation in her back teeth—a sensation that began to grow painful the longer it persisted.

On the bed, Cory shifted in his sleep but did not wake.

The house creaked.

The walls seemed to be breathing in and out all around her.

She thought of the broken shards of glass tucked away in that trash bag in the hall. The way they'd hung there, suspended in midair the night before.

*Tink.*

Ellen McBride silently backed out of the room.

# CHAPTER TWO
# THE DOOR

## 1

Around the time Ellen McBride was stirring awake upon a mattress of unwashed laundry in the basement of her home, a retired heart surgeon named Michael Danver stepped from his multimillion-dollar waterfront McMansion to survey the damage left behind by the storm, and noticed something inexplicable—something that would ultimately and irretrievably change his life forever.

The Danver house was a fashionable white stone affair sporting a three-car garage, marble arcade columns, and a state-of-the-art burglar alarm system. The refrigerator was always stocked with Perrier, and there was an expansive (though largely untouched) library along the west wing of the house. The sound system was one of the best that money could buy, and there were speakers piped throughout the house that, on Sunday evenings, hummed with the strains of Michael Danver's favorite jazz records. Miranda, twelve years her husband's junior, possessed a closet full of fashionable tennis whites and sensible, name brand shoes. Even Clementine, Miranda's bright orange Pekingese (with whom Danver shared a mutually contemptuous relationship), enjoyed a lushly upholstered doggie bed beside the Danvers' stone hearth, yet slept between them in their marital bed each night. Theirs was one of only thirteen homes in the suburban Maryland neighborhood of Mariner's Cove that sat perched on the edge of a bluff overlooking the Chesapeake Bay. The rich section of the Cove, as people liked to say. Danver had purchased the house over a decade ago, and although Miranda, in her restlessness, often prattled on about relocating to some other part of the country—like a shark, Miranda Danver considered a lack of continual forward momentum akin to certain death—Danver himself was content with his life within the walls of the white stone house on Bay Road.

At a sturdy sixty-nine years of age and only a year into his retirement, Michael Danver still woke up at five fifteen every morning without the assistance of an alarm clock. His morning routine had not varied in his retirement: he would rise out of bed, take a four-minute shower beneath a brisk spray, dress in a pair of simple slacks and a bland but not inexpensive Charles Tyrwhitt button-down shirt, swallow a handful of vitamins, then head downstairs for a breakfast consisting of nothing but black coffee and unbuttered wheat toast. The coffee machine was automated, and if he timed things correctly (which he always did; that was just his nature), the machine would finish percolating just as Danver, whistling some off-key jazz standard, retrieved a hefty ceramic mug from the cupboard above the sink.

It used to be that, after breakfast, his day would truly begin: the drive to Johns Hopkins in Baltimore, where fighting traffic was the only undignified part of his day. Now, however, it seemed like the only scheduled part of his day—the only part that seemed to have any purpose, to have a beginning, middle, and end—was concluded after he finished his wheat toast and his cup of coffee. For the first few weeks following his retirement, he found himself deliberately prolonging this simple morning ritual, to the point where he would keep refilling his coffee cup and found himself pressing an index finger to all the crumbs of wheat toast that remained on his plate, then leveraging that finger into his mouth, until there wasn't a single crumb left. Anything to prolong the inevitable drudgery that promised to follow.

"What will you do today?" Miranda would ask him when, hours later, she would find him still seated at the kitchen table, working through a crossword puzzle and a third or fourth cup of coffee.

"Anything I want, I suppose," would be his lackluster response.

They had carried on that little stage play for the first few weeks of his retirement. It had even been funny the first couple of times. But the more Michael Danver became aware of the fact that he actually had *nothing to do*, the more their little charade began to grow stale and to grate on his nerves. To her credit, Miranda was at least observant enough to quit asking the question. Instead, she would tell him how well she had slept the night before (usually with the aid of a sleeping pill) or something equally innocuous while filling her own cup of coffee. They had been married for just shy of fifteen years—this was Michael Danver's second go-round on the matrimonial carousel, with the previous marriage best left forgotten—and it was what Danver (and, he supposed, Miranda) would consider a good marriage, although they never commented on such a thing to each other. Sure, they'd had their arguments, their disagreements, but overall, Dr. Michael Danver had no pressing complaints.

Most of their marriage's good fortune Danver had always attributed to the long hours his profession had demanded of him, though he had never actually said this aloud, and certainly not to Miranda. But deep in his heart he knew that to be true. And like some self-fulfilling prophecy, throughout the past year, he had come to find himself growing increasingly irritated by every little thing around the house, resulting in petty quarrels with Miranda over whatever trivial thing happened to incite his ire in the moment. Miranda, to her credit, would only put up with so much. She told him to take up golf, or woodworking, or maybe go to a matinee downtown a couple times a week to stave off boredom. While he agreed that those were all good suggestions, Danver never did any of those things.

This morning signaled the first alteration to Dr. Michael Danver's schedule in recent memory. By the time he climbed out of bed (Miranda beside him in her eye mask, sprawled on her back, silent and motionless as the dead), he was surprised to find, after glancing at his cell phone on the nightstand, that it was already well past seven o'clock. Strands of some disremembered nightmare still clung to him, tacky as a spider's web, as he ratcheted out of bed then staggered to the bathroom where he jostled the light switch only to find that last night's storm had knocked out the power. In the dark, he struggled to unleash an uncooperative sputter of urine into the bowl. Two minutes later, he attempted to recall elements of last night's dream as he stood scrubbing his scalp beneath the tepid spray from the showerhead—but no details of the nightmare came to him; just a lingering sense of unease bordering on apprehension that, for someone like Dr. Michael Danver, retired heart surgeon, was a foreign and wholly unsettling sensation.

He came downstairs to find the coffee machine dormant given the powerlessness of the house. Most likely the whole block was out. Goddamn storm, screwing with his morning routine. So, forgoing his large mug of piping hot coffee, Danver passed through the French doors at the rear of the house and walked out onto a sandstone patio that was littered with severed tree limbs, some random garbage, and the Bridgeports' cheap plastic lawn furniture. One at a time, Danver collected the cheap lawn chairs and ferried them over to the waist-high hedgerow that stood on the demarcation line between their two properties. He proceeded to toss the furniture over the hedgerow and onto the Bridgeports' lawn, wincing against the early morning sunlight as he did so.

When he was done, he strode out into the yard so he could scrutinize the damage to the house. All the windows were intact, although he counted three missing shutters up on the second story. A section of the gutter had been pried away from the house and hung now at an aggrieved angle, although it still appeared to be in one piece. Everything else seemed to be tiptop. They had gotten off lucky, considering how violent that storm had sounded.

Where the hell had that storm come from, anyway? There'd been nothing about it on last night's weather report.

*Fucking meteorologists,* he thought, flossing a stiff finger across the freshly shaven pocket of flesh between his lower lip and chin. *Must be nice to have a career where you're only expected to be accurate fifty percent of the time. Try that on an operating table sometime, will you?*

He turned and gazed down the slope of his back lawn, straight out to the edge of the cliff and out across the tumultuous, slate-gray expanse of the bay. A chilly summer breeze rippled his thinning salt-and-pepper hair. He could smell the remnants of the storm on that breeze, an orgy of brine and saltwater and oysters and all manner of things churned up from the murky brown depths of the bay. He headed in the direction of the water and stopped at the place where his property canted steeply toward the surf. Upon the edge of the bluff, he stood looking out at a parade of roiling whitecaps in the cove below with both his hands planted firmly on his hips.

That was when he saw it.

And the sight of it confounded him.

*What in the world are you doing out here?*

It was a door.

A door standing straight up out of the water.

A peculiar thing to see, for sure. In fact, it looked false—like something superimposed on a movie screen, a substanceless thing fashioned from fractals of light that he might just put his hand straight through, unimpeded, if he were to touch it.

He was surprised by the laugh that juddered up the channel of his throat. He even looked around, as if to find someone who might share in the peculiarity of this moment with him, but he was alone.

Where had it come from? How had it wound up out there on the water, standing perfectly straight, like he could just stroll out upon those frothy whitecaps, waltz right up to it, turn the knob, and enter—

—well, whatever was on the other side.

*What a strange idea,* he thought, and for the first time since trying to remember his nightmare, a wave of quiet unease passed through him.

There was nothing on the other side, of course. It was just a door, likely wrenched from someone's house by gale force winds in the night, only to perfectly wedge itself upright in a sandbar in the middle of the cove.

Right?

Suddenly, and despite the fact that his sockless feet were clad in chalk blue Sebago boat shoes, he was overcome by the compulsion to climb down the sheer face of the bluff and out to the water's edge in order to get a better look at the thing. In fact, that was all he wanted in that moment—to have just a better look, and nothing more.

The footpath leading down to the water was comprised of loose sand with spools of tree roots arcing out of it, and persisted in the face of decades of erosion—or perhaps because of it. Danver maneuvered his way down like someone negotiating a minefield, cautious where he stepped.

When he reached the water's edge, sweating and out of breath, he brought up one hand to shield the sun's glare from his eyes. He could see the door better from this proximity, yet standing here on the shore, so close but still so far from it, left him feeling queerly, inexplicably anxious. He bent forward and cuffed his pants to just above the knees, then pulled off his boat shoes and set them on a rocky precipice before stepping out into the water.

It was the middle of July, but the water still held the lingering chill of a cold spring. The silt between his toes, fine as powder, was damn near icy. The door was just a handful of yards out from shore, but the water was too dark, too turbulent, and it was deeper than he would have thought given how much of the door stood exposed above the surf—

*Wedged in a sandbar for sure . . .*

—and Danver, as he waded out and as the water rose past his knees and up to his waist, could no longer see the bottom. He knew, from periodic low tides, that there were jetties of rock down here, not to mention whatever else the storm had seen fit to deposit or churn up beneath the surf—booby-traps of broken glass or jagged twists of rusted metal. Hell, he'd once reeled in a discarded TV antenna while trolling for rockfish from his johnboat. Not to mention crabs and water snakes and whatever else lurked beneath the surface. It made good sense to turn back, return to the house and slip on a pair of old sneakers just to be safe. Yet he couldn't quite bring himself to take his eyes off the door in that moment, as if it might just wink out of existence if he happened to look away.

Before he could wrap his head around why he was even doing this, he was standing before the door, close enough to touch it. It was stained a dark brown beneath which the natural grain of the wood was visible, and it was divided into four topographical rectangles—two side-by-side on top, two side-by-side on the bottom—giving it some character. A pitted brass doorknob extended from a simple metal plate. Given its height, at least a good twenty inches of the door was most likely buried in the sandbar at Danvers's feet, which explained how it was being supported in such a fashion.

He heard a sound then—or, more accurately, *felt* a sound: a high frequency buzzing that caused his back teeth to ache. He even opened his mouth and pressed a finger to his left molar, as if to quell the pain. But then the sound (or the feeling, or whatever it was) was gone, so quickly he questioned if it had been there at all, and thought maybe it was actually the frigidity of the water that had caused the pain in his back teeth.

Danver reached out and jiggled the doorknob. It turned freely, and he could see the latch slide in and out of the thin metal plate along the interior frame of the door. He could see, too, where the door had been wrenched free from its hinges, leaving a trio of splintered indentations behind in the wood. He walked around to the other side of the door, his bare feet churning up clouds of brownish silt that turned the water into chocolate milk all around him, and realized that he had been staring at the *back* of the door, at the side that would go on the *interior* of a house. On *this* side of the door, four black iron digits were affixed to the woodwork: 1183. Someone's address. He reached out and traced each number with a forefinger. The iron numerals were gritty with sea salt and pitted like the doorknob.

"Where'd you come from, my friend?" he said to the door, unaware in that moment that he was speaking aloud. "Who do you belong to?"

Then he waited, as if the door might respond.

As if the door might say, *You.*

He reached out, gripped the door at both sides, and proceeded to wiggle it back and forth like a loose tooth. It budged only slightly. Danver grew certain that, with a little more force, a little more *effort*, he would be able to pry the thing clear of the sandbar.

*And then what?* said a small voice at the back of Michael Danver's head. *Go house to house, up and down Bay Road, all throughout Mariner's Cove, looking to see who has lost a door? Check the entire neighborhood? Look at every house on every block, straight out to the goddamn highway?*

Michael Danver was a pragmatic fellow. He knew that he could eventually find the house this door belonged to by searching street addresses with the corresponding numbers—1183. But he also knew, on some deeper, cloudier plane of thought, that he would not do that.

*You,* the door might have said. *I belong to you.*

Danver gave it some thought. Sure, he could pry it loose from the sandbar, but it was a heavy oak door, and the post-storm current might strip it from him and cast it out to sea before he managed to recover it. Moreover, how the hell would he carry something like that up the sheer face of the bluff unaided?

Anyway—

Why the hell would he *want* to?

Another humorless chuckle clawed its way out of his throat. What the hell was he thinking? Why was he out here, waist-deep in this cold, dirty water, obsessing over some piece of junk that had been blown in by last night's storm? Was he really that goddamn bored with himself?

*Take up golf, take up woodworking,* Miranda had urged him.

*Perhaps, with the proper equipment, it would be possible to haul it up the side of the bluff . . . maybe a rope-and-pulley system . . .*

Michael Danver shook his head, as if to clear it of silly thoughts, then proceeded to climb back up the face of the cliff.

## 2

Miranda was fixing herself a breakfast shake in the kitchen when Danver came in. She had been blessed with good skin, lucid hazel eyes, and still cut a nice figure. She sat on the board of various charities, campaigned for local politicians, and maintained an annual VIP membership to the Kennedy Center. A few years ago, she started a local arts and culture magazine called *Look There!*, a free monthly publication that collected all the local events in the area, from sports to bake sales and theater productions, and that subsisted solely on advertisements. Miranda was still in the clutches of life, constantly busy, that aforementioned shark progressing on the sheer will of its forward momentum. Whereas Danver felt restless and aloof in his retirement, Miranda appeared to have cultivated such a varied repertoire of extracurricular activities that any inkling of boredom, let alone free time, had been summarily and mercilessly beaten into submission.

"Is there much damage?" she asked without looking at him.

"No, not—"

"Goddamn it."

"What?"

She was pressing buttons on the blender.

"Oh," he said. "The power's out."

"Right. I knew that. I forget." She slumped against the countertop, her eyes glued to her phone now as she scrolled through something, still not looking at him. "How long do you think that will last?"

"I don't know."

She opened the fridge and took out a bottle of Perrier.

"Probably shouldn't open the fridge so things don't spoil," he said.

Miranda made a noise that established she didn't much care what his opinion was on the matter. At her feet, Clementine cocked his head and glared at Danver with unmasked contempt. Two machinegun yips fired out of him.

"Anyway, no," Danver continued, clearing his throat. "Not much damage at all. A couple of shutters are missing from the second story windows, and the gutter is a bit bent out of shape, but that's about it."

"They're probably halfway across the Atlantic by now, those shutters." Still staring at her phone, she carried her bottled water into the living room and sat down on the sofa. Clementine bounded after her and hopped up beside her on the sofa cushion.

"I guess we got off lucky," he added. Although that strange, high-pitched buzzing in his ears had not returned, he opened his mouth and prodded his left molar again without even realizing what he was doing. It was as if the sound—the *vibration*—had embedded itself inside him, like a poison.

"Well," Miranda said, still scrolling through her phone, "that was certainly some storm last night. I had to take an extra sleeping pill. And even then, I had the craziest dreams."

Danver tried to recall what his own dream—his own nightmare—had been about, but failed. Yet just thinking about it caused his back tooth to throb again. He went to the liquor cabinet, removed a bottle of Chivas and a lowball glass, poured a splash, then stood staring at the amber liquid with something akin to numb detachment.

"Michael, it's not even noon yet." She was looking at him for the first time since he'd come into the house. "What are you doing?"

"My tooth hurts," he said, and knocked the Chivas down his throat.

"And you're all wet! What happened to you?"

He glanced down, as if he'd forgotten what had transpired out there and where he'd been. His pants were still cuffed above the knees, his clothes dripping wet and stained with a brownish hue from the bay.

"There's a door down there, you know," he said, matter of fact.

"A what?"

"A door. Down in the water. Someone's front door."

"You mean from a *house*?"

"Yes. That's what it looks like, anyway."

Both her eyebrows arched as she glanced back at her phone. "Well, I've heard strong storms have the power to drive a blade of grass through the side of a barn." Then she frowned. "No, that can't be right." She looked back at him, nodded at his bare feet, and at the trail of wet footprints he'd inadvertently stamped across the hardwood floor. "Clean up that water, will you? And stay out of the river, for God's sake, Michael. That water is unclean, particularly after a storm. You know that. They always close Sandy Point after a bad storm. All that runoff and whatnot."

From the couch, Clementine barked at him: a sound as trifling and pathetic as a tricycle horn.

He was about to say something more about the door, but then decided not to.

It felt wrong.

Like spilling a secret.

## 3

He couldn't shake it from his mind.

*Where did you come from?*

*What are you doing here?*

*Why have you—*

## 4

By lunchtime, and with Miranda already out of the house pursuing one of her numerous enterprises, Danver found himself bumbling among the clutter in his three-car garage. Holiday decorations were corralled in one corner, various lawn implements hung from a pegboard on the wall, and an assortment of forgotten items were jumbled together in schizophrenic piles. After some fumbling around, he located a pair of Miranda's gardening gloves on a shelf and several yards of sturdy rope coiled like a rattlesnake on the floor beside some bags of mulch and grass seed. There were a pair of unused golf shoes on a shelf, a gift from Miranda from her time spent urging him to find a hobby, and he grabbed those, too. The cleats would likely provide better traction in the silt of the cove. Tucking the gardening gloves into the rear pocket of his slacks, he carried the coil of rope back out into the yard.

He'd already run the playbook in his head: he'd loop one end of the rope around the door and tie the other around his waist while attempting to jostle the door free of the sandbar. The door would be heavy, no doubt about that, but if the current decided to fight him for it once he'd pried it loose, it would be tethered to him. And the thing should float, too, so he'd be able to use the rope to pull it back toward shore with minimal difficulty.

*And then what?* spoke a thin, wavering voice toward the back of his head. *What's the point of all this, anyway? Why is this door stuck in your head like a seed between your teeth? Why did you wait for Miranda to leave before you did anything about it?*

He shook his head, chasing the voice away.

The *point* of why he was doing this wasn't important.

The *door* was important.

He could see it now, as he gazed down the slope of the bluff and out into the cove. A door, standing up like it was set there on purpose.

Beckoning.

"Hey, doc."

The voice startled him.

Donnie Bridgeport stood on the other side of the hedgerow, attempting to right a stone birdbath that had presumably toppled over last night during the storm. He looked chipper, despite somehow also looking hungover.

"Hello, Donnie."

"One hell of a storm last night." Defeated, Donnie dropped the birdbath back to the ground with an audible thump. His black hair was tied back in a ponytail and he was dressed in faded jeans and a Guayabera shirt unbuttoned nearly to his navel. There was a cigarette tucked behind one ear and when he turned to look at Danver, a toothy grin stretched across the lower half of his overly tanned face. "You guys have much damage?"

"No."

"Guess we got off easy. I mean, did you hear that wind? Sounded like Armageddon." He pointed in some vague direction out over the bluff and across the cove. "And the lightning? It hung right out there over the cove, flashing over and over again, like some freaky Morse code or something. It was wild, man. I've never seen anything like it."

Danver, who had already begun his descent down the footpath, attempted to tune him out.

"Where're you going, doc? What's with the rope?"

Danver's first inclination was to lie to Donnie, or maybe just tell him to take a hike. But when he craned his neck and peered back up at the man, Danver could see his neighbor staring with a look of confusion at the door down there in the cove, rising straight up out of the surf.

"Jesus," Donnie mumbled. "Would you look at that . . . ?"

In that moment, Danver felt the need to stake his claim on it before Donnie got any bright ideas.

"I found it. I'm going to . . . to retrieve it . . ."

"Is that a *door*?"

"Don't worry about it," Danver said curtly.

"How the heck is it standing upright like that?" Donnie bladed his hand, as if to illustrate the definition of upright.

"It's wedged in the sandbar."

"Who do you think it belongs to?"

"Me," Danver said. "It's mine."

"From the house?" Donnie glanced over at the Danvers' house, as if to locate a door-shaped hole in the structure.

"It's mine *now*," Danver corrected. "I found it."

Donnie frowned, rubbing his forehead and squinting against the daylight. "So you're gonna climb down there and . . . do what?"

*Just go away,* Danver willed him. *Just go away and leave me alone. Don't you have cheap plastic patio furniture to put away?*

"Are you wearing golf shoes?" Donnie asked, nodding at Danver's feet.

"Donnie, if you don't mind, I'm in the middle of—"

—and then he lost his footing and plummeted straight down on his ass. The loose soil beneath him tumbled down the footpath in a compact little avalanche, and Danver began sliding down the face of the bluff after it. The rope came unspooled and he scrambled to find purchase in the crumbling dirt with his fingers, the cleats of his golf shoes digging trenches in the earth but failing to prevent him from sliding further.

"Doc! Doc!"

He felt Donnie snatch up one of his wrists and arrest his fall.

"Jesus," Danver gasped. His heart was trampolining in his chest and he'd broken out in a greasy sheen of sweat. His ass hurt, too, and there would probably be a nice bruise there by the end of the day. With Donnie's assistance, he climbed back to his feet, the rope now slung about his shoulder like a bandolier.

"You'll break your neck going down there," Donnie said.

"I've already done it once today."

Donnie shook his head. "I don't get it, doc. What's the urgency?"

*I don't want you to get it,* Danver thought. *I don't want you even thinking about it, do you understand?*

"I'll be more careful," Danver said, and yanked his wrist free of Donnie Bridgeport's grasp.

## 5

At the bottom of the hill, Danver waded back out into the water and moved slowly toward the door. The water gradually rose above his knees before reaching his waist. Donnie had followed him down the footpath, no doubt worried that Danver might take another header, and the younger man lingered now along the shoreline, watching.

Small, foamy waves lapped at the door which stood against the backdrop of a stunningly blue and cloudless sky, that pitted brass doorknob catching glints of sunlight that sought out the most vulnerable parts of Danver's eyes. As Danver approached, his shadow rose against the wood, and for a moment he was overcome by the curious thought that perhaps his shadow might get snared in the whorls of the wood grain; that it might, in some way, become trapped upon the door—

*(within the door behind the door inside the door)*

—forever.

A silly notion, yes . . . yet Michael Danver was not prone to such speculative fancy, so it felt like some alien entity suddenly infiltrating his brain.

"You okay, doc?" Donnie called from the shore.

Danver flapped a dismissive hand in Donnie's direction.

*How did you get here, my friend?*

*What is your purpose?*

He wound one end of the rope around the door—once, twice, three times. Then he tied the other end of the rope around his waist.

"You sure you wanna lash yourself to that thing, doc?" Donnie shouted from the shore.

Danver ignored him. He fished Miranda's gardening gloves from his back pocket—they were already soaked from the bay—and he gritted his teeth as he tugged them onto his hands.

*Just like wiggling a loose tooth,* he thought as he gripped the door on both sides and proceeded to rock it back and forth.

Back and forth.

Back and forth.

He felt the door come free of the sandbar and rise buoyantly upon the surf. His heart, too, felt buoyant in that moment—or at least something akin to a welling of exhilaration in his chest. The weight of the door caused it to fall backward, despite Danver's hold on it; the damn thing was too heavy and it crashed to the surface of the water, spraying Danver's face with droplets that tasted like saline. He pawed the water from his eyes just as he felt the rope around his waist grow taut. The door was being carried away from him on the surf in mesmerizing undulations, a seesaw on the sea, a *seasaw*, and Danver could feel the strength of the current tugging him further out into the cove.

He gripped the rope in both hands and pulled back.

The door bobbed.

He began reeling it toward him.

Thinking, *If the rope comes loose, I will swim out after it and bring it back to shore.*

Aware at the same time that doing so would likely be impossible.

*If you've come here for me, then* be *here for me.*

There were thoughts shuttling through his mind and he possessed hardly any awareness of them. Thoughts like—

*(buzzing)*

—lightning zigzagging through the labyrinth of his gray matter. Too fast for him to grasp and make any sense of.

But the door came to him: hand over hand, he pulled on the rope and drew the door closer to him.

Closer.

*Closer.*

And then he was pulling it toward shore, at first by the rope, like a leash to a pet, but then he bent down and gripped it, lifted it from the surf, felt the cleats of his golf shoes drive deeper into the silt, felt the incredible weight of the large, wooden, waterlogged door, and the ache in his spine, the bruise forming on his ass, and through all of that, the inexplicable buzzing in his back teeth.

Before he realized what was happening, Donnie was rushing toward him through the surf, bare feet kicking up fans of foamy tide and dark brown sand. Just as the weight of the door was about to drive Danver to his knees, Donnie gripped the other side of it and took half the weight off him. The ache in Danver's spine diminished even if the buzzing in his back teeth did not.

By the time they wrangled the door to the shore, both Danver and Donnie were breathing heavily and sweating like a couple of prizefighters, bent at the waists with their hands on their knees.

"Do you think you can help me carry it up the side of the hill and to the house?" Danver asked. He didn't really want Donnie involved, but knew he wouldn't be able to carry it up the footpath on his own.

"I don't get it, doc," Donnie said. He was looking at the door strangely, Danver thought. "Why're you breaking your back over this?"

Danver sighed. Closed his eyes. Shook his head, as if to clear it of smoke. "I just want to get this thing up to the house, okay? Can you give me a hand with that?"

Donnie shrugged, then reached for the place behind his ear where his cigarette had been previously, but was no longer. "You got it, doc. Whatever you want."

They each grabbed a side and carried it horizontally up the face of the bluff. Donnie was younger and stronger so he took the lead; twice,

Danver dropped his end, and the door slammed to the earth with a resounding wallop that seemed to echo for far too long within the confines of Michael Danver's skull.

Eventually, they reached the top of the bluff, and together they carried the door around the side of Danver's house toward his garage.

"One-one-eight-three," Donnie said, reading the metal numerals on the front of the door. "You know, doc, this thing isn't from any of the houses on our street. No one out here's got a four-digit address."

"Doesn't matter," Danver muttered. They crossed into the shade of the garage and Danver said, "Here, here," the second *here* wheezing out of him as if from some punctured wind instrument.

They lowered the door and propped it like a lean-to against the interior wall of the garage. Danver searched around the garage, located two paving stones, and used them to chock the bottom of the door to prevent it from sliding and falling.

"How do you think it happened?" Donnie asked.

"What do you mean? How did *what* happen?"

"Well, I mean, you know, a storm tearing off someone's front door? That's a little bizarre, don't you think?"

"It was a bad storm."

"Yeah, but still—how does, like, *wind* grip around someone's front door and just yank it off like that? Not to mention dropping it straight down into the bay standing upright like that. Fucking wild, man."

"I don't know, Donnie."

Donnie shrugged, looking instantly disinterested. He produced another cigarette from a pack in his back pocket and smoked it in the entranceway of the garage. Watching him, Danver's mind filled with images of blackened, diseased lungs.

"So now what?" Donnie asked.

"Now?" He rapidly blinked his eyes, then considered the question. For some reason, he suddenly felt strange, like maybe his blood sugar was low.

"I mean, what was the point of all this?" Donnie waved a hand at the door leaning against the wall of the garage. "I don't get it. Why'd you want to bother dragging this thing in here?"

Just then, the light in the ceiling of the garage came on.

"Well," Donnie said, grinning. "Look at that. I thought it'd be hours before the power came back on."

Danver stared at the glowing fixture above his head.

Felt the buzzing in his back tooth grow stronger.

"I guess this old door's good luck," Donnie said.

## 6

Once Donnie had left, Danver lowered the garage door, then proceeded to clear some space from the empty garage bay. This was where Miranda usually parked the Escalade, but the other two bays were occupied with Danver's two vehicles—a sleek, black Lexus LC 500 whose vanity plate said HARTDOC and, in the farthest bay, a forest-green 1967 Mercury Cougar which had once belonged to Danver's father. The door, leaning against the wall of the garage where he and Donnie had propped it, kept attracting Danver's attention; his eyes kept shifting in its direction, observing it from various angles in the poor lighting of the garage. When he had finished packing all the randomly horded items onto various shelves or into crowded corners of the garage, he dragged two sawhorses into the center of the cleared space.

The door watched.

He went to it, gripped it in both hands. It was heavy, but somehow, he managed to carry it over to the sawhorses and lay it down across them horizontally. Those pitted iron numerals shone beneath the dull, solitary light in the center of the ceiling.

The door studied him.

He studied the door.

And after a time, he pressed the side of his face down upon it.

His ear.

As if—

*—to listen.*

# CHAPTER THREE
# SYMBOLS

## 1

Raj Subador was dying. What else could it be?

It never occurred to him earlier that morning, as he laced up his Nikes, popped in his earbuds, and stepped out of his Plainview Street bungalow for his morning run, that he would end the day in death. Who would think such a thing? The fresh, crisp, chilly morning air, the neighborhood still asleep at such an ungodly hour, the procession of quaint little homes along Plainview still dark in these early, pre-dawn moments (though likely due to the power outage after last night's storm)—who in their right mind would think that death was waiting for them just around the corner?

It was roughly a four-mile loop that wound him in and out of the neighborhood streets of Mariner's Cove. Raj preferred to go early in the morning, when the streets were still dark and quiet and few neighbors were out. The air was always cool against his skin, and he rejoiced in the soft sigh of the wind in the trees. He knew every bump and groove and pothole that made up Plainview Street, the gradual incline of Bay Road with its string of million-dollar homes between which he could glimpse the silvery shimmer of moonlight upon the Chesapeake. He knew that the dog who resided in the barn-red house on Tamarack Way—a furtive, anxious fellow who looked like he might have a touch of pit bull in him—stayed out all night and would bark at Raj as he chugged past the chain-link fence that encircled the property. There was a house on Capshaw Street where the windchimes tinkled like champagne flutes. There were the year-round Christmas lights in the windows of the house on Jolene Street. There was a duplex on Poplar Station Road whose backyard was cluttered with what appeared to be props scavenged from a miniature golf course—a three-foot-tall windmill, a papier-mâché gorilla, a duo of mechanized sunflowers in top hats and sunglasses. There were overturned johnboats in front yards, tackle boxes and fishing rods left abandoned on front porches, decorative life preservers hanging above garage doors. His run took him along a portion of the shoreline, where the night-song of small toads hidden in the reeds was still in full orchestration. It took him, too, through Gladstone Park, where the enormous water tower rose up beyond the trees, startling against a still-dark sky, and looking like some otherworldly spacecraft with its ring of white lights around the circumference of the water tank.

The world was an insulated little capsule and Raj Subador was its only occupant.

That was how he fell in love with running.

On this morning, by the time he reached the wooded outskirts of Gladstone Park and the first strains of daylight began poking through the trees, something funny was going on in Raj's head. He had nearly completed his four-mile circuit around the neighborhood, and while he'd felt invigorated by the post-storm chill in the air for much of the run, he thought the fogginess building in his head might, at first, have something to do with dehydration or low blood sugar.

Two fingers to the pulse at his neck, Raj counted in his head while Brahms issued through his earbuds. The path beneath his feet surrendered to spongy brown mulch and then grass. He had been thinking of the day's drafting work that lay ahead of him when that bank of mental fog rolled in, leaving him feeling dazed, his mind strangely muddled. Something felt *off.* Was he a little dizzy, too? He realized the early morning sun was blotted out and he was standing in a pool of shadow. He looked up and saw the massive Gladstone Park water tower looming above him. Sunlight burned around the edges of the tank like a solar eclipse.

*Sun shouldn't be that high this early,* he thought. It took him less than an hour to complete the four-mile run, and he was often back home before daylight broke along the horizon. He glanced at his wristwatch, but the digital face was nothing but a jumble of blinking digits. Maybe the battery was dying.

He wasn't sure how long he stood there with his head craned back, but when he blinked and finally turned away from the tower, Brahms had quit playing in the earbuds and the morning had grown considerably brighter and warmer. He turned and looked back in the direction he had come, at the tail end of the four-mile loop he'd been running nearly every morning for the past year—a four-mile loop that had become as intimate to him as the interior of his own home—and realized that he didn't know where he was.

Where was he?

He uttered a humorless laugh rich with distress. Disorientation tightened noose-like around his throat.

*Something is wrong with me.*

*Something is happening to me.*

He took a step forward and nearly lost his balance as the world, like the floor of a funhouse, seemed to tilt to one side beneath his feet. With mounting dread, he wondered if he was having a heart attack, or maybe a stroke. If he was, he—

A sudden pain knifed through the center of his skull. The ferocity of it dropped him to his knees in the wet grass. He dug the earbuds from his ears and clutched instinctively at both sides of his head, as if to keep his cranium from splitting down the middle. The pain came again . . . and again . . . and again. An unrelenting surge. It pulsed through the gray matter of his brain in synch with his panicked heartbeat.

Not a heart attack, not a stroke, but another terrible word flashed in bright neon through Raj's head as he struggled to rise to his feet—*aneurysm.* In his goddamn *brain*, this time. The word terrified him. He managed, unsteadily, to ratchet to his feet, but the searing, white-hot pain in the center of his skull drove him straight back down to the earth.

A bright star burst in the center of his head. It opened like the mouth of a tunnel, like a widening pupil, the center of which looked as black and unwelcoming as an underground cave. He shook his head and rapidly blinked his eyes, and that star dispersed into shimmering raindrops of light.

*I'm dying.*

*I'm dying.*

*I'm—*

There was a squat stucco building just a few yards away—a maintenance shed affiliated with the park, the words MARINER'S COVE COMMUNITY ASSOCIATION stenciled on the side. Yet the words meant nothing to him in that moment—they were nonsensical glyphs on a frieze that he could no longer comprehend. Gibberish, just like the digital readout on his watch. The image of the shed doubled then trebled as Raj, his eyes filling with water and his brain still resonating with the afterimage of that exploding star, stared at it. For some inexplicable reason, he felt it necessary to make it to that building in order to stop the pain in his head, or to at least find some dark corner of solace, of shelter, so he proceeded to crawl toward it through the wet grass and muddy soil on his hands and knees. However, when the pain struck again, he crumpled to the ground, gasping for air like a fish on the deck of a boat. He caught a whiff of lilac; caught a whiff of his own sour perspiration. He rolled onto his side, and then onto his back, still gasping.

Something was boring through that black tunnel at the center of his mind. It was nothing he could see or even imagine—just a sensation lingering below the surface of his consciousness, though with unwavering certainty. His body suddenly felt as though it were being tickled by a thousand feathers. He went numb.

In that moment, he thought of a snake. He could see it winding its way through the damp grass, navigating the natural undulations of the earth, its body as iridescent as the carapace of a beetle and possessing the rainbow sheen of an oil slick. In his confusion, he thought that maybe *he* was the snake, his body convulsing along the muddy ground. It was true: some part of his brain was demanding his broken body comply and begin to weave itself serpentlike along the earth in search of—

What?

Salvation?

Just as a bank of darkness, dense as sackcloth, shrouded over his brain, an image materialized at the center of Raj Subador's mind: not so much the image of a snake, but of a thing very closely related to one, or at least as close in proximity as Raj's simple human brain, desperate for interpretation, was able to decipher. He watched it emerge from the black mouth of the tunnel in the center of his brain. *Snake*—an image that seemed to scream out in a blaze of phosphorescent light and rain down like smoldering embers from a fire.

And the last conscious thought that shuttled through Raj Subador's head before he blacked out was:

*It . . .*

*is . . .*

*so . . .*

*terribly . . .*

*big . . .*

## 2

A crescent moon.

An infinity symbol.

The crude, hieroglyphic rendition of a human being.

*And on and on and on and . . .*

## 3

He awoke on his back, gasping for breath. Not dead. High above his head, a series of interlocking tree branches, blurry and distorted, slowly reconciled themselves and took on sharper focus. Beyond that canopy of trees, the sickly, washed-out gray of the sky gradually returned to a bright, cloudless blue.

Raj felt his heart punching against his ribs. Each exhalation exited his body in an achy, labored rattle. He was outside, though he could not recall exactly where, or how he had gotten here. There was a swirling mist of confusion roiling around inside his head, and it even took him a moment to remember his name.

*What is this? What happened?*

He remained lying motionless on the ground, feeling the wetness of the grass soak through his T-shirt. Too frightened to move.

*What the hell happened?*

*Where the hell am I?*

Took a breath.

Braced himself.

Slowly, he sat up in the grass. His skin felt raw and tacky with sweat, and his T-shirt adhered to his chest like clingwrap. There was a dull throbbing at the center of his head—had he fallen and bumped it on a rock?—and his entire body felt jittery and traitorous. It wasn't until he looked beyond the tree line and saw the tank of the Gladstone Park water tower that he remembered where he was and, to some degree, what had happened to him.

He was cautious climbing to his feet. But the world around him remained steady. He touched his head, his face, and could feel no bumps or cuts or anything of that nature. The fog in his head was already beginning to clear, too.

He was okay. He must have just passed out.

He looked around, as if to find someone who might corroborate such a fact, but this remote and wooded section of Gladstone Park was deserted. He was the only living soul out here, as far as he could see.

*I just overdid it, that's all. Pushing myself too hard. Possibly dehydrated.*

As he brushed dirt and bits of dead leaves from his clothes, he happened to glance over at the maintenance shed. He knew it should have said MARINER'S COVE COMMUNITY ASSOCIATION along the side of the shed, but instead, those words—those *letters*—had been replaced by a string of strange and incomprehensible symbols. To Raj, they looked like characters from some ancient Egyptian language, things carved in distant stone monoliths, arcane and somewhat ominous, stenciled right there on the side of the building. He pressed the heels of his hands against his eyes and rubbed furiously. But when he looked again, those strange symbols were still there. Unchanged.

He wondered if there was something wrong with his eye again.

Last summer, he'd woken up very early one morning to find the world around him distorted and twisted out of shape. That was back when Marco had still been living with him, and he'd woken Marco up sharply, jostling him in bed, trying to keep his voice calm because he didn't want to sound histrionic, but Christ, his *eye* was fucked up, his *vision*, so then it became, "Marco, Marco, Jesus, something's wrong with my eye, I can't see right, something's wrong, something's happened, I don't know what's going on," and Marco had switched on the lamp beside the bed, since it was still dark out, both of them wincing at the suddenness of the light, and Marco had braced Raj's face in his hands, his palms cool against Raj's fevered cheeks, and he had stared deep into Raj's dark, terrified eyes, studying him, maybe judging him a little, and saying, ultimately, "There is nothing wrong with your eyes," to which Raj had exclaimed, "Everything's bent out of shape," and then he'd rolled out of bed to call 911. There *had* been something wrong—he'd suffered an aneurysm in the blood vessel of one eye due to unchecked high blood pressure—but that didn't seem to earn him any favor or pity from his boyfriend. He supposed there had been one too many things between them at that point. It was soon after the aneurysm that Marco had left for good.

But this was different. The aneurysm had been like a blurry dent in the center of his field of vision, causing things to appear wavy, distorted, or sometimes not all there. What he was seeing now, however, he was seeing with perfect clarity, even if none of it made any sense to him: those nonsensical symbols stamped on the side of the maintenance shed stood in sharp relief.

Something that looked like a crescent moon.

An infinity symbol.

A whirlpool swirl.

Other less identifiable sigils.

Raj shook his head, as if to clear his vision. But those strange symbols persisted. He looked down and realized that at some point, he had lowered himself to a kneeling position upon the dirt footpath that wound through the wooded section of Gladstone Park, as if in supplication . . .

His right index finger was weaving back and forth, back and forth, reproducing one of those shapes—the infinity symbol—in the mud.

# 4

By the time he returned to his modest house on Plainview Street, he was no longer Raj Subador. Not fully. Something else had slipped inside him and corrupted a small but vital aspect of him. Invaded him, though snuggly, like a glove. Worst of all was that Raj possessed no knowledge that this corruption had occurred. Even as his mind twisted and changed and opened like a lotus flower, he had no concept of it, no understanding . . . except for a vague sense of confusion that seemed to cloud his thoughts from time to time throughout the afternoon. Those symbols cycloned inside his head, a jumble of nonsense rebounding off the interior walls of his skull. Whenever he tried to think his way through them, they impeded his thought. Suffocated it. Drowned it out. He noticed, too, that every once in a while, his back teeth would feel like they were vibrating right down to the roots, shaking in their sockets, and they would begin to ache.

He'd attempted to read the street signs on his way home—that much he could remember doing—but just like the words on the side of the park's maintenance shed (and the flashing digital numbers on the face of his wristwatch), they made no sense. They weren't *words*, weren't *letters*. Not from any alphabet he was familiar with, anyway. Same with the numbers on every mailbox he passed: indecipherable nonsense.

By the time he reached his house, he sat exhausted on the front steps and pulled off his running shoes. Those symbols kept buzzing around inside his head. There was a label stitched to the tongue of his shoe, but whatever language that was now printed on it was not meant to be read by him. Same with the doormat, which should have read, simply, WELCOME, now appeared as a collection of alien text, impossible to translate.

Some part of him struggled to fight through the fog in his brain. There was work to be done, a drafting project that he needed to complete by the end of the week for a big client, but once he adjourned to his home office, he found that he could not decipher the text on the digital blueprints on his computer screen, could not navigate the CAD program because he could no longer understand it. He picked up the TV remote and saw that the numbers and words had been replaced with squiggly lines, infinity symbols, and blocky rectangles.

"Help me," he muttered to the empty house.

He was thinking of Marco.

Maybe even calling out to him, despite him being gone.

Marco would've known what to do.

He went to the bathroom, sat on the edge of the tub, and strapped the cuff of his blood pressure machine to his left arm while he set the unit down on the toilet lid. The machine switched on and the cuff tightened around his bicep. When the machine beeped and the pressure in the cuff released, the screen was nothing but a jigsaw of bright red nonsense he was powerless to decipher.

In that moment, the terrified and desperate part of Raj Subador that was struggling to breach the fog was finally swallowed whole. And by lunchtime, he was idly doodling those strange symbols first on a notepad he kept beside his laptop and then on the desktop itself. A jumble of glyphs that resembled crescent moons, an infinity sign, a stick figure with a spiral for a torso, and many others. He hardly registered that he was doing this, or that he was doing anything at all.

When he finally glanced down and saw what he was scribbling, there was no surprise or fear or even a solitary element of concern in him. There was only a mounting sense of urgency to continue transcribing the symbols that were now boiling furiously in his head.

Symbols he did not comprehend in any way, shape, or form, other than in the single-minded conviction that they were, above all else, of the utmost importance.

*The symbols, the symbols, the symbols . . .*

At times, it felt like there was something alien alive inside his skull, an indecipherable thing sharing that tight space with Raj's own mind. A thing coiling itself around his cerebral cortex, tightening like a—

*(snake)*

—noose.

Whatever it was, it kept him focused. He located a black felt-tipped marker in a kitchen drawer, then proceeded to reproduce the odd symbols on the walls of his house. When he came upon a hanging picture frame—he and Marco last summer at the Grand Canyon, sunglasses on, gaudy souvenir T-shirts, grinning with their arms around each other like they'd be together forever—he printed straight onto the glass without giving it a thought. He was so completely preoccupied that when he cracked his big toe against the base of a credenza, bruising the bone and splitting the nail, he did not notice. There was nothing else in the world that mattered in that moment except the symbols, fed to him by that continuously flexing, alien muscle inside his cranium. And the feeling—the *drive*—would only grow stronger over the next few days.

Suddenly, Raj Subador had a very important job to do.

# CHAPTER FOUR

# "SHOW ME"

## 1

Later that evening, as a tray of manicotti—Cory's favorite meal—baked in the oven, and while Cory soaked in the tub, Ellen McBride stepped out onto the back porch with her cell phone. The power had come on at some point during the afternoon, all the lights in the house and the TV switching on simultaneously, but Cory hadn't woken from his slumber in his bedroom. She hadn't disturbed him, had let him sleep, and instead went about cleaning up the rest of the house, the yard, and ultimately stapling a sheet of heavy-duty plastic over the shattered kitchen window. She'd call somebody about that in the morning. For now, her mind was occupied by weightier thoughts.

The evening was chilly. The storm had brought down a good number of trees, and somewhere in the distance she could hear the chirr of a chainsaw rivaling the chorus of summer crickets in the yard. Next door, Mr. Zachs's porch lights flickered.

She found her brother's phone number in her contacts, and the little icon beside his name that showed she still had his number blocked. It had been about two years since she'd last spoken to him. A conflicting mixture of emotions overwhelmed her in that moment, as she stared down at the glowing screen of her phone. As much as her brother had been in the wrong back then, did she have any right to insert herself back into his life now? What kind of signal would that send? What did that make *her*? She vacillated on this as she leaned against the porch's railing and watched the sun slowly setting beyond the trees.

When she went back inside, she found Cory peering through the window of the oven door. His dark curls were wet from the bath and brushed neatly to one side, and he was wearing an old Race for the Cure T-shirt that had once been hers. She saw that he had also set the dining room table while she'd been outside, contemplating things.

"Looks ready," he said, still staring through the oven window.

"Should be." She pulled on an oven mitt then took the tray of manicotti from the oven and placed it on the stovetop. "Let's let it cool for a couple minutes, yeah?"

"Sure," Cory said. "Can I have a Coke?"

"All right."

He opened the fridge and rummaged around for a can of soda.

Ellen went to a high cupboard and pulled down a half-empty bottle of cheap red wine. She poured herself a hearty glass, then carried it over to the dining room table. "Come have a seat. I want to talk to you."

He peered at her from overtop his Coke, eyes as big as saucers.

She waved a hand at him and motioned toward the chair in front of the empty place setting beside her. He came reluctantly, his eyes on hers, that can of Coke clutched in a death grip in one hand. When he sat, he did so in silence, and even the chair legs were soundless as they moved along the hardwood floor.

They stared at each other without speaking for what felt like a long time.

"Hey," she said eventually, reaching out and squeezing his hand. "Can we talk about last night?"

"You mean the storm?"

She felt herself make a face. "Well, no. Not the storm. Not exactly."

Cory's eyes jittered over in the direction of the kitchen, and to the broken window above the sink, now covered in a sheet of plastic.

"Last night," she said. "When the window broke and those bits of glass . . . well . . ." She didn't know how to say it, so she just came out with it: "How did you do that?"

He said nothing; only stared at her, his eyes impossibly large, his mouth pressed into a firm line. He suddenly looked much older than his ten years, and this realization caused a pang of sadness to resonate through her body.

"Did you know you could do it?" she asked.

He nodded slowly.

"How long have you been able to do stuff like that?"

His eyes skirted away from hers. He stared down at his can of Coke, one finger playing with the aluminum tab.

"Do you not want to talk about it?" she asked.

In a small voice, he said, "I feel weird."

"Why's that, baby?"

"Because I kept it a secret from you for so long."

*For so long.* How long? She thought of the lights flickering in the house, the TV spontaneously turning on and surfing through channels without anyone touching the remote. "How long has it been going on?"

Cory's small, narrow shoulders rose to points as he shrugged. "For a while, I guess. I don't know exactly. I don't really know when it started."

"Why would you feel weird about it?"

"I don't know. I mean, I guess . . . I guess it's like the time I hid my dirty laundry in my closet," he said, still not making eye contact with her. His thumbnail kept using the tab on the soda can as a diving board—*plunk plunk.*

"How's it like that?" she asked.

Still not looking at her, he said, "Too much time had passed for me to know why I hid it from you in the first place, and so I just felt bad about it and didn't really know what to say."

"So, you feel bad about hiding this from me, too?"

"I don't know." His voice was barely audible. "I don't know how to feel about it."

"Are you scared?"

"No."

"Are you . . . worried about something?"

"I'm worried that it might change things."

"What things? What do you mean?"

"I'm worried it might make normal situations different."

"Like how?"

"Like maybe you'll start to think about me in a different way."

She reached out, took his chin in her hand, turned his face toward hers. His eyes locked on her eyes, and she could see all the brilliant spangles of color in his irises, the delicate black fans of his lashes. Her boy. "I could never think differently about you, Cory. You're my kid and I love you, no matter what. Do you understand me?"

Silently, he nodded. She released him and folded her hands together on top of the table.

"Does it happen when you're upset? When you're frightened?"

"Sometimes."

"Like you're losing control?"

"I don't know. I think maybe it started that way."

"Are you frightened that you can do things like that?"

He looked at her. "Are *you*?"

It was such an adult thing to say, or maybe it was just the way he said it, that Ellen took a moment before responding. "No, baby. It doesn't frighten me. It doesn't frighten me at all. I just don't want you to be scared when it happens."

"I'm not scared."

"No? Not even a little bit? Having those things happen without any control?"

He frowned, a crease forming between his eyebrows. "It doesn't just happen. I can control it."

"You can?"

He glanced back at his can of Coke. "I'm hungry, Mom."

"You can control it? It doesn't just . . . happen . . . when you're angry or upset? When you get emotional?"

"It happens when I want it to happen," he said, matter of fact. "Can we eat?"

"Show me," she said.

Cory's eyes shifted back in her direction. There was a cold calculation in them in that moment, and once again he appeared much older than his years.

"Show me," she said again, and slid a fork across the table toward him.

He turned his gaze on the fork. Stared at it. His finger stopped plucking at the tab on the soda can. In fact, his whole body seemed to freeze. To stiffen. That vertical divot between his eyebrows appeared to deepen the slightest bit.

"Can you?" she asked. "Can you make it move? Even just a little bit? Can you make—"

The fork jumped on the tabletop.

*Cli-clang!*

"Oh," she said, and pulled herself back against her chair. She even brought a hand up to her mouth, as if to stifle any further sound. The metallic clink of the fork striking the tabletop still resonated in the room and in her ears. "Wow. Okay."

That vertical divot between his eyebrows deepened further.

On the table, the fork began to quiver. A metallic *rattle rattle rattle.*

"Jesus," she said.

*Rattle rattle rattle.*

Vibrating.

Then it began to whirl in a circle, like a board game spinner. The sound of it rotating along the wooden tabletop was steady and hypnotic. Dronelike.

"Jesus, Cory, that's—"

The fork came to a dead stop. It felt like all the air had been sucked out of the room. As she stared at it, the fork pivoted upward until it stood vertically with its tines pointing toward the ceiling. She glanced at Cory's face, saw the intensity of his stare, his brow suddenly beaded with sweat.

The fork began to rotate—slowly at first but then quickly gathering momentum until the tines became a blur. It sounded like it was drilling into the tabletop.

"Okay, okay, okay," she said, suddenly realizing that she had bolted from her chair and was standing at the head of the table, hands pressed to the sides of her face like someone who had just witnessed something either wholly horrifying or terribly, unspeakably grand.

The fork froze in mid-spin. Slowly, Cory—Cory's *mind*—lowered it back down to the tabletop. It touched down with hardly a sound. Then, a second later, it slid across the table and tucked itself right up against Ellen's plate.

For a moment, it felt as though she couldn't breathe.

"Are you still so sure?" he asked, staring up at her, his face eerily expressionless.

It took her a moment to find her voice. "Am I still so sure about what, baby?"

"That you're not scared," he said.

She went to him, ran a hand along the back of his head. His hair was still damp from the bath, but she could also feel a prickling perspiration running along the warm nape of his neck. It was then that she realized the hairs along her own arms had stiffened, and that her entire body felt like it had just had a current of electricity travel through it. She looked toward the center of the table and could see a miniscule hole in the wood, from where the tapered handle of the fork had drilled down past the lacquer.

"No, baby. I'm not scared." A timorous laugh quaked out of her. "I don't know *what* I am, but I'm not scared."

"And you don't think I'm weird or something?"

"No, love. I could never think that of you." She kissed the top of his head, which smelled clean and of shampoo. "I'm amazed by it, Cory. It's amazing to me. I've always been amazed. I want to understand. How does it work? How does it happen? Do you just . . . focus on something? Concentrate?"

"I don't really know. It's hard to explain. I just think about it and then it happens. It's like there's this thing in my head making it happen. A little thing that comes awake and does what I tell it to do."

"A little thing that comes awake? What does that mean?"

He frowned in concentration. For a moment, Ellen thought the fork might start spinning again. "You know the garden gnomes? The ones in the back yard?"

Caught off guard by this non sequitur, she hesitated before nodding her head. There were four or five of the little terracotta figures in the garden out back, each one sporting a jaunty, colorful dunce cap and a white beard. They had come with the house, and she'd just left them there.

"That's what it's like," he said. "Like a little garden gnome in my head, coming awake and doing the things I tell it to do. Like I'm not even the one doing it."

"Like moving stuff around?"

Cory nodded.

"Does anyone else know you can do this?"

He looked up at her. His finger had gone back to plucking the tab on the soda can, but it stopped now.

"Tell me the truth," she said, a sinking feeling in her guts.

Not taking his eyes off her, Cory slowly shook his head.

"No? Are you sure?" she pressed. "No one else besides you and me knows you can do this? It's very important that you're honest with me right now."

"No one else knows," he said. "I swear, Mom."

"Not even your friends? Not Davey and Winona across the street?"

Again, he shook his head. But this time he averted his eyes.

Did she believe him? She wanted to. That plummeting sensation in the pit of her stomach persisted.

She took their plates from the table and carried them into the kitchen, where she loaded them up with manicotti. Her hands wouldn't stop shaking and there was a slight tingling sensation running along the surface of her flesh.

"Mom?"

"Yes, baby?"

"You said you were amazed by it. You said you've *always* been amazed."

She'd let that slip, hadn't she? And he'd been astute enough, even in the middle of all this, to catch it.

"When I was a little girl," she told him, "I had a great aunt named Patty. She was grandma's older sister, and she passed away a long time ago, back when I was still just a girl. She used to come and visit for a week every summer when we lived over the bridge. As a kid, I remember her sitting in front of the radio for hours and guessing song after song in the moments before they played. I thought it was some kind of really cool parlor trick at first."

"What's a parlor trick?"

"It's like a stunt or a spectacle. Something that appears to be legit but it's really just a trick. It wasn't until later, when I was a little older, that I realized it wasn't a trick at all. Aunt Patty had a special gift. She was clairvoyant, at least as far as music on the radio was concerned."

"What's that?"

"Clairvoyant? It's the ability to see things a little bit into the future. Or maybe just an intuition about things that are about to happen. Like a heightened sense, you know?" She was about to say more—she felt it right there on the tip of her tongue, straining to come out—but then she stopped herself at the last second. She didn't want to go there. Instead, she said, "Aunt Patty could do other things, too. Things like you just did with that fork, although not nearly as impressive."

"She could make things move around without touching them?"

"Small things. A drinking glass, a paper napkin. She once rolled one of your uncle's Matchbox cars along the kitchen table."

"Did it scare you?"

*He keeps asking that*, she realized, *which maybe means* he *is scared.*

"No way!" She tried desperately to brighten her face. "I used to beg her to do it so I could figure out *how* she was doing it, as if it was something I could learn. And Aunt Patty would laugh and pretend she didn't know what I was talking about, but then she'd do it anyway, only this time with a wink. But—and listen to me here, Cory—I'll never do that with you. It's your own private gift. Do you understand? You can keep it to yourself, if that's what you want to do with it."

"Can *you* do it?" he asked. He sounded hopeful, and the sound of that hopefulness was nearly heartbreaking to her ears. "Did you ever learn?"

She carried their plates to the table and set Cory's down in front of him. "No, baby. I don't think that's something anyone can just learn. I wouldn't even know how to summon the power. I think it's a gift some people are born with, like you and my old Aunt Patty. And even some of those people who're born with it are better at it than others."

"What do you mean?"

She placed her own plate down then sat in her chair. Picked up the fork and held it up between them so that she was staring at him between the metal tines. "You were able to do that very easily. You could control it. I don't think Aunt Patty was ever able to do it that well." She set the fork in her plate then hid her hands beneath the table so that Cory wouldn't see them shaking. She wasn't thinking of Aunt Patty in that moment, of course. "That's why it's important that we keep this a secret between us. Do you understand why that's important?"

"Because people might want me to do something bad."

"Yes. Exactly. Or maybe they'd just want to take you and learn how you can do the things you can do."

"Take me where?"

"Away," she said. She made certain to keep her voice firm. "Away from *me*, Cory."

"Oh."

"I'm not trying to scare you, Cory, but I want you to understand just how important this is."

Cory was staring at her, his eyes wide. She reached out and caressed the side of his face. His skin felt warm.

"Mom?"

"Yes, baby?"

"What I did last night with the window?"

She nodded for him to continue.

"Well, it's never happened that way before."

"What do you mean?"

"I mean," he said, "I knew the window was about to break before it did. Just like Aunt Patty knowing the songs that were gonna come on the radio."

Ellen nodded. She suddenly felt very cold.

"I think it's getting stronger," he said.

## 2

That night, after Cory had gone to bed, Ellen finished the bottle of red wine while seated at the dining room table, staring at the fork. *She* concentrated on it, but the fork did not move. Never could. Yes, Aunt Patty had been able to predict songs on the radio, but it had been Ellen's brother who had moved drinking glasses across countertops, and who had willed a Matchbox car to roll across her bedroom floor. She didn't want Cory to know that part, though. Not after everything that had happened.

Kept staring at the fork. Rubbing her temples while narrowing her eyes. Thinking, *Spin around for me, why don't you?*

After a while, she began to feel foolish. And a little lightheaded.

She heard Cory call out in his sleep, so she got up and went to his bedroom door to peer in at him. He was still asleep, though the sheet was twisted about his small frame. A fitful dream, she supposed. And on the heels of that, she wondered what her son's dreams might look like, what things might be stirring to life inside his head. *You know the garden gnomes? The ones in the back yard?* She could feel the hair along her arms prickling to attention, so she crept silently back down the hall toward the dining room. Once the last drop of wine had been emptied from her glass, she fished her cell phone from her pocket and pulled up her brother's contact info.

She was thinking of the photo on Cory's bulletin board, her son propped up on her brother's shoulders, the two of them caught forever in mid-laugh. For a brief time, her brother had been nearly like a father to Cory.

*Goddamn you.*

She unblocked her brother's number, then called it.

Pressed the phone to the side of her face.

It was hot against her sweaty flesh. When she looked down at her hand on the table, she saw that it was trembling.

A sterile robo-voice came on the line to inform her that the number she had dialed was no longer in service. Couldn't say she was surprised, knowing him. And maybe that was for the best. Maybe this would have been a mistake.

*Goddamn you.*

As if she expected anything different.

She disconnected the call.

# CHAPTER FIVE
# MIZUCHI

## 1

A little over three thousand miles west of the suburban Maryland neighborhood of Mariner's Cove, a recovering addict named Brian Russo opened his eyes. He had spent the better part of his adult life accustomed to waking up in unconventional locations—unfamiliar apartments, the backrooms of bars and strip joints, small-town jail cells, an alleyway or two, and on at least one occasion, he'd come into a state of semi-consciousness while splayed on his back on the cold marble floor of an otherwise empty cathedral. He had awoken folded like a paper doll behind the wheel of his own vehicle more than once (and at *least* once behind the wheel of someone else's vehicle), blessedly propped up on the shoulder of the road with the engine still idling, as if God Himself had seen fit to take the wheel and ease him to safety while he lay slumped and unconscious in the driver's seat. He'd roused himself to some semblance of awareness in haylofts and barns belonging to shotgun-wielding farmers in midwestern No-Man's Land, straw in his hair and with his clothes stinking of cow shit. On some of these occasions, the face that gawped down at him, prodding him with a shoe or the elongated barrel of a shotgun, was just as unfamiliar and inhospitable as the location itself. He'd been robbed, beaten, and gotten into fights along the fetid waterfronts of downtown Baltimore, though the details of these occurrences were always hazy and disjointed upon waking—scattered pieces of a jigsaw puzzle that were never meant to be assembled. All he had were the scrapes and bruises to confirm those things had actually *happened.*

But that was the old Brian Russo. It had been approximately two years since he'd been that person—a guy whose mouth always tasted of vomit and whose clothes perpetually reeked of day-old sweat; a guy who'd been tossed out of Vegas casinos and roadside diners with equal measure; a miserable cretin who'd suffered from everlasting shakes and a jittery, nervous-eyed countenance. So, when he opened his eyes on this particular morning, he found himself in his own bed. Which, in a way, had become the most unusual thing of all.

The first few months of sobriety had been the toughest. The drugs were easier to quit than the booze—he still craved the booze—and he'd suffered through what seemed like countless setbacks and relapses before he found himself shambling forward for a time along what his AA sponsor liked to call the Straight and Narrow. It had been his hope that once he'd gotten over the proverbial hump, things might begin to level out in steady, measurable increments—that he might begin to feel *normal* again, whatever the hell that meant. When was the last time he'd felt normal? He couldn't remember. In fact, what the hell *was* normal? He'd been zombie-walking through most of his adult life, cotton-mouthed and sweat-sticky, and greeted upon waking by a raging hangover like some dedicated if not particularly trusted friend—all of these things for so long that "normal" had become an alien concept.

There *was* no proverbial hump: that was something that took some time for him to learn. Sobriety had no finish line, unless you counted death as the ultimate finish line; there was only continual forward momentum, a tortuous Bataan Death March of clear-headed abstinence, one foot in front of the other with no visible line on the horizon. What's that old saying about a journey of a thousand miles beginning with the first step?

The trick, he'd learned, was to forget about the notion of a finish line. Just get it out of your mind. Sobriety was a slow and never-ending crawl, flat on your belly like a snake, and you had to learn to be grateful for every agonizing inch of ground gained. And after a time—and if you're lucky—the clarity of the world might just reveal itself to you.

This morning felt different. He rolled over and winced at the unforgiving California sunlight knifing through his apartment windows. His meager belongings were packed into cardboard boxes and stacked by the front door of the tiny one-room efficiency. He hadn't had a sip of alcohol in over a year, but there was a cottony pulsing in the center of his head that felt very much like a hangover. It worried him.

*A bad dream*, he thought. He couldn't remember the last time he'd had a dream of any variety that he could recall upon waking, yet this one's pulsating afterimage seemed to resonate with alacrity behind his eyes. And it left behind the residue of anxiety like a foul taste in his mouth.

Perhaps the nightmare had been nothing but the accumulation of stress over the move and the new job that waited for him clear across the country, in New York. That certainly made sense. The nightmare itself made no sense—as it quickly faded from him, he found he could only now recall the vague memory of some impossible ouroboros constricting in a never-ending gyre. It had been a snake, an enormous one, and it had been either running from or chasing something. Or someone.

He sat up and looked around the sparse apartment. Mr. Ming had been kind to rent him this dump so cheaply, and had been kinder still to employ him while he struggled to find his footing on the west coast after . . . well, after all that had transpired back east. The gig in New York wasn't anything spectacular, but it was a doorway to get him back on track to the thing that had once been his lifeblood. The Straight and Narrow.

At least, he hoped.

## 2

His apartment was above Mr. Ming's Chinese restaurant, which was where he not only worked but typically ate his lunch every day. The place was empty this afternoon—it really didn't start to fill in until dinnertime—so Brian was the only patron. He took a seat at the counter, glancing out the wall of windows that looked out upon the steamy blacktop of El Segundo. He watched idly as women in biking shorts strutted by on cell phones and vehicles glided silently along in the blazing white heat of midday. Across the street, a young man with bleached hair broke off bits of a hotdog bun which he tossed to a gathering of frenzied gulls on the streetcorner.

Lily came over, poured him a glass of ice water, and smiled prettily at him. She was one of Mr. Ming's daughters, a wry creature in her early twenties whose expressions always indicated the knowledge of some great truth much more advanced than her physical age. Now, Lily's smile faltered as she set the water pitcher aside. She studied his face.

"You look like you're deep in thought," she said to him.

"Do I?"

"It's not a familiar look for you."

Brian laughed. "I thought you were going away this weekend," he said.

"Kai is sick. Father needed me here today."

"But what about your trip? Lake Tahoe with your friends? You've been talking about it for months."

"There'll be other trips," she said. "Couldn't leave the old man in the lurch."

"You should have said something to me. I would've covered for you."

She laughed. Her father, kind as he was, refused to let Brian work behind the bar or even as a server, because, according to him, people came to Chinese restaurants to be fed and waited on by Chinese people. Not by whatever Brian Russo was.

"It's okay," Lily told him.

"Yeah, well, I know you were looking forward to it, and now I feel bad for you."

"Lake Tahoe isn't going anywhere. Unlike you. How long will it take you to drive to New York City?"

"About a week, if I commit to ten-hour days behind the wheel. But I'm in no rush. The job doesn't start until the fall, when the students come back from summer break. It'll give me some time to find a place to live, get myself together."

"I'm proud of you, you know."

"It's just some low-key gig at a college radio station. No big deal."

"Still," she said, a sly smile overtaking her face, "it's what you're meant to be doing. Not washing dishes and delivering meals and all that stupid bullshit. You're very good at the radio thing."

"Yeah? How would you know?"

"I've listened to your shows."

"How the hell did you manage that?"

She lifted her cell phone from behind the bar and wagged it at him. "There are old recordings of your shows online. Didn't you know that?"

"I did not," he said, and rubbed the scruffy side of his face with the palm of one hand. "I surely did not."

"Who's the Air Man?"

It had been years since he'd heard that moniker. Something about it unsettled him. "An enigma wrapped in a riddle."

Lily frowned. "I don't understand."

"No one does. You're not supposed to understand the Air Man."

She shook her head, confused but smiling at him nonetheless. But then something behind her eyes went dark. "There's something bothering you," she said, studying him more closely now. "I can see it in your eyes, man."

"You think you know me so well, huh?"

She leaned her elbows on the bar. "Tell me what it is," she said.

"Just a bad dream."

"I like bad dreams."

"You do?"

"I like having them and I like hearing about them."

"No one likes having bad dreams."

"I do." She looked insulted.

"If you say so."

"Tell me," she insisted.

"I dreamed of a dragon," he said.

"Well, that's fitting. It's the Year of the Dragon, you know." She jerked a thumb over her shoulder, to where the statue of a jade dragon sat on a shelf among a bunch of ceramic sake cups. "What exactly was this dream dragon up to?"

"I don't really remember now, except that I woke up covered in sweat and feeling anxious." He shrugged, his mind hazy with the memory of the nightmare. "Maybe it wasn't even a dragon. Maybe it was a snake. I can't really remember now."

"What was it doing in the dream?"

He considered, recalling so little of it now, except for a great spiral of coils, forever rotating, rotating, rotating—more a feeling than an actual image, now that he sat and thought about it. But wasn't that the way with all dreams?

"The snake, or the dragon, or whatever it was, it was moving fast," he told her. "It was either chasing something or *being* chased. I couldn't tell. It's just the feeling I got." He shook his head, suddenly embarrassed. "I don't put a lot of meaning in stuff like that."

"Stuff like what?"

"Dreams."

Lily shrugged, as if to show indifference in his belief. Brian had known her for about a year and a half, and had been working for her father here at the restaurant for much of that time. She had witnessed him relapse on just one occasion, when he'd come through the restaurant drunk and belligerent because he'd lost his keys and his cell phone, and Lily had ushered him through to the back of the restaurant and up the stairs to his apartment before her father could hear him upsetting the customers. She'd had a spare key and had unlocked the apartment door for him, had followed him inside, and had watched as he flopped down on the mattress which lay on the floor in a slant of moonlight. He assumed she had likely removed his shoes for him, because his feet had been shoeless the next morning, his Nikes set neatly on the floor at the foot of the mattress. She had never mentioned what had happened to him, nor was she aware of the extent of his addictive behavior; she'd never known him at his worst and he never told her about his past. But she was smart—smart enough to know that there was something dark and dreadful and haunting about the night he'd come through the restaurant drunk and shouting, something that ran deeper than a single evening of too much drinking. He knew that she noticed the way his hands always seemed to tremble, and how he always drank a glass of ice water with his lunches instead of a beer. There were things that the booze and the drugs had done to him that he'd never be able to shake, no matter how long he remained sober: the wear and tear of his poor decisions was etched not just on his flesh but carved straight down to the bone. He knew Lily could see it festering inside him like a disease.

"Dreams have many meanings," Lily said. "They say if you dream about a creature being chased, it may mean someone close to you is in danger."

"Yeah? Who says that?"

"My grandmother, for one."

He smiled humorlessly at her. He wanted to say that he no longer had anyone in his life who might be considered close to him, who would reach out whether they were in distress or not. He'd alienated anyone who had ever meant anything to him years ago. And in the stark, shameful light of his sobriety, he found he couldn't blame them. Not one bit.

"What else can you remember?" Lily asked.

Additional pieces of the dream were drifting back to him now. "I remember something about water. Like, maybe the snake was *in* water? I don't know, Lily, it's all really hazy to me now."

"It sounds like Mizuchi."

"What's that?"

"A water deity that takes the form of a serpent. Mizuchi is mentioned in the chronicle *Nihongi*. It breathes poison on the land, killing all people who pass by it."

"Sounds like a bad dude in need of a breath mint."

"My grandmother used to tell my sister and me the story when we were kids. In the story, Mizuchi was defeated by a warrior named Agatamori, a descendant of the *Kasa-no-omi*. In *Nihongi*, Agatamori cast three gourds into the water, which floated, and he challenged

Mizuchi to sink them. Mizuchi was an arrogant prick who couldn't resist a challenge, so Mizuchi changed form to sink them, and as it did, Agatamori killed it. So I guess you don't have to worry too much about it. Mizuchi is dead."

"Well, that's a relief," Brian said.

"When do you leave for New York?" Lily asked.

"Right now," he said, and set some cash on the bar, even though he hadn't eaten anything.

"That's too soon! My father will be upset he missed you."

"Your dad knows. I'm sorry, but I've never been good with goodbyes."

"There's nothing good about goodbyes," Lily said.

"You're right. Come around and give me a hug."

She came around the bar and hugged him.

"Say goodbye to Kai for me, too," Brian said. "And tell your dad thanks for everything. He's a good man."

"He thinks you're a good man, too. Deep down inside, I guess." She smiled, winked at him. "He says you seem like someone who's brave and honest. Someone who will do great things one day."

"I'll settle for keeping out of trouble," he said, and left that place.

# 3

Brian Russo drove east through the desert. All his worldly possessions, which amounted to very little, were boxed up in the back of the Soundwave, which was the name he'd given to the old conversion van. It was a 1994 Chevrolet, jet-black, except for the mural of howling wolves airbrushed along the sides. He bought it two years ago, after arriving in California, with what little money he still had to his name. He figured he could sleep in it if it came to that . . . and that was exactly what he'd done for the first couple months out here in the Golden State. He got it for a song, and the airbrushed wolves on the side spoke to him, because they reminded him of the Air Man. The Air Man had once owned a leather motorcycle jacket with a pack of howling wolves embroidered on the back. In the early days, the Air Man had started every broadcast off with a howl.

The Air Man, whose actual name had been Gary Manheim, had been in his mid-forties when Brian, who had been only twenty-one at the time, had started working as an intern at the Rockville, Maryland radio station. With his long, silvery ponytail and stark black cowboy hat with alligator teeth stitched into the band, the Air Man was truly larger than life. His face—hawkish, weather-worn, with startling aquamarine eyes—was plastered on billboards up and down the Baltimore beltway, and his whiskied voice was instantly recognizable whether it was on the radio or on the other end of a phone at three in the morning, speech slurred, police sirens whirring in the background. Brian had once heard a radio executive comment that the Air Man's voice was what driveway gravel would sound like if you poured honey over it and taught it to speak. However you'd describe him, there was something ubiquitous about him, as if the Air Man was a thing that had existed long before the beginning of time, and would continue to perpetuate long after the planet was swallowed up by the sun.

"*Communion*," the Air Man had said on one particular evening as he lay slouching in a booth of some Baltimore bar, a Lucky Strike propped behind one ear, his coke nail tap-tap-tapping on the sticky tabletop. Brian had shown up to drive him home but, as had become their custom, wound up staying and drinking with him for the remainder of the night. "That's the business we're in, Russo. I'm not fucking talking about *communication*, man. That part's bullshit. I'm talking about *communion.* It's a goddamn spiritual condition. We're cosmic fucking preachers, you and I."

"I'm not preaching anything," Brian reminded him. "I'm doing production bullshit behind the scenes. *You're* the preacher, man."

"And it's not just a radio show," the Air Man continued, as if he hadn't heard Brian speak. He ran one broad index finger around the rim of his whiskey glass. The fingernail on his pinky was elongated to a claw and painted black. His knuckles were bejeweled with pewter rings, one of which looked like a tiny skull with ruby eyes. "Take radio waves, for example. Do you know what radio waves are?"

"Waves of sound."

"You fuckin' imbecile, *no*," said the Air Man, though with no real animosity. In fact, he was grinning at Brian, his teeth no different than the sharpened incisors of a wolf. Quite often, Brian hypothesized that the Air Man *was* part wolf . . . or at least the possessor of some lupine characteristics. That rim-running finger popped up beside the Air Man's hawkish snout, and its tip glistened with whiskey. "They're waves of fucking *light*, not sound. People don't realize that. Our speech, it's carried in those waves, buoyed by them, like apples in a goddamn barrel of water. If you could see them, they'd look like the crinkly black-and-white static on an old television set. Sometimes, you know, I think I *can* see them."

"Really?"

"So," the Air Man went on, "what do we do?"

"What *do* we do?" Brian asked.

"What we *do*," said the Air Man, that index finger still propped up beside his nose, "is we crank a few knobs, radiate a few dials, tweak and praise the tower. All hail the holy fuckin' tower, am I right? And then you know what you've got?"

"What?"

"Only the biggest goddamn megaphone in the history of the modern world. Yet, see, it's a megaphone dispersing *light*. Look at us, Russo. You and me, kid, we're capable of throwing up to three motherfucking kilohertz into the stratosphere while reclining in cushioned office chairs, sipping Irish cappuccinos, doin' some blow during commercial breaks—"

"That's mostly you," Brian interjected.

"—and patting down our shirt pockets for our last pack of Lucky Strikes," the Air Man said, not to be interrupted. "You and me, kid, we're traveling through the stars on chariots of fucking light born from our own mouths and our feet never even leave the ground."

"You," Brian said.

The Air Man frowned. Groused, "Whaaa?"

"You," he repeated. "Not me. I'm not the one on the air."

The Air Man flapped a hand at him. "You're missing the goddamn point, kid."

"Then what's the point?"

The Air Man leaned closer to him from across the table. "What we do for a living, Russo, is commune with the whole fucking universe by speaking in sharp, flashing pulses of literal *lightning*. We're proselytizing on a daily basis to the fucking cosmos, my man. Is there any other profession on earth closer to being God? Think about it! Fuck doctors, fuck pastors and poets and propagandists—*we're* the real deal, kid. You and me. I've been doing this for over two decades, Russo. My voice on the air. Think about that. Those beams of light travel on, ad infinitum. Just how far do you think my traveling lightshow is by now?"

"What do you mean by 'far'?"

"Into space. The fucking vainglorious cosmos. Lightning fired from my throat in order to *commune* with whatever exists out there in all the vastness of space."

Brian had opened his mouth to say something in response, but the Air Man was already rising from the booth, his red, glassy eyes surveying the scant crowd of career alcoholics and scantily clad waitresses sidled up to the bar. He wended his way toward the restroom, where he stayed for an inordinate amount of time while Brian ordered them each another round. When the Air Man finally returned, his eyes were still red and glassy, but there was a renewed vigor in his step. He dumped himself into the booth then slid a small plastic baggie of cocaine over to Brian.

"The sky is literally the limit, Russo," the Air Man said.

Brian took the baggie and did his own disappearing act into the restroom. When he returned, he found the Air Man smoking a cigarette despite the NO SMOKING sign hanging above his head, and there was the distinct impression of a lipstick kiss-mark high up on his left cheek which decidedly had not been there earlier in the evening.

"It's all about magic," the Air Man said, as if there had been no break in their conversation. "That's what I'm here to teach you, Russo."

"Maybe I already know something about magic," Brian retorted. The coke was already shuttling through his system; he could feel his heart beginning to race while sweat flooded into his sneakers. This had become a routine with them, and although Brian recognized the pitfalls on the horizon, he was powerless to derail it.

The Air Man exhaled a plume of cigarette smoke toward the ceiling. "Is that right?" he drawled, his shiny silver eyes narrowing. "What do you know about magic, Russo?"

The Air Man's empty whiskey glass was still on the table between them. Brian focused his gaze on it, and he sensed the Air Man following his stare. He summoned in his mind the thing that he always summoned, a thing that he had learned to summon during his childhood, the spark of a distant star, and the rocks glass slid several inches across the tabletop. It left a contrail of moisture in its wake.

"That," said the Air Man, seemingly indifferent, "is one hell of a good trick, kid."

Some months after that, the radio station moved the Air Man's show from midnights to the morning rush hour. The Air Man did not *do* mornings; it was a sentiment he'd made abundantly clear during his increasingly contentious meetings with the radio station's head of programming. But the Air Man did not have much of a leg to stand on: despite a growing listenership, he'd been responsible for a few FCC lawsuits lately, and the head of programming thought switching the Air Man to morning rush hour might ensure he'd be on better behavior (or at least not show up drunk). Ultimately, the Air Man had conceded, though under one condition—that "the Kid," Brian Russo, would co-host the show with him.

"I don't know how to host a radio show," Brian had explained to him one evening while seated at some other nondescript bar in downtown Baltimore.

"Co-host," the Air Man corrected. "And anyway, you don't have a choice, because, see, *I* don't have a choice. I don't trust myself to do mornings. They shouldn't either, but they're all a bunch of shortsighted, pencil-pushing corporate slugs. So, I'll need you to pick up my slack, Russo, of which there will be plenty."

"Gary, I don't—"

"I need someone *there*, kid. You get me? Anyway, you wouldn't be the host, or even the co-host. You'd be . . . like, my sidekick. Get it?"

"I don't know." He'd already done a bump of coke earlier in the night and his eyes suddenly felt like they were about to jitter out of their sockets. In fact, they felt too big for his skull: like a couple of jellyfish about to wobble down his cheeks. Across the table from him, the Air Man was growing incrementally more and more wolflike.

"You're not *hearing* me, kid. Check it out: *you don't have a fucking choice.*" The Air Man cleared his throat, dug a pouch of something out from the inner lining of his motorcycle jacket, and said, "Anyway, I've already had them rename the show."

Three weeks later, *Mornings with the Air Man and the Kid* was on the air.

*The Kid.*

It was a hit. Soon, Brian Russo's face joined the Air Man's rugged mug on all those billboards around the city. They went into syndication after their first year, were heard in over two dozen markets, and there was suddenly money to be had. If things were also beginning to spiral out of control, Brian was unaware of it at the time. True, the Air Man had become increasingly unreliable and insouciant, but Brian had found his own groove and was able to pick up much of his mentor's slack on the air when necessary. He had a *knack* for this radio shit, a *talent* for it. He felt buoyant and unstoppable, just the way the Air Man had described it to him that night in the bar: *Is there any other profession on earth closer to being God?* Their nights were now free, and they spent them in a dizzying haze of alcohol and drugs and women. Sometimes they never went to bed, and would arrive at the station after a night of binge drinking to do their show, popping speed and snorting junk up their noses to keep themselves awake and on fire. They frequented strip clubs and dive bars, and there was always someone—or a group of someones—more than willing to buy them round after round after round. Brian bought a sports car and didn't have it for a week before he wrapped it around a tree, miraculously walking away with just a superficial bump on his head. He began to accumulate DUIs, collecting them like baseball cards, and a few drunken disorderly charges. He engaged in some physical altercations at his local watering holes (and once with a police officer), but what did any of that matter? It was part of the gig, wasn't it? It was part of what made the Kid shine. That giant face of his was always peering down at him from between the buildings in Rockville, in downtown Baltimore, all the way out on the Eastern Shore.

*The sky is literally the limit, Russo.*

There had been an intern at the radio station named Vicki Parsons whom he had dated for a few months until too many failed romantic encounters prompted her to say, "You know, you should think about going to rehab." She was a bland, clinical girl of twenty-two, with an earnest face and the calculating brown eyes of a barn owl. She rarely joked, so he had known right away that she had meant what she said. So, he had broken up with her.

One evening, while he and the Air Man were at a bar entertaining a drunken cadre of young coeds from a nearby college, the Air Man slid an empty rocks glass toward the center of the table and said, "Hey, Russo, how 'bout you show these fine young ladies that wicked magic trick you do."

Brian's head was spinning. His heart felt like a jackhammer smashing his ribs to powder.

He stared at the empty rocks glass. Concentrated on it. Focused.

Nothing happened.

The women went "woo-hoo!" as if this was all some gag, and even the Air Man had a stupefied grin plastered to his face, one wolflike incisor gleaming beneath the dim, smoky lights of the bar.

He concentrated some more.

Focused.

Couldn't move the glass.

*He couldn't move the glass.*

"Your nose is bleeding, kid," the Air Man muttered, nodding casually in Brian's direction.

Brian looked down and saw a constellation of red splotches on the tabletop. He brought a hand up to his nose and his fingers came away slick with blood.

"Great trick," one of the women crooned. "A spontaneous bleeder!"

The laughter that followed felt like a cannon blast within the confines of Brian Russo's skull.

He went home that night, set up a line of empty shot glasses on the kitchen counter, and stared daggers at them. Not a single one budged. And when he finally surrendered in defeat, he looked down to find the front of his shirt covered in a spackling of blood, and little red droplets on the floor between his bare feet.

Late one afternoon, after they'd gone off the air, Brian was approached by the head of programming, a thin, mealy-mouthed character named Houseman, who pulled him into a small room and closed the door. "We're taking things in a new direction," Houseman told him. Then he opened a portfolio, and showed him the mockup design for a new show called *Russo After Dark.*

"I don't get it," Brian said.

"Gary's finished here. We're gonna tell him before he leaves today. We don't expect him to take it well, so we're planning to run repeats of the show all week, starting tomorrow morning."

"You're *firing* him? You can't do that."

"We've approached him about going to rehab. He told us to go fuck ourselves. He keeps racking up these FCC fines and we told him we'd hold him personally and financially responsible for them, but he didn't care. His mind is fried."

"But the show's doing great."

Houseman frowned. "Were you even in the same studio this morning?"

This morning *hadn't* been great: the Air Man, still a bit inebriated from the night before, was barely conscious for the first forty-five minutes of the show. During a commercial break, he vanished to the bathroom, a bit more pep in his step. By hour two, he was rambling about the vainglorious cosmos, which turned into *screaming* about the cosmos, which turned into him smashing a chair on the console. Brian, who admittedly hadn't been feeling top of his game himself, ate up airtime with some longwinded anecdotes and fielded calls from listeners, only to have the Air Man grow restless with Brian's blathering and pick fights with the callers. The kid working the board through the glass couldn't dump the slew of curse words that erupted from the Air Man's mouth fast enough.

"You know how he is. We've gotten over this kind of thing before," Brian said, and in his swampy, muddled mind, this sounded like a reasonable retort.

Houseman snapped the portfolio shut. "It's all just too much, Brian. This whole thing is a powder keg. We never know what he'll say or do, or if he'll even show up half the time. He was tweaked out of his mind all morning on the air, for Christ's sake."

"I'm holding it down."

"*He's* holding *you* down. You've got a promising future in this industry. You're *good*. Don't hitch your cart to Gary's horse."

"He *made* my fucking cart!"

Houseman visibly recoiled. He sidestepped toward the door. "You can do the new show on your own or you can pack up your things today, too. Take an hour or so to think about it, will you?" Before leaving the room, Houseman scanned him from head to toe. "And clean yourself up, will you? You don't look much better than he does."

Brian went down to the station's cafeteria where he pounded cup after cup of black coffee. His hands shook, he craved a drink, and his head felt like it was filling up with steam. He wasn't sure how long he'd been sitting there when he looked up and saw the Air Man standing before him. Decked out in his trademark cowboy hat, leather motorcycle jacket, and rings of polished pewter, he looked like some creature summoned from the depths of Brian's imagination. He even had a moment to consider whether or not Gary Manheim, a.k.a. the Air Man, was, in fact, a real person.

"They tried firing me, so I quit," the Air Man said. His eyes were as big as light bulbs and there was a purplish bruise at one corner of his mouth. There was a dryness to his lips that was severe enough to create audible little clicks when he spoke. His signature clothing no longer looked rakish and cool; he was too thin and swimming in that motorcycle jacket with the wolves on the back, and the brim of the cowboy hat caused a shadow to fall across his face that made him look gaunt and soulless. The Air Man reached into his jacket pocket and took out a pack of smokes. "Come with me, Russo."

"Where?"

"Wherever. What does it matter? We can go to the fucking moon, kid. Sail between the stars."

Brian shook his head and looked down at this coffee. "I don't think so."

The Air Man came around beside him and gripped his shoulder. His fingers felt like the talons of some predatory bird. "You and me, kid—we'll be gods."

Brian just kept his eyes down. The Air Man's wolfish countenance was reflected on the surface of the coffee that Brian clutched with both hands. "I'm sorry, Gary, but I really don't think so."

He waited for the Air Man to grow angry, to become irate, to pick up a chair and send it sailing across the cafeteria like he'd done back in the studio. But all that happened was that talon-strong hand loosened its grip and slid slowly off Brian's shoulder.

"Go fuck yourself then," the Air Man said. Simple as that.

When Brian eventually looked up, it was to glimpse his mentor striding on his boot heels out of the cafeteria, wallet chain swinging like a hypnotist's pocket watch from the sagging seat of his faded blue jeans.

Brian eventually *did* go to rehab, but it had nothing to do with what the intern Vicki Parsons had said, or even with what had gone down with the Air Man. Instead, the producer of *Russo After Dark*, Mark Wells, had approached him about Brian's own increasingly undependable and erratic behavior, both on- and off-air. "You need to spend some time in a facility, man. You need to clear that fuzz out of your head and dry out."

They had been having lunch at a pub in Rockville, and Brian couldn't help but hoist his vodka tonic and salute Mark with it as he spoke.

"It's not even a big deal," Mark went on. "There's no stigma to it anymore. My brother-in-law has gone three times, and he manages a successful hedge fund."

"Three times, huh? Sounds like it really does the trick."

"I'm being dead serious here, Brian. Forget liver cancer. Forget cirrhosis and hepatitis and whatever crazy, irreversible damage you're doing to your body. I've never known you to be the kind of guy to think too far into the future, so let's focus on the here and now."

Brian sipped his drink then set it down. He smacked his lips, placed both palms flat on the table, and exhaled a breathy, "Ooooookay."

"Your bullshit is going to get you fired," said Mark. "You keep this shit up, the suits are gonna quit putting up with it."

"Come on, Mark. The ratings are great. We've made *Talkers* Heavy Hundred. And you saw the Arbitron ratings."

"No one's questioning the show's success," Mark assured him. "But you know how the suits are about these things. Not to mention the sponsors. You can't start alienating your sponsors, Brian. No one wants to field calls from the goddamn FCC on a monthly basis, not to mention soccer moms who happened to catch you drop the F-bomb on the air when they're hauling around a carload of kids. Did you forget so quickly what happened to Gary?"

"Good old Off the Air Man," Brian mused.

"This isn't a joke," Mark said. "That shit with the councilman—"

Brian waved a dismissive hand. "Hey, fuck that guy."

"You've been cited with a willful violation of Section 73.1206 of the Commission's regulations by broadcasting that councilman's telephone conversation without authorization."

"How do you remember all those wacky numbers?"

"Because I deal with them on a weekly basis due to your bullshit,

Brian. That's how." Mark opened his briefcase and placed a stack of papers on the table between them.

"What's this?"

"Challenge Broadcasting is considering coming after you civilly to recoup these fines, citing your deliberate and continual disregard for company policy."

"Yeah, that sounds like me." His drink was low and he was scanning the crowd for their waitress.

"You're not Howard Stern, Brian. Hell, you're not even Gary Manheim when he was at the top of his career. You could have been, maybe, but you thought living this way"—he nodded in the direction of Brian's near-empty vodka tonic—"was more important."

"Christ, Mark. It's bullshit. They're just trying to hassle me."

"You either do a stint in rehab or get buried under these fines and lose your job. And if you think it'll be a cakewalk to get picked up by some other station, I can promise you that won't be the case. So, not such a tough decision, if you ask me."

He mulled it over for less than ten seconds. Watched the Air Man smash that chair down on the console in his mind's eye.

"Fuck it, fine, I'll go to fucking rehab. You happy?"

"Oh, I'm giddy, can't you tell?" Mark muttered, tucking the paperwork back inside his briefcase.

He did the twenty-eight days. And for a time, things were okay. Or at least he fooled himself into believing that—believing that he could still knock some drinks back or do a bump of coke without repercussions. Pot to mellow him out at night, speed to kick his shit into gear come morning. The same old routine, but with a slightly different paint job. Like he was fooling the entire world.

Somewhere in the midst of all that chaos, he'd met a woman. She was a stunner, with auburn hair, bright green tiger's eyes, and a killer figure. She was also the opposite of all the other women Brian had gone out with previously, primarily due to the way she made him feel about himself. Her name was Donna Holmes and she was an advertising executive for a small company out of Columbia, Maryland. He had found her pragmatism and dedication to her job endearing, the perfect ying to his yang. Conversely, she had thought him charming in his quirkiness and rising celebrity, and frequently claimed that he made her feel younger, freer, happier than she had felt in a long time. They dated casually for two months before deciding to become exclusive. Five months into that exclusivity, they began talking about more serious things. Out of nowhere, she seemed to get hung up on the fact that she was older than him, if only by a couple of years. "My mother was nearly five years older than my pop, and my pop still had the good sense to die first," he had told her, grinning. They had been at a nice restaurant in the Little Italy section of Baltimore. She was on her first and only glass of red wine; he was on his third glass of Dewar's.

Yet a year into that relationship, it became apparent that Donna's concerns over the discrepancy in their ages had little to do with the fact that Brian was physically younger than she was, but that he was trapped on some hazy merry-go-round of booze and drugs that had stunted his maturity. She had asked him to cut back on his drinking; he had refused. She had asked him to seek help and go to rehab again, to which he had explained that his "problem" was defined not by how he felt about himself but by other people's haughty judgments. She had asked him to consider all of what she was asking of him, for the sake of their relationship and his own health; drunk when this conversation had taken place, he had knocked some empty bottles off the kitchen counter, given her the finger, then marched out of her apartment.

She didn't respond to his calls for the next three days. When he finally caught her coming up the walk after work—he had been perched on her front stoop for over an hour in the cool, gray, misting rain—she had stopped short and just glowered at him. There was a confluence of emotions etched there on her face, but the one that stood out most to Brian Russo was the fear that he could suddenly see behind her eyes. Her fury with him, he could understand. Her disappointment and regret and sorrow, sure. But fear? He had never laid a hand on her.

"I just wanted to see you," he said. "I just wanted to talk to you."

"There's nothing we need to say to each other."

"I thought we were going to get engaged. You know, like we talked about."

"So did I."

"So what? You're saying you've changed your mind? We're done? Just like that?"

"Things change." Then she frowned and looked away. "Or maybe they don't."

"Don't do this," he begged. "Let's straighten things out."

"I want a partner. Not someone I have to look after, like a child."

"Just give me a chance." He rose up off the steps. He was cold, wet, shivering, and couldn't look more helpless if he tried. Yet she backed away from him, that look of fear flashing once again behind her eyes.

"Please," she said, her voice hardly audible. The umbrella she carried cast a darkness over her face. "Please don't do this. I just want to get inside."

"I love you," he said.

Donna shook her head. "No," she said. "No, you don't. If you did, we wouldn't be here. I've put up with a lot of stuff from you because, Brian, *I* loved *you.* So, I know what that's like. And I would have stuck by you if you really wanted to beat this and get help. I really would have. All you had to do was *want* to beat it. All you had to do was be brave enough to *try.* Love is bravery. So, yeah, I know what it means to love someone. And you don't have it for me."

"Donna . . ." He came down the steps, reaching out to touch her, but she drew away from him. "Why do you look so afraid?"

"Because I *am* afraid," she said.

"That's ridiculous. I've never laid a hand on you. I've never hurt you. I never would."

"You have."

"I meant not physically."

"What's the difference?"

"The difference is I've only been hurting myself," he said.

She made a sound that sounded like a sad, pitiable laugh. "If you believe that, then you really are hopeless . . ."

"I can change," he said—that desperate, clichéd phrase.

"I hope you can," she said. "It just won't be with me."

"Donna—"

"Please," she said, cutting him off. He could see that she was crying now. "Please move out of the way. I don't want to see you again. I just want to get inside. Please."

He had stepped aside and watched her enter the apartment. He remained on the sidewalk for nearly ten more minutes, getting soaked as the rain began to fall in sheets, holding out hope that she might open the door and rescue him. Forgive him. But that did not happen. Eventually, he turned away and headed up the block, hands wedged into the soaking wet pockets of his jeans, his long, stringy hair hanging in dripping tendrils in front of his eyes. Two blocks away, when he glimpsed the welcoming neon lights of Nat's Pub on Water Street, he went inside.

He was fired on a Monday. He thought of the Air Man appearing before him in the cafeteria, looking like a skeleton wearing people clothes. Eyes like light bulbs. Something about that memory caused a tightness to form around Brian's throat, and he staggered down the hall of the radio station and out through a fire exit to a back alley to gasp for air. And when he finally caught his breath and looked up, he could see his own massive face grinning down at him from a billboard across the street.

He never bothered going back inside to clear out his office.

When the blackouts began, he had been surprisingly unconcerned. If he woke up in a strange place with no memory of how he had gotten there, well, that was just the cost of doing business. There were no worries when some club bouncer slapped him awake, having found him passed out under a table or propped unconscious against a urinal in the men's room. Some nights, he'd find himself wandering the streets of Baltimore for hours because he was too fucked up to remember where he lived. When he could no longer pay rent, he lit out for parts unknown, desperate to lose himself among the human detritus in various, shady parts of the country. When he ran out of money, he sold his car and hitchhiked.

"I used to be able to move things with my mind," he explained to some woman at a bar one night.

"Me too, fella," she'd replied.

He was missing Donna, and so he used the last of his cash to hop a train back to Maryland. He kept hearing her voice in his head saying, *Love is bravery.* But when he got there, he found himself too terrified and ashamed to visit her. Instead, he found himself standing on the front porch of a ranch-style house in a quaint, suburban neighborhood called Mariner's Cove.

The door was opened before he could knock.

Without a word, Ellen McBride took one look at him then pulled him into a sisterly embrace.

## 4

He was reminded of all this bleak history as he drove due east through the desert along a vast, dark, empty ribbon of asphalt. Clipped to the visor above the steering wheel was a photo of Brian with his nephew on his shoulders. The pure joy on both their faces was unmistakable.

It was the photo that abruptly jarred an additional piece of last night's nightmare loose: an unwavering certainty that the serpent from his dream had, in fact, been chasing his nephew.

Cory.

# CHAPTER SIX
# THE GNOME

Some men armed with chainsaws were standing beneath the midday sun, slicing up the tree that had fallen across Mr. Zachs's front lawn into big wooden cartwheels. Cory watched from the bay window of his house, his legs drawn up underneath him as he sat perched on the cushioned bench within the window's curved alcove. He could see Winona Orem sitting cross-legged in the grass on her front lawn across the street, her head cocked at a curious angle as she, too, stared at the men. Above the peaked roof of the Orems' house, the sky was so bright and blue and cloudless, it was as if the storm had been nothing more than a dream.

Cory's own dreams had been frighteningly vivid the past couple of nights. Upon waking he could remember very little detail, except for a singular recurring image. An avid reader, he had read *The War of the Worlds* and had even seen the movie; it was one of those Martian war machines that kept surfacing as the central image in all of these nightmares. A thing that resembled an iron spider, impossibly tall, and under whose ominous shadow Cory was powerless to outrun. He had gotten too old to crawl into bed with his mother after suffering a nightmare, so upon waking in the middle of each night, he'd remained in bed, the sheets pulled tight to his chin, his heart pounding, and his body swaddled within his pajamas feeling slick and oily with sweat.

Now, just thinking about that giant steel spider from his dreams caused the gnome inside Cory's head to stir.

He imagined it as one of those garden gnomes in the back yard because that was the closest thing he could compare it to when he tried to think hard about it and ferret it out, although he knew that wasn't exactly right. Just like he knew the thing haunting his recent nightmares wasn't actually a Martian war machine or a giant mechanical spider, but rather something his mind couldn't quite comprehend. These were just the closest things he could compare them to.

The night of the storm, the gnome had shown him the kitchen window imploding moments before it actually had. Not really in an image, though, like something projected onto a movie screen, but more like the flexing of a muscle that *told* him it was going to happen then caused in him a reaction. He'd thrown his hands up to arrest those jagged blades of glass in midair as if by instinct. Similarly, when he went to move the fork that his mother had placed before him on the dining room table, he felt the gnome come awake and flex like a muscle, same as normal. If, of course, any of this could be called normal.

It started months ago, and not with the movement of objects with his mind, but with a heightened sense of "premonition"—a word he had eventually looked up online. He and his mom had gone out on a Saturday evening for one of their "date nights" (which was what his mother called them, much to Cory's embarrassment). The night had started with pizza at the Pink Penguin, which was his favorite because they always globbed on the cheese, followed by a movie at the Harbor 9 Cinemas. It was after the movie had let out and he and his mother were walking across the darkened parking lot toward their car when Cory happened to look up and spot a man. He was disheveled, with his hair in unruly corkscrews and the collar of his polo shirt tugged up at one corner. He didn't look homeless but there was a distinct sense of disassociation coming off the man, one that any person could sense whether they possessed any special abilities or not. The man was weaving between two parked cars and appeared to be patting down the thighs of his jeans, the way someone might if they were looking for their car keys. Yet Cory instinctively knew this man was not feeling around for car keys. He knew, inexplicably yet unequivocally, that none of the cars in that parking lot belonged to this man. As he followed his mom down a row of parked vehicles toward their car, Cory turned his head to continue staring at the man. He felt it, all right—that low-res hum, as if all of a sudden he was walking not through a movie theater parking lot but the main thoroughfare of a nuclear power plant. The flesh on his arms pricked into sensitive knobs and he felt a tingling at the base of his spine. Across his brain, like a roadwork sign on the side of the highway, blazed the word *DANGER* over and over again. It was as if something inside his brain had awakened and opened its eyes to alert him to this fact.

It was at that point that the man had looked up and met Cory's stare. The man's jittery movements ceased, and he looked suddenly like some hapless forest creature hypnotized by the glare of oncoming headlights. Even from their considerable distance, Cory recognized insanity blazing in the man's eyes.

*He's either done something horrible or he's about to,* was the next thing to rocket through Cory's mind. *Maybe anyone who takes a good look at him would see that, but they wouldn't know it the way* I *know it. They wouldn't feel it the way* I *can feel it.*

The man's eyes had remained on Cory as Cory climbed into the car. When his mom pulled out of the space and motored across the parking lot to join the mass exodus of vehicles leaving the movie theater, Cory turned around in his seat and, looking out the rear windshield, was terrified to see the man was *still* staring at him.

That time, there was no resolution to the story, no evidence that his feelings toward the man had been right. However . . .

Another time, he had gone to a local farm and petting zoo with Davey, Winona, Kip Ransom, and their parents. The petting zoo stood on a large plot of farmland where, far in the distance, sat a ranch house with a collection of ancient TV antennas on the roof. Closer toward the road had been three separate barns, one of which housed pigs, another horses, another cows and sheep. In between the barns were fenced areas where goats and chickens were kept. There were little gumball machines filled with oats where, for a quarter, you got a handful of feed which the goats would eat directly out of your hand. As they walked from one barn into the next, Cory's friends yammering on about one thing or another while their parents talked in low voices behind them, Cory was accosted once more by the electrical vibe of foreboding. It was similar to the sense he'd gotten from the strange man in the movie theater parking lot, only this time, he could not readily see the source of it. But then movement in his periphery caused him to jerk his gaze upward, where he spotted a pair of legs clad in filthy overalls dangling from a hayloft. The legs belonged to a boy who looked just a few years older than Cory, with longish brown hair, a hefty build, and dark, shifty eyes. The boy was already staring down at Cory when Cory looked up at him, and that dark gaze caused the thing inside Cory's head—the gnome—to stir. The boy was burning pieces of hay with a lighter as he watched Cory and his friends parade through the barn. Tendrils of smoke spiraled up from the burning strands of hay before going out. Cory had paused for a moment, still staring up at the older boy while everyone else remained oblivious to him. It was enough to make Cory wonder if he was seeing an actual human being up there or if the older boy was, in fact, a ghost. Once he smelled the burning hay, though, he knew the boy was real, which was when he realized he had been *hoping* the boy was a ghost. The gnome flashed that word across his brain again—*DANGER*—and Cory began to feel his skin crawl. When the older boy's lips parted in a humorless grin that exposed an uneven file of teeth the color of turpentine, Cory quickly averted his eyes and hurried after his friends toward the barn's exit.

Some days later, he and his mother had been watching the evening news during dinner when a report came on about a tragic fire that had occurred at that very same farm. The fire resulted in two of the three livestock barns burning to the ground. A number of animals had died in the inferno and two firemen had been injured. The fire chief was interviewed and explained that they were looking into arson as the cause of the fire. Then various members of the family were interviewed, and they were all distraught and teary-eyed, except for the farmer's son, whose meaty face and dark, shifty eyes had been immediately recognizable to Cory the moment he appeared on the screen.

"Big fire," was all the boy seemed capable of saying to the reporter, his eyes lost in some dalliance while he kept glancing over his shoulder at the heap of wood that lay smoldering in the background. "Big fire. Real big fire."

Lately, the gnome—or whatever the heck it truly was—seemed to be on heightened alert. And while he'd lied to his mother about some things during their conversation the night before, he'd been telling the truth when he told her he thought the gnome in his head was getting stronger.

Not that he felt guilty about lying to her: *she'd* also been lying to *him*. It had something to do with the story she had told him of Aunt Patty—some of it resonated with truth while other parts had resonated, well, falsely. Like his mother had deliberately changed up some of the details so that he wouldn't know the truth. At the time, Cory had roused the gnome and had instructed it to reach out and gently poke his mother's thoughts. It was an almost tactile sensation, like pressing a finger to the pliable surface of a bowl of Jell-O. He had felt a part of his mother's mind yield to the gnome's prodding finger. She hadn't seemed to notice.

It was the first time he'd ever tried to breach someone's mind, and he wasn't sure the gnome could actually do it. Turned out, the gnome couldn't see things very clearly with that poke—for Cory, it was like watching shapes move behind a panel of frosted glass, only in his own mind—but it was enough for him to discern that the thing his mother had been keeping from him had not been about Aunt Patty but about Uncle Brian. He'd instructed the gnome to poke a bit deeper, aware that this was some form of violation of his mother's person space, personal *thoughts*, but doing it nonetheless. He could suddenly sense that while Aunt Patty *had* guessed those songs on the radio, it had been his *uncle* as a boy who had moved the drinking glasses and the Matchbox car with his mind. Why had his mother lied to him about that part? He forced the gnome to dig deeper and found himself surrounding by other, murkier thoughts that presented more like emotions having to do with Uncle Brian's drinking. Anger on his mother's part. Anger and sorrow.

He'd been too cautious to have the gnome linger inside his mother's head for too long, so he'd extracted that poking finger before he could properly see whatever else she might have been keeping from him.

Outside on Mr. Zachs's front lawn, those guys with the chainsaws were standing in a cloud of sawdust. Cory pressed a palm against the window and could feel the windowpane vibrating from the sound of the saws. He barely heard his mother come up behind him.

"I have to meet some clients and show a house today," she said, tying her hair back in a ponytail. She was dressed in beige slacks and an untucked white blouse, and despite the weariness that was so clearly imprinted on her face, Cory thought she looked pretty. "In fact, I'm showing houses all week, but I'll mostly be in the neighborhood, and I won't be gone for too long. Maybe we can do Pink Penguin for dinner one night, if you want."

"I want to talk to Uncle Brian."

She paused in the middle of adjusting her ponytail.

"Please," he added.

"Why? What brings this up?"

He rolled his shoulders.

"I don't think so, Cor," she said, and then slipped into the kitchen.

Cory climbed down off the window bench. From the kitchen doorway, he watched his mother gather up a collection of brochures off the counter, a bottle of water tucked under one arm.

She must have sensed him standing there. "It's not a good idea," she said, not looking at him.

He just stared at her.

Exasperated, she stopped fumbling with the brochures and just rested her palms flat on the counter. Still not meeting his gaze. "Listen," she said. "I know you and Uncle Brian were close. And I understand that as a young boy who's got no father figure around, that going through . . . well, going through changes . . . that you might have questions about . . . well, about anything . . ." She cleared her throat, then turned to face him. Smiled wearily, though he could tell she was frustrated and at a loss for how to talk to him about this. "Jesus. What

I'm trying to say is that it's just you and me, kiddo. Always has been, always will be. So, if you need someone to talk to, then talk to me. I'm here. Okay?"

"Can I talk to you now?"

She glanced at the clock on the microwave, then down at the brochures fanned out along the countertop. "Yes, of course," she said.

"That thing about moving drinking glasses and toy cars and stuff," he said. "It was really Uncle Brian who could do that, right?"

A look of surprise washed across her face. He thought about peeking inside her head again to see the thoughts shuttling around in there, but didn't dare do it in that moment. Anyway, the stiffening of his mother's posture was all the confirmation he needed.

"I want to talk to him," he repeated.

"Well, you can't," she said flatly, regaining some composure. "Whatever questions or worries you might have, we'll figure them out together. You and me."

"That's not fair."

She looked at him, eyes narrowing the slightest bit. That ponytail had been hastily tied, and a strand of his mother's long, flaxseed hair now hung down, bisecting her face into two distinct halves.

"The answer is no, Cory. That's final."

"Mom—"

"I wouldn't even know how to reach him. It's been two years."

"It's not fair!"

The brochures slid off the counter and scattered to the kitchen floor. A second later, the bottle of water dropped out from beneath his mother's arm as well, bounced once between her feet, then rolled toward the refrigerator. His mother turned to him, and he knew she was wondering if he'd made those brochures slide to the floor or if it had been the gentle breeze blowing against the loose section of tarp still taped over the kitchen window.

She gripped him about the shoulders. "I'm your mother. It's my job to protect you. I won't let anything bad ever happen to you. Do you hear me? I won't let anything bad happen to you ever again."

"But—"

"We're done talking about this," she said.

She kissed his forehead, then bent down to gather up the brochures from the floor. He could see that her hands shook, and he suddenly felt guilty for pressing the issue. He got down on his hands and knees to help her.

Inside his head, the gnome opened its eyes. Just as the gnome had done the night before, it prodded at the air between Cory and his mother. Less like touching the surface of a bowl of Jell-O this time and more like inserting an index finger through the tenuous surface of a soap bubble. Only the bubble didn't burst but instead allowed the gnome's probing mental finger momentary access. Fleeting, fragile, but there, nonetheless.

For a millisecond, Cory thought he could sense what his mother was feeling.

Helplessness.

"Hey," she said, glancing at him as they both collected the fallen brochures. "The night of the storm. You said something like, 'It found me. It's trying to get me.' What did you mean by that? What did you think was trying to get you?"

"I don't remember," he said, which was another lie. He was just too embarrassed to say it out loud.

*The Martain war machine.*

*The iron spider.*

Inside his head, the gnome closed its eyes and went back to sleep.

## CHAPTER SEVEN

# "HAVE YOU SEEN THE INSTRUCTIONS?"

## 1

The door between the garage and the house opened and Miranda appeared, framed in a rectangle of surprisingly harsh, surprisingly bright light from the hallway. Danver winced, as if he'd inadvertently looked at the sun. He quickly pulled an old bedsheet over the door, which was still propped upon the two sawhorses in his garage looking like something about to undergo surgery, before she could get a good look at it.

"What have you been doing in here, Michael? You aren't even showered yet."

"Showered for what?"

"We're going over to the Harrisons' tonight, remember? I told you at lunch."

He had no recollection of discussions about the Harrisons. He had no recollection of lunch, period.

"It's their annual luau. How could you forget?" She frowned. "It's so dark in there. What in the world did you do to the windows?"

She was referring to the windows in each of the three garage doors. Yesterday afternoon, he had cut up some brown paper shopping bags and taped them over the windows, so that no one would be able to see in.

"Oh," he said, wiping his hands down the thighs of his pants. His palms were sore and had given way to a crop of blisters from his constant cleaning and polishing of the door. "The sunlight's too harsh on my eyes."

"And I suppose the plan is to keep my Escalade parked in the driveway while you take up all this space in here, doing whatever it is you're doing?"

He wasn't taking up that much space, but he didn't think it was really the *space* Miranda was commenting on—it was the overall *strangeness* of the setup in here. Sure, he knew it. The door beneath the sheet was occupying only one of the three garage bays, but he had dragged over his workbench and a metal shelving unit so that he could clip work lights to them and angle their beams on the door while he cleaned and polished it. The way the lights were angled on the sheet which now covered the door, it looked like an operating table. He'd been in here toiling away all day yet only now did he realize how bizarre this arrangement might look to an outsider.

*That's you, Miranda,* he thought then, looking at her standing there in the doorway, dressed in a smart silk blouse and linen slacks, her hair pinned back, her cheekbones freshly rouged. *An outsider.*

Clementine scurried into the garage, looped once around Danver's ankles, then barked at the door beneath the sheet.

"Go on," he told the dog. "Get."

"What in the world have you been working on in here for the past couple days, anyway?" She was glowering at him from the doorway while fumbling with a tennis bracelet that she was trying to clip to her wrist. "What's under that sheet?"

"It's nothing. I'm just tinkering."

Clementine growled at the door but did not go near it. Seemed afraid of it, in fact.

"Well, whatever it is, I'm glad to see you're finally tackling a hobby." She patted her thigh and the dog bounded up the stairs and back into the house. "Don't forget to shave, too. You've got that white sandpapery look."

She left, taking the harsh light with her.

# 2

There were already a dozen people at the Harrisons' when Michael and Miranda Danver arrived that evening. Tables were set up on the flagstone patio out back, and some of the men were playing volleyball in the yard. Ken Harrison was manning the outdoor wet bar, festive in a Hawaiian shirt and straw sombrero. He was flirting with Mia Bridgeport, equally nonchalant in cut-off denim shorts and a canary yellow bikini top. With her year-round tan, toothpaste-commercial smile, and ridiculous fake breasts, Mia looked just as proficient as any woman Danver, back in the days of his adolescence, had ever glimpsed between the glossy pages of men's magazines.

"She's perfectly starved for attention, that girl," Miranda commented to him, already halfway through a gin and tonic. With Miranda, drinks tended to materialize in her hands as if by magic. "It's really quite pathetic. Did I tell you she submitted an article to the magazine?"

"Mia Bridgeport did? What's it about?"

"A grave injustice, apparently. She's concerned that the Mariner's Cove Oyster Princess is a title too rigidly reserved for teenage girls. Can you imagine? She's proposed an additional designation, one that would no doubt incorporate her own demographic."

"What demographic is that?"

"Married, with fake tits."

"That's a bit harsh."

"She'll want her own title, too, I suppose," Miranda continued. "Oyster Queen, perhaps? Oyster Shooter? Take me to your Oyster Bed?"

"You're in a rare mood tonight," he quipped.

Miranda's humorless laugh was all the response he needed.

Chinese lanterns strung around the perimeter of the Harrisons' backyard winked on, a patterned array of reds and greens, and the men in the volleyball pit cheered. The Harrisons' teenage daughter—a dour, pale-skinned bulimic whose name Danver could never remember—ghosted across the patio toward the sliders. Her stringy black hair hanging in her face, she looked like she'd just stepped out of a Japanese horror movie.

Donnie Bridgeport strutted over to the Danvers, a Budweiser in one hand. "Hello, Miranda. Hey there, doc. Beautiful night, huh?"

"It's wonderful," Miranda said. "And I must say, Mia looks lovely tonight. I remember when I could wear a bikini top like that."

"Ah, you're still lovely," Donnie said, kissing the side of Miranda's face. "How about you, doc?"

"I've never worn a bikini top, Donnie."

Donnie laughed, his mouth full of veneers. He took a chug of his beer, then said, "Figure out a use for that door yet?"

Danver felt a muscle spasm above his left eye.

Miranda asked, "What door is this?"

"Piece of junk," Donnie said. "Me and the doc, we fished it out of the cove a couple days ago, right after that storm. We used our *ingenuity.*" The fool actually tapped his temple with an index finger. "Ain't that right, doc?"

Danver summoned a smile to his face that felt like a prosthetic.

"A *door*?" Miranda said, confounded. She looked at Danver. "Is that the thing you're keeping hidden under that sheet in the garage? That thing you've been obsessing over like some mad scientist while my car is parked in the driveway?"

"I'm not obsessing over anything," Danver said.

"It's like he's trying to bring Frankenstein's monster to life in there," Miranda told Donnie. "It's all very suspicious and clandestine. And it's a *door*? Like, a regular old *door*?"

"I told you about it," Danver grumbled, growing increasingly irritated. "Morning after the storm. I told you—there's a door down there."

"You should've seen it, Miranda," Donnie said, as if Danver hadn't spoken a word. "The thing was standing straight up out of the water behind my house, like you could turn the knob and just walk right through it."

"And where would that lead you?" she asked, grinning at Donnie over the rim of her gin and tonic.

"To places vast and unknown!" Donnie professed, spreading his arms wide. Beer sloshed from the neck of his bottle onto the Harrisons' patio.

"Is my husband causing trouble?" Mia asked, joining them. She wore a cocktail umbrella tucked demurely behind one ear.

"I was just telling your husband how lovely you look tonight," Miranda said. Then she looked around the yard. "Where's Olivia?"

"Ken said she wasn't feeling well," said Mia.

"And he still went ahead with the party?"

Mia shrugged. Then she cocked her head and made a perfect *O* with her mouth, but no sound came out. She had her platinum hair pulled back into a sporty ponytail and wore no makeup. Her bronzed cleavage was spangled with tiny brown freckles and appeared to sparkle with glitter. She was staring directly at Danver.

"Oh," Donnie said, sounding as if he'd been stung by a wasp. "Oh, oh—doc—"

"Oh," Miranda parroted, and took a step back from Danver.

"What is it?" Danver said. They were all staring at him now.

"Your nose, doc," Donnie said, pointing at Danver's face. "It's leaking like a sieve."

Danver felt a tickle along his sweaty, brine-tasting upper lip.

Mia grabbed a fistful of cocktail napkins from the nearby bar and thrust them at him. He clutched them in a ball and blotted his face. The napkins came away sodden with blood.

"What is going *on* with you lately?" Miranda said. "You've had a nosebleed for the past two days."

"Hay fever," Danver said, then nearly choked when he swallowed a glob of bloody mucus.

"Gotta put your head back, doc, and pinch your nose," Donnie suggested.

"No," Ken Harrison said, ambling over from behind the bar. Everyone turned to look at him. "You have to put your head *forward* and stick a wadded Kleenex between your gum and upper lip."

"I thought you were supposed to put your head between your knees?" said Miranda.

"I'm a fucking heart surgeon, I can handle a bloody nose," Danver said. It was perhaps a bit too aggressive, because both the Bridgeports as well as Ken Harrison all seemed to take a step back and said nothing further.

"Go inside and clean yourself up, dear," Miranda said to him.

Still blotting his nose with the napkins, Danver detached himself from the others and crept into the Harrisons' house through the rear slider. He passed through the kitchen and down the hall to the bathroom with his head back in order to staunch the bleeding, feeling his way with one hand along the wall. In the bathroom, he cleaned up, then stood for a while examining his reflection in the thick-framed oval mirror above the sink. A muscle spasm in his lower left eyelid made it look as if he was winking at himself.

Sure, his nose was bleeding, but it didn't hurt. His back teeth, on the other hand, felt like someone was taking a jackhammer to them. Every time he inhaled too sharply, the pain grew worse. It was as if the nerves were exposed, although when he opened his mouth before the Harrisons' bathroom mirror and examined his molars, they appeared to be fine.

Wincing, he rummaged through the Harrisons' medicine cabinet. When he came upon a bottle of aspirin, he shook a few into his hand, popped them in his mouth, then slurped up some water from the faucet. He splashed cool water on his face, too, then went back out into the hall.

A sleek black snake lay coiled on a bed of bone-colored gravel inside a terrarium that sat on a table in the hall. There was a heating lamp shining through the top of the terrarium, causing the pattern of scales along the snake's spine to shine. Danver bent the slightest bit at his waist and peered in at the creature. He knew nothing about snakes, and only saw them on occasion in the wild when he was out in the yard and spied one wriggling through the underbrush. The snake in the terrarium was spooled around itself, its arrow-shaped head resting atop its coils. A pair of eyes, shiny as twin dollops of India ink, seemed to collect Danver's own gaze with all the authority of a tractor beam.

*No, not a snake, but something close. Something similar. Something that would make me think of a snake, because that's the closest thing I know to compare it to . . .*

The thought accosted him out of nowhere, leaving him unsure as to its meaning. The snake was not a snake? It made no sense . . . yet something about it tickled the back of his brain, connected somehow to the strange dreams he'd been having lately.

There was a reflection in the glass of the terrarium: a figure framed in a lighted doorway at Danver's back. He stood and turned to see Olivia Harrison standing in the doorway, gazing out at him with dim, unfocused eyes. She was not dressed for the party, but rather wearing a pair of old sweatpants and a T-shirt. The short bob of her hairdo stood in corkscrews, as if she'd just awoken from a nap.

As Danver stared at her, Olivia retreated back into the room without uttering a word. Danver saw her shadow—elongated and distorted—swim across a section of garish wallpaper before that disappeared, too.

He went to the open doorway and peered into the room.

It was a small parlor, with a bookshelf against one wall and an upright piano sitting at an angle in one corner. The walls were outfitted in ugly fleur-de-lis wallpaper and a smattering of tiny pictures in gold frames. Olivia Harrison stood in the middle of the room, staring down at what looked like a camping chair, the foldable kind with a canvas seat and no back. As if sensing Danver's arrival in the doorway, she turned and faced him.

"I keep trying to get up and leave the room," she said, her voice a monotonous drawl, "but I can't seem to do it. It's funny, you know? I've got a party to get ready for, the guests will be here any minute, yet I can't seem to get my . . ."

She lowered herself onto the camping chair with an audible sigh. Her feet were bare, and Danver could see her toes curling into the weave of the carpet; it appeared to him as such an intimate gesture, for whatever reason, that he was suddenly embarrassed for her.

"And once I sit down, it's like I can't get up again," she said. There was a dryness to her voice, an audible abrasion—someone crawling through the desert dying of thirst.

Danver just stared at her. He had become aware of an incessant buzzing in the center of his head, one that was steadily increasing in volume and somehow connecting to the throbbing pain in his molars. He thought of the door hidden away in his garage and was desperate to get back to it. He didn't like leaving it unattended.

"Every time I try," Olivia went on, her moist eyes jittering in Danver's direction, "I just sit right back down again. Isn't that funny? Isn't that *strange*?"

The buzzing in his head growing louder still, Danver felt like he was ascending through an archipelago of boiling, roiling storm clouds. Snippets of last night's dream struggled to return to him.

"Ken is very concerned about me," she said. "He thinks I'm sick. Who knows? Maybe I am."

Danver manifested a smile, sweat collecting within the fleshy pockets of his face, then took a step backward into the hallway.

"Wait," Olivia said. There was an urgency in her voice that did not comport with the medicated look on her face. "Have you seen the instructions?"

"Instructions for what?"

Oliva Harrison's eyes grew even more distant. Slowly, like someone in a trance, she shook her head. "I'm not sure," she said, her voice slow, like a record being played at the wrong speed. "I don't know what they mean. But I've seen them. They're all over the neighborhood. It's like someone keeps going around in the night and leaving them for us."

"Why would someone do that?"

Olivia just shook her head.

"I don't know what you're talking about," Danver said.

"You need to look for them. We all do. They're . . ." She faltered, as if hunting for the right word. "They're *important*."

"Should I go get Ken?" Danver asked.

"Ken thinks I'm ill. Thinks I'm sick. Is that what you think, too?"

"No," he said. He was thinking about the door again. That snake curled upon itself in that terrarium in the hallway, too. "No, Olivia. I don't think you're sick."

"You'll keep an eye out for the instructions?"

He nodded. "I will."

"Good man."

Danver waited a moment more, watching as Olivia Harrison's head lowered on her neck in slow, lethargic increments, her distant gaze focused on something beyond the carpet at her feet. Uncomfortable, he slipped quietly back down the hall, past the snake, through the kitchen, and back outside into the cool summer evening.

Instead of rejoining the party, however, he snuck around the side of the Harrisons' house, squeezed himself through a space in the hedges, then came out on the sidewalk that ran parallel to Bay Road. The evening had cooled, and the sky had transitioned to a depthless purple hue. Stars were already poking through the firmament out over the bay. The Harrisons' house was only a few doors down from his. As he stood on the curb, the perspiration dissipating from his cooling flesh, he looked up Bay Road and could see his home unimpeded and without difficulty, lighted from within and superimposed against the backdrop of the night sky on the crest of the bluff. It brought him a measure of peace to stand there watching his house, knowing that everything looked fine from here. Knowing that the paper bags were still taped over the windows in the garage doors so that no one could peek inside.

The buzzing in his head was gone.

His back teeth no longer ached.

"Hey, sport," said Ken Harrison as he came around to the front of the house. A glass of scotch clinked against his wedding band. Donnie Bridgeport tottered along a step or two behind him. Both men joined Danver on the curb as Ken dug a pack of cigarettes out of the breast pocket of his obnoxious Hawaiian shirt. At least he had ditched that ludicrous straw hat. "You still having trouble with the old schnoz?"

"It's fine now," Danver said, flossing an index finger beneath his nose.

"Not to get on your case, Michael, but are you sure it isn't anything more serious? Healthwise, I mean? You've been looking a bit pale and undernourished lately."

"I'm fine."

Ken offered him a cigarette, but Danver declined.

"Ah, that's right," Ken said. "I don't suppose heart surgeons smoke.

Even retired ones."

Danver, who was standing in a puddle of industrious blue light issuing from a nearby streetlamp, felt suddenly exposed to them in a way that he couldn't readily comprehend. His head was beginning to throb again, though the buzzing in both his skull and his molars remained silent.

"I saw your wife," he told Ken. "She didn't look too well, either." The *either* had been automatic, and he silently hated himself the moment the word slipped out of his mouth. It felt like an acknowledgement.

"She's been off lately, for sure," Ken said, leveling his booze-bleary gaze on him. "She's been sick the past few days and we nearly wound up canceling the party. Could also be menopause."

"Man o' war," Donnie said, as if in his own conversation. Donnie turned to Danver. "Do you own a firearm, doc?"

"A what?"

"A gun." Donnie pointed a finger-gun at him and mimed pulling the trigger.

Danver had a compact revolver tucked away on the top shelf of their bedroom closet, but he said, "No."

"This guy's going all NRA on us now," Donnie said, cocking a thumb at Ken Harrison.

"There's nothing wrong with wanting to protect yourself and your home," Ken said. He smoked, and ash from his cigarette blew into his glass of scotch. "A number of houses have been burglarized in the Cove over the past year, and it's only a matter of time before that sort of thing makes its way to this street. I don't relish the idea of waking up in the middle of the night to a large black man in a ski mask standing over me holding a knife."

"Jesus Christ," Donnie said, chuckling. "So, it's a black man, is it, in this deranged fantasy of yours, Kenny? Yes, of course it is. And how would you know the fellow's black if he's wearing a ski mask?"

"You're missing the point," Ken said.

"I'd like to know how you're going to shoot this mask-wearing black man as he stands over you with a knife, too," Donnie went on. "You gonna sleep with an AR-15 under your pillow?"

"I've been traveling from one corner of this country to the other my entire career," Ken said, "and I can tell when bad elements begin to creep into an area."

"Maybe so," said Donnie, "but there are no bad elements in Mariner's Cove."

Ken Harrison shook his head. His ice cubes clinked together in his scotch glass as a smug smile stretched across the terrain of his face. Danver noticed Ken's daughter sitting on the front steps of the house behind the two men, the glowing cyclopean ember of her own cigarette a solitary pinpoint the darkness beneath the portico.

"You have to keep your eyes open, Donald, and pay attention to the small details," Ken explained to Donnie. "It starts with a little graffiti in Gladstone Park, some spray paint on the playground up at the high school. Then packages start disappearing from people's porches. Some cars get broken into in the middle of the night. Then there're a few break-ins out by the highway. Next thing we know, this tidy little bayside community of ours becomes a whisper on the circuit."

Donnie laughed. "The hell does *that* mean, 'a whisper on the circuit'? Sounds like a Dylan song." He crooned the phrase while snapping his fingers, decidedly more Sinatra than Dylan.

"Bad elements, they talk," Ken said, ignoring him. His smile had vanished, and his face had grown tight, somber. "That's what it means. There's a whole underground network. They find a community that seems like an easy mark, and the word spreads. Bad elements. Next thing you know, we're infested. They slip in through the cracks."

"Jeez, man," Donnie said, waving a hand at him.

"Don't be so obtuse, Donnie. Here—take a look right here. Do you see?" Ken stepped off the sidewalk into his yard and pointed at the stamped concrete. Beneath the light of the streetlamp, Danver could see that a child had decorated the sidewalk with colored chalk symbols.

"So what?" Donnie said, also staring at the sidewalk. "I don't get it. What's the big deal?"

"It used to be no one came down Bay Road unless they lived here," Ken said. "This street ends in a cul-de-sac, a dead end. But the past couple days, I've come out to get the mail or drag the trashcans to the curb, and this is what I find, all over the sidewalk."

"Big deal," Donnie said. "Some kid was playing hopscotch."

But it did not look like a hopscotch grid to Danver. The drawings, done in stark white chalk, looked like crude little hieroglyphics of some unknown origin and meaning. And for whatever reason, in his head, he heard Olivia Harrison ask:

*Have you seen the instructions?*

It rang there like the strike of a gong.

"You're missing my point, Donald-san," Ken continued. "There are no kids living on Bay Road young enough to do something like this. Chalk drawings on the sidewalk? We're talking six-year-olds, Donald. My daughter's the youngest scamp on the block and she's fifteen."

"Sixteen," Ken's daughter corrected from the front porch, her voice startling the three of them.

"So what?" Donnie barked, waving a hand at Ken.

"*So,*" Ken articulated, "it means that *strangers* have been matriculating into our comfortable little community. This has never happened before. It's a glimpse into the future. It's the slow creep I've been talking about. Bad elements, graduating their way toward us, virulent as a plague. It's an invasion."

"A whisper on the circuit," Donnie said, smirking.

"Increment by increment," Ken said, ticking at the air with an index finger. He finished his cigarette, crushed the filter on the sidewalk, then announced that he was heading back to the party.

"I'll be there in a minute," Danver said, and watched both men disappear around the side of the house again. He could hear raucous, drunken laughter back there. He thought one of the loud, obnoxious voices belonged to Miranda.

"It's not a kid," said a voice behind him.

Danver turned around to find Ken Harrison's daughter standing there, her long hair draped over one eye. Her pale skin looked luminous in the moonlight.

"What?" Danver said.

"My dad's wrong. It's not some kid who did this." She nodded at the chalk drawings on the sidewalk.

"Then who did?"

"A man. Some man."

"A grown man was making chalk drawings on the sidewalk?"

"I saw him," said the girl. "I came out here early this morning for a smoke on the porch. It was still dark out, but I saw him crouched right there, scribbling on the sidewalk with a piece of chalk."

"Who was he?"

"Beats me. I didn't get a good look at him. Like I said, it was still dark." She nodded her head in the direction of Bay Road. "He left a bunch of them all the way up the block. Go walk and see for yourself."

"Was he someone who lives around here?"

"Like I said, I didn't see him."

"Did you tell your father?"

"Why should I?"

"It's very strange," Danver said. He was staring at the chalk drawings again—those unusual symbols that, he suddenly realized, looked almost familiar to him. Had he seen them somewhere before? No; that was ridiculous. Still . . . they struck him like a song he may have heard in his youth, mostly forgotten but freighted with a hint of familiarity.

One of the chalk drawings in particular caught his attention. A large rectangle with four smaller rectangles inside it, two at the top and two at the bottom.

Danver felt something lurch in his chest at the sight of it.

He pointed at it and, to the girl, said, "What does that one look like to you?"

She looked down. Shrugged. "I don't know."

"Think about it. What does it look like?"

She said, "A door?"

"That's right!" Danver exclaimed, feeling a grin peel its way across his face. He was aware of a nervous energy beginning to infiltrate his body. "A door! Right. Very good."

When he finally looked up, he found that the Harrison girl was gone, and he was alone on the sidewalk. Much time had passed.

## 3

Once Miranda was fully unconscious beside him in bed, barricaded behind her sleep mask and a wall of pillows, Danver peeled away the blankets, quietly swung his legs around to the side of the bed, then insinuated his knobby, calloused feet into a pair of fleece-lined Gucci slippers.

He felt jumpy, his mind a cauldron full of snakes. When Clementine sat up and whined from the foot of the bed, Danver, startled, nearly launched out of his pajamas. He hushed the dog then crept out of the bedroom.

Downstairs, he stood for a long time in the center of the house in the dark. At the end of the hall, he could see the closed garage door, and imagined *his* door on the other side of it.

*Maybe,* said a tiny, ageless voice from the back of his head, *this isn't something that's good for you. Maybe obsessing over a door isn't healthy.*

He wondered if he should just get rid of it . . .

. . . yet that thought caused a tremor of panic to vibrate up through the core of his body.

*No,* he thought.

*Can't.*

*Never.*

In the garage, the door lay supine across the two sawhorses beneath the bed sheet, just as Danver had envisioned it a moment ago. He turned on the garage's feeble overhead light and then all the work lights so that the covered door took on the aura of an operating room again. With a magician's flourish, he whipped the sheet to the floor.

It was unrecognizable from the thing Danver had dragged out of the cove days earlier. He had cleaned it up, scraped the silt from its locking mechanism, scrubbed the algae from the wood, applied several layers of polish, buffed the brass knob and the iron numerals to a dull shine.

He ran a hand along its dark wood and its particular pattern of grain, unique as fingerprints, and that looked to his eyes as if there were symbols—were messages—embedded in the wood. Hidden there, just for him to decode.

*Have you seen the instructions?*

*They're* important.

He grabbed a flashlight from his workbench then went back through the house and out the backyard sliders. The night had grown cold, and a strong wind lashed at the trees between his property and the Bridgeports'. He crossed the street, the wind rippling his pajamas, and scurried in the direction of the Harrisons' house. He clutched the flashlight in one hand but had not yet turned it on; high above, the full moon, grinning like a skull, cast enough light on the ground to unfurl a shadow, long and distended, ahead of Danver on the pavement.

He turned on the flashlight once he reached the Harrisons' property. Kneeling on the sidewalk, he shined the light on the chalk drawing of the door. Yes, it was undoubtedly a door—*his* door. Yet it was the group of symbols that had been drawn *beside* the door that Danver now focused on. Together, the symbols looked like some sort of mathematical equation:

He traced a finger along each symbol in the equation—the equal sign, the infinity symbol, the shape that resembled a lowercase *m*. And was that what it was? An equation? Equals infinity m? How did he know that? Moreover, what did it *signify*, and how was it related to his door?

A gust of wind funneled down Bay Road, rattling the foliage and dispatching small tornadoes of leaves across the Harrisons' front yard. The sound was like the aggrieved moan of an animal hiding wounded in a cave.

A feeling: like something tightening inside his head . . .

Suddenly, Danver understood.

## 4

He arrived back at the house out of breath, adrenaline surging through his body. In his excitement, he made some racket coming through the back door which alerted Clementine, whose black, oil-spot eyes appeared glistening at the far end of the hall just as Danver entered the house. As he headed in the direction of the garage, Clementine pursued him down the hall, the dog's claws clacked on the hardwood floor.

In the garage, Danver dug through his workbench until he located a simple flathead screwdriver. He took it over to the door, his respiration coming in gasps now, his armpits swampy. Goddamn, but his heart was racing. He ran a hand down the entire length of the door—from the bottom to the four metal numerals at the top—just as Clementine ran in frantic circles around his ankles.

Danver wedged the screwdriver under the number 1, the first of the four digits. He worked the screwdriver up and down, up and down, until the nail surrendered from the wood and the number 1 was free.

Clementine growled then snatched the bottom of Danver's pajama pants in his mouth. He shook the dog loose, and Clementine ran in a circle around the door, barking.

"Quiet, you. Hush."

He repeated the process three more times: on the second number 1, the number 8, the number 3. Once they were all free and there was a collection of bent and rusted nails scattered on the floor at Danver's feet, he rearranged the numbers atop the door so that they resembled, as closely as possible, the enigmatic equation printed in chalk on the sidewalk in front of the Harrisons' house:

There.

Jesus, *there*: look at it.

Danver took a step back. His breath was puttering in labored gasps. The screwdriver fell from his hand and clattered to the cement floor.

This was *right.*

Whatever it was, this was *right.*

Clementine barked once—sharply—at the door again, then scurried behind Danver, as if afraid of something. The dog snatched up the hem of his pajama pants once more, tugged at them while growling.

"I said *quiet,*" Danver groused through gritted teeth, and then jerked his leg away from the dog.

Clementine slid across the cement floor and disappeared beneath the door.

And was gone.

Danver took another step back. He said the dog's name, patted his thigh. Approximated a toothy whistle.

Clementine did not reappear from beneath the door.

Grunting, Danver lowered himself to his hands and knees. The cement floor was chilly through the thin fabric of his pajama pants.

The dog was not under there.

"Clementine," he said, the timbre of his voice risen now. "Here, boy."

Nothing.

Well, not *quite* nothing—that buzzing was back, droning on in some distant corner of Michael Danver's head, and causing his back teeth to ache.

He picked up the screwdriver that he had dropped and rolled it beneath the door. When it breached the door's shadow, the screwdriver rolled *into* it, as if over a ledge, and disappeared.

Still on his hands and knees, Danver did not move for several seconds, perhaps a full minute. Perhaps even longer—who's to say? The practical, analytical part of him suggested going back into the house, locking the garage, and then burning the door in the yard first thing in the morning. But since the storm, the practical, analytical part of Michael Danver's brain—the part that had seen him through years of medical school and in the performance of countless open-heart surgeries—had become less and less prominent. In this moment, it was like a small voice muttering through a static-laden A.M. radio station. And it was being drowned out by the buzzing that was steadily swelling in his head.

He crawled toward the door then stopped, just as the top of his head connected with the door itself. *Bump.* The space between the door and the garage floor, as well as the rectangular shadow of the door stretching out along the cement, did not look unusual. In fact, it looked like a perfectly normal shadow. Nonetheless, he extended a hand along the floor, feeling the pebbly grit along the surface of the cool concrete. He paused just before his fingertips reached the edge of the shadow, but then continued.

A chill radiated up his arm. It wasn't wholly uncomfortable, except for the fact that it shouldn't have been emanating from the shadow at all. He inched his hand further and watched as his fingers vanished *into* the shadow, straight through the floor of the garage.

When he was just a boy, eleven or twelve, he had helped his father rewire the old farmhouse. The circuit breaker was old and unlabeled; his father had thought he had shut the power in a particular part of the house, but he had been wrong. It was not a sudden jolt of electrical current that had bolted up Danver's arm as he pried the socket from the wall with a screwdriver at his father's behest, but a numbing matriculation that took him several seconds to realize what was going on. Electricity trickling through the center of his arm, a numbness in his fingertips. A chill in the bone. His father had yanked his hand away before Danver even knew what was happening.

The feeling inside that shadow was very much the same.

Danver jerked his hand out and fell backward on his ass.

He brought his hand up to his face. Wiggled his fingers. Everything was in proper working order, every digit accounted for. The icy numbness had vanished the second he'd withdrawn his hand from the shadow.

*No, not a shadow,* he thought, *but a space beyond the shadow.*

He wanted to scream, but what ratcheted up his throat was a brittle, humorless laugh.

Then the lights blew out, dousing him in darkness.

# CHAPTER EIGHT
# GEORGETTE AND ALEX

## 1

Georgette Braswell was worried.

She had been concerned for several days now, ever since the morning after that terrible storm, when she'd found Alex standing in his underwear on their front lawn. She'd glimpsed him through the bay window very early that morning, just as she'd filled her coffee cup—her husband just standing there in the middle of the yard among downed trees, overturned trashcans, broken sections of their neighbors' lawn furniture. In his underwear.

She'd gone to the window, her mind struggling to reconcile what she was seeing. Opened the window and shouted to him. Alex hadn't responded, hadn't even heard her. She'd hurried out the door and stumbled through the wreckage in their yard, all matter of discarded debris from last night's storm, still calling out his name. His body a roadmap of gooseflesh and reddened from windburn, he had been staring off into some hazy distance, his dark eyes unfocused. In a trance, it seemed like. Georgette had slapped his face, and that seemed to do the trick. Awareness flooded back into her husband's eyes. He staggered backward, disoriented and groping at the air as he fell over a trashcan and into a tangle of tree limbs on the front lawn, cutting himself up in the process.

What had it been? Sleepwalking? According to Alex, he'd had no memory of getting out of bed and going outside. After coming inside, he had gone into the bathroom and soaked in a warm bath at

Georgette's insistence while she contemplated making a phone call to Dr. Fasil. Alex had never sleepwalked in his life, as far as she knew. And that faraway look in his eyes when she'd approached him out in the yard, like he'd been in some sort of trance . . .

It had frightened her.

It was nothing, Alex had later assured her. No, he'd never sleepwalked as a child, not to his knowledge, but it was just a single incident—should they really be that concerned? It was likely stress-induced, he'd told her; there was always some measure of stress related to Alex's job.

She wanted to believe him. But there had been other things she'd observed throughout that week, too. Smaller stuff: an uncharacteristic brusqueness, a disquiet almost, around Georgette and the girls—an overall detachment from the family in general, really. He hadn't touched her in bed all week; he appeared to fall asleep the moment his head hit the pillow. A change too drastic to simply be attributed to stress. Yet Georgette couldn't put her finger on it. There was a falsity about him now—that was how she thought about it. As if this man living in her house and sharing her bed all week was someone just pretending to *be* Alex Braswell.

Now, as Callie and Denise ate a late lunch in front of the television in the living room, the house phone rang. Usually, the only people who called on the landline were telemarketers, but Georgette answered it, nonetheless. It was Joe Peyser, one of Alex's coworkers at DelMar Tech, whom Georgette had met on a few occasions at company cookouts and work events. Surprised to hear his voice on the line, the first thing that jumped into her head was, *There's been an accident.* Despite Alex having spent the past several months behind a desk, given his new position at the engineering firm, she knew he often slipped out into the field to examine the progress of specific projects on the ground. Some of those sites could be dangerous, she knew. Just hearing Joe Peyser's voice on the other end of the line, coupled with that creeping yet ill-defined premonitory vibe she'd been hauling around with her ever since the morning after the storm that *something was wrong with Alex*, Georgette was suddenly certain something awful had happened to her husband.

"Hey, Georgette, I'm real sorry to bother you but I've been trying like heck to reach Alex on his cell, and he's not answering."

"Did you try his office line?"

"I'm *at* the office," Joe said. "Alex hasn't been in all week. Everything okay out there at the house?"

She did not answer right away. From the living room, she could hear *Miraculous: Tales of Ladybug & Cat Noir* coming from the TV. She heard Denise's high-pitched giggling, too.

"Hello? You still on the line, Georgette?"

"All *week*?" she said, her voice cracking on the last word. "He hasn't been in the office *all week*?"

There was a hesitation on the other end of the line—the barest hint of one, but it was there, nonetheless.

"That's right, ma'am," Joe said, a hair more cautious in his approach now, Georgette could tell. "Given the storm and all, I thought maybe I should check in with you folks, make sure everything was copacetic. It's not like Alex to miss a day, and when he does, he usually phones in ahead of time."

Georgette's face felt hot. She eased herself down on a kitchen chair and turned to stare out the bay windows. Remembering Alex out there in his underwear, gazing up at something she could not see just above the tree line, a lost expression on his wind-reddened face. Across the street now, the Lacey boy was riding his bike in the driveway. Going in circles, circles, circles.

"*Are* you okay, Georgette?" Joe asked.

"Oh," she said, snapping back to reality. "We're fine here, Joe. Everything at the house, I mean. I appreciate the call."

"Well, that's good. But listen, you should let Alex know that Tom McKeel's been asking about him. I don't want your husband to be caught with his pants down."

She couldn't help it—she thought of her husband standing in his boxer shorts on the lawn.

"You sure you're okay, ma'am?"

She weighed what she was about to ask, knowing it wasn't her place, even if Alex *was* her husband. "Joe, has Alex had any problems at the office lately? I'm worried about him. He's seemed unusually stressed."

"Not that I'm aware of. But he's carrying a lot of weight on his shoulders after the promotion. Stress is part of the job."

"Right. Okay." This gave her little solace.

"You *sure* you're okay, Georgette?"

"We're fine here, Joe. Everyone is fine. Alex is probably at a site somewhere. He isn't home. I'd keep trying him on his cell phone if I were you."

She remained sitting in the kitchen chair for some time after ending the call, watching the Lacey boy across the street describe never-ending circles on his bicycle. *Circles, circles, circles,* she thought, her mind suddenly abuzz with the word. *Circles, circles, circles.*

This was likely a misunderstanding, of course. An easy explanation that she would laugh off once she realized what it was. What *was* it? She checked her phone, opened the calendar app. Maybe he had scheduled some appointment for today that had slipped her mind? Georgette, always too busy with the girls' hectic schedules, could have easily forgotten about it.

The month of July, like all months, was full. Chiropractor, dance rehearsals, oil changes for the cars, orthodontist appointment, mammogram, bills due, swim club, book club, sailing club, pick up dry cleaning, an HOA meeting, grocery store, bank, playdates, hair appointments, potlucks, bake sale, hot yoga (if there was time): their lives summarized in a series of thirty-one gridded squares on the glowing white screen of her iPhone. But today, this random weekday, existed as a solitary empty square. Unpopulated. Conspicuous in its emptiness. An outlier, really.

Alex standing on the lawn in his underwear.

Alex staring up at the sky, not hearing her call his name.

*Why aren't you at work?*

When she finally turned away from her phone, she saw Denise, their six-year-old, standing in the kitchen doorway with an empty plate in both hands. Absurdly, she was wearing a metal colander on her head like a helmet.

"I ate the whole thing," Denise said proudly.

"Even the crusts?"

"Even the crusts."

"What's with that silly thing on your head?"

"It's mine," Denise said.

"Are you playing astronaut or something?"

"I'm not playing anything. It's not a game." Denise pushed her plate into the sink, then asked, "Can I have a snack now?"

"You just had lunch."

"I'm still hungry."

"What kind of snack?"

"Cookies."

"How about some fruit instead?"

Denise put a finger to her chin and said, "How about *half* of fruit and *half* of cookies?"

"You drive a hard bargain, but okay, sister. Go inside and I'll bring it in for you."

Denise gave her a thumbs up—a gesture she'd learned from Alex—then went back downstairs to the living room.

Georgette washed her face at the sink, still hearing the echo of Joe Peyser's voice in her head: *Alex hasn't been in all week. Everything okay out there at the house?* No, things were not okay out here at the house. She'd lied to Joe Peyser. If her husband hadn't been at work all week, where the hell *had* he been?

*Where are you?*

She felt her stomach twisting into knots.

She set to work cutting up an apple, dusting the wedges with cinnamon, then shaking a couple of Oreo cookies onto a fresh plate. She brought the snack down into the sunken living room, where Callie, their twelve-year-old, was watching some sort of adolescent soap opera, her bare legs slung over an arm of the recliner.

"This is not age appropriate!" Denise tattled, pointing at the TV.

"You're right," Georgette said, plucking the remote from Callie, who moaned in disapproval, and switching it back to one of Denise's cartoons.

Denise, still wearing the colander on her head, cheered from her perch atop the ottoman. Georgette handed her the plate of snacks.

Callie moaned. "I'm tired of watching all this baby stuff. She always gets her way."

"Go outside and play," Georgette said. "I'm sure your friends are all sitting around doing nothing, just like you. Go do something together."

"When can I get a TV for my room?"

"I think you stare at screens enough as it is."

Denise giggled at something on the TV. It was then that Georgette noticed something unusual about the colander perched atop her younger daughter's head: namely, that Georgette owned two aluminum strainers, and that the one on Denise's head was neither of them. Georgette tapped it with a fingernail, *tink tink tink*, and said, "Where did this come from, anyway?"

"Ugh, she's so weird," Callie commented, occupied now with her iPad.

Georgette plucked the colander from Denise's head to examine it.

"Hey!" Denise reached for it. "That's mine!" In her zeal to snatch it back, she sent the plate of apple slices and Oreo cookies tumbling to the carpet.

"Look what you did!" Callie exclaimed, pointing at the mess. "Mom, look!"

"Give it back!" Denise shouted, rising to stand on the ottoman so that she was Georgette's height. She gripped the colander in both hands and yanked it from Georgette. Shocked by her daughter's brazenness, Georgette watched as Denise plunked the metal strainer back onto her head. Then the girl got down on her hands and knees and picked up the pieces of apple and cookies, placing them one by one back on the plate.

Across the room, her legs still slung over the armrest of the chair, Callie was staring at Georgette, a look of shock on her face. For once, Georgette's older daughter was stunned into silence.

"Where did you get that thing, Denise?" Georgette demanded, more firmly now.

"I found it."

"*Where*, Denise?"

"She found it in the yard," Callie answered, still staring at her mother while the screen of her iPad flashed in her lap. "We think maybe the storm dropped it there."

"How does a colander blow out of someone's house?" Georgette said.

"You're right, Mom," Callie intoned, suddenly reengaged with her iPad again. Back to the old, dismissive Callie Braswell. "You figured us out. We stole it from Home Goods. That, and a Lamborghini."

"Don't be smart, kid."

"Whatever," Callie muttered.

"Denise, this thing is filthy. It's got bits of dirt stuck in the holes. Why are you bringing in junk from outside? And wearing it on your *head*, no less?"

"It's not junk," Denise said. Her plate restacked, she crawled back atop the ottoman, her eyes glued to the television screen across the room.

"It *is*," Callie retorted before Georgette could respond. "Mom's right. Mom, it was half buried in the dirt, and she just dug it up. Probably had worms and bugs and *poop*—"

"There's no poop!" Denise yelled back.

"—and whatever else in it," Callie finished, unfazed.

"It's *treasure*," Denise countered, scowling at her sister while not taking her eyes off the TV. "It's *important*."

"It's garbage," retorted Callie.

"It's mine and I'm keeping it," Denise said, and that was the final word. She set down her plate of snacks in her lap and stared up at Georgette, as if to challenge her.

"Hey," Georgette said. "What's with the eyes?"

"It's *mine* and I'm *keeping* it," Denise repeated.

Georgette sighed. "Well, at least let me go upstairs and wash it for you. Okay?"

Denise's lips puckered and slid to one corner of her face. Deep in thought, she eventually acquiesced. "Okay. But then bring it right back."

"All right."

"Promise?"

"I promise," Georgette said.

Denise removed the colander from her head. Before handing it to her mother, she studied it, running her fingers along the pattern of little holes. *Lovingly so*, Georgette thought. Then, somewhat reluctantly, she handed it to Georgette.

In the kitchen, she washed the colander at the sink then set it on a dishtowel to dry. After wiping her hands, she grabbed her cell phone and went down the hall to the master bedroom. She closed the bedroom door and dialed Alex's number.

*This is silly,* she thought. *He's going to answer. Of course he will. Alex always answers his phone when I call. He'll say he's at a site and will give Joe Peyser and Tom McKeel a call as soon as possible, and that this was all some miscommunication, a misunderstanding, and that he's been at work all week, because where else would he be? He'll say he'll be home early for dinner, too. Maybe he'll bring flowers.*

The call went straight to voicemail.

For some reason, she thought of Alex then as he was when she'd first met him, at a bar in Georgetown. Alex with a group of friends, leaning one arm against the brass rail of the bar, this good-looking white boy, not her usual type, dressed incongruously in a charcoal blazer and a Rush T-shirt, his faded jeans threadbare at the knees, and how he'd made eye contact with her from across the bar, *bam*, like a zap of lightning. She had been there with friends, some girls from the university, and she'd said, hey, said, hey, I'm gonna get another drink, which was her attempt at wandering closer to the guy in the blazer and the Rush T-shirt slumped casually against the bar chatting with his friends while keeping one eye on her (she could tell), and she'd thought, *He could be anyone, anyone at all,* and that was likely true, because anyone could be anyone and he could be—

She stopped herself.

Across the bedroom, the mirrored door to the closet stood open. A file of Alex's suits was all she could see.

She went there, smelling each suit jacket and folded pair of pants, inhaling every single one, wondering where each individual suit had been this past week. A charcoal Hugo Boss jacket that smelled faintly of smoke; a navy-blue jacket with faux brass buttons, captain-like, that gave up the aroma of nothing more than laundry detergent; a gray pinstriped job that possessed the vaguest fragrance of Alex's aftershave.

Where was he?

What was going on with him?

What was he *doing*?

She looked toward the clothes hamper next and saw his black dress socks balled up on the floor beside it. One of Alex's suits was folded atop the hamper, the pants on top of the suit jacket.

She felt like a thief and a traitor as she made her way over to the hamper and lifted his folded suit pants to her nose and inhaled.

They smelled of cloth.

She picked up the jacket next, but the jacket smelled no different. She was about to set it back down when she noticed something bulging from within the side pocket. It was roughly the size of a baseball, whatever it was, its size causing the flap of the pocket to jut out like the open door of a mailbox.

She reached her hand inside. She expected to recoil from it, even if there was nothing repulsive about it—this was how on edge she was in that moment—but she didn't. The odd texture of the thing incited her curiosity, and her fingers explored its somewhat pliable, baseball-shaped surface with intrigue, not repulsion, until she finally yanked the damn thing out and looked at it.

It was a ball of white string. A ridiculous thing to find hidden in the pocket of her husband's suit jacket, all things considered. What did it mean? What was its significance?

She tried to feel relieved about it. What had she *expected* to find, anyway? She stuffed it back inside the pocket and was about to dump the jacket back down onto the hamper, when she thought she should check the *other* pocket.

Inside, she found a small spiral-bound notepad, the kind her old English professor at Georgetown University used to keep tucked into the breast pocket of his shirts. Holding her breath, she flipped it open, not sure what she expected to find—a woman's phone number or the address to some sleazy motel? But what she found was a peculiar little drawing, sketched crudely in pencil, of what appeared to be an ovoid shape beneath which several long, spindly legs extended. To Georgette, it looked like a child's rudimentary drawing of a spider.

She flipped to the next page and stared down at the drawing of a large rectangle with smaller rectangles inside it. On another page, she found that same rectangle only with what now looked like an upside-down triangle taking up its lower half. Another page showed a series of numbers linked together in some indecipherable calculation. Another page was filled with intersecting vertical and horizontal lines so that the whole page was divided into grids. She flipped through the next several pages and found that same grid formation on each one, obsessively reproduced over and over again. It seemed the entire notepad was filled with these odd, cryptic sketches, calculations, and gridded hashmarks.

*It's for work,* she rationalized. *These are schematics and sketches for work. He's a goddamned engineer, for Christ's sake.*

Unsure how she should feel, she tucked the notepad back inside Alex's jacket pocket. Then she sat on the edge of the bed, her cell phone still clutched in one hand, her palm sweaty. At the corner of her vision, reproduced in the mirrored door of the closet, Georgette's reflection sat, vague and indistinct as a ghost. They looked at each other, but the creature in that mirror was too pitiful to stare at for much longer than a passing glance, and Georgette quickly averted her eyes.

## 2

The girls had dance class later that afternoon. As was her custom, Georgette dropped them off at the studio then walked across the plaza to a small Mexican restaurant for a margarita and some chips and salsa while she waited for the classes to let out. Tina Jarrett was already there, perched on a stool at the bar and scrolling through Facebook on her phone. Tina's daughter Jessica was in Callie's dance company, so this weekly rendezvous between the two moms wasn't unexpected—had become something of a ritual, in fact—yet Georgette, in her frazzled state, found herself desperate to avoid her friend's company. She slipped past Tina and took up a stool at the far end of the restaurant, where she hoped the curve of the bar might preclude Tina from seeing her. When the waitress slid a menu in front of her, Georgette held it in front of her face like a shield for good measure.

Tina Jarrett found her anyway.

"What are you doing all the way over here?"

"I didn't see you." Georgette smiled wanly as her friend slid onto the stool beside her.

Tina was attractive, slightly older than Georgette, and a lifelong swimmer with a body to match. She commanded an athletic disposition—always prettily plain-faced, no makeup, with her mousy brown hair pulled back in a severe ponytail, and her high cheekbones a natural bronze color. She dressed in form-fitting workout clothes and neon green Under Armour training shoes, too bright to look at for any extended period of time. Despite their friendship, Georgette had always felt a bit too frumpy and unsorted around the woman, her shirts always misbuttoned, her bulging faux-leather handbag perpetually stained from spilled ketchup or A.1. Steak Sauce, and jampacked with crayons and breath mints and tampons and nothing remotely sexy.

Tina ordered them both a margarita on the rocks, no salt on the rim, then tumbled into a diatribe about some potluck dinner she'd gone to last weekend with her husband. Georgette smiled and nodded and pretended to listen. She kept checking the time on her phone, willing the minutes to tick by more quickly than they were.

"Level with me," Tina said at one point, and the sudden shift in her tone caused Georgette to blink and stiffen, as if rousing herself from a nap. "What is *wrong* with you?"

Just hearing the question ignited something very close to a sob to swell up inside her. She felt it buoy up the column of her throat but fought it back down before she made any sound. Until that moment, she hadn't realized just how desperate she was to talk to someone.

"It's Alex," she said, and then she told Tina Jarrett about Alex's sleepwalking, his lack of interest in her and the girls all week, and how she'd received that inexplicable phone call from Joe Peyser earlier that afternoon informing her that Alex hadn't been to work all week. "He even comes home later than usual each night, which makes me wonder now what the heck he's been up to."

"Do you think he's seeing someone?"

"What do you mean?"

"Having an affair, G. Do you think he might be having an affair?"

She waved the sentiment away, shaking her head. Tried to impart the preposterousness of such a comment by pantomime. "No, of course not. Alex wouldn't do something like that. An affair? No way."

"Oh, you're such a Pollyanna. You think everyone pisses rosewater and farts daffodils. Half of what goes on in this neighborhood would shock you to pieces if you knew."

"That's not true. I know plenty."

"Did you know Zola Croft has been sleeping with that guy Larry who owns that window and door company? Or that Julie Stern has been carrying on with the guy who does their yard for over a year now . . . *and that her husband knows about it and gets off on it*?"

"Oh, stop," she said. "That's not true."

"They're swingers. I'm talking gold star upside-down pineapple spouse-swappers. Only she's the only one swapping. He just watches."

"Cut it out," she said, waving Tina off. Of course, Tina herself had carried on with her current husband behind her first husband's back, so maybe she knew what she was talking about, even if she was wrong about Alex.

Though hadn't that exact thought crossed her mind earlier that day? Wasn't that why she'd sniffed all his clothes, dug around in the pockets of his suit jacket? She couldn't deny that she'd been searching for evidence of infidelity.

"Have you talked to him about any of this?" Tina asked.

"Just in general. I said I was worried about the sleepwalking thing—I mean, it was so *strange*, T—but he just sort of brushed it off. I didn't know about the work thing until today. I mean, I'm sure there's a plausible explanation. I'm sure I'm worrying about nothing."

"But you *are* worried," Tina said, not a question.

Georgette looked down at the archipelago of ice cubes in her margarita. Of course she was worried. She wouldn't be having this conversation if she wasn't worried. And the worry was clouding her mind—not just occupying her thoughts but anesthetizing them, a cool bank of fog rolling in off the sea to leave her disoriented and fumbling and blind.

Was it possible Alex could be having an affair? Really? It seemed so out of character for him. But then again, wouldn't every wife say that about her husband? What wife would say, yes, an affair, that sounds exactly like something he would do? No wife, that's who. Every wife must think the same way, a collective thought, cult-worthy, a hive mind of thought, all coming back to the same singsong mantra: *Not my husband*. Still . . . *Alex*? In that instant, she was flooded with a host of regrets: maybe he resented her for never going back to work once the girls were older and in school fulltime; maybe he'd grown bored with the perfunctory, utilitarian nature of their dwindling sex life ever since Denise had been born; maybe he was simply at that crossroads of male middle age where he'd grown dissatisfied with the life they'd created together and was hungry for something new and exciting.

She found that thinking about those things only made her angry. Not angry at the suggestion of infidelity per se, but at the utter *injustice* of it all. Hadn't *she* sacrificed? Hadn't *she* grown equally as . . . well, not dissatisfied, not disillusioned, she wouldn't say those things, but she'd certainly grown *stale* in her marriage. A marriage was like a garden, sure, but a marriage was also like one of those fish that suction to the underbelly of a shark, too. After a while, you're just stuck to something bigger and more powerful, a thing carving its own passage through murky depths, and suddenly you're just along for the ride, a mindless thing that feeds and suctions and subsists as the possessor of no unique and individual thoughts, dreams, hopes, desires. After all, she'd given up her career to stay home and raise the girls. She'd stopped playing the piano, stopped visiting old friends, stopped going to the gym. Who had the time? She used to *do* things, used to *enjoy* things, goddamn it. A love of books and music and movies that no longer seemed to have any place in her current life. In her current headspace. She'd once met Joyce Carol Oates at a book signing in Owings Mills. She'd once gotten drunk and made out with a complete stranger at a friend's house party. She'd once had a nice figure absent of stretch marks and dimpled cellulite. Who allowed Alex to have a monopoly on resentment, anyway?

"Nearly half of all marriages end in divorce," Tina said.

"I don't think that's it," Georgette said, though her mind was still racing through the possibilities. She felt cheated, felt discarded. A thing happens to a woman when she becomes a mother. She was a woman usurped by motherhood. She'd been a living, breathing organism at one point, irretrievably replaced by an idea, a concept, a conceit. A construct. She'd let motherhood override womanhood. Should she be blamed or applauded for it?

*Christ,* she thought, head spinning. She felt a migraine coming on. And for some inexplicable reason, she thought of the colander that Denise had been wearing on her head earlier that day.

"I think I need to freshen up," Georgette said, and quickly excused herself for the restroom.

## 3

Alex returned home around a quarter after nine, well after Georgette and the girls had finished dinner. Callie was in the shower and Denise was already in bed when he came through the door, and it was as though he'd planned it this way; all week, he had appeared to avoid all social interaction with his children. With Georgette, too.

Seated at the table with a glass of wine, her bare feet propped up on an empty chair, she watched him lumber through the kitchen and set his briefcase on the counter.

"Well, hello," she said. "Busy day at the office?"

"Same old," he said, stripping out of his suit jacket and tossing it over the back of a chair. Alex had always taken pride in his appearance, his suits always tailored and neat, sometimes even with a pocket square to match his necktie. The past week, however, he'd looked like a wrinkled mess. He had even worn the same suit and tie—and dress shirt—to the office two days in a row. Or, if not the office, then to wherever the hell he had been going all week. He'd stopped shaving, too, and his face had taken on a slack, lifeless appearance, the bristle darkening his cheeks. To Georgette, he looked like a corpse some voodoo priestess had magicked back to life.

*He does not look like a man having an affair. He looks more like a man contemplating suicide.*

"Are you hungry? I made chicken soup. I can reheat it for you."

"Not hungry."

"Have you eaten anything today?"

"Had a big lunch."

"At the office?"

He looked at her.

"Joe Peyser called the house today, looking for you. Said you hadn't been in the office all week. Said Tom McKeel was looking for you, too. No one knew where you were."

Alex's gaze hung on her. His corneas looked milky and yellow. He didn't say anything.

"Where've you been all week?" she asked him, point-blank.

His nostrils flared as he exhaled. "Are you getting at something here, Georgette?"

"I'm getting at just what I'm asking. And I'm asking where you've been going all week, if it hasn't been to the office."

"That's pretty presumptuous of you."

She was momentarily rattled by the impudence of his response. "Is it? I called your cell phone today and you didn't answer. You used to always answer your phone when I called. Or at least you'd call me back when you'd see you've missed a call from me."

"I left it in the car today."

She frowned. "You left your cell phone in the car all day."

"I've had a lot on my mind lately," he said, pulling his jacket off the chair. He went down the hall to their bedroom and Georgette followed him. While he undressed, he said, "Sometimes I'm at the office and sometimes I'm on-site somewhere. You know that. Joe and Tom know it, too."

"Is there some trouble at work?"

"No trouble at all."

"Is it something with your health? Something you're not telling me?"

"I'm as healthy as a horse." He thumped a lackluster fist against his chest, though his eyes looked dead.

"Are you having an affair?"

He was sitting on the edge of the bed, unlacing his shoe when she asked him the question. He paused now and looked up at her. There were dark rings around his yellowing eyes and his jawline was patchy with beard stubble. Again, she saw that he did not *look* like someone who was having an affair.

Nonetheless, she braced herself for his answer.

"How could you ask me that?"

"Because something hasn't been right with you, and I want to know what it is. I'm worried about you."

"Are you still stewing on that sleepwalking thing? I told you it was no big deal."

"It's not just the sleepwalking thing, Alex, or whatever the hell that was. It's *everything*. It's the way you've been with the girls all week. Or, more accurately, the way you *haven't* been. Even when you're home it's like you're barely here. We go to bed, and you roll over like you're disgusted by me. I stare at your back all night. And I can tell you're not sleeping. You toss and turn and sometimes even cry out in your sleep, like you're having terrible nightmares."

"That's not true," he said, twisting off his shoe. He massaged his foot through his sock, toes flexing.

"You haven't actually answered my question."

"What question is that?"

"Are you having an affair? Are you seeing someone? Yes or no."

"Of course not. Come on. You know me better than that."

"I thought I did."

"Listen," he said, pointing a finger at her. "Don't get all high and mighty, all right?"

"Jesus. You're pretty goddamn defensive for a guy who's done nothing wrong."

"Son of a bitch," he said, and he suddenly looked like he wanted to jump up off the bed and punch a hole in the wall. But he didn't; in fact, she watched as he struggled to regain his composure, breathing deeply, heavy lids over those dead black eyes. Very calmly, he said, "I'm sorry. I'm just stressed out. Can't a guy just have a bad week at work?"

"Is that really what it is? Do you want to talk about it?"

"No."

"Have you actually been *going* to work?"

"For fuck's sake," he said, voice rising.

"Keep your voice down."

"Don't tell me what to do. You've asked me questions and I've answered them. Now can you please leave me be? I've got a headache, and I need to go to sleep."

"It's not even nine thirty."

"My *head* hurts," he said, the words coming out on a whoosh of breath. Perspiration glistened on his forehead. She saw that his hands were trembling. "Look, Georgette, I'm sorry I yelled," he said, his voice cool and measured now, though she could tell it was taking much effort to keep it that way, "but my head hurts and I need to sleep. You're right, I've been sleeping poorly, and it's catching up to me. I just need to sleep. Is that okay?"

She stared at him.

"I promise you there is nothing wrong," he said. "Okay?"

"Okay," she said, not believing him, and left the room.

# 4

Once everyone else in the house was asleep, Georgette stepped into a pair of running shoes then went outside. It was fully dark, the moon a wicked-looking scimitar behind a thread of black clouds. A misty rain hung in the air; she walked through it as if passing through a curtain of ice-cold beads.

Alex's Camry was parked in the driveway, glistened beneath the glow of a nearby streetlamp. His car keys in her hand, she unlocked the driver's door and climbed inside behind the wheel. She didn't know what she was looking for out here, but some suspicion bordering on intuition had roused her from sleep and told her to check the car. Whatever Alex was doing—wherever he had been going all week—there might be evidence of it in the car.

But there was nothing here, except for the faint yet pungent odor of man-sweat. Had he stopped showering, too? Would a man stop shaving and showering if he was having an affair? Maybe she was over-thinking things. Maybe she was stressing herself out over nothing, that her conversation earlier with Tina had set her off course, and the truth was exactly as Alex had said it—he'd just been having a tough week at work, nothing more.

She checked the glove compartment, but there was nothing unusual in there. She ran her hands under the seats, combing her fingers through the gritty carpeting in the foot-wells, finding nothing but granulated pebbles, a couple of pull-tabs from soda cans, and the plastic lid from a Styrofoam coffee cup.

*What exactly did you expect to find?* a voice inside her head spoke up. *Some evidence of infidelity? Some woman's missing earring snared in the fire-retardant fibers of the carpeting? A love letter with a lipstick kiss beside some woman's signature?*

She wasn't sure, but she believed that whatever was going on with Alex, it transcended infidelity. She kept picturing him standing on the lawn, staring at the sky, his bare chest and thighs reddened and wind-chapped from the cold, his eyes unfocused as if under a hypnotist's spell. What if he hadn't just gotten up that morning and wandered outside? What if, in actuality, he'd roused sometime in the *night*, and had been standing out there for hours in the storm until she happened to find him come morning?

The thought chilled her.

She climbed out of the car and stood for a few moments in the rain. It was coming down harder now, the sound of it on the car's roof like artillery fire. She looked up and down the block, as if to anchor herself to reality before she lost her mind with worry and supposition. Across the street, the houses were all cookie-cutter split-levels just like theirs, some of them completely dark, others with only the vaporous blue flicker of television light flashing in an upstairs window. There had been a strange symbol chalked on the pavement in front of their house earlier that day, but it looked as though the rain had washed it away.

She went to the rear of the car and opened the trunk.

She expected to find the usual suspects inside—a spare tire, a jack, maybe a tangle of jumper cables. Instead, she found several plastic shopping bags. She peered inside one of the bags and found that it was filled with large balls of twine. These were not dissimilar to the ball of string she'd found in his jacket pocket earlier that afternoon, although she could not fathom why he was hauling these things around. She looked in a second bag and found that this one also contained twine. It was the tough, sturdy kind, like a very thin rope. A third bag *did* contain rope, or what looked like clothesline, anyway. The bag also contained spools of duct tape, a pair of scissors, several pairs of latex gloves, and a bone-handled hunting knife that she had never seen before. Her concern mounting, she searched every bag, and found that each one of them contained either more balls of twine or spools of duct tape . . .

Except for the final bag, which looked bulkier, and emitted a smell of sour perspiration ten times worse than she'd smelled inside the car. She peeled open this bag, her hands shaking, and looked inside.

They looked like old rags at first, but as she proceeded to remove each one out of the bag, she realized they were articles of clothing. A few T-shirts and two pairs of suit pants, each one streaked with dirt and reeking sourly of body odor.

Georgette stuffed the clothing back in the bag, shut the trunk, and hurried back to the house through the rain.

In the foyer, she stepped out of her wet sneakers, the sweaty soles of her feet squeaking on the hardwood floor. She felt momentarily lost. She thought of the man asleep in her bed, a man who wore an Alex Braswell mask. Unease rippled through her in unstoppable waves.

She noticed that he had left his briefcase on the floor along the kitchen wall. She went to it, picked it up, and found it disconcertingly lighter than she would have thought. Setting it on the counter, she turned on the meager yellow light beneath the microwave, then popped open the clasps on the briefcase.

Held her breath—

*Don't be silly, now . . .*

—and opened it.

A handful of towels were inside—old face- and hand-towels, once kept in the garage for washing the cars and cleaning up messes.

They were still cleaning up messes, she saw.

Each one, streaked with dried blood.

It took her several tries to pack the towels back into the briefcase and latch the clasps, her hands were shaking so badly. She set the briefcase back down on the floor where Alex had left it, then went to the sink.

The colander that Denise had found in the yard was still sitting on the kitchen counter. Its rounded aluminum hull radiated with moonlight coming in through the window over the sink. Georgette extended a hand toward it—her hand had ceased shaking now—and set her moist, sweaty palm against the cool metallic hull.

It felt as if it strummed with an electrical current. From every hole in the colander, she imagined she could feel a numbing, tingling sensation caressing the palm of her hand, like some magical gas leaking out of it. Or like a humming that she felt throughout the marrow of her bones, her *teeth*, rather than heard. In fact, it was almost as if—

"What are you doing?"

She jumped and made a catlike sound as she spun around.

Alex stood in the hall, a silhouette against the screen of windows in the foyer.

"I couldn't sleep," she said. "Was getting some water."

The silhouette did not move. It stood there, featureless. She could hear it breathing. Was it still wearing the Alex mask or was its true face lain bare before her, hidden now only in darkness? Watching her with its own true eyes? A face that would set her screaming if it came into the light.

Just as she felt panic tightening about her throat, she glimpsed one of the bloodied towels from Alex's briefcase still on the counter. In her frenzy, she had missed one, hadn't put it back. She grabbed it now and tucked it beneath the colander, so quickly she didn't think the thing pretending to be her husband had time to notice.

"You're all wet," the silhouette said. It did not move closer to her but remained there cloaked in darkness. Its face could literally look like *anything.*

"Am I?" She made a show of glancing down at herself. Had he seen the bloody towel? Had he watched her hide it beneath the colander? Could he sense that she had gone through his briefcase, his car?

The silhouette grunted: a sound that suggested this maybe-Alex knew she was lying about something.

"Okay," she said, "you caught me. I went out and had a cigarette."

"In the rain?"

She shrugged. "I can't control the weather."

"You quit smoking months ago," the silhouette said.

"I found one left in an old pack. Had a moment of weakness."

"A moment of weakness," the silhouette echoed, its voice dry.

"Alex," she said—

*(maybe-Alex)*

—but she could not find the words to continue.

The thing pretending to be her husband receded quietly back down the hallway.

She didn't realize she was holding her breath until she exhaled with enough zeal to weaken her knees. Recalling the bloody towel, she lifted the colander—

—but there was nothing beneath it.

The bloodied towel was gone.

# CHAPTER NINE
# SIDEWALK CHALK

## 1

*(COME OUT COME OUT COME OUT)*

Cory's eyes flipped open. He was slouched against the armrest of the sofa in the living room, the TV tuned to Cartoon Network. There was a half-eaten plate of Tostino's Pizza Rolls on the couch cushion beside him, and a formidable kink in his neck from having fallen asleep after lunch in an awkward position.

"Mom?"

No answer: the house was empty. She had gone to show another house earlier that afternoon, he suddenly remembered, and likely hadn't returned. Yet he'd sworn some voice had shouted to him—

*(COME OUT COME OUT COME OUT)*

—and roused him from his nap.

He shut the TV off and called out for his mother again. But again, the house remained silent. He went to the dining room and peered out the bay window to see if his mother's car was in the driveway, but it was not.

A buzzing, static-laden hum drifted into his head. It sounded like the whirring of an electric saw, but the men cutting the tree in Mr. Zachs's front lawn had finished their work days ago, and he couldn't see anyone else outside. Well, except Winona Orem: as was her daily custom, the girl was sitting cross-legged on her lawn across the street. As he stared at her, that buzzing sound once again seeped its way into his head. It was enough to provoke the gnome into wakefulness; Cory could abruptly feel it lying in the meaty canyon at the center of his brain, alert.

Something felt *wrong*.

At the front door, Cory dug his feet into his Crocs then stepped out into the bright sunshine. Even though the men with the chainsaws had long since left Mr. Zachs's property, there was still a sawdusty haze clinging to the air. Maybe someone *was* sawing something somewhere. As Cory crossed the street, he glanced up and down the block, but could see no one. The buzzing in his head had subsided, too. Maybe he was just hearing imaginary things.

Winona Orem looked up and smiled at him as he approached.

"Cory! That big tree fell down!"

"Yeah, I saw it."

"Men came and cut it up!"

"I saw that, too."

Winona was perched crisscross-applesauce on her front lawn, an assortment of toys scattered in the grass around her. She had her favorite ragdoll in her lap, an old and tattered thing that she never left the house without. At eleven, Winona was a year older than Cory but the girl acted much younger and went to a special school. Cory had known her and her brother Davey nearly his whole life, and the Orem siblings were two of only a handful of kids in the neighborhood Cory felt he could call friends.

"That poor tree!" Winona shouted, pointing to the place on Mr. Zachs's lawn where the tree had once lain. The stump was the only thing that remained, its surface smooth as a tabletop from the workmen's chainsaws.

"Well, it's gone now, Winona." Despite the smile on the girl's face, Cory could see that she'd recently been crying: her cheeks were blotchy and red and her eyes still sparkled with tears. "What's the matter? Why were you crying?"

"Because it is so sad! Those men came the other day and cut it up into all those pieces."

"It's just a tree," he said, stepping up on the sidewalk.

"But trees are *alive*." She swiped a fresh tear from her cheek and pointed at the sidewalk at Cory's feet. "Don't step there!"

He glanced down and saw a series of hastily sketched chalk drawings on the pavement. He hopped over them and onto the grass.

"Did you hear that big storm the other night, too?" she asked him.

"Yeah, I did."

"That's what made the poor tree come down."

"Yeah, I guess."

"Did it scare you?"

He cleared his throat and said, "No way."

Yet he was remembering the iron spider that had chased him out of his nightmare the night of the storm—how he thought, in his sleep-addled mind, the thing had actually been outside, driving its massive lodgepole legs through sections of the house. The way the roof had creaked and the wind had roared as his mom roused him from sleep and dragged him down the hall, it was as if that terrible bit of alien machinery had broken through the wall of his subconscious only to arrive in the real world.

He thought, too, of the gnome flexing in his brain like a secret muscle.

"It scared *me*," Winona confessed.

"Yeah, well, the storm is long gone, Win. You don't need to be scared of it anymore."

She looked at him quizzically. "Are you sure?" Then she brightened once again. Her smile was radiant and addictive, despite the sparkle of tears still in her eyes. "Did you come to say hello to me today, Cory?"

"Sure," he said, smiling back at her. No need to explain that why he'd *really* come out here was because of the strange buzzing noise, and the voice he was so certain he'd heard speaking right up against his ear while he napped on the couch—*come out come out come out.* Like a playground chant during hide and seek. *Come out, come out, wherever you are.*

Just thinking of it caused the gnome to stir about inside his head again. Its movements felt small and furtive and confined within the vast galaxy of Cory's mind. He glanced down at Winona, who was smiling to herself while parading her ragdoll around the grass. He let the gnome extend a poke in her direction. Unlike touching his mother's mind, which had felt like pressing against a film of Jell-O that first night and then sliding through the skin of a soap bubble the following night, breaching Winona's mind was more like passing through a wisp of gossamer filaments, like the tacky strands of webbing excreted by silkworms. Through that web of silk, Cory picked up on loud colors, delicate smells, the sliding of checkers across a checkerboard, Beatles music, and sitcom theme songs, all jumbled around inside Winona's head. Just as peaceably as it had entered her mind, the gnome withdrew its probing finger and retreated back into the dark cave of Cory's skull.

"Is she still bawling about that stupid tree?" It was Davey Orem, Winona's brother and Cory's best friend, coming across the lawn while staring at his cell phone. He had gotten the phone last year for his birthday, and it had become an appendage since then, never leaving his hand.

Winona looked over at her brother and shouted, "It's dead! It's dead!"

"Maybe *people* died, too," Davey taunted. "Ever think of that? Maybe little puppies and kittens and goldfish all died in the storm, too, Win."

Winona clamped both hands to her ears and squeezed her eyes shut. A fresh tear skittered down her cheek.

"Cut it out, Davey," Cory scolded him. To Winona, he said, "Hey. Please don't cry, Win. Come on. Davey's just messing with you."

She looked up at him, her round face pulled downward in a scowl of pure agony at what her brother had said.

"It isn't true," Cory told her. "No one died. No one was even hurt."

"You don't know that," Davey cut in, nonchalant.

Winona howled.

"Cool it, Win," Davey said, finally glancing away from his cell phone and down at his sister. "Cory's right, I was only joking." He looked to Cory. "Make the doll dance, will ya? It'll shut her up."

Cory looked down at the ragdoll that lay in the damp grass between Winona's feet. It was an ugly thing with stitching for a face that, for whatever reason, Winona had named Showtime Corner. He glanced over at Davey and said, "I don't know if I should . . ."

"Don't be a jerk about it," Davey groused, already peering back down at his phone, disinterested.

Cory poked a finger into Davey's mind and glimpsed a whirlwind of charcoal-gray storm clouds. He quickly withdrew, uneasy about his friend's agitated and erratic thoughts. On the heels of that, he found himself feeling like a thief, or at least like some violator who has trespassed into a place—into many places—he wasn't meant to be. In that moment, it occurred to him that maybe it wasn't *right* for him to poke around inside people's minds.

"Pleeeeease, Cory, *pleeeeease*," Winona whined, scooping the ugly doll off the ground and hoisting it into the air above her head. Another big, sloppy tear spilled down the side of her face.

Cory glanced up and down the block. They were the only three people out here, as far as he could see. Of course, he was recalling what his mother had told him the other night, about not letting anyone else know about what he could do. But Winona and Davey weren't some bad guys looking to take advantage of his special gift. Besides, Winona and Davey *already* knew. He'd lied to his mother on that score.

"Okay," Cory relented.

Winona cheered, then set Showtime Corner on the lawn, just a few inches from her grass-stained knees.

Inside his head, Cory once again called out for the gnome. The gnome responded, and Cory felt the now-familiar widening inside him as the gnome separated both hemispheres of his brain. In that moment, the inside of Cory's skull felt as wide and unbounded as the universe.

One of the doll's floppy legs rose off the ground. An arm followed suit. A moment later, it was upright in a parody of standing. As Cory fine-tuned his focus on the doll, it began to twirl in a circle, much like the fork had on the dining room table the other night. The doll's lifeless, stitched-together limbs flapped and flopped while its head lolled from one side to the other.

Winona cheered, clapping her hands.

The doll spun, pirouetted, twirled. When Cory felt the last of his energy drain from him, Showtime Corner completed the routine with a commendable bow, then dropped back down to the ground, motionless once again.

"Hooray!" Winona cried. She scooped up Showtime Corner and hugged the doll, her smile radiating. All trace of her former misery appeared to have fled. "That was a really good one, Cory! The best one yet!"

"Wow, yeah," Davey said. He'd been impressed enough to look up from his phone, and now he nodded with appreciation, a look of approval on his round and sweaty face. "Jeez, man, you got really good at that."

"Yeah, I guess I did," he agreed, feeling slightly lightheaded. It was the most disciplined, controlled dance he'd had the doll do yet, and something about that didn't sit well with him for some reason. He pressed a palm to his forehead and found that, despite the heat of midday, his skin felt cold and clammy.

"Thank you, thank you, thank you, Cory!" Winona sang, still squeezing the ugly ragdoll to her chest.

"You're welcome, Win," Cory said, returning her smile. Her simple joy was infectious. He looked over at Davey and asked, "Have you been hearing some strange buzzing sounds out here?"

"Nope." He was engrossed in his phone again, blunt little fingers tapping on the screen.

"What about someone calling out?"

"What do you mean?"

"Saying 'come out, come out,' over and over again."

Face still buried in his phone, Davey said, "Nope."

"Well, okay," Cory said. He smiled one last time to Winona before turning to head back across the street. "Don't stay out in the sun for too long without sunscreen, Win."

"And don't step on the chalk!" She pointed once again at the drawings on the sidewalk.

This time, Cory took a closer look at what was scribbled there.

Not a hopscotch grid, not a rickety conga line of stick figures holding hands beneath a rainbow. None of the things Winona typically drew, in other words. These chalk drawings, all done in a sterile, emotionless white, were of symbols. That was the only way he could think of them. To Cory, they looked like Egyptian hieroglyphics, which he'd once seen photos of in a book.

"What do they mean?" he asked Winona.

Winona shrugged. She was still cradling Showtime Corner to her chest. "I don't know, but I do not like them."

"Didn't you draw them?"

"No!" She shook her head emphatically. "No way!"

"Then who did?"

"A man."

"What man?"

"A strange man. A man with messages on his face."

Cory frowned. "What does that mean?"

Winona's mouth hung open in an O as she simply repeated, with more emphasis, "*Man* with *messages* on his *face*." As if Cory was about the dumbest kid on the block.

Cory turned to Davey. "What does she mean? A man with messages on his face?"

"Huh?" Davey said, looking up from his phone and blinking the sun from his eyes. He was stockier than Cory, with sweat stains darkening the armpits of his Pokémon T-shirt. "What are you talking about?"

Cory shook his head. "Never mind."

He peered farther up the block and saw another grouping of similar symbols sketched onto the sidewalk up ahead. He thought he saw a third grouping of them right in the middle of the street, down by the stop sign at the intersection of Cloister and Capshaw.

"Why did you tell me not to step on them if you didn't draw them?" he asked Winona.

"Because they're bad," she said, bouncing Showtime Corner in her lap. "Because they're ugly and nasty and I don't like what they mean."

"What do they mean?"

"Oh," she said. "I don't know. But it isn't good."

He glanced back down at the symbols sketched at his feet. He could not make heads or tails of them, yet something about them bothered him on some deep, inexplicable level just the same. He slipped his own cell phone from his pocket—a cheap phone that Davey made fun of, that couldn't even search the internet—and took a photo of them.

"Take one of me! Take one of me!" Winona bellowed, smiling from ear to ear.

He snapped a photo of Winona, too.

"Am I fancy, Cory?"

"You're always the fanciest, Winona."

"Yay!"

He hurried back across the street, ditched into the house, then came out through the garage wheeling his dirt bike. It was a lime green Diamondback Cobra with a six-speed twist shifter and stop-on-a-dime handbrakes—his most prized possession, even though his mother had gotten it in less-than-mint condition at a yard sale. He unhooked the helmet from the handlebars and strapped it to his head. As he hopped on his bike, he waved to Winona. She beamed a smile at him then waved right back.

He coasted to the end of the block and eased to a halt at the intersection. Yes, there were more strange symbols here, although different than the ones that had been chalked onto the sidewalk in front of the Orems' house. They were larger, too, as if the person who'd drawn them wanted people to notice as they drove by. It occurred to him that it had rained last night, so whoever had drawn these, they must have done so very early this morning. They upset him for some reason, made him feel queasy in the pit of his belly, although he had no idea why. He took out his phone and took pictures of them, too.

*Sssssss,* he thought, unsure what it meant or where the thought had come from. In fact, it didn't feel like his thought at all, but more like some errant notion he had somehow managed to harness straight out of the atmosphere. Like snagging a boot while fishing. *Ssssss . . .*

*(snake)*

*. . . ssss . . .*

He nudged the gnome awake. The gnome needed little instruction; it guided him through the neighborhood on his bike, an internal compass leading the way. It was as if the gnome knew where all the chalk drawings were on every street corner. Cory took pictures of them all.

*Ssssss . . .*

Something was wrong. Cory sensed this right away. The farther he biked from his house, the greater the wrongness became. It wasn't just the chalk drawings, which seemed to be plentiful, scrawled on nearly every sidewalk beyond Cloister Road, and sometimes in the middle of the street, too. Something felt wrong in the overall resonance of the neighborhood. A low, dark hum beneath the surface of things. It was like in music class, when the instruments weren't properly tuned: you could hear the music and tell what the song was supposed to be, but it all sounded sour.

By the time he reached Poplar Station Road, he was overcome by that same throb of unease that had struck him upon coming awake the night of the storm. Instead of retreating from the sensation as he'd done on that night, however, he let the gnome approach it. The gnome reached out and probed it, like poking something with a mental stick.

Whatever was out there, it poked back.

The force of it caused Cory to skid off his bike and fall to the pavement. With his knees gashed and his bike wedged in the gutter, front tire still spinning, he rolled onto his backside and peered across the road to the entranceway of Gladstone Park. There were more chalk drawings on the asphalt driveway that served as the entrance to the park, but he didn't want to go over there and take a look. Something about getting too close to the park suddenly frightened him.

That *sssssss* in his head transitioned into a low buzz—*sssszzzzz . . .*

More cautiously this time, the gnome reached out and stroked the ether. Something massive and indecipherable was strategically hidden on the other side. Not behind a soap bubble or a film of Jell-O or even a silkworm's gossamer strands, but shored up behind a curtain of impenetrable chainmail. The gnome couldn't penetrate it, couldn't glimpse the massive thing crouching there on the other side.

*Sssss.*

*Zzzzz.*

The agitated bleat of a car horn caused him to jump. Cory scrambled out of the street just as a vehicle slowly swerved around his fallen bike then motored on down the road. He glanced down and saw that the stinging in his knees was because he'd dashed them along the pavement in the fall; bright red rivulets of blood trickled down both his shins.

Trembling, he got back on his bike and raced home.

## 2

By the time he coasted back up his driveway, Cory's heart was slamming against his ribcage and his T-shirt clung wetly to his back. His knees were still bleeding and he was trying to remember if there was peroxide in the bathroom medicine cabinet. Davey and Winona were no longer in their front yard across the street, and for that Cory was grateful, because he felt very jittery and unlike himself. Something, he knew, was wrong. Even if he didn't understand it.

He retrieved a bucket and scrub brush from the shed out back, filled the bucket with dishwashing soap and warm water from the kitchen tap, then carried it across the street to where those strange symbols were sketched on the sidewalk in front of the Orems' house.

Furiously, he scrubbed away the chalk drawings. Then he went up the block and scrubbed the symbols away from the sidewalk there as well. Then he went to the intersection and, on his hands and knees like an old washerwoman, took the brush to those larger symbols, too. At one point, a car took the turn too fast; the driver laid on the horn and swerved to avoid striking him, but Cory was so immersed in what he was doing that he hardly noticed. He also did not realize that he had gouged open his knuckles on the blacktop from scrubbing too hard until he'd finished and actually saw the blood there, just like his knees.

Once the chalk drawings were gone, he stood, panting, and felt a false pang of security in what he'd done. Once, his mother's car had started to make a strange clanging noise, and she'd only smiled sadly and turned up the radio because she couldn't afford to have it fixed. That was what this felt like to him now: turning up the radio. Still, it was better than having to look at those eerie chalk sketches, that was for sure.

He was halfway around the side of his house to return the bucket and scrub brush to the shed when he saw Mr. Zachs standing on their property line. Cory waved but kept his head down, embarrassed, and moved quickly to the shed. Mr. Zachs did not wave back. He did, however, turn his head to follow Cory's progress toward the rear of the house. The gnome in the center of Cory's skull blinked its shining, silver eyes and stirred, sensing the older man's stare.

Cory glanced over his shoulder at Mr. Zachs, who stared at him so intently that it caused Cory to pick up his step and hurry into the shed.

There was a small window in the wall of the shed, curtained with spiderwebs. After setting down the bucket and scrub brush, Cory peered out the window and at Mr. Zachs, who hadn't moved from where he stood on the property line except to pivot his head in Cory's approximate direction. Could Mr. Zachs see him through the shed's window? Cory didn't think so, yet he also couldn't be one hundred percent sure.

*What's wrong with him?*

A moment later, it occurred to him that he had a way of finding out.

The gnome reached out and peeked inside Mr. Zachs's head.

## 3

A crescent moon.

An inverted triangle.

An infinity symbol.

And above all else: the hissing of a snake merging with the buzzing cacophony of a colony of bees . . .

## 4

The next thing Cory knew, he was regaining consciousness on the gritty floor of the shed. He sat up, his skull aching—he had slammed it against the lawnmower when he passed out—and leaned against a wheelbarrow as he climbed to his feet.

He peered back out the smudgy window.

Mr. Zachs was still there. Staring at the shed.

*That's not Mr. Zachs.* It was a realization that struck him like a mallet to a gong. He had seen with the gnome's eyes what had been inside Mr. Zachs's head: a raging, swirling storm. Mr. Zachs was no longer himself. Not fully. Something else—some living, conscious poison—had taken up residence inside Mr. Zachs, even if Mr. Zachs didn't know it.

And whatever it was, it meant Cory harm.

There was no doubt about that part.

Cory took a breath, counted silently to ten, then sprinted across the yard to the back deck. He threw open the slider and rushed inside, quickly slamming shut and bolting the door. Then he went around to all the other doors and windows in the house, locking each one in turn, and drawing the curtains closed.

He had a cell phone that did not get the internet but did allow him to text and make calls. In case of emergencies, his mother had said, knowing that he would sometimes have to be left home alone while she worked. *Emergencies, right,* he thought, and fired off a text message to Davey Orem across the street:

> Are you still home?

He didn't have to wait long for Davey's response; the kid's face was always buried in his cell phone.

> Yea you wan 2 cum over?

Cory typed:

Look out your window.

He went into the dining room and over to the curtains that he'd drawn across the large bay window that looked out upon Cloister Road. He parted the curtain only an inch, enough for him to peek out and spy the Orem house across the street. A moment later, Davey's face appeared in an upstairs window. In Cory's hand, his cell phone buzzed:

What am i looking 4?

Cory typed:

Can you see Mr. Zachs?

Waited. Waited.

The phone buzzed with Davey's response:

yes

Cory asked:

Where is he?

Waited. Waited.

Waited.

He was staring down at the screen when Davey's response came through:

standing at your front door

Just then: a series of rapid little knocks resounded on the front door. Cory let the curtain swing closed, his breath catching in his throat. He dropped his phone on the floor.

The voice on the other side of the door was muffled but undeniably Mr. Zachs's: "Cory? Are you all right in there, son?"

Heat prickled his flesh.

"Cory? Hello?"

More of those rapid little knocks.

*Bump bump bump bump bump.*

He kept a baseball bat in the hall closet; he grabbed it now then returned to the foyer. All was quiet on the other side of the door, but he could still sense Mr. Zachs standing out there. He thought about poking him with the gnome again, but he hadn't liked what he'd glimpsed on the first go-round, and didn't want to see it again.

The doorknob moved the slightest bit. He tightened his grip on the baseball bat.

"Cory? I know you're in there." The sandpapery sound of a hand brushing against the outside of the door. "I watched you go in. I watched you close all the curtains. I thought it was a strange thing to do."

Cory took a step back from the door.

"I just want to make sure everything is okay, son. I would feel terrible if I didn't check in on you, knowing your mother isn't home, and that sometimes she works long hours to put food on your table and clothes on your back."

Another furtive step backward.

"Do you hear me, Cory? If you aren't feeling well, son, I can help you."

Again: small movements of the doorknob.

"I'm here to help."

*Go away*, Cory willed him, tears welling in his eyes. *Go away, go away, go away.*

"It's just me, Cory. Can you hear me?"

Two gentle knocks. *Bump bump.* Barely audible this time, much like the diminishing, singsong quality of Mr. Zachs's voice on the other side of the door.

"Why don't you come on out, son?"

*(COME OUT COME OUT COME OUT)*

"Go away!" he shouted back, his grip tightening around the baseball bat.

"I just want to make sure you're okay."

Cory didn't respond. He backed up against one wall, sweat pooling in the palms of his hands that were still wrapped around the hilt of the bat. He thought that if he had to, he might be able to have the gnome *do something* to Mr. Zachs, although he didn't want to think about that, didn't want to imagine what the gnome could do if provoked, if Cory needed it to—

Silence.

He waited, panting, sweating. Listened. Got the sense that Mr. Zachs was no longer there but couldn't be sure.

He saw his cell phone on the floor of the dining room, right where he'd dropped it. He rushed over to it now, still clutching the bat, and snatched it up off the floor. Hastily, he texted Davey:

> Is he gone?

Held his breath. A drop of sweat slipped into his eye, stinging him there.

The phone buzzed with Davey's response:

> no. hes still there.

Followed by another message:

> at front door

Yet not making a sound.

*Go away, go away, go away.*

Cory typed:

> What is he doing?

Davey responded:

> just standing there

*Go away, go away, go away.*

The gnome could do things to him if it came to that.

The gnome was getting stronger and stronger every day.

*No,* he thought, and fought back a sob. *No, I don't want to think about that. I don't want to do something like that.*

Silence on the other side of that door.

Except—

*(COME OUT COME OUT COME OUT)*

—that buzzing sound ringing once more in his head.

In his hand, the phone vibrated with another message from Davey:

he is walking around to the side of the house

Followed by:

this is wierd what is he dooin?

The side of the house.

The broken window over the sink.

He rushed to the kitchen. The plastic tarp that his mother had nailed over the window above the sink rippled in the soft midday breeze. One loose corner even flapped, revealing snippets of daylight beyond.

He kept waiting for Mr. Zachs's shadow to darken that pale bit of plastic from the outside, for the shape of a hand to materialize and to peel the plastic away. For Mr. Zachs to come clambering through the window, over the counter, and into the kitchen.

He hurried back into the dining room and dragged a chair into the kitchen, set it facing the window. The chair legs left black scuff marks on the tile, but Cory didn't care. Still clutching the bat, he climbed onto the chair. His whole body felt hot and prickly with sweat.

After a time, he texted Davey:

Where is he now?

To which Davey responded:

cant see him

That side of the house wasn't visible from Davey's bedroom window.

The phone vibrated again with another message from Davey:

whats this all about????

Cory texted back:

He isn't Mr. Zachs anymore.

Davey:

what does that mean???

Cory:

I don't know. Something strange is happening.

He waited for Davey to text back and ask what he meant, but no further texts came.

That plastic over the window rippled.

Winks of daylight from that one fluttery corner.

Cory remained in the chair for an unknowable length of time, clutching the baseball bat to his chest with his cell phone in his lap while his knees kept bleeding and his ruined knuckles left behind crimson smears along the sweat-dampened fabric of his shirt.

# CHAPTER TEN

# THE TRENTON HOUSE: LITTLE GIRL LOST

## 1

Ellen arrived at the old Trenton house on Poplar Station Road for a showing fifteen minutes early. After parking in the driveway and climbing out of her car, she waved to Pamela Guerin who stood in her front yard across the street, then went up the brick walkway to the front door. She punched in her code, took out the key, and accessed the house.

The place smelled stale, so she cracked open some windows and lit a few scented candles. She opened the blinds on the remaining windows to get some natural light in the place. With a few minutes to spare, she went around making sure the place looked clean and presentable, that the lights and appliances still worked, and that the mousetraps she'd placed strategically in the basement were empty and shunted from view.

There was a sitting room at the rear of the house, an addition that was windowed on three of its four sides. Ellen noticed one of the windows was ajar; the screen had been popped out of the frame and lay in the grass outside. She noted the treads of Converse sneakers on the carpeting and a solitary cigarette butt, bent at a right angle, inside the candle jar that she'd set in here during her last visit. She jimmied the window open further and stuck her head out. Beside the screen, there were more cigarette butts in the yard as well as a few crushed cans of Natty Boh.

Her mind was elsewhere. With Cory. Still thinking about all that had transpired over the past few days. Still worried about him, and left with the unsettling sensation that he'd not only been able to move that fork with his mind, but that he'd somehow siphoned from her the information about Brian that she'd been unwilling to tell him. She wondered if there were things Cory was able to do—things beyond the abilities of Aunt Patty and Brian—that he was keeping from her.

*I'm worried about you, baby.*

Fifteen minutes after their scheduled appointment time, the Mayers were a no show. No calls, text messages, or emails from them, either. Strange. Ellen gathered her handbag off the kitchen counter, blew out the scented candles, then closed up all the open windows. As she headed back down the driveway toward her car, a champagne-colored minivan pulled up along the curb.

Warren and Angela Mayer were in their mid-thirties. They were healthy, spry, beachgoing. Their five-year-old daughter, Luna, was a vibrant blonde with luminous aquamarine eyes. Ellen had been working with them for a few weeks now, showing them a handful of houses in the area. This was the first house she'd planned to show them in her own neighborhood, a prospect that the Mayers seemed delighted by at the time. Now, this late for their appointment, Ellen wondered if they'd changed their mind for some reason.

"So sorry we're late, Ellen," Angela said as they all emptied out of the minivan. "It's been a morning!"

"No problem at all. I've got all day. Let's have a look."

She ushered them through the house. Warren and Angela commented positively every step of the way, but Ellen knew this was their typical modus operandi; she had shown them four or five other houses earlier in the summer and while they'd had nothing but positive commentary to espouse during every viewing, they ultimately had passed on each one over some miniscule, inconsequential issue or another.

Little Luna was the only one acting out of sorts. On the occasions Ellen had met with the Mayers, Luna had whirlwinded through rooms, climbed on furniture, and generally pestered her parents so that Ellen got used to taking an Advil prior to each meeting. Today, however, Luna trailed desultorily behind her parents as they ambled from room to room. She kept her shiny aquamarine eyes trained on her bright pink sneakers and very rarely raised them to meet Ellen's curious gaze.

"It's a lovely house," Angela commented.

"It's a nice street," Warren agreed.

"Well, it's a great neighborhood," Ellen told them. "I can attest to that firsthand. I've been living in Mariner's Cove for nearly a decade now."

"Is there a beach we can walk to from here?" Warren asked. They were upstairs in the master bedroom peering out the windows that looked down upon a wooded backyard.

"There is, but it's mostly rocky shore and mud this far in from the bay. You wouldn't necessarily want to lay out beneath an umbrella, but you can go fishing and take kayaks in and out. There is a main community beach off Slope Hill which is more for swimming, but it's maybe a mile or so up the road. There are . . ."

She paused as Warren Mayer placed a hand against one wall and arched his back like a cat. His skin had gone pale. For one dreadful moment, Ellen thought he might be sick all over the carpet. The day was hot but the house was kept cool, yet there were beads of perspiration glistening upon the ridge of Warren's forehead.

"Are you feeling okay?" Ellen asked him.

"A little touch of vertigo there for a sec," he said after a moment. His lips made a dry, smacking sound as they came apart. "You know, I've been feeling it coming on ever since we got off the highway. Go on, what were you saying?"

"Oh, uh," she began, not sure where she'd been in her speech. "There are marinas along the shore, too, where you can dock a boat. Do you guys own a boat?"

"Not at the moment, but we've been planning on getting one," Warren said enthusiastically, perhaps overcompensating for the grim, pasty look on his face.

"We've been *discussing* it," Angela interjected, more diplomatically. She had one of the house's brochures in her hand and was fanning an exposed area of prickly red flesh just below her neck. She was looking a bit pale, too.

"Are you not feeling well, either?" Ellen asked the woman.

"I'm fine, I'm fine," Angela responded . . . although she didn't *look* fine. If vertigo was contagious, Ellen would have thought she'd caught it from her husband. "It's just been a long, stressful week. Go on, Ellen. We're listening."

"Also," Ellen said, "there are so many kids in this neighborhood, and there's Gladstone Park just up the block here. Perfect place for you and your daughter to play." Ellen looked around, and for the first time, noticed Luna was no longer with them. "Where is she?"

Both Angela and Warren seemed to just realize their daughter was missing, too.

Warren peeled his hand away from the wall and called out, "Luna? Sweet pea?"

His voice echoed through the mostly empty house.

"She's had a rough morning," Angela said to Ellen, her voice a conspiratorial whisper. "Nightmare after nightmare last night. That's why we were late this morning. She didn't want to come out here. It got to the point where we had ourselves a little freakout session."

As Warren stepped out into the hallway still calling his daughter's name, Ellen said, "Freakout session?"

"She faints when she gets upset," Angela explained. "She's prone to it. It's not like she holds her breath until she passes out like some obstinate child; it's more like she just gets so riled up that her body flips a switch and, poof, the whole thing just shuts down. Like a circuit breaker."

"What shuts down?"

"Well, Luna," said Angela. "Her. Her body."

"Oh."

"It's not as unusual as it sounds. Happened to me as a girl, too."

Warren returned to the bedroom, still looking a bit green around the gills but also flummoxed now, too. "She's not answering me. I don't think she's still in the house."

"Well of *course* she's still in the house, where else would she *be*?"

Angela said, pushing past both Ellen and Warren and marching out into the hallway herself. She was still fanning that exposed patch of upper chest with the brochure. "Luna! Luna! You come here right now, young lady! Do you hear me? Enough games!"

"Do you hear your mother?" Warren called out, hands cupped around his mouth. His voice echoed over the second-floor landing like someone shouting across a canyon:

*. . . other . . . other . . . other . . .*

The three of them searched the other rooms on the second floor, but Luna was in none of them.

"This is absurd," Angela said. She was clearly growing agitated while her husband was looking more and more concerned.

"Maybe if we split up," Warren suggested, already slinking down the stairs to the first floor.

Ellen followed him, leaving Angela to steam in the upstairs hallway. The front door was still closed, yet Warren pulled it open and stepped out onto the brick stoop. "Luna! Luna Marie Mayer!"

Ellen wove through the kitchen, the living room, a quaint little sitting area near the back of the house. The back door was still locked, so the kid couldn't have gone out there.

Angela's voice, distant and shrill from the second-floor landing: *"Where are you, Luna? Where are you hiding?"*

Hiding? Was that what the kid was doing? Was this some sort of game to her?

*She didn't look much in the mood for games,* Ellen thought, recalling the way the girl had quietly moved in step behind her parents when they'd first entered the house, a look of grave disquiet on the kid's face. Given how her parents had looked in the upstairs bedroom just moments ago, Ellen wondered if the Mayer family wasn't dealing with the sudden onset of a stomach bug, maybe food poisoning. Either way, she thought it was time they all got out of the house.

*She didn't want to come out here. It got to the point where we had ourselves a little freakout session.*

Ellen yanked open closets and cupboards. She executed a second pass through the kitchen, the living room, the quaint sitting area. The house was empty and unadorned, so there *was* no place to hide. Where had the damn kid gotten off to, anyway?

*Basement.*

The thought struck Ellen at the same time her eyes fell upon the basement door. It was closed, and tucked in a niche in the wall between the kitchen and the main hallway, much like the basement door at Ellen's own house. Had Luna gone down there, would she have also closed the door behind her? Moreover, what reason would a five-year-old girl have for going down into a strange basement by herself? Weren't little kids frightened of basements?

*She isn't down there and she isn't anywhere else in this house. She's vanished, swallowed up, and we'll never find her. I'll be here all night dealing with the police. They'll put this kid's picture on the six o'clock news and people will talk about her disappearance for weeks, for months, and then they'll all just forget about her. Except Angela and Warren will never forget. They'll always keep looking. And I won't ever forget, either; I'll always drive by this place wondering what happened, and believing I've glimpsed her pale white ghost-face peering out at me from some darkened second-story window . . .*

Of course she wasn't down in the basement: there was a barrel bolt on the door, the bolt engaged. It was locked.

Still—

Ellen slid the bolt, opened the door, and descended the stairs.

## 2

It was a small, unfinished basement with a washer and dryer crowded beside a large utility sink. Luna was down here, her back facing Ellen, standing before the sink. The single exposed bulb above their heads merged their shadows along the concrete floor as Ellen came down the final step and entered the room.

"Luna," she said, her voice low.

The girl didn't respond, not right away. Instead, the silence was punctuated by the steady, metronomic drip from of the faucet of the utility sink.

*Plink.*

*Plink.*

*Plink.*

"Luna," she said again, a bit more sternly.

Her back still facing her, Luna said, "I kept my eyes closed."

"What do you mean, honey?"

"I kept my eyes closed," she repeated. "I kept them closed when I went through."

"Through what?"

"The space," she said. "The crack."

"What space? What crack?"

"I don't like this place."

"This house?"

"This whole place. It makes me feel funny."

*Plink.*

Ellen came up beside her. Luna was staring intently at the drops dripping from the faucet, which formed a murky puddle at the bottom of the basin. Ellen saw what looked like a slight sunburn along the left side of the child's face, something she hadn't noticed before.

*Plink.*

*Plink.*

"I don't like that water, either," Luna said.

Ellen bent down so that she was at eye level with the little girl, even though the girl was still staring straight ahead at the water dripping from the faucet. Softly, Ellen asked, "What don't you like about that water?"

Luna turned and faced her. The girl's eyes were glassy with tears and they seemed to jitter about in their sockets. That left side of her face was as bright and red as a slap. In a voice barely above a whisper, Luna said, "Something is in it."

"What? What's in it? Tell me."

The girl seemed to consider, her bright blue eyes ticking upward in concentration.

*Plink.*

"It's a . . . *snake* . . . I think . . ."

"In the water?"

"Something like that."

"What did you mean you kept your eyes closed when you went through? Went through what? What crack? Luna, how did you get down here with the door locked?"

*Plink.*

*Plink.*

"Luna?" She shook her gently by the shoulders.

The girl said nothing.

"Here you are!" Warren boomed, his frazzled, rambling shape suddenly filling the basement doorway at the foot of the stairs. The sound of him caused Ellen's heart to leap into her throat. Warren shouted up the stairwell to let his wife know they'd found their daughter, then he hurried over to the girl, clearly dismayed. "What were you thinking, running off like that?"

"I don't think she's feeling well," Ellen said.

Warren clamped a hand atop his daughter's shoulder, gave her a subtle shake. Clarity seemed to flood back into the girl's aquamarine eyes; she blinked, stared up at her father, and then over at Ellen. "Yeah, she looks really flushed," Warren agreed.

"Luna, honey, how'd you get down here?" Ellen asked her. She kept thinking of the barrel bolt, engaged. Impossible that it would somehow latch behind her.

Luna looked around, as if suddenly uncertain about her surroundings. "I went in one door and came out another," she said simply.

"What door?" Ellen asked.

"Yeah, well, don't do that kind of thing again," Warren interrupted, stepping on Ellen's question. He gathered up his daughter's hand and dragged her toward the stairs.

"What door?" Ellen asked again, still standing there.

Luna stopped and glanced at her from over one shoulder as her father tugged her by the hand toward the stairs. As Ellen stared back, she saw the girl's eyelids flutter and the eyes themselves roll back in their sockets. An instant later, Luna's body went limp; Warren's hand still clutching hers, she spooled to the floor at his feet rather than fell.

"Jesus," Warren muttered, gathering his daughter up in his arms. When he looked over and saw the expression on Ellen's face, he said, "She does this all the time whenever she's stressed out. It looks worse than it is. She'll come to in a minute."

But Warren didn't wait around the basement for his daughter to come to: he was already carrying her up the stairs, his own gait perceptibly wobbly and uncertain.

Before following them, Ellen reached over and tightened both taps on the faucet of the utility sink.

*I don't like that water, either. Something is in it.*

*It's a . . .* snake *. . . I think . . .*

The drops stopped dripping.

## 3

Once the Mayers had left, Ellen crossed the street to Pamela Guerin's house. The older woman was still in her yard, staring off toward some indeterminable point on the horizon. Pamela was in her early seventies, with her weighty bosom stretching taut the fabric of her floral-patterned housedress, and her exposed calves a jumble of fat blue varicose veins. Her silvery hair was pulled back in a bun, but loose strands blew like tinsel across her face. It looked as if she hadn't moved since Ellen's arrival.

"Hi, Pam. How's things?"

The older woman started at the sound of Ellen's voice. She turned around, a hand to her breast. There was a storm cloud of confusion in the woman's gray eyes. Pamela's mouth unhinged, revealing a file of small, even teeth. Spittle glistened in one corner of her mouth. A vertical crease appeared between her eyebrows, deep as a trench.

Ellen frowned. "Everything okay, Pam?"

"I am . . . trying to . . ." But Pamela's voice, creaky as an old wooden gate, trailed off. She was staring at Ellen as if trying to remember who she was. Then she cleared her throat and said, "Oh. Ellen McBride. *Ellen. McBride.* Hello. Hello!"

"Is everything okay, Pam?" Ellen asked again.

Pamela Guerin smiled. "Everything's *fine*, dear. Just wonderful, really." Her penciled eyebrows arched. "Did you sell the Trenton house yet, dear? Were those the new owners I saw leaving?"

"I don't think so."

"Shame. It's such a nice house. I thought it would go quickly. Seems to have been standing there empty for an eternity now."

"Have you noticed any kids from the neighborhood hanging out there?"

"What do you mean?"

"I think some kids are breaking it, using it as a party pad."

"A party pad? Lord. No, I haven't seen anyone. Say, Ellen, can I ask you something?"

"Sure."

Pamela withdrew an item from the pocket of her housedress. She extended it toward Ellen, but when Ellen reached for it, Pamela retracted her arm, as if suddenly changing her mind about giving it to her. Instead, she just held it up.

"Does this look like anything to you?" the older woman asked.

Ellen peered at the item cupped in Pamela Guerin's arthritic hands.

"Pam, it looks like the wheel off a shopping cart."

"Yes, yes," Pamela said, "but does it *look* like anything to you? Anything more than just an old shopping cart wheel, I mean."

"I don't understand."

"I found it *right there*," Pamela said, pointing at the concrete birdbath in the center of her yard. An oval of moss-green water reflected the summer sky. "It was the morning after that terrible storm.

Do you remember the storm? I came out here, and there it was, right in the birdbath." Something suggestive of a grin manipulated the lower half of Pamela Guerin's face, but there didn't seem to be any humor in it. "Isn't that *strange*?"

*No stranger than what just happened in the house across the street,* Ellen thought, still shaken, but did not say. She was still trying to puzzle out how Luna had gotten down into the basement with the barrel bolt on the basement door engaged.

"Even stranger than that," Pamela continued, "is that no birds have come back. Not since the storm. Have you noticed? Not to the birdbath, at least. Not since this old shopping cart wheel was in it. Do you find that peculiar, Ellen? Do you find that *strange*?"

She kept emphasizing the word *strange*, and for some reason, it was making the hairs stand up on Ellen's arms.

"How long have you been standing out here in this heat, Pam?"

Pamela appeared to consider this. The crease between her eyebrows sharpened to an exclamation point. Sweat rolled down the sunburned sides of her face. "I guess . . . I guess I can't really say . . ."

"Why don't I take you inside where it's cooler? Make us some lemonade?"

"You know, I'm fine, dear," Pamela said. That humorless, mechanical grin reappeared. "It's a nice idea, you making lemonade, dear, but I made a pitcher of iced tea just yesterday, and do you know what? It tasted funny." She frowned. "Or was that the day before? Either way, I think something was wrong with the water."

"Why do you say that?" Ellen asked. Suddenly, she was back in the basement of the Trenton house, little Luna saying, *I don't like that water, either.* Saying, *Something is in it.*

Pamela Guerin flapped a dismissive hand at her. She slipped the wheel of the shopping cart back into the pocket of her housedress. "Do you know what, Ellen? I think I'll go inside and watch some *Wheel of Fortune.*"

"Good idea," Ellen said, already retreating back across the street. "You have a good day, Pam."

After she got in her car, she watched Pamela Guerin in the rearview mirror, still standing motionless in the middle of her yard. Gazing once again toward some indeterminable point on the horizon.

"Go inside, Pam," Ellen muttered to the woman's tiny reflection in the rearview mirror. "Go inside, go inside, go inside . . ."

Across the street, Pamela Guerin lifted her head, looked around as if suddenly realizing where she was, and then hurried into her house.

# CHAPTER ELEVEN
# PINK LINES

## 1

There were several decent restaurants within a five-mile radius of Mariner's Cove, but Sarah Miller did not work at any of them. She worked at Hollywood BBQ, the only eatery in a mom-and-pop strip mall that was situated along U.S. Route 50. The food was just mediocre and there was decidedly nothing remotely "Hollywood" about the place—no meals named after celebrities, no retro movie posters on the walls, no kitschy L.A. motif. It was just a drab little shoebox with a couple of fryers in the back and a phalanx of booths outfitted in sticky crimson vinyl. It had once been a Hollywood Video, and the restaurant's owners, given to extreme parsimony, decided it was more economical to alter the existing sign than commission a new one. Hence, Hollywood BBQ. End of story.

Sarah Miller was nineteen years old, a dropout from the local community college, and one of three waitresses on staff this evening. She was the current Employee of the Month, and had been for the past three months, although considering her competition, such an accolade was no big shakes. Melanie Yodell, thirty years Sarah's senior, was sweet as pie, though she had a penchant for screwing up orders; meanwhile, Roberta Ducette, whose dour demeanor Sarah would have ordinarily deemed a virtue, smoked so much dope that by the end of her shift she was little more than a mindless zombie maneuvering about on an invisible track, eyes red, glassy, and heavy lidded. Sarah had worked here on and off throughout high school, and now, having unenrolled from the community college, she had, with a sense of doomed resignation, picked up the reins again. College, she knew, was not for her; she had only initially enrolled at her father's behest, and because she had no other options after graduating high school. Hollywood BBQ was certainly not a career. But money was tight, and she wanted to get out there and earn some. Sure, dropping out of community college had made her feel like a first-class loser, but really, what was the endgame there? Get an AA degree and transfer to a state university? Then what? Anyway, they didn't have the money for that. Regardless, Beatrice Hope, the floor manager, was more than happy to have her back on the schedule, and Sarah was already well on her way to Employee of the Month for August when her world came crashing down around her.

Locked in a stall in the women's room, pants around her ankles and the toilet seat cool against her buttocks, Sarah stared with almost incomprehensible dread at the slender white stick of the pregnancy test. The *positive* pregnancy test. According to the instructions on the box, that was what the double pink line meant—*positive.* As in, there was *positively* a fucking *baby* inside her.

"Well, shit," she uttered. Her own voice sounded foreign and echo-laden to her ears in that rectangular chamber of the bathroom stall. She tried to keep calm and stay cool about it, but her heart felt like a large stone rolling against the inner wall of her ribcage. Her flesh was suddenly tacky with sweat.

Someone entered the restroom. Sarah held her breath, as if fearful of being caught in some immodest act. She clenched the pregnancy test in one hand like a shiv.

"Sarah, honey? You in here?" It was Melanie Yodell.

Sarah cleared her throat. Couldn't she get a moment's peace in this godforsaken place? "Uh, yeah, Mel. I'm in here . . ."

"What's the matter, doll? You eat the special or something?"

"Just give me a minute, will you?"

"Beatrice needs you on the floor. Dinner rush."

"Just a minute," she reiterated, struggling to keep the tremor from her voice.

"If it's the mensies, I got an extra tamp in my purse."

Sarah closed her eyes, her face growing hot at the irony. "I'm good, Mel. Thanks."

"I'll buy you a couple more minutes, doll."

"Thank you."

Sarah heard the restroom door squeal closed again. Above her head, the automatic air freshener went *ffft.* She caught a whiff of lilac.

*Not pregnant,* she thought, tugging up her jeans and retying her apron. *The test was faulty. You're supposed to take more than one to be sure, right?*

She buried the white plastic stick deep in the restroom waste bin, then stood before the spotty mirror attempting to fix her hair. Splashed cool water on her face. Her hands were shaking.

If she *was* pregnant, then it was Doolie's fault. She'd had sex with no one else, just Doolie, and even *that* particular act, which she and Doolie had engaged in less than a dozen times in the back of his work van, one of her legs propped up on a power washer and rugburn imprinting along the base of her spine, could scarcely be worthy of procreation. Shane Doolman was twenty-three; he played bass in a (fairly awful) progressive rock band called Trembling Hamster, power washed houses during the week, and smoked pot with the regularity of someone who was being paid to do so. He still lived at home with his mother in an apartment in Glen Burnie, a sad, squalid place Sarah had only visited once and was happy never to return to again. Shane Doolman quoted Tarantino movies, and possessed a shelf of hardbound Dungeons & Dragons guides in his bedroom, although he swore he hadn't cracked one open since middle school. He was a geek, and somehow Sarah, in her flawed logic, had mistaken geekdom for a prophylactic.

But no: she wasn't pregnant. The test was faulty. It was a mistake.

It had to be.

*Although,* countered a small voice in her head, *those furiously changing hormones would account for the terrible dreams you've been having lately.*

That was true. Changing hormones might even account for the strange preoccupation that had overcome her ever since the night of that violent storm, as well. Since that night, she had cultivated an obsession for wire coat hangers. She had been finding them strewn about the neighborhood—snared in bushes, lying on the pavement, dangling like party decorations from tree branches. It wasn't just the ubiquitous nature of the coat hangers that troubled her; it was her inexplicable fascination with them, a desire to *have* them. She began collecting them, extracting them from the bushes, gathering them up off the pavement, plucking them like ripe fruit down from the tree branches. How had they gotten there, anyway? Who had deposited them there? Had the storm tossed them there, scattering them willy-nilly about the neighborhood, explicitly for her to find? Well, however it had happened, she now had a whole cardboard box full of them hidden in her bedroom closet, buried beneath an old Winnie the Pooh sleeping bag. It was a compulsion, that need to collect, something she was powerless to *not* do . . . yet she couldn't explain *why*, and that troubled her even more than the act of collecting itself. Now, gazing at her grim reflection in the restroom mirror, Sarah Miller felt some slight sense of relief in her ability to blame such craziness on a little fibrous collusion of cells multiplying exponentially inside her womb. If, in fact, that was the case.

It felt as if God were taunting her.

Out on the floor, she cleared a few tables, then got caught behind the register. A woman came in and ordered two fried chicken dinners to go. Sarah rang her up without comment, but when she ultimately looked up at the woman, she felt a spark of recognition go off in the back of her head. No, she did not know this woman, had never seen her before . . . yet something about her seemed familiar to Sarah. *Probably just someone I've seen around the neighborhood,* she rationalized, and yes, that was probably true. But nearly half the people who came into this place were from Mariner's Cove, and she was always recognizing faces even if she didn't know their names. Those vague recognitions had never bothered her before; they barely even registered with her, to be honest. So why was this woman making such an impression upon her? Perhaps this, too, could be attributed to a tide of rapidly changing hormones caused by the thing growing inside her. If a fetus could obligate her to collect the coat hangers and suffer a series of hallucinatory nightmares, then maybe it could also mess with the wiring inside her head, lending importance to something that was otherwise benign.

The woman standing in front of the register was named Ellen McBride. The name meant nothing to Sarah as she glanced at it on the woman's Visa card, yet she couldn't shake the sensation that there was something undeniably . . . *familiar* . . . about this woman.

*Maybe I've seen her in a dream,* she thought. Because her dreams had been pretty crazy lately, too. In last night's dream, she was a child again, holding her father's hand while they stood on a street corner in Chinatown in downtown Washington, D.C., watching a parade go by. This was something that she and her father had done in real life many years ago, so in a sense, the dream was also a memory. She stood there clutching her father's hand while men wearing an elaborate and colorful Chinese dragon costume danced down the center of H Street, past the shops with cooked ducks in the windows and beneath the elaborately decorative Friendship Archway. In her dream, she stared mesmerized by the large, golden head of the dragon, eyes like emeralds, crepe streamers blazing from its hinged and flapping maw, the jaw unhinging in synch with the men's jaunty footsteps, gaping, gaping, yawning, sneering, laughing.

Sarah rang up Ellen McBride's order, then handed her back the credit card. She told Ellen McBride it would be about a ten-minute wait, and Ellen McBride—

*(who is Ellen McBride?)*

—smiled and said no problem, she'll just wait over here.

Sarah looked down.

Her hands were trembling, and the black nail polish on her fingernails had been gnawed to patchy flakes.

"You okay?" It was Eric Rhodes, who stood stapling receipts together behind the counter. He was tall and good-looking in that Midwestern football hero sort of way—a look that Sarah had never been particularly attracted to, in all honesty—and he seemed like a nice enough guy.

"I don't know," she said truthfully, still staring down at her hands.

"Are you feeling sick or something?"

She considered this. Found that she actually wanted it to be true. "Maybe. Is something going around?"

Eric shrugged. "Beats me. But I'll tell you, Beatrice had the Hershey squirts yesterday. She'll deny it but it's true, swear to God. I know because I got stuck with bathroom duty at the end of my shift, and boy, I nearly quit."

One corner of Sarah's mouth tugged upward in something close to a grin. "Beatrice talks so much shit, I wouldn't be so certain which end those squirts came out of."

Eric laughed. "Good one. See? You look better already."

Maybe she looked better, but she felt like the inner workings of her body were coming loose. She dug her phone out of the rear pocket of her jeans and saw that there was still nearly four hours left on her shift. God, she couldn't get out of here fast enough tonight. Before putting the phone away, she typed into the search engine:

Is abortion legal in Maryland?

Google's response:

Yes, abortion is legal in Maryland. The state's constitution enshrines a broad right to abortion access, meaning abortion is legal at all stages of pregnancy.

*Enshrines,* she thought. The sheer audacity of such a word suggested abortion was some inalienable right. But was it for *her*? If it came down to it, was that something she could go through with?

Her head was beginning to spin.

"You doing anything when you get off?" Eric asked, noticing her checking her phone.

"Was just gonna go home and watch TV." She tucked the phone back in her jeans. When she looked up, she found herself glancing at

Ellen McBride, who stood waiting at the far end of the counter for her food. Why was this woman's familiarity so troublesome to her?

"Hey," Eric said, the stapler in his hand going *chu-chick*. "How old are you?"

"What?"

"It's just, I got a pair of concert tickets for this weekend but you gotta be twenty-one. It's at a club in Baltimore. My friend's band is playing."

"What are you doing?"

His eyebrows arched. He looked suddenly embarrassed. "What do you mean?"

"You're asking me out? On a date?"

"Oh, what? A date?" The tips of his ears turned red. "No, no, nothing like that. I mean, like, just as friends. Whatever. It's just, I've got this extra ticket . . ."

"What kind of music?"

"Pretty bad music."

She thought of Shane Doolman's terrible band. They never played clubs, just in a basement at someone's house. Sarah had gone to a practice and had pretended to be impressed.

"I'm nineteen," she said. "But I got a fake ID. Maybe I'll go."

"Okay, great. Just let me know."

When Ellen McBride's to-go order was ready, Sarah brought the food out from the kitchen herself. Ellen McBride thanked her then left. Through the wall of plate glass windows, Sarah watched the woman stride across the parking lot toward her car. That needling in her head persisted. Despite the dinner rush, Sarah told Roberta to cover for her, that she needed a cigarette. Before Roberta could protest, Sarah ditched out the back door of the restaurant, and into the alley where she had a clear shot of the McBride woman's car. She watched the taillights flash, the reverse lights come on as Ellen McBride backed out of her parking space. When the car pulled forward and headed out of the parking lot toward the street, Sarah walked to the mouth of the alley so she could see in which direction the woman drove. She saw the turn signal come on, and Sarah watched as Ellen McBride pulled onto the highway. The taillights dwindled in the encroaching darkness, threatening to fade altogether, but not before Sarah saw the vehicle take the exit for Mariner's Cove.

*How do I know that woman?*

Moreover—*Why do I fucking care?*

After all, there were more important things for her to be worrying about at the moment.

She dug a cigarette from her apron pocket, lit it. She puffed once, then gave consideration to the fact that perhaps the pregnancy test had been *right*. Which meant that there was a baby inside her right at this very moment. *Not a baby*, she reconciled. *A fetus. A zygote.* Trying to think of all the clinical terms for the damned thing that she'd been taught in high school biology. *Blastocyst. Embryo. Just not a baby. Anything but a baby.*

"There *is* no baby because the test had been wrong," she muttered to herself, suddenly feeling chilly despite the summery warmth that still hung in the air. Nevertheless, she tossed the cigarette onto the ground then crushed it out with her sneaker, unfinished.

## 2

Twenty minutes later, she decided to call it quits for the night. Ever since she'd peed on that stick—even before that, really—it had felt like a storm was slowly gathering in the center of her body. Her skin kept going from hot to cold, hot to cold. Friends kept dinging her phone with random nonsensical texts, so much so that Sarah had ultimately muted the damn thing before it drove her insane. She told Beatrice she wasn't feeling well, then clocked out early for the night.

Before leaving, she went to the backroom where the employees kept their personal belongings. It was a cramped little office with a slouching wooden desk in one corner, a corkboard bristling with flyers hanging askew above it, and a long wooden bench against one wall that looked like something one might find in a high school locker room.

Metal hooks hung from the wall over the bench, where employees hung their coats in the winter and their baseball hats and beach towels in the summer. Beneath the bench were purses and shoes and someone's ratty old canvas sandals. No one worried about theft around here, even though sometimes the registers didn't add up at the end of a shift. Sarah had given up carrying a purse long ago, opting instead for her old JanSport backpack with the Ramones and Urge Overkill patches sewn on it, which she now snatched from one of the hooks on the wall.

There was also a closet in here, which was really just a slender niche in the wall with no door. Before leaving, Sarah paused in front of it. Stood there, hands fidgeting. The closet's interior was painted a garish purple and there was nothing inside except a horizontal bar on which hung a cluster of plastic and wire hangers. For several heartbeats, Sarah stared at those coat hangers. As she stared, she gnawed unconsciously at her lower lip. Then, before she knew what she was doing or why she was doing it, she unzipped her backpack and proceeded to stuff the coat hangers inside. No, not all the coat hangers: just the wire ones.

"Hey," Beatrice said, startling her.

Sarah jumped, and spun around to see the woman standing in the doorway. Had Beatrice witnessed her stealing the hangers? Furiously feeding them into the open maw of her backpack? Was such a thing even a *crime*?

"Hey," Sarah said back, her voice cracking. "What's up?"

"Mel's asking for Saturday off. Something to do with her kid. You feel like covering her shift?"

"Yeah, sure."

Beatrice's eyes narrowed at her, as if Sarah has said something suspicious. Beatrice Hope was a robust and chesty woman with a beehive of dyed black hair and the severe, painted-on eyebrows to match. "Boy, you really don't look so good, honey. What do you think it is?"

*I think I might be pregnant and I've been having terrible nightmares and I steal wire coat hangers for no conceivable reason.*

"Just tired, I guess. Run down."

"Go home and get some sleep," Beatrice said, and then she retreated back out into the hall.

Without saying goodbye to anyone, Sarah vanished out the back door of the restaurant and out into the employee parking lot. Roberta Ducette and Tyler Coombs, one of the cooks, stood beneath a streetlamp sharing a joint. Sarah marshaled across the parking lot toward her car, head down, not interested in attracting her coworkers' attention. She drove a piece of shit Ford Festiva that she had bought from a cousin of hers for about three hundred bucks. It was a fucking roller skate with a steering wheel, but at least it was hers. She climbed into the driver's seat, tossing her backpack on the passenger seat where she heard the wire hangers jangle together in there. She jabbed the key into the ignition, cranked it. The Festiva's engine made a *whir-whir* sound, but the car did not start.

"Oh. Oh, don't you be dead. Don't you be dead on me tonight, you son of a bitch."

She cranked the key again. This time, the engine didn't even go *whir-whir.* The dome light brightened briefly then went dark.

"Fuck you," she growled at the car.

She wanted to scream.

She wanted to break down and cry.

Maybe, if the car *had* started, she would have just driven the son of a bitch off the Bay Bridge. End of story.

A tapping against the driver's side window startled her. She turned and saw Eric standing there, peering in at her. She rolled the window down.

Eric said, "Car trouble?"

"It won't start. Do you know anything about cars?"

"No, not really. Sorry."

"Goddamn it." She yanked the key out of the ignition and fought off the urge to send it sailing out through the window and over Eric's head.

"I can give you a ride home, though," Eric offered. He lived in her neighborhood.

"Is your shift over?"

"I'm on break."

She glanced at the backpack in the passenger seat. Thought of the wire hangers inside it, tangled up together. What the hell was wrong with her?

"Yeah, okay," she said. "Thanks."

She got out, slung the backpack over her shoulder—

*(jangle jangle)*

—and followed Eric to his ride. It was a nice-looking pickup truck, black as an oil slick, with shiny chrome bumpers. Beneath the streetlamp, Roberta Ducette and Tyler Coombs spotted them and began catcalling.

"Ignore them," Eric said, going around to the passenger side of the truck and opening the door for her. "They're morons. Watch your step."

She climbed into the cab. The wire coat hangers in her backpack clanged mutely together but she didn't think he noticed. Eric shut the door then strode around to the other side, climbed in beside her. The interior of the truck smelled clean and of pine-scented air fresheners, unlike the interior of Sarah's Festiva, which smelled perpetually of greasy fast food and cigarette smoke. Eric coasted out of the parking lot with appreciable ease.

Sarah said nothing. She was sweating in her skin, despite the comfortable temperature of the truck's cab. She assumed the silence was uncomfortable for Eric, though, because he asked if she minded if he turned on the radio. She said she didn't, and a Mumford & Sons song came on.

"You like this music?" he asked.

She casually covered up the Ramones and Urge Overkill patches on her backpack. To be polite, she said, "It's okay." Then she remembered something. "What day did you say your friend's band is playing?"

"Saturday."

"I have to work."

Eric glanced at her. His face had taken on a cool gray hue in the fading daylight coming through the truck's windshield. "Oh. I didn't see your name on the schedule."

"Melanie's got something going on with her kid, so I told Beatrice I'd cover her shift."

"Oh, right. Well, that sucks."

"Yeah. I'm sorry."

"It's okay. I just thought it would be something fun to do. Maybe some other time."

"Sure." She glanced out the passenger window, and at the lighted houses along Spruce Street, the clusters of crepe myrtle and windblown willow trees crouched in the darkening spaces between the houses. "Do you mind if we make a pit stop? I need to grab something from the Walgreens."

"Yeah, sure, you got it," Eric said, and spun the wheel.

## 3

She told Eric to wait in the truck while she ran in. When she came back a few minutes later, climbing up into the passenger seat as Eric lowered the volume of the music on the radio, the last strands of daylight were beginning to drain from the sky. She snapped her seatbelt into the place, the plastic Walgreens bag on her lap suddenly the most conspicuous thing in the world.

Eric reached for the gearshift, but Sarah said, "Wait. Please. Okay?"

"Okay."

He was staring at her, but she was looking straight ahead, right out the truck's windshield, even though she could feel his eyes on her.

"Feels good to be out of the neighborhood, is all," she said, more to herself than to him.

"Yeah," he said anyway.

She knocked a knuckle against the passenger window. "Can I roll this down? Get some fresh air?"

Eric hit a button and the window descended. The evening air spilled into the cab of the truck, cooling the sweat along Sarah's flesh.

Eric nodded at the plastic bag in her lap. "You okay?"

"Uh, I needed some sleeping pills," she said, surprised at how easy the lie came to her. She quickly unzipped her backpack and stuffed the plastic bag containing the pregnancy test inside, careful not to let Eric catch an eyeful of the coat hangers hidden in there. "I've been having a tough time sleeping lately. Terrible nightmares." This part, at least, was the truth.

"No kidding?" he said. "Me too."

"Yeah?"

"I keep having dreams about these weird symbols. And when I wake up, I can't stop thinking about them. They make me feel . . . I don't know . . . funny, I guess."

"Funny how?"

"Like my mind is on fire."

Together, they laughed nervously.

"Seriously, though," he said, "I even went online, to Reddit and Facebook and wherever, because I thought I was losing my mind, and wanted to hear what other people had to say."

"What'd they have to say?"

"Nothing. It was hopeless. There was no point. Those dreams made me feel so . . . so helpless, yet anxious at the same time. Christ, I don't know how to say it."

"No, I understand. It's okay."

"What's even creepier is that I started seeing those symbols in real life. Around the neighborhood, I mean. Someone's made chalk drawings on—"

"I've seen them, too. They're all over the Cove."

"Right. Right. So, what do you think they mean? Like, what purpose do they serve? It can't just be a gang of roving teenagers vandalizing shit for no reason. It's all too . . . too *deliberate*."

She thought of her coat hangers, but said, "I don't know."

"I started to convince myself that maybe they had all been there longer than I thought, and that I'd seen them, like, subconsciously, and that would explain why I was dreaming about them. But then the dream changed, and it's been the same nightmare every time, and I keep having it. Pretty much every night. What's that called when that happens?"

"Recurring."

"Yeah, Recurring. A recurring dream. Or nightmare, in this case. That."

She glanced at him. "And . . . ? Don't leave me hanging, man."

Eric said, "Well, in the dream, I'm like, part of some . . . I don't know . . . some group. You know, like it's me and a bunch of other people, only I don't know who they are, and we're all just crawling around this . . . this giant . . . I don't know how to describe it . . ."

"Hive," Sarah finished.

He looked at her. Said, "Yeah." Said, "Hive." Said, "How do you . . . ?"

"I've been having the same dream."

She watched Eric's eyebrows knit together the slightest bit. "That's not . . ." Then he grinned, shook his head. "You're messing with me."

"It's this big, beige-colored ball hanging in the sky," she said, "and there are all these people, like, clinging to it. Sometimes some of them lose their grip and fall and I can hear them screaming all the way down until they hit the ground."

The grin faded from Eric's face. He was slowly shaking his head, his eyes locked on hers. "Yeah, that's the . . . the same thing I've been dreaming about," he said, his voice filled with what sounded like a mixture of awe and fear. "Only my dream starts off with me wandering through the woods. There are other people around me, but they're mostly hidden behind the trees. I can't see their faces. But I get the sense that we're all being . . . I guess, drawn to the same place."

"Right," she said. "To the hive. It's right up there in the sky, above the trees. And there are people crawling all over it like insects. It sort of breathes like a lung—I can see it expanding and contracting, like something alive. Or maybe there's something alive *in* it, you know? In the dream, I'm drawn to it, just like all the other people around me, and just like the people clinging to it. And then I'm suddenly clinging to it, too. We're all just . . . clinging to it . . . for dear life. Like it's so important we need to protect it."

"Jesus, Sarah." He released a nervous, shuddery breath. "You know, it never occurred to me that it was a hive until you just said it."

*It's not really a hive,* she thought out of nowhere, uncertain as to what such a thought meant. And then on the heels of that, she was remembering the parade and the Chinese dragon from another dream which had also been a memory from a different time.

"This is impossible," Eric was saying, still shaking his head. "How can two people be having the same recurring dream? What does that mean? The fact that you and I are, you know, both having it . . ."

"I don't know," she said, "but there's been a lot of crazy shit happening lately."

"Yeah? Like what else?"

She thought about the coat hangers in her backpack and what might be a living thing insider her uterus. "Forget it," she said. "I don't want to talk about it right now. I'm freaked out enough as it is."

"Me too," Eric said.

Across the street, a string of streetlamps came on.

"Come on, let's go," she told him. "You need to get back to your shift."

## 4

They spent the drive back to Mariner's Cove in relative silence. Sarah could tell Eric was still struggling to comprehend how the two of them happened to share a dream, but that he was likely too unnerved by the whole thing to ask any further questions. For that, Sarah was grateful; her mind was already filled with enough worry, she didn't need to spook herself any more than she already was.

She'd been riding with her eyes closed and her head against the headrest, the cool evening breeze feeling good along her flesh. But now, as they crossed back into the neighborhood, she was aware of a strange sort of pressure overtaking her. It was as if her skin had shrunk just the slightest bit around her body. By the time they pulled onto her block, her molars had begun to ache.

Eric pulled up outside her house. He geared the truck into park, but left it idling. He was late returning from his break, but he didn't seem to mind. "Hey," he said. He was looking at her profile, she could tell, even if she wasn't looking at him. "You're not messing around with me, right? You've really been having that same dream?"

"How would I know the details of your dream if I didn't dream it, too?"

It was a logical thing to say, but she could tell it made him even more uncomfortable. She couldn't blame him.

"Right," he said, and exhaled audibly.

She looked at him and smiled miserably. "Maybe something in that restaurant is poisoning us. Maybe we're all suffering from some shared barbecue-induced hallucination. When you go back tonight, check the expiration date on the ground beef."

Eric's expression turned grim. "Are you joking? Please be joking."

"Or maybe it's just some strange coincidence."

"Do you think?"

"I don't know."

"It's freaking me the hell out."

"It's freaking me out, too."

"And it's not just the dream," he said. "But, like, after I wake up from having it, I've got this strange sensation that . . ." His voice trailed off.

"That what?"

"Forget it. It'll sound like I'm crazy."

*I'm the one collecting wire coat hangers for no apparent reason,* she thought. *Don't tell me about crazy.*

"Go on," she urged him. "Tell me."

"Well, sometimes right after I wake up, it feels like a part of that dream is still there inside my head. I don't mean, like, the memory of the dream still lingering. It's more like something from that dream has followed me out of it and it's still moving around inside my head. You know what I'm saying? Like, there's *me* in there, same as always, but at the same time, there's also something *else*." He was staring at her, his eyes pleading.

"I don't think that's crazy at all," she told him.

"No?"

"That's a classic barbecue-induced hallucination, all right."

"I'm being serious, Sarah. You don't find this totally fucked up?"

"It's totally fucked up for sure."

"Should we tell someone?"

"Who would we tell?"

"Jesus, I don't know." His hands were gripping the steering wheel so tightly his knuckles were white. "My parents would think I'm on drugs. Cops wouldn't believe us."

"Why would the cops care?"

"I don't know. I'm just thinking out loud." He looked at her again. Intently. "You're much calmer about this than I am. Why is that?"

She didn't want to tell him.

"Hey," she said instead. "Thanks for the ride."

"You aren't freaked out?"

"I said I was."

He glanced at her backpack. Then met her eyes again. "Everything okay with you? Whatever other stuff is going on, I mean?"

"I'm peachy. Thanks again for the ride," she said, and climbed out of his truck.

She hurried up the walkway toward her house, her head down, one strap of her backpack slung over a shoulder. She could hear the wire coat hangers clanging around in there, whispering in their secret coat hanger language.

She entered the house and kicked off her sneakers in the front hall just as her father's voice greeted her from the living room: "Is that you, kitten?"

"It's me."

One hand tightening on the strap of her backpack, she poked

her head into the living room to find her father seated in his recliner beneath the tepid yellow glow of a floor lamp. Classical music played softly on the stereo. He had a notepad balanced on one thigh, his Bible beside him on an end table beside a glass of red wine, and he was tapping a ballpoint pen against the armrest of his chair. Sarah knew he was working on one of his sermons.

He peered at her from over the rim of his glasses. Smiled. "I thought you were closing tonight."

She made a face. "Wasn't feeling well."

"Oh? What's wrong?"

"Just my stomach."

"Oh, no," he said, looking genuinely concerned. David Miller was a pastor at the United Methodist Church on Terrace Avenue. He was a simple, kindhearted man who had never remarried after the death of Sarah's mother from cancer a few years back. He was not the type of man to disown his unmarried daughter for getting pregnant at nineteen—at least, she didn't think he was—but she knew the weight of his disappointment might very well kill her.

"Don't worry, Dad. I'll be okay."

"Well, in that case, I don't suppose you're hungry. There's leftover roast beef in the fridge. Pretty darn tasty."

"I'm okay. I think I'm just going to go to bed early."

"Smart idea. Get that rest. Goodnight, kitten."

"Goodnight, Dad," she said, then hurried up the stairs to her bedroom.

There, she unzipped the backpack and dumped the stolen coat hangers onto her bed, along with the Walgreens bag. The hangers clattered unmusically. What the heck was she doing? What was wrong with her? If she truly was pregnant then maybe this strange new obsession could be explained away. Heck, she'd heard stories of pregnant women eating rocks and dirt and rolled up bits of paper, so how did that compare with some compulsory need to collect wire coat hangers?

*But there* is *no baby. That test was faulty.*

Her eyes drifted toward the Walgreens bag.

*There is no baby.*

She gathered up the hangers and carried them over to her closet. With her foot, she drew back the Winnie the Pooh sleeping bag to reveal a cardboard box filled with even more hangers. So many she could no longer count them just by looking. She dumped the new hangers into the box with the old ones.

*What is wrong with me?*

Even now, just staring at them all in there, she wanted to run her hands over them, to touch them, caress them. Throughout the day she fantasized about unwinding the braided hook at the top of each hanger and straightening them into slender wire rods. In fact, she had done that on a few occasions, untwisting the hooked part of the hanger so that it sprung open, then bending it so that it became a somewhat straight rod of metal. She could never iron out all the kinks from where it had been bent so that it was perfectly straight, but she didn't think that mattered; it just felt good, like some near-sexual release, to unwind them and straighten them out.

She had no idea why she'd been doing this, except that it was an obsession. And a small and still-dwindling part of her understood that she should probably be afraid.

*It's more like something from that dream has followed me out of it and it's still moving around inside my head,* Eric had said back in the truck. *Like, there's* me *in there, same as always, but at the same time, there's also something* else.

*There's sometimes something else inside of me, too, Eric,* she confessed, if only to herself, now that she was within the relative safety of her own home. *It came in with the storm and it's taken up residence in one dark corner of my brain. Sometimes, I think I can almost see it, and when I do, I think of—*

She thought of the men in the Chinese dragon costume in downtown D.C.

Emerald eyes.

Decorative mouth flapping open on a hinge.

And then for some reason she thought of that woman from earlier,

Ellen McBride, who had come into the restaurant and ordered two fried chicken dinners to go. Who was Ellen McBride? Why did it matter? How was any of this connected?

*Two chicken dinners,* she thought, her head suddenly reeling.

*Two.*

She picked up the Walgreens bag from her bed and shook the box containing the pregnancy test out onto the bedspread.

*One test might be faulty, but two . . .*

She scooped up the box then went down the hall to the bathroom. She could still hear her father's classical music down there on the stereo, a tempered orchestral piece that should have soothed her but instead caused a tremor of anxiety to ripple through her. In the bathroom, she stripped her jeans and underwear down to her ankles then sat on the toilet. She was thinking about coat hangers, coat hangers, coat hangers. And dreams of the hive.

*. . . and it's me and a bunch of other people, and we're all crawling around this . . . this giant . . . I don't know how to describe it . . .*

She peed on the stick then set it on the corner of the sink. Waited, watching the time on her cell phone, while still seated on the toilet.

*. . . there's* me *in there, same as always, but at the same time, there's also something* else *. . .*

When the time was up, she looked at the stick. One line would mean not pregnant. Two lines, just like the test she'd taken earlier, would mean she was pregnant. Two lines: one for each consciousness residing inside her.

*. . . but at the same time, there's also something* else *. . .*

There were three pink lines on the stick.

# CHAPTER TWELVE
# SPRAY PAINT

The transmissions were being received through his teeth. A chronic, incessant buzzing that travelled along the main sensory nerve of his face, radiated across his lower mandible, and pumped what felt like a constant surge of electricity into his molars. It was so powerful, he thought that if he touched a finger to a lightbulb, he might cause it to glow.

The symbols were what was being transmitted, of course. They filled his head day and night, cluttered his thoughts, invaded and corrupted his consciousness. He could no longer see letters or numbers for what they were—whenever he looked at them in the pages of a book, on a computer screen, on a road sign or mailbox, they appeared to him as those same immutable symbols and nothing more. Not that he understood what those symbols were supposed to be, either; he was equally as illiterate to them as he was, now, to the English language.

But that didn't matter.

What mattered was that he, too, was a transmitter.

He rummaged around in his garage, collecting cans of spray paint from a shelf. He worried the chalk wouldn't last if another storm came through, or if someone decided to take a hose to the symbols sketched on the sidewalk at the front of their house. The notion that all his work could so easily be washed away terrified him. He didn't want to fail in his mission. Yet—

What mission?

Who—or what—was transmitting the symbols to *him*?

*Doesn't matter. Doesn't matter. Only the symbols matter. Only getting them down, passing them on, transmitting . . .*

Whoever or whatever was transmitting those symbols to him through his teeth, they were also beginning to guide him as to where *he* was supposed to transmit them. It had started out completely random and indiscriminate, with him scribbling those symbols in his house and on his flesh, before printing them in chalk throughout the neighborhood, wherever it felt right. But lately, whoever or whatever was transmitting those symbols to him, they were also beginning to guide his hand, suggesting places for him to sketch a particular symbol. It wasn't so much a voice in his head as it was an instinct, a reflex, that overcame him with undeniable authority.

And still, a vestige of his previous mind would sometimes think:

*Maybe I'm going crazy.*

*Maybe I'm dying.*

He couldn't remember the last time he'd slept or ate a meal. Sometimes, he would try to focus on the thing that was sending him these transmissions, but instead, he found himself thinking of the time Marco had discovered a slender black snake crawling into a birds' nest in their garden, and how Marco had gotten a long stick, scooped it up, and tossed the snake out into the grass.

The symbols had to be conveyed. If he was the conduit to get it done, then so be it. The symbols were all that mattered.

Spray paint.

Spray paint was *permanent.* He uncapped a can of bright orange paint. Shook it so that the little ball clanged about inside. The interior of Raj Subador's house was positively brimming with those arcane symbols—he'd printed them on the walls, carved them into the hardwood floors, had even drawn them in permanent marker on his face, arms, chest—but the walls of his garage were relatively barren. He raised the can of spray paint and—

*(sssss)*

—sprayed a vertical line straight down the wall in orange neon.

He blinked at it, then sprayed two curved semicircles, one atop the other, along the right side of the straight line.

There was something familiar about the shape. It wasn't one of the symbols, yet it somehow also *was*. For a moment, the pain in his back teeth lessened even as his nose began to bleed.

Had he still been able to comprehend the alphabet, Raj Subador would have recognized the symbol for precisely what it was.

The capital letter B.

# CHAPTER THIRTEEN
# "I THINK SOMETHING IS HAPPENING TO EVERYONE"

## 1

Ellen pulled into the driveway, the aroma of the fried chicken dinners in their little boxes on the passenger seat having filled the interior of the car. Despite that, she found upon arriving home that she wasn't very hungry. She could see that Cory had drawn the drapes closed across the bay windows at the front of the house, and that he'd lowered the shades on all the other windows, as if afraid someone might come along and try to peek inside.

Patrick McBride—Cory's father and Ellen's husband—had been ripped from their lives in a fatal car accident so long ago now that Ellen had stopped wondering what advice he might offer in any given situation, had he still been alive; however, as she sat behind the wheel of her car, engine idling and engulfed in what should be the comforting scent of fried chicken, she wondered now what advice Patrick might impart. What would Patrick do in this situation for his son?

*He wouldn't know what to do because he wouldn't understand it,* she knew. *Not in the way Brian would understand it.*

At one time, anyway. Before he drank it away.

How had her son been keeping this a secret from her? How long had she noticed the lights blinking or dimming throughout the house when he'd come home from school? How long had she been hearing books slide off the bookshelf in his bedroom in the middle of the night while he tossed and turned in his sleep? Maybe things had been happening for even longer than she realized—even longer than perhaps *Cory* realized—only she hadn't noticed. It was like water seeping through cracks in a dam. She should have been more observant. More vigilant.

*Maybe I should take him to a therapist,* she thought now, though on the heels of that, she envisioned items in some psychiatrist's office spontaneously levitating or rearrange themselves on shelves. *No, I can't do that.*

The sun was setting and shadows were being stretched between the houses along Cloister Road, yet she could suddenly see Mr. Zachs from next door standing in the web of darkness between their two houses. He was at the bottom of the stairs that led up to the side door of Ellen's house, staring up at the kitchen window that was still covered in plastic.

She turned off the car, grabbed the dinners off the passenger seat, then climbed out into a breezy summer evening. She paused midway up the driveway, and instead of going up the walk to the front door, stepped around to the side of the house to where Mr. Zachs was standing.

"Hey, Mr. Zachs. Everything okay?"

Apparently startled by the sound of her voice, Mr. Zachs jumped, then whirled around in Ellen's direction. His face was red and glistening, as if he'd just come back from a run. He blinked his eyes in rapid succession, and the whole thing would have been comical if it wasn't so damn *weird*.

"Oh," he said, then cleared his throat. "Hello, Ellen. Hi. How . . . how are you?"

"Just getting back from showing a house and picking up some dinner. Is there something I can help you with?"

"Well, I don't want to upset you and I'm sure it's probably nothing, but I thought I heard your son calling out to me while I was in the yard. I didn't see your car, so I assumed you were working, and figured the boy was home alone. So, of course, I knocked"—he nodded toward the side door—"but he didn't answer."

"Oh." A pang of distress pulsed in her chest.

"Maybe it's just me," Mr. Zachs said, grinning apologetically now.

"Maybe I'm just mis-hearing things. These old ears, you know? I'm sure he's fine and I was just overreacting. I don't want to upset you, Ellen."

She went up the stairs to the side door, the one that led into the kitchen. The door was locked, so she jabbed it with her key, then swung it open and onto a dark and silent house.

"Cory?"

She dumped the dinners on the counter along with her purse then switched on the lights. Behind her, Mr. Zachs came up the stairs and peered through the doorway.

Cory materialized at the other end of the hall, clutching a baseball bat over one frail shoulder. Both his knees were bloody.

"Cory, what are you doing? What's going on?"

She went to him, ran a hand through his hair. She tried prying the baseball bat from him, but he refused to let it go. He was staring past her, down the hall and at the rounded, beet-faced shape of Mr. Zachs who was still standing in the open doorway.

"Why are all the lights off and the drapes drawn?" she asked him.

"Everything okay in there?" Mr. Zachs called from the doorway.

"Everything's fine," she returned. "Thank you, Mr. Zachs."

"Is there something I can do for the boy?"

The curios in the China cabinet began to vibrate.

"He's fine," she said. "We're both fine. Thank you again."

"Go home!" Cory shouted at him, and rushed to the door. He slammed it just as Mr. Zachs staggered backward and retreated down the steps, a look of consternation on his round, sweat-jeweled face. The moment he slammed the door, the ceiling lights flickered.

"Cory, what the heck is going on with you?"

"That's not Mr. Zachs." Still clutching the baseball bat, he hurried over to the kitchen counter and peeled back a flap of the plastic over the window so he could peer out into the side yard.

"Baby, what are you talking about?"

"Shhhh," he said, still staring out through the flap of plastic.

Ellen closed her eyes. Took a deep breath. The scent of the fried chicken smelled nauseating now. In a softened tone, she asked, "Were you calling for help? Did something happen? Mr. Zachs said he heard you."

"No."

"Tell me," she begged. "Tell me what's going on, Cory. Please."

He made a clicking sound in the back of his throat. When he turned to face her, she could still clearly see the fear in his eyes. "Mr. Zachs was lying. I wasn't calling for him. *He* was calling for *me*, only not with his words."

"What does that even mean?"

"He was talking in my head. He kept saying *come out*."

"In your head," she said flatly.

"Like, I could hear what he was thinking, and he *knew* I could hear it. He was talking to me with his mind."

She felt the world begin to unravel beneath her feet.

"I shut off all the lights and closed the drapes so he couldn't see in. But then he knocked on the front door and tried to get me to open it. I told him to go away. But he kept telling me to *come out, come out*."

"That's because he said he heard you shouting or something," she explained to him. "He was coming over to see if you were okay."

"No! That isn't true."

The lights flickered once more.

The curios rattled in their glass coffin at the far side of the dining room.

"Here," he said, and dug his cell phone from his pocket. He handed it to her with one trembling hand. "Look at the text messages between me and Davey. Davey saw him, too. He was texting me from across the street while Mr. Zachs was trying to get into the house. Read them, Mom!"

She opened the texting app and scrolled through a series of messages between Cory and Davey Orem. She read only a couple before she sighed and set his phone on the dining room table. "Yes, Cory, he was here at the door, knocking. He told me as much. I want to know why you're holding a bat and thinking our elderly neighbor is trying to break in and get you."

"Because he's not our neighbor, Mom. Mr. Zachs isn't Mr. Zachs anymore."

"What does that even *mean*, Cory? I don't understand any of this."

"I looked inside his thoughts."

She shook her head, not comprehending. "What?"

"It's something I found out I can do now," he said. "Or, at least, the gnome can do it. If I concentrate, I can . . . like, peek inside someone's head. But just for a second, and it's not very clear. I did it to Mr. Zachs today, when I saw him outside, and there was . . . was something else *inside* him . . ."

"I don't know what that means. I can't understand any of this." She sat down in one of the dining room chairs before she fainted.

"I don't know, either, Mom," he said.

And he began to tremble.

## 2

They ditched the fried chicken and had great heaping bowls of ice cream instead. There was a Jim Carrey movie on TV, but they were only half watching it. When they were finished with their ice cream, Ellen was comforted by her son's head coming to rest on her shoulder. She could feel the soft labor of his respiration along her arm.

"I want to tell you about my bike ride today," Cory said, "but I don't want to scare you."

"You won't scare me."

"It scared *me*."

She muted the television.

He told her about the strange symbols he saw chalked on the sidewalk outside Winona Orem's house, and how they'd made him feel . . . funny. The symbols themselves meant nothing to him—they were just a collection of nonsensical shapes—but their presence made him uncomfortable. He showed her the pictures he'd taken of them on his phone. He told her that there were additional symbols sketched farther up the sidewalk and even in the road, and despite the uneasy way they made him feel, he felt compelled to see just how many places those symbols had been drawn. So, he had gotten on his bike and coasted up and down the streets of Mariner's Cove. Sure enough, he found they were everywhere: etched onto sidewalks, in the middle of the streets, drawn on people's driveways, even along the brick siding of some houses.

"What about them bothered you so much?" she asked him. She was still scrolling through the photos of them on Cory's phone. Strange and arcane, yes, but nothing inherently off-putting about them. Hell, she'd probably stepped right over them on the sidewalk without even noticing.

"I don't know," he said. "I can't explain it. It was like the same feeling I got when I peeked inside Mr. Zachs's head, only then, I hadn't peeked yet, so I didn't know. I just felt they were . . . important somehow. And . . . well, like dangerous, maybe."

"You keep saying you peeked inside Mr. Zachs's head," she said. "Do you mean you're sensing something about him? Like, you're getting a bad vibe or something?"

"I mean exactly what I said. I peeked inside his head and saw what looked like a really bad storm in there."

"In his head?"

"In his mind."

*Jesus Christ*, she thought. *What the hell is going on around here? What's happening to my baby?*

"And then earlier, when you told me Mr. Zachs was . . . was talking to you, only he wasn't using any words . . ."

"That's the only way I can describe it."

"Okay." The word creaked out of her.

Cory looked up at her. "Do you believe me?"

"Yeah, baby. I believe everything you ever tell me."

"Have you seen them? The symbols?"

"I don't know," she said. "But I haven't really been looking for them."

She felt he wanted to say more but didn't quite know how to do it.

She urged him to continue, giving him a comforting squeeze around his shoulders.

"When I got to Gladstone Park," he said, "the bad feeling got stronger. I tried to think real hard about who had drawn those shapes all over the neighborhood, but something stopped me from seeing. It knocked me off my bike."

She frowned. "Someone knocked you off your bike? Who?"

"Not someone," he said. "It was just like a feeling in my head. Like, I pushed a little bit to send my thoughts out there, and something very big pushed back."

"In your head," she said.

"Yeah. In my head. The same way I made the fork spin around."

"And now you think Mr. Zachs is somehow . . . connected . . . to these chalk drawings?"

"Not just Mr. Zachs," he said in a small voice.

"What do you mean?"

"I think . . . I think people are . . . *changing.*"

"Changing how?"

"The way Mr. Zachs is different in his head now. I think something is happening to everyone. I can feel it all over the neighborhood. Behind doors. In houses. People watching me on my bike. It scares me."

She was worried about him. No question he possessed a unique ability, just like her brother and her aunt had, but this recent bout of paranoia and anxiety—his irrational fear of Mr. Zachs and a series of crude chalk drawings on the sidewalk—was something altogether different. Maybe she *should* take him to a therapist.

"Have *you* noticed people acting weird?" he asked her.

"No, baby, I haven't," she said . . . yet even as she said it, she thought back to earlier that day—to little Luna Mayer disappearing in the Trenton house only to wind up in the basement despite the locked door, followed by the peculiar conversation she'd had with Pamela Guerin about a shopping cart wheel—and knew that what she'd said to him wasn't entirely true. Not wanting to frighten him further, though, she decided not to say anything.

Beside her on the couch, Cory glanced down at the melting clump of chocolate ice cream in his bowl. Black curlicues of hair hung down over his eyes.

"What else?" she said, because she could tell there was more.

He muttered something inaudible.

"What?"

He said, "I don't want you to think I'm a freak."

"Baby, I could never think that about you. I've told you that already."

"It's what you *say.* You're my mom, so you have to say it."

"Listen to me." She reached over and lifted his chin, so that he was peering out at her from behind that fringe of curly black hair. *Patrick's hair.* "I'm worried about you. *That's* my job, because I'm your mom. Do you understand? I'm worried, just like any mother would be, but I don't think you're a freak, baby. I don't think anything bad about you in this world. I promise."

His eyes were filling up with tears.

"Do that thing," she said.

"What thing?"

"The thing you said you did to Mr. Zachs. Go on. See inside *my* head. You'll know I'm telling the truth."

"No." There was a fearful look in his eyes. "I don't want to do that to you."

"It's okay. Just this once. Take a little peek. It'll make you feel better. You'll see."

He wrapped his arms around her and pressed his face to her chest.

"Did you do it? Did you see?" she asked.

He just hugged her more tightly.

And she hugged him back.

## 3

Later that night, after Cory had gone to bed, Ellen set both the empty ice cream bowls in the sink then poured herself a glass of wine. She turned off the TV and sat in the darkened living room, her mind exhausted but still reeling. Cory's phone was on the coffee table, so she picked it up, and slowly scrolled through the photos he'd taken of the chalk drawings out in the street. She felt nothing from looking at them, of course—just some nonsense scribbled there by neighborhood kids, most likely. Nothing more nefarious than that.

*I looked inside his thoughts.*

Christ, she was worried about her son. Yes, she'd seen what he could do with the fork, but this thing about peeking inside people's heads? Worried that Mr. Zachs was no longer Mr. Zachs? The old neighbor speaking to him telepathically? It sounded like the ravings of a crazy person.

*Where are you, Brian?* And on the heels of that thought: *Would you even be able to help if you were here?*

She was still angry at him for what he'd done, but she couldn't help wondering if she might not feel as lost as she did if he'd still been in her life. In both their lives.

*Are you even still alive?*

It was a terrible thought, but something she had considered on more than one occasion over the past two years.

And for a moment, Brian was there—an amalgam of Brian in his youth and Brian as an adult. A composite that, blessedly, contained only the good qualities of her brother—the rakish smile, the twinkle in his eyes, the goodness that had always been in him, even if, over the years, it had been tamped down by drugs and alcohol.

*Where are you, Brian?*

*I'm right here, sis.*

She glimpsed him soaring through a midnight sky freckled with the shimmer of countless stars. He left behind a contrail of glitter in his wake.

# 4

She awoke on the sofa, her neck kinked, her head throbbing. It was well past two in the morning, according to the clock above the TV. She lay there for a moment catching her bearings, her empty wine glass on the table, her heart strumming rhythmically in her chest. The low, soothing hum of the air conditioning in the walls filled her ears.

After a time, she got up and placed the empty wine glass in the sink beside the ice cream bowls. Then she went around the house switching off the lights. When she reached the bay windows, she was tempted to leave the drapes drawn, but something—

*(I think something is happening to everyone)*

—urged her to open them.

She did.

And at first, she could see nothing but the fat, pearlescent face of the moon and the string of lighted streetlamps running the length of Cloister Road.

But then she saw the figure of a man, crouched low to the ground, at the foot of their driveway. She thought he was doing something to her car, but then she realized he was too far from the vehicle, and was in actuality bent over at the lip of the driveway—

The man stood and stared straight at her through the window.

Ellen's breath caught in her throat.

Beneath the glow of the nearest streetlamp, she could see his face and bare chest were covered in cryptic black sigils, like a tapestry of tattoos. She thought maybe she recognized him, too . . . but then the man ran off into the night before she could identify him.

She stood there for a moment longer, wondering if a part of her was still asleep and dreaming.

Pamela Guerin's voice came back to her from earlier that day: *Do you find that peculiar, Ellen? Do you find that strange?*

—Yes.

She most certainly *did* find this peculiar. She most certainly *did* find this strange.

Stepping onto the porch, she found the night had cooled the air considerably, causing a chill to ripple through her body. Hugging herself, she crept down the walk and descended the length of the driveway, eyes searching the darkness for any sign of the mysterious figure with a face full of tattoos. But except for the crickets, she was alone.

She paused at the foot of the driveway, her shadow elongated on the pavement against the glow of the streetlamp at her back.

She looked down, and it was there at the bottom of their driveway that she saw it, hastily rendered, over and over again, not in chalk but in shining neon spray paint:

# CHAPTER FOURTEEN

# CORY/BRIAN

Cory McBride, snared in the clutches of a terrible nightmare in which he was being pursued through the ink-black streets of Mariner's Cove by a giant mechanical spider, tossed and turned and, at one point, just moments before the massive arachnid leveraged down upon him with a telescopic arm as thick as a telephone pole and capped with gleaming, knifelike pincers, forced the gnome to open its eyes wide, and unleash a strident scream into the cosmos—

*(!!!UNCLE BRIAN!!!)*

—and Brian Russo, who at that very moment was traveling across the Texas panhandle beneath a canopy of stars, heard the scream, *felt* the scream, shuddered as it seared through the center of his brain then dissipated like the twinkling tendrils of fireworks throughout every single cell in his body. So powerful was his receipt of this dispatch that his vision went temporarily blurry and his entire body shook. The van he was driving veered off the road where its front passenger tire encountered a jagged and sizable boulder. The sound of the blowout was like the report of a starter's pistol, and the subsequent rumbling along on the flattened tire, *fwhump fwhump fwhump fwhump fwhump*, was what thrust him back into some semblance of awareness. He rolled the van onto the shoulder of the desolate desert highway and ultimately brought the vehicle to a full stop. With his entire body still shaking, and his head—his *mind*—still resonating with the echo of that scream, he just sat there behind the wheel, hot and cold at the same time, and with a terrible premonition suddenly and intractably seated at the center of his brain.

*Sssss . . .*

PART TWO

# HIVE MIND

I pace upon the battlements and stare
On the foundations of a house, or where
Tree, like a sooty finger, starts from the earth;
And send imagination forth

William Butler Yeats
"The Tower"

*Comes down like a wisp of smoke coursing through the night-streets, snakelike whisper-shushing,* sssss, *in all directions simultaneously: straight out along the pebbly shores of the darkened Bay Road, where the sharpened blades of the tide crest moon-shiny while edged in silver, and where night-steam rises into the atmosphere as the bay water cools and turns ink-black; where, too, a woman stirs fitfully awake, certain she has just heard the distant barking of her missing dog, and rouses the husband beside her, who, for hours now, has done nothing but stare at the cold, black panel of ceiling while obsessing over a door secreted away in his garage, feigning sleep, desperate for sleep's cool, anesthetizing fingers to caress and subdue his racecar, thunder-rocket mind; where his wife leaps from the bed and searches the house, guided by the vague, phantom barks echoing from some remote and indistinguishable distance, chasing the plaintive yips of a pet whose disappearance (to her, at least) remains a mystery; comes hijacking slipstreams and cruising the shoulders of switchback, sand-swept roadways, sweeping down the gritty, potholed slaloms that become Cloister Road, where the streetlights flame-flicker and unseen windchimes tinkle from a porch buried deep in the darkness; where a boy, bed-sweaty, tosses in the throes of a nightmare, and where his mother, just down the hall apiece, dreams of a swirly, serpentine adversary, a thing which pulses with a grand heartbeat of white, spangled light; straight out to Plainview, a rush of homes, speedy-by, each one luminescent beneath the blazing orb of a moon glimpsed through the interlocking fingers of barren, desiccated tree branches, not a presence but a wisp, a delicate and barely audible* sssss; *the furtive shudder of the willow boughs along Tamarack Way; the mournful baying of a dog, or possibly a fox, tucked in the darkened crook between two duplexes on lonely Capshaw Street; a solitary pinwheel spinning wildly in a yard on Jolene Street despite the absence of wind; the young girl who climbs from bed and hunts down what she perceives to be a metal space helmet, placing it on her head, only to remain standing there in the center of her darkened house, staring at nothing and everything all at once; comes across Gladstone Park, too, and how the trees tremble and the tall grass ripples like soundwaves spreading out into the stratosphere; how the moonlight drips down the side of the tank of the water tower at the far end of the park and seems, if for just a moment, to project some unearthly, ethereal reflection of a thing not quite there; comes down Macadam Street silent except for a whisper, much like sand shushing along the pavement, or the leaky hiss of hot air, a sound going* sssss; *through the back lots behind a stone carriage house on Macadam, where a man whose body is covered in swollen red welts snores in a recliner beneath the stars, and where a colony of bees, typically dormant at this time of night, swirl in a frenzy above his head as if his mind has given birth to the thought of them, an entire cyclone of bees, a blendered shriek of them, the air itself alive with the drumming, buzzing cacophony of their multitudinous wings, sensing that something,* something, *isn't as it should be; and farther still, where an old woman does not sleep, and instead stands before a paper calendar that's pinned to a corkboard in her kitchen, a free wall calendar that also serves as a menu for a Chinese takeout joint off the highway, and where, at the top of the calendar menu, printed in bloodred script, it says—*

YEAR OF THE DRAGON

*—and the woman merely nods her head and thinks, with a fuzzy mixture of confusion and approbation,* yes yes yes yes yes, *while weighty and solid in the pocket of her housedress resides the metal caster from a shopping cart; and there, farther up the road apiece, a lone figure crouches upon the sidewalk, much in the way a devil may perch upon the slumbering form of a maiden while the pupilless mare looks on; a lone figure frantically spilling ideas onto*

*the concrete, unburdening in a mad, obsessive rush: a jumble of thought given form given purpose.*

*Have you seen the instructions?*

*Can you hear the sound?*

*Back to where the houses creak, and tornadoes of dead leaves carve aimless passage down narrow alleyways. Back where the swings squeal on rusted chains that hang from backyard swing sets and where something weaves stealthily through the dark, twining between trashcans and bushes and propane grilles alike. A squirrel freezes in mid-lope along the crenelated spires of a fence, alert; an owl's eyes flash with a transcendent inner light; the mournful, distant baying of the dog (or fox) has finally transitioned into the unmistakable cry of unbridled lunacy.*

*Comes, too, a group of teenagers traversing much like the whispery wisp itself through the darkened, unseen corridors of this quiet, slumbering, nighttime suburban neighborhood—comes down poorly lighted roads and through yawning gaps in fences and trees. There: a cherry-red Nissan, or perhaps some sort of hybrid vehicle, maybe a Prius, causes them to go motionless as it passes by. Headlights wash along the blacktop, taillights briefly guttering. Is it stopping? Have they been seen? No: it glides onward until the darkness swallows it whole.*

*Because they come from different directions to congregate at this particular location—an empty house—the presentation suggests nothing more than a fortuitous accident. But that is not the case: they have been coming here, descending upon this vacant house on Poplar Station Road, vulture-like, for several nights now. They call it* abandoned, *for the sheer fact that no one has lived here for some time, although they all secretly understand that* abandoned *is not the most accurate descriptor for such a place.* Abandoned *denotes something that has been left behind for good. That is not the case with this place. There is a FOR SALE sign staked into the front lawn, and the house itself—the old Trenton place, which is how one of them knows it—remains as dark and silent as a subterranean tomb. It is merely a* house where no one lives for now, *and one of the teenagers, a boy, his entire life existing right now, in this moment, within a burst of sound, removes the screen from a rear window of the house, much as he has done a handful of times the past several nights after discovering that the house was* abandoned. *He drops the screen to the grass in a soundless whump. Pries open the window while, at his back, the congregation bustles with anticipation.*

*A ritual.*

*Sacred, maybe.*

*They are here to party—to drink beer and smoke pot and feel each other up—and one of the girls on this evening has a knot caught in her throat. She wants to have sex with one of the boys—it will be her first time—and she is nervous and not completely certain yet strangely determined in a way, too. She tries to convince herself, making mental columns, pros and cons, while thinking of this particular boy's hands on her, touching her, squeezing her breasts, perhaps sliding inside the waistband of her jeans.*

*Comes the wisp wisping by, sssss, and she whirls around, certain there is someone—*

(something)

*—right behind her, creeping up on them through the woods. But she is alone, the last teenager in the queue as her friends have filed through the open window of the abandoned—*

(empty)

*—house.*

*A chill ripples through her. Her senses are heightened, she knows, because of the carnal fantasies on her mind. She is overwound.*

*A hand extends through the open maw of the jockeyed-up window. The girl, whose name is Tatum Klass, grips it and uses it to help haul her over the sill of the window and into the vacant house.*

*Someone has brought beer. Caps are popped, bottles bandied about. The girl, Tatum, has been in this house only twice, but knows that the boys have frequented it more often. Nearly nightly, or so they claim. The boy she likes—a boy from Terrace Avenue named Mike Bliss—has just cracked a joke and everyone is giggling while still trying to be quiet. They don't turn on any of the lights in the house for fear that someone watching from the street might see, so they linger in dark, encapsulated rooms. She runs a hand along a wall to find her way into the next room, like a blind person. Which she nearly is in this lightless place. Fingers trailing along the drywall. Walls exist if only to prevent rooms from becoming infinite. Is that thought her own? She wonders. It seems the house is heady, or maybe that's just the pot smoke. Or her nerves.*

*Mike Bliss rolls into a dark room of his own. She watches him, a shape shifting about in the dark ahead of her. He's alone, perhaps deliberately so. Tatum's heart races. Are there beds upstairs in any of the bedrooms? Is this even a good idea?*

*Mike Bliss. He's got a vibe. Baggy clothes, shaved ridges on the left side of his head, matching the nick in his left eyebrow. He's not into sports. He's into cigarettes. He's into girls, too. He likes music. His playlists, which he's shared with her (and some other girls, Tatum knows), are eclectic, the* Donnie Darko *soundtrack his latest infatuation, but he prefers old technology to streaming; he wears those old-fashioned headphones with the orange foam over the speakers, and with a cord, a wire, trailing down his chest to a clicking, clacking Walkman. He plays tape cassettes like someone from a different time, a different generation, thinking who he is. Even now: that ridiculous Walkman clipped to the waistband of his jeans, slender black cord bisecting the front of his T-shirt, some ancient cassette trundling through warbly music issuing from those silly orange caps of foam. They're around Mike's neck now, so she can hear the music, too—just barely—as she trails one hand along the wall of the darkened house on Poplar Station Road in pursuit of him. It's Van Halen or some band like that—some band her own father listens to—and she follows the sound of it like a guide rope. That music is breadcrumbs leading the way. That music thrums with the same electric, anticipatory energy that thrums through her in this moment. In this place.*

*He's moving up the stairs toward the second floor of the house now. Is he taunting her? Seeing how much he can get away with, how much of herself she's willing to surrender unto him? She knows she should turn back and join the others, yet her heart is still galloping in her chest, she's still envisioning his hands squeezing her breasts and running down the dungareed swell of her buttocks, and that music—*

*—yes, definitely Van Halen—*

*—beckons her.*

*She follows him up the stairs. It is only when she is halfway up, or maybe two-thirds of the way up the stairs, and Mike Bliss is a mere smudge in the darkness along the second-floor landing, that she senses the wisping wisp once again—a murmuring susurration in her ears, or maybe even in her head. For a moment, she is thinking of the summer many years ago when she'd gone swimming with her brothers in the river behind the house and then the next thing she knew, she was face to face with the periscopic head of a water moccasin. How she had been terrified, and how the water moccasin had submerged itself, and she swore she could feel it weave its pulsating, muscular body between her legs. The memory of that event—and the murmuring sound that, for some reason, has summoned it—is enough to cause Tatum to pause, one hand on the banister, and peer over her shoulder and back down the stairwell. She stares at a spot of moonlight on the floor below for what feels like an impossible length of time. It shines like water in moonlight. Her heart is still beating with great fervor, but for a different reason now.*

*"Hey," Mike Bliss says from someplace above her. "You coming?"*

*She's coming.*

*Comes in after her, right on her heels,* sssss, *a tendril of sentient cobweb clinging to her, diaphanous filaments continually grazing against the nape of her neck. Her cognizance of* something there *strengthens* . . . yet there is nothing there.

*Mike Bliss takes her hand. His palm is cool. Hers is sweaty, and makes her self-conscious. He tugs her gently toward him in the dark. A moment later, his lips are on hers. His upper lip is sandpaper-rough and he's wearing too much body spray. His tongue pokes between her teeth and she pokes back, though a touch more reticent. Another part of him is poking, too; she can feel it against her upper thigh. Can she do this? Will she do this?*

*Mike Bliss mutters something she does not understand into one ear. This close, she can hear the music more clearly, can feel the orange discs of foam vibrating against the soft flesh of her neck. Another sound, too, somewhere in the distance behind the music, yet somehow also right here with her, nearly a part of her, or maybe just a part of this house, or maybe coming directly from the lips of Mike Bliss:*

. . . sssss . . .

. . . sssss . . .

. . . sssssssssssss . . .

*She feels dizzy.*

*Lightheaded.*

*Her back teeth begin to hurt.*

*"C'mon," says Mike Bliss. He disengages from her and pulls away. Advances farther down the hall. He's walking funny, like something is wrong with his leg, or maybe his pants are too tight.*

*Mike Bliss slips through an open doorway at the far end of the hall.*

*Tatum watches him go.*

*She still hears the music from his Walkman.*

*Still hears the* sssss . . .

*. . . or at least believes she does.*

*Diaphanous filaments.*

*A ritual.*

*Sacred, maybe.*

*She goes to the doorway of the room that Mike Bliss has entered. It must be a bedroom. The house is so dark, but what else could it be up here on the second floor? She whisper-shouts his name, but he does not respond. She enters the room, which is barren of furniture and dark except for a triptych of moonlit panels on the carpet.*

*The room is empty.*

*"Mike?"*

*Again: no answer.*

*Comes up against her,* sssss *and* sssss, *but she is too preoccupied now to notice. Instead, she stands there alone in this empty room—a room she has just watched Mike Bliss disappear into. Disappear? Why in the world would she think of it that way? Why* disappear?

*There is a closet. Of course there is. The door is closed. Is he hiding in there? On the other side of that door? Mike Bliss with his knuckles wedged between his teeth to stifle a laugh, the cord of his headphones trailing down the front of his T-shirt. She does not stop to think* why *he might be hiding in there attempting to stifle a laugh, but instead goes to the closet, grips the cool brass doorknob. In that moment, she is certain that Mike Bliss is* not *behind this door, but instead it is the water moccasin, or whatever type of snake it had been all those years ago, ratcheted to its full height and ready to strike the moment she—*

*She opens the door.*
*The closet is empty.*
*The* room *is empty.*
Sssss.
*For the first time, she realizes she is no longer hearing Van Halen.*

# CHAPTER FIFTEEN
# HORLA

## 1

Headlights appeared on the pitch-black horizon. Brian Russo brought up one arm to shield his eyes from the glare while holding out his other arm, thumb extended in the classic hitcher's pose. The car didn't even slow down as it blew by him, the wind from its passage rippling his clothes and hair while pelting the airbrushed wolves on the side of the conversion van with a buckshot blast of highway debris. The stink of its exhaust hung in the air long after the car had vanished down the road. It was only the third or fourth vehicle he'd seen since the van had blown a flat tire, and at this point he wasn't holding out hope for speedy salvation.

No cell service out here in the middle of this godforsaken desert landscape. No pinpoints of light to indicate civilization on the horizon, either, no matter in which direction he looked. Occasionally, he'd hear the all-too-near holler of a coyote, and decided it was best to hang close to the van, at least until daylight began to crest over the mesas in the east.

That eruption in his head—it had come out of nowhere and had shaken him down to the foundation of his soul. It had sounded like a child's plea for help, and the clarity of it had been so great, that after he'd pulled the limping van with the flat tire onto the shoulder of the road, he'd searched the back of the van for a stowaway. What had it been? Some errant radio signal amplified by the fillings in his back teeth? No, that was bullshit. It had been a voice—a child's voice—and it had called him by name.

*Not just by name*, he thought. *That voice called me Uncle Brian.*

And the only person in the world who had once called him that had been his nephew, Cory.

So: not an errant radio signal. What, then? A particularly malicious brain tumor bent on using his own personal shame to drive him mad before it killed him? He might even deserve such a fate. Of course, the simplest answer was a lack of sleep. He couldn't even do the math to figure out how long he'd been awake behind the wheel. No wonder his think-box was going haywire.

Another set of headlights appeared over the western rise. Brian leaned out from the shoulder of the highway and watched as the vehicle approached through the darkness. Without holding out much hope, he popped up his thumb as the vehicle's headlights drew closer.

It was a decades-old Chevy Impala the color of bone with tinted windows and no hubcaps. It slowed down then glided by like a shark, until its taillights blazed a devilish red and the whole thing rocked to a standstill along the shoulder of the highway, perhaps fifteen yards ahead of where Brian now stood. A cloud of desert dust puffed up around it. Surprised by the driver's willingness to stop, Brian hurried toward it and approached the driver's side window just as it descended.

"Hey, thanks for stopping," Brian said.

Behind the wheel sat a man of about fifty years of age, with great peppery sideburns trailing nearly to his jawline. He wore reflective aviator sunglasses even though it was pitch-black out, and a Dr Pepper cap tugged low on his head. A toothpick swiveled from one corner of the man's mouth to the other. Beside him in the passenger seat was a woman who looked about twenty years younger than the good Dr Pepper—closer to Brian's age—and wore a skimpy tank top with Hello Kitty on the front. She leaned forward, placing her hands on the dashboard, and Brian could see that she wore a lot of silver rings on her fingers.

"You having some bad luck out here at this godforsaken hour, my friend?" Dr Pepper asked.

"You could say that." Brian jerked a thumb over his shoulder in the direction of the van. "Blew a tire and didn't have a spare."

"Sucks," said the man. "Where you headed?"

"Right now, I'd settle for the first motel on the map. I figure there's nothing I can do about that tire tonight. I can call for a tow truck in the morning and hopefully get back on the road without much trouble."

"You don't got a cell phone?" the woman in the passenger seat asked. She spoke with a Midwestern twang.

"I do, but it can't get a signal out here."

"Well," said Dr Pepper. "Can't say I know when the next motel's gonna come by, but we'll give you a lift until we find one. How's that sound?"

"Like a godsend," Brian said. "Thank you. I was starting to get worried I might be eaten alive by coyotes out here if someone didn't come along soon."

Dr Pepper grinned. "I guess there are worse ways to go. Hop around to the other side and climb in."

Brian hurried to the other side of the car just as the passenger door popped open and the woman climbed out. She was slim almost to the point of emaciation, and her hipbones, which were clearly visible in the space between her low-hanging denims and her too-short tank top, looked as sharp as bullhorns. One side of her head was shaved to a buzz cut while the other side unfurled in a cascade of bleached hair that looked decidedly pale blue in the moonlight.

"Gonna be a bit of a tight squeeze, I'm afraid," she said, standing by the open passenger door, her hips cocked. She nodded toward the rear of the car. "Got a bunch of luggage back there so it's three to the front. Lucky for you I wore my good perfume."

He peeked in one of the back windows and saw that the Impala's back seat was jampacked with large black garbage bags that looked fit to bursting. He considered asking if they could move the stuff to the trunk, but then thought that might sound unappreciative.

"Come on, sugar, I ain't gonna bite."

Brian smiled and nodded . . . then realized she had gotten out because she wanted *him* to sit in the middle. "You don't want to sit next to . . . ?" He jerked his head in the general vicinity of the driver.

"I gotta sit by a window 'less I get carsick. And that ain't pretty for no one."

"Right. Okay."

He slid past her and crawled into the car. The Impala had bench seats, so at least he was grateful for that small bit of luck. The woman piled in after him and Dr Pepper was already pulling back onto the highway before she'd fully closed the door.

"Where you from?" the woman asked. She had her window open a crack, filling the car with the tunneling sound of rushing wind.

"California."

"Where you headed?"

"New York."

She laughed. "In that van? You're lucky you got this far!" She slapped his thigh.

"What about you guys? Where're you from?"

"Oh," she said. "Halfway between here and there." There was a singsong quality to her voice, and when she finished speaking, she laughed again. "What's your name, anyway?"

"Brian."

"Horla," said the woman. She reached over and extended her right hand, which Brian shook, albeit awkwardly given the confines of the front seat. The three of them were packed shoulder to shoulder.

"That's a unique name," he said.

"I'm a unique gal."

"Does it mean something?"

"It's my name!"

"I mean, does it, like—"

"It's from a Guy de Maupassant story. Do you know who that is?"

"Not a clue."

"He was an author and a playwright. Sort of like the French version of Poe. He tried to take his own life by cutting his throat, but ultimately died of syphilis while he was institutionalized. Unlike Poe, who just had the good sense to die of unknown causes, but likely drank himself to death."

"Poe bastard."

Horla made a creaking sound way back in her throat. Her eyes went wide. Then she broke out into a toothy grin and slapped his thigh again. Brian thought he'd never seen a mouth so wide. "Wait, that's a joke? Hey, that's a good one! I like it." She leaned forward and, to the driver, said, "Check it out, we picked up a funnyman!"

"What's in New York?" asked Dr Pepper.

"A job."

"What do you do?"

"I'm in broadcasting."

"What's that call itself when it's at home with its feet up?"

"Well, I was a radio disc jockey once. Hit a bit of a rough patch, and now I'm trying to get back into it."

Horla laughed. "This whole stretch of highway straight out to Oklahoma is a bit of a rough patch, fella."

"Terrestrial radio is a dead medium," declared Dr Pepper.

"Probably why I'm so suited for it," Brian said.

Dr Pepper didn't respond to that; he merely flexed his fingers around the Impala's steering wheel.

Something was not right here. He realized the driver hadn't introduced himself and Brian decided he didn't want to engage in too much more conversation with either one of them, so he kept his hands in his lap and his eyes straight ahead.

"Ain't you gonna ask what I do?" Horla said.

"What do you do?"

"I'm a contortionist. I can slide through tight spaces. We've got some plastic tubes in the trunk that you wouldn't think a cat could crawl through. I can get through 'em, easy peasy. I also perform feats of human endurance and bodily curiosities."

"Not tricks," commented Dr Pepper. His face was mostly hidden behind those aviator glasses and the brim of his ballcap. "Not illusions."

"That's something," Brian said.

"I can bend metal rods in my mouth," Horla said. Her breath reeked of weed.

"Reinforced rebar," Dr Pepper clarified. "She also eats glass bottles and pounds nails into her face."

"Wow," Brian said. "And what about you?"

Dr Pepper just grinned but said no more. He never took those aviator glasses off the road.

"The shoulders are the widest part of the human body," Horla went on. "Wait, watch this." She exhaled more marijuana breath into Brian's face as she held one arm straight out in front of her. Her fingertips touched the windshield. Slowly, she rotated her arm until it completed a full 360-degree rotation.

"Jesus," Brian said.

Horla laughed again.

"Does that hurt?"

"No, sir."

Dr Pepper said, "Quit freaking him out."

Horla unwound her arm and placed her hands in her lap.

A few blessed moments of silence. Still no lights on the horizon.

"My real name's Jennifer, you know," Horla said. She wrinkled her nose to show how little she appreciated her birth name.

For the first time since Brian had gotten into the car, Dr Pepper turned his head. Even with the sunglasses on, Brian could tell he was glaring at his female companion with disapproval.

"It's just not a good performer's name," Horla continued, oblivious that Dr Pepper had shot her a look. "You know what I mean? Jennifer. Jennifer. Jennifer. Jennifer. Jennifer. Plain Jane, right?"

"For a contortionist, I guess so," Brian said.

"Jennifer. Jennifer. Say it over and over again like that it starts making no sense."

"You got expensive broadcasting equipment back in that van of yours?" Dr Pepper asked. The question seemed to come out of nowhere.

"No. Just my voice."

"What's that mean?"

"Just that I'm a disc jockey. I talk."

"Ah, right. Well, I was just asking, since it'll be on the side of the road overnight. Wouldn't want to leave a bunch of expensive equipment unattended."

"Hey," Horla said, squeezing Brian's thigh. He thought he might have a bruise there come morning. "I also read palms, you know. Want me to do you?"

"You're just full of talent," Brian said.

She stuck out her lower lip but she looked like she was only pretending to be insulted. "Are you making fun of me, mister?"

"I don't make fun of anybody."

"So?" she said, and she actually clasped her hands between her breasts like a pleading schoolgirl. "Will you let me?"

"I don't see why not. What do I have to do?"

"Which is your dominant hand?"

"My right."

Horla held out a slender white palm toward him. "Then give it here, pal," she said.

He placed his right hand in hers, palm up. Her thin fingers closed around him gently. Her fingers were very cold. Corpse fingers.

"The dominant hand is the window to the conscious mind. It's what we call the 'realized personality.' Yours is a fire hand," she said, looking closely down at his palm. How she was able to see anything in the dark of the car with only the dim dashboard light for illumination was a question for the ages. "See? You've got a rectangular shape to your hand. And look—the length of your palm to the wrist is greater than the length of your fingers."

"What does that mean?"

The girl frowned. "Not sure. It's an interesting observation, though, right? But wait—see this?" She touched the tip of an icy index finger to one of the crosshatched lines of his palm. "This is your love line."

"Like, it says who I'm going to marry or how good I am in bed or something like that?"

"No, silly. It's your emotional life, not your love life."

"It's poorly named, then."

She gripped him with both hands and pulled his palm closer to her face for a better examination. Like someone looking for a splinter, Brian thought.

"What?" he said. "Is something wrong?"

"It has a lot of gridding and chaining," Horla said.

"What's that? Is that bad?"

"Are you creative?"

"If you consider being a disc jockey creative."

"Hmmm." She traced another line. "See that? This one's your head line. It tells me what I've already figured out the moment I saw you standing on the shoulder of the road—that you act on impulse rather than rational thought."

"I know a lot of people who would agree with that assessment."

"Lastly," Horla said, "this is your life line."

"Uh-oh. Looks pretty short."

"Everybody thinks that. But really, the length of your life line has really nothing to do with your mortality. It's a total misconception."

"That's a relief."

"Instead, it reflects major life changes, like cataclysmic and life-altering events."

"Am I due for a life-altering event?"

She tilted her head so that she was looking directly into his eyes now. Hers were the black and haunting eyes of a shark, with hardly any whites exposed, and he thought that he could see himself reflected in them, her face so close to his.

"Maybe you are," she said, not pulling her gaze from his. "I think that maybe you are."

"It could be something good, right?"

"Sure."

"But?"

"I didn't say 'but.'"

"No," he said, "but you're thinking it."

It was then that he turned his hand over so that their palms were touching. He interlaced his fingers with hers and she willingly closed her fingers around his hand. The heat from his hand had begun to warm her flesh. It seemed to bring heat into her face, too.

Brian stared into her eyes. They became less like shark eyes, the irises diminishing until much of the white swam back into focus. It was all a trick of the poor lighting inside the car, Brian knew . . . yet something about this whole exchange suddenly felt powerful nonetheless.

Ever so slightly, Horla's head cocked to one side. An expressionless serenity came over her face. Her mouth hung open the slightest bit, as if she was being put in a trance.

Brian said, "Your name isn't Jennifer. Not really."

He sensed more than saw Dr Pepper turn his head again and look at them.

"Your real name is Merritt," Brian went on. "You hated that name so you went by your middle name, Jennifer, for most of your life. You're from Lipscomb, Kansas."

She just kept staring at him with that medicated look on her face.

"Hey," said Dr Pepper, but Brian ignored him.

"You *are* a contortionist, and you used to perform at county fairs and even once at a nightclub in Vegas, which is where you met Dr Pepper here. But now, the two of you rob people. That's not luggage in those trash bags in the back seat. The two of you picked me up tonight because you were going to rob me, too."

He felt the car begin to slow down.

"You were going to drive me out in the middle of nowhere, take my wallet, and leave me stranded. Then you'd double back to my van and take whatever you wanted."

"Hey," Dr Pepper said again. There was less authority in his voice now.

The car eased to a stop in the middle of the road.

Brian uncurled his fingers and released the woman's hand. The instant he did so, she blinked repeatedly, as if coming out of a hypnotic stupor. She smiled at him the way a lover might, dreamily and starry-eyed, and for one crazy moment, Brian thought she might reach up and caress the side of his face.

"Get out," Dr Pepper said. "Get out of the car."

"No," Brian said. He pointed toward the horizon, where daylight was beginning to creep over the mesas. He could see the lights of civilization there now, too: low and simmering along the misty ground like a mirage. "Drive me there and then I'll get out."

"No. I want you out of the car right—"

Brian turned his head and looked at him. He didn't need to see the guy's eyes behind those reflective aviator shades to know he was terrified.

"Drive," Brian said.

## 2

They dropped him off in the parking lot of a combo gas station and A&W restaurant. The woman who called herself Horla was quick to jump out of the car—that medicated serenity had fled her system by now—and she kept a wide berth as Brian himself climbed out. Before she could hop back in, Brian peered in at Dr Pepper and said, "It's not a good idea to mess with my van. Just keep that in mind as you two head back out on the road. You got me?"

"Yeah, whatever," the man muttered. Then he barked at Horla/Jennifer/Merritt to get back in the fucking car.

Brian watched the Impala speed away so fast that it fishtailed out of the parking lot and kicked up a plume of dust once it hit the highway.

Every ounce of strength immediately drained from Brian's body. He collapsed to the ground on his hands and knees, his head reeling. He couldn't explain what the hell had happened in that car—what the hell had come over him to allow him to suddenly know those things about that woman—and the mystery of it all left him feeling unanchored, depleted, and even a little bit frightened. He had never done anything like that in his entire life, not even back when he could move shot glasses with his mind.

This was something else.

He thought of that child's voice that had boomed through his head and wondered if that had something to do with this. The voice that sounded so much like Cory. The voice that had called him Uncle Brian.

"You okay, man?" someone called from one of the gas station pumps.

"I'm fine, thanks. Just got a little lightheaded."

Gradually, Brian stood. He was still weak and his hands were shaking. He took a deep breath and looked across the parking lot to where a rundown motel stood behind the A&W. The sun was rising, he'd been up for what felt like days, and he knew that if he didn't rent a room and go straight to bed, he'd go find someplace to drink.

He crossed the parking lot, his sneakers crunching over bits of white gravel that looked like teeth. Inside the motel, an elderly man sat reclining in a chair with a newspaper opened before him. A pair of half-moon reading glasses were perched at the end of his nose. As Brian came in, the man's gaze shifted in his direction, strangely suspicious beneath a duo of massive gray eyebrows.

With what felt like his last remaining bit of strength, Brian Russo said, "I'd like a room, please."

# CHAPTER SIXTEEN
# STINGER

## 1

Jeremy "Stinger" Stuckey had brain damage; he was convinced this was true.

The evening of the terrible storm, he had been out in the back lot securing the Tower with ratchet straps when a strong wind sheared a heavy branch from a desiccated oak and dropped it on him. The thickest section of the branch—about the size of an Easter ham, he later estimated—struck him on the left shoulder, but the remainder came down on his head. Later, when he came to, he was lying on the ground beneath a tumultuous evening sky that needled him with freezing rain. Something was banging around inside his head—percussive and repetitive hammer strikes, *wham wham wham*, on a steel drum.

Like some creature emerging from a swamp, he had lurched half blind through the pelting rain and gathering wind toward the house, spidery tendrils of dark red blood oozing down his forehead from a fresh wound and leaking into his eyes. In the bathroom he shared with Queenie, he examined the head wound in the spotty mirror, Queenie's adjustable shower stool and a jungle gym-like system of handicapped bars reflected behind him in the glass. With the blood streaking down his pallid face, he looked like some graveyard ghoul from a horror movie. The branch had opened a wound in his scalp that he knew required stitches. But since he wasn't about to drive himself to an urgent care facility or ring for an ambulance in the middle of what was probably a goddamn hurricane, he cleaned the wound with a bottle of peroxide. A pink waterfall cascaded down the bridge of his nose and pattered into the bathroom sink, the drain of which was scuzzy with soap scum, clipped black hairs, and the shorn, yellowed crescents of Queenie's fingernails. He pressed a gauze pad to the wound then secured it in place by wrapping his head with a second gauze bandage, so that by the time he'd finished he looked like someone suffering from a toothache in an old black-and-white movie.

The following day, at the behest of Queenie, he went to an urgent care facility where he was attended to by an attractive young nurse with an endearing little mole on her upper lip. There wasn't much she could do for the wound at this point, since it had already begun to close up, but she did make sure it looked clean and then reapplied a fresh bandage. She'd heard of people breaking their necks or even dying after being struck on the head by a falling tree limb, she informed him, so she considered him to be very lucky. At the time, Stinger had no reason to suspect brain damage, so he had not asked the attractive young nurse with the endearing little mole what the odds were that he now suffered from such an affliction. But now, given all that had been transpiring, he wished he had.

At first, the brain damage manifested in a series of vivid, claustrophobic nightmares, where Stinger, the sole survivor of some nonspecific apocalypse, struggled to construct a new Tower to add to the one he kept in the back lot behind the house—or perhaps to replace it. Yet with no wood or tools at his disposal in this apocalyptic world, he had to assemble the thing with discarded tin cans, lengths of rope, an old roller skate, a fishbowl, a cowboy hat, a shopping cart, a used condom, an empty Campbell's soup can, and a shoe. Instead of a cinderblock platform, which served as the foundation of the original (actual) Tower, he balanced this dream-state abstraction on a quartet of spindly, telescopic spider legs. It never held together, and his failure would thrust him from these nightmares, frazzled and anxious and wound up like a bullet fired from a gun.

But nightmares were nightmares, and not inarguable proof of cerebral trauma.

That proof came when the bees began talking to him.

## 2

If asked, Stinger would attest to liking many things in life. He liked baseball—watching it, not playing it. He liked cold cans of National Bohemian, though he had never turned away a beer for being room temperature. He liked the 1967 Mercury Cougar that he sometimes spied motoring throughout the neighborhood, and even fantasized on occasion about following the elderly driver of that sweet car home, overpowering the old fellow in a physical altercation (Stinger was always more physically proficient in his fantasies than he was in real life), and taking the car for himself. He liked women, particularly if they were younger than him, and he *really* liked Marybeth Maysall, the twenty-something-year-old cocktail waitress who lived in the duplex next door. He liked any music so long as it was Motörhead. He liked a good pair of hand-stitched cowboy boots, although he had never owned a pair. But mostly, Stinger liked bees.

Jeremy Stuckey was just two years old the first time he'd been stung by a bee. He had been seated at a picnic table in the back yard of their house on Macadam Street eating a peanut butter and jelly sandwich and just generally minding his own—

*(beeswax)*

—business when a honeybee landed on the edge of his plate. Two-year-old Jeremy Stucky watched in astonishment as the bee scuttled around the edge of the plate before crawling atop the other half of his sandwich. Jeremy grew entranced by the alternating black and yellow-brown stripes along the honeybee's abdomen, the fuzzy, scratchy-looking hairs that made up its winged thorax, the compound eyes that looked like the finest, most delicate meshwork ever created.

Little Jeremy Stuckey reached out, plucked the honeybee off his sandwich, and popped the sucker right into his mouth.

The boy's yowls of pain alerted his grandmother, Glenda-Rae, who arrived to find her grandson's face a blotchy, tear-streaked mess, at the center of which was a gaping, reddened hole that was the boy's mouth.

Not knowing what she would find, Glenda-Rae reached inside her grandson's mouth, located a twitching lump stuck to the inside of her grandson's cheek, and pulled the thing out. Realizing what it was, she herself cried out, and dropped the honeybee back onto the boy's plate where it continued to twitch for a few more seconds before it died.

A globule of greenish mucus bubbled from the bee's rear end, which meant it had detached its stinger. Glenda-Rae reached back into her grandson's mouth, probed around the inside of the boy's cheek—the flesh there was already beginning to swell—and located the stinger. She tweezed it out of the tender flesh just as the boy, in his pain and fear and confusion, chomped down on her fingers.

Howling right along with her grandson now, Glenda-Rae snatched her hand out of the boy's mouth like someone who'd nearly gotten caught in a mousetrap. Whatever became of the stinger became a point of speculation in the Stuckey household for years to come, but there was no need for speculation on Glenda-Rae's part: the boy had swallowed it. Case closed.

Jeremy, too young to have much memory of that incident despite the occasions when his grandmother would recount it, wouldn't learn about the bee's propensity for stinging until a handful of years later.

When Jeremy was nine years old, he had gone wandering through the wooded lots behind the old stone carriage house where he lived with Queenie and Glenda-Rae. He had no friends or siblings, so he often spent time by himself in these woods, peering at the squirming, blind insects under rocks, or scooping up brine shrimp buried in the cool brown silt of the creek beds. On this particular day, he had been winding his way deep through the trees when he happened to look up and spy a curious thing: a brownish, skull-sized mass clinging to the bole of a white oak. Whatever it was, its surface appeared to be undulating, as if it was a thing alive. A curious kid by nature, Jeremy had gathered up the longest, sturdiest stick he could find, and had proceeded to swat at the thing stuck to the tree. It took only one good whack before the thing detached itself from the trunk of the tree and dropped down squarely on Jeremy Stuckey's head.

The pain came from everywhere all at once. His body instantly ablaze with stinging hot pinpricks of fire, Jeremy shrieked and swatted at his face, his neck, his exposed arms and legs. There were *things* crawling all over him, *things* that were puncturing his pink, sunburned flesh with tiny, barbed stingers. The pain reached a point where he could no longer distinguish the individual places where those things were stinging him, but instead felt like his entire body had been lit on fire. He ran screaming and half blind through the woods, the air around him swarming with those terrible stinging *things*, his body crawling with them just like the thing he'd whacked out of the tree had been crawling with them. Somehow he managed to find his way back to the old stone carriage house, where he proceeded, in a feverish panic, to slam his palms against the back door of the house. His screams were the high-pitched, reedy bleats of a goat.

"Well, I suppose this means you're not allergic," Glenda-Rae said later, as she daubed his body with a cotton ball soaked in calamine lotion. Previously, she had taken a pair of tweezers and extracted from his swollen, weepy flesh a series of miniscule harpoons, delicate as eyelashes, which she dropped into the kitchen sink, one by one. He stood there in nothing but his underwear, arms outstretched like Jesus on the cross. His flesh was on fire and there were countless red welts all over his face and body. He sobbed while Glenda-Rae pressed that cold swab of cotton against the burning red bumps stretching taut his flesh while, across the room, Queenie, his mother, already a sizeable woman in a formless floral muumuu, looked on. And while Glenda-Rae had ultimately laughed at the ordeal and called him Stinger from that day until her death, Jeremy's mother Queenie, her face a perpetual scowl of disapproval, never did.

The incident did not scar him, as it might have for most other little children. He became fascinated by the bees' unmitigated sense of self-preservation. After he learned that bees died after they stung (and learned that it was only the female honeybees who could sting), his admiration of them only increased. It was a literal fight to the death. Stinger Stuckey, who even at a young age constantly felt like he was the butt of some cruel, cosmic joke, could really appreciate that level of dedication.

One might reason such a traumatic event in his ninth year would have fostered a healthy fear of bees, and for a while that was true. But as he got older, his curiosity about the insects overshadowed any apprehension he'd harbored toward them. When he would see one in the yard, he would follow it (albeit at a safe distance) until it ultimately returned to its hive. For the most part, the hives were all pretty much the same: tiny, honeycombed phalanxes nestled in the bores of trees or clinging to the eaves of someone's house. He marveled at the collective consciousness that had instructed each individual bee to attack him simultaneously. When he'd run from them, desperate to claw his way back to the house, they had collectively known to follow. And when they ultimately dispersed, they did so in a single-minded black cloud. It seemed to him that one brain controlled them all. Was that true?

If his preoccupation with them became too invasive, they would sting him, which didn't matter much—as he grew older, he would say, with a gruff sort of laugh, that it was the cost of doing business—for he just needed to flick them away, pluck out the stinger, and apply some salve on the swollen area when he got home. Simple as pie. Sometimes the pain even felt good.

He learned that there were many kinds of bees, that they came from different places around the world and came in different colors and patterns, and that some of them were even stingless. He learned that their ability to fly could not be explained by physics, suggesting they violated the theories of aerodynamics. (This only amplified his curiosity—a bug that defied science!) He learned that there were three different types of honeybees, which were the most common bees in the suburban Maryland neighborhood of Mariner's Cove: drones, workers, and queens. Drones were male, stingless, and stupid. Even the word *drone* made them sound like mindless zombies or idiots. Workers were female, and they displayed a wide range of behaviors, and their daily routines included feeding the other bees, receiving nectar, foraging, cleaning up around the hive, and sometimes they would even assume guard duty, defending the hive against potential attackers, sort of like military personnel. Lastly, there was the queen, whose existence intrigued Stinger the most because his mother shared this bee's name.

(He supposed that if Queenie had possessed a husband—if Stinger had possessed a father—then their lives might have been vastly different, but that was not the case. Stinger had no idea who his father was, and Queenie never spoke of the man. The queen bee, Stinger knew, was impregnated through a ritualistic mating flight, during which she may mate with as many as twenty drones. This dance occurred only once in a queen's life, which would explain why Stinger was an only child, and which could further attest to why no one seemed to know the identity of Stinger's father.)

Stinger was twenty-eight years old, and he still lived with Queenie in that same brick carriage house on Macadam Street. The house had been in their family for generations, long before Mariner's Cove existed as a community, and long before a string of duplexes popped up along either side of it. The carriage house resided on several undeveloped lots that Queenie, in her misplaced wisdom, had refused to sell to developers over the years, leaving them with an abundance of property but very little money.

In the lot farthest from the house, Stinger had constructed and maintained a beehive. The hive looked like a set of wooden dresser drawers stacked one atop another and coated in a wash of white paint. Inside every drawer was a brick of honeycomb, each tiny hexagonal cell filled with either pollen, larvae, or the trembling golden diode of raw honey. This single hive housed anywhere from 40,000 to 60,000 honeybees.

He had started out a couple years ago by ordering a queen and a few thousand workers and drones online (his mother had thought him crazy). It had taken him a while to get the queen excluder right, meticulously readjusting the width of the mesh links in the wire screen so that each opening was wide enough for workers to pass through but small enough so that the queen could not. He had also cultivated an immunity to their stings, for the topography of his arms, neck, and face were frequently covered in red, shiny knobs of stung flesh.

Stinger took great pleasure in his hive. Stylistically, it was what was typically referred to as a Langstroth hive, although Stinger preferred to think of it simply as the Tower. After a long day of manual labor—mowing lawns and performing various repairs at homes throughout Mariner's Cove; ever since he was a teenager, he'd become something of a neighborhood gun-for-hire—Stinger would recline in a lawn chair, his skin shiny, red, bumpy, and hotly throbbing, his fingers tacky with propolis, and watch the airborne residents of the Tower go about their daily routines. He would often wonder about the complex bustle underway inside the Tower. After a few beers, he would imagine the queen on a tiny silver throne, tended to by workers adorned in royal garb, their stingers fashioned into arrowheads affixed to the tips of tiny spears. He pictured the workers, thousands upon thousands of them, scuttling over one another, driven solely by a joined mentality to heat or cool the hive, to communicate the location of food, and tend to the ever-growing brood within those whitewashed walls. As he closed his eyes and sank into comfortable inebriation, a six-pack of National Bohemian in the grass beside his lawn chair, Stinger envisioned a sky blackened by a blanket of countless drones in search of mating partners, the vibration of their collective wings no less imposing than the rumble of a Blackhawk's rotors in the air.

In the days following the terrible storm, and as the nightmares continued, he sensed that something was not right. The wound in his scalp continued to ache. Outwardly, it looked to be healing just fine, yet Stinger knew looks were often deceiving. He had begun to wonder if the wound had started to reopen in places, microscopic tears invisible to the naked eye whenever he glared at his lumpy, inflamed reflection in the bathroom mirror. Was it possible that some external, intrusive poison or noxious gas was slowly ingratiating itself into his skull via the ragged gash in his scalp? That would explain the recurring nightmare. That would also explain the persistent hum he often heard echoing in some deep recess of his brain.

No, not a hum . . .

A *buzz.*

One morning, as he sat at the kitchen table shoveling down a bowl of Cinnamon Toast Crunch (his favorite), the buzzing in his head reached such a crescendo that his eyes began to water. He pressed a hand to the bandaged wound in his scalp as he scooted back from the table. At the center of the table was a fruit bowl, the contents brown, withered, and dressed in a nimbus of bluish mold. A solitary honeybee appeared between a gap in the rotting fruit. It traversed the terrain of a furry blue banana where it met up with a second bee. A third descended from the dusty chandelier above the table and landed on the rim of the fruit bowl, its wings twitching.

It was not unusual for them to gain access to the house, often hitching a ride on his clothes when he returned from visiting the Tower. Yet this impromptu congregation made Stinger uneasy. They seemed to move—to vibrate their wings—in rhythm with the pulsing buzz inside his head. Not an airborne poison or noxious gas, but a *sound* created by the decisive and unified vibration of honeybee wings . . .

A fourth bee, zigging through the air as if on an invisible wire, buzzed by Stinger's head before landing on the back of his hand. It twitched and turned in circles—

*(circles circles circles)*

—then waggle-danced across the landscape of his hand. Stinger looked up and saw the bees in the fruit bowl were doing the same thing.

Communicating.

Stinger lifted his hand to eye-level. Quietly, he said, "You talking to me, fella?"

The bee waggled, its abdomen convulsing. It went still for a moment . . . and then plunged its barbed stinger into the porous flesh along the back of Stinger's hand. It was a quick, hot pinch. Stinger let the bee wriggle, impaled in his skin. When it finally managed to detach itself, it was with a globule of greenish mucus purling from its striped abdomen. It left its own stinger planted in Stinger's flesh.

Stinger flicked the bee from his hand, then plucked out the stinger. He grabbed the bowl of fruit—the bees spiraled up into the air at his approach, a dizzying clot of them—then tossed the fruit out into the backyard. When he turned back to the house, he saw that the vinyl siding was crawling with bees. They all moved with jerky, communicative movements. The drone of their buzzing harmonized with the raucous din in his head.

He decided to visit the Tower to see what the hell was going on. Was the hive in danger? Was that what they were trying to communicate to him? Yet as he approached through the wooded lot, a feeling of apprehension gathered like a muscle tightening in his chest. Bees clouded the air around him, lighting on his clothes, his skin. He swatted them away, cognizant of their electronic mutterings in his ears and filling up the inside his skull. He wanted to push on, but the air became so dizzyingly infused with bees that he wondered if this was some kind of warning in and of itself—that they were warning him *not* to proceed.

The *Tower* was not in danger.

The Tower *was* the danger.

He ran back to the house to attend to his multitude of fresh stings.

## 3

The nightmares persisted. And with them, a sound not unlike a power tool whirring in the center of his brain, one that seemed, preposterously, to articulate his name, his birth name, in what sounded disconcertingly like Queenie's voice—*ZZZZZZZEREMEEEE*...

## 4

He was pummeled awake by a dream so vivid that his hands continued to manipulate the air in front of his confused, sleep-bleary eyes just as they had been a moment ago in his sleep. He lay in bed, his breathing erratic, his bedsheets swampy with sweat. The curtains were drawn over his bedroom windows, but even the barest glint of sunlight peeking through the part in the curtain hurt his eyes.

From downstairs, there came a knock at the door. He pulled on yesterday's clothes then slunk down the hall, pausing only a moment outside Queenie's bedroom door to intercept the mechanical, labored sounds of her breathing. Then he continued down the stairs.

Doug Winslow stood with his hands on his hips, perspiring on the porch. He looked garrulous in a bright pink polo shirt forcibly tucked into a pair of khaki shorts and with a vividly white Titleist visor tugged down over his square head. He was the president of the Mariner's Cove Community Association, and his visits to the Stuckey household were frequent in the summer months, since the MCCA paid Jeremy to upkeep the various community properties and beachfronts. Winslow's red face glistening with moisture, he informed Stinger that there was trash and fallen tree limbs strewn about Gladstone Park, and that they had been there for several days, ever since the big storm, and what the hell had Stinger been up to lately, anyway? Before Stinger could formulate a response, Doug Winslow added, "There's also a bees' nest hanging from one of the eaves on the maintenance shed. Figured you'd be the perfect guy to get rid of it."

"Hive," Stinger corrected.

"What?"

"It's not a nest, it's a hive."

As if summoned by magic, a single honeybee appeared in the air, and then proceeded to circumnavigate Doug Winslow's enormous crimson head. Winslow jerked back and nearly fell backward off the stoop. He yanked his visor from his head and swatted at the air with it.

"I can't believe you still mess with these damn things," Winslow said, his voice having risen a tick in agitation at the sight of the honeybee.

"That's not one of mine."

"I'm looking into it. That beehive you've got in that back lot has got to be against community ordinances or something."

"How? Bees are good for the environment."

"They sting."

"Not unless you bother them."

"And what happened there?" Winslow asked. He was peering at the poorly healing wound along Stinger's scalp.

"How would you know there's a hive back there unless you've been trespassing on my property?" Stinger said, ignoring Winslow's question and ogling stare.

Winslow scowled. "You know, we're going to have a good, long conversation someday, you and me."

"Sure," Stinger said, thinking he wouldn't mind conversing with Doug Winslow via the blunt grammar of his knuckles.

Still swatting at the air with his visor, Doug Winslow jigged off the porch then hurried to his MG that was parked in the street. "Just get your ass down to the park, clean the place up, and get rid of that bees' nest. They've already stung a couple of kids. I don't need any more emails from angry parents."

Stinger just nodded but didn't say anything more.

In the street, Winslow folded himself into his tiny car. The MG belched black smoke, and then he sped away.

Stinger stepped out onto the porch. He saw nothing at first, but then on closer inspection, he could see that there were bees creeping along the screens of the second-floor windows of the house. Most prominently on Queenie's bedroom windows, in fact. From here, he couldn't tell if they were inside or outside the house.

He didn't know how long he stood there staring at the bees until the sound of a screen door slamming snapped him from his reverie. Next door, Marybeth Maysall came out of her house. She was wearing some hotsy totsy nylon shorts and a T-shirt that put her bare midriff on prominent display. Stinger watched her appreciatively as she meandered down the driveway to the mailbox. Twice he had asked Marybeth Maysall out on a date. The first time she had laughed and said how sweet he was and that she found him to be just about the funniest guy on Macadam Street, but then she had gotten into her shitty little Kia, and drove away without actually responding to Stinger's invitation. The second time, he happened to catch her sunbathing on a towel on the other side of the hedgerow that separated their two properties. He had risen up from behind the hedgerow like a perfect periscope, and when he opened his mouth and asked the question, Marybeth had jerked her head up off the towel and emitted a startled little hiccupping sound. She had been lying on her stomach in a bikini, the back straps of the bikini top undone so as to not leave tan lines, and when she jumped up a little, Stinger had gotten a healthy eyeful of her miraculous cleavage. That time, she'd just gathered up her towel, held it against her chest, and hurried into her house.

Now, as he watched Marybeth come back up the driveway clutching a stack of magazines and newspaper advertisements, he cleared his throat and said, "Hey there, Marybeth."

Evidently startled, she froze midway up her walk. She jerked her head in his direction, a strand of chestnut-colored hair sweeping across her forehead. She wore no makeup today, which was all right, because Stinger wasn't really fond of women who wore too much makeup.

"Oh," Marybeth said, swiping the loose hair from her forehead and tucking it behind one ear. "You startled me, Jeremy."

He ambled down the stoop and in her direction. "I got some free passes to the mini golf place up the highway. What do you say? Feel like some putt-putt?"

"No, I don't think so."

"They're good for whenever. I mean, they don't got an expiration or nothing."

She gave him what he knew to be a piteous smile. It made him angry but he maintained his composure. "I'm really not a golf person."

"Miniature golf," he corrected. "You know, the little windmills and stuff?"

"Yeah, yeah, I know what it is. I'll see you around, 'kay?"

"Well, okay. Sure. Take care."

He watched her mount the porch steps, her legs long and tan and coltish, and he was somewhat pleased that she turned and glanced back at him over her shoulder before slipping back inside her house. Above her doorway, two strips of aluminum siding were missing, revealing bone-colored wood and Tyvek paper exposed to the elements. He supposed it had happened during the storm.

A white-hot *zap* alongside his neck: Stinger slapped a hand to the spot, and felt the wriggling of a honeybee beneath his palm. He plucked the thing from his neck, its stinger still impaled there, a greenish globule of goo bubbling from the insect's abdomen. Absently, he flicked the bee away, then dug the stinger out of the tender spot in his neck.

For some reason, he felt funny.

## 5

Before driving out to Gladstone Park, Stinger checked on Queenie.

No longer capable of moving about the house on her own, Queenie was entombed in the back bedroom like the hideous creation of a mad scientist. It was a room of bleak consequence, where the shades were perpetually drawn, and the crusty jumble of bedsheets surrendered a fetid odor suggestive of missed appointments with the toilet at the other end of the hall.

Stinger cracked open Queenie's bedroom door, and the stink wasted no time accosting his nose. He registered her enormous bulk heaped upon the bed, limned in the half-light that blazed against the thin vinyl window shades. His ears registered the *sssst* of the oxygen tank and the answering wheeze of his mother's hapless lungs. As his eyes adjusted to the gloom, he focused on one massive forearm beached above the bedsheets, a slab of colorless dough textured like crepe bunting, a frowning divot the only evidence of an elbow.

"Mother?"

He'd whispered it so softly.

As if he didn't truly want her to know he was there.

The only response: the *sssst* of the oxygen machine, followed by an exhalation of Queenie's labored breath.

Stinger slipped back out into the hallway.

## 6

There were bees in the cab of his GMC pickup. He noticed them on his drive to Gladstone Park, crawling along the perimeter of the rearview mirror. One campaigned the length of the cracked plastic of the dashboard, its twitching, waggling abdomen unfurling some secret, coded language. Somehow, one had gotten trapped inside the pickup's instrument panel, and for a moment Stinger watched as it traversed like a tightrope walker the trembling needle of the speedometer.

He arrived to find Gladstone Park unusually empty for such a nice summer day. Stinger hardly gave it any thought; the buzzing in his head was back, harmonizing with the sounds of the bees in the cab of the truck. In fact, it wasn't in his head, he suddenly realized, but resonating right there in his back teeth—his goddamn molars. The sensation was not unlike a dull toothache. When was the last time he'd been to the dentist? Christ, he couldn't remember.

He parked along a gravel path that ran behind the backstop of the park's baseball diamond. Stinger liked Gladstone Park. He had come here often as a boy to shoot squirrels with his grandmother's pellet gun (this was before Glenda-Rae died, cirrhosis of the liver, painful and grueling, skin as yellow as parchment, eyes like runny egg yolks). As a teenager, he had come here to drink stolen beer and fumble around in the back seats of cars with some of the less discerning girls from the local high school. Though he was not the type of person to think in sentimental terms, he had lost his virginity right here in Gladstone Park when he was sixteen years old. He had done it with Eloise Llewellyn, who'd only been a freshman at the time, right behind the clubhouse in the grass on the far side of the baseball diamond. He had convinced her to do it by giving her a pack of unfiltered Camels, which it turned out she couldn't smoke because they were too harsh and incited her asthma. As he sat now behind the wheel of his truck gazing out across the field, Stinger absently wondered what had become of old Eloise Llewellyn. *Probably married and fat and with a brood of awful, ugly children*, he guessed.

Another bee zippered across his field of vision. Distractedly, he swatted it away. Then, once it passed, and for just a moment, his eyes locked on the chain-link backstop of the baseball diamond while his hands dropped off the steering wheel and fell limply into his lap.

*Wait a minute . . .*

A thought needled into his head.

*Well, isn't that . . . ?*

That chain-link fence . . .

Had the bees planted the thought there?

*No,* he corrected himself, *not the bees. The Tower. It was the Tower.*

Yet when he tried to summon a visual of the Tower in his mind, something he'd seen nearly every day for the past two years, ever since he'd constructed it, he found that he couldn't. Or, more precisely, he found that the image that came to him was of a different sort of tower altogether. One that was both alien and familiar to him all at once. One that, for Stinger Stuckey, defied definition.

His mind returned to when he'd constructed the Tower's queen excluder—how he'd had to resize the links in the screen over and over until he got it correctly. He thought, too, of his nightmare, and the terrible fury with which he had to cobble together that dream Tower using bits of garbage and discarded junk in that postapocalyptic wasteland. It would be possible to accomplish this feat if he could *wrap*—

A splotch of blood fell into his lap. He looked up at his reflection in the rearview mirror and saw a thread of bright red blood drooling from his left nostril. With little concern, he swiped his thumb beneath his nose, smearing a crimson streak across his upper lip.

He wondered if something was indeed broken inside his head.

## 7

He eased the truck along the bumpy gravel drive that cut through the back end of the park and wound in the direction of the maintenance shed. There was an electrical substation back here, a medieval-looking arrangement of transformers, bus bars, and surge arresters. The whole station was barricaded behind a chain-link fence capped with concertina wire and a sign that read DANGER – HIGH VOLTAGE. Again, his eyes were drawn to those diamond-shaped links in the fence, much as they'd been drawn to the baseball diamond's backstop. Inexplicable the way the sight of it suddenly filled up his mind.

Once the maintenance shed revealed itself to him, piecemeal, between the trees, he parked the truck and dripped out of the cab and into the bright sunshine of midday. The maintenance shed was a rectangular stucco building with a metal door on one end and a small wire-mesh window high up in the eaves. Inside the shed were generators, road cones, sawhorses, the old Mariner's Cove neighborhood sign which had been replaced at least a dozen years ago, a riding mower, a chainsaw, countless spools of extension cords, cans of paint and turpentine, and innumerable other items which, in Stinger's estimation, would never be utilized in a million years. In fact, as far as he knew, he was the only person in the whole community who ever went in there; the sole keeper of the neighborhood's forgotten history, the neighborhood's buried secrets.

A cool breeze rattled the surrounding trees as Stinger walked the circumference of the building, searching for the hive. Finally, he saw it: a helix of grayish papier-mâché dangling fruitlike from beneath the eave. It was roughly the size of a basketball, for Christ's sake, and it was absolutely *crawling* with wasps.

"Moron," Stinger mumbled, referring to Doug Winslow, who apparently didn't know bees and wasps from his own asshole.

Stinger Stuckey despised wasps. Bees were mathematical, harmonizing in their actions, united in their movements and thoughts as if controlled by a singular brain. Bees went about peacefully gathering pollen and nectar, which they used to feed their brood and fertilize flowers. Bees stung only when provoked, and they were not afraid to surrender their individual lives for the safety and betterment of the colony. Wasps, on the other hand, were sleek, black, carnivorous hunting machines, which often stung without provocation. They ate bees.

He ambled back to the truck where he tugged on a pair of work gloves. He grabbed a hoe from the truck bed, returned to the shed, and knocked the nest loose from the eave, piñata-style. The thing spiraled through the air and landed softly in the grass, rolling a bit before coming to a stop. Wasps gusted into the air in a snarl of black, whirring wings. Stinger felt something tickle the nape of his neck; he slapped a hand to it, but his palm came away clean.

He knew there was a gallon of gasoline in the shed, which he could use to burn the nest, so he returned to the truck, yanked the keys from the ignition, and found the key to the shed's padlock on his keyring. He went around to the door . . .

. . . then froze.

Someone had spray-painted a series of hashmarks in blinding pink neon on the door of the shed:

He stared at those hashmarks, suddenly and inexplicably mesmerized. He wanted to reach out and touch them, but feared his fingers would smudge the paint, because it looked fresh. Just staring at those hashmarks reminded him once again of the queen's excluder that he'd struggled to get right when building the Tower. They reminded him, too, of the diamond-shaped links in the chain-link backstop back by the baseball field.

When he blinked his eyes and cleared his head, he was aware that the sun had drastically repositioned itself in the sky, and that he had cultivated a formidable tan along his bee-stung forearms. How long had he been standing here, staring at the hashmarks on that door? He grabbed the can of gasoline from the shed and doused the wasp nest with it. Wasps patrolled the air in a frenzy, so Stinger was quick about fishing a lighter from his pocket and setting the whole goddamn thing ablaze.

The next thing he knew, the nest was a smoldering clump of gray ash in the grass and the wasps—most of them, anyway—had fled for safer locales. Again, the sun was in the wrong place in the sky; Stinger shielded his eyes from the brunt of it while peering into the sky, but the sun was tucked behind the tank of the Mariner's Cove water tower just beyond the tops of the distant trees.

*What the hell is happening to me?*

*How long have I been standing out here?*

He was afraid to check the time on his phone.

## 8

That evening, he brought Queenie's dinner to the back bedroom, though a part of his mind was still out there in Gladstone Park, staring fixatedly at that chain-link backstop behind home plate. What was the Tower trying to tell him? He didn't know.

Queenie was awake, her massive bulk avalanched against the headboard and a dam of sweat-yellowed pillows. Her pale, doughy skin was refracting the sickly bluish glow from the flickering TV across the room. The whole place stank of shit.

Stinger swiveled the aluminum arm and food tray from the side of the bed and positioned it across Queenie's vast, surging body. He had constructed the tray himself from an old desktop which he'd fitted to a retractable arm and attached to the side of Queenie's bed. He'd always been mechanically inclined, had always been someone who liked to learn new things. He'd graduated at the top of his class in high school and had even received an academic scholarship to the University of Maryland, but of course, he couldn't leave his mother behind. She had no one to take care of her.

Queenie's head rolled in his direction. Her eyes were dusty marbles.

"I can't stand the heat in this house," she groused.

"It hasn't been that hot, Mother," he said, cutting up her Salisbury steak.

"You keep the air turned off and the windows open in the middle of summer, that's the problem. You do it to punish me. Don't think I can't tell, Jeremy."

"The air is on, and the windows aren't open, Mother."

"Don't lie to me. Those bees keep getting in here, too. I killed two of 'em with my Nora Roberts." She rolled her head to acknowledge the stack of hardcover library books piled on a chair within arm's reach; the fleshy dewlap quivered below her chin.

Finished cutting her steak, he kissed Queenie's sweat-jeweled forehead—his lips came away salty—then switched on the bedside lamp. He removed the stack of books from the chair and set them on the floor.

"Smells lovely," she said, leaning over the dinner he had prepared for her: Salisbury steak, buttered bread rolls, a steaming tureen of pasta, a wedge of huckleberry pie sprinkled with powdered sugar, and a large thermos of chocolate milk. Her medication, too—a plastic cup filled with countless bicolored capsules and chalky horse pills.

His mother's Bible was on the nightstand beside the lamp; he picked it up, then sat down in the chair. Queenie watched him, her swollen white face bisected by the rubber oxygen tube that snaked beneath her nose. Her eyes turned to black slits as she ate, reminding Stinger of how a shark will roll its eyes back when going in for a kill, her whole face framed by loose gray strands of brittle, lank, unwashed hair. The part in her scalp was startlingly white, crusty with dandruff, and reminded Stinger of an infected surgical scar.

"Deee-lish," she said, shoveling a forkful of Salisbury steak into her mouth. Queenie smiled as she chewed, her chin glistening with grease. It was a grotesque manipulation of her features, the heavy jowls ratcheting upward as if by hydraulics, the dull black shark eyes thinning to cheery, pencil-thin crescents. The oxygen, like a serpent on the floor beside her bed, went *sssst.* "Your head looks better, too."

He brought a hand up to touch the wound at his scalp. Said, "Thanks."

"You see? Aren't you glad I made you get those stitches?"

"Sure," he said, even though he hadn't gotten any stitches.

While Queenie ate, Stinger read her the parable of the prodigal son. By the time he finished the story, Queenie had cleaned her plate and sucked down about a gallon of chocolate milk from the thermos.

"My good boy," she said, and pushed the retractable arm and food tray out of the way. She lifted her massive arms off the bed. Fat swung pendulously from her forearms, pronounced as batwings. "Come."

He went to her, bent forward into her sweaty, fetid embrace. The smell of her made him lightheaded, made him want to gag. As much as he hated to admit it, he knew she would require another bath soon. He would have to set aside an evening, and likely purchase another six-pack of Natty Boh to chase away the memory of that repugnant ordeal.

"There, there," she said, her breath hot as a gas fire against his ear. "Put the air on, will you, Jeremy? It's so hot in here."

"All right, Mother," he said, even though the air was already on, and set the Bible down beside her on the mattress.

"That's my good boy." Queenie's hand rubbed his back, leaving a damp arc along the fabric of his shirt. "Love you, Jer-Jer."

"Love you too, Mother," he said, then he extracted himself from her sweaty embrace.

He was halfway down the hall when his mother emitted an ear-piercing shriek. Stinger rushed back into her room to find the bedsheet pulled taut up to Queenie's ample bosom, her face a rictus of terror. Queenie's temples burned a bright red.

"What? What is it?"

A part of him thought she was dying of something—suffering a stroke or a heart attack, maybe—but then she pointed to the foot of the bed.

Stinger did not see it until it moved, its tiny body describing a zigzag pattern over the massive ridge of Queenie's sheeted left leg.

A bee.

"Jeremy! Jeremy! Get it *off*! Oh, *JERE—*"

*(ZZZZEREMEEEE)*

"*—MEEEE!*"

Without thinking, he reached out and plucked the honeybee off the sheet, pinching it between his thumb and forefinger. It sank its ovipositor into the pad of his thumb, but Stinger hardly noticed.

"This is what happens, Jeremy! This is what . . . what happens when . . . when you disobey your . . . your mother!" Queenie cried between gasps for air. Beside her bed, the oxygen tank went *ssst-ssst*. Angrily so.

"It's fine, Mother," he said, backing toward the doorway, the bee still pinched between his fingers.

"It is *not* fine! We have *talked* about this, Jeremy! I have never been stung *in my life*, boy! I could be *allergic*! I am *ill*, Jeremy. I am *unhealthy*! Do you know what a bee sting might do to me? Are you trying to kill me?"

"Of course not, Mother," he said. The bee wriggled between his fingers so he popped it like a grape.

"You're so—"

*Ssst.*

"Mother . . ."

"*—selfish . . .*"

*Ssst.*

One of her enormous arms came around and whipped her dinner plate in his approximate direction. Stinger flinched, and the plate shattered against the wall.

*Ssst-ssst.*

Her body trembling and her face beet-red, Queenie gasped for breath between sobs. Stinger remained standing in the doorway to make sure she was okay, until she scowled at him and told him to get the hell out of her sight, he was so selfish he made her physically ill. Satisfied that she would not asphyxiate, Stinger left the room, closing the door behind him.

Out in the hall, he smeared the remains of the bee down the thigh of his pants. He adjusted the thermostat, set the air to a brisk fifty-seven degrees (for Christ's sake), made sure all the windows were closed (they were), then ventured out to visit the Tower.

He was aware, as he advanced through the wooded lots toward the Tower, that the chorus of buzzing at the center of his—

*(teeth)*

—head had risen in pitch and stridency. Feverish, almost. *Dispatches from the Tower*, he thought, and wondered if that was, in fact, accurate . . . or if something had gotten knocked loose in his head and was simply rattling around in there, likely due to the tree limb having fallen on him. Should he go back to that urgent care place, demand an X-ray? Maybe that attractive nurse would be there.

And then he came upon it, a thing no less formidable than a stone idol in a breach of jungle. Godlike; looming.

The Tower.

Honeybees swirled before it in a dense fog. They lit upon the flesh of Stinger's exposed arms, and several of them buried their barbed stingers into his skin. He was so accustomed to this by now that he hardly noticed.

*Zzzzzt zzzzzt*—inside/outside his head.

The swarm parted as he approached the hive, then closed around him, enveloping him, swallowing him up. Cocoonlike. Their strident, bristling bodies danced around him, erratic as sparks of light. Together, they formed something almost—

*(snakelike)*

—serpentine in the air.

Sour breath juddered out of Stinger's constricted throat. Another step closer to the Tower. Raw honey glistened between two drawers, bleeding out like some—

*(headwound)*

—mortal injury.

He dropped to his knees and placed a hand on each side of the wooden Tower. A sleeve of bees rolled up each arm.

"What?" he asked, his voice cracking. His throat burned. Bees crawled about on his face. He was thinking of his dream, that crazy dream. "What is it? What are you saying? What are you trying to tell me?"

They crawled down the back of his shirt and got tangled in his hair.

*"What are you trying to tell me?"*

He leaned forward and pressed his sweaty forehead against the wooden drawers of the Tower. Honey collected in his hair and glazed his brow. He closed his burning eyes—

*(ZZZZEREMEEEE)*

—and the image that flashed across the screen his mind was not of bees, but of something he could not fully describe or discern or fathom, except to liken it, in his own pedestrian way, to a northern water snake he had once seen as a child cutting across the smoked glass surface of the Chesapeake Bay.

## 9

The Tower explained what the spray-painted hashmarks meant, and then it told him what to do for the time being. Everything else, the Tower promised, would be revealed to him in time.

## 10

That night, beneath the cover of dark, Stinger drove back out to Gladstone Park. With a pair of bolt cutters, he clipped away the chain-link fence that made up the backstop of the baseball diamond. He cut the fencing into smaller sections, which were easier to handle, then rolled each of them up into tubes. He secured them with bungee cords in the back of his truck. When he was done, the muscles in his shoulders ached from the work and the palms of his hands bled from cuts where the chain-link had carved shallow trenches into his flesh.

The buzzing a steady drone in both his head and his back teeth now, he drove back to the stone carriage house on Macadam Street where he awaited further instruction from the Tower.

## CHAPTER SEVENTEEN

# PURSUIT

### 1

It was the sound of Alex's alarm on his phone that roused Georgette from sleep. It was early—a quarter to five in the morning, according to the glowing red numerals on the clock beside the bed—and the bedroom was still dark. She rolled over to find Alex's side of the bed empty. Sitting up, she could see that he wasn't in the master bathroom either, because there was no strip of light running along the bottom of the door, which was how she could always tell he was in there getting ready for work. On the nightstand next to Alex's side of the bed, the cell phone alarm kept up its incessant, mechanical *reet reet reet*, until she leaned over and shut it off.

The whole house went silent. In that moment, Georgette was overcome with the certainty that she was the only living thing inside this house, and that her husband and daughters had, in some form or fashion, vanished from existence while she'd slept in the night.

She climbed out of bed and drifted ghostlike down the hall in the dark. Both her daughters' bedroom doors stood open, and she couldn't help but pause outside each one, holding her own breath until she could hear theirs. She knew she was acting irrationally—that her mind was operating in some traitorous fashion to her logic—but she couldn't help it. In fact, she couldn't remember the last time she had felt more helpless.

Alex was standing in the living room in the dark. He was dressed for work in a suit and clutching the handle of his briefcase as he gazed out the front window and out into the moonlit yard, his back to her. His body was silvered in moonlight, and his head was cocked at an angle that suggested maybe he was looking up at something high in the trees or perhaps in the sky. Just like the morning she'd found him on the front lawn. She said nothing as she watched him now, her body growing hot and prickly beneath her nightclothes, the beat of her heart gathering momentum within the confines of her chest.

Alex stood there for an inordinate amount of time, not moving.

She, too, stood and watched him in silence, and with each passing minute, she sometimes opened her mouth to speak his name, but each time decided against it in the end. Perhaps, she thought, the two of them might stand here until the end of time, Alex staring toward some unknown line on the horizon, Georgette staring at *him*.

But that did not happen: just as the first striations of daylight began to seep up over the property fence, brightening the atmosphere beyond the living room window, Alex turned. It was still dark in the hallway, so Georgette did not think he could see her, although she was able to catch a glimpse of *him* before she retreated farther into the shadows of the hallway—a man who looked twice Alex's age, with a mask for a face that seemed to droop off the skull, and there were shimmery tracks of tears leaking down from the corners of Alex's eyes.

*Jesus,* she thought, her heart and mind racing. *Jesus, what's wrong with him?*

She withdrew farther down the hall before he could see her, cloaking herself in darkness. She heard the footfalls of Alex's work shoes coming into the hall, *clack clack*, and then she saw him move across the mouth of the hallway like some motorized thing rolling along a conveyor belt. A moment after that, she heard the front door open then close, following by the muted scuff of his shoes along the gritty walkway that curled around the front of the house. A moment after *that* and she heard his car door slam.

*Follow him.*

It was so basic a command that she did not question it. She headed down the hall to the foyer, patting around in the darkness for her own keys, but unable to find them. Her purse was on the small table in the vestibule; she rummaged through it like a thief, sunglasses, tampons, a tin of breath mints, her wallet, but no keys. She glanced up and out one of the front windows and could see Alex seated in the driver's seat of his car, both hands gripping the steering wheel, but not moving.

*What the hell is he doing?*

She spun around and was about to bolt into the kitchen—she'd left her keys on the counter, she suddenly realized—when she was startled by Denise standing there in the dark. Her eyes were wide, her gaze laser focused on Georgette. She wore that goddamn spaghetti strainer on her head again.

"Jesus, baby, you scared me. What are you doing out of bed?"

"I had a funny dream."

Georgette plucked the colander off her head, then administered a swift kiss to the side of her daughter's face. Denise's flesh felt hot and clammy against her lips. *Maybe everyone in this house is getting sick. Maybe that's all it is. Delirious with fever.*

"Go back to bed," she instructed as she hurried into the kitchen and snatched her car keys off the counter. "It's still early. And I have to run out for a minute, but I promise I will be right back."

As she passed by the front windows, she saw Alex's car backing slowly out of the driveway and into the street. The headlights blinked on, and for a moment, Georgette felt spotlighted in their glow like an inmate sneaking along the perimeter of a prison yard bent on escape.

"Go," she admonished her daughter one last time.

Denise turned and disappeared back down the darkened hallway.

Georgette stepped into her shoes then slipped out onto the front porch.

The summer air was cool this early in the morning. As she watched the taillights of Alex's Camry roll slowly down their street, she hurried across the lawn toward the driveway and to her own set of wheels—a boxy Chevy Equinox with dented quarter panels. Pine-scented air fresheners hung perpetually from the rearview mirror and there was an Evanescence disc stuck in the CD player. Denise's car seat was strapped in the back, and there were the girls' toys and books and some grease-stained McDonald's bags in the back seat, too. It was their everyday car, the thing they'd taken on countless family adventures to theme parks and museums and aquariums and birthday parties. Alex called it the Shwagon, an affectionate portmanteau for "Shit Wagon," because it was always in such disarray, but for Georgette, it had always felt comfortable and of home. As she climbed into it this morning, however, it had never felt more alien to her. Almost hostile. Much like her marriage. Much like Alex.

When she reached the stop sign at the end of their street, she looked in both directions. The taillights of Alex's car were growing smaller on her left, so she took the turn, spinning the steering wheel with one hand. She glanced down and realized she was still holding onto the colander with her other hand, its dented aluminum dome patterned with holes, its weight in her hand feeling somehow significant. She flashed back to the night before—how she'd hidden the bloody towel beneath this thing only to find that it was gone once she went to retrieve it—and wondered, once again, if she was *also* losing her shit, much like her husband.

*Maybe there's a gas leak on the block. Maybe that storm broke open a gas line and we're all slowly being poisoned. Maybe it's messing with our heads, slowly driving us all toward madness.*

She tossed the colander on the passenger seat, wanting to be rid of it . . . though her eyes hung on it a moment longer than they should have.

Up ahead, Alex's taillights took another left turn. When she approached the intersection, she followed.

*This is not the way to the highway. He should have taken a right turn if he was heading to work.*

But she already knew he wasn't heading to work. Still, a left turn would send him deeper into the neighborhood. Had she still believed he was having an affair, this would have forced her to consider he was seeing someone *in their neighborhood*, maybe even someone Georgette knew and was friendly with. But after the past twenty-four hours and

Alex's increasingly bizarre behavior—not to mention his deteriorating hygiene—she no longer believed this was about infidelity.

She realized she was driving too fast and thus following Alex's car too closely. This early in the morning, theirs were the only two vehicles navigating the streets of Mariner's Cove, so she backed off and let some distance grow between them so that Alex wouldn't grow suspicious and maybe even recognize the Equinox in his rearview mirror.

*I could probably crash into him right now and he wouldn't even notice.*

Up ahead, Alex took another turn that cast him onto a curving ribbon of asphalt that would wind him deeper into the community. Georgette was thinking about those bloody towels again, and the items she'd discovered in the trunk of his car—the balls of string and duct tape, the latex gloves and coils of rope. The bone-handled knife.

She had been so preoccupied in wanting to know what the hell was going on with him, she never stopped to think if she *should* know. What if whatever he was doing would irrevocably change them? And not just her relationship with him, but change their entire family? She thought, then, of Callie snoring peacefully in her bed, and Denise's wan face as she stared up at her in the darkened hallway just moments ago. She thought about how different things would be if Alex was no longer in their lives.

*I have to know. I can't keep living this way.*

For whatever reason, she glanced down at the passenger seat, and at the colander sitting there. Before she had time to think about what she was doing, she picked it up . . .

. . . and placed it atop her head.

A part of her thought she might just disappear into it, much like the bloody towel had done. Maybe that would solve all their problems: for her to just disappear. She sensed an errant thought zip through her head—a thought that felt more like someone else's than her own—that suggested what happened with the towel *could happen again* under the right circumstances. Yet she did not know what those circumstances might be. She did not—

*I'm going crazy.*

She laughed, though a tear trickled out of her left eye and raced down the side of her face, hot as magma. Glancing at her reflection in the rearview mirror, she realized how—

*(right)*

—ridiculous she felt. No: it was more than just that. The colander atop her head felt like some sentient thing capable of reading her thoughts. Or, more accurately, capable of transmitting thoughts *to her.*

"I'm losing my fucking mind, all right," she muttered, and tossed the thing back onto the passenger seat.

## 2

She lost sight of him somewhere along that twisty strip of roadway. Once she realized this, she slowed whenever she came upon the entrance of another street, peering down that street to see if she could spot the Camry's taillights. But they were never there. Had he realized she was following him? Had he lost her on purpose? Should she just turn around and go back home?

A column of panic stiffened within her.

She came out onto Poplar Station Road just as a string of streetlamps along the sidewalk winked off in the burgeoning morning light. A car shuttled by on the next street over, collecting her attention, but it was a shuddery white pickup truck belching clouds of black exhaust from its tailpipe. Not Alex's Toyota.

She closed her eyes for a moment, then spun the steering wheel. The Shwagon lumbered over a curb and headed back in the direction she had come. Another side street appeared—she didn't know all the street names this deep into the neighborhood, rarely ever came this way—and she took it, spying a string of darkened homes to her left and a swath of tall trees and thick bushes to her right. Farther still, and the trees were suddenly on both sides of the road, arching up over the roadway to create a tunnel that blocked out much of the pinkening dawn light. Any houses she spotted nestled back beyond those trees were uniformly dark, their windows shuttered, their porch lights off. That same feeling that had accosted her upon waking to Alex's alarm—of being the only living person inside their home—struck her again, more profoundly this time, because she suddenly felt certain that she was the only living creature in all of Mariner's Cove in that moment. Every house vacant, the great sweep of woods devoid of wildlife. The cool, slate-gray waters of the bay beyond the neighborhood as sterile and inhospitable as a canyon on an alien planet.

Alone.

She drove until the road emptied her onto another intersection. To her right stood the open fields of Gladstone Park, listless and desultory at this bleak hour, and suddenly she knew where she was. She'd done nearly a complete circuit, in fact, and was facing back in the direction of their home. But where had *Alex* gone?

*He's disappeared. Just like everyone else. I'm here alone.*

But then she saw Alex's Camry parked up on a patch of grass along the shoulder of Gladstone Park that, in the midst of summer, was infused with the tiny yellow satellite dishes of buttercups and the swaying, fuzzy-headed helmets of dandelions. Georgette rolled slowly past the Camry, wincing because she was suddenly certain that Alex would see her as she drove by. But Alex was not in his car. She continued to roll up another block before parking against the curb, turning off the engine, and climbing unsteadily out of the Equinox.

The air was no longer cool and fresh. The swampy smell of the nearby bay was assaultive—a fetid, scummy odor reminiscent of dead fish. The sun wasn't even fully up yet, but she could already tell it was going to be a hot one.

Something felt wrong. Not just with Alex, but right here, right in this spot. In her soul, perhaps. She stood there beside the curb, hugging herself despite the encroaching heat. Twice, she peered in through the Shwagon's window at the colander that still sat on the passenger seat. Thought of Denise materializing before her in the dark, frightening her, that damn thing perched atop her head like a space helmet.

What had Denise said about the thing when Georgette had first asked about it?

*It's important.*

She happened to glance down and noticed a peculiar drawing on the sidewalk at her feet done in bright orange spray-paint. At first, she thought it was a tic-tac-toe board, but then she realized she was wrong. It was, in fact, a grid of hashmarks:

She had spied that same drawing in the small notepad she'd found in Alex's jacket pocket yesterday. That symbol, repeated over and over, page after page, among a host of other strange symbols. It occurred to her in that moment that this *same* symbol had been the one written in chalk at the foot of their driveway earlier in the week, which last night's rain had seen fit to wash away. Had Denise drawn it there?

*No.*

Now, the sight of it caused Georgette's throat to tighten.

There were more symbols sketched in the street and some on the opposite sidewalk, too, she could see. Some were rendered in chalk, though now faded from last night's storm; others were done in more bright orange spray paint. Each one unnerved her. She crossed the road not to get a better look at them, but to study the shape of a figure she suddenly spied cutting across the field at the far end of Gladstone Park.

Alex.

*Where the hell is he going?*

She pursued him across the field, the distance between them so great that even if he happened to turn and look back toward the road, he might not see her (and even if he did, he might not recognize her).

He was carrying his briefcase, which struck her as odd—or, more accurately, which struck her as just one more odd element added to this entire incomprehensible ordeal. She watched as he vanished into the dark swell of trees toward the far end of the park.

*Whatever it is he's doing back there, I need to catch him doing it.*

She wasn't sure what that could be, but she knew that there was no way to get him to have a conversation about it with her, no way to get him to confess. It was all just too bizarre. No—she had to see with her own eyes just what the hell was going on.

*I want to tell you a story, Mommy.* It was Denise's voice, sounding off like an explosion in the center of her head. In fact, the force of it—the *actuality* of it—was so monumental, it momentarily stopped Georgette dead in her tracks. Not a memory of something Denise had said to her in real life, but her actual *voice*, as if the girl were speaking directly to her right now. Georgette pressed fingers to both temples as Denise said, *Do you want to hear it, Mommy? It's a good story, and very important. Once upon a time, a snake got lost . . .*

Georgette shook her head to clear it of her daughter's voice. It broke apart like static. She didn't want to hear it, didn't want to sink further into whatever madness this was. Disorientation filled the gap where Denise's voice had just been, causing Georgette to look around, unsure why she was standing ankle deep in wet summer grass in a field at the ass end of Gladstone Park in the early hours of the morning, before the sun had fully risen. But it was a fleeting disorientation, and she quickly recalibrated. There was a strange, inebriating fog quickly gathering in her head, and a buzzing sound to go along with it. Her molars suddenly ached. So badly, in fact, that she opened her mouth and pressed an index finger to each one, as if she could stop them from hurting by the sheer application of pressure.

She glanced once more toward the trees. There appeared to be an Alex-shaped opening carved through the foliage in his wake, dark as pitch yet beckoning her to follow.

She pursued her husband into the trees.

## 3

The woods were dense and buggy, the air humid from the recent rain. The smell of pine sap coupled with the earthy aroma of rich, dew-dampened foliage invaded her nose. Gnats congregated out of a near-militant determination in front of her face, getting snared in her eyelashes and in the slick saline tracks that had moistened her cheeks. There was a sponginess to the earth this deep into the woods, and twice her sneakers were nearly sucked from her feet as if by a vacuum.

After just a few minutes of wandering among the trees, she realized she had gotten turned around. She couldn't tell from which direction she had just come, or in what direction she had been heading. She kept listening for birds with a sort of desperate hopefulness, thinking their chatter might imply some goodness here, but nothing pervaded except the incessant buzzing of insects orbiting her head and adhering to the sweaty pockets of flesh along her face. Once again, she felt utterly and completely alone.

And then the trees parted. There was a clearing up ahead. She paused, her heart thundering so loudly she believed she could hear its contractions like drumbeats in her ears. Breath rasping from her throat, she peered through the bristly pine boughs.

The clearing was actually a gritty oval of asphalt salted with bits of white gravel. The massive legs of the Mariner's Cove water tower rose up from the circumference of the oval and stretched up to the water tank that stood at a dizzying height off the ground. It looked like some giant robotic insect spirited down from the stars . . .

. . . and there, directly beneath it, stood her husband.

Alex was doing . . . *something* . . . that she could not quite understand. Although she could describe it to anyone who might have asked clearly enough: Alex was weaving a web of string around the legs of the water tower. It was the string she had seen in the trunk of his car, she realized, only now it had been wound around the legs of the water tower so that it created a sort of—

*(hashmark)*

—meshwork encircling the tower's base. Alex stood inside of it, weaving the string into a latticework, bracing it around the stanchions of the tower, winding it in and out of the grid that was already there, much like a caterpillar spinning a cocoon around itself, or a spider constructing a web.

There was an intensity with which Alex worked. A single-minded focus, his brow furrowed, his dedication unwavering. She could tell just by looking at him. He appeared coldly possessed, going about his work with a frantic sort of devotion that was nearly hypnotic. He'd removed his suit jacket, necktie, and dress shirt—they hung absently from a nearby tree branch, limp as sloughed skin—and there was a triangle of perspiration at the center of his plain white undershirt. He didn't even notice her standing there observing him.

"Alex."

Her voice was a ringing bell in that otherwise silent clearing.

Alex froze. He looked up at her through the meshwork of criss-crossed string. When his eyes found hers, locked on hers, Georgette discovered she hadn't the strength to muster another word.

"Georgette. Georgette."

There wasn't even the barest inflection in his voice. It *was* Alex's voice, but at the same time it seemed robbed of some vital nuance, stripped of its former essence. Foreign in some way, and not to be trusted.

Again: "Georgette."

Because it was always *G*, never *Georgette*, never her full name.

This stranger wearing her husband's face speaking to her as if she, too, were a stranger capable of being fooled . . .

She was aware—just barely—that she had begun shaking her head back and forth, as if to respond in the negative to some question she hadn't yet been asked. She was similarly aware that she was taking small, furtive steps backward, retreating from whatever spectacle her husband was creating, was constructing, at the base of this water tower.

"Georgette," Alex said again, and this time he came right up to the meshwork of string that now seemed to serve as a barrier between them. As if he was some animal trapped in a cage of his own design. He reached out and curled a set of fingers around the string, which remained taut though bowed slightly at the weight of him. Then he lowered himself first to his knees before actually lying on the ground, his movements calculated and slow. She didn't know what he was doing until he actually did it: there was a two-foot gap between the paved ground and where that latticework of string began, and Alex rolled himself underneath it. And then he was standing before her, brushing bits of mulch and flakes of dead leaves off his clothing and out of his hair. Sweat glistened on his face.

"What is this?" The words whooshed out of her. She felt them—a physical expulsion of something not quite poisonous but damn close. There was an ache in her chest, and she seemed unable to fully catch her breath. "What's . . . what's going on? What the hell are you *doing*?"

"Georgette," he said—

*(please stop saying my name like that)*

—and took a step toward her.

She took another step back.

"Hey." He held up his hands as if in surrender. As if in defeat. He was wearing a pair of latex gloves, condom-looking, runnels of sweat dribbling down his wrists.

"What the fuck are you doing out here?" she said.

"Babe, you shouldn't be—"

"What the fuck are you *doing*, Alex? What *is* all this?"

Alex's black eyes hung on hers. His gloved hands were still up, as if in supplication . . . but then she realized he wasn't trying to calm her with such a gesture, but was instead attempting to impede her view of what he had been doing at the base of the water tower. That massive spider web of string . . .

"You shouldn't be here, Georgette." That calm, even-keeled voice. He took another step in her direction. "It isn't ready."

"What isn't ready? What are you *doing*?"

She could see his briefcase on the ground behind him, beneath the tree branch where his suit jacket, shirt, and necktie hung. The briefcase was open, and she saw that it was filled with more balls of string and latex gloves. And all those bloody towels, too.

"Something very important." He stripped off the latex gloves, *snap snap,* and for the first time, Georgette noticed that the palms of his hands were raw and abraded, crisscrossed with their own meshwork of thin red lines.

*Rope burn,* she thought.

Had he been so distant with her lately that she hadn't noticed his hands were ruined like that? Conversely, had *she* been so distant with *him*?

What was going on here?

"Alex." She held up her own hands and took another step back.

"It's not perfect . . . I know it's not . . . I mean, I just can't seem to get it right . . . but it's very important, Georgette. It's *very* important."

"Tell me what it is. Tell me what you're doing."

"I'm building . . . I mean, I'm *trying* to build . . . to *construct* . . ." Some nonspecific confusion briefly clouded his eyes. He glanced over his shoulder, as if to remind himself of what he'd been doing. "I'm trying to build . . . *something.*"

She shook her head. "What?"

"It's . . . " His voice trailed off, lost in thought or perhaps simply overwrought by the prospect of thinking. Then something seemed to occur to him: his eyes brightened, and he dug around in his pants pocket until he found what he was looking for.

It was the small spiral-bound notepad that she had found in his jacket pocket the day before. The notepad with all the strange drawings and equations in it.

"These," he said, opening the notepad to the first page. "These are clues. Like, puzzles pieces, you know? Someone has been leaving them for me to find, and I've been copying them down every time I see one. They're all *over* the place." He showed her the first page, and she remembered finding it and looking at it the day before—the ovoid shape from which a series of spindly legs descended. Something that, at the time, had reminded her of a spider. "This was the first one," he said, thrusting the notepad so close to her face that she flinched and drew back from him. "It took me a while to figure out exactly what it was," he said, his yellowed eyes jittering in their sockets, "but then I realized it's *this*."

He turned and swept a hand toward the water tower.

She took another step back, this time to bring the entire water tower into focus. A spherical tank suspended high atop a collection of insectile legs. Indeed, the shape of it resembled the rough sketch in her husband's notepad.

"But this was just one clue." Alex's moist, tallow-colored eyes still trembled in their sockets. He flipped frantically through the notepad, tiny pages rifling by, *flit flit flit*. When he came upon the page he was searching for, he held the notebook up for her to see again. "This is another." He had flipped past all those pages of hashmarks that she knew were in there only to land on a page that showed a combination of both—of the spider-like image of the water tower with the grid of hashmarks at its base. "It's like, I was given one image by itself, and then *another* image by itself, and then both images *combined*. Do you understand? I'm trying . . . I've *been* trying . . . I guess, to recreate . . . to *duplicate* . . . to *make* . . ." He was running out of breath just talking.

"Your nose," she said.

"Oh." He touched a set of fingers to the tributary of blood that was trickling out of his right nostril. Then he went to the briefcase, scooped up a towel, and blotted his face. The notepad still held out in front of him, he walked back toward her, his eyes locked on hers.

"I don't understand," she said. "Where did these drawings come from?" She reached out to take the notepad from her husband's shaking hand. He let her have it, then turned back around to stare up at the water tower once she'd taken it, the bloody towel still pressed to the lower half of his face. It occurred to her in that moment that the very top of the water tower was visible above the tree line across the street from their house . . . and upon realizing that, recalled the way he'd been standing that morning in the dark before the living room window, gazing hypnotically at something up in the sky. The same way he'd been standing on the front lawn the morning after that terrible storm. She looked at the notepad, turning slowly from page to page, paying closer attention to everything scrawled in there now. "You said someone was . . . was leaving these drawings for you . . ."

"Yes, yes," Alex said quietly. Breathlessly. There was a measure of excitement in him, or possibly exhaustion, that caused his breath to rasp from his throat. He kept dividing his attention between her and the water tower—back and forth, back and forth. "Yes, yes. All over the neighborhood."

"What do you mean?"

"Sketched in chalk at first. More recently, I've seen them in spray paint, I guess so the rain won't wash them away. They're everywhere, Georgette. On the streets. On the sidewalks. On the sides of buildings and the doors of mailboxes."

"Like the ones out there," she said, and nodded her head in the approximate direction of the street, where she'd seen those drawings for herself just moments ago.

"Yes! Right! Exactly! They're all over, babe." He flipped the bloody towel over one shoulder then reached out and gripped her high on her arms with both hands. His fingers dug painfully into her flesh. "It's a puzzle." Then he shook his head, as if to clear it of incorrect thoughts. "No, no—it's not a puzzle. That's too simplistic. They're more like . . . like instructions."

"Instructions for what?"

Alex's eyes, which had been focused on the notepad in Georgette's hand for the past thirty seconds or so, now darted up to meet her stare. "I don't know," he said ultimately . . . and Georgette couldn't deny the pity she suddenly felt toward him, for he suddenly sounded so wholly and inconsolably dejected. "I just don't know."

"Alex . . ."

"But it's very important." His eyes were on fire again. "Very important."

Something weakened in the center of Georgette's body. She wrapped her arms around herself as her vision blurred. A sob erupted from her as she dropped the notepad to the ground. In her mind, she could hear those same words coming out of Denise's mouth when she talked about the colander: *It's important.*

"Hey," Alex said, rubbing her forearms. His hands were cold, the palms rough. "Hey, hon. Honey. Georgette? Babe? Don't. Don't be upset."

"Christ, Alex." Her voice shook. She covered her face with her hands.

"Hey," he said again, wrapping her up in his arms; she could smell the days' old sweat on him, and distantly, she wondered when he'd last showered. "It's fine. Everything will be fine. In fact, I'm glad you're here. I'm glad you know about this now. I was coming apart, you know? Thinking something was wrong with me. I didn't know how to tell you. I didn't know how to explain it to you, even though I wanted to, but now that you've seen it, babe, well . . ." His voice trailed off.

She sobbed quietly against the crook of his neck. "I can't believe this."

"Shhh."

"Don't tell me that. Don't tell me shhh." She pulled away from him, pawing the tears from her eyes. "What about your job?"

"It doesn't matter."

"How can you *say* that?"

He pointed up at the water tower. "The job isn't important anymore. This is the only thing that matters now."

"Yeah? What about your daughters, Alex? What about your family?"

He faced her, grinning. The look of him terrified her. In that moment, he couldn't be further from the guy in the Rush T-shirt and blazer whom she had met all those years ago in a Georgetown bar. "It's all connected, Georgette. Don't you see that now? We're all a part of it."

She just shook her head as more tears streamed down her face.

"You just don't see it yet," he said.

"No," she responded, shaking her head. "No, I don't. Not at all. Not a fucking bit. I don't see it."

"But it's true." He bent down and picked the notepad up off the ground. There was dirt on it, which he brushed away. Then, delicately, he turned the pages until he found the one drawing he was looking for. Once again, he held the notepad out toward her.

Reluctantly, she took it.

Looked down at the page.

Sketched in pencil was the drawing of an upside-down bowl-shaped semicircle flecked with tiny holes. Like a helmet, but only *just*.

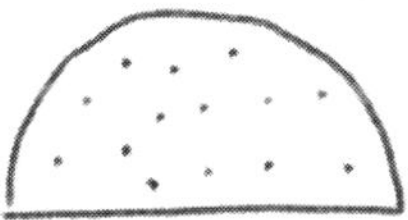

She knew what it was. At this very moment, the thing was sitting on the passenger seat of the Equinox, parked along the curb just outside Gladstone Park.

The colander.

"Us," Alex said, his breath hot and sour in her face. "You see, Georgette? We're all a part of it."

# CHAPTER EIGHTEEN
# THE BROKEN WINDOW

A man came to replace the broken window over the kitchen sink. Cory watched him from the hall, a middle-aged fellow in gray workpants and a dark blue work shirt with his name embroidered over the breast—LARRY. Cory's mom knew the man from the neighborhood, and Cory thought maybe he'd seen him around a few times, too.

He kept looking at Cory from over his shoulder while he worked.

Cory woke the gnome. It stretched wide within the canyon of Cory's brain, a sensation not dissimilar to a lung inflating. He could feel how much stronger the gnome had grown, even in just the past few days. The gnome reached out and grazed the membrane that was this man Larry's consciousness—

—but found it could not penetrate the barrier.

Struck against it like a wall.

A closed door.

A shuttered window.

Larry the window man turned and stared at Cory. His eyes narrowed the slightest bit despite a grin that slowly stretched across the lower half of the man's face.

*He felt it. He felt the gnome try to get inside his head. He felt it and he stopped me.*

When he was finished, Larry the window man cleaned up his tools, threw the sticky sheet of plastic into the trash, then said goodbye to Cory's mother. His work boots thunked along the floor as he ambled to the front door.

He winked at Cory before he left.

## CHAPTER NINETEEN

# THE TERRIBLE THING THAT HAPPENED

### 1

For the first time in many years, Michael Danver dreamt of his father. In the dream, Hal Danver was sitting in his study which was at the rear of Michael Danver's childhood home, a place he was forbidden to enter unless beckoned there. Hal was seated in his plush wingback chair—the same chair in which he would eventually take his own life with a bullet to the brain. The study was dark, except for a tall lamp in one corner which shed only the slightest amount of dull yellow light onto a blank spot on the burgundy carpet. When Danver arrived in the doorway, Hal smiled at the sight of him, then reclined with an audible sigh. There was a window at his back, a swipe of heavy curtain drawn across it. Hal reached out and swept the curtain aside, to reveal a blackened, storm-riddled landscape. Dead leaves and bits of debris slammed against the windowpane. In the distance, Danver could discern a large structure, ovoid in shape, and seeming to hover above the ground. As he stared at it, the structure began to glow with a bluish, ethereal light.

"Door becomes chair," his father said. "Take it there."

And then, suddenly, Michael Danver was standing *beneath* that great glowing structure, as a storm raged all around him. The glowing bluish light reached an intensity that even in his dream was too harsh to look at. He turned away, shielding his eyes from the glare, just as an explosion erupted above him, and things—pieces of metal springs, giant steel gears, aluminum poles and rods, angry javelins of wrought iron—rained down all around him.

In the dream, Michael Danver screamed.

## 2

*Wake up.*

Not so much a voice in his head as a needling urgency prodding the base of his spine.

*Wake—*

Michael Danver opened his eyes. Or, more precisely, consciousness returned the world to him, since his eyes had already been open for some time now. For a moment, he thought he was still dreaming—that he'd somehow transitioned from crawling along the outer shell of a massive skull-shaped structure floating unanchored in the air to standing right here in the middle of an open field. It was early enough so that the sun wasn't fully up, and a swimmy sort of mist hung in the cool dawn air.

Danver didn't know where he was. He looked down to find his feet bare. He wiggled his toes, the dewy grass damp and good-feeling against his hot, prickly skin. He was wearing a pair of silk pajama pants and a white V-neck undershirt; when he glanced down to take inventory of these clothes, he noted a tidy little constellation of blood arced across the front of the undershirt, the red so vivid against the backdrop of white that it looked like a bit of abstract art.

Where *was* he?

The last thing he remembered was standing before the door in his garage, sanding it with a fine-grade bit of sandpaper. Clouds of wood dust had filled the garage and had filled Danver's lungs, too, because, in his eagerness to prep the door, he'd neglected to wear a mask.

Prep the door for what?

He had no clue.

He looked down at his hands now. They'd once been the sterile, well-kept tools of a surgeon; now, they were calloused, rough, abraded.

They felt overlarge and clumsy. Unrefined and crude. He'd extracted countless splinters from the hardening pads of his fingertips and from the tender meat of his palms ever since he'd rescued the door from the cove and continued working on it. How he'd tweezed those slender scimitars of wood from his flesh.

He supposed he was a different kind of surgeon now.

Around him, the mist cleared. He could see straight across the field now and out toward Poplar Station Road, and the string of duplexes on the far side of the street. He was in Gladstone Park, he suddenly realized, although how the hell he'd wound up here was beyond him. Had he walked all the way here in his sleep? Had he even *gone* to sleep? Whatever events had transpired between him sanding the door in his garage and rousing into consciousness right here in this park was lost to him.

Movement in his periphery. He swung his head toward the baseball diamond in time to see a young black woman walking pointedly across the field. Not in Danver's direction, but in the direction of the woods that made up the farthest perimeter of the park. As Danver watched, the woman stopped and stood there, staring ahead at nothing specific that Danver could discern. He watched her for some time, faintly aware that his back teeth were beginning to ache, to vibrate in his jawbone. Across the field, the woman opened her mouth and slid a pair of fingers inside. As if her teeth suddenly ached, too.

A tremor of unease rattled through him.

Because there was something not only unsettling about all of this, but also something . . . *something* . . .

Familiar?

Across the field, the woman's spine seemed to stiffen. Her hand fell away from her mouth. She looked around, appearing about as disoriented as Danver had been just a moment ago, but she didn't see him where he stood, partially hidden by a stand of trees and the dissipating fog.

*I don't think this is the first time I've wandered out here in my sleep.*

He watched as the woman crept into the trees and vanished.

# 3

He walked all the way from Gladstone Park back to the house on Bay Road, a good three miles, and while he was in better than decent shape for a man his age, he arrived at the edge of his property sweating, out of breath, and with the soles of his bare feet aching.

Someone had spray painted a symbol in the middle of his driveway.

He stood staring at it, a peculiar sigil that had been sprayed in neon orange paint, for so long that by the time he pulled his eyes from it, the sun had repositioned itself in the sky above his head and he could still see the symbol burned on his retinas like the afterimage of a flashbulb's explosion. The symbol itself appeared to be a variation of the door symbol he'd been seeing printed in chalk on the sidewalks and streets up and down Bay Road over the past several days, only instead of a large rectangle with four smaller rectangles inside it (the symbol of the door), this was a large rectangle with a strange, inverted triangle near the bottom of it. And not a perfect triangle, either, because a pair of legs seemed to extend from the bottom point:

Some vague, untethered nook of Michael Danver's consciousness knew that he was supposed to know what this symbol meant, yet when he tried to *grasp* its meaning, he found the revelation of the thing eluded him. Why was it floating there, just out of reach? Moreover, who had spray painted this symbol on his driveway?

He thought about what Ken Harrison's daughter had said to him the night of the Harrisons' luau, something about witnessing a man chalking those odd symbols onto the sidewalk up and down the block. Thinking this, Danver peered over his shoulder at the Harrisons' house across the street—

—and there was Olivia Harrison, standing on the front stoop. Her hair was an unkempt rats' nest, and she was wearing the same sweatpants and ratty T-shirt she'd been wearing the night of the luau, when he'd found her hiding in the back room of their house. She was staring right back at him.

Danver's back teeth began to ache.

Across the street, Olivia Harrison touched the left side of her jaw. Just like the woman in Gladstone Park had done.

A buzzing in his head.

A buzzing in his *teeth.*

In his mind, he could hear Olivia Harrison asking, *Have you seen the instructions?*

Danver glanced back down at the symbol spray painted on his driveway. That inverted DayGlo triangle superimposed atop the bright orange image of a door.

*His* door.

He looked back across the street at Olivia Harrison.

*Yes,* he thought, and felt that thought transmit through the space between them, closing the distance until they were of one mind.

*Yes.*

*I have.*

*I've seen the instructions.*

The bleat of a car horn caused him to jump. He spun around and saw Miranda's shiny black Escalade idling in the street. The driver's side window eased down, and Miranda flapped an agitated hand at him, soundlessly instructing him to move out of the way. Danver stepped onto the lawn as Miranda pulled the Escalade into the driveway.

He glanced back across the street at the Harrisons' house, but found that Olivia Harrison, like something skittish frightened by Miranda's arrival, had already retreated back inside her home.

"Where've you been?" Danver asked as Miranda climbed down

from the Escalade. She slammed the door shut as if irritated about something.

"Out looking." She sounded exasperated, and with a ballcap and sunglasses on, Danver knew she was hiding how haggard she looked. She'd been up most of the night hearing the phantom barks of her missing Clementine.

"Out looking for me?"

"What?" she said, confused. "I was out looking for Clementine."

It had been a handful of days since the dog had . . . well, disappeared . . . and Miranda had been on edge ever since. She'd made posters and hung them up and down the neighborhood; she called Doug Winslow, who was the president of the Mariner's Cove Community Association, and asked that a notice be placed in the weekly blotter and on all of the neighborhood's social media sites; she drove the streets of Mariner's Cove three times a day—once in the morning, once in the afternoon, once in the evening—with the window down, calling for Clementine to come home.

"I thought I heard him again last night, you know," she said. "I tried to wake you, but you were dead asleep."

Danver hadn't been dead asleep; in fact, he had just climbed into bed beside her a few minutes prior to her coming awake, having spent the entire evening and some early hours of the morning in the garage with the door.

"I got up and searched through the whole house, calling his name," she went on. "Do you think it's possible he's gotten himself trapped behind a wall?"

"I don't see how."

"Or maybe . . . I don't know . . . up in the attic?"

"That's not possible."

"It's just that I'm so *certain* I can hear him, although I can never seem to pinpoint where the sound of him is coming from. Poor Clem, he sounds so very far away, but also very close."

"Probably a neighbor's dog you're hearing."

"No. It's not that."

"Or part of a dream."

Miranda eyed him up and down as he stood there, barefoot and in his pajamas, in the grass. As if just now seeing him for the first time. "Is that blood on your face and shirt?"

He reached up and was surprised to feel a tacky rivulet of blood below his left nostril. He glanced down at the smudge on his fingertips then at the constellation of blood drops on his undershirt.

Miranda redirected her gaze to the symbol spray painted on their driveway. "This has gotten out of hand," she said.

"The symbols?"

"All of it. The graffiti all over the neighborhood lately, and now right here at our home. Poor Clem lost somewhere. Not to mention the fact that I've got to keep my car in the driveway because you've got some top-secret project going on in the garage." Her eyes narrowed at him. "You've been acting so *strange* lately."

It occurred to him now that he'd left Miranda alone in the house with the door while he'd gone off sleepwalking through the neighborhood. He didn't like that. It made him uncomfortable to think that all she had to do while he was gone was go into the garage and she would see it there, splayed out across those two sawhorses like someone on an operating table. Would she have touched it? Would she have tried to make it her own?

Would she have knelt down and slipped a hand into that dark, bottomless shadow beneath the door?

Danver felt his heart begin to race.

"We're having dinner with the Jacobis tonight," Miranda said, "so whatever is going on with you, kindly snap out of it." She disappeared into the house.

Danver cast one final glance at the Harrisons' house across the street. From where he stood, he could see the same symbol that had been spray painted on his driveway had also been spray painted in that same hideous neon orange on the Harrisons'.

# 4

The door was just as he'd left it: laid out across those two sawhorses and covered by an old paint-splattered sheet in the garage. A wave of relief washed over him at the sight of it. He peeled the sheet off, and there it was, smooth from his excessive sanding, the fine, threaded grains in the wood like tendrils of smoke trapped in statis for all eternity.

*What makes you think Miranda hasn't been in here?* came a paranoid little voice toward the back of Danver's head. *What makes you think she hasn't taken that sheet off and seen the door and all the love and care you've given it? And not just this morning, as you were out traipsing around the neighborhood in your pajama pants. She lives in the house with you and it's not like you've been in the garage twenty-four hours a day. In the brief and infrequent periods where you've found some sleep, what makes you so sure she hasn't crept down to the garage to see what you've been working on for all this time? You are a fool, Michael Danver, to think she hasn't seen it. And if that's the case, then there's a chance she understands it better than you do. What if she understands it better than you? What if she understands its purpose? Meanwhile, you keep sanding the door and staring longingly at it while time slips away from you in great barreling rolls.*

*Don't be a fool, doc.*

He wasn't being a fool; he'd been *cautious.* He'd been wary and alert. In fact, just yesterday he'd installed a deadbolt on the interior garage door, one that required a key to unlock from both sides. The door was locked now and would be locked later when he left this place. Cautious. Alert.

Except—

*Except you didn't lock it before your little sleepwalking expedition this morning, did you?* countered the voice.

And that voice was right: he hadn't.

*She wouldn't come in here,* he rationalized. *She would have no reason to come in here. Why in the world would she come in here?*

Still, panic rippled through him as he stared at the door.

*What are you supposed to be?*

*What is your purpose here?*

*Tell me.*

He went to a rank of metal shelves, heavy with tools and various items he'd stowed away there when clearing space for the door. Rummaged around, that neon orange symbol once more flashing across his brain. There was a spool of blue painter's tape on one of the shelves; he tore off strips then laid the strips across the lower half of the door in a mimicry of the inverted triangle. The shape of it looked right, but it didn't *feel* right. Frustrated, he peeled the tape off then returned to the shelves, where he located some rods of rebar. Each one felt sturdy in his grasp. He placed them, one by one, along the lower half of the door. Once again, the *shape* of it looked right, but something about it didn't *feel* right. What he *felt* was—

—a timorous yet mounting buzzsaw sound in the center of his head.

In his *teeth.*

*Donnie Bridgeport has been lurking around the house more than usual, too,* the paranoid voice continued, as sweat began to pool beneath Danver's arms. *He's seen the door. He keeps telling people about it. He knows it's in here. Like a fool, you'd asked him to help you carry it in.*

In here? Where was *here*? Because Danver was suddenly standing beneath a massive structure floating high above the neighborhood, his clothes rippling and his hair blowing back in the gale force wind. There were others all around him, men and women and children, each one similarly gazing upward in a unified sense of awe—

No, he wasn't staring up at anything. He was back in Gladstone Park, bare feet on the dewy grass, sun in his eyes. He felt a runnel of blood tickling his upper lip. He looked up, wincing at the sun, just as a collection of random junk came falling from the sky. The items crashed to the earth all around him, so forcefully they pounded craters into the ground. The door came down, too—*his* door—plummeting straight down from the sky and wedging itself into the earth. It stood there poking up from the ground in much the same way Danver had found it poking up from the sandbar in the cove behind his house the morning after that terrible storm.

*And Donnie likely told Mia, and Mia's got such a big mouth, she's likely told half the women on Bay Road, maybe even half the residents of Mariner's Cove, and even if she didn't, Donnie had spoken of the door the night of the Harrisons' luau, and even then . . .*

How many people knew about the door?

He blinked his eyes and found himself sitting cross-legged on the garage's cold concrete floor. He had a sense that some time had passed, although he couldn't be sure how much. From this vantage, he could see the dark shadow on the floor beneath the door. The discarded strips of painter's tape lay nearby, rolled into a crude and useless ball. He leaned over and flicked the ball across the floor.

It skidded along the concrete then vanished down into the shadow.

A moment later, something came *out* of the shadow.

Danver watched it float into the air like an ember rising from a bonfire. It spiraled lazily toward the ceiling, circled the single light fixture, then descended until it came to rest atop the door.

It was a bee.

"Jesus," Danver said, heart pounding. "Where the hell did you come from?"

It crawled along the length of the door before taking once more to the air. Danver watched it spiral around the garage, the distant buzzing of its wings matching the distant buzzing in Danver's head and jaw, until it landed on the floor less than ten inches away from him. As he stared at it, the bee scuttled across the floor until it reached the edge of the shadow.

Danver held his breath.

The bee slipped over the edge and vanished back into the shadow.

Danver's heart pounded. He rolled onto his hands and knees and crawled slowly toward the door, staring at that dark, rectangular space beneath it. Where had that bee come from? Where had Clementine gone?

He came right up to the edge of the shadow and peered down into its black, limitless depths.

He reached out, poked the tips of his fingers into that impossible darkness, much as he had done previously. His fingers sank down into it and he could feel them go instantly numb. This time, however, he did not retract his hand so quickly. In fact, he reached deeper, feeling that numbing chill elevate up his hand and past his wrist.

That buzzing in his head.

In his *teeth*.

What if there was an entire secret world down there? A secret world operating beneath the surface of what some might call the *real* world, undetectable to those who weren't sharpened like scalpels in order to cut through the veil and glimpse it? What if there were inner workings, things like metal cogs and wheels and pistons and bolts and screws and tightly wound springs, much like those that had rained from the sky in one of Danver's nightmares, down there? Most people, he knew, were blind to this knowledge. Maybe because they were afraid to look.

Should he lean forward, put his *head* into that dark space?

What would he see?

What revelations awaited him down there?

Danver clamped his jaw to prevent his aching teeth from shaking out of their sockets. He leaned farther over the shadowy opening beneath the door, his right hand still down there, straight past the wrist, marinating in that lightless, rectangular void . . . although he couldn't feel it, the damn thing had gone so cold and numb.

Looked down into it.

Like staring into a black hole.

Brought his face down to it.

That rectangular black hole, so close. Less than an inch from the tip of his nose now, in fact.

*I can put my head right down into it, see what's going on down there. Maybe that's the endgame to this whole thing, the point and the purpose of the door.*

Something about that seemed right.

Rang true.

Like a child about to submerge himself in water, Michael Danver took a deep breath and squeezed his eyes shut.

He felt the icy chill overtake him the moment he pressed his face into that vacuum of space—not just numbing the flesh of his face but filling as with ice water the curved bucket of his skull. That cold, pins-and-needles sensation coursed along the snakelike ridge of his spine then spread through his internal organs, his limbs. He felt the cold of it fill his ears and, despite holding his breath, infiltrate his nostrils. His lungs.

He wanted to open his eyes and *see*—

—but he was suddenly too afraid.

*(endgame endgame endgame)*

He jerked backward, withdrawing from that terrible place. As he did so, he smacked the crown of his head hard enough against the underside of the door to make the rods of rebar jump, roll across the length of the door, and ring out along the concrete floor of the garage like a series of weighty chimes as they fell.

*"No no no no no—"*

Held his breath.

Bit down on a ridge of knuckle.

Then, inevitably: a soft knock at the interior garage door, followed by Miranda's muted inquiry: "Is everything okay in there?"

"Fine!" he shouted, then dialed it down. "I'm fine. Everything's fine. I just . . . I just dropped a few things."

He watched the doorknob jostle.

"Why is the door locked?"

"Is it?" he said, although he knew damn well that it was. And if Miranda had noticed he'd installed the deadbolt, she had the good sense not to say anything about it.

"You've been in there for hours," she said. "What are you doing?"

"Cleaning," he said, which was the first thing that came to his mind. "Straightening up. Clearing things out and making some space."

"I want to put the Escalade back in the garage tonight."

Danver struggled to his feet, bracing himself against one of the sawhorses. The back of his head throbbed where it had smacked up against the door.

"Michael?" she said, knocking gently on the door again. "Do you hear me?"

Though the feeling had returned to his whole body the moment he withdrew from that dark opening in the floor, he could still feel the residual effects of it, as if he'd inadvertently acquired some virulent disease from the atmosphere of that cold and hopeless place. Except that there *hadn't* been any atmosphere. It had been like poking his head into a vacuum-sealed tube.

He decided it was a good thing he hadn't opened his eyes.

"Michael?" Miranda said from the other side of the door.

"I'll be out in a sec."

He waited, holding his breath. After a moment, he heard Miranda's footfalls retreat down the hall.

Danver closed his eyes. He could feel every molecule of his body vibrating at once. For some reason, his teeth were getting the worst of it.

When he opened his eyes again, he found himself staring at the rectangle of perfectly black space beneath the door.

A *doorway* beneath a door.

But to where?

He felt jittery. Cold and numb. In his bones.

What if he'd opened his *eyes* in there?

Hands shaking, Danver gathered the sheet off the floor and covered the door once again.

Like a body.

## 5

At Miranda's behest, Danver climbed into the shower then got dressed in a simple pair of slacks and a white button-down shirt. He didn't know where the dinner with Guy and Gaye Jacobi was supposed to be, nor did he care: he kept wondering if he should tell Miranda that he wasn't feeling well, maybe coming down with a cold, so that she wouldn't make him leave the house.

*Maybe Ken Harrison was right,* he thought, standing in his bedroom closet while buttoning the cuff of one shirtsleeve. *Maybe bad elements have already slipped in through the cracks. They might be outside right now, lurking along Bay Road, waiting for people to leave their homes so they can gain entry.*

They'd find the door.

Even with the deadbolt locked and the key in Danver's pocket, they'd find a way in.

*Cracks,* Danver thought absently, patting down his pants pocket to ensure that, yes, the key to the deadbolt was there. *Cracks everywhere. Bad elements slipping in. Need to be careful. Need to stay alert.*

He glanced at the shelf above the rank of button-down shirts and pleated slacks. There was a shoebox up there, and inside it was the small revolver he had purchased just last year. Home protection. Miranda had scoffed, claimed there hadn't been a robbery in the neighborhood for years. She'd tossed statistics at him about homeowners being more likely to accidentally kill their spouse than any would-be burglar.

The gun made him think of his father.

Two weeks after his son's graduation from medical school, Hal Danver, seated in a faux leather chair in his home office, elected to take the back of his head apart with a nickel-plated Smith & Wesson revolver.

It was his father's voice that came to him now, an urgent, synaptic spark that pulsed in the center of Danver's brain:

*—the door the door she's found the door—*

Yet the deadbolt key was still in his pocket.

*Don't be a fool. There are other ways. Bad elements always manage to slip in through the cracks.*

"Jesus," he muttered, then hustled out of the bedroom and down the stairs. Two at a time, really, his mind so singularly focused on the door, the door, the door—

At the end of the hall, the door leading to the garage was still closed. Danver breathed a sigh of relief . . . but then wondered if Miranda hadn't swiped the key from his pants while he was in the shower, only to return it to his pocket so he'd be none the wiser. Was she in there with it right now?

He hurried to the garage door, his bare feet clapping along the hardwood floor. Gripped the doorknob, tugged on it.

The door did not open.

The deadbolt was still engaged.

Relief . . . but only for a moment.

*Don't be a fool,* came Hal Danver's voice again. *You've forgotten something so basic, haven't you?*

"Have I?" he said aloud, already digging the key out of his pocket. He slid it into the lock, turned the bolt.

Opened the door.

And he *had.*

He *had* forgotten something.

So goddamn *simple.*

Miranda was standing in the middle of the garage. She'd yanked the sheet off the door—it lay balled at her feet now—and was staring down at the door, one hand resting atop its smooth, sanded surface. Behind her, the exterior door of the garage bay stood open, and in her hand was the remote.

*(fuckfuckfuckfuckfuck)*

"You shouldn't be in here," he said, coming down the stairs.

"I wanted to see what you've been doing in here," she said, a tremor of anger in her voice. But not just anger—confusion, too. "I wanted to know what this *obsession* is all about. What is it? *This?* This piece of driftwood garbage?"

She slapped her palm against the door.

It rocked on the sawhorses.

"Don't do that," he warned her.

"Don't tell me what to do. I've got a right to know what goes on in this house. And I don't like the way you've been acting. Something is *wrong* with you, Michael. Something is—"

*"Get out of here!"* he roared at her.

Miranda's eyes blazed at him. Her face dared him. Through clenched teeth, she said, "Don't you *dare* tell *me*—"

A sound, then.

An almost *not-a-sound.*

Because what reverberated out of the shadow beneath the door was undeniably the sharp, popgun *yip!* of a small dog.

Danver watched as Miranda's gaze swung toward the shadow beneath the door. She opened her mouth, fresh lipstick already applied so that he could hear the smacking sound of her lips parting, suddenly so loud in Danver's ears.

"Clem?" she said, her voice suddenly small. Confused. Still staring at that black, rectangular hole in the floor. "Clementine? Baby?"

"Miranda—"

She bent to kneel down on the floor.

*"No no no, goddamn it, no,"* the words—a prayer, really—issuing out of his lungs upon a shuddery gust of hot air as he thrust himself in her direction.

Miranda jumped back, one hip knocking against the door propped up on those two sawhorses. It wobbled, nearly in slow motion, *whump whump*, then tipped over—

*"No no no no please, no no—"*

He shoved Miranda out of the way, heard her body crash against the metal shelving unit, and as items began raining down from the shelves, and the shelving unit itself tipping forward, the *door* kept tipping, tipping, tipping—

*"—no no no no—"*

—and as he grappled for it, pawed at it, digging his fingernails into the wood surface to prevent it from toppling to the floor, all of it in under a split second, it did just that: the sawhorses slewed off in opposite directions as the door slammed down against the concrete floor of the garage, loud as a mortar explosion, just as the entire shelving unit collapsed on top of it. Danver watched in horror as the doorknob ejected from the wood and went bouncing across the floor in a series of discordant, metallic clanks.

He crawled on his hands and knees over to the door. It was buried now under the fallen shelving unit, and beneath a heap of tools, broken pottery, gardening equipment, and a few lumpy bags of mulch. The doorknob lay several feet away, seeming to shine with a preternatural light that could have just been the sunset beyond the open garage door reflecting in the brass.

"Goddamn it, Miranda, look at what you've . . ."

But his voice trailed off.

Like the door, Miranda lay beneath the weight of the shelving unit.

Motionless.

## CHAPTER TWENTY

# DISPATCHES FROM THE TOWER

### 1

Stinger opened his eyes to find himself staring at the blazing white face of the sun. Sweat leaked down his face. He ran his fingers along the ground and realized he was lying in a patch of dewy grass. His body ached, and his skin felt strangely loose, as if it was too big for him—a skeleton in an oversized man-suit. His tongue was a slug in his mouth, swollen and dry. As he closed his eyes, molten tears spilled down the sides of his face. The sun's afterimage sizzled on the undersides of his eyelids.

A moment earlier, he had been soaring down a gloomy, hexagonal tunnel, where the walls glistened with a golden, viscous fluid, and vibrated with the incessant droning of countless unseen honeybees. He'd been on autopilot and uncertain of his destination, although he understood that it was imperative he arrive there. And when he did, he found himself in a dark, suffocating chamber, his own hot, fetid breath breathing back against his face.

It was there, in that chamber, that the Tower informed Stinger of his destiny.

Things, it seemed, were beginning to swim into focus.

His wet shirt clinging to his body, Stinger sat up in the damp grass and saw that he was lying in the wooded clearing just a few yards away from the whitewashed tower of the Langstroth hive. The air positively *strummed* with honeybees. Groggily, Stinger glanced down at the exposed flesh of his arms and saw his skin studded with bee stings. There were too many to count, and a number of them wept blood. Others glistened with a gelatinous bead of urine-colored fluid.

*Poison,* Stinger thought.

He was wearing cargo shorts, which left his legs below the knees exposed. Several bees still wriggled in the mostly hairless, shiny tracts of his shins, the tapered, sunburned swell of his calf muscles. Many of their barbed stingers were still embedded in his feverish flesh. As he stared, a single honeybee crested the rise of his left kneecap; Stinger watched it for a time with a primate's sense of dim inquisitiveness before flicking it away. Then he ran his hands up and down his legs, smudging those twitchy, impaled bodies into smeary greenish tracks of goo along his skin.

He kept thinking about what the Tower had told him. Kept thinking about traversing that hexagonal corridor, a series of corridors, and how the walls had wept with golden tears of honey. How he could hear the cacophonous buzzing of bees all around him moments before he emptied into that lightless chamber at the center of the hive, where the bees' buzzing unified into a collective, singular voice. His physical body had still been out here, unconscious in the grass, of course; it had only been his *consciousness* that had been allowed inside the Tower. His *mind.* Which was why his skin now tingling from sunburn and was lumpy with the swollen red knobs of countless bee stings. But the Tower's godlike voice still clung wetly to his brain. A single throbbing, pulsating word, lighting up like a neon sign and filtering through the smudgy gray bulwark of Stinger's brain:

**ENDGAME**

And he knew what it meant.

No time to think about that now, however. He felt sick from the bees' venom, and he could tell he was dehydrated from having his body lying out here for however long in the heat of midday. Possibly for hours.

Standing proved unexpectedly problematic. His legs felt about as dependable as broomsticks and the world around him spun with a sort of drunken glee. The colors of the day struck him as overly bright and painful to look at, the multitude of summer flower like fireworks frozen in mid-explosion. When he managed a single lumbering step forward, he felt a numbing reverberation travel up his leg, his spine, and straight into his skull, where it detonated with all the riot of cannon fire.

He staggered back through the woods, intermittently swatting at the air redolent with bees, until he arrived back at the house. He passed through the rear slider, then latched it, as if bees might unify and somehow pry open an unlatched sliding glass door. Then he shuffled down the hall to the bathroom where he flicked on the light, only to cry out at the sudden, eye-stinging brightness of the single fixture above the mirror.

Anyone could die from too many bee stings—you didn't have to be allergic—but Stinger felt incrementally overcome by a strange calmness that precluded any concern as he gazed at his ruinous reflection in the bathroom mirror.

His face was a topography of welts and oozing red hillocks. A few stingers still protruded from the swollen purplish knuckles along the ridge of his jawline. He leaned in closer to his reflection and proceeded to pluck out all the stingers with his fingers, dropping each stinger, one by one, into the sink, in much the same way Glenda-Rae had done for him all those years ago. His eyebrows were puffy, and threatened to occlude his vision. They looked like lumpy caterpillars above his pale gray eyes.

He turned on the tap and shoved his hands under the cold stream. It felt good. The palms of his hands were lacerated and sore, but that had nothing to do with the bees. That was from cutting up the chain-link fencing of the baseball diamond's backstop.

He washed his face, which ached him and felt like alien terrain. Then he patted cold water along the sweaty, feverish nape of his neck. He stuck out his tongue. It looked dry, cracked, swollen. Sahara-like. Could be dehydration, could be the bees' apitoxin shuttling through his circulatory system.

Despite this, Stinger felt himself at ease. That one word imparted to him from the Tower possessed, for Stinger, all the meaning of the world. Things, it seemed, were beginning to become clear.

Of course, he knew it really wasn't the *Tower* that had spoken to him. Christ, he wasn't crazy. *Something* had summoned him into that clearing. *Something* had called to him. *Something* had used the Tower as a conduit to transmit its message. Whatever it was, it had revealed itself (to a degree) and Stinger's purpose (also to a degree) to him back in that dark, chamber-like room inside the Tower.

*Endgame.*

Stinger moped back down the hall and into the kitchen, where he guzzled two large glasses of water, not caring that much of it spilled down the front of his shirt. Absently, as he poured himself a third glass of water from the tap, he wondered if he had swallowed any bees while lying unconscious in the grass.

The last thing he remembered before being summoned out into the clearing was bringing his mother lunch. A ham and cheese sandwich on rye with a bowl of Campbell's chicken noodle soup, half a bag of cool ranch Doritos—the fucking *family-size* bag, not one of those little individual bags you get from vending machines—two cans of Pepsi, and two packets of Lorna Doones. After using the motorized switch beside the bed to raise the mattress, he had set the food tray down in front of her, then had quickly fled the room. He did not stay around to watch her eat as he normally did; he did not read her a parable from the Bible while she slurped up her soup and peppered her chest with cookie crumbs. She'd even commented on it ("No story today, Jer-Jer?"), but despite the routine, he found he couldn't do it. For the first time, the thought of reading Bible passages while Queenie choked down her meal felt like an inconceivable proposition. Queenie ate like some monster from a storybook, her mouth packed with oversized bites, her thin lips smeared with mayo and speckled with crumbs, while she took intermittent hits of oxygen. Stinger realized that he couldn't stand watching her eat—didn't even like the sound of it, that dry *muck-muck* lip-smacking sound—and he had departed for the room to drink a beer and watch some TV until she called him to come and take the food tray away.

That had been when the voice had summoned him. Right there, as he sat slumped and with his legs splayed in the recliner before the television, a can of Natty Boh balanced on one knee. A voice that sounded like an echo that sounded like a gunshot that sounded like Our Lord and Savior:

*(HAVE YOU SEEN THE INSTRUCTIONS?)*

At first, he'd thought the voice was coming from the TV.

*(HAVE YOU SEEN THE INSTRUCTIONS?)*

But then he somehow realized that the voice was coming from outside—that the quality of that voice contained the same collective *buzzing* quality as the colony of bees. The bees were speaking to him. Or, more accurately, *something* was speaking to him *through* the bees. That was what he'd thought at first.

Curious, he had wandered out of the house, crossed through the trees, and came out into the clearing to find the atmosphere nearly black and solid with bees.

That was when he had passed out, and his consciousness was ferried into the Tower. Not the bees, but the Tower: something was speaking to him through the Tower.

*For how long?* he wondered now, gazing out the window above the kitchen sink and at the dizzying array of bees swarming about out there. *How long was I lying in that grass? How long did my consciousness spend crawling through the honeycombed chambers of the beehive? How long did it take to tell me what I needed to hear, to show me what I needed to see?*

He went back down the hall then paused outside Queenie's closed bedroom door. He stood there for a while, hearing the occasional hiss of his mother's oxygen machine. Finally, he cracked the door partway open. Queenie's TV was on, the volume muted, the glow from the set casting his mother's enormous bulk in shades of electric blue light. The food tray from lunch was still there, tipped to one side near the foot of the mattress, a scatter of crumbs and a smear of something dark and greasy on the bedspread. She looked like the carcass of a beached whale that someone had covered up with a sheet. The whole room stank of feces.

He knew she was alive because he could still hear the Darth Vader rasp of her oxygen tank. Stinger watched as one massive, fleshy forearm rose slowly with each labored inhalation. Black bits of food clung to the cheese-white skin of the arm. The sheer volume of that massive arm abruptly turned Stinger's stomach. Queenie's skin, he knew from occasionally sponging her down in the tub, was like sacks of latex filled to bursting with Jell-O.

It occurred to him that this was the first time he found himself disgusted by his mother's condition. He had been taking care of her for so long that he had never actually stopped to think about it. But now, and for whatever reason, it was as if he was truly *seeing* his mother for the first time. And the sight of her repulsed him.

As he stared from the doorway, the black bits of food on Queenie's arm moved. Stinger blinked, astounded. He was already in the process of convincing himself that it had been a trick of the flickering television light when one of the black specks *crawled up the length of her forearm* and disappeared around a fold in the bed sheet.

Stinger reached for the wall switch and flipped on the bedroom light. He winced, the light horribly, invasively bright. Through his bleary, stinging eyes, he saw the black specks on his mother's arm moving in frantic little dances. Those specks weren't food at all.

They were bees.

Had he been careless and left the sliding glass door open as he followed that inexplicable voice out into the yard? No, the door had been closed when he'd returned to the house. These bees had gotten in another way.

He approached his sleeping mother, the *gaah-wisssst* sound of the oxygen filling the cramped little bedroom. Quick math told him there were six . . . no, seven bees wiggling upon his mother's arm. He reached out and, one by one, plucked each of the bees off her flesh. Between his fingers, each bee squirmed and wheeled its legs, but none of them deigned to sting him. He made his other hand into a loose fist and, like a magician performing some magic trick, poked each bee one at a time into that fist. He held them loosely in his palm, careful not to squish them.

And then there it was—the first sting. This one took him on the fleshy pad of his palm, a quick and hot needle prick. There were two more bees frolicking at the edge of the sheet now, up near his mother's bosom. Where had they come from? Stinger picked one of the bees off the sheet—the damn thing let him do it willingly enough, just as the others had—and he stuffed that one, too, into his already throbbing fist. Then he pinched up the final one and filed it away with the others.

A second sting . . . and then a third. Pain at first, of course . . . but an anaesthetizing ecstasy followed. His hand hotly tingling, Stinger leaned his head back and, for a moment, stood there in the glow of the muted television with his eyes closed. To an observer, he might look like a man in mid-prayer.

A man in ecstasy.

Thirty seconds later, he carried the fistful of bees to the sliding glass door at the rear of the house. He unlatched it then slid it open only wide enough to thrust his fist outside. He opened his palm and shook the bees off him. The bees spirited away into the afternoon. All except one.

He retracted his hand and closed the slider. Brought his open palm up to his face. The honeybee squirmed, its barb planted deeply in the fleshy mound just below Stinger's thumb. The bee's legs scrabbled, and its wings went *zzzp-zzzp* as they fluttered ineffectually against the tender red love line that bisected Stinger's palm.

He reached out and plucked the struggling honeybee from his palm. The insect's barb went with it—it didn't stay lodged in Stinger's flesh, as they sometimes did—and the bee's legs continued to cycle almost comically in the air. Stinger brought the bee close to his face to examine it. He knew that even if they didn't leave their stingers behind, often when they stung, the ovipositor became unmoored from their hindquarters so that a snotty viscous fluid bubbled out, and the bee would eventually die. You had to look closely to see it, Stinger knew.

It was there this time, too. But it wasn't the dollop of greenish fluid leaking from a tear in the bee's abdomen that collected his full attention. This bee, it seemed, was unique in a way that Stinger, given all his experience around honeybees, had never seen before.

It had two heads.

Yes. He could see it clear as day. And when he rubbed at his eyes with his throbbing left hand to clear his vision and be sure, the two-headed bee remained. He wasn't seeing things, wasn't hallucinating.

"You're a special gal," Stinger said, absently flipping the latch on the sliding glass door again. Tweezing the two-headed bee between his thumb and index finger, he carried it into the kitchen while finding it difficult to take his eyes off it. He located a jelly jar in one of the cupboards, punctured holes in the tin lid with the point of a steak knife—a difficult task to accomplish one-handed—then unscrewed the lid, and dropped the two-headed insect inside. He quickly screwed the lid back into place then held the jelly jar up to his face. Inside, the bee did the Curly Shuffle before going still. Its two front legs pawed futilely at the air. "Hey," Stinger said, so close to the jar that his breath momentarily fogged up the glass. "Don't die, pretty gal. It'll be okay. Hang in there."

He thought of the word the Tower had relayed to him.

Thought about what it meant for him.

The changes that were coming.

The changes that were already here.

"Hang in there, old gal."

Breath fogging up the glass.

## 2

His bedroom was small, and hadn't changed much since he'd been a teenager. There were still the same old movie posters on the walls—Burt Reynolds in *Smokey and the Bandit*, Charlton Heston in *Planet of the Apes*, Cronenberg's *Videodrome*—among posters of some of his favorite bands, like Motörhead, Kix, and AC/DC. There was also the iconic poster of Bo Derek from the movie *10*, upon which an adolescent Stinger had meticulously drawn, in red felt-tipped marker, a pair of large nipples.

He set the jelly jar on the nightstand beside his bed.

Bent down and peered in at the thing.

It was still alive, wriggling there at the bottom of the jar.

*Changes coming.*

*Changes here.*

Still feeling feverish and woozy, Stinger was about to climb into bed when he caught a glimpse of Marybeth Maysall through his bedroom window. Through *her* bedroom window, too, which faced his side of the house. A canopied bed took up most of Marybeth's bedroom. There were the expected dressers and an armoire, along with a full-size beveled mirror in one corner by the closet.

Marybeth herself was in the room. She was dressed in a pair of gray running shorts that hugged her ass, and nothing else. Her back was facing him, smooth and unblemished, and despite his wooziness, Stinger felt himself become instantly aroused.

*Turn around,* he willed her. *Turn the fuck around so I can see you.*

Marybeth Maysall turned around.

She was bleeding from the nose and holding what, to Stinger, looked to be the front wheel of a tricycle.

Without opening her mouth, Marybeth's voice closed the distance between the two of them, only to detonate in the center of Stinger's skull:

*(WE HAVE TO DO SOMETHING THIS IS IMPORTANT WE HAVE TO DO SOMETHING PLEASE)*

Stinger felt his body go rigid.

*(CAN YOU HEAR ME CAN YOU HEAR ME I TURNED AROUND)*

Stinger thought, *Yes.*

Thought, *I can.*

Thought, *I can hear you.*

Marybeth cocked her head at him, the way a curious dog might.

The wheel of the tricycle was still clamped in both her hands, the rubber fat and black, the spokes a gleaming white. A pair of black plastic pedals extended from a crank that ran through the center of the wheel. Behind the wheel, Stinger could see her breasts.

*(I HEAR YOU TOO WHAT IS HAPPENING WHAT IS GOING ON?)*

Stinger thought, *I think I know.*

*(TELL ME)*

*I don't know how to say it.*

*(HAVE YOU SEEN THE INSTRUCTIONS?)*

*They're not instructions.* Stinger could feel his own nose begin to bleed. His molars felt like they were vibrating in his jaw, too. Painfully. As he realized this, he watched as Marybeth brought a hand up to her own jaw, as if she shared in his pain. *They're not instructions.*

*(TELL ME TELL ME)*

*They're blueprints.*

*(BLUEPRINTS BLUEPRINTS FOR WHAT TELL ME PLEASE)*

*Blueprints for building . . . something.*

*(WHAT?)*

*I don't know.*

*(HOW DO WE BUILD IT?)*

*I don't know.*

*(HOW DO YOU KNOW THIS?)*

*The Tower told me.*

*(WHAT IS TOWER?)*

*It's a hive. A colony. A collective consciousness.*

*(IS IT ENDGAME?)*

Stinger's whole body stiffened.

*(IS IT ENDGAME?)*

His back teeth felt like someone was taking a drill to them and he could feel the blood from his nose running in a salt slick over his lips.

*(IS IT ENDGAME IS IT ENDGAME TELL ME PLEASE IS IT ENDGAME?)*

*It is*, Stinger responded. *It's endgame.*

And a split second after that, a swirling, shifting cloud came barreling out of some black tunnel . . .

. . . and Stinger collapsed to his bedroom floor, unconscious.

## 3

In that dark chamber, a thing shifted and spoke, and despite the frantic, unmistakable mounting cacophony of the buzzing of many bees, the image that leapt into his mind in that sightless black antechamber, was that of a snake.

## 4

He came thrusting into consciousness some unknowable amount of time later to the trilling of his cell phone. He sat up, head spinning and muscles stiff, and found that he had been splayed out on his bedroom floor. His body was clammy with sweat. He scrambled to his feet and snatched his cell phone off the nightstand, right next to a jelly jar he had some vague memory of placing there.

It was Doug Winslow on the phone.

"I'm at the front door," Winslow said, clearly annoyed. "Been knocking. What the hell are you doing?"

"Gimme a sec," Stinger said, and disconnected the call.

He bent and peered down into the jelly jar on his nightstand. There was a dead bee at the bottom of the jar. Had he put it in there? Stinger leaned closer to the jar, nearly pressing the tip of his nose against the glass.

Damn thing had two heads.

Some fuzzy recollection drifted back to him. He glanced over at his bedroom window, the curtains partway open. Strangely, he had an image in his head of Marybeth Maysall, topless and communicating to him with nothing but thoughts, while standing there holding the wheel of a tricycle as blood dribbled out of her nose. He went to the window now, some part of him half expecting to see her still standing there, topless and bleeding. But her bedroom, from what he could see of it, was empty. No doubt he had dreamt the whole thing.

Doug Winslow was perspiring on the front stoop when Stinger peeled open the door.

"Jesus, boy, what the hell happened to you?"

Confused, Stinger said, "Huh?"

"Your face." Winslow studied him with his slitted, piggy eyes. "You're stung all over."

"Am I?" Stinger glanced down at his arms and saw that his flesh looked like braille. He felt woozy, but bits and pieces from earlier in the day were slowly filtering back to him. Only thing was, he couldn't remember if those things had actually *happened* or if they'd all been parts of a dream or hallucination influenced by bee venom. "Just a few stings."

"A few stings? You look like goddamn Quasimodo."

*Can you read my mind?* he thought.

"I'm telling you, Stuckey, those bees have got to go."

"Was there something you needed, Mr. Winslow?"

"Some son of a bitch cut down all the backstop fencing from the baseball field down at the park."

"Oh," Stinger said.

Thought, *Can you read my mind, you fat cocksucker?*

"It's probably some neighborhood kids," Winslow prattled on. "But listen, Stuckey, I don't have the time to dick around with this. I'm putting you in charge. I want you to get to the bottom of it."

"The bottom of it?"

"Are you just gonna stand there and repeat everything I say?" Winslow demanded.

"Well, what exactly do you want me to do about it?"

"I want—"

*Can you hear my thoughts, you chubby piece of shit? I know damn well what happened to your sacred chain-link fence.*

"—I want you to figure out who did it," Winslow said. "I want to know who these kids are. I want to know their *names.* I want to know where they *live* so we can hold them *accountable.* This shit drives me up a wall. No one wants to pay community dues just to have some local delinquents going around tearing the place apart. You get me?"

"Sure," Stinger said.

"My guess is they're the same kids responsible for marking up the streets and sidewalks."

"You mean the chalk marks?"

"It was chalk at first," Winslow said, his face growing redder and redder as he spoke. "Past couple days, it's been spray paint. Shit's gotta stop."

"You want me to clean up the paint?"

"I want you to find out who's doing it! We're here to cure the ailment, not the symptoms."

"Sounds like you should call the police," Stinger said . . . and then immediately regretted it. After all, he knew damn well who had cut down all that chain-link fencing down at the park. The Tower had told him to do it. His hands were bloody with the work of it, like some tragic Shakespearian character.

"Oh, trust me, I've already notified the police. But they're not going to do anything over a little neighborhood graffiti."

"Well, what am *I* supposed to do?"

"For starters, you can research security cameras. Inexpensive ones, but ones that work. We'll put them down at the park. See what we see."

"Is that even legal?"

*You fat fuck . . .*

Winslow frowned. "What are you, Perry Mason? Just look into it."

"Okay. Anything else?"

"Yeah," Winslow said, and for a moment it looked like he was attempting to look past Stinger and into the darkened—

*(chamber)*

—foyer of the house. "Go see a doctor about those welts."

"Sure thing," Stinger said, and offered Doug Winslow what must have been a rather hideous, suppurating grin.

## 5

After Winslow left, Stinger changed his clothes then meandered over to Marybeth Maysall's house, where he knocked on her front door. Marybeth's Kia wasn't in the driveway, but he hoped she was home. No answer, so he knocked again. Glanced up at the missing siding above the doorway, the exposed Tyvek paper. It looked like a flesh wound.

*Are you in there, Marybeth?*

*Can you hear me?*

*Can you hear me thinking in your head?*

*Did I dream it, or had it actually happened?*

She never came to the door, and Stinger eventually left.

## 6

Before heading to Gladstone Park, he hopped in the GMC and sped out of Mariner's Cove toward the highway. His headache cleared considerably by the time he merged onto the main thoroughfare, so he popped a Slayer album into the dash and cranked the volume. He unrolled the windows and allowed the hot summer air to whip through the pickup's cab. Suddenly, and despite the fact that his face and body were covered in bee stings, he felt the best he had in days.

There was a hardware store tucked in the shopping plaza off the highway, right next to Hollywood BBQ. By the time he parked and climbed out of his truck, Stinger was feeling at the top of his game. His skin still itched and burned, and his face ached and felt too tight around his skull, but his head was clear—clearest it had been in days, maybe weeks—and his thinking sharpened like the blade of a carving knife fresh from the whetstone. It was like waking in the night to a fever that had just broke, and all the normalcy of the world filtered back into his system, infiltrating all the minute nooks and crannies of his anatomy. He was feeling so good, in fact, that he realized just how hungry he was.

He'd been taking care of his mother, preparing her meals and cleaning up the place, that he'd been neglecting himself for far too long. When was the last time he'd eaten a decent meal? The trashcan back at the house was full of empty beer cans, sure, but when was the last time he'd ingested any actual *food*?

He stepped through the bell-jingled door of the hardware store and wended, head down, through the aisles. When he located what he was looking for—a heavy duty padlock and key—he took it to the counter.

"Lord, son, that's some face," said the old-timer behind the register. He was gazing at Stinger as if he was some curious specimen under a microscope. "The hell happened? Poison oak?"

"Poison something," Stinger muttered, then thought, *Can you hear me, old man? Can you hear my thoughts?*

"Calamine lotion should do the trick," the old man said. "Pharmacy's two doors down."

*I know where the pharmacy is, you grizzled piece of shit. I'm there at least twice a week for Queenie's bullshit. Have you ever had to clean out bed sores with rubbing alcohol? Have you ever had to disinfect a wound on your mother's body because it got infected with literal shit? Have you ever had to make sure maggots haven't collected in an open wound?*

"Good idea," he said to the old-timer as he dug money from his wallet.

Back outside, he tucked the padlock into the pocket of his utility pants, then wandered into Hollywood BBQ. The smell of the place caused his stomach to growl audibly—so audibly, in fact, that a pair of women standing by the hostess stand turned and stared at him. When they saw the ruined topography of his face, they looked away in horror. What had Doug Winslow called him? Quasimodo.

*Can you two bitches hear me?*

The women did not turn to look back at him again.

He placed an order to go, then stood in the restaurant's vestibule while he waited for someone to bring it to him. He kept looking down at his hands, and at the collection of bee stings along the tender flesh of his palms. Abrasions, too, from having cut down all that chain-link fencing the other night. That metal chain-link was sharp and dangerous. It liked to scratch. It liked to bite.

His food was brought to him by an attractive girl, maybe nineteen or twenty, with raven-black hair and the smooth, unblemished complexion of a runway model. She smiled prettily at him as she handed him his to-go bag. Stinger thanked her, then thought—

## 7

*(I WOULD FUCK YOUR BRAINS OUT)*

Sarah froze. Those words had just come barreling through her skull, so clearly it may have been someone shouting into her ear. A man's voice. *This* man's voice? This dirty, gangling man with the ruinous face, reeking of days' old sweat and looking like someone had set his face on fire then put it out with a rake? *This* man?

Stunned into silence, Sarah Miller watched as the man with the red, lumpy face grinned a terrible grin, then lumbered back out into the daylight.

Eric's hand fell upon her shoulder before she could think a thought back at the man in return. "You okay?" he asked.

"Yeah," she responded, but felt very far from okay.

## 8

The drive back to Mariner's Cove was less agreeable than the drive to the hardware store had been. The closer he came to the neighborhood, the more he became aware of a nearly physical weight pressing down upon him. Not just down on his body, either, but upon his *mind*. He'd been eating his takeout barbecue sandwiches and blasting Slayer, windows down, slipstream of air soothing his burning, bee-stung flesh, feeling pretty damn good. But then he happened to spy the top of a water tower cresting above the trees on the other side of the highway. It snared his attention, his eyes glued to the thing while the interior of the GMC filled up with the stink of vehicular exhaust. Someone honked at him, and he realized he'd inadvertently slowed to about ten below the speed limit. Farther ahead, the top of another water tower—this one sky-blue—poked above the tree line. He couldn't explain why the sight of these things caused such anxiety in him, but he also couldn't deny it.

When he took the exit off the highway, the top of a third tower revealed itself to him. Its white, domed tank rose like the moon beyond a complex of condominiums. These things were all over the place, yet for some reason he was only just now *seeing* them. And for some reason the sight of them made him think of the chain-link backstop. Made him think of the voice that spoke to him from the beehive, too.

Minutes later, as he took the exit to Mariner's Cove, the sandwich meat felt like it was curdling in his stomach. He tossed the remainder out the window, then rolled it up, sealing himself in that motionless, vacuum-sealed cab of the pickup truck. The music suddenly hurt his head, so he switched it off.

He thought of the Langstroth Tower saying, *Changes are coming.*

Saying, *Changes are here.*

He slowed the pickup just as the entrance to Mariner's Cove filled up his windshield. The driver behind him—some prick in a black Tesla—laid on his horn then zoomed around him. More vehicles filed by, one after the other, each driver oblivious that the operator of the GMC pickup with the MCCA decal on the door was about to collapse into a full-fledged panic attack. Stinger pulled the pickup onto the shoulder of the road.

Something was wrong with him.

Something was *wrong* with him.

Gasping for breath, he cranked the ignition off. The whole truck shuddered then went still.

Stinger sat there perspiring in the driver's seat for several minutes, vacuously watching the traffic shush by. He kept jerking his gaze toward the sky, expecting to see the formulation of roiling black storm clouds building above the neighborhood. The sky was clear blue and cloudless, yet he couldn't shake the premonition that something . . . *storm-like* . . . was rolling closer and closer.

He tried to imagine the storm, but instead, his mind summoned the visual of a sleek black snake weaving itself through tall grass. A thing with obsidian eyes and a musculature that pulsed and beat and throbbed like a heart. And when it rose up out of the grass and opened its mouth, a spume of dazzling bluish white light spilled out, light as cold as arctic ice, and when it washed over Stinger, it cooled those feverish welts and numbed his entire body.

*Changes coming.*

*Changes here.*

He realized in that moment that he wasn't nervous about *returning* to Mariner's Cove, but instead worried he might not be allowed back *in*. As if there was some invisible shield that would prevent him from turning down Poplar Station Road and motoring right past the decorative sign that read:

"Fuck this," he muttered, then twisted the key in the ignition.

The GMC rumbled to life.

He eased back onto the roadway and coasted into Mariner's Cove with no ill effects.

Relief washed over him, damp and smelly as perspiration.

Yet that buzzing was back inside his head.

## 9

He drove straight to Gladstone Park and took the dirt access road behind the field to the maintenance shed. It was a nice day, and while the park grounds remained empty, there were some kids out playing in the street, a woman pushing a stroller, someone's black Lab sprinting after squirrels. Stinger fired a mind-shout out to them all—*Hey, you motherfuckers, can you hear me?*—but from what he could tell, it went wholly unnoticed. No one heard him.

Had that whole thing with Marybeth Maysall been a dream? He'd had some doozies lately, no doubt about that. Or had they actually shared some sort of telepathy while she'd stood there topless holding a fucking tricycle tire?

*Insane.*

The maintenance shed revealed itself through a web of summer trees. To Stinger, it looked like a stucco mausoleum.

Perhaps the exchange with Marybeth had been a dream, or perhaps even a venom-induced hallucination, but he was confident that what had happened at the Tower had not been. What the Tower had *told* him. What it *meant*. Spoken in a language that had been nothing but the furious buzzing of bees' wings, yet somehow Stinger was able to comprehend it. That had been all too real. Something, it seemed, had tapped Stinger's head like a keg and, instead of draining him, had filled him with an alien drive and momentum, a complex motivation that made no sense to the uninitiated but, Stinger was sure, would come to make perfect sense to *him* in time. And that was all that mattered.

Stinger blinked. Cleared his head. He glanced at the clock on the GMC's dashboard and saw, with some surprise, that he had been sitting behind the wheel in front of the park's maintenance shed for nearly forty minutes now. How was that possible?

He glanced up and met his unsightly reflection in the truck's rearview mirror. His eyes were bloodshot and droopy-lidded, the whites threaded with fine crimson hairs. His brow was tender and lumpy from the bee stings, and there was a reddish, waxy pallor to his cheeks. He stuck out his tongue and could see a swollen pink nodule on the left side, where a bee had no doubt crawled into his mouth and staked its abdominal barb while Stinger had been unconscious and blissfully unaware; he kept feeling that uncomfortable lump against the roof of his mouth.

Disgusted by his reflection, he averted his eyes and instead found himself gazing upward at the top of the water tower that rose above the treetops of the park. It stood like something in a movie superimposed against a flat azure sky.

Stinger slipped out of the truck. The utility pocket of his Blaklader workpants bulged with the padlock he'd bought. Unlike back at the shopping center, where Stinger had enjoyed the fresh air and sunshine, the air here in the wooded section of the park felt thick and heavy. Whenever he breathed, it was like inhaling glue. Cicadas made mechanical noises in the trees; the sound seemed to echo in the center of Stinger's cotton-stuffed head.

There was already a padlock on the maintenance shed door. Stinger had the key to it, but so did Doug Winslow and the rest of the MCCA board members. He undid the old padlock now, then tossed it into the underbrush. It gave him more than just a modicum of satisfaction to do so.

Flakes of rust rained down on his face as he entered the shed. The blackness of the interior of the shed was almost absolute, save for a vertical sliver of daylight that cut through a high window at the back of the shed, where motes of dust swirled.

Stinger tugged on a pull cord and a single exposed lightbulb above his head winked on. The dreamy aromatics of gasoline rushed to greet him, a smell he had found nearly ambrosial since earliest childhood.

The chain-link backstop was in here. Stinger had cut it up into manageable sections and rolled each section up like you would a carpet. They were held in this shape by a series of bungee cords, six separate sections in all, stacked in a pyramid toward the rear part of the shed—three chain-link rolls on the bottom, two atop those, and the final roll at the very top. It had been an exhaustive effort, and he'd sliced up his hands pretty good in the process, but he'd gotten it *done.* He'd done the Tower's bidding and had asked no questions.

*Changes coming.*

*Changes here.*

Even now, and after what the Tower had told him while he'd been passed out in the clearing, he still had no idea what purpose these rolls of chain-link served. Yet he was relieved to find that they were still here, and that no one else had come along and taken them.

As if granted a sign from above—quite literally—a fat black carpenter bee descended from the ceiling rafters a mere two feet in front of Stinger's face. It moved with the jerky, halting mechanics of something fitted to the tip of a long piece of metal wire. Dipping and bobbing, it emanated a steady droning sound that reminded Stinger of the garbage disposal back at the house when it wasn't functioning properly. The carpenter bee hovered momentarily in front of Stinger's face, and when Stinger blew gently onto it, the bee fled, carving a clumsy swath through the musty air before disappearing into a knothole in a wooden beam that ran horizontally across the cinderblock wall at the opposite end of the shed. Spools of industrial chain hung from the beam so that the wall itself looked like part of some primitive torture device. Stinger negotiated around a riding mower, cans of flammables, a rototiller, and a tower of bright orange construction cones until he reached the far wall. The chains had been here for years—he'd seen them without really *seeing* them—and they were laden with rust. To Stinger, they looked like the type of chains that might be attached to the anchor of a sailboat. Cobwebs clung to them like death shrouds.

As he stared at the chains, the carpenter bee reappeared from its bullet hole and ascended lazily into the air. Stinger watched it with a sense of raptness, the way someone might afford their undivided attention to a lecturer. The bee approached the exposed light bulb and proceeded to thump against it as if striving to get at the glowing filaments housed within the glass. The bee's shadow, grotesquely large, mimicked its movements along the cinderblock wall.

The bee went *tamp-tamp-tamp* against the bulb.

Stinger closed his eyes. The light from the bulb was too much for him to look at. His skull felt as if it were filled with cotton balls and the skin of his face felt too small for his skull.

*Tamp-tamp-tamp.*

He thought then of the strange dreams he'd been having lately, in which he desperately tried to construct a hive out of random items left behind in some apocalyptic landscape. Even now, he could feel the same sense of anxiety and desperation he felt in the dream overtake him.

*Tamp-tamp-tamp.*

There were a few panels of aluminum siding stacked in one corner of the shed. He gathered them under one arm, carried them back outside—Christ, the sun was suddenly so *bright*—and dumped them in the bed of the pickup truck. Back at the maintenance shed, he closed the door then took the new padlock from his pocket. He stripped it out of its packaging, then looped the padlock through the eyelet on the door.

From now on, he'd be the only one with a key to this place.

Instead of heading back to his truck, he walked a bit farther through the trees. Mosquitoes were out in full force; he swatted distractedly at them as he pushed his way through the underbrush. Eventually, he came out onto a clearing and found himself standing at the base of the Mariner's Cove water tower.

It was an imposing structure. There were eight stanchions that supported the tank above, plus a wide center post, twice as girthy as the legs, that ran up the middle and attached to the base of the tank high above. Stinger had wandered out here once or twice in the past, always marveling at the sheer enormity of the thing—you saw water towers all over the place in coastal Maryland, but always from a distance, maybe from the highway, and never up close to see just how enormous they really were—and now was no different.

Well, it was a *little* different.

For one thing, someone had encircled all eight of the tower's legs in a webbing of thick white string. Very strange. It looked like a tedious and time-consuming task, the purpose of which was not clear to Stinger, although he couldn't help but marvel at the crosshatched design that the strings made. A weave of string, really. Anyone else looking at that latticework of string might have thought of a spider's web, but to Stinger, he thought the shapes made by the intersecting lines of string looked like the honeycombs in a hive.

"Someone's been busy," he said aloud, moving slowly around the base of the tower. At one point, he stopped and stared straight up toward the top of the tank, so many countless yards above him in the air. In that moment, he was reminded of the carpenter bee thumping futilely against the light bulb in the maintenance shed, and that's when he realized that the hive he was desperate to construct in his dream was not a hive at all, but the Mariner's Cove water tower.

The revelation struck him like a smack across the face.

Sure, it had looked different in his dream—more organic, like an actual beehive—but the *shape* of it was unmistakable. The size and grandeur of it. *This* was the thing he'd been dreaming about. *This.*

The *real* Tower.

*And some busy little bee has been here toiling away,* he thought. He reached out and plucked one of the taut lines of string like a musician plucking the string of an upright bass. He even heard it emit a bass-like sound—a low, resonant hum that lasted for only a few seconds, but whose presence was undeniably significant. *Some busy little bee has been out here working very, very hard. Very, very diligently.*

A peculiar sensation overcame him in that moment. It took him several seconds to realize it was a sense of homecoming.

He continued walking around the base of the tower, occasionally testing the tautness of the strings by plucking them and liberating similar discordant tones. After a time, he wondered if the tones were really just in his head and that they actually made no sound at all.

For a while, he sat cross-legged at the base of the tower, the weave-work of strings against his back. Mosquitoes feasted on the suppurating welts along his arms, face, and neck. Gnats collected in the moist corners of his eyes. Stinger felt like a human banquet.

That dream. That thing he was frantically *building* in his dream. He couldn't shake it. What did it mean? What did it have to do with what the Langstroth hive had told him?

He climbed to his feet and dug out a pocketknife. The string wrapped around the legs of the water tower was so taut, it made an audible *thwing!* when he cut through it. The string dropped limply to the ground like cobwebs at his feet. He passed beneath the shade of the tower, fumbling with a ball of keys on his belt now. The water tower's wide center post had a door with a tapered handle, something that didn't really stand out unless you were looking for it. When he found the appropriate key, Stinger unlocked the door and wrenched it open. It felt like prying open the hatch of a submarine.

He stepped inside and found himself at the bottom of a long, vertical chamber. The atmosphere felt airless. Beneath his feet, the floor was a concrete slab, the chamber itself a hollow chute. There was a ladder clinging to one wall that went straight up, but it was too dark up there for him to see anything.

Yet he didn't need to see—he *felt* something.

"Hello?"

His voice echoed throughout the giant metal tube: *hello . . . hello . . . hello . . .*

His teeth were vibrating.

He'd never been in here before, yet he was overcome by such an unshakable sense of familiarity in that moment that it nearly dropped him to his knees. He kept his head far back on his neck and continued to gaze to the top of the chamber. Far above him, the pipe narrowed to a dizzying pinpoint of darkness.

Was something up there?

For whatever reason, his mind summoned the image of a rat snake, which he often saw in the summer months carving passage through the wooded lots behind the carriage house. Once, he'd nearly been bitten by one.

No, not a snake.

Not really.

It was just the closest thing that his mind was able to summon.

When he stepped back out into the daylight, he saw that the sun had repositioned itself dramatically in the sky. He had no idea how long he'd spent in the dank metal throat of the water tower, gazing up into the pit of darkness above his head. At least his teeth had stopped hurting. As he skulked back to his truck, he paused one last time to glance back at the meshwork of string that was still wound around seven of the eight legs of the water tower.

It meant *something*...

It felt *familiar*...

Right there, teetering on the edge of his brain.

He wouldn't realize what the string was supposed to be until later that night, when he would wake up screaming.

## CHAPTER TWENTY-ONE

# A UNIFIED FRONT

### 1

First things first: they had to get rid of the girls.

Alex's mother lived in Northern Virginia, which was just a little over fifty miles from Mariner's Cove but, given the perpetual snarl of beltway traffic, Georgette knew it would take them nearly two and a half hours to get there. She packed lunches.

Callie was indignant. She complained about having to leave her friends in the middle of summer vacation to spend an unknowable amount of time with her grandmother, and on such short notice. Denise, on the other hand, did not seemed derailed by this sudden turn of events at all. In fact, she cheered when Georgette told her that she'd be spending a few days with her grandmother, and then she'd hurried into her bedroom where she methodically packed up her belongings in a small Smurfette duffel bag, humming some TV show theme song under her breath. It wasn't until Alex and Callie were already belted into the Shwagon and Georgette was lacing up her sneakers in the foyer that Denise came over to her and said, "I can't find my helmet."

She was talking about the colander, of course. What Georgette's mother would have called a spaghetti strainer.

"Well, we don't have time for that," Georgette said. "Get your shoes on. Dad and Callie are already in the car."

"I can't go without my helmet."

"Denise—"

"It's *important*."

*Yes,* Georgette thought. *I know it is.*

"If it's not in your room, then I don't know where it is," Georgette said. "I can't be responsible for keeping track of all your things."

Denise's eyebrows knitted together. Her mouth turned into a lipless frown. Something in her eyes seemed to intensify, like a fire burning out of control. "Liar," she said.

Georgette blinked. "What did you call me?"

"Liar." She repeated it without hesitation. "You're a liar. You know where it is, but you won't tell me."

"That's ridiculous. Why would I hide it from you?"

"Because you want it for yourself. Because you know how important it is."

"Listen," Georgette said. "Don't you talk to me that way. Now go get your bag and get in the car before—"

"No! I won't!"

Again, Georgette was taken aback. The kid was balling her fists, for Christ's sake. It wasn't like Denise to act this way.

"I want it! I want it! I want it!"

"The heck is going on?" Alex said, darkening the front doorway.

"She's being a little bitch," Georgette blurted, then immediately regretted it. It was as if someone else had momentarily taken over her mind and body, controlling the words that came out of her mouth. She quickly recalibrated, and turned to Denise, but Denise didn't even seem to have noticed. She was still standing there with her fists balled, that obstinate scowl carved deep across her face.

"Mommy took my space helmet, and she won't give it back."

"I'm sure that's not true," Alex said. His hands were jittery and restless at his sides.

"It is! I know it! She won't let me have it."

"I don't have your goddamn helmet!" Georgette shouted back, and again, in an instant, she regretted it. She was on edge. She kept thinking about the water tower. All that crisscrossing string surrounding its legs at the base. It had been a whole day since they'd been away from there and she felt like a junkie dying for a fix.

"How about this?" Alex said. "If we find your space helmet, I will drive it over to you at Grandma's so you'll have it. Okay?"

Denise was watching him with a calculation that made her seem much older than her years. Her eyes kept shifting between Alex and Georgette, back and forth, back and forth, and it was making Georgette uncomfortable.

"Fine," Denise said, relenting, but not happy about it. She backed down the hallway—literally *backward*, as if to keep eyes on both her parents—then slipped into her bedroom to retrieve her duffel bag.

"Hey," Alex said. "Do you think you can drive?"

"Drive?"

"My head is all swimmy," he said. The whites of his eyes looked jaundiced, too, and his hands still fidgeted at his sides. "I got no sleep last night."

She knew. Georgette had similarly suffered a chaotic dream the night before, which was the primary reason she wanted the girls—Denise in particular—out of the house and away from Mariner's Cove. In the dream, she and Alex and several others had been navigating through a dense swath of woods in the dark. It was Gladstone Park—she realized this in the dream—yet there was something different about it, nefarious almost, because just being there was making her dream-self anxious. Her dream-self charged through the woods, driven by some inexplicable need, something akin to a ravenous hunger. Alex advanced rapidly beside her, and when she glanced down, she saw Denise there, too, pushing her own way through the trees; she wore the colander on her head, its stainless-steel hull gleaming with moonlight. In the dream, Georgette, Alex, and Denise came out upon the clearing at the base of the water tower. Alex's string was no longer wrapped around the legs of the tower, although *something* was there in its place, albeit too hazy in that dream-state for her to discern exactly what it was. She saw others standing around the base of the water tower, each of them gazing upward at the water tank that glowed a pearlescent white in the moonlight. In unison, they dropped to their collective knees as if in supplication. Then, in the dream, there was a flash of white light, followed by a shockwave that had thrust her into wakefulness. She'd bolted up in bed, a scream lodged in her throat, her body tacky with perspiration. Alex had been sitting upright beside her, panting as if he'd just run a marathon, no doubt having just suffered the same dream. They'd shared a look in the dark.

"Denise was there with us," she'd said. Her voice was a hoarse rasp, and the pounding of her heartbeat filled her ears. "Did you see her, too?"

"It was just a dream," Alex had told her, touching the side of her face.

But, of course, it wasn't.

## 2

Alex's mother wanted them to stay for dinner before heading back on the road, but Alex politely refused. He lied and said he and Georgette already had dinner plans, and then he pecked his mother's cheek in a sad approximation of a kiss. Georgette, who by this point felt like an imposter who wasn't fooling anyone, gave her mother-in-law a sturdy one-armed hug, then systematically hugged both girls. Callie hugged her back in her typical disinterested, halfhearted way. Hugging Denise, however, was like hugging a hitching post. The girl didn't even bring her arms up in an embrace, the way she had with her father. Georgette was remembering her dream, and how Denise had run through Gladstone Park in the night like some pygmy warrior, that goddamn colander whirling freely about on her head. When Georgette pulled away, she was chilled by the look on her daughter's face—an expression of unmitigated distrust. As if her youngest daughter had just caught her in the midst of some heinous untruth.

## 3

They didn't speak aloud to each other the entire drive home.

At one point, as the Shwagon idled in bumper-to-bumper traffic, Georgette found herself thinking, *What will happen with work?*

*(WORK ISN'T IMPORTANT RIGHT NOW)*

*What about the bills? The mortgage?*

*(NONE OF THAT MEANS ANYTHING UNLESS I FIGURE THIS OUT)*

*We,* she corrected him. *We figure it out. The two of us.*

*(YES WE YES)*

*It feels different being so far away from the neighborhood. Like things are almost back to normal. My head feels clearer than it has in days. Weeks, even. Do you feel it, too?*

*(WE CANNOT LOSE SIGHT OF WHAT IS IMPORTANT THE TOWER IS IMPORTANT)*

*Yes, I know.*

*(THE TOWER IS IMPORTANT)*

*I know that. But* why *is it important? What are we doing out there?*

*(SOLVING A PROBLEM)*

*What problem?*

*(I DON'T KNOW I HAVE TO PUT IT ALL TOGETHER THERE ARE THINGS THAT I STILL DON'T UNDERSTAND MY DREAMS HURT MY HEAD AND I HAVE TO PUT IT ALL TOGETHER)*

*My dreams hurt my teeth.*

*(MY TEETH MY TEETH MY TEETH TOO)*

*We shared that dream last night, didn't we?*

*(BEEN HAVING THAT DREAM AWHILE)*

*I haven't. It's new to me.*

*(THAT'S BECAUSE YOU'RE A PART OF IT NOW)*

*What exactly am I a part of?*

A simmering silence in her head.

Then:

*(ENDGAME)*

*What's endgame?*

*(I DON'T KNOW)*

She turned and looked at him.

*Are you hearing me? Is this really happening?*

He turned and looked at her, too.

*(IT IS A BUZZING)*

*But you understand me, don't you? Just like I understand you? Hearing each other's thoughts in our heads? We're having a conversation right now without talking, aren't we?*

*(YES)*

*It's been happening for a while now, hasn't it? It's how you knew Denise was arguing with me when you were in the car.*

*(YES)*

*It's how we were able to share that dream.*

*(YES)*

*Something is happening to the two of us.*

*(YES)*

*A change.*

*(ENDGAME)*

*What is that?*

*(I DON'T KNOW)*

*We should be scared, shouldn't we?*

*(I DON'T KNOW I DON'T KNOW)*

*But we can't stop, can we?*

*(NO WE CANNOT CANNOT)*

*Because whatever this is, it's important.*

*(YES)*

*Maybe I'm scared. Maybe I'm exhilarated, too.*

*(YES YES)*

*Will you hold my—*

He reached down and held her hand.

## 4

When they arrived home, Georgette hurried straightaway to her bedroom closet, where a large hatbox sat on a high shelf. She quickly took down the box, opened it, and eased herself down on the edge of the bed as she stared at the colander she'd hidden inside.

*Because you want it for yourself,* Denise had said. *Because you know how important it is.*

And she did.

She didn't know why, but she knew it was important. The same way Denise knew it. The same way Alex—

## 5

—had drawn the shape of the colander in his notepad.

*(WHAT DOES IT MEAN WHAT IS ITS PURPOSE?)*

He was standing in the spare room at the back of their house—a room that sometimes functioned as his home office, sometimes served as a guest room whenever his mother would come for an overnight visit. It was sparsely furnished with a small bed, a desk and chair, and a closet that, for now, was mostly packed with winter clothes.

His notepad was in his hand now. All those symbols, painstakingly copied from the graffiti he'd seen all over the neighborhood, interred within those pages. It had been a compulsory need that defied explanation, an obsession he'd been unable to control or even comprehend. When had he glimpsed the first symbol? Days ago? Weeks? Who had drawn them there, all over the neighborhood? Why had they spoken to him so profoundly? They were all crammed in his head now, fighting for space, and Alex was desperate to interpret their meaning.

He was *missing* something, damn it.

He blamed the thing inside his head. He knew it was really *that thing* which was obsessed with the symbols, *that thing* which allowed him and Georgette to share each other's thoughts, read each other's minds, infiltrate each other's nightmares.

*Does that mean the consciousness is inside her, too?* he wondered.

And on the heels of that came her response:

*(THERE IS SOMETHING IN MY HEAD IT MAKES MY*

*TEETH HURT THERE IS NOT ENOUGH SPACE FOR US BOTH IT IS IN ME IT IS IN YOU)*

Alex felt a slick of perspiration forming between his shoulder blades.

He went to his desk and took out a pad of graph paper and a black marker. He proceeded to recreate the images from his notepad on the graph paper, one symbol per page, larger than he'd been able to draw them in that tiny notepad. When he was done, he pinned each page to the wall, one at a time, until he had neatly wallpapered one full panel of sheetrock in graph paper. He had seen TV shows where cops were tasked with piecing together bits of evidence that had been shredded or otherwise damaged, and that was what this felt like now. Once the wall was covered in those pages, he took a few steps back to survey them all. The pieces were all *there*, they just weren't *right*. He was missing something.

*(I AM MISSING SOMETHING TOO)*

*It will come to us eventually,* he answered her, even if he wasn't so sure whether he believed that or not.

Studying the images on the wall.

Scrutinizing them.

He unpinned a sheet of graph paper and repositioned it, replacing its empty space with another sheet from a different section of the graph-paper mural. Moving pieces. Rearranging. Schematics. He was an engineer, for Christ's sake; it was what he did for a living.

Studying.

Scrutinizing.

He wasn't sure how long he busied himself with this fruitless preoccupation, but the shadows in the room had shifted considerably by the time he glanced down and saw that his nose had bled onto his shirt. Pinching his nostrils, he went down the hall and washed up in the bathroom, then gazed at his reflection for an inordinate amount of time. He tried to see the eyes behind his eyes. Thought, *I'm not really me.* Thought, *I'm providing the body, but something else has infested my mind.* In that moment, he thought of himself in just the way he thought of the drawings now pinned to the wall of the spare room at the back of the house—one small piece of a greater, consequential whole. Just what that meant, however, he had no idea.

He wandered aimlessly through the house, uncertain if he was hungry or thirsty, tired or exhilarated, sleepwalking or wide awake. He found Georgette seated at the kitchen table, the waning daylight coming through the front windows casting a dazzling white serpent down the contours of her back. She had the metal colander on the table in front of her. He said nothing as he stood in the kitchen doorway and watched as she slowly spun the colander around, around, around, gradually building up momentum. The colander's curved base made a whirring sound against the wooden tabletop. *Circles, circles, circles.* For some reason, the motion of it struck him as indescribably *right.* Eventually, Georgette looked up at him, her eyes bleary and filled with a rising level of confusion. It was as if she didn't immediately recognize him. Was she seeing that alien *thing* inside him? The same thing that was inside *her*?

When the colander stopped spinning and the sound of it whirring against the tabletop died, Georgette asked, "How long will we stay away from the tower?" It sounded strange to hear her voice in the otherwise silent house.

"I don't know. I can't keep going back and winding that string over and over. It isn't right and it's causing me to lose my mind. I need to figure out what's wrong first."

"But I want to *be* there," Georgette said.

"I do, too," he said. Indeed, it felt like he'd been holding his breath in the time he'd been away from it. "I'm just hoping some time away will give me fresh perspective. Sometimes you have to step away from something to see it in a different light."

He watched as Georgette got up off the chair. She put the colander on her head as she meandered past him and into the living room. There were no lights on in the house and dusk simmered beyond the windows like smoke from a fire. She came to rest in front of the window that looked out onto the front yard. Winged maple seeds spiraled to the ground on the other side of the window—what Alex and his brothers had called "helicopters" when they were younger. Thinking this usually brought a smile to his face. But not today.

Not looking at him, Georgette said, "I can't quite . . . figure it out." The words seemed to strain from her. She removed the colander from her head and, holding it like a bowl, peered down into it. She was frowning.

"You'll get it," he assured her, although he wasn't sure why he'd said this. He wasn't sure of anything at the moment. "We'll both get it."

"These holes," she said, lifting the colander and holding it up in front of her face so that it reminded Alex of a fencing mask. "They're meant for something."

"Draining spaghetti," he said.

Georgette laughed. It was a dry, sharp sound, and there was no humor in it. The sound of it made Alex think of someone crunching dead autumn leaves beneath their shoes. "I'm being serious. What if we never figure it out?"

"We'll figure it out. Don't worry."

"You don't sound too convincing."

"It's not a choice," he said. "We *have* to figure it out. Don't you feel it? Don't you feel that desperate drive to do it?"

"It's like we've . . . what?"

"Been chosen," he said.

"Right. But I keep wondering, Alex—*for what*?"

He just offered her a tepid smile.

"Hey," she said.

"Yeah?"

"How come you call me Georgette now instead of G?"

"Do I?"

"You haven't noticed?"

*Maybe it's not me doing it,* he thought.

*(MAYBE IT'S NOT)*

She turned away to stare back out the window and into the yard. Across the street and beyond the distant trees, the top of the Mariner's Cove water tower was visible. In the fading daylight, it looked like something from a science-fiction movie.

"Let's go right now," she said. "To the tower. Before it gets fully dark."

He looked at her just as she turned and looked at him. Tried to see whatever was hiding inside her head behind her eyes, same as he'd done with his own reflection in the bathroom mirror.

"I think we should go," she insisted. "Something in my head—in my *teeth*—is telling me we should go."

"Then let's go," he said, and gently kissed the side of her face.

## 6

They arrived at the tower to find that someone had torn down all the string.

Alex stopped short, his sneakers grinding into the bed of woodchips that surrounded the base of the tower. Panic jangled through him. Beside him, Georgette said, "Oh, no . . ."

The string was gone. All of it. Looking around frantically, Alex saw the nearby bushes were decorated with it, and that lengths of string hung from tree branches and lay scattered in squiggly swirls atop the underbrush. Whoever had done this, they'd made a mess of the place. Whoever had done this, they—

Someone was approaching through the trees.

A man in workpants and a sandy-colored mullet emerged. He was hauling something large and cumbersome behind him that dragged along the ground. When the man looked up, Alex saw that his face was a ruinous landscape of bulges, welts, and red, swollen knobs. An angry-looking cut was visible poking down from the man's hairline.

To Alex Braswell's utter astonishment, the man smiled at him.

"Well," the man said, "if this isn't the busy bee." Then he turned and nodded politely at Georgette. "A pair of bees, more like it."

"Who the hell are you?" Alex asked. His whole body was trembling, and he felt suddenly like a rocket about to explode into space. "What the hell are you doing here?"

"I'm fixing your mistake," said the man with the ruined face. Then he stepped aside and waved a hand over the large and ungainly item he had been dragging through the woods. When Alex didn't approach, the man waved him over and, still smiling that awful, lumpy smile, said, "C'mon. Don't be afraid. Take a look."

Alex reached down and grabbed Georgette's dangling hand. Together they approached the man, stopping just a few feet from him but close enough so that Alex could get a good look at the item that lay at the man's feet.

It looked like a rolled up chain-link fence.

And at the sight of it, something clicked inside Alex Braswell's head.

"Shit," he muttered. "Holy . . . fucking . . . shit . . ."

The lumpy-faced man's smile widened. "You've been using string, but string won't cut it," said the man. "First of all, it needs to be metal. Second, ain't no way you're gonna recreate the exact design. String is too pliable. It's like when I was building the queen excluder—you'll fumble around forever with the spacing but likely never get it right."

"The what?" said Alex.

The man bent down and poked his finger through one of the links in the fence. "It's either a square turned on its side or a diamond shape," the man continued, "but personally, it reminds me of a cell. You know—like in a beehive."

"How . . . how did you know?" It was Georgette who asked this, as Alex had not yet recovered his voice.

"To come here?" the man said. "To use the fence instead of the string? I guess the same way you folks got here. It just sort of called to me." The man absently scratched at a collection of red, weeping welts along his arm, which immediately began to bleed. "We're part of the same hive, aren't we." It was not a question.

"Pieces of the same puzzle," Georgette said.

"Parts of the same machine," Alex said, finally finding his voice.

"Sure are," said the man. He extended a hand toward Alex for a shake. There was dried blood beneath the man's fingernails and fresh blood running in threadlike tributaries down his arm. "I'm Jeremy Stuckey. But you can call me Stinger."

They shook hands.

## CHAPTER TWENTY-TWO

# SARAH AND ERIC: A COMMUNION

### 1

She was nursing an orange soda in one of the booths at Figaro's, her backpack full of fresh new coat hangers at her side, when Eric Rhodes came in. She had her earphones in and was listening to The Cramps on her phone when she saw him. A vague flutter awoke in her belly, and although Sarah knew it was way too early to feel the life that was growing inside her, she couldn't discount the possibility that she just had. She turned off the music as Eric dropped down opposite her in the booth.

She had texted him earlier, asked if he'd meet her after his shift at Hollywood BBQ. He'd responded right away that he would, and he looked all bright and sunny now, as if she'd asked him here on a date. For all Eric knew, maybe she had.

"Hey, you look really nice," he said.

She appreciated the compliment, but knew it was bullshit: she was dressed in her typical attire of black concert tee, faded jeans, metal jewelry.

"Is this place any good? I don't think I've ever eaten here." He was looking around at the décor, fingers drumming on the tabletop.

"I didn't ask you here to eat," she said.

"Yeah?"

"I want you to sleep with me."

He looked at her. He was fresh-faced, his neatly combed hair still damp from the shower he'd likely taken after his shift so that he didn't smell like smoked meat. "What?" he said, and the expression on his face suggested he thought she was playing some trick on him.

"It's not how it sounds. Hey, let me get you a soda."

"What? Uh, no, I'll get my own," he said, starting to get out of the booth.

"Sit," she told him, and was already up and headed toward the counter. She bought another paper cup and filled it with orange soda at the fountain, not knowing if Eric liked orange soda or not. When she returned to the table with his drink, he was still wearing that perplexed look on his face. She suddenly felt bad for him.

"Listen," she said, setting his drink down in front of him and sliding back into the booth. "Something really weird happened to me the other day. I wanted to tell someone about it and the first person I thought of was you."

"Why me?"

"Because we've been having the same dream."

His gaze dropped, as if he was suddenly ashamed—or maybe afraid—of their shared talent. He pulled the cup of orange soda toward him but didn't drink any.

"It happened at work," she said. "You even came over to me afterward, and I thought maybe you could sense something was wrong."

He shook his head. "I don't remember."

She said, "A man came in and ordered some food. He was a strange-looking guy, and his face and arms looked like they were covered in bee stings. When I brought his food to him . . ." She trailed off.

Eric said, "What?"

"When I brought his food to him, I heard his thoughts."

Again, Eric said, "What?"

"I heard what he was thinking, Eric. It was directed straight at me. I heard it clear as a bell, right in my head. I think he *wanted* me to hear it."

"Okay," he said. His fingers had stopped drumming on the table. He leaned back in his seat and exhaled a breath that caused the tuft of sandy hair curling over his forehead to flutter. His eyes were having trouble meeting hers.

"He's been in our dreams," she went on. "I don't know who he is, but after I saw him that day at the restaurant, I see his face clearly when I dream. It's like I needed to see him in real life before I could see him in my nightmare."

"Sounds like some Freddy Krueger shit."

"He's there with us in the woods. And he's there with us as we're all standing beneath that big thing that's hanging in the air."

Eric shook his head. "I don't recognize anyone in those dreams except for you."

"That's because you *know* me. Think about it, Eric. We didn't realize we were in each other's dreams until we talked about them and made the connection. And now I see you in them, and you see me. That's my theory, anyway."

"So now this guy with the bee stings is in your dreams, too?"

"Yes."

"And you . . . you heard what this guy was *thinking*?"

"Yes."

"What was it?" Eric asked. "What was he thinking?"

Sarah leaned back in her seat, too.

Thought, *I would fuck your brains out.*

Eric visibly bucked in his seat. He looked like someone who'd just been poked with the business end of a cattle prod.

"Jesus," he said, a breathless whisper. "Jesus, Miller. I just . . ." He reached up and pressed his fingers into both sides of his head, as if to prevent his skull from splitting down the middle. "Was that . . . ? Did you . . . ?" He took a long chug of the orange soda then, more calmly, said, "I just fucking heard you in my head. How the hell did you do that?"

"Try it," she told him. "Do it back to me. I think maybe you can."

"I can't. I don't know—"

*(HOW TO DO IT I CAN'T)*

She grinned at him.

Eric did not grin back. He looked petrified, frightened.

"I don't understand," he said.

"I don't, either. But something is happening. We're in each other's dreams and we can hear each other's thoughts. That guy from the restaurant is in my dreams now, too, and I could hear *his* thoughts."

"But *how*?"

She laughed. "I don't know!"

Heads turned in their direction.

"Which brings me back to why I asked you to meet me here," she said, her voice lower. "I swiped some sleeping pills from my dad's medicine cabinet. He used to take them after my mom died, and they work pretty well. I want to see if you and I fall asleep together, if we can . . . I don't know . . . communicate in our dreams. Maybe actually manipulate the dreams themselves. Try to figure out what's going on, what all this means."

His gaze slipped away from hers again.

"What's the matter?"

He shrugged.

"Are you scared?"

"Come on," he said, his voice laced with false bravado.

"Then what's the problem?"

"It's just silly."

"It's silly that we can communicate with our minds and that we've been sharing the same recurring dream? Because I think it's pretty fucking incredible."

"It's just, there's got to be an explanation."

"You got one?"

Eric said nothing.

"Me either," she said. "So what do you say? Can we give it a try?"

Eric looked over his shoulder, as if waiting for someone. She could tell just how uncomfortable he was—in fact, she thought she could *feel* it. Maybe there was no limit to what she and Eric could do now. She and Eric and the bee-stung guy.

She needed to *know.*

"Yeah, all right, Miller," he said, and got up from the booth. He scooped up his soda. "Let's go."

## 2

*(WHAT DOES IT SOUND LIKE TO YOU?)*

*Like a buzzing.*

*(ME TOO BUT I CAN UNDERSTAND IT SOMEHOW)*

*I feel it in my teeth.*

*(SO DO I IT'S LIKE THEY'RE SHAKING AND THEY HURT WHEN THEY SHAKE)*

*I think that's how we're able to do it.*

*(THROUGH OUR TEETH?)*

*Maybe there are rules. Ways for these things to happen.*

*(WHO MAKES THOSE RULES WHO MAKES THESE THINGS HAPPEN?)*

*I don't know.*

*(HOW IS THIS EVEN POSSIBLE?)*

*I don't know. Are you really so scared?*

*(NO I DIDN'T SAY I WAS SCARED I NEVER SAID I WAS SCARED)*

*I'm sorry, I didn't mean to think that last part into your head.*

*(I'M NOT SCARED I'M JUST CONFUSED AND DON'T UNDERSTAND)*

*I'm confused and don't understand, too.*

*(DO WE HAVE ANY CONTROL?)*

*Over what we send to each other and what we don't?*

*(I DON'T WANT SOMEONE PEEKING AROUND IN MY HEAD ARE YOU ABLE TO PEEK AROUND IN MY HEAD ARE YOU ABLE TO LOOK AT STUFF IF YOU TRY REALLY HARD?)*

*I don't know.*

*(I DON'T WANT TO ASK YOU TO TRY)*

*People's thoughts should be private.*

*(I JUST DON'T UNDERSTAND)*

*Are you able to peek around in my head?*

*(I DON'T KNOW I DON'T KNOW IF I SHOULD)*

*Try and tell me what it feels like it if you can do it.*

*(I DON'T KNOW)*

*It's okay. I'll think of a color but not transmit it to you and you see if you can tell what it is.*

*(LET ME SEE LET ME TRY I DON'T KNOW IF)*

*If?*

*(IF)*

*You don't—*

*(THERE)*

*What?*

*(GREEN)*

*Jesus Christ.*

*(GREEN GREEN GREEN GREEN GREEN)*

*I can see it. I can see you flashing the color.*

*(NOT ME IT'S YOU YOU'RE FLASHING THE COLOR)*

*I don't know. I don't know.*

*(OH)*

*What?*

*(NOTHING NOTHING)*

*Tell me.*

*(NOTHING)*

*What's—*

*(LET'S STOP STOP I DON'T LIKE DOING THIS I DON'T WANT TO DO IT ANYMORE)*

## 3

She was sweating and the interior of Eric's truck smelled funny, like she could smell the frying of their synapses as they'd communed telepathically during the drive.

Eric shifted nervously in the driver's seat. "Let's not keep doing that, okay?"

"Yes, I heard you," she said, and looked immediately down at her cuticles.

"It's just, I don't think people should be rummaging around in other people's heads. You know?"

They drove a bit farther.

"See here? Right up here? This place has been empty for years," Eric said. "Used to be a family called the Trentons who lived here, but I don't remember much about them. My little brother comes here sometimes with his friends to, you know, hang out and do whatever."

"Have *you* been here before?"

"Once or twice."

"With a girl?"

He glanced at her as he drove, his face darkening in the fading daylight.

"You don't have to answer that," she said, giving him an out.

"Only once," he said anyway.

"I said you didn't have to answer."

He shrugged one shoulder. "I don't mind telling you."

"Did you have sex with her?"

He said nothing.

Sarah laughed. "Oh, so now you're taking me up on my offer not to answer. I see how it is." When she saw him squirm in his seat, she said, "Hey. I'm only joking. I didn't mean to embarrass you."

"You didn't embarrass me."

*But I did,* she thought, and hoped he didn't hear it.

They slowed in front of a vacant house with a FOR SALE sign on the lawn. They were still on Poplar Station Road, which was the main street that ran through the neighborhood, but so far down the street that the roadway narrowed and the houses all looked considerably older. Even the trees were taller and fuller back here. She had never come down this way, never had a reason, and it almost didn't feel like they were still in Mariner's Cove.

*No, that's not right,* she thought. *I would know if we left the neighborhood. Because something is happening here, something that is fueling all of this, whatever it is . . .*

Again, Eric glanced at her.

"What?" she said.

"I heard you," he said. "In my head."

They parked about a block or so away from the house so that they wouldn't draw attention. Eric hopped out of the truck and hurried around to the passenger side to help her out of the cab. She let him, even though she thought it was a little ridiculous. Her backpack slung over one shoulder, she followed him to the tailgate of his truck. She had thrown her Winnie the Pooh sleeping bag in her car before heading to Figaro's, and it was in the bed of Eric's truck now. Eric yanked it out and tucked it under one arm. Together, they walked up the block toward the vacant house. There was another house across the street from it, clearly occupied: warm yellow lights simmered in nearly all of the windows.

"Come on," he said, and she felt his hand grope for hers in the dark. She let him take it, and she followed him up the driveway of the empty house at a quick clip. Instead of going to the front porch, Eric led her around to the back of the house. There was a screened-in porch here, up against a swell of black trees. Crickets trilled in the grass. Eric handed her the sleeping bag, then popped the screen from the sill. With little effort, he jockeyed open the window.

"What kind of line do you use to lure some hapless chick into this place and coax her out of her panties?"

"Jesus, Miller, your dad's a pastor. Who taught you how to talk that way?"

"The internet."

"Here, let me help you," he said, reaching for her hand again.

"I got it." She tossed the sleeping bag through the open window, then she arched one leg, and then the other, over the sill. The room was dark and smelled like stale cigarette smoke. It made her crave a cigarette, but then she thought about that fibrous little twist of tissue multiplying exponentially inside her womb. She hadn't smoked a cigarette since she'd taken that second pregnancy test. And that one had been messed up, too. Three pink lines? Since then, she'd thought about getting a third test, or maybe even going to one of those clinics to find out for sure, but she just couldn't bring herself to do it. Once she knew with one hundred percent certainty, she would have to make a decision, and it was a decision she wasn't sure she'd be able to make. Besides, her mind had been occupied with more otherworldly pursuits lately. Something about those dreams, something about those wire coat hangers . . .

She forced herself to stop thinking, worried that she might inadvertently transmit those thoughts to Eric. But Eric didn't seem to have heard her; he followed her in through the window, then patted down the pockets of his jeans to make sure he hadn't lost his keys.

"Where do we go?" she asked.

"Well, this floor is laminate. Might be a little uncomfortable, even with the . . . what is that, Winnie the Pooh?"

"You sound pretty judgmental for a guy who wears a Mickey Mouse watch."

"Hey, man, it was a gift from my grandmother."

"When you were five?"

"Six, actually. But now who's being judgmental?"

She suddenly sensed how close he was to her in that dark room, could smell his cologne, his body spray, his deodorant. She waited to see if he would take her hand again, but he didn't.

He moved past her and opened the door that led into the main part of the house. She picked up the sleeping bag and followed him. Inside, it was stuffy and hot. There was no circulation to the air, and each time she inhaled, it felt like breathing in steam.

"There are probably carpets in the bedrooms upstairs," Eric suggested.

"That's it," she said. "That's the line right there."

Eric laughed, but said, "Quit it, will you, Miller? We're about to sleep together. Show a little couth."

Eric was right: they found a carpeted bedroom upstairs. She unzipped the sleeping bag and splayed it open on the bedroom floor. Then she dug out a bottle of water and the tube of her father's sleeping pills from her backpack. Eric, who was watching her with his arms folded across his chest, said, "What are those, coat hangers?"

She looked up at him. The room was dark—they hadn't turned on any lights for fear someone might notice from the street—and only half his face was visible in the moonlight coming in through the partially shaded windows. "They are," she said. "I can't explain it, but I take them whenever I see them. I even stole a bunch from the employee closet at work."

"Why?"

"I don't know. I just feel compelled to do it. I feel like a drug addict."

"You think it's connected to everything else? The dreams and the . . . the thoughts in our heads?"

"It's gotta be," she said. "It all started happening around the same time. Is there something like that for you?"

"I'm not collecting coat hangers, if that's what you mean."

"What about anything else?"

He was silent as he considered it. "No," he said finally. "No, nothing like that."

She found she did not believe him.

She opened the bottle of pills and shook some into the cupped palm of her hand, then extended her hand to him.

"How many do I take?" he asked.

"Try two."

"What if that doesn't work?"

"Then try three."

"Jesus, Miller, don't people overdose and die on this stuff?"

"You gotta take like a whole bottle for that to happen. And even then . . ." She shrugged.

"You're pretty nonchalant for someone doling out narcotics."

"It's not heroin, man."

"Yeah, well, you gotta start somewhere . . ."

He picked two pills from her hand. She handed him the water bottle, and he unscrewed the cap. But then he stood there, not doing anything else, as if waiting to see if she'd take the pills first.

She popped two pills into her mouth, slid the rest back into the bottle, then took the bottle of water from him. Two hearty gulps and the pills were gone. She handed the water back to Eric, and he swallowed his pills, too.

"If the real estate agent finds our corpses here in the morning," he said, "I'm blaming you."

"No worries, I'll take the heat."

They both lay on the sleeping bag, side-by-side, hands laced atop their stomachs. For several minutes, all she could hear was their commingled respiration. After a while, Eric said, "I don't think I can fall asleep on command."

"Give those pills some time to work."

"What exactly is the point of all this again?"

"If we're dreaming together, maybe we can communicate with each other, too, the way we did back at the restaurant."

"And then what?"

"And then we see if we can control ourselves."

"In the dream?"

"Yes, in the dream. Because that's all they've been—dreams. I can't control what I do, I'm just along for the ride. But maybe if we're able to link up on the other side . . ."

"The other side," Eric muttered, and chuckled.

She turned and looked at him. Stared at his profile outlined in moonlight. "What's so funny?"

"You're very serious about this whole thing."

"It *is* serious. I just want to figure out what's going on."

"What if *this* is the dream and whatever we're doing in those woods is reality?"

"Don't get all metaphysical on me now."

"But what if I'm right?"

"Then you win the kewpie doll. Now close your eyes and stop talking."

"*You* stop talking."

She smiled to herself in the dark.

And felt his hand find hers.

## 4

Then she was there, running through the woods in the dark, swatting branches and sharp, pointy limbs from her face. Her backpack jounced on her back, the near-musical chime of the wire hangers inside just as loud her footfalls tromping through the underbrush. She was alone, just as she always was, but when she finally reached the clearing in the middle of the woods, she could see many other people standing in a rough semicircle, each one gazing up at something they could not see clearly hovering up there in the midnight sky. This was the dream as she'd always had it, except that once she and Eric had discussed it, he was always here right beside her in the swirling mist.

Eric was not here this time.

She projected a thought to him: *Can you hear me?*

But then she was high above the earth, clinging to the side of some monstrous structure floating in the atmosphere. All the other people were clinging to the thing, too, and some of them occasionally lost their grip and plummeted to the swirling black mist below; she could hear their screams fade as they fell.

Someone was scrambling along the shell of the structure, coming down from the very top at a quick, insect-like pace in her direction. She braced herself as the figure approached, and she saw the swollen, bulging terrain of his face, teeth chattering like some windup toy, eye sockets radiating with a mindless white light.

*You've been a busy little bee,* said the bee-stung man. And then he pointed to a word written on the side of the giant metal object that they were both clinging to:

**Come join us!**

And written below that in cruder, angrier text:

It was then that she lost her grip and fell backward, backward, backward, until she—

## 5

—screamed.

And sat up, her back stiff as a wooden plank. Her heart was racing, and her clothes were damp with perspiration. For a moment, she forgot where she was, but then she turned and saw Eric lying next to her. He stirred and his eyelids fluttered open. She dug her fingers into his shirt and rocked him back and forth.

"I'm awake, I'm awake," he muttered, propping himself up on his elbows. He glanced at his Mickey Mouse watch. "Jeez, it's almost midnight."

"You weren't there," she said. "You weren't in my dream. I tried to call out to you—I was able to do that, at least—but I couldn't tell if you heard me."

"I didn't hear you."

"*He* was there."

"The guy whose mind you read at the restaurant?"

"Yes. And he said something to me, then pointed at some words written on the side of whatever that big thing is that we're all hanging onto."

"What words?"

"'Come join us,'" she said. "And another one that said 'endgame.'"

"That's creepy."

"Why weren't you there?"

"I don't know." He sat up, hugging his knees to his chest.

"What did you dream about?"

"I don't know. I don't remember."

"Seriously? You've been having the same dream every time you fall asleep!"

"Maybe the sleeping pills messed with my head. Maybe I didn't dream at all."

"Well, *I* still had the dream. I don't understand why *you* wouldn't."

"I don't know the science behind it, Miller. What do you want from me? I played your game, all right?" He picked up the water bottle, chugged half of it, then offered it to her. She shook her head, so he screwed the cap back on then climbed to his feet. "We should get out of here before we get caught."

*He's lying,* she thought, then quickly shielded the thought from transmitting from her head to his. *I don't know why, but he's lying to me. He's hiding something.*

"Come on, Miller," he said, rocking her backpack with the toe of his sneaker so that the hangers chimed. He was hugging himself as if he was cold, despite the stale humidity in the house. "Let's get out of here."

She grabbed her things, rolled up the sleeping bag, tucked it under her arm. Unlike before, Eric did not help her with any of the items. He wasn't even waiting for her; he was moving several paces ahead, quickly, his hurried footfalls descending the stairs causing the wooden risers to stress.

"Hey, will you slow down?"

"Huh?" he said, not even bothering to look back at her over his shoulder.

"Are you angry about something?"

"Me? I'm not angry at all. Why would I be angry?"

"Then slow down!"

He came to a full stop somewhere in the middle of the house. Without any furnishings, a house was characterless, Sarah realized, where any room possessed the potential to *be* any room.

She came up to him in the dark. He stood a good ten inches taller than her, and she felt comical standing so close to his chin in the moment, but she did so anyway. It was too dark to see his eyes, though she remembered the way his eyes always glowed with a dull white light in her—

*(their)*

—dream.

"You're different now," she said, point-blank. "Something happened to you while we were sleeping."

"I don't know what to tell you, I don't remember dreaming."

"Then what's wrong?"

He shifted uncomfortably in the dark. She reached out and put a hand on his arm, and he glanced down at the touch. There was nothing warm and inviting about the glance, so Sarah withdrew her hand.

"I know we can't help what dreams we have," Eric said, "but we *can* help what we do to each other. I'm talking about that telepathy stuff."

"What about it?"

"I don't like it, Sarah," he said, and she noted that this was the first time that she could recall him using her first name and not just calling her Miller. "It feels wrong. It feels . . . I don't know . . . invasive. Like we're trespassing on someone else's property."

Sarah gave him a coy grin and spread her arms, to indicate the house they were currently occupying.

"Cut it out," he said. "You know what I mean."

She nodded. "Yes, I know. But as long as we give each other permission—"

"Well, I'm revoking that permission. Okay?"

Her throat suddenly felt dry. "Okay."

"I think we both need to be more careful about things from now on."

"Careful about what?"

"All of it," he said. "Whatever's happening. What's that one word you said you saw in your dream?"

She thought for a second. "Endgame?"

"Right. So we both need to stop treating this whole thing like it's some kid's game and take it more seriously."

"All right, sure," she said, mostly because he was stressing her out talking this way, and possibly because some of what he was saying made sense. "If that's what you want."

"What I want," he said, "is to get out of this house and go home."

He turned and continued through the house toward the screened-in porch where they'd gained access through the window. Sarah followed, clutching the rolled-up Winnie the Pooh sleeping bag to her chest now, and smelling its floral-scented detergent from the wash. She paused again, just briefly, when she thought she heard a low and muffled moan emanate from somewhere within the house. It sounded far away and aggrieved, like someone was in pain. She looked around, realizing she knew nothing about this house, which was fairly large, and nothing about who may or may not come visiting such a place in the middle of the night.

Eric's hand on her shoulder, causing her to jump—such a classic horror-movie cliché, she couldn't help but unleash a peal of nervous laughter after the fact.

"What are you doing?"

"I thought I heard something."

"Let's *go*."

They left.

# CHAPTER TWENTY-THREE
# ERIC THE LIAR

Sarah had been correct, of course, although Eric could not tell her such a thing. They drove back to Figaro's in relative silence, the streets of Mariner's Cove mostly empty at this late hour. Figaro's was in a plaza just on the outskirts of the neighborhood, halfway between Mariner's Cove and the highway, and it was mostly dark now, too. Eric spied Sarah's dumpy little car right away, since it was the only car still in the plaza's parking lot. He sidled up next to it but did not get out to open her door like he had back at the Trenton house.

"Thanks for humoring me tonight," she said.

He smiled at her, and hoped it didn't look as false as it felt. She looked absolutely stunning sitting there in the passenger seat of his truck, backlit against a row of lampposts that were strung along the perimeter of the parking lot. They cast a spectral blue haze around her, making her look like some divine creature from ancient mythology.

"Well, goodnight," she said, popping open the passenger door and hopping out. Eric heard the wire hangers in her backpack clang together just before she slammed the door closed.

*I can't explain it, but I take them whenever I see them. I even stole a bunch from the employee closet at work.* And then she'd asked, *Is there something like that for you?*

No, he wasn't collecting coat hangers. He wasn't collecting *anything.* Except maybe bad thoughts.

He watched her climb into her roller-skate of a car, watched the taillights flash, then waited as she pulled out of her spot and puttered toward the road. He followed, but at a slow enough pace to ensure she'd create distance between them.

*I'll think of a color but not transmit it to you and you see if you can tell what it is.*

He had sent his thoughts as a response into her head, and had been greeted by that ceaseless buzzing sound that he'd been feeling in his back teeth for some time now, followed by a burst of bright green light that flooded his skull like a noxious gas. Green. He'd seen it.

He'd seen something else in there, too. Or, rather, he'd *sensed* it. Things traveled along in that incessant buzzing telephone line and sometimes, he thought, you couldn't control what was transmitted and what was received. For Eric, in that moment, he caught one word that was also an idea that was also a concept all tied together by fear and anxiety, pumping at the center of Sarah Miller like a second heartbeat:

*baby*

He could even sense that separate consciousness inside her, much in the way he had often been feeling a separate consciousness inside *him.* Only this one was different. There was nothing alien about it. Nothing remotely nefarious. Just Sarah's anxiety over the thing. Which meant she already knew about it.

She didn't know he had sensed the baby. Which made him wonder how much *she* was able to glean from inside *him* without him knowing. And that troubled him. Troubled him *deeply.*

*You weren't there,* she had said. *You weren't in my dream. I tried to call out to you—I was able to do that, at least—but I couldn't tell if you heard me.*

*I didn't hear you.*

That part, at least, was true.

*Maybe the sleeping pills messed with my head. Maybe I didn't dream at all.*

That part was not.

In his previous dreams, yes, he'd been right there with Sarah, running through the woods toward a moonlit clearing where they'd join a mass of faceless people, each of them staring up at some great contraption in the sky. Those dreams had always been laced with a sense of panic and distress, as though he was somehow the prey for some great, unseen predator. But now, that dream had changed. He was no longer running through the woods, but crouched silently in it. Hiding. Masking himself. Not so much prey as the predator itself now. And through those trees was a house—a simple house, possibly somewhere in this very neighborhood, although he had never seen it before in real life. Just a quaint, single-story house nestled there in the dark with the curtains drawn and the warm interior lights making those curtains look like brightened movie screens.

He couldn't tell Sarah about this new dream because it made him feel disgusted with himself upon waking. It made him feel like he was . . . well, a bad person about to do a bad thing. And he didn't want her poking around inside his head, either, in the event she was able to glean something about that dream just like he'd inadvertently gleaned that she was pregnant. He didn't want her to know that, in the dream, he had one thought relentlessly and inexplicably tickertaping over and over again as if on repeat:

*the boy the boy the boy the boy the boy the boy the boy*

## CHAPTER TWENTY-FOUR

# SOMEWHERE IN A MOTEL IN THE MIDDLE OF NOWHERE

Like the shaking of pennies in a tin can, Brian Russo, his mind rattling, bolted awake in the dead of night feeling like someone was standing on his chest. He gasped for breath and could feel the jackrabbit urgency of his heart slamming against the interior wall of his ribcage. Beneath him, the motel mattress felt spongy with perspiration.

The fleeting tendrils of a nightmare actively withdrawing from his memory, he tried to grasp onto the few remaining filaments with a sort of ardent desperation. A nightmare about Cory, his nephew, though the details were already becoming hazy. He'd suffered plenty of nightmares involving Cory soon after the incident back in Maryland, roughly two years in the past now. The outcome of the incident in those nightmares had been a hundred times worse than what had happened in real life (though they *could* have happened), and they were a big part of why he'd managed to remain sober for so long. This nightmare, however, despite Brian not remembering much about it, resonated differently. Cory shouting for him from some dark, subterranean space? Something to do with a serpent, too, he thought now, struggling to recall the details . . . although that could have just been the influence of Lily Ming's story about the water deity Mizuchi.

Cory had been on his mind quite a lot lately. He thought he could feel the boy's presence clinging to him throughout each day and night—a veritable tingling in his Swadhisthana.

*I hope you're okay, Chicken Little.*

Across the motel room, his reflection stared back at him from a mirror on the wall. He was mostly a black and amorphous blur in the glass, except for the small star that glowed with a dull yellow-green light at the center of his chest.

## CHAPTER TWENTY-FIVE

# PROTECT THE DOOR

### 1

It had been an accident. Even now, Danver couldn't say exactly how it had happened, only that he'd come into the garage to find her there, and that there'd been some sort of . . . altercation . . . that had caused the door to slide off the sawhorses and the shelving unit to come down on his wife. Had the shelves not been so overstocked with junk to make room for Danver's project, the weight of the thing coming down may not have been that severe. Yet as it happened, he had found that a metal strut from the shelf had fallen on the back of Miranda's neck. Some other item that had come cascading off the shelf had struck her in the head, opening up a gash that bled profusely along the concrete floor of the garage. At the time, Danver had only stared down at what had happened, and at the lifeless body of his wife, unable to comprehend. When reality finally rushed back to him, he pulled the shelving unit off her body as best he could, but it was too heavy, and it kept slamming back down. Finally, he just dropped to his knees in Miranda's pool of widening blood and called her name over and over and over again. He didn't need to be a doctor to know she was not going to answer. Not ever.

The door leading out to the driveway was still open, just as Miranda had left it. Danver could see the Bridgeports' house next door, some lights on in the upper windows. Like someone in a dream, he drifted over to the switch on the wall, tapped it once, and stood there as the garage door began to shudder closed. As it was halfway down, Danver spotted Mia Bridgeport standing on the other side of the hedgerow, her eyes locked on his, and some detached part of Danver's mind would later recall having a conversation with her, although that couldn't have been the case, because that garage door was closing, closing, closing. It took what daylight remained with it.

He had left the garage then, only to find himself pacing helplessly about the house like a dementia patient, a sob caught midway up his throat but unable to burst free. Seven or eight times he picked up the phone in the kitchen, knowing that he needed to call the authorities, an ambulance, somebody, but each time he placed the receiver back on its cradle without dialing. Authorities *would* come if he called them, and they would certainly come walking through his house. They would want to see the body, which was in the garage . . .

. . . with the door.

At some point during all of this, he happened to look down at his hands and saw they were red, as if from a very bad sunburn. More disconcerting was what looked like an earthworm, perhaps an inch and a half long, lying on the top part of his left hand. As he stared at it, he saw the earthworm's body convulse, its wet outer skin shiny. He prodded it with the finger of his other hand and saw it bend like a guitar string but it did not fall off his hand. In fact, it seemed attached to the top of his hand from both ends. A leech, sucking at his blood?

It *was* his blood: it wasn't an earthworm at all, but a section of his radial artery protruding from the skin. He could see his own lifeblood pumping through the slender tube in dark purple pulses, in synch with his heartbeat. He went to the kitchen, took a butterknife from a drawer, and carefully slid it beneath the artery. He was able to lift it a bit off his hand, watched it thin as it stretched, and saw that both ends of the artery were still tucked beneath the dermal layers of his right hand where they belonged. There was no pain, no visible wound, no feeling like something was out of the ordinary. Just that inch and a half strand of artery looping up from the back of his hand. He thought of tree roots that bow out of the ground. He thought, too, of an article he'd read about how sea cucumbers turned themselves inside-out when frightened.

There was a first aid kit beneath the sink in the ground-floor bathroom. He found some gauze and wrapped it around his hand, then sat on the edge of the closed lid of the toilet while greasy bulbs of perspiration wrung out from his pores. He'd put his hand in that hole beneath the door. Both hands, yes, but this hand in particular had been in there longer. Christ, he'd put his *head* in that hole beneath the door, too. Thinking this, he got up and examined his face in the bathroom mirror. Tugged down his lower eyelids to expose the conjunctiva. Pushed the tip of his nose up to scrutinize his septum.

Satisfied that nothing else seemed out of the ordinary, he had gone back into the garage and, with much effort, hoisted the shelving unit from his wife's body. Tools, metal canisters, boxes of carpentry nails, planks of blond wood, countless other items clattered to the floor all around Marina's body as Danver hastily excavated her. Once she was free, he turned her over and could see the slack, open-eyeness of her lifeless face. That gash in her head looked like something from a horror movie—a vertical crease straight down the center of her forehead—although the blood had ceased pumping out of it. How had she sustained such a wound? The shelving unit had come down on her from behind. Had she turned her head the last second before it drove her to the floor? Had something like the steel toolbox or a hammer come sliding off the shelf to punch that bloodied divot into her head?

In the end, he bound her up in a death shroud, which was actually the old bedsheet he had been using to cover up the door. Then he carried her up to the second floor of the house and into the master bedroom. When he laid her down on her side of the bed and rolled her covered body from his arms, it was as if a great chasm had opened between them, and he was being shuttled against his will through never-ending darkness that was so cold it froze his skin.

He covered her with the additional sheet that was already on the bed, then the bedspread, then he pulled down the shades over the bedroom windows. There was some of her blood on his shirt, so he unbuttoned it, tossed it in the hamper. In his slacks and undershirt, he climbed into bed next to her. Even though her body was still covered in a multitude of sheets and blankets, he couldn't bring himself to lie down beside her—that much he could *not* do—but he was content to sit upright with his back firm against the headboard.

He remained that way for minutes, hours, days. He couldn't be sure. Time seemed less than inconsequential: it seemed nonexistent. At one point, there came the honk of a car horn outside in the street, followed by someone rapping on their front door. He ignored these things at first, but then the knocks on the front door persisted. Could it be the police? Had someone in the neighborhood witnessed what had happened? Donnie and Mia?

Like someone operating on autopilot, Danver rolled out of bed, slunk downstairs, and opened the front door to find Guy Jacobi standing on the porch wearing a sports coat and necktie. Behind him, the Jacobis' jet-black Mercedes idled in the street, Gaye Jacobi grinning like a loon and waving from one of the windows. For a split second, Danver thought he was dreaming, and even considered reaching out and poking the lapel of Guy Jacobi's sports coat just to see whether or not his finger might pass right through it.

"You're not even dressed," Guy said, making no effort to mask his consternation.

"Dressed for what?" Danver heard himself say.

"Dinner. The four of us have got reservations at Cattleman's. Didn't Miranda tell you?"

"Oh," Danver said. "Right. Jeez, I'm sorry, Guy. Miranda and I have the flu."

"*The flu?*" Incredulous.

"Yeah," Danver said. "The summer flu. I'm afraid we'll have to take a raincheck."

In the street, Gaye, oblivious to the conversation taking place on the porch, gave a quick tap on the Mercedes's horn. Still grinning like some psychiatric patient, she waved at him, and shouted, "Hi, doc! Hey, there! Let's get this show on the road!"

"Well," Guy said, shuffling a step backward, as if Danver's fictitious illness might be contagious. "I hope you both feel better."

Danver closed the door then stood there in the gloomy vestibule for an uncountable amount of time. He thought about the door in the garage, *his* door, and how its doorknob had flung free of its frame when it slid off those sawhorses and hit the floor. It was still in there now, just lying on the floor of the garage. He thought about the blood in there, too. Miranda's blood, from her mysterious head wound.

*Miranda.*

He crept back upstairs and climbed into bed with her.

## 2

In the periods where sleep overtook him, he was shuttled through a black and endless void, a lone meteor hurtling through space without so much as a single distant star to provide any light, any hope, any guidance, or any indication that he wasn't hopelessly and irrevocably alone.

This dream transition into a different one, where he wandered lost through his childhood home until he ultimately discovered his father, Hal Danver, seated in a faux-leather armchair in his study at the back of the house. His father had the nickel-plated revolver pressed to his temple this time, unlike in other versions of this dream. Grinning a skeletal grin, Hal leaned forward and pulled back the curtain once again on the window to reveal a storm-blackened landscape against which a massive structure loomed like something otherworldly. The thing looked like a giant mechanical spider, and Danver could see strange, arcane symbols now scrawled like hieroglyphs along its metallic hide. In the dream, Danver went to the window for a better look, because, yes, there were also *words* printed there, crude like graffiti, and he found he couldn't make out what they said. It was in that moment that his father let the curtain whisper back into place. In a voice that was not his own, Hal Danver said, *"Door becomes chair. Take it there."* Then he imparted one final word to his son, before sticking the barrel of the revolver into his mouth and pulling the trigger, spraying the black, cherry-sauce clumps of his brains against the wall.

*"Endgame."*

Now, as the midday sun brightened against the window shades of their master bedroom, and with Miranda's body growing ever colder within the sheet and beneath the heavier bedspread, Danver could no longer ignore the implication of those nightmares. The door was still in the garage. It was summoning him, and despite his grief, he needed to tend to it.

With Miranda dead, there was no reason to confine the door to the garage. Danver dragged it into the living room, where he propped it against one wall. The hole where the doorknob had been looked to Danver like an empty eye socket. It hurt him to see the thing in such a tragic state. He went and got two kitchen chairs, which he set them up in the middle of the living room. With some difficulty, he managed to suspend the door horizontally across the chairs, much as he'd done with the sawhorses. But the seats of the chairs were lower than the sawhorses, and the shape of the shadow beneath now looked different.

Danver knelt down and inched his bandaged hand toward the shadow. When the tips of his fingers reached the edge, he took a deep breath then inched his hand farther.

But his hand did not go any farther.

His fingers did not slip inside that shadow.

They did not go *down*.

"No," he said, shaking his head. He could feel beads of sweat popping out along the furrowed ridge of his forehead as he crouched there beneath the door on his hands and knees. "Please, God, no. Come back. Don't do this."

What had changed?

Was it the missing doorknob?

He hurried back into the garage and located the doorknob—both sides of it, one for the front, one knob for the back—and carried the pieces, along with the toolbox that may or may not have punched a dent into Miranda's skull, back into the living room. The wood was splintered, but he was able to work the doorknob back into place, to seat it, and to screw it firmly to the frame. There.

Dropping back onto his knees, he rolled the screwdriver beneath the door. It rolled straight across the shadow and came to a rest there.

It did not disappear.

It did not fall *away.*

The fucking door was broken.

—*What are you going to do about it?* asked Hal Danver.

"I don't know."

—*You can't fuck this up, Michael.*

"I know that."

—*This is very important.*

"I know that!" His fists were balled and there were hot tears slipping down the sides of Michael Danver's face. He glanced around the dimly lit living room but could not see his dead father anywhere. Probably a good thing, considering the way he'd gone out. "What are you even doing here? You're dead. How did you get here?"

—*Through a crack,* said Hal Danver. *There've been many cracks forming. I'm surprised you haven't noticed.*

As if this made all the sense in the world, Danver nodded. His vision was blurry with tears, but for a second, he thought he could discern the shape of his father slumped in one corner of the living room in a wingback chair, mostly cloaked in shadow. Danver pawed the tears from his eyes, and the visage disappeared. Yet his father's voice persisted.

—*You need to prepare the door, Michael. You need to get it ready.*

"Get it ready for what?"

—*Endgame.*

"What's that? What's endgame?"

Nothing.

"Dad?"

But his father was gone.

His hands trembling and his bottom molars beginning to hurt, Danver poured himself two fingers of Chivas into a crystal glass. He took a sip, then migrated over to the stereo system that was ensconced in the living room wall. It was an impressive unit, with a quartet of Coltrane Supreme speaker towers outfitted in Swedish wood with a

50mm diamond mid-range driver connected to a custom Marten amplifier and a 150-disc CD changer. Danver selected *Liebman Plays Puccini: A Walk in the Clouds*. He closed his eyes as the initial filaments of music filtered, crisp and uninhibited, through the speakers. He allowed the music to wash through him, scrubbing him clean. For a while now, it had felt like there had been *two* beings inhabiting his body, a foreign consciousness right there alongside his own. One that remained mostly hidden in the dark recesses of Michael Danver's psyche, but there nonetheless, even if he could only sense it but couldn't see it. He stood there swaying to the music with his eyes closed, the crystal glass of Chivas pinched loosely between the thumb and middle finger of his left hand. When he remembered that this had been Miranda's favorite Liebman album, his eyes sprung open and he quickly turned the stereo off.

Someone was knocking on the door again. Confused, Danver ambled over to the door lying supine across the kitchen chairs and put his ear to it. *What worlds are inside you? What universes do you contain?* It was only after several minutes had passed that Danver, ear still to the door, realized the knocking must have come from the *front* door.

The hair along his arms bristled.

He was thinking of Donnie and Mia Bridgeport again. Had they seen what had happened in the garage? Did they know what he had done? Mia had been standing there staring at him as he'd lowered the garage door: was it possible she saw what had happened to Miranda? He kept thinking that he had some sort of conversation with Mia in that moment, just as the garage door was shutting, but he couldn't remember any details about it. Besides, she'd been too far away to engage in any discussion. For all he knew, he'd dreamed that, too.

Danver finished off his drink, set the empty glass upon the wet bar, then wandered down the hall to the front door. He was no longer thinking it might be Donnie and Mia Bridgeport on the other side of that door, nor even the police, but perhaps Miranda herself would be standing there. She would be perfectly fine and happy to see him. If his father could—what had he said?—come *through a crack* and in order to have a conversation with him, shouldn't Miranda be afforded the same luxury?

But when Danver opened the front door, no one was there. On the porch, some deliveryman had deposited a stack of magazines—the latest issue of Miranda's publication, *Look There!*—bundled together with twine. He bent down and stared at the cover of the magazine at the top of the stack. It was a photo of black storm clouds sweeping in off the bay, heading toward the craggy hillside studded with tiny white homes that was the cusp of Mariner's Cove. The photo unnerved him.

Before heading back inside, he happened to glance across the street, and at the Harrisons' house. Oliva Harrison mirrored him, standing on her own front porch, staring back at him. She was still dressed in an oversized T-shirt and sweatpants, her hair an unruly tangle of knots and corkscrews. She held something in her hands, pressed against her abdomen just below the line of her breasts. From such a distance, he couldn't tell what it was.

The buzzing in his head grew louder.

No, not in his head.

His back teeth.

He snagged the stack of magazines by a loop of twine and tossed them into the house. The twine snapped when they hit the floor and the magazines fanned out along the vestibule like a deck of cards. Danver hardly noticed. He shut and locked the door behind him, and then realized that anyone—Olivia Harrison, Donnie Bridgeport, literally *anyone*—could now see the door through any of the floor-to-ceiling windows that made up the back of the house. Frantically, he went around pulling the drapes closed, and making sure all the windows as well as the sliding patio door were latched.

Hal Danver was once again seated in the wingback chair. It was as if the gloominess of the room, with all its curtains drawn, facilitated his reappearance—as if his father did not wish to be seen clearly. But Danver could see him clearly enough: the man's head was cocked at a curiously impossible angle, a gaping wound along one side of his head so fresh that tendrils of grayish smoke still unfurled from it. Danver caught a whiff of gunpowder.

—*Her death was unfortunate,* Hal Danver said, *but it was an accident. You can't let it serve as a roadblock, Michael.*

"I just want to lie down and close my eyes for a while."

—*There's no time for that.*

Danver felt a sob threaten to break free of his throat. Even at sixty-nine years old and after a successful career as a well-respected cardiac surgeon, he did not want to cry in front of his father, no matter if the man was dead or not.

—*Stop that. This isn't about Miranda, Michael. This isn't about you, either. This thing is bigger than you. It's bigger than all of you.*

"The door," Danver said, glancing at it now as it lay horizontally across the chairs. "I think it's broken."

—*It's not,* said his father. *You've just closed up one of the cracks. The cracks shift and move and don't necessarily always stay in the same place. Not until everything becomes anchored. But it doesn't matter right now, Michael. The cracks are just a side effect of everything that is happening. They're not important.*

"Then what's important?"

—*That you finish what you started.*

"And what's that? I don't even know what I'm doing anymore." He rubbed a tear away from his eye with the heel of his hand. "I don't think I ever did."

—*I can't tell you,* said his father. *You have to do it on your own.*

"Why won't you just say what it is I have to do and then I'll do it?"

—*Because I'm mostly in your head, Michael. I can't know what you don't know. For the most part, anyway. I can only urge you to move forward.*

Danver shook his head. Another tear slipped down the side of his face, hot as candle wax. "You said you came through a crack."

—*I did. It happened when you put your head there.*

"My head where?" he said, but the instant those words were out of his mouth, he understood what his father was talking about: how he'd closed his eyes tight and submerged his head into the shadow beneath the door. "Oh," he said now, as if all of this suddenly made perfect sense. "I get it."

*—Do you?*

"What would have happened if I opened my eyes in there?" Danver asked.

*—You would have gone mad,* answered his father. *That world is not for you.*

"It's for the dragon," Danver said. Even as the words issued from his mouth, he did not know what they meant.

The slumped, broken-headed shape of Hal Danver approximated a subtle shrug of his shoulders.

*—If that's how you see it,* he said.

Something else Danver saw: the dark silhouette of a person moving like a shadow puppet behind the wall of drapes at the back of the house. Had it not been so bright out he might not have noticed, but the figure was backlit by the midday sun and cut a stark and nefarious shape, like something carved from wood or stone and projected onto a screen.

"Who is that?" He realized he was asking his father, so when no response came, he glanced back at the chair. Hal Danver was gone, as was the smell of gun smoke in the air.

*Protect the door,* Danver thought.

He rushed upstairs and into the master bedroom, all too aware that Miranda was still there on the bed wrapped in sheets and buried beneath the bedspread. He averted his eyes so that he wouldn't see the shape of her, could pretend she wasn't there, and instead went straight for the walk-in closet. That shoebox on the top shelf: he took it down and tore off the lid.

The revolver gleamed, the blue-black of Superman's hair.

Danver hurried back downstairs, just in time to see that dark man-shaped silhouette retreat from the drapes. Danver peeled away a section of the drapes and peered out through the glass slider. He saw Donnie Bridgeport standing on the patio, looking up at the second story of Danver's house. Looking directly at the windows of the master bedroom, Danver could tell.

*He knows. He saw.*

Donnie's gaze swung down and met Danver's eyes through the glass. A roguish grin appeared.

*Either that or his wife saw and she told him. She was staring daggers at me as that garage door came down . . .*

"Hey, doc." Donnie's voice sounded muted on the other side of the glass, which, Danver thought, was an improvement.

Danver unlatched the door and slid it open a few inches. Hot summery air rushed in through the—

*(crack)*

—opening. He kept the revolver by his side, hidden from Donnie's view behind the drapes.

"Hey, doc. Didn't mean to be lurking around."

"What is it?" Danver asked.

"I've got some downed tree limbs in the yard that I wanted to cut up, but my electric saw just shit the bed. I was wondering if I could borrow yours."

*He's lying*, Danver thought.

"What do you say, doc?" Donnie's smile could have been on a billboard.

"I can't," Danver said. "I'm . . . I don't feel well. I've come down with something. I'm ill."

That billboard smile vanished just as quickly as it had arrived. "That's awful, doc. What is it?"

"I don't know. Could be the flu, could be COVID. I've got a fever, chills. Best to just stay away. I'd hate to get you sick."

"Right, right, no doubt about that, doc. You should be in bed."

"That's what I'm planning to do."

"Maybe if you opened your garage I could just go in and grab it, though?"

*He's testing me. He knows.*

"The garage is a mess, Donnie. You'd never find it. I'll see if I can dig it out for you later and run it over."

"Hey, no, no—not if you aren't feeling well. Maybe if Miranda happens to—"

"Miranda isn't home."

"Oh, okay. Well . . . uh, you know what? Forget I asked. Don't worry about it."

Danver pulled his head back in through the crack in the door.

"Anything I can do for you?" Donnie called.

*Just go the fuck away*, Danver willed him. Said, "No, thank you, Donnie."

"Well, all right. Feel better, okay?" Donnie raised a hand then stepped down off the porch. Danver watched him cross over the mulch of the weedy flower bed until he vanished around the side of the house.

Danver's heart was thundering in his chest. He let the drapes swing back into place then hurried to the side of the house where he peered through the slatted blinds of another window. His breath fogged up the glass as he waited for Donnie to reappear. To make sure the son of a bitch was actually headed back home.

*Protect the door.*

*Protect the door.*

*Protect the—*

Donnie materialized on the far side of the hedgerow, his linen shirt rippling in the summer breeze, one hand raking a set of fingers through his hair. Before he went back inside his own house, Donnie cast a final glance over his shoulder back in Danver's approximate direction.

*He knows.*

*Protect the door.*

He'd told Donnie that Miranda was out, yet her Escalade was parked in the driveway. He was being careless. In the living room, he set the revolver atop the wet bar, knocked back one last pour of Chivas, then went into the garage to clean up Miranda's blood and square everything else away to make room for the Escalade. Just as Miranda had wanted.

## 3

When he was done, he returned to the living room to find Donnie Bridgeport's silhouette clinging to the drapes again.

*Protect the door.*

"You son of a bitch," Danver muttered. He looked around for where he'd left the revolver, finally locating it atop the wet bar. He snatched it up in his bandaged hand and hurried over to the drapes. He yanked them aside and was startled to find Olivia Harrison standing on the other side of the glass.

Danver unlocked the slider and pulled it open. "Olivia. What the hell are you doing here?"

"I knocked on your front door, but you didn't answer."

"I was in the garage."

He looked at the thing she was clutching to her chest. It was the camping chair she had been sitting on the night of the luau, folded up. He saw her eyes tick down toward the gun in his bandaged hand, but he did not bother to hide it behind his back. His molars were buzzing again. Beelike.

"I think I'm supposed to be here," she said.

She pulled open the camping chair, and Danver did not need to reexamine the spray-painted symbol on his driveway to realize that Olivia's camping chair, when open, was the shape of an inverted triangle.

"Jesus Christ," Danver muttered. "Come in, come in. Hurry." Hurry, because he didn't want Donnie Bridgeport seeing Olivia standing there, didn't want that nosy, spying son of a bitch slinking back over here.

Olivia shuffled into the house. She was wearing sandals, their rubber soles shushing along the polished hardwood floor. Danver could smell her—a whiff of unwashed hair and sweat-soured flesh—and deduced that she hadn't bathed in quite some time. Not that he could judge.

She paused in the middle of the living room when she laid eyes on the door.

"Is that it?" she asked, her voice low and reverent.

"Let me get a drill and some screws," Danver said, and he hurried back into the garage. He'd righted the shelf before pulling the Escalade into the garage, and he went to it now, rummaging around the jumble of tools there until he located a box of screws and his electric drill. When he returned to the living room, he saw that Olivia had placed her camping chair on the door, and that she was staring at it with her head cocked, much like a curious dog's.

"That looks right," Danver said, marveling over the sight of the camping chair on the door. It looked just like the symbol that had been spray-painted on his driveway. On the Harrisons' driveway, too.

"It does," Olivia agreed. She spoke quietly and breathlessly, like someone at the feet of a great deity. "I suddenly feel so . . . so . . ."

"Relieved," Danver finished.

"Excited," she countered. Her eyes were bright. For a moment, she looked like her old self, the woman who ran PTO events and was a judge for the annual Oyster Princess competition every Fourth of July.

Grinning, Danver plugged the drill into the outlet, then leaned over the door with some screws poking out from between his lips. It was a good drill, and it drove the screws straight through the aluminum legs of the camping chair and right into the wood of the door. When he was done, he stepped back to survey what he had done. Olivia stood a few feet away from him, vibrating excitedly like a live wire.

The shadow beneath the door suddenly looked darker.

Deeper.

Danver had one remaining screw still poking from his lips; he plucked it out, looked at it, then tossed it toward the shadow beneath the door. It *tink tink tink*ed along the hardwood, then disappeared completely beneath the door.

"How . . . ?" Olivia said.

Danver dropped to his hands and knees. He crawled to the edge of the shadow, his dead father's voice returning to him inside his head now—

*(that world is not for you)*

—but he didn't care. Miranda was dead and there were other things waiting for him on the other side of this world. A world behind a world beneath a world beyond a world. Down there, he would not be blind. He would not be one of the drones. How many people knew the truth of it? How many mechanical beings were there *right now* negotiating their mindless way through the hidden, underground tunnels, a system of tunnels, a complex network of them, each one like a wire in a machine, a machine, a machine—

"Michael?"

Danver peered around at Olivia from over his shoulder. He'd forgotten she was here.

"Are you okay?"

"You should go home," he told her.

She blinked rapidly, as if roused from a trance. "Wait, what? Go home? But we just *made* this . . ."

"Leave through the front door. I don't want Donnie to see you going around the back."

She took a few furtive steps in his direction—his direction and the door's. Her eyes were locked on that impossibly dark shadow beneath the door. It looked like a trapdoor in the living room floor. She lifted one leg, balancing like a flamingo, and removed her sandal. Casually, she flipped the sandal at the shadow beneath the door. The sandal vanished.

"It's not a garbage chute, for Christ's sake, Olivia."

"What *is* it?"

*It's a crack,* he thought. *It's how Dad came through. Other things, too. A doorway to the world behind a world beneath a world beyond a world.*

"A crack," he heard Olivia say, and it took him a moment to realize she was reading the thoughts from his mind as clearly as if they were printed on a banner above his head. "Whose dad?"

A pulse of pain shuttled through his bottom teeth. Had he said something about his father aloud?

"I said to leave, Olivia. I don't want you here."

"You can't make me." She was still staring at the shadowy portal on the living room floor. "We're in this together, Michael. We've *created* this together. It's important. Can't you feel how important it is?"

*I know how important it is.*

"So do I! I've been reading the instructions. You can't—"

"Get the fuck out of here."

"I don't *want* to leave! You can't make me! That's my *chair*!"

"No." He stood with a grunt. "Door becomes chair. It's a transition. *That's* what was written in the instructions, you dumb cunt, so if you've been reading them and expect something different, then you've been reading them *wrong.* The door is mine. It's *always* been mine. So now the chair is mine, too. This is how it's supposed to be."

"I don't—"

She stopped so abruptly, it was as if her voice had struck a wall. Danver looked down and realized that he had picked up the gun again at some point; he wasn't aiming the thing in her direction, just holding it loosely at his side, but the implication was clear.

Olivia's eyes narrowed. A moment later, Danver felt a physical *thump* against the interior walls of his skull, followed by another pulse of pain in his lower teeth.

"Is that what you did to Miranda?" Olivia asked. "Did you use a gun or . . . something else?" She took another step in his direction, more measured this time. Her one remaining sandal thumped mutely on the hardwood floor. There was suddenly something predatory about her. "I can't see it clearly, but I can see it, and I know you've done something to her, Michael. Is that it? Did you use the gun? Did you shoot her?"

The hand holding the gun trembled. Danver felt his heart begin to gallop in his chest. He had lived all sixty-nine years of his life harboring minimal fears, but his two greatest—no doubt due to his life's experiences—were suicide by handgun and dying of a widow-maker heart attack. Now, he wondered if he might not just succumb right here and now from the latter.

Even Olivia could feel it—literally. She placed a hand over her own heart, her small breasts rounding out the fabric of the ridiculous

Care Bears T-shirt she was wearing. "I feel it, too, you know," she said. "Your fears, your anxiety. As you can probably feel mine. See? We're connected."

"You don't know anything about Miranda."

"Don't I?" One of her eyebrows arched knowingly. "You're going to fuck this up, doc," she said. The brightness in her eyes had fled, as had the cold calculation; she was seething at him now, and when she spoke next, it was through gritted teeth. "You don't even know what you're doing."

"Do *you*?" he countered. "Do *you* know what's going on, Olivia? If so, please tell me. Don't keep it a secret. Don't keep it to yourself. Share with the class!"

She said nothing. She didn't know. Danver could suddenly sense her lack of knowing in her head, radiating outward and filtering into the air, crackling there in the space between them, clear as if she was speaking to him aloud. His back teeth vibrated like tiny tuning forks in his gums, and he watched as Olivia brought up a hand and pressed it against the side of her own jaw. As if she shared his pain much like she shared the racing palpitations of his overtaxed heart.

For a moment, he thought she wouldn't leave, and he began wondering exactly what he might do about that. But then she put her head down and marshaled down the hall toward the vestibule. Her footfalls were uneven, one sandaled, one barefooted. The gun still in his hand, Danver followed her at an unhurried pace. By the time he reached the front hall, he saw her slip on the glossy spread of magazines splayed out there on the floor; she fell backward on her ass, her remaining sandal flying off her foot, and Danver thought he could hear her teeth knock together in her head. She scrambled to her feet and was out the door quicker than Danver would have thought her capable. She left the door open to a wall of blinding daylight and a lone sandal on the floor of the foyer.

The buzzing in his teeth was beginning to fill up his skull, vibrating the tiny hairs inside his ears. He'd hoped it might subside once she left, but it only seemed to be gaining strength.

*Protect the door.*

*Protect the door.*

He sensed her return before he actually saw her come barreling back through the front door, her eyes blazing, fingernails clawing at the air in front of her face. Magazines were churned into a whirlwind beneath her feet, pages tearing, glossy inserts fluttering into the air.

"*Mine!*" she screeched. "*It's mine!*"

She bolted past him and down the hall. Danver's back struck a wall, a picture frame fell, and suddenly the buzzing in his head was interrupted by a transmission of thought, booming through his skull in Olivia Harrison's shrill, plangent voice—

*(IT'S MINE IT'S MINE IT'S MINE IT'S MINE IT'S MINE)*

Danver regained his footing and sprinted into the living room. He found Olivia there, attempting to pry the camping chair from the door. Her jostling was causing the door to wobble on the chairs, and Danver was suddenly terrified that if the door fell again then the portal beneath the door might become a regular shadow once more, and maybe next time he wouldn't be able to get it back. He wouldn't let that happen.

He gripped Olivia high on the forearm—

*(MINE MINE MINE MINE MINE)*

—and yanked her away from the door. She staggered backward with such force that she struck the far wall. The stereo system burst to life, spilling Liebman from the speakers. A swatch of hair swinging pendulously in front of her face, Olivia shrieked and launched herself at him again, fingers fashioned into claws and slicing at the air.

Danver felt the revolver buck once, twice, three times in his hand. He heard each explosive report, saw three distinct sparks explode from the barrel of the gun in the periphery of his vision. He smelled smoke and tasted cordite at the back of his throat.

A spray of wood above the bookshelf.

A toppled speaker tower, silencing the music.

Olivia Harrison collapsed to a heap on the living room floor just as—

## 4

—Sarah Miller buckled forward, clutching at her belly, *the baby the baby the baby*, something was wrong, something had suddenly broken inside her, the sharpness and suddenness of such a white-hot, searing pain the indication that something was terribly wrong inside her, while—

## 5

—Pamela Guerin, running an old shopping-cart wheel up and down a wall calendar with the phrase *Year of the Dragon* printed across the top in blood-red letters, the wheel going *squeak squeak squeak*, as the pain abruptly pierced her abdomen and she uttered a gasping, throaty cry of surprise, while—

## 6

—Raj Subador's eyes flipped open, a burst of fire igniting in his gut. He sat up from his living room floor, knocking over canisters of neon spray paint, his walls a vast, collective missive of indecipherable sigils, his skin similarly marked, palms dusty with chalk, cuticles neon with spray paint, face and chest freshly tattooed, the backs of his hands and straight up his arms inked, too; all those symbols made permanent so that he'd never forget them, never forget them, never forget them, as he felt the burning fire in his belly bloom outward, rivaling the buzzing transmissions in his teeth, his mind and body screaming, and as—

## 7

—Stinger, standing beneath the shadow of the Gladstone Park water tower, suddenly bent at the waist from a fierce and sudden pain that was perhaps contagious, for both Alex Braswell and his wife Georgette buckled forward, too, moaning aloud, all of them, hissing with sharp and sudden intakes of air, while—

## 8

—many, many other residents of Mariner's Cove felt it, too, in just the way that—

## 9

—Danver felt it: a white-hot iron poker thrust through the center of his abdomen. He clutched his own belly while, on the floor, Olivia moaned and rolled onto her back. There was now a spreading crimson stain in the center of that ridiculous Care Bears T-shirt.

The silence that followed was nearly as loud as the gunshots. His whole body suddenly trembling, Danver dropped the gun on the floor. He staggered over to the sofa, his legs made of rubber, and dropped his weight onto the cushions. Forget the buzzing in his back teeth: it now felt like his guts were boiling.

On the floor, Olivia moaned again, then went still.

"Jesus," Danver muttered, a breathless whisper. "Jesus Christ . . ."

—*It was necessary,* came his father's voice. *It had to be done.*

Olivia Harrison lay on the floor, vacant eyes staring at the ceiling, upon a spreading pool of blood.

—*Things are moving very quickly now, Michael. You were correct: door becomes chair. You've always been a smart, smart boy.*

His father had never called him a smart, smart boy.

Danver opened his mouth to say something—to say anything—but the only thing that came out was a pathetic, creaking sob.

—*Do you know why I killed myself all those years ago, Michael?*

Though his vision was now blurry with tears, he thought he could see Hal Danver slumped in the wingback chair at the far end of the room again. Masked in shadow.

—*It's because I was a failure. Do you want to be a failure like me, Michael? Is that what you want?*

In a barely audible voice, Danver said, "No."

—*No. Of course not. That's why you went to medical school. That's why you've achieved so much success in your life. No one wants to be a failure. It's better you shot that woman in the belly and stopped her craziness than become a failure and blow your own head apart like your old man. Don't you agree?*

Danver said nothing.

—*Don't you agree, Michael?*

"Sure, whatever," he said, his voice cracking. His whole *body* felt like it was cracking. The pain in his stomach had disappeared, which he took to mean Olivia Harrison was now dead. "Yes. Right. Sure."

—*Now get rid of her,* said his father.

Danver swiped tears from his eyes. "What?"

—*You heard me, boy. Get rid of her.*

"How?"

But it was a stupid question.

*Comes whispering-ways down the corridors of minds, sleek and bullet-speedy, resplendent in a cloak of blinding, invisible light, a sense and semblance contracting with all the authority of a cosmic heartbeat: a consciousness tethered, world-heavy, invading and burrowing within the coalmines of these cerebral honeycombs, all of it with a soundless and a godlike laugh, a cool yet comforting embrace, whipping through the cracks formed by the sudden and jarring collision of two worlds, up through the foundation and out the doorless entryway of an abandoned, decrepit house on Jolene Street, to a shopping cart tipped on its side in a wooded lot, strangled by vines, one rusted caster missing, through the vast cavernous channels where bees travel and speak in their secret emotive language, to the singsong chiming of thin metal wires seemingly singing from everywhere, everywhere, and above all else, the instruction to assimilate, to adapt, to metamorphose . . .*

*. . . to come join us . . .*

# CHAPTER TWENTY-SIX

# THE TRENTON HOUSE REVISITED

## 1

Ellen was in the process of uploading photos of a new home on Terrace Avenue to the Multiple Listing Service website when there came a knock at the front door. She was seated at the dining room table on her laptop, so she happened to glance out the bay window and saw a police car parked down by the curb. She got up, opened the door, and found two uniformed officers standing on her porch.

"Hello, ma'am. We're looking for Ellen McBride."

"That's me. What's the matter?"

Her first thought was of her brother Brian.

"Ma'am, are you the real estate agent of record for 2929 Poplar Station Road?"

The Trenton house.

"I am," she said.

"Are you aware that some neighborhood kids have been breaking in there at night and hanging out?"

"You know, I had an inkling. Did you catch them?"

"In a manner of speaking," said the officer. He glanced at his partner, who hadn't spoken a word yet, then said, "These kids broke into the house a few nights ago and one of their friends disappeared. The boy hasn't been home since, and his parents had filed a missing persons report. We thought maybe his friends were covering for him at first, like maybe he was hiding out at one of their houses, but turns out they were all just as worried about him as his parents. One girl in particular told us he went to one of the upstairs bedrooms and just, well . . ."

"He disappeared," piped up the other officer. Stubbly black crewcuts, white faces, Ray-Bans, both young men could have been mirror images of each other.

"Oh," Ellen said, blinking at them. "I'm sorry to hear that. But what exactly do you need from me?"

"We need to search the house," said the first officer. "Just have a look around. The real estate listing said you were the realtor, so we figured you'd have the key."

"Yes, I do," she said, "but should I call the Trentons first? They're the homeowners. I think they're in Europe, last I heard, but I think . . . I mean, do they need to give you permission or something? Legally, I mean?"

"It's a missing boy, ma'am," said the second officer. "Exigent circumstances. It's a courtesy we're even here. We just thought this was better than breaking the door down and notifying you after the fact."

"Oh," she said again. This was new territory for her. "Yes. This is better than breaking down the door, absolutely. Right, okay. The key is in a coded lockbox on the front door. I'd prefer to come with you, though. The house, it's my responsibility. I'd feel funny just giving out the code and letting—"

"It's fine, we can drive you," said the second officer. She could tell they were in a hurry.

"Let me just tell my son."

She invited them inside, but they chose to remain on the front porch. She went down the hall and poked her head into Cory's bedroom. He was seated with his back toward her, scribbling something at his desk.

"Hey, Cor," she said, and he jumped, startled. He rustled the papers around on his desk, as if to cover up what he was doing. "There are a couple of police officers here. They need me to go unlock a house so they can check it out."

"Police officers?" He hopped down from his chair, went to his bedroom window, and peered out. "Yeah, there's the police car. Jeez."

"It's no big deal, Cory. I'll just be gone maybe fifteen minutes. Are you going to be okay alone for a while?"

He turned from the window to face her. "Are you sure they're real cops?"

"Of course they're real cops."

His lips thinned.

Something tingled at the back of Ellen's head. "Why do you think they might not be real cops?"

He seemed to consider this. His silence began to unnerve her. Finally, he said, "Never mind."

"Do you want to meet them?"

Again: a beat of contemplative silence.

"Cory?"

"I'm okay, Mom. It's fine."

"Okay, baby. I'll be back soon."

She blew him a kiss then drifted back down the hall where the cops were waiting for her.

## 2

Sitting in the back of the police car, she asked, "Who's the boy that's gone missing?"

"Michael Bliss. Fifteen years old. Folks live out on Tamarack." This was the driver, who motored the police car down Cloister Road toward Capshaw at a hurried pace.

"When did this happen?"

"A few nights ago. Took a while for one of the boy's friends to come clean about breaking into the house. No one wanted to get in trouble."

"Will they?" she asked.

"Will they what, ma'am?"

"Get in trouble."

"Depends on how this all plays out."

"Well," she said. "I hope it's nothing serious."

The Trenton house was hot and stuffy. Ellen lingered in the front hall as the two officers filed into the house. When they took their Ray-Bans off, she could see one had brown eyes, the other had blue.

"We're just going to look around the place, see what we can see," said Officer Blue Eyes. "Do us a favor and stay right here until we come back, okay?"

"Sure." She supposed they didn't want her accidentally messing up any potential evidence.

Officer Blue Eyes meandered down the hall in the direction of the kitchen while Officer Brown Eyes slowly ascended the staircase to the second floor. Ellen apprised the equipment on his belt along with the bulkiness of his bulletproof vest and absently wondered how they worked a shift lugging all that gear around in the dead of summer, let alone how they chased perps through alleyways and wrestled with drunks and whatever else they did.

The last time a pair of police officers had shown up at her front door, they had been there to tell her Patrick, her husband and Cory's father, had been killed in an automobile accident. She still had a bit of a Pavlovian reaction to finding cops standing on the other side of her front door, but she thought she was keeping it together well enough now.

She hadn't liked that Cory had been distrustful of them. She was worried that these newly discovered abilities of his had triggered in him a level of paranoia that she'd have to be cautious to keep in check. Even when Larry Kotara from down the street had showed up at the house to replace the kitchen window, Cory had lingered at a safe distance in the hallway, scrutinizing the man while he worked. After Larry had left, she'd asked him if there'd been some problem with him, something Cory didn't like about him, but Cory had just shaken his head and wandered back into his bedroom. His distrust and paranoia had extended beyond Mr. Zachs, it seemed, and she wasn't sure why.

Did she really think he could read minds? Or . . . how had he put it? Peek inside someone's head? She wasn't sure. True, Aunt Patty could guess a string of songs on the radio, but that had been the extent of her talent, as far as Ellen was aware. And Brian had never possessed such an ability. Maybe what Cory *thought* was him peeking around inside someone's head was just him being hyperaware of someone's demeanor and emotional state. An empath.

*He knew I was lying to him about Brian*, she thought now. *He knew Brian had the same ability even though I deliberately omitted that from my story.*

She'd done so because she hadn't wanted Cory to think that having such abilities had any nexus, any link, to the demons that had haunted her brother. And to be honest, she didn't know if that was true or not. Maybe it had been Brian's ability to move small items with his mind that had caused him to fall into ruinous addiction. Or, on the other hand, maybe it had all been a coincidence. Either way, she hadn't wanted her son arriving at that conclusion and worrying that his future held nothing but despair and self-destruction. She hadn't wanted him to think he had some disastrous, drug-addicted future waiting for him on the horizon.

"Looks like they've been coming in through a window at the back of the house," said Officer Blue Eyes as he ambled back down the hall. "Screen is in the grass, and the window isn't closed all the way."

"You know, the last time I showed this house, the five-year-old daughter of the couple I was showing it to vanished."

The officer glared at her. "What?"

She laughed nervously. "I mean, we *found* her, but we had to search around for her."

"Where'd you find her?"

"In the basement."

"There's a basement?"

"Well, yeah," she said. "The door is sort of hidden in a niche in the wall. Can I show you?"

"Absolutely."

She led him to the door and saw that the slide bolt was still engaged. Ellen disengaged it and pulled open the basement door. A sliver of darkness appeared, and a moment after that, a jumble of houseflies swarmed out. No, not houseflies.

Bees.

"Jesus!" Officer Blue Eyes jumped back, swatting at the air. "I'm allergic to these things."

Ellen peered down the basement stairwell, straight into the dark.

She called, "Hello?"

Still fanning the air, Officer Blue Eyes triggered the radio strapped to his shoulder. "Hey, come down here. There's a basement." To Ellen, he said, "Don't go down there, lady."

But she was already moving down the stairs, one hand brushing along the railing in the dark.

"Ma'am," Officer Blue Eyes called after her.

She could hear the buzzing of bees down here, too, the sound so prominent she grew a bit concerned at just how many there might be. At the bottom of the stairs, she flipped on the switch. The small basement burst with light.

Bees swarmed in the air, moving like small, inanimate objects affixed to invisible wires. Dozens of them. How the hell had they gotten down here?

There was the washer and the dryer, the utility sink whose faucet still dripped murky water into the basin even though she'd tightened those taps the last time she'd been down here. The unfinished walls with their tufts of pink insulation visible, the electrical work and ductwork networked through the walls and along the ceiling, the exposed copper pipes.

A sound among the buzzing: the soft, cottony hiccup of a whimper.

Ellen knelt down and peered beneath the utility sink. What at first looked like a jumble of unwashed laundry reconciled itself into the shape of a teenage boy curled on the floor in a fetal position. Knees hugged to his chest, ankles crossed, the boy was staring out at Ellen with eyes whose irises were just as white as the sclera, while the pupils were no bigger than pinheads. His face looked sunburned, and she could see a dark, spidery network of veins throbbing in his temples and crisscrossing his cheeks, fine as sewing thread.

*They look like they're on the outside of his body*, she thought, a tremor of revulsion barreling through her.

Urgent footfalls on the basement stairs.

"Christ, there's bees everywhere," said Officer Brown Eyes. Then he shouted up the stairwell: "Stay up there, Eddie, unless you wanna put that EpiPen to use!"

"Here," Ellen said, pointing at the boy beneath the sink. "He's here. Right here."

Officer Brown Eyes bent down beside her. "Holy shit," he said. "Hey, kid, you okay? Michael Bliss? Can you hear me?"

The boy beneath the sink said nothing. Despite those unsettling, wide-staring eyes, Ellen couldn't tell if the boy was even conscious. Or was even alive. The backs of his hands that were clutching his knees to his chest were strung through with strange purple threads. Ellen leaned forward and thought they looked like veins. On the outside.

"Gimme your hand, kid," the officer said, extending a hand of his own.

The boy did not move.

"What's wrong with his eyes?" the officer asked, maybe to her, maybe to the ether.

"He didn't keep them closed," Ellen said, the words out of her mouth before she could comprehend what she was saying. A moment later, she was thinking of what the five-year-old girl, Luna Mayer, had told her when Ellen had found her down here: *I kept my eyes closed. I kept them closed when I went through.*

Into his radio, Officer Brown Eyes told his partner that they found the kid and to call for an ambulance. Then he reached slowly beneath the utility sink and laid a gentle hand on one of the boy's knees.

The boy started screaming.

## 3

Officer Blue Eyes, deathly allergic to bees, volunteered to drive Ellen back home while the paramedics loaded the boy into the back of an ambulance. Ellen got into the passenger seat of the officer's police car just as Mr. and Mrs. Bliss pulled up in front of the Trenton house in an SUV. The boy's mother was amphetamine-thin and looked frantic, while the father strode long-legged across the yard waving his hands above his head like someone trying to signal a taxi. The boy himself—Michael Bliss—was strapped to a gurney near the open rear doors of an ambulance, his strange, discolored eyes unblinking despite the glare of the midday sun.

Ellen was grateful to not be around that scene for much longer. She sat in the passenger seat of the police car as Officer Blue Eyes, whose first name was Eddie and whose last name—Grayson—was pinned to the breast of his uniform, drove at a slow pace back down Poplar Station Road. She felt a warm, throbbing pain on her arm. She looked and saw the swollen red knob of a bee sting stretching taut the flesh beside her right elbow. It must have happened back at the Trenton house, although she hadn't felt it at the time.

"What do you think happened to him?" she asked the officer.

"Drugs, probably. Did you see his eyes?"

Ellen didn't know what sort of drugs might suck the pigment out of someone's irises, nor make someone's veins erupt through their flesh, but she didn't bring this up.

*I kept my eyes closed. I kept them closed when I went through.*

"What have you been doing there?" he asked, nodding down at Ellen's hands that were in her lap.

"What do you mean?"

Another nod of his square head. He was maybe in his late twenties, and with his sunglasses off, she thought he looked familiar. Like someone she'd seen around the neighborhood. "Your fingers," he said. "They're all bloody."

She glanced down at her hands. There was dried blood around several of her cuticles and her fingernails had been gnawed straight down to the quick. "Nervous habit," she said, suddenly self-conscious.

"They could get infected, you know, biting 'em like that." He shrugged, then added, "Not too sanitary, either."

She felt it was a strange thing for a cop to say.

"Do you live in the Cove?"

"You know, I was born in this neighborhood," Officer Grayson said. "When my folks retired to Florida, I moved back into the house where I grew up."

"Oh? Where, exactly?"

"Little green cottage on Jolene. Mom comes back to visit every summer and hangs geraniums from the porch. A nice touch to be sure—that's Mom for ya—but then I'm stuck watering them for the rest of the year."

She wasn't familiar with the house he'd described nor the surname Grayson, but that didn't mean anything; Mariner's Cove was a huge neighborhood and there were plenty of residents whom she did not know.

"Do you think your partner will lock up the house before he leaves?" she asked.

"The house?"

She frowned to herself. "It's just that I'm responsible . . ."

"Oh, sure. Right. The house. No problem there. Don't even have to worry about it."

She kept seeing that kid curled up beneath the utility sink. "I don't think I'll be able to sleep tonight."

"Kids do drugs, crazy shit happens. That basement door was locked from the outside, right? Which means the kid didn't just wander down there on his own. Which *means* one of his friends must have locked him down there."

She thought he might be wrong about that, but she said nothing.

"Whatever the case," the office concluded, "those kids are going to have a lot to answer for now." He looked at her. "You said you had a son, right?"

Had she? Yes, she supposed she'd mentioned that she had to tell Cory she was leaving with them, right?

"I do," she said. She was staring down at her bloodstained cuticles again.

"Good lesson for a kid to learn early," Officer Grayson said.

"What lesson is that?"

"Fuck around and find out," he said, then gave up a sharp, barking laugh.

A minute later, they pulled up outside her house. She caught a glimpse of Cory peering out at them from his bedroom window before retreating. She also noticed that the curtains were drawn over the bay window at the front of the house again, which was not how she'd left them.

Officer Eddie Grayson turned and looked at her. Stared, really. Then he slid the cruiser into park. Before she could pop the handle on the passenger door, he jerked his head in the direction of Mr. Zachs's house next door. "What's the deal with that guy?"

Ellen craned her neck and saw Mr. Zachs sitting on a lawn chair on his front lawn. Strange in and of itself—she'd never seen him sitting out there like that before—but stranger still was that he was facing her house and dressed in nothing but a white terrycloth bathrobe.

"His name is Bert Zachs," Ellen said. "He's lived next door to us for years. Never had an issue. But lately . . ." She shrugged, not knowing how to explain that her son had recently become wary of their neighbor for some inexplicable reason.

"If he's bothering you and your boy," said the officer, "I can have a talk with him. Set things straight."

She felt her eyebrows arch. "Straight?"

"Lay down the law. Tell him to leave the two of you alone."

"Oh," she said, and felt a sigh as potent as a yawn buoy out of her. Cory's paranoia was contagious. "I don't know if that's necessary. It's nothing like that. He's harmless."

"Hmm," said the officer.

She slipped out of the car, then poked her head back in before closing the door. "Will you let me know how things turn out?"

A small vertical line formed between the officer's eyebrows. His face was sweaty and the cleft in his chin glistened with moisture. She was trying to picture this guy watering geraniums and found that she couldn't.

"Things?" he said.

"With the Bliss boy."

"Oh. Right. Sure. The Bliss boy. *That* boy. Absolutely. I'll personally keep you posted, ma'am. Count on it."

She didn't necessarily feel good about the way he'd said that, but she thanked him nonetheless, then closed the passenger door. She stood there as the officer put the car in reverse and backed up in front of Mr. Zachs's house. Mr. Zachs, perched on that lawn chair in his bathrobe and bare feet, did not even appear to notice. When the officer got out of the car and ambled over to Mr. Zachs, the older man appeared visibly alarmed at his approach. As if he'd been asleep with his eyes open in that lawn chair and was just startled awake.

## CHAPTER TWENTY-SEVEN

# CEILING STARS

He was not stupid: he knew his mother deliberately parked her car lower in the driveway now in order to hide the fact that someone had spray-painted *the boy the boy the boy* over and over again on the blacktop there; he'd gotten down on his hands and knees one afternoon and peered underneath the car to see it. He tried to search Mr. Zachs's head to see if he had been the one to do it—Mr. Zachs had taken up in a chair in his front lawn and spent his days just staring at their house now, which made Cory feel all the more uncomfortable—but Mr. Zachs's head was nothing but a black, whirring tornado, same as last time Cory had peeked, and he couldn't glean any information from him. It was a like a TV tuned to a dead channel. The gnome didn't like to linger in there, anyway.

Maybe it had been the window repairman who had spray-painted those words on their driveway. Cory could still remember trying to peek inside that man's head only to have the gnome stopped dead in its tracks. The man—Larry—had *sensed* Cory's gnome attempting to gain access, and he had *stopped* it.

Then grinned.

And just moments before his mother had left with those two police officers, the gnome had tickled the interior of Cory's skull with a feather. Something wasn't right. He'd gone to the window as the cops led his mother to their police car, and let the gnome reach out and poke the mind of one of the officers. The information there was hazy, possibly due to the distance, but the gnome discovered that the officer wasn't feeling well, and hadn't since he'd arrived in Mariner's Cove, and frankly he just wanted to end his shift and go home. Nothing out of the ordinary there. But when he sent the gnome to poke the mind of the *other* officer, he was met by that same roadblock, that same mental dam that Larry the window guy had put up to prevent him from prying inside his mind. As Cory watched the officer slip into the police car, he caught the sight of him glancing up at the house and looking precisely at Cory's bedroom window. As if he sensed Cory's presence.

Seated now at the desk in his bedroom, he pulled up the photos he'd taken of the symbols on his phone, and scrolled through them one by one. They still bothered him on some deep, subconscious level, but he had no idea why. However, he had read enough young adult detective novels to know that sometimes when something gnawed at you for some inexplicable reason, it often meant that it was a thing there to be solved, like a clue or the missing piece of a jigsaw puzzle that required assembly. So that was exactly what he decided to do: he sharpened a pencil with his Wolverine pencil sharpener, then pulled out a pad of tracing paper from his desk drawer. He studied the images on his phone, then traced each symbol onto its own sheet of paper. He did this diligently, his tongue propped in the corner of his mouth, his ten-year-old brow furrowed in concentration. When he was done with a particular drawing, he set the page aside and moved on to a fresh sheet of tracing paper, and proceeded to draw the next symbol. He did this over and over and over again, until he heard the front door close on its frame at the far end of the house.

"Mom?" he called, his voice echoing throughout the otherwise empty house.

On his desk, his phone buzzed.

A text from Davey:

come out

Those two words instilled within him a seed of fear that made the hair along the nape of his neck go prickly and stiff. He could still hear Mr. Zachs repeating them over and over inside his head as the man tried to get him to open the front door.

come out

His mother poked her head in his bedroom. "You doing okay, baby?"

"Yeah. What happened with the police?"

"Hey, you know your mom. Everybody needs my help. I'm practically a superhero around here."

He gave her a smile, but he knew she was covering up something. Something she didn't want him to know. Why had the police come to the house? Why had he sensed something . . . off . . . about one of them?

"What are you doing?" she asked, coming into the room.

"Just drawing." He absently slid one hand over the pages so that she wouldn't be able to see them.

"What are you thinking for dinner?" she asked.

He thought about Mr. Zachs sitting in that chair on his front lawn, watching their house. He thought, too, of all those symbols spread around the neighborhood, chalked in the street, spray-painted on signs and mailboxes, those two words—

*(the boy the boy the boy)*

—emblazoned on their driveway.

"Let's go out for dinner," he suggested, wanting nothing more than to get away from the neighborhood for a while. He summoned up some enthusiasm and said, "Pink Penguin!"

His mother pulled a face, tongue lolling out. She even crossed her eyes, trying to make him laugh, which he knew was her way of pretending she wasn't so stressed out and upset. She kept saying she wasn't scared, but he knew that she was. Lately, she'd been biting her fingernails until her fingers bled. "Pink Penguin again, dude? Seriously?"

"It's my favorite."

"All right. Just let me jump in the shower."

When she left, he looked back at the symbols he'd reproduced on the tracing paper. He saw that the way he'd drawn them, all those symbols, they could all overlap, could fit together snuggly just like pieces of a puzzle, or even individual sections of some machine. This brought to mind the Martian war machine from his nightmares. Was that what they were meant to be?

He placed the pages atop each other then held them all up in front of the gooseneck lamp on his desk. The lamplight shining through, the symbols all layered perfectly together. They somehow seemed to *fit.* Their assemblage meant nothing to him—it looked like nothing specific, and there was no *ah ha* in his head upon seeing it—yet there was an undeniable harmony to the way the symbols seemed to engage one another. Even at ten years old, Cory could see it.

His phone buzzed again. Another text from Davey, urging him to come out. That phrase did not sit well with Cory. He texted Davey back:

> What's going on?

Davey responded:

> lets play cory

Then:

> come out come out come out come out come out

*Wherever you are,* Cory thought, then texted back:

> Stop being weird. I think those drawings on the sidewalk mean something.

Davey responded:

> tell me what they mean

Cory considered the sketches he'd made on the tracing paper, splayed out now on his desk, and texted back:

> I think they're pieces of a puzzle. I think they all go together somehow.

To which Davey texted back:

> come out come out come out

Something wasn't right. He was about to text Davey back, but then he stopped himself. Thought for a minute. Wrote:

> You're texting the same thing Mr. Zachs has been saying to me. In my head, I think. Why are you saying it now?

He hit send.

Then waited.

Waited.

Waited for Davey to respond.

When he didn't, Cory got up from his desk and went to his bedroom window. He peeled a section of the shade away and peered out across the street at the Orem house. He was worried he might find Davey sitting out there on his lawn, staring at the house, much like Mr. Zachs was currently doing next door. But there was no sign of Davey across the street. Not even the silhouette of him in his bedroom window. The Orem house looked sleepy and dark, like no one was home.

Cory needed help. He knew this on some subterranean level. Something was happening in Mariner's Cove and Cory felt like he and his mother might very well be involved somehow.

*No, not just involved,* he thought, scanning Cloister Road for any sign of Davey Orem. *Maybe we're the target.*

But of what? And for what reason?

He needed help.

*Uncle Brian.*

Cory turned away from the window and looked over at the corkboard above his desk. There was a photo pinned to the board of him on Uncle Brian's shoulders. He was old enough now to understand Uncle Brian had some sort of problem with drinking alcohol, and that his—

*(car accident)*

—drinking had soured the relationship between his uncle and his mother. Uncle Brian had lived with them for a time two years ago, but after the—

*(car accident)*

—incident, Cory's mom had forced him to leave. There'd even been a fight, an argument, and he remembered his mother refusing to even let Uncle Brian back in the house after the incident. Cory remembered sitting on his bed crying silently while his mother shouted at Uncle Brian. And once Uncle Brian left, he could hear his mother weeping audibly and slamming cupboards and doors.

He looked up at his ceiling, and at the constellation of glow-in-the-dark stars glued there. Uncle Brian had put them there during the time he'd stayed with them. The morning after, Cory had woken up in bed with a star stuck to his forehead. He hadn't noticed at first, wandering out into the living room where his mom and Uncle Brian were having their coffee, the star, unbeknownst to him, still stuck to his forehead. Uncle Brian had thought this to be just about the funniest thing in the world, and he started calling him Chicken Little, because, ha ha, the sky was falling. Cory, a little embarrassed at first, eventually warmed up to the name. He'd even punched a hole in the plastic glow-in-the-dark star and threaded an old shoelace through it, making a necklace for his uncle.

*Does he still have it? Does he still wear it?*

Cory hadn't wanted Uncle Brian to leave, but he'd been young, and what could he say to stop his mother? How could he express how he felt? His father had died in a car accident so long ago that Cory had no real memory of the man, so for the time Uncle Brian had stayed here with them, it had been almost like he'd had a father, or something very close to one. At the time, he hadn't understood any of it. Even now, he wasn't too sure he understood it.

He climbed onto his bed and laid his head against his pillow. Reaching over, he pulled the shade down over his window, making the room not completely dark but somewhere in the vicinity of gloomy. Above him, those stars glowed with a cool, yellow-green hue. He stared at them for a long time, and when he finally closed his eyes, the pattern of them remained glowing on the underside of his eyelids. He felt the gnome stir within the vast canyon of his brain. *Find Uncle Brian,* he instructed it, and the gnome did a curious thing: instead of extending outward as it did when Cory wanted to probe someone's head and get a view of their thoughts, the gnome retreated to some deep chasm inside him, way back within the far reaches of Cory's brain. It wasn't hiding from him—Cory could tell if the gnome was ever skittish about anything, and it rarely was—but it was hunkering down, ruminating, contemplative.

A pencil rolled off Cory's desk.

Tracing paper rippled like ocean waves.

The bulb in the gooseneck lamp grew brighter, brighter, brighter, until the filament pop-sizzled and the bulb went dark.

*Please please please please please,* he thought, eyelids still squeezed shut, sweat spilling down the sides of his face. He centralized all his thoughts into the *idea* of Uncle Brian, the sheer *concept* of him. He didn't know if that was how it worked, but it was all he could think of to do. *Please please please please please.*

Because he knew something bad was headed his way.

And a part of him also knew that only Uncle Brian could help him.

# CHAPTER TWENTY-EIGHT
# A PSYCHIC DISTRESS CALL

## 1

Brian Russo needed a drink. It had been five hundred forty-seven days since he'd fallen off the wagon, when Lily Ming had to assist him into his one-room apartment above her father's Chinese restaurant, and every day since then had been a struggle to stay sober, but he had done it. There was always the persistent tickle at the back of his throat, the gulping urge to crack open a bottle of something, of anything, and take a drink. Just one drink. Maybe two.

Since that relapse, he'd been able to stave it off. But look at him now: maneuvering skittishly along the outskirts of some Podunk town in Illinois or Indiana or wherever the hell he was at the moment, trolling for a lighted beer sign in a smoky window, a tavern that promised two-for-one shots, a fucking Mexican restaurant with margarita specials, or anything that possessed even the remotest possibility of serving alcohol. He knew his resolve was weak, and if he waltzed into any of those establishments, he would sidle up to the bar and order whatever the fuck he thought might quelch the desperation that lingered in the back of his throat.

Why was the drive to drink suddenly so all-encompassing? Because he was losing his mind? Hell, if he was going to self-destruct, he might as well enjoy himself in the process. The dreams were bad enough: a cross-country migration plagued by a series of paralyzing, kaleidoscopic nightmares, where he'd jerk upright in whatever seedy motor lodge bed he had rented for the night, panting as if he'd just gone ten rounds in a heavyweight title bout. Sometimes with a nosebleed. But even in his waking hours, while driving or having lunch at some rest stop along Route 70 or wherever the hell he was, he was constantly sensitive to the fact that something from those nightmares was seeping into the real world. Bleeding in through cracks, much like the demons that had come for him in the rehab facility, which he had been thinking about lately, too. The nightmares themselves were awful enough, but worse was the nearly physical sensation that they left behind upon waking. The residue. Something about those nightmares felt deliberate. Something about them felt . . .

Felt . . .

Well, fuck. What did he know? Was he really going to flush eighteen months of sobriety down the toilet because of a few bad dreams? A sizzle in his brain in Denver, Colorado; a scream snared in the trap of his throat in Topeka, Kansas; jolting awake with a blistering case of the night-sweats in Columbia, Missouri, or wherever the hell he'd been at the time: it seemed like every leg of his journey had been plagued by some barely remembered nightmare.

But they weren't just nightmares, were they? They weren't just bad dreams.

He flipped down the visor and glanced at the photo of Cory on his shoulders. Jesus Christ, if it didn't feel like there was something out there in the ether reeling his thoughts back toward the boy, over and over again . . .

He saw it up ahead: a slouch-roofed building in a gravel parking lot, a Budweiser sign in the window. It was the only building in the whole plaza, as if it gave off bad vibes that had caused all the other local businesses to pack up and move away. The sun was setting behind the building, causing a nimbus of radiant light to surround it. The place looked illuminated for his convenience.

He pulled into the lot, pine-scented air fresheners and plastic dashboard hula dancers rocking as he applied the brakes. Shut down the engine. His mind was reeling and his skin was beginning to crawl, so he sat there in the van for a while thinking about the inside of that bar and not moving. Thinking about the bar itself. Thinking maybe one drink wouldn't matter because there was no one here to know about it except himself. And he certainly wasn't anyone to pass judgment.

He permitted himself one last glance at the photo clipped to the visor before hopping out of the van.

The place was quiet, with just a handful of patrons scattered about and keeping to themselves. No jukebox, no music, so it wasn't totally cliché, but Brian still felt a pulse of . . . well, let's be honest . . . of familiarity and comfort just walking through the door. No denying it now: it felt like coming home. Last time he'd been in a bar had been eighteen months earlier, and poor Lily Ming had seen to his wellbeing before her father discovered what a degenerate he was. What a fucking slouch, what a fucking perpetual disappointment. The only way to rid himself of those nefarious thoughts now was to drink them away.

There was a little glass display case beside the entryway filled with T-shirts, shot glasses, beer steins, and mugs with the bar's name, Giddy Up, on them. There was a deck of playing cards in there, too, with the painting of a Conestoga wagon on the box. Above the display case was a taxidermy snake, skin as black as tar, curled around a forked branch. It hung on a wooden plaque on the wall at eye-level, so that Brian recoiled the slightest bit upon seeing it, mistaking it for alive.

The bartender was cute: slim-waisted, busty, and with a fringe of raven-colored hair arcing over her sleek, black eyebrows that hinted at a darker, gothic side. Twenty-five, tops. Brian sat, smiled at her, drummed a set of fingers on the sticky, lacquered bar top.

"What'll it be?" asked the cute bartender.

Brian had already taken inventory of the booze along the wall behind the bar. "Jameson." Just saying it caused him to salivate.

"Neat or on the rocks?"

"Dealer's choice."

She grabbed a fresh rocks glass and a bottle, poured the drink, then set it down in front of him on a coaster that had some law firm's logo on it.

"What's that?" she asked, nodding at his neck.

He glanced down, not sure what she was talking about at first. But then he saw it dangling there just below the hollow of his throat, where it had been for the past two years: a plastic glow-in-the-dark star on a length of shoestring. Even now, it glowed a cool yellow-green in the dimness of the bar.

"A little souvenir from my nephew," he said.

"That's sweet. How old is he?"

He did the quick math in his head. "Ten, now. Though he was eight when he gave it to me."

"Are you traveling to see him?"

"How do you know I'm traveling?"

"This is a local dive, honey. I've never seen you in here before. What's your nephew's name?"

"Cory."

"Cute name."

He was thinking of Cory's voice booming through his head, the barrage of nightmares he'd been suffering, weighing down on him like rusted, broken armor.

He stared at the whiskey in the rocks glass, which he hadn't yet touched. Just stared. How easy it was to fall back into old habits. How simple it was to look down and see his pitiable reflection looking back up from the surface of the whiskey in that glass.

What the fuck was he doing?

"Do you think . . ." he began, but then he found that he couldn't complete the thought.

"Do I think what?" the bartender asked.

He considered. Waved a dismissive hand. Wasn't sure exactly what he'd meant to say. Something inside his head felt funny, like a blister growing and growing and growing until it threatened to pop: he could feel the pressure of it building against the interior walls of his skull.

"You doing okay there, buddy?" the bartender asked.

"I think I've got a migraine coming—"

A bolt of lightning caromed through his cerebral cortex; he felt it not as pain but as a vast, propulsive light, ever-expanding. Within that light was a tornado of sound and thought, of wind whipping, coming—

*(PLEASE COME PLEASE UNCLE BRIAN PLEASE)*

—from nowhere and everywhere all at once. He clutched his head in both hands and winced.

"Jesus," he uttered, and leaned back on his stool. His vision went blurry with tears. The sound that whined and tittered out of him must have sounded like a laugh, but it was far from it.

The bartender leaned over the bar, her face coming to rest mere inches from his own. For a second, he thought she was going to kiss him, ridiculous as that would have been. But the expression on her face told him otherwise.

"Your nose is bleeding, man," she said.

He glanced down in time to see a dollop of blood plink through the surface of the whiskey in the rocks glass.

"Shit."

She handed him a wad of napkins from behind the bar, which he used to blot his bleeding nose. As he did so, he glanced around the room, eyeballing all the other patrons who were hunched over tables or curled like vultures on their barstools. When he saw that the bartender was still staring at him, he said, "Did you hear that?"

"Hear what?"

"I . . . I don't know . . ."

He looked at the balled up, bloodied napkins in his hand.

Looked at the whiskey, too, with its drop of blood simmering on the surface.

He was losing his fucking mind, all right.

In a trembling voice, he said, "Hey, listen, I'm sorry, but I can't drink this. I'll pay for it, but can I get a Coke instead? And maybe a menu? I should probably eat something."

She was looking at him funny now. Why wouldn't she?

"No prob," she said, and slid away from him.

His brain was broken.

He was falling apart.

He'd had an AA sponsor back in El Segundo, a pock-faced, sallow-skinned fellow named Gideon, and Gideon always said, *Sometimes the desire to drink outweighs the desire to live. Don't forget that, and don't give in to it.*

When the bartender returned with a menu, he said, "Hey, where am I?"

"I thought planet Earth, but now I'm wondering," she responded.

"Like, the name of the town. This town. This state. I don't know where I am."

"You're in luxurious Gideon, Indiana, man."

"Well, that's one hell of a coincidence."

"Yeah?" she said, though didn't ask for an explanation as she rolled down the bar to see to another customer.

He took out his phone and googled AA meetings in Gideon, Indiana. Found one for later that evening in the basement of the Baptist church on Decatur Street, which was only a few blocks over from the bar, according to the map. That was a little over an hour from now. He could wait it out. He'd be okay. He'd make it.

*That was Cory's voice I just heard in my head. Cory's voice calling my name again.*

Was it an aneurysm? Was he dying?

The bartender returned with a glass of Coke and a menu.

"You know, I'm not very hungry anymore," he said, sliding the menu back to her. "I think I'll just sip on this Coke for a while."

"You're a man of strong convictions," she said, slipping the menu back beneath the bar. "Just let me know if I can get you anything else."

"In fact, you can," he said. He lifted the wad of paper towels and blotted his nose again. The bleeding had already begun to slow. "I'd like to buy one of those shot glasses in the display case by the door. The deck of cards there, too."

"Hey, whatever you want, man," she said. But she was still looking at him funny.

Brian didn't care: his head was still reverberating with the disembodied child-voice that had cannonballed through his skull and so he barely heard her anyway.

# 2

After attending the AA meeting, he rented a dingy little room at a motor inn along Interstate 70. His appetite had returned, so he grabbed some fast food and devoured it while sitting upright on the uncomfortable little bed, watching infomercials on TV. When he was done eating and sucked the last of the Diet Coke through his straw, he shut off the TV, stripped down to his underwear, and carried a small plastic giftbag with him into the bathroom.

He turned on the cold water tap in the tub but didn't put in the stopper. The sound of running water sometimes helped, but even that had been years ago, and it had stopped working for him ever since that distant star in his head had winked out of existence. Nonetheless, he listened to the stream of cold water rushing into the tub and gurgling down the drain for a while, just standing there in his underwear with his eyes half closed, his skin prickling into gooseflesh, and that little plastic giftbag in one hand.

After a time, he sat cross-legged on the bathroom floor and opened the bag. He took out the shot glass first, setting it on the rim of the tub. It had the name of the bar, Giddy Up, printed on the side in a stylized red font that resembled a length of rope. He took out the deck of playing cards next, peeled away the cellophane, then shook the deck out into the palm of his hand. That Conestoga wagon looked like it might roll right off those cards and onto the bathroom floor. Absently, he shuffled the cards for an unknowable amount of time.

He kept hearing that voice—*Cory's* voice—inside his head. What exactly had he experienced back at the bar? A psychic distress call from his nephew halfway across the country? That hardly seemed likely. On the other hand, they say people often smell burning toast or oranges when they've had a stroke, so why not hear voices from the past instead? It seemed just as plausible. Because thinking his brain might slowly be breaking down made a whole lot more sense than . . . well, than whatever else it could mean. Maybe the effect of all those drugs was finally catching up to him.

But it wasn't any of those things.

He knew that it wasn't.

He didn't have Ellen's number in his current phone; her number had vanished the night he'd gotten drunk and lost his previous cell phone. Anyway, she'd blocked all his calls long ago, so she likely wouldn't have answered had he called. He had no other way to reach her, to speak to her to see if Cory was all right.

It was a full day's drive from here to Ellen and Cory's house in Maryland. What was the name of their neighborhood, again?

"Mariner's Cove." He said it aloud to the empty bathroom.

He set the cards down on the bathroom floor then focused all his attention on the shot glass. No distant light ignited in the farthest reaches of his skull, but he attempted to move the glass nonetheless. The sound of the running water soothed him, assisted him, but it was futile: he stared at that glass for so long that by the time he quit, his head was aching and his nose was dribbling blood in a shiny crimson thread down the center of his bare chest.

He picked up the deck of cards next. Shuffled it one more time for good measure. Then he concentrated on the top card. Put a finger on it, as if he might glean something from it simply by touch.

Thought, *Ten of diamonds.*

Turned the card over.

Suicide king.

He went through the whole deck this way, one card at a time. And when he was done, he started over. And when he was done again, he started over again.

## 3

He was nodding off with his head against the toilet seat, the deck of cards splayed out like an accordion along the bathroom floor, when he finally decided to stop for the night. He shut off the water in the tub, dropped the shot glass back into the plastic giftbag, and gathered up the cards. His back had gone stiff, causing him to wince as he rose on unsteady legs.

When he stepped out of the bathroom, he saw daylight burning down the part between the window drapes. He'd been in that bathroom the entire night; no wonder he was so exhausted.

There'd been no more disembodied voices shouting in his head. Now, in his exhaustion, what had happened back at the bar seemed as insubstantial as one of his nightmares. Yes, it was a full day's drive to his sister's place in Maryland, but he doubted she'd welcome him with open arms. Besides, he had a job waiting for him in New York.

*Sleep on it*, he told himself, dropping down onto the bed. The mattress was stiff and unyielding, but he was so tired that he didn't care. *Sleep on it and see how you feel when you wake up. Make a decision about what to do once you wake up—Maryland or New York? The lady or the tiger? But not now. Now is for sleep. Now is for stopping the pounding in your head. Decisions are best left for tomorrow. Besides, Cory is fine. This is all just a manifestation of your guilt, you son of a bitch. That's all it is.*

*That's all.*

He fell asleep trying to convince himself of that.

# CHAPTER TWENTY-NINE

# RIGHTNESS: GEORGETTE, ALEX, AND STINGER

## 1

*There is rightness here,* thought Georgette Braswell. *So good, so good.*

It was still early enough in the morning so that the sun hadn't fully risen, though the eastern horizon was striated with bands of pink and orange that bled through the dense foliage of the heavy summer trees. Georgette had no idea how long the three of them had been out here toiling away at the base of the water tower—she'd lost all concept of time, it seemed—yet she thought this might have been the second sunset she'd witnessed since she and Alex had joined their odd new companion here in the woods of Gladstone Park. They'd been working nonstop, serving themselves up as a glistening, sweat-seasoned banquet for hordes of bloodthirsty mosquitos. (They paused only once, when they were all suddenly and inexplicably overcome by a sharp, iron-hot pain in their bellies; but whatever had caused it, the pain had quickly dissipated.) Georgette's arms were braille-like and itchy with mosquito bites, as were Alex's; they both kept absently swatting at the air and slapping their hands against the bloodsuckers impaled in their flesh. Still, she didn't think they looked even half as bad as the man who called himself Stinger.

She wasn't sure what to make of Stinger, except that he *had* solved Alex's problem. After their serendipitous meeting, he'd taken them to a storage shed in the woods where he'd been hoarding additional rolls of chain-link fencing. Alex had dropped to his knees at the sight of them, had run his hands over their rusted links, eliciting a vague jangling sound that seemed to echo against the cinderblock walls of that confined, tomblike interior. Stinger had seemed pleased by Alex's perceived supplication before those rolls of chain-link, and even Georgette had to admit that something about it had just felt so *right*.

Now, they had spent unknowable hours rigging the sections of the chain-link fence into place around the base of the water tower. It was tedious, difficult work, the chain-link sections themselves continuously curling or falling over and just overall refusing to cooperate. After growing frustrated with these struggles, Stinger hoofed it back to the storage shed only to return with some bungee cords and heavy-duty chains, which they used to secure the sections of fencing around the tower's legs.

How Stinger could have shared the same obsession with her husband, Georgette did not know. In fact, how she *herself* had found herself sucked into Alex's obsession remained a mystery to her. She wondered if it had something to do with the dream she and Alex had shared the night after she'd followed him to the water tower and discovered what he'd been doing with all that string.

Georgette stood at the base of the water tower. Wincing at the javelins of sunlight breaking through the trees, she took a few steps back, shielding the glare from her eyes as she looked up. The water tower was a tremendous thing, particularly when standing right beneath it. How was it possible to live so close to something for so many years without ever really *seeing* it? She supposed that was the way of things—that you never really looked at the trees you drove past on your way to work, or the names of all the streets once you left your neighborhood. Autopilot.

The intricacy of the water tower surprised her. Prior to this strange business, had she been asked to draw a picture of the Gladstone Park water tower—or any water tower, for that matter—she would have simply sketched a cylindrical tank held aloft on tripod-like legs. But this close, she could see that there was much more to it than that. There was that phrase printed along the side of the bone-colored water tank, something she had seen nearly every day of her daily life that she had become oblivious to it. Only now, given their current circumstance, did the missive on the tower appear to have deeper meaning:

MARINER'S COVE
*Come join us!*

There was a railing and a narrow walkway that wound around the circumference of the tank, adorned with tiny lights. At its top sat a crown of antennas connected to a braid of cables that trailed down the side of the tank and down one of the legs. It looked like a bit of space-age machinery, something from a Ridley Scott film, and looking up at it now, she began to feel that same tremor of anxiety that she'd also felt in her dream.

*It's like I'm dreaming right now,* she thought, *and none of this makes a goddamn bit of sense. Yet there is rightness here. We are moving in the right direction, making whatever it is that we're supposed to make. I can't explain it, and I don't even understand it, but I can certainly* feel *it.*

She backed up now until her buttocks struck the wooden split rail fence that surrounded the large, graveled floor beneath the tower. She lowered herself onto the top rail and sat there, somewhat content. Beneath the soles of her sneakers, the ground seemed to hum as if with some buried current. An electrical substation sat just beyond the trees, she knew, but she also knew that this subtle, current-like hum moving through the ground and in the air and through her bones had nothing to do with it.

She cradled the colander in both hands.

It was *hers* now. It felt *right.* Perhaps having taken it from her daughter was the reason she'd shared that first dream with Alex—was the reason she'd suddenly been *incorporated* into that dream herself. Yes, Denise had been there, too, and she'd been wearing the colander on her head as a helmet, but maybe that was just a residual dream-state afterimage. In truth, she couldn't explain *any* of this. All she knew was that she and Alex were where they were supposed to be, doing what they were supposed to be doing. And that she was glad the girls were now far enough away from all of it. At least for a while.

Alex and Stinger were halfway up the legs of the tower to the tank at the top. There was a steel ladder that descended from the tank that ran flush against one of the tower's legs, and Alex balanced upon one of the rungs of the ladder now while bracing a section of chain-link fence into place. Like a monkey or maybe a rat, Stinger had forgone the ladder and had simply scaled the sections of chain-link that were already fixed into place around the base. Stinger carried lengths of that heavy chain looped around his shoulder, which he and Alex used to tie the fencing into place, secured between two of the tower's legs.

To Georgette, the whole thing resembled a science project she had made with her father when she was in the fifth grade. It was one of the few good memories she had of her father, the hours spent together at the kitchen table constructing a model volcano out of chicken wire and papier-mâché. When it was completed, it spewed a bubbling torrent of baking soda from the top, which her father had dyed orange with food coloring. She had won first prize in the science fair that year, and when she'd returned home from, her father had hugged her and said, "Good job, Georgie, good job." Somewhere, back at the house, she still had the ribbon.

She looked down at the metal bowl in her hands. It was dented in places, but she had buffed it to a commendable shine. The distorted reflection of her face stared up at her, nothing more than a Picasso of blurry colors and an undisciplined outline. Lifting it up, she held it against the horizon so that the rays of the early morning sun bled through the colander's holes, as if they were countless stars that she had unwittingly caught at the bottom of the metal strainer.

It was around noon when Alex and Stinger climbed back down from the tower. They spoke in low voices to each other while staring up at their handiwork, their hands on their hips, eyes squinting against the sunlight. There hadn't been enough chain-link to reach all the way up to the tank itself, but they'd come damn close. Absently, Georgette wondered if the next step would be to cover it in papier-mâché then pour baking soda into the tank. *Good job, Georgie. Good job.* This thought made her giggle behind her hand, momentarily attracting both her husband's and Stinger's attention.

"I'm exhausted," Alex said, ambling over to her. He'd quit wearing the latex gloves because they made his hands sweat, not to mention it was too difficult to manipulate the sections of fence, but his palms, outstretched for her to see, were lacerated and bleeding. Stinger came up behind him, peering absently down at his own hands. Sweat cloaked them, and their faces were sunburnt and wind-chapped, which didn't help the already grotesque appearance of Stinger's lumpy face. The guy looked like he'd recently been pelted by BBs shot from an air rifle. She had noticed, while working alongside him on the lower tier of fencing, that each time he flexed his muscles to wrestle a section of the chain-link fence into place, a mixture of blood and greenish pus would ooze from the heads of the swollen red nodules along his arms. Georgette would have found this revolting had there not been so much work to get done. The work was more important than anything else.

Also, the colander. That was of supreme importance. Unfortunately, she didn't know what she was supposed to do with it yet, or even *why* it was important.

"What do you think?" Alex said, out of breath. Each time he inhaled, the divot at the base of his neck deepened. Georgette could see bloody handprints along the hips of his jeans. Those thick and uncooperative metal wires were bastards, all right.

"I think it looks great," she said.

"No," Alex said, shaking his head. He peered back at the monstrosity they'd spent the past however many hours constructing. "It looks *right*. I mean . . . doesn't it?"

"It does," agreed Stinger. "Wish we had more fencing, though. It seems like it should go all the way to the top." He rubbed at his welt-lumpy chin. "There's a fence up by the elementary school. I could drive by there tonight with some bolt cutters."

"There's fencing around the electrical substation just past those trees, too," Georgette suggested, nodding her head in that direction.

"That's right," Stinger said, his eyes widening. A grin curled one corner of his mouth. "It's got barbed wire at the top, so we'll just have to be careful."

"Do you really think it needs to go all the way to the top?" Alex asked. He had removed the small notepad from his rear pocket and was flipping through its pages now.

"I do," said Stinger. He didn't bother to look at Alex or the notepad. He was staring up at the tower.

"So do I," said Georgette, and Alex glanced at her. Despite the exhaustion and sweat on his face, his eyes sparkled like diamonds. Wasn't it so recently that she had thought something wrong with him? She couldn't remember the exact details now, which seemed funny. Anyway, it was silly and pointless to consider such a thing now. Alex had never looked so happy, so healthy. *So right*, she thought.

Alex nodded, and she thought she saw a faint smile playing at the corners of his mouth, too.

"What about this?" Georgette asked, holding up the colander again so that the sunlight could dazzle its way through the grid of tiny holes.

"Or what about any of this other stuff, for that matter?" Alex said, glancing back down at his little notepad. "That colander is only one item represented in these drawings. What about all the other ones?"

"It'll all come together," promised Stinger.

"I think I want to go back home and work on the puzzle some more," Alex said. He seemed sad to say it, like a kid who knows it's time to leave the candy store. Georgette watched as he glanced forlornly up at the tower. "I mean, I think it's necessary."

"There's a lot of stuff that's necessary," said Stinger.

*He talks so confidently, like he knows more than he's telling us,* Georgette thought, deliberately transmitting the thought into Alex's head. Alex's gaze flicked briefly in her direction, then returned to the images in his notepad. Stinger, on the other hand, turned to face her and let his gaze linger much longer. The sight of him looking at her made her body grow cold.

"We're missing so many pieces," Alex said, turning the pages of his notepad. "How do we find them?"

"We'll find them," Stinger said. "Here, let me see that notepad."

Alex handed Stinger the notepad and Stinger riffled hurriedly through the pages, as if he was searching for one drawing in particular. He possessed none of the reverence that Alex did when he went through the pages. Ultimately, Stinger stopped on a specific page and held it out so that Alex could see it. Stinger asked him what it was supposed to be.

Alex shrugged. "That's the problem. I don't know what *any* of them are supposed to be. I think it looks like a beachball."

"A beachball?" said Stinger.

"Let me see it," Georgette said, setting the colander in her lap. Stinger handed her the notepad (she was careful not to let his fingers graze hers) and she looked at the drawing. A circle with a series of spokes crisscrossing at the circle's center:

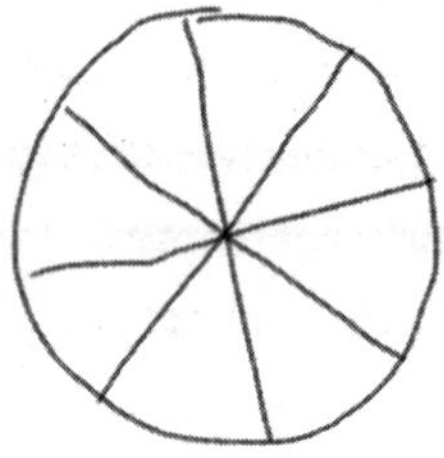

It seemed pretty obvious to her.

"It looks like the wheel of a bicycle," she said. Then she looked up sharply at Alex. "The girls have bikes in the garage at home. We could take one of the wheels off, bring it here."

"I don't think it works that way," said Stinger, plucking the notepad from Georgette's hand. She saw that he had left bloody fingerprints on the page. "Things are already set in motion. Those other pieces are out there already, and they're like . . . charged, you know? Primed and ready to go. Just like your colander."

"Primed by what?" Georgette asked. She recalled the bloody towel disappearing beneath it, and she wondered why such a thing hadn't happened again.

Stinger shrugged. He looked suddenly disinterested.

"Maybe instead of finding these pieces," Alex suggested, "we find the person who's been drawing them all over the neighborhood. That might explain a lot."

"We'll get there, for sure," Stinger said. "Can I hang onto this?"

"My notepad?" Alex said. He seemed unsure how he should answer and even glanced briefly at Georgette as if to seek guidance. But then he said, "Yeah, okay. I've got other drawings of them back home. I've been sketching quite a bit lately."

"What about my colander?" Georgette wanted to know.

"Beats me," Stinger said, tucking Alex's notepad into the rear pocket of his workpants. Some of the welts along the left side of his face and neck had begun to bleed again. It seemed he couldn't stop scratching them. "Maybe we won't know until more of it comes together."

"And how do we do that?" Alex asked. "Bring all the pieces together, I mean."

After a moment of deliberation, Stinger said, "I think I might have an idea." Then he looked Georgette and Alex over. Georgette thought Stinger's eyes looked yellow, even more so than Alex's. She didn't like how long they seemed to linger on her, either. "In the meantime," he announced, his voice gruff, "why don't you folks head home and get some rest? We've been at this for a while, and we're all exhausted."

"I'm not tired," Alex said . . . yet the words nearly wheezed out of him. They hadn't eaten or slept, and Georgette suddenly realized that they were all probably dehydrated, too.

"You can work on your puzzle at home," Stinger suggested. "After all, what good is finding all the remaining pieces if we don't know how they fit together?"

Georgette's eyes scaled back up to the top of the water tower, which now looked so much like the beginning stage of her fifth-grade science project, and thought, once more, *There is rightness here. So good, so good.* They were on the right track, whatever that track might be.

She grabbed Alex around the wrist and said, "He's right. Let's go home for a bit."

## 2

Once they were walking across the baseball diamond toward Poplar Station Road, and well out of Stinger's earshot, Georgette said, "He can hear our thoughts, too, you know."

Alex glanced at her, and she was reminded of the way his eye sockets glowed with a dim, electric light in her nightmare.

"I just assumed he could," Alex said, and then said nothing more.

## 3

They made love for the first time in months, and with a frenetic, ravenous compulsion that channeled their earliest days as newlyweds. Afterwards, reeking of sex, they collapsed in a heap of tangled, sweaty limbs on the mattress where they slept like the dead.

## 4

It was the same dream as before, only this time Denise was no longer in it. Even in her dream-state, this realization flooded Georgette with relief. And when she touched her head, she found that it was *she* who wore the colander as a helmet.

## 5

Sometime later, when Georgette awoke, she found Alex's side of the bed empty. She leaned over and saw that the colander was on the nightstand next to her side of the bed. Just where she'd left it.

Naked, sore, and gratified, she climbed off the sodden mattress and glided across the floorboards to the bathroom. There, she filled up the sink with cold water then stuck her whole face down into it. The frigid temperature caused the flesh along her back and arms to tighten and the small hairs along the nape of her neck to stiffen. She remembered her dream, and how Denise had no longer been there. Stinger had, though—she recognized him readily enough as she and Alex broke through the trees of Gladstone Park and stepped out into the clearing that housed the water tower. Stinger, with his lumpy, bug-stung face and weeping sores, turned his head and grinned at her from across the moonlit clearing. His eyes glowed like fireflies.

Back in the bedroom, she tied a silk robe about her frame, though not before examining her reflection in the mirrored surface of the closet door. She had lost at least fifteen pounds over the course of a handful of days. *That's what no food for days on end will get you,* she thought to herself as she lashed the belt of her silk robe about her waist. *Crash diet and exercise regimented by stress, compulsion, and obsession. Not to mention vivid nightmares and dose of telepathy.*

Down in Alex's study, she found her husband standing before the wall that was papered with sketches of symbols on sheets of graph paper. Alex was still naked from their lovemaking and, upon walking into the room, she was surprised and a bit embarrassed to find that he was still in a state of arousal. Yet Alex didn't seem to notice; he stood with one hand on his hip while he rubbed at his forehead with the other, scrutinizing the collage of drawings pinned up on the wall before him.

"I thought I had it . . . but then it left me again," he said, still rubbing his forehead.

"You had a dream, didn't you." It wasn't a question; she knew this with certainty.

He looked at her. His shadow was behind him, stretched out along the far wall in a panel of fading daylight. The shape of it reminded Georgette of those long-limbed aliens at the end of *Close Encounters of the Third Kind.* "I had the same dream as you. Again."

"Not exactly the same," she corrected.

He nodded. "That's right. Denise wasn't there anymore."

"That's good, isn't it?"

"I don't know. I hope so."

"That guy Stinger *was* there."

"Right." Alex sawed a finger back and forth across his chin. "I guess everyone else in that dream is someone, too. I tried to see their faces, but they were all blurry."

"Maybe you can't see their faces until you meet them in real life."

"Anything's possible at this point, I guess." His eyes jittered away from her and returned to the drawings on the wall. His erection bobbed like an angler's lure. He folded his arms across his chest and said, "I can see a pattern here, but it doesn't make any sense. It comes together for me when I'm dreaming—a different sort of dream than the one you and I are having together—but when I wake up . . ."

"You can no longer remember it," she finished for him.

"That's right."

She pointed to one of the drawings. "You know, the more I look at—"

The phone in the living room rang, startling them both. It rang again. After it rang a third time, Georgette realized she and Alex were both just standing there staring at each other like a couple of fools, so she darted into the living room and scooped up the portable from the kitchen counter.

"You're not answering your cell phone," said a woman's voice over the line.

"Uh, hello?" Georgette stammered. "Who's this?"

"Are you kidding me? What the heck is going *on* over there, G?"

Georgette blinked. Her eyeballs felt dry and itchy. "Tina?"

"Why haven't you been answering your phone?"

She swallowed a dry lump in her throat, then said, "I guess I had the ringer turned off."

"Jesus." Tina Jarrett exhaled loudly into the phone. "Are you alone?"

"Alone?"

"Is Alex there, or is he . . . well, out?"

"Alex is here. Was there something you wanted, Tina?"

"Seriously, G? I've been calling your cell and leaving you messages for days. I even came by the house, but no one was home. Not even the girls."

"They're staying with Alex's mom for a while."

"Where have you been?"

"Just busy, I guess."

"Do you know the sort of things that have been whirling around in my mind? I even considered calling the police."

"Calling the police for what?"

"I thought maybe you'd confronted him and that he'd pulled, like, a goddamn murder-suicide or something heinous like that. I know it sounds like an overreaction, but blame those true crime docuseries on Netflix."

"Confronted who? I don't understand."

"Alex! Do you not remember the conversation we had about him not showing up at work? Running around having an affair?"

*Jesus Christ,* she thought.

Her molars were beginning to ache.

"Right, Tina," she said. "I remember. Alex and I talked. Everything is fine. He isn't having an affair."

"Everything's *fine*? What did he *say*? What the hell has he been up to when he's not at work?"

"It was just a misunderstanding."

"Tell me what happened, Georgie. What's going on? You don't sound like yourself."

"I'm very much myself," she said, "and everything is fine. You don't have to worry."

"I'm coming over."

"No!" It came out fiercer than she would have liked, but she didn't think Tina noticed. She softened her tone and said, "No, hon, we're fine. We've got some things to take care of, but I promise you I'll get in touch with you soon and fill you in. We can do drinks in Annapolis."

"Are you sure? Because something is off."

"I'm positive, Tina."

"Even that," she said.

"What?"

"You never call me Tina. You always call me T. We're G and T, babe. Gin and tonic. What the hell is going *on* with you? Say 'chardonnay' if you're being held against your will."

Georgette felt a vein throb at her temple. "Listen, I appreciate the call. But I promise, everything is perfectly fine."

"Yeah, okay," Tina said, audibly resigned. "But if you need anything, you give me a shout."

"I will."

"And check the ringer on your goddamn cell phone."

"All right, I will. Goodbye."

Georgette had just hung up the receiver when the phone trilled again, startling her all over. A bulb of perspiration dripped down from her hairline and stung her right eye. She considered not answering but then decided that might not be wise. She didn't want Tina Jarrett sending any police officers to the house.

This time, she was surprised to hear Callie's voice on the other end of the line.

"Hey, Callie. What are you doing calling me?"

"It's been days, Mom. When are you and Dad coming to get us?"

Days? How many days? Didn't they drop them off yesterday?

Georgette took a breath. "Aren't you having fun at Grandma's?"

"Denise wants to come home. She's being *terrible.*"

"I'm sure that's an exaggeration."

"Mom, no."

"Is she there?"

"Yes."

"Put her on, please."

"Okay, hold on . . ."

Georgette heard Callie pull away from the phone and mumble something to someone—presumably Denise—who must have been standing close by. When Denise came on the phone, she said, "I want my space helmet."

A sinking sensation overcame Georgette. She felt as if she was crashing through floors of a skyscraper in an elevator whose cables had just been severed. And although she knew exactly what Denise was talking about—of course she did—she said into the receiver, "What space helmet is that, Denise?"

"You know what it is. You took it from me. I want it back."

"We haven't found it, Denise. Like your dad promised, once we do, he'll drive it out to you and—"

"*Liar!*"

Georgette jerked the phone from her ear, wincing.

"You are a *liar*, Mom! *You* have it! *You* have it and *you* don't want to give it to *me*!"

"Denise, you need to watch your tone with—"

"It's *mine*! I found it!"

"Denise—"

"Come get me! I want to go home! I don't want to stay here anymore."

Denise's shouting was making her teeth hurt even more. The phone still pressed to her ear, she wandered down the hall and entered the master bedroom. The colander was still where she'd left it on the nightstand. She sat on the edge of the bed, the bedsprings creaking, and placed the colander in her lap. The hem of her silk robe was cut just below the buttocks—it was one of those sexy Victoria's Secret numbers Alex had given to her quite a few Christmases ago—so that her thighs were exposed. The metal bowl felt cool and relaxing against her bare and fevered flesh.

"You have it right now, don't you?" Denise said. Her voice had gone calm, and eerily adultlike.

"I told you," Georgette said, "I don't know where it is."

"Yes, you do. You have it right now. You're touching it. I can tell."

*Stay out of my head,* Georgette thought.

"It's mine," Denise said.

*No,* Georgette thought. *No, Denise, you're wrong. It's* mine *now and you just better deal with it, kiddo. Now quit fucking around with me on this phone because your father and I have serious business to deal with.*

Silence on the other end of the line.

As if Denise had heard her.

"And if you don't behave for Grandma, I'll leave you there for good."

More silence. Not even the sound of her daughter's labored breathing.

Then Alex's mom came on the line, sounding concerned: "Georgette, is everything all right?"

"I'm sorry she's being such a handful, Candace. I've told her to cut it out."

"Oh, it's fine. I was more concerned about you and Alex. You've missed some nightly phone calls with the girls. We were all starting to get worried."

Again, she wondered how many days ago she and Alex had dropped them off. Time suddenly felt malleable, stretching like putty. She wanted to ask Candace, but knew that she couldn't.

"And I certainly don't mind them staying here," Alex's mother went on, "but do you happen to have a timeframe for when you're planning to come pick them up?"

Georgette coughed into one fist. An excuse came to her, so sharp and sudden it was as if someone had just spoken it directly into her ear: "I'm sorry, Candace. Alex and I have the flu."

"The flu!" The woman gasped audibly.

"That's right," she said, deliberately trying to sound more nasal now. "The summer flu. We've been in bed."

"Oh, that's just awful. I'd hoped you both were having some quality time alone without the girls for a change."

"Quality time with a fever of a hundred and two," she responded dryly.

"That's just terrible. How's Alex? Can I speak with him?"

"He's asleep."

"You poor kids."

"We'll be okay. You don't mind keeping them for a little while longer?"

"Don't worry about it, dear. You two just concern yourselves with getting better."

"Thanks, Candace."

Georgette disconnected the call, then sat staring at the receiver in her hand as though it had just materialized out of thin air. She waited a full minute, counting out all sixty seconds in her head, expecting the phone to ring yet again. But it didn't. And even if it had, she probably wouldn't have answered it this time.

*I want my space helmet*, she thought, placing the colander on her head. She gave it one good twirl and felt her hair twist and tangle beneath it, tugging at her scalp. When she looked across the room and spied her reflection in the mirrored closet door, she couldn't help but smile at how preposterous she looked. It never occurred to her that maybe she should be terrified.

## 6

By the time she returned to the spare bedroom at the back of the house, Alex had removed all the graph paper from the wall. Still naked (though his erection had abated), he was sitting cross-legged on the floor, working a pair of scissors around one of the drawings. He had already cut out a few others, and these were lined up on the floor in front of him. They reminded Georgette of how she and the girls made snowflakes out of construction paper every Christmas, then decorated them with glitter and multicolored puffballs, which, for whatever reason, the girls referred to as angel boogers.

"Hey," she said. She still had the colander with her, only now she held it loosely in one hand and down at her side. "How long have the girls been at your mom's?"

"Huh?"

"How many days?"

"Uh, I don't know. One? Two?"

"I don't think that's right." She frowned. "What are you doing?"

"They're puzzle pieces, right? So, then they need to be cut out and actually *made* into *pieces*." He said this in one great whooping declaration while scissoring at the paper in a frenzy.

"Don't cut off your fingers," she warned him, only half joking.

"What were you going to say?"

She blinked, suddenly lost in some deep gray mental fog. "What are you talking about?"

"Before the phone rang," he said. He didn't look up at her, didn't stop cutting. "You were going to say something. What were you going to say?"

"Oh!" It came back to her in a tidal wave, mostly because she spotted one of the sketched symbols on the floor right next to Alex's naked left foot. It was one of the drawings Alex had already cut out, though its design made it difficult for him to cut cleanly along the lines. To Georgette, it looked like a child's crude drawing of the sun—a perfect circle with long, spidery lines coming off it in all directions. There were similar drawings of suns hanging on the refrigerator in the kitchen, done by Denise: fat yellow orbs hanging in azure skies above undulating green valleys populated with flowers of all colors. The only difference was that the interior of *this* sun was speckled with dots. It looked diseased.

She bent down, picked it up, examined it more closely. On second thought, she thought it looked more like a germ than a sun:

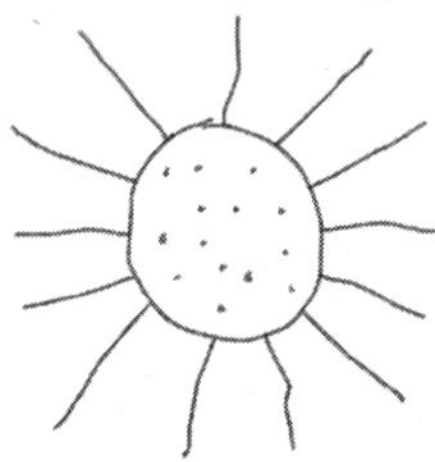

"What?" Alex said, sitting up on his knees and leaning his face against her thigh. His cheek was prickly with beard stubble and the smell of their lovemaking still hung around him in a cloud.

"What does this look like to you?" she asked.

"A sun," he said. "But with chickenpox."

"Yes. Okay. But what do you think it is? Like, what is it supposed to represent?"

"I have no idea."

Georgette set the colander on the floor. She placed the speckled paper sun inside it then gave the colander a gentle spin. It wobbled as it rotated and made a soft whirring sound against the laminate flooring.

"It's my colander," she said.

"No, no, no," Alex said. He grabbed the stack of pages off the floor and began rifling through them. When he found the drawing of the semicircle, or half-moon, or whatever it was, similarly flecked with dots, he held it out to her. "You said *this* was your colander."

"Yes. It is."

"But then how—"

She said, "They both are."

She pulled her eyes away from the rotating paper sun just quick enough to see the reaction on her husband's face. His features softened and his yellowish eyes grew wider. His jaw went from tense to slack. She watched as his lips parted the tiniest bit.

"I just assumed each drawing was its own individual thing," he said, peering back down into the revolving bowl on the floor. When it slowed, he reached down and gave it another wobbly spin. "It never occurred to me that there might be duplicates. Like, the same few items, but seen from different angles."

"Yes," she said. "The drawing in your hand is the colander but seen from a side view. This drawing"—and she pointed to the spinning speckled sun at the bottom of the stainless-steel bowl—"is the colander seen from above."

"Or below," Alex offered. "Yeah, I see it now. I get it. But then what are the lines supposed to be? The . . . uh, the sunbeams coming off it?"

"Whatever piece of the puzzle fits together with the colander," she said. It was like she was gleaning all this information through a crack that had suddenly split open in her brain—a crack no different than a crack in a wall through which she might glimpse bits and pieces of a room but never the full picture.

Slowly, Alex lowered himself back down onto his haunches. Georgette noticed that his penis had begun to stiffen again, as if her revelation had excited him on some carnal level. Desire struck her out of nowhere, and she knelt in front of him and reached between his legs.

She gave his thickening cock a squeeze. Alex appeared to hardly notice; he was combing through the pages of graph paper again, this time with a deliberate slowness, studying each page. Again, she watched as a fresh revelation brightened his features.

"I'm a fucking moron," he said, his own voice just barely above a whisper. On the floor beside them, the colander slowed until it stopped spinning altogether. "I'm a goddamn engineer with a goddamn master's from Tech, and it took me this long to finally realize it."

"What's that, baby?" she said again, and it was beginning to sound like the call-and-answer chorus to some sleazy burlesque tune.

He picked up another one of the cutouts off the floor. This one was the sketch of what appeared to be a door—a simple rectangle with four smaller rectangles inside it, two on top and two on the bottom. As she watched, Alex folded the cutout of the door in half so that when he held it up between his thumb and forefinger, it was bent at a right angle in the shape of a capital L.

"The door is a chair," he said, letting the paper cutout flutter to the floor. "They maybe start out as one thing but then change—are *supposed* to change—into something else."

"The door is a chair," Georgette repeated, no longer paying attention. "The tower is a volcano."

"Huh?"

She shook her head, kissing his rough cheek. There was rightness *here*, too. "Never mind. It's nonsense. Nonsense from old dreams, really. What aren't?"

"They're like assembly instructions," Alex said, marveling over the other cutouts on the floor in front of him. Between his legs, his penis was as rigid as a fencepost.

"So assemble," she told him.

"Yeah," he said, the word issuing from between his lips on a warm, breathy wave.

"But first," she said. "Me."

She climbed on top of him.

## CHAPTER THIRTY

# OF PURPOSE AND DESTINY: A VOICE FROM THE BEEHIVE

## 1

Once the Braswells left, Stinger lingered about the clearing, peering occasionally up at the water tower and at the great cream-colored tank with the dark green words scrawled in what must have been ten-foot-tall letters:

MARINER'S COVE
*Come join us!*

The thing they had done might have reminded Georgette Braswell of her fifth-grade science project—he'd gleaned that much from a quick rummage around inside her head—but to Stinger, there was no question about it: they had spent the past day and a half constructing a hive.

This realization brought a smile to Stinger's distorted face. His skin was sunburnt, the bee stings all pulsed with their own individual heartbeats, and his throat felt parched and abraded. Yet he couldn't help but smile. He was part of a new brood now. A three-person brood to begin with, sure, but Stinger had faith that things were about to get considerably . . . well, *bigger* . . . soon enough. Destiny was in motion. He could feel it in the spongy grayness of his marrow. The voice from the beehive had told him as much.

Abject horror did not dawn on him until he had finally come

out of the woods, as if leaving the Tower behind had swept aside a curtain of daydreams to reveal a plane of harsh reality. Queenie. He had forgotten about her, had left her home alone without any food or assistance for a full day and night.

"Shit," he uttered, and hoofed it to his truck.

There were no kids in the park this afternoon—it was a bright and sunny day, but it was also too damned hot—so Stinger shortcut it across the baseball field toward Poplar Station Road. The pickup truck jounced over the curb and he cracked the top of his head against the ceiling of the cab. A car horn blared as he emptied into the street, and Stinger quickly spun the wheel, narrowly avoiding a Volkswagen Beetle.

When he reached the old stone carriage house on Macadam Street, an extra finger of guilt prodded him in the spine. He wondered if he could go to jail for neglect. Worse—what if Queenie was dead? People could survive for a day and a half without food, of course, but what about water? Or what if the goddamn oxygen tank ran dry and she'd suffocated? Desperately, he tried to remember if he'd left one of Queenie's thermoses besides her bed on the nightstand. He couldn't recall whether he did or not. He also couldn't remember the last time he'd changed out her oxygen tank.

*Fuck fuck fuck.*

The truck thundered up the driveway and Stinger hopped out of the cab without bothering to shut the engine off. When he shoved himself through the front door, he was accosted by the eye-watering stench of bodily waste, not to mention the rotting trash in the kitchen he had neglected to take out for the past week or so. The interior of the house felt as thick and humid as a sauna.

Just how long had he been working on that water tower with that married couple, anyway? Had it really been since yesterday? Had they really worked all through the night and into the next day?

Had it been even longer?

Bees zigzagged in the front hall. Stinger waved them away as he moved quickly through the house. Queenie's bedroom door stood open, and Stinger braced himself for what he might find upon entering that room. A death chamber, to be sure. He imagined Queenie's face swollen and black, lips split and caked in dried blood from dehydration, a silvery rivulet of spittle hanging suspended from one corner of her purpled mouth. In fact, he could smell the death of her the nearer he drew to that open bedroom door—the ripe, sickly sweet stink of evacuated bowels and fresh decomposition. Yet as he approached the bedroom doorway, he heard the familiar, comforting sound of the oxygen—*sssst.*

The room was dark except for the glow of the muted television. An evangelist with too-white teeth and a chunky gold pinky ring was silently, animatedly proselytizing on the screen, and for one chilling moment, Stinger thought the man's eyes leveled directly upon him as he entered the bedroom. He thought he could read the evangelist's lips, too: *come join us.*

He switched on the small bedside lamp and was startled to find that Queenie had been staring at him in the dark. Her face wasn't all that different from the face of her corpse in Stinger's imagination—the chapped, scaly lips and the tightrope of spittle running from her lower lip to the sodden pillowcase—yet he could see that she was alive and alert.

"How you doing, Ma?"

With some effort, Queenie drew her lips together. The rolls of fat beneath her chin were studded with fine black hairs. There were sleeves of cookies on the nightstand along with several cans of diet soda, plus her water thermos within arm's reach. She hadn't starved after all, although judging by the smell, she'd definitely shat herself.

She said something, but her voice was so dry and raspy, Stinger couldn't make it out. He reached for her water thermos, but she levitated one massive, cheese-pale arm and shoved the thermos onto the floor.

"Come on, Ma," he said, picking it up.

"You left me," she said. "I don't want to die in here."

"You're not dead, are you?"

Her eyes followed him as he negotiated around the bed and jimmied open a window to get some fresh air into the room. A smattering of honeybees clung to the outside of the screen; he flicked them off, one by one. Behind him, the oxygen tank went *sssst*.

"You were gone so long," she said.

"I wasn't," he retorted, although in truth he had no idea how long he'd been gone.

"Why would you leave me here like that?"

"I came back, didn't I? Are you hungry?"

She turned away from him. The hair at the back of her head was a rat's nest. "You just want me to die."

Stinger said nothing as he flicked the final honeybee off the screen. He could hear them all buzzing about out there just beyond the window. Or maybe that buzzing was in his head, in his teeth. He didn't know for sure.

"What did I ever do to you? I was a good mother. You're just disgusted by me."

Through the screen, he could see down into Marybeth Maysall's front yard, the empty lounge chair covered in a beach towel out there beside the hedgerow. He recalled something having transpired between him and Marybeth recently, something that brought to mind the word *communion*, although he couldn't be sure exactly what it had been now. Or if it had been real at all, or just a part of those strange dreams he'd been having lately. He tried to extract exactly what the incident had been, but his mind was too scrambled with the growing, strumming sound of the bees for him to get any real thinking done.

"I'm right, aren't I, Jeremy? You're disgusted by me."

He turned and looked at her. Queenie's colossal breasts pulled taut the fabric of her gigantic T-shirt as she shifted upon the mattress. Despite the open window, he caught another whiff of shit.

"Let's get you cleaned up and then I'll make you something to eat."

"How can I eat when you're so awful to me, Jeremy? How can I eat when you leave me lying in my own filth for days?"

He wanted to close his eyes and smash his head against a wall. He wanted to scream until his throat ruptured and bled. Instead, he slipped out of the room upon a wave of Queenie's wails and protestations. The buzzing in his head was growing louder, causing his bottom molars to radiate with a dull, persistent pain. In the bathroom at the end of the hall, he gathered up the implements he needed to clean his mother up—a fresh diaper and pad, a spray bottle of water and soap solution, a plastic tub of disinfectant wipes, rubber gloves, a dry towel, a garbage bag—and carried them all back into Queenie's bedroom.

"Do you think this is a good life for me?" She hadn't shut up, despite overtaxing the oxygen tank on the floor beside her bed—*sssst, sssst, sssst.* "Do you think I wanted this medical condition? Do you think I asked God for to be this way? I used to live a normal life, in case you don't remember, Jeremy. And my best years were spent tending to *you.* So now this is my cross to bear."

*My cross, too,* he thought, and just before he stripped the sodden, piss-smelling bedsheet from Queenie's massive, reeking body, he prayed to find that her diaper had contained most of the mess.

## 2

When it was done, he stood beneath a tepid stream in the shower, scrubbing every sore and tender inch of his body. He thought a relaxing shower might calm the buzzing in his head and make his teeth stop throbbing, but it didn't.

In his bedroom, he climbed into a fresh pair of cargo pants and an AC/DC concert T-shirt. As he dressed, he peered down at the two-headed bee inside the jelly jar on his nightstand.

*You could mean anything,* he thought, staring at the deformed honeybee. *You could symbolize my divergence—leaving one hive in favor of another. Or you could have served as an omen, telling me I was to meet that couple, the Braswells, the two-headed man-and-wife creature, and together we would begin setting the stage for the endgame. You could even stand as a symbol for me, for myself, transitioning from an old life into a fresh new one: the divided man, the splitting of personalities, the creation of duality, metamorphosis. Two of me in one body.*

These ruminations surprised Stinger.

*Maybe it's not me,* he considered. *Maybe it's the other consciousness inside me.*

The bee at the bottom of the jar began slowly pinwheeling its legs.

Stinger unscrewed the cap and watched as the bee spiraled lethargically into the air. It circled the bedroom a couple of times then shrank its orbit until it was circling Stinger's head.

That buzzing in his brain.

That ache in his molars.

Stinger opened his mouth, and the two-headed bee flew inside.

## 3

He realized he'd left the truck running in the driveway, so he sauntered outside and yanked the keys from the ignition. The GMC rumbled then died. Alex Braswell's little notepad was right there atop the dashboard; Stinger scooped it up and flipped casually through each page until he located the drawing he was looking for. He tore it out, stuffed it into his pocket, then tossed the notepad on the driver's seat.

He dropped the truck keys in the pocket of his cargo pants then scooped out the slats of aluminum siding he'd taken from the maintenance shed from the back of the truck. There was an A-frame ladder and a toolbox back there, too, which he also hauled out.

He carried the items through a part in the hedgerow then laid them down on the lawn beside Marybeth Maysall's lounge chair. Her Kia was not in the driveway, but he climbed the front steps and knocked on her door anyway. When Maybeth did not answer, he carried the ladder to the porch and set it up beneath the section of the house where the siding was missing. Despite the ache in his teeth, he whistled while he worked.

When he was done, he stepped back to survey his handiwork. The color of the replacement siding wasn't a match, but at least it would prevent weather and animals from getting into the house.

*We had a conversation with our minds, Marybeth,* he thought now, suddenly remembering the memory that had been eluding him earlier. Or maybe it was the two-headed bee inside him that was remembering for him. *Just like I was able to hear that Braswell woman's thoughts as we were working on the water tower, you and I had a full conversation without ever opening our mouths and uttering a single word.*

He remembered, too, the item she had been holding as she stood topless on the other side of her bedroom window, bleeding from the nose.

Stinger removed the slip of notepad paper from his pocket. The symbol on it had been drawn with a black marker, and it was so basic a rendering that it was nearly childlike. Yet looking at it, Stinger knew exactly what it was, just as he had when he'd first glimpsed it from over Alex Braswell's shoulder as the guy had flipped through those notepad pages.

The unmistakable front wheel of a tricycle.

Stinger folded the slip of paper and fed it through the mail slot of Marybeth Maysall's front door.

## 4

At suppertime, he prepared Queenie a simple microwaveable meal which he carried into her bedroom on her favorite John Wayne dinner tray. She pretended she wasn't hungry when he set it down in front of her, but he knew that she was. When he turned and sauntered back toward the door, Queenie said, "You've stopped reading the Bible to me while I eat."

He paused in the doorway.

"It's because I disgust you," she said. "It's because you can't stand to be in the same room with me any longer than you have to."

Slowly, Stinger turned around.

Queenie's narrow eyes hung on him; he could almost feel the weight of them, like a physical thing. Like the two-headed bee that was now buzzing around inside him, whispering its thoughts to him, he felt like he was being torn in two directions at once.

"Do you remember when Glenda-Rae died?" Stinger asked, reverently enough.

Queenie's eyes narrowed further, as if sensing some deception about to take place.

Stinger sat in the folding chair beside his mother's bed. At his feet lay the silver O2 canister with its clear plastic tube snaking all the way up to the underside of Queenie's nose; on the nightstand near Stinger's elbow, partially concealed behind a fortress of empty soda cans, Danielle Steel paperbacks, and wax-paper sleeves of Ritz crackers, was Queenie's beloved Bible.

"You said you heard the Voice of God speaking to you through the TV," he said.

Queenie frowned. Her eyes shifted over to the Bible that still sat on her nightstand. "What are you doing? Jeremy, I don't like this . . ."

He lifted a finger to his lips. "Shhhh," although he thought it came out more like the buzzing of a bee . . .

. . . or maybe the hiss of a snake.

*Sssss.*

Queenie closed her mouth. The oxygen tank went *sssst*, which, in a way, *also* could have been a snake.

"You said God spoke to you and told you not to worry, that everything was going to be okay, because He had given you a son, and that your son would never desert you. That you would always have someone to take care of you because your son—because *I*—was here to do it."

Queenie turned away from him, her gaze shifting toward the ceiling. She was being obstinate and sulking, not wanting to hear him, but Stinger didn't care and carried on nonetheless.

"You said it was my divine purpose. And whether I believed that or not, I *did* stay. I've always stayed. I've taken good care of you, Mother. For all this time, and despite what *I* may have wanted, I've stayed and taken good care of you."

He watched as his mother's lips thinned.

"Well, now I've heard a voice, too."

She turned her head in his direction. Her eyes sparkled. "The Voice of God?"

He considered this, but ultimately shook his head. "No, not God. Something else. Something strong enough to cause cracks in our world whenever it speaks."

"Jeremy, I don't—"

"Dragon," he said, cutting her off. He hadn't realized it until now, and his mind still couldn't summon a visual of it, but that was the word that leapt into his brain, unbidden. He wasn't even sure why he'd said it. "The voice of the Dragon."

"What dragon? What are you talking about?"

"Endgame," he said. "I'm talking about endgame, Mother. Changes are coming, and I've been selected as the one to usher them in."

"What does that even *mean*?"

He leaned forward in the chair, hands clasped and dangling between his knees. "It means I've finally got agency, Mother. I've finally got a purpose and a destiny that doesn't concern you. I've finally been given an endgame of my own."

"I don't like that word, Jer-Jer—*endgame.* It scares me. It sounds dangerous."

He shrugged. Said, "Maybe it is. The Dragon said people may try to stop me. That no matter what, it was my job to keep the Hive safe. Protect the Tower."

On the floor by his foot, the oxygen tank went *sssst.* Queenie stared at him now as if watching something ugly and peculiar being reeled out of the sea on the end of a fishing line.

"I don't understand," she said eventually. "Where did you hear that? Where is all this coming from?"

"My teeth," Stinger said, and rose up off the chair. He went over to the window—the bees were back, crawling all over the outside of the screen—and saw how the light in the sky had changed. Dusk was coming in like a tide. He turned and headed toward the door. "Eat up,

Ma," he said. "I'm going out for a bit later tonight. I've got things to do once it gets dark."

"And for how long this time?" she called after him. "Will you even come back this time?"

"I'm coming back," he told her.

"Maybe you will, maybe you won't. Eventually, you won't. You're just summoning the guts."

He said nothing to that.

"You're just waiting for the moment when you can walk out of this house and leave me here alone to rot, and then I'll be—"

He closed her bedroom door.

Back in the living room, he dropped himself down on the sofa, killed half a jar of peanut butter, then slept for a little over an hour.

## 5

When he awoke, it was to a strident humming in his jaw: a reverberation that radiated along the bones of his skull like someone hammering upon them with tiny wooden mallets. Pain burrowed down to the root. He sat up, his neck stiff. His throat was still sore so he got up and guzzled three full glasses of tap water while standing before the open door of the refrigerator so that the cool air could wash over his itchy, lumpy, sunburned flesh.

Queenie was asleep with the TV on. She'd eaten all the food on the John Wayne dinner tray, including the jellied cherries that she claimed tasted like Dimetapp. It was that same evangelist on the TV, his overlarge white teeth as big and broad as a billboard. The TV was still muted, but again Stinger thought he could read the evangelist's lips.

*Come join us.*

He slipped out of the house, the truck's keys jangling in one of the loose, oversized pockets of his cargo pants. The evening air was dizzy with bees, fuzzy with them, and he thought that if he inhaled forcefully enough, he'd suck a whole snarl of them down into his lungs.

*Come join us.*

Propped behind the steering wheel, he dug Alex Braswell's notepad out from under his ass. He ran his thumb along the pages so that they made a zipping sound, *zzzzzt*, then opened it. He wended casually through the pages, soaking up each strange symbol sketched in graphite or sometimes blue or black ink. Some of the earlier ones looked like Braswell, that busy bee, had taken his time with: they were more finely culled, more detailed, and sometimes even shaded so that they appeared to be three-dimensional. But the drawings near the end of the pad were nothing more than hasty scribbles. A few of them he couldn't even make out. But he knew he had what he needed, so he tucked the notepad into one of the many pockets of his cargo pants, then started up the truck. The growl of the engine fought for dominance over the buzzing of the bees inside Stinger's back teeth. His scalp itched, and when he reached up to scratch it, he could feel honeybees squirming about up there, snared in his hair. He rolled down the window, shook the bees from his hair. There was a greasy Baltimore Ravens cap with an angler's hook bent over the bill on the passenger seat. Stinger snatched it up and tugged it down over his eyes. Then he backed out of the driveway.

Yes, he had heard the Braswell woman's thoughts, and he had also caught snippets of Alex Braswell's thoughts as well, although less clearly. The woman—Georgette, wasn't it?—was more clearheaded than her husband. Stinger wasn't sure why this was the case, although he wondered if maybe Georgette was a late addition to the plot. Maybe whatever consciousness was living inside him and Alex Braswell had not fully occupied Braswell's wife. This made him think of the two-headed honeybee again. *That's what it means,* he thought, *that's the symbolism. All those heads coming together to accomplish a singular job. Thinking as one.*

Hive mind.

It wasn't a question of locating the other items; it was a matter of bringing together all the other busy bees who likely already had them. That was what the voice in the beehive—the Dragon—had entrusted him with: endgame. He just had to bring everyone together.

And Stinger thought he knew just how to do it.

## 6

He drove out to Gladstone Park with the radio blasting Rage Against the Machine. It was early evening and there were a few loathsome teenagers loitering just outside the park grounds when Stinger pulled up, but they paid him no attention and seemed to steer clear of the park itself. Once more, he cut across the baseball field, the truck's tires spitting out great plumes of dry, orange dust, and toothy bits of gravel. He rolled onto the path that wound through the trees and ultimately rocked to a stop once the maintenance shed appeared on the other side of the leafy boughs. The brand-new padlock he'd cinched to the door gleamed like a silver bullet fired from a gun in the fading daylight. Despite the pain in his teeth, Stinger grinned.

Inside the maintenance shed he heard more buzzing—not just in his head and in his teeth—and looked around for bees, but didn't find any until he glanced down at his left shoulder and at the crawling yellow-and-black apostrophes there. They clung to him like epaulets.

There were several cans of paint on the shelf along the back wall of the shed. The shelf was actually just a couple of planks of wood nailed together and bracketed to the wall and the cans were all mismatched gallons, some of which were probably a decade old. He certainly hadn't bought most of them, nor could he ever remember using them to paint anything. He had no preference for a specific color and didn't really care how old the paint was, so he wound up pulling down from the shelf whatever was most within reach.

Stinger set six cans of paint into a wheelbarrow, along with a screwdriver. Hanging on a pegboard above the shelf of paint cans were half a dozen paintbrushes, nearly all of them cruddy and stiff and useless, as well as a crusty roller on a long pole. He stood a better chance painting with the rubber sole of his shoe. But then he remembered his equipment in the back of his pickup truck.

Humming the Rage song under his breath, he rolled the wheelbarrow out into the waning daylight. The sun seemed harsher than it had just minutes ago, like it was putting up a good fight in its final few moments. After digging around in the toolbox in the bed of the pickup, he collected two brand-new paintbrushes, still in the packaging, as well as a new paint roller that he snapped onto the pole he'd found in the shed. He tucked the brushes into the rear pocket of his cargo pants, right next to Braswell's notepad. Then, still humming, he pushed the wheelbarrow around the side of the maintenance shed and into the woods.

He paused only once, and that was to peer down at the patch of scorched earth where he had doused the wasps' nest with gasoline before setting it ablaze. He only paused for a second, maybe two, before continuing through the trees. Something about that patch of burned grass tickled something deep at the base of his skull.

It was a hot and breezeless evening, and his clean T-shirt was already damp with sweat, but Stinger was in a good mood.

## 7

It was fully dark by the time he finished. He did not know what time it was when he got back in the truck to return home—the clock on the dashboard hadn't worked in over a year now—but he guessed several hours must have passed. He hoped Queenie was already asleep for the night, because he didn't feel like dealing with that noise back at home. Besides, his shoulders and the small of his back ached, and his entire musculature was sore from what he'd spent the past several hours doing. Still, his spirits were high.

He noticed Marybeth Maysall's tiny champagne-colored Kia motoring along in front of him as he coasted down Poplar Station Road. He followed her until she pulled into her driveway, and then he coasted the rest of the way and pulled into his. He peeled the sweat-dampened Ravens cap from his head, tossed it on the passenger seat, then ran his trembling, paint-splattered fingers through his hair while examining his reflection in the rearview mirror. He looked like hell, and he knew it, but he also knew that he and Marybeth now had some sort of special connection.

She was standing on her front lawn when he hopped out of the GMC and strolled over to the low hedgerow that separated their two properties. Her Kia was still idling in her driveway with the driver's door standing open. Marybeth stood within the glow of the Kia's headlights in her cornflower-blue waitress outfit, hands on her hips, as she stared up at the front of her house.

"Howdy," he said, amiably enough.

"Did you do this?" Her voice was sharp, tinged with disapproval. She jabbed a finger up at the front of her house. She was pointing to the spot where Stinger had replaced the missing aluminum siding earlier that day.

"Oh, yeah. Well, I found some extra siding and I thought I'd . . ." His voice trailed off. He wondered if she was remembering the nonverbal conversation they'd had while staring at each other through their respective bedroom windows. How she'd been topless, bleeding from the nose, and clutching a tricycle wheel to her chest. "I thought I'd do you a favor, is what I mean, Marybeth."

"Don't." It came out nearly as a bark. "Don't do me any favors, Jeremy. It's not . . . it's not *normal* . . . for some stranger to just come and fix up your house when you aren't home. Do you understand?"

"I'm not some stranger."

"It isn't romantic, okay? I know you think it is, but I'm telling you it isn't."

He felt something like a knot tighten deep in his chest. "I was just trying to do something nice."

"It's creepy, okay? It creeps a girl out when some guy she hardly knows does something like—"

"We've known each other for years," he said.

"Just cut it out, Jeremy. Okay? I'm not your girlfriend."

He shrugged, hoping he looked unaffected, like this was no big deal, when in reality he felt a hot flash of shame. That knot in his chest tightened. "Sure, Marybeth, no problem. Whatever you want."

Her eyes lingered on him. He wondered if she might also be remembering—or trying to remember—their telepathic conversation. He thought about transmitting a thought into her head right then, but decided it might *also* be a thing she'd consider creepy and unromantic. Besides, the buzzing in his own head had reached such a crescendo that he could barely hear the chirping of the crickets in the grass, let alone think straight.

He watched her go to her car, shut down the engine, and turn the headlights off. When she disappeared into her house, he remained standing there at the edge of her property breathing heavily. The two-headed bee was slamming around inside him, plunging its stinger into all his vital organs—his lungs, his liver, his heart. The damn thing was in his head, too, or at least the sound of it was: shaking apart the foundation of his skull and making his bottom molars feel as tender as raw nerves.

He returned to his house before Marybeth could come back out clutching the drawing of the tricycle wheel he'd stuffed in her mail slot. He was careful not to make noise closing the front door, not wanting to wake Queenie at the far end of the house if, in fact, she was asleep. He was still parched, so he went directly to the kitchen sink, filled a drinking glass with water from the tap, then gulped it down. He repeated this process two more times until he began to feel somewhat more like himself. From down the hall, he could hear the familiar, pressurized *sssst* of his mother's mechanical respiration.

The buzzing in his head had turned into a tornado of white noise, causing tears to spill from the corners of his eyes. He leaned over the kitchen sink, hands on either side of the basin, and let loose a tightrope of silvery drool.

He felt his way to the sofa in the dark, where he lay down and folded his trembling hands atop his heaving chest. The buzzing voice of the Dragon from the beehive had been strong enough to drive cracks between their worlds, Stinger knew, which was how the two-headed honeybee had gotten here in the first place. Now, the bee was buzzing around inside him, pushing him toward the cusp of madness.

In fact, it felt like there was more than one bee in there, maybe a whole tornado of bees, an entire colony, black and snarled and metastasizing like a cancer.

Stinger unhinged his mouth. Lips stretched taut, he exhaled toward the ceiling. He heard the buzzing travel up from his guts, down the length of his arms and legs, and drain quickly from the dented ovoid bowl that was his skull. The bees all gathered in his lungs, and when he exhaled a second time, they vomited out of his open mouth and spewed upward until they splashed themselves along the ceiling. The buzzing was no longer in Stinger's head, but here in the room with him, swarming in the air and crawling on the drywall. Bees everywhere . . .

. . . until they weren't.

Because at some point, they had fled for wherever two-headed bees from some other plane of existence flee. And all around him, the house went blessedly silent.

*A crescent moon.*

*A door.*

*The wheel of a tricycle.*

The Dragon had granted him a reprieve. Likely, because the Dragon was pleased with him and needed his help, even if Stinger himself didn't quite understand what all of that entailed. Because after what he'd done tonight in Gladstone Park, he was pretty sure the remaining pieces would start falling into place very, very soon.

# PART THREE

# ALL HAIL THE DRAGON, ALL HAIL THE TOWER

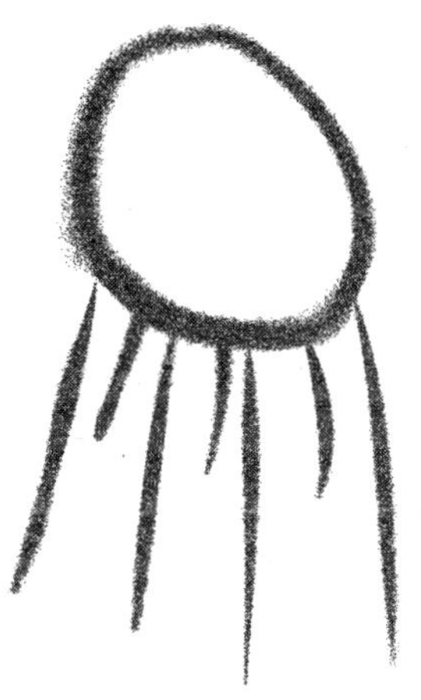

Doodle, doodle, doo,
The princess lost her shoe;
Her highness hopped,
The fiddler stopped,
Not knowing what to do.

UNKNOWN

*Goes skim-skimming* sssss sssss *across the treetops, wind-tricky, before sinking down, down, carving passage through channels of liveable suburbia, bobbing and leaping and loping from place to ephemeral place, from mind to ephemeral mind, a thing that is a notion as mysterious and infinitesimal as the spark between synapses, the electrical pulses of brainwaves, weaving snakelike and single-minded through the ever-widening cracks, where the bleed-over of worlds has a smell like raw honey and a consistency like the delicate yet persistent flutter of tiny insect wings,* zzzzt zzzzt *with its* sssss sssss, *and swoop-swooping lower, lower, unseen, undetected, a reality unstable but existing, a radiant band of pure energy, of pure thought, of pure consciousness, and here, seated right here, let us see, a figure of pasty white turned kiln-red by the sun, unkempt, longish fingernails digging into the wooden handrests of a beach chair or maybe a lawn chair or maybe whatever kind of chair it might be called, bare toes tightening into curls in the warm summer grass, a transmission humming in this man's bottom back teeth, a buzzing, a communique, a coded message, and here his head turns as the droplets of sweat spill down his temples and shimmer like diamonds along the ridged creases of his forehead, the perceptible tic of an eyelid, the narrowing of the eyes themselves as the pupils dilate to take everything in, all of it, devour it, predatory, while one corner of the thin, skin-peely mouth tugs upward in an approximation of dim, distant understanding, or so it may appear to the uninitiated, as this figure, this man, this Bertrand Zachs, as he is known by name, content in the bland banality of what he has been doing all this time, content in knowing that it is of the utmost importance even if he cannot articulate a single cognizant truth about what he is doing, cannot say* why, *driven only by obsession, this man, this Bertrand Zachs, this sagging bag of bones and sun-peely flesh, whose neck is thick with sweaty folds, whose underarms sprout black, wiry kudzu, whose exposed shins somehow remain blindingly white and patchy with spider-leg hair and a thin, purple cascade of blood vessels, watches in confused delight or perhaps abject horror—he himself is uncertain—as a smelly, rattletrap conversion van with wolves airbrushed on the side pulls up along the curb of Cloister Road, arrives, materializes, becomes thus, belching clouds of black exhaust from a vibrating tailpipe, rolling, roiling, thumping, lumbering, coming finally to a stop just past Bertrand Zachs's own house, right in front of the McBride house next door, a house that is a home that contains the world, that contains the engine, the motor, the key, the heart, THE BOY THE BOY THE BOY THE BOY THE—*

## CHAPTER THIRTY-ONE

# A (SORT OF) HOMECOMING

### 1

Brian switched off the ignition and the van shuddered then died all around him. Through the windshield, the afternoon was sunny, the sky a cloudless blue, yet there was a perceptible sense of doom that hung low: Brian Russo could feel it as a firm, immovable lump in the back of his throat.

Once he'd made up his mind that he was coming back here, he'd been nervous and anticipatory throughout the drive, but something had happened—something funny, something strange—as he entered the neighborhood of Mariner's Cove that made his previous anxiety seem like nothing. He'd even pulled over to the shoulder of the road upon entering the neighborhood, his head suddenly spinning, his heart thundering in his chest. It wasn't just the guilt, the regret, and the reticence to look his sister in the eyes again: it was something even more than that. In the animal kingdom, this would have been a clear warning, STAY AWAY, but people were sometimes the dumbest animals, and he had kept driving regardless. Anyway, he attributed it to nerves and nothing more.

Ellen and Cory's house looked the same as he remembered.

It had been about two years since he'd last been here. At what was inarguably the lowest point of his adult life, Brian had arrived on that doorstep, shaking, sweaty, and itchy all over. He must have looked like hell come home to roost. But his younger sister had embraced him. She'd brought him into her home, put on a pot of coffee, and went to work making him a sandwich while he attempted to scrub away at least a modicum of his shame and degradation in the shower. Later, at the dining room table, his hands had shook as he leveraged the sandwich she'd made him to his mouth. The reflection wobbling on the surface of his coffee was that of a hopeless, soulless, strung-out wretch.

He was now sober and had been for the past eighteen months, yet returning to this house, he could feel all that old wretchedness pressing down upon him once again. He'd spent six months living within those walls with Ellen and Cory, six months that saw him complete a stint in rehab, get a job bussing tables at a local restaurant, and forming a close bond with his nephew. He saved up money and bought an old beater that he drove to and from work, and his healthier lifestyle saw him shed the doughy bulge around his waist. He began to *look* healthier, to *feel* healthier. And not just physically, but mentally and spiritually, too. He'd spent days with the boy playing board games, teaching him to ride a bicycle, drawing pictures of spaceships and planets and aliens. He'd glued an entire constellation of glow-in-the-dark stars to the boy's bedroom ceiling, and when Cory had woken up the following morning, one of the stars had been stuck to the center of his forehead, earning him the nickname Chicken Little. He'd also spent evenings on the back deck talking with Ellen for hours after Cory had gone to sleep, reconnecting with her, talking about their lives, their hopes and dreams and past sorrows. Ellen sometimes spoke of her husband, Patrick, who'd been killed in a car accident when Cory was very young. In turn, Brian told her about Donna, the woman he'd lived with in Baltimore whom he'd wanted to marry, and how she'd rightly ended that relationship with him because he'd been such a trainwreck of a human being. Ellen had listened with compassion and empathy, sometimes reaching over and gripping his hand in hers as he spoke. He loved his sister, always had, but his lifestyle had necessitated a growing distance between them until he'd cleaned up his act. He loved Cory, too, and cherished those six months he'd spent with the boy.

The house on Cloister Road in the bayside neighborhood of Mariner's Cove had been good to him.

Yet there was a gene residing deep within Brian Russo that was perpetually bent on self-destruction. It was almost inevitable, and Brian often felt powerless to control it. *We are who we are, and we'll be that way until the day we die,* the Air Man had been fond of saying, and it became a sentiment that Brian, too, began to believe with unwavering faith. One afternoon, after finishing his shift at the restaurant, he wound up having a few drinks with some of his coworkers. Nothing extravagant—just a few beers, and *Christ* they felt good going down—and he was far from drunk by the time he drove his beater back to the house on Cloister Road. Ellen was out showing a house and Cory was depressed about some kids bullying him at school. Wanting to cheer his nephew up, he took him to the Pink Penguin, Cory's favorite eatery, for pizza and ice cream. Cory had brightened right up, and it did Brian's heart good to see it. In fact, he was feeling so good that he ordered a beer. Then another. They played some arcade games while Brian drank yet another. Yeah—feeling pretty good, all right.

It was dark by the time they drove home. He'd taken his eyes off the road for just a split second, and when he looked back up, he saw the glowing red taillights of the car in front of them filling their windshield. He jerked to the shoulder, tires squealing as he stamped on the brake. The whole car lurched, Cory shrieked from the back seat . . . and then they dipped down into a shallow ravine that Brian hadn't known was there.

There had been a police officer a few cars back who had witnessed the whole thing. The world suddenly became an alternating swirl of red and blue lights. For a moment, Brian Russo didn't know where he was or what had happened. Then he could hear Cory sobbing from the back seat of the car. Brian craned his head around and saw the boy buckled into his seat, hanging at an angle due to the slanted pitch of the car. He was cradling his right arm against his chest. The bone had not pierced the skin, but Brian suddenly knew without question that it was broken.

Cory was taken to the hospital while Brian was detained, questioned, and ultimately failed the breathalyzer. Not by much—he'd only had a handful of beers, or so he explained to the officer administering the test—but it was enough.

It had been enough for Ellen, too. She'd only had one stipulation about him living with them, and it was that he stayed clean and sober. The audacity of him putting her son's life in danger—she railed at him, shouted, even sobbed. His heart had broken watching her, knowing just how wrong he was, knowing that he'd inflicted this upon his sister and his nephew. And what if it had been more than just a broken arm? What if it had been so much worse?

Ellen had lost her husband Patrick to a drunk driver.

This was not lost on him.

She told him to leave and never come back.

Yet here he was.

His hand reached up and fondled the ball of keys still dangling from the van's ignition. He could crank it back over, pop a U-turn, and continue on to New York. Ellen would be none the wiser. But in that last moment he thought of the nightmares he'd been having, and of that strange, Cory-like voice that had rocketed through his head.

One of the twelve principles of AA was Awareness—paying attention to your thoughts and feelings and to seek guidance from a higher power. He couldn't deny the dreams or the voice-shouts in his head that had caused his nose to bleed, but he also couldn't ignore the overall sense of encroaching doom that seemed to hang around him like a dark cloud since he'd left California. It was as if the closer he came to the east coast—the closer he came to *Cory*—the more powerful this sense of doom became.

He couldn't just drive away. Even if Ellen refused to let him into the house, he'd at least want to know if Cory was okay and to gain some peace of mind.

He pulled the keys from the ignition and got out of the van just as the front door of the house opened. Ellen stood there in the doorway. Her face was expressionless except for a touch of incredulity at the sight of him. There was that persistent lump in the back of his throat again, but he advanced slowly up the lawn in her direction, nonetheless.

Cory suddenly appeared beside her, then burst into a sprint in Brian's direction. Brian felt his knees go weak just as the boy leapt into his arms. They hugged each other tight, Brian burying the side of his face against the boy's neck. He could feel tears threatening his eyes.

Cory gripped him tighter, then whispered with hot, sugary breath into Brian's ear: "You heard me calling."

"Yeah, Chicken Little. Yeah, I did. I don't know how, but I did." He set his nephew down then took a step back. "Come on, let me get a look at you."

Cory beamed a smile at him then turned back to his mother and waved her over. Ellen came rigidly, her arms now folded protectively across her chest. She returned her son's smile, but when her eyes fell upon Brian's again, he could see the conflicting emotions behind them, and could see his own shame and humility reflected back at him, too.

"Man, he's gotten so big," he said as Ellen approached.

"Takes after his father," she responded, running her fingers through the boy's curly hair.

Brian didn't know if she'd meant to bring up Patrick as a way of setting expectations—letting him know that she still blamed him and detested him for putting her son's life at risk—or if it had just been an automatic response, something she likely said to anyone who might make a similar observation about her son.

"Hey!" Cory cried, pointing at Brian's chest. "You're still wearing it!"

Brian glanced down and saw the glow-in-the-dark star necklace dangling between the open buttons of his sleeveless flannel shirt. "Every single day," he told the boy.

"Really?"

"Would I lie to you, Chicken Little?"

"It's good to see you, Brian," Ellen said. She finally lowered her arms and leaned in, kissing him quickly on the side of his unshaven face. He wanted to hug her but was too nervous; instead, he offered her what felt like a sad excuse for a smile. She turned and glanced at the house next door, where a man in a bathrobe sat in a chair watching them. "Let's go inside, yeah?"

## 2

"I've been sober for eighteen months now," he said, the two of them seated around the dining room table with fresh mugs of coffee before them. In the kitchen, Cory was whipping up a pot of macaroni and cheese, and was dancing to whatever music was in his head while his socks slid back and forth along the kitchen tiles.

Ellen glanced over her shoulder at Cory, who was within earshot at the stove, but Brian shrugged his shoulders. When she turned back around, the smile he gave her this time felt more genuine.

"I don't mind if he hears, as long as you don't," he said.

To Cory, Ellen said, "Why don't you put on some music, you dancing fool?"

"Good idea!" Cory shouted back, then summoned some classic rock on the little black hockey-puck speaker that sat on the kitchen counter.

Her voice a touch lower, Ellen said, "I never spoke badly about you after you left. I want you to know that."

"I'm sure that broken arm didn't help him think too fondly of me." His throat tightened just saying the words.

"Bones heal." But she said this with a look of distaste on her face.

"Did he ever ask about me?"

"For a while after the fact, yes. I just told him you needed to see a doctor to get help. That was all I said. After a while, he stopping bringing you up." She must have realized how that sounded, because her lips went thin and she stared momentarily down at her coffee. When she glanced back up at him, Brian could see tears standing in her eyes. "You look good, Brian. I'm glad to see it. And I'm happy to hear you've gotten yourself together."

"Listen," he said. "I owe you an apology. I owe you more than that, I guess, but I did want to say I'm sorry. I was fighting a lot of demons back then—I guess I still am, in some ways—and I let that fight cloud my judgment. You and your son mean the world to me, El, and I've suffered with what I've done every day since it happened. You had every right to say to me the things you did that day, and you've got every right to still hate me for it now—"

"Brian—"

He held up a hand. Took a breath. "I just want you to know that I see that now. And that I'm sorry."

She nodded. Those tears still glittered in her eyes but refused to fall.

"I don't hate you, Brian. I hate what you *did.* I'm just glad you're in a better place now."

He realized that wasn't necessarily forgiveness, but he'd take it.

"Now don't take this the wrong way," she said, clearing her throat, "but what are you doing here?"

He glanced at Cory through the doorway where he was scooping macaroni and cheese from the pot on the stove into three big bowls.

"I was leaving California on my way to New York for a job," he said, "and I kept having this feeling that something . . . well, that something was wrong with Cory. That maybe he . . ."

"He what?"

"That maybe he needed help."

She eased back in her chair. The tears had vanished from her eyes; there was now a distant look in them, as if she was suddenly lost in some deep reverie.

"Has he been okay, El? Is something going on?"

She looked at him. "Yes," she said flatly. "Something is going on. In fact, it's almost unbelievable that you're here right now."

He felt a sinking sensation in the pit of his stomach—a feeling not dissimilar from the one he'd felt as he'd taken the Mariner's Cove exit off the highway and passed the neighborhood's welcome sign. "Tell me."

She seemed to consider this before admitting, "I don't know how to tell it."

"Just say it, El."

She glanced back at Cory who was still shoveling spoonfuls of mac and cheese into the bowls, then said, "Remember those things you used to be able to do when you were younger?"

"Yes." He didn't need her to expound on that.

"Cory can do those things, too."

Brian felt a hot, prickling sensation creep up from the small of his back. He was again remembering—or trying to remember—his dreams. No details, no specifics, only the notion that Cory had been in danger, with something akin to a dragon pursuing him through the darkness.

"I think he needs you, Brian. I think you showing up here—"

"It wasn't just chance, El. It wasn't *just* a feeling I had, or a couple of bad dreams."

"It wasn't?"

"He *called* me."

"Called you?"

"Called *out* to me." He tapped an index finger to his temple. "Inside my head. I know that sounds crazy, and I wasn't even sure about it until I was hugging him on the lawn, and he said, 'You heard me calling.' I got a chill, El. This whole time, I thought maybe I was losing my mind."

Ellen's eyes shone with tears again. She brought a hand up to cover her mouth but then lowered it again. In nearly a whisper, she said, "What's going on with him, Brian?"

Brian shook his head and was about to say that he didn't know when Cory came into the dining room holding a bowl of mac and cheese in each hand. He was grinning from ear to ear, and Brian himself didn't have to be a mind reader to know that this was the happiest Ellen had seen her son in quite some time.

# CHAPTER THIRTY-TWO
# BABY TALK

## 1

The baby was trying to tell her something. Was it even a baby yet? Could it be called that while it was still inside her, and so early in the game? Sarah didn't know. Similarly, she didn't know just how far along she was: she'd missed only one period, which should have arrived two weeks earlier. The last time she and Doolman had had sex had been about a couple weeks before that, give or take, although she supposed she could have gotten pregnant the time before that, which had only been about two weeks prior to the last time. Two weeks here, two weeks there. She, too, felt too weak, ha ha. She felt that if she couldn't find at least a modicum of humor in all this, she might just jump off the Bay Bridge.

Still: the baby was trying to tell her something.

Those wire coat hangers that she had obsessively straightened out into long, bowing wands? She began to lay them atop one another on her bedroom floor, a bunch of them horizontally overlaid by a bunch vertically, forming a sort of crosshatch, a giant tic tac toe grid. She obsessed over this grid in the same fashion she obsessed over the coat hangers, although something inside her felt *different* this time. It was as if this particular obsession, unlike with the collecting of the hangers, was being transmitted from someplace other than her own mind—from the fetus straight into her brain, it felt like. She thought of how a mother's body shared nutrients with the fetus via the umbilical cord, but could that same mysterious umbilicus also serve as a conduit for the fetus to transmit things to *her*? Not nutrients, of course, but perhaps *information*? Perhaps an unshakable *obsession*?

That perfect grid of vertical rods atop horizontal ones, each thin wire meticulously spaced the same distance apart, forming a network of perfect little squares. Yet something about it seemed *wrong*. The fetus spoke to her and relayed that it was unhappy. Displeased. Was it possible for a fetus to feel those things?

She reached down and widened the space between two of the vertical wires. Wider, wider, like parting a curtain made of chainmail. Wider, wider . . .

. . . too wide.

The whole thing was ruined.

*What the fuck am I doing?*

She forced herself to stop and buried the straightened coat hangers at the back of her closet.

Things were getting too far out of hand.

Sarah Miller stood now at the far end of the downstairs hall where she watched her father as he ate lunch by himself at the kitchen table—a tuna salad sandwich, a pickle spear, and a glass of milk. He wore the cuffs of his white dress shirt rolled to his elbows, kept his posture rigid, and gazed dreamily out the kitchen windows at the vibrant beds of begonias, violets, tulips, and bougainvillea out there swaying in the sun. Her mother had planted all those flowers, and despite receiving no care and attention from Sarah or her father in the two years since her mother's passing, those flowers continued to blossom and flourish.

She loved her father but had no understanding of him. A man whose career—whose *life*—was laid bare at the feet of unwavering faith, even as his wife had rotted away from cancer and ultimately died in the upstairs bedroom they'd once shared. He still slept in that room, in that bed. Sarah had been thinking a lot about that sort of thing lately—life and death. Life, because of what was growing inside her, of course; death, because inevitably that was where everyone eventually ended up. How her father could maintain his religious conviction after Sarah's mother had died in such a cruel, painful, and undignified fashion, she had no idea. She'd wanted her father to renounce God, much as she had. She wanted him to show some human emotion. Instead, there was just one less plate set at the dinner table, one less stocking hung from the hearth at Christmas. There were framed photos of them on the walls of the house, the three of them depicted in happier times. She could say that she missed those days—it was easy to do so in hindsight—but Sarah had never been particularly fond of childhood. The only thing she missed about those times, aside from her mother, was the simplicity that came with the theoretical invincibility of youth.

Her father seemed to sense her standing there: he turned and looked at her, his eyes going comically wide for just a second, then he offered up a smile pocked with a dollop of mayo in one corner of his mouth. His profile silvered by the sunlight coming in through the kitchen windows, he happened to look pious and otherworldly in that moment. For a split second, she wondered if maybe *she* was the one who'd been misled about God.

"You certainly slept late," he said around a mouthful of tuna salad. "Are you feeling all right?"

"Feeling fine."

"Are you hungry? I can whip something up."

"No, thanks."

She made a beeline for the cupboard, took down a glass, filled it with water at the sink. She hadn't eaten properly since she'd taken that first pregnancy test and didn't have the stomach for it now. She brought the glass of water to her lips . . .

. . . then paused, watching as the aerated bubbles rose to the surface like shooting stars. A thought accosted her then—

—*there's something in the water*—

—but it was so fleeting that it carried no logical weight and so she didn't stop to think about it. She downed the glass of water in three hearty gulps.

"Interesting earrings," he said, examining her from the kitchen table.

"Thanks. I made them."

"Are they . . . ?"

"They're pieces of coat hanger," she said. To keep some of the coat hangers with her at all times, she'd cut some into sections with a pair of bolt cutters she'd found in the garage, and fashioned them into jewelry—an uncomfortable set of rings, a necklace that, admittedly, looked more like orthodontal headgear, and these ugly, corkscrew-shaped earrings. Each earring was several inches long, but she wound them like a spring so that they each made a spiral hanging from her ears. It made them look more decorative.

"Myra and I are headed to Ellicott City today for some antiques shopping and then dinner," he said. "Did you have any plans?"

"I'm working. It's on the calendar."

"Is it? I stopped looking."

The calendar was from a local Chinese restaurant, the words *Year of the Dragon* printed at the top in garish red font, and it was kept on the inside of the pantry door. It was where they both used to outline their schedules for one another, but over the past year, and as Sarah grew more despondent, she had ceased using the calendar, petulant about allowing her father to know her whereabouts like she was some parolee straight out of prison. But after she'd peed positive on the first pregnancy test (and peed three pink lines on the second, whatever the hell that meant), she had reverted to some desperate childish rendition of herself, and found that she was surprised to find comfort in old familiarities. So, she had begun using the calendar again.

Yet she wasn't actually going to work today.

She had other plans.

"Do you want me to have Myra pick me up?" her father asked. "This way you can take the Tank."

The Tank was a 1963 Ford Thunderbird which, aside from his Bible, was perhaps David Miller's most prized possession. He had let her drive the Tank on only a handful of occasions, and he had been seated right beside her, shoulder to shoulder, on the long bench seat every time. She assumed he was offering up the Tank now because she'd been having trouble with the Festiva lately, but also because he was likely trying to mitigate some of the tension that had begun to form between them over the past several days. She couldn't tell him about the pregnancy tests, couldn't tell him about her obsession with coat hangers and how she and the jock from the restaurant were communicating telepathically while sharing the same dreams. So she did what any nineteen-year-old girl would do and kept avoiding him like some virulent disease.

"I don't think I need the Tank," she said, "but thanks anyway."

"Hey, listen, can I talk to you?"

She had transitioned over to the refrigerator, door open, rooting around for a can of Diet Coke, when he said this. Her back stiffened, and she closed the refrigerator door and looked at him. Said, teenagerly, "What?"

"I'd like you to consider going back to school in the fall. If that means you have to cut back on your hours at the restaurant, I'm willing to help make up the difference. I've got some money squirreled away."

"I don't know, Dad . . ."

"You're a smart girl, Sarah. I'd like to see you take advantage of every opportunity. You can't work at a barbecue joint forever."

She shrugged. Said, "Why not?" Though the prospect of working at a place like Hollywood BBQ for the rest of her life made her want to eat a gun.

"Listen, kitten, it's your life. I'm just here to help guide you to make smart choices. Choices that you won't regret later. Just promise me you'll think about it."

"Sure," she said, but had no plans to do so.

She watched him finish his meal, then rise from his chair with a labor that seemed reserved for a much older man. He set his plate and glass in the sink, kissed the side of her face, then shuffled down the hall and up the stairs.

She looked at the cross that hung on the wall, next to an old family photo. Heard those empty scrabbling claws of absolute devotion somewhere inside the walls of this house, the foundation, the dark spaces of the attic. Life was futile. What the fuck did community college matter? What the fuck did *any* of it matter?

Still, she felt her face grow hot as she stared at that cross.

Her eyes: a little blurry.

Later, after her father had left in the Tank to pick up his girlfriend and drive to Ellicott City, Sarah went upstairs to the bathroom. With the shower running to fill the room up with steam, she cried a bit while perched naked on the edge of the tub. After that, she called Hollywood BBQ and called out sick. Beatrice wasn't happy about it—they'd been short-staffed all week—but she recalled that Sarah had been feeling under the weather lately (and likely heard the residual stuffiness from her crying in her voice), so she didn't make a federal case about it. After that, she called Shane Doolman's cell phone. She wanted to know if he'd be around later today, because suddenly, Sarah Miller felt like burning down the world. The phone rang, rang, rang, until an automated voice informed her that Doolie was unable to take her call and to leave a message at the tone. Sarah hung up without leaving a message. She thought about firing off a text message, but in the end, she decided against it. She had a pretty good idea where he was and what he was doing—it was band practice day—and she liked the idea of a sneak attack. Anyway, she felt like ruining Doolman's afternoon; it might make her feel better.

The spray of the shower felt good against her skin, until a thought, errant and without logic, accosted her:

*(there's something in the water)*

The same illogical nonsense that had come to her down in the kitchen.

And for some reason, it made her angry.

After she showered, she pulled on a pair of black jeans, a Rob Zombie T-shirt, and laced up her Doc Martens. She lied and told herself that everything was normal and that she was feeling pretty good, but then that urge to assemble those straightened coat hangers into that massive tic tac toe grid overtook her yet again. So, there she was on her hands and knees upon the plush carpet of her bedroom floor, lining metal rods into rows and columns, making the world's biggest and strangest goddamn hashtag. After however many minutes of this madness, she collected the rods and stuffed them back in her closet. Enough was enough. She had to stop. If nothing else in her life mattered anymore, why did those goddamn hangers? Her head felt fuzzy and like her brain was fighting for space inside her skull. She hoofed it down the stairs, taking them two at a time.

The Festiva started up on the first crank, so at least the world wasn't taking a total shit on her today. But before she pulled out of the driveway, she was overcome by the strange compulsion to take some of the hangers with her. The impulse was so strong that it seemed impossible to drop the car into gear and reverse out of the driveway without retrieving some of the hangers from the house first. So that was exactly what she did: she ran back inside, loaded a stack of them insider her JanSport backpack, then carried them back out to the car. She felt instantly calmer with the backpack on the passenger seat next to her, and realized the ridiculous bullshit jewelry she'd made herself wasn't doing its job.

At one point she slowed down outside her father's church. It was a modest brick building with a small parking lot that sat at the intersection of Terrace and Goodall. To Sarah, the building had always looked more like a nursery school than a church, what with its quaintness of stature and the paper cutout of children's hands on all the windows. Of course, the exception was the cross on the roof's spire: no doubt about what that meant. There was also a large sign posted in the grass at the entrance to the parking lot—a sign that had been there for as long as Sarah could remember, except she felt herself truly noticing it now as if for the first time:

**PREGNANT? ALONE? SCARED?**
COME JOIN US
GOD CAN HELP

There was a phone number below that, but Sarah ignored it. She wasn't about to call some church or some pregnancy hotline. But the sign *did* cause something inside her chest to flutter about. Pregnant? Check. Scared? You bet. Alone?

That one gave her pause.

And no, it had nothing to do with that idiot Doolman whom she'd so stupidly, carelessly allowed to knock her up. Instead, she was thinking of her father, and of the photos of her dead mother that still lined the walls of their home, as if the woman might just come waltzing through the front door after a day of running errands at any moment.

She thought of the baby inside her.

*Alone?*

There'd been that sharp, burning pain that had pulsed through her womb the other day as she was getting out of the shower. She thought she was having a miscarriage and had plunked herself down on the toilet, terrified at whatever mess might spill out of her. But nothing had happened, and the pain had fled her with the same expediency as it had arrived.

Fuck, she wanted a smoke.

Instead, she stepped on the gas and drove off.

## 2

Panic didn't touch her again until she was about to drive out of the neighborhood. In fact, it arrived so unbidden and abrupt that her entire body seemed to gush sweat all at once. She sensed her muscles tense to the point that they felt like metal rods in her arms and legs, no different than the ones hidden at the back of her bedroom closet. Trembling, she pulled the car over onto the shoulder of the road and slammed it into park. Ahead, she could see the sluggish crawl of weekend beach traffic along the highway just beyond the entrance—or, in her case, the *exit*—of Mariner's Cove. It was in that moment that she could no longer deny that she had been feeling this same sense of panic for a while now, albeit to a lesser degree, every time she left the neighborhood. It had been there every morning as she left for work, followed by a subtle relief upon returning later that evening. Until this morning, it had only manifested as an unsettling stir in the center of her chest. Now, however, she could no longer deny that *something was wrong*, that maybe *something was wrong with her*, because she was having a difficult time breathing.

The car shivered then died.

"What? No, no!"

She cranked the key in the ignition over and over, but was rewarded with nothing but a dim buzzing—

*(buzzing)*

—sound. After the fourth crank, not even that: just a click, then dead silence.

"Oh, fuck you!"

Her first instinct was to call her father, but then realized he was with Myra in Ellicott City for the day. She took out her phone, scrolled through her contacts. It occurred to her that she didn't have many friends—an observation that, strangely, hadn't occurred to her until just this moment. Her friends from high school had mostly flitted off to colleges around the country, and she didn't consider fifty-year-old Melanie Yodell or pot-smoking Roberta Ducette from the restaurant to be friends.

She stopped scrolling when she came to Eric Rhodes's name. He wasn't working today, she knew. Yet did she want to call him? She got the sense that she'd pushed him away after that night in the Trenton house, when she'd basically forced him to take sleeping pills and then invaded his privacy by firing off telepathic messages straight into his cranium, which had made him uncomfortable. Christ, she'd freaked the poor son of a bitch out. Could she really call him now?

For a moment she considered walking all the way back home, a trek that was over a mile and would prove torturous in this heat. In the end, and before she knew what she was doing, she dialed Eric's number and had the phone pressed to her ear as it rang.

"Hey, Sarah."

*Not Miller,* she thought. *He's stopped calling me Miller. Something's changed between us, all right. Something's happened.*

"Are you home?" she asked.

"Yeah. What's up?"

"My car's dead. I'm at the entrance to the neighborhood, on the shoulder of the road. Do you think you could come get me?"

To her chagrin, he laughed. "That car! You need a better set of wheels, man."

"I'll put that on the to-do list."

"I'll be right there," he said, and hung up.

She cranked down the windows to get some fresh air into the vehicle then reclined her seat several inches. Her eyes drifted to the glove compartment. She reached out and unlatched the door, which dropped open like a mouth in surprise. Paper napkins, tampons, a tin of mints, a pair of cheap sunglasses—a bunch of that shit fell onto the passenger seat of the car. Something else, too: a pack of smokes. Marlboros. There was even a neon green plastic lighter tucked tidily inside the pack's cellophane sleeve.

The sight of them settled her nerves a bit, so she reached for the smokes. Felt the cellophane crinkle against her palm. Could feel her mouth watering for the taste of one . . . but then for some reason—

*(pregnant? alone? scared?)*

—she paused. It was silly, really: if nothing mattered and everything eventually ended in death, what did one cigarette mean for a fetus that may or may not be growing inside her? Nonetheless, she leaned over and stuffed the pack back in the glove compartment and slammed it shut.

Closing her eyes, she took a series of deep breaths until she was able to stabilize her breathing. When she opened them again, she found she had dragged her backpack into her lap from over on the passenger seat, had unzipped it, and was caressing the jumble of wire hangers inside with both hands.

This made her feel better. In fact, this made her feel *good.* She pulled up Spotify on her phone, pumped up the volume, and listened as Joey Ramone came on, shouting about Sheena being a punk rocker.

## 3

What Sarah didn't notice as she sat there with her eyes closed and her music playing was that a pair of teenage boys donning matching black slacks, sleeveless white button-down shirts, and loose black neckties had just entered the community of Mariner's Cove intent on spreading the Good Word of the Lord. It was a route both boys took once a month, knocking on doors, chatting with the friendly residents, and leaving pamphlets tucked into the doorframes or in mailboxes. But on this day, and for no discernable reason, both boys paused simultaneously in the middle of the road, looked around at the tightly packed houses that flanked them on either side of the wide street, then turned back around and retreated toward the highway. They said nothing to each other about this sudden change in plans: in fact, the change did not seem to register with either of them at all. They simply walked along the shoulder of the highway until they came to the next community, and neither of them ever considered why they'd turned around and fled from the quaint, quiet neighborhood of Mariner's Cove in the first place.

## 4

She felt herself burst into wakefulness to the sensation of a hand nudging her gently on one shoulder. Eric Rhodes stood before the open driver's side window of the Festiva in a pair of reflective sunglasses. For a split second, Sarah caught her reflection in the lenses, and thought she looked like a reanimated corpse, startled by the touch of his hand on her shoulder.

"Thanks for coming," she said, and switched the music off her phone. She pulled the keys from the ignition, then grabbed her backpack as she crawled out of the car, slamming the door behind her.

"You know, we can set it on fire, collect the insurance money," Eric suggested.

"Don't fucking tempt me."

They got in his truck and Eric made a U-turn in the street. "Where were you headed?"

She'd been headed to Doolman's house, where he'd likely be practicing all afternoon with his bandmates, to unload the burden of this pregnancy on him, but she sure as hell wasn't going to say that to Eric. Instead, she muttered something about having to run some errands.

"I can drive you around," he offered. "I've got nothing going on."

"No way."

He hoisted one shoulder, as if it was no big deal. "Just saying."

Was she being too hard on him? Was she angry that he'd gotten upset with her at the Trenton house and had acted funny on the drive home? Was this some form of payback to make her feel better?

"Hey," she said. "Are we okay?"

He glanced at her. "What do you mean?"

"I feel like something's changed between us."

"There's a 'between us'?"

That made her feel like shit. "You know what I mean."

"Everything's fine." Another nonchalant hoist of the shoulder.

"You sure?"

"Of course, Sarah."

*Sarah. Just Sarah now.*

They drove the rest of the way to her house in silence. When they got there, Eric pulled his truck into the driveway. She offered a curt thanks, then hopped out of the cab before he could say anything. As she hustled her way to the front door, she heard the truck's engine go quiet and the driver's side door close.

Eric came up the walk, fiddling nervously with his keys.

"What?" she said. Her tone was no different now than it had been earlier that afternoon when she'd spoken with her father in the kitchen about college.

He was thinking about how to say whatever it was that was on his mind. She thought about poking her way into his head and seeing if she could suss it out herself, but didn't for two reasons—one, because she didn't know if she could; and two, she'd promised him that she wouldn't.

"I guess," he said, staring down at those fidgeting hands, truck keys jangling, "I guess I just wanted to say that if there's anything bothering *you*, that, you know, you could come and talk to *me* . . . I mean, if there was something . . . if you . . . if you wanted . . ."

She'd heard the beginning of what he'd said, but the rest was lost in a buzzing wash of white noise. She wasn't even looking at him anymore, either, but instead out past her front yard and the street and beyond the houses on the other side of the street. She was looking at the steel tank of the Gladstone Park water tower looming behind a fringe of verdant summer trees. It wasn't just the tower that had caused her breath to catch and had relegated all that Eric Rhodes was saying to the verbal equivalent of white noise.

It was what someone had *done* to the tower.

"Oh my God," she said, the words slipping breathlessly up her throat. She pointed, and Eric ceased talking and looked across the street, not seeing what she was seeing at first, but that didn't matter: she felt something *connect*, felt something spark to life inside her head.

She grabbed Eric's hand and dragged him out into the street.

## CHAPTER THIRTY-THREE

# SAFE CAMP: WELCOME TO THE HIVE

### 1

"Look!" Alex shouted, his voice a sudden, sharp crack filled with awe. They had just left the house and were pulling up to the intersection of Jolene and Tamarack when Alex jumped on the brake, causing the Camry to rock to a standstill in the middle of the road. He slammed a hand against the driver's side window as he stared out. "Georgette, look!"

"What are you—"

Alex jumped out of the car, and she scrambled out after him. He was backing up onto the curb, his eyes locked on something high on the horizon. Georgette followed his gaze to the massive bone-colored tank of the Gladstone Park water tower that rose above the line of trees and stood against the afternoon's stark blue and cloudless sky. To Georgette's disbelief, someone had gone up there and painted over the words on the tank in a muddy brown wash of paint:

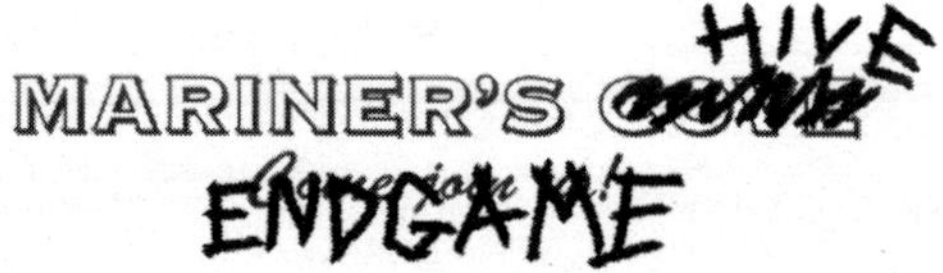


Whoever had written this had also reproduced the symbols from Alex's notepad along the outer walls of the water tank with that same ugly brown paint. The symbols were tremendous, several feet high. They looked as if they'd been magicked there by the Hand of God.

*No, not God,* Georgette thought, her grip tightening onto the colander that she was clutching now between her breasts. *Stinger. Stinger did this.*

"Endgame," Alex marveled.

"He's calling everyone to the tower," she said, and she could hear that her own voice was now filled with a sense of awe, too, and barely louder than a whisper. She wasn't even sure Alex had heard her or, for that matter, if she was even speaking to him aloud or with her mind. "He's summoning the colony." She did not know why she had chosen that word—*colony*—but once she'd said it, she knew it was right.

A vague smile breaking across Alex's face, he said, "Jesus Christ, Georgette, we're—"

*(WE'RE REALLY DOING IT AREN'T WE?)*

"—really doing it, aren't we?"

She could hear his words both out loud and inside her head simultaneously. She didn't even know if he was aware he was doing it. She simply nodded and said, "We are."

She wasn't sure how long the two of them remained standing there staring at the top of the water tower in the distance before she realized they were not alone anymore. Two additional people had joined them—a girl of about nineteen or twenty, dressed all in black and with smudgy streaks of mascara running down her cheeks, and a young man who was maybe only slightly older. The girl wore a backpack and she was gripping the straps that came down around her shoulders with both hands. As the girl met her eyes, Georgette saw that she wore peculiar earrings that looked like bronze-colored bits of wire curled into snail-shaped spirals. For some reason, they reminded Georgette of Christmas decorations.

"Sorry." The girl's voice was edgy, suspicious, and Georgette wasn't sure what she was apologizing for. The girl nodded in the direction of the water tower in the distance. "Did you guys do that?"

Georgette said, "No, but I think we know who did. What're your names?"

"Sarah Miller," said the girl.

"I'm Eric Rhodes," said the boy. Georgette felt him studying her. "I think you used to give me piano lessons when I was a kid. Mrs. Braswell, right?"

"Eric," she said, suddenly remembering the young boy he'd been—towheaded, freckle-faced, unable to grasp the concept of reading sheet music or, in truth, the concept of music, period. "Yes, I remember you. You can call me Georgette. This is my husband, Alex."

Alex said nothing; he'd already lost interest in the two newcomers and was back to staring at the water tank rising high above the trees at the far end of Gladstone Park.

The girl—Sarah—said, "Are you guys going there now? To the water tower?" She was staring at the colander Georgette was clutching to her chest, and Georgette's first instinct was to hide it behind her back, the way a child might. But she resisted.

"Yes," Georgette answered. "What's in your backpack?"

"You've brought something, haven't you?" This was Alex, speaking up for the first time, though his eyes were still trained on the water tower. "What did you bring?"

Crazily, Georgette thought of the Biblical tale of the Magi, and how those three wise men had allegedly followed a star to Bethlehem bearing gifts for the newborn Son of God.

Sarah slipped the straps of the backpack off her shoulders then cradled the bag against her chest as she unzipped it. When she pulled back the canvas flaps to reveal what was inside, Georgette saw what looked like a lunatic jumble of metal wires twisted about in there. For a moment, that rat king of wires gleamed in the sunlight.

"What are those?" she asked the girl.

"Hangers. For clothes."

Georgette nodded, as if this made all the sense in the world. When she looked up at the girl's face again, she noticed that Sarah Miller was still staring intently at the colander Georgette held against her chest. Protective of it, Georgette bladed her body so that the colander wasn't too exposed.

"I think," Sarah began, her voice distant and dreamy, but then she trailed off leaving the sentiment unfinished.

Georgette nodded at Eric. "What about you? What did you bring?"

"I didn't bring anything."

Georgette found this suspicious, but she didn't say anything more about it.

"I think there's someone you both should meet," Alex said. He stepped back down into the street and with his eyes still locked on the water tower, made his way to the open car door. When he finally turned to look at the rest of them, Georgette could see that queer little smile still fermenting there on his lips. "Get in the car and we'll take you," he told them.

## 2

When Sarah saw the couple standing in the middle of the street staring up at the water tower, it was as if some great bolt turned and clacked into place. All concerns over her pregnancy fled from her, and in that moment, the only thing that mattered was the wire coat hangers. That word—ENDGAME—that had been painted overnight on the water tank was a message to her; the moment she saw it she knew she had to go there—was *destined* to go there. It felt like she was being summoned. And she had let go of Eric's hand and hurried up the block to meet these two strangers who seemed to be looking upon the water tower with the same sense of destiny. She even managed to catch the fleeting buzz of one of their thoughts humming through the air—

*(WE'RE REALLY DOING IT AREN'T WE?)*

—as she approached.

Now, with Sarah and Eric in the back seat, the man—Alex Braswell—drove them in a circuitous fashion around the park until they came out along a nameless stretch of road that ran through a dense strip of trees. There were quicker ways to get to the park, Sarah knew, but she had a sense that Alex was driving in—

*(circles circles circles)*

—such a fashion as to confuse anyone who might be following

them. It was a ridiculous thought, really—this wasn't some old spy movie where they were trying to give some unseen pursuer the slip—and anyway, who the heck would be trying to follow them?

Of course, *she* had found them, had spotted Georgette and Alex . . . and likely would have followed them had Alex not told them to get into their car. She needed to go to that water tower.

They parked off the road in a patch of weeds then they all climbed out of the car. Sarah followed the Braswells through the woods, careful of her footing while ducking beneath low-hanging boughs. They walked in silence, though Sarah's head was burning with questions. Like Eric, she thought she recognized the woman from the neighborhood, thought she might have two young daughters that she sometimes took to the park or down to the beach at the end of Slope Hill in the summers. She didn't recognize the man. Nonetheless, there was a feeling of absolute and undeniable *correctness* about their chance meeting, and of the sound of that mental bolt turning—*clunk!*

She glanced over her shoulder to find Eric lagging. He looked glum and uncertain, and she wanted to call out to him to keep up, but also didn't want to interrupt the silence. Despite Eric's discomfort with the act, she transmitted a single thought to him—

*Are you okay?*

—and that was when the Braswells both stopped dead in their tracks. Eric looked up, too, his eyes wide, his face expressionless.

*(WE CAN BOTH HEAR YOU)*

The thought was stronger and more direct than the fleeting one Sarah had managed to snatch out of the air by accident as she'd approached them in the middle of the street. This time, it sounded like it was both Alex and Georgette speaking in her head in unison, and the strength of that thought caused a dull, pulsing pain to radiate through the nerve endings of her molars.

Eric took a step backward. He was slowly shaking his head.

"Eric," Sarah said.

"No." He held up a steadying hand. "Tell them, Sarah. I don't like it. I don't think we should be doing things like that."

"Things like what?" Georgette asked.

"He doesn't like the telepathy," Sarah explained.

"Oh, honey," Georgette said, moving past Sarah and advancing toward Eric. "It's just part of the becoming."

"The assimilation," Alex said from the front of the line.

"Come on, sweetie," Georgette said. She held out a hand toward Eric. "Come join us."

Sarah felt her back teeth throb again. She braced herself for another telepathic missive, but nothing happened.

She watched as Eric took hold of Georgette's hand.

Georgette smiled prettily. "See? We're all in this together."

"Endgame," Alex said.

"Endgame," Sarah heard herself repeat.

"Come on," Alex said, turning around and continuing his journey through the trees.

Eventually they stepped into a wide clearing surrounded by trees. The Gladstone Park water tower, in all its tremendous glory, stood at the center of the clearing, pious as the Tower of Babel. Its base surrounded by a splintery wooden split-rail fence, and the ground at the base of the tower alternated between cracked pavement and powdery white chips of gravel. She'd never been this close to a water tower before, and the sheer enormity of it was breathtaking.

She saw that the legs of the tower were swaddled in chain-link fencing. Why she should focus on this right away, she couldn't say—for all she knew, the legs of *every* water tower across America were housed behind a chain-link fence—but for some reason this stood out to her as . . . well, as something important.

"It's so big," she marveled. She took a few more steps toward it, until the tank at the top blotted out the sun and she was cast into shadow. Staring straight up at it like that had a dizzying effect on her, and she couldn't look at it for very long. She felt the woman, Georgette, come up beside her. Sarah asked, "Did you guys do that? Put that fencing up around it like that?"

Georgette said, "Yes. With some help."

Sarah nodded. "It's mostly right," she said, not really sure why she was saying it or what it meant. It *felt* right, maybe. She was thinking of the baby inside her, and how it had been forcing her to make that grid of straightened wires on her bedroom floor—a design that looked nearly identical to the chain-link fencing, she now realized.

"What do you mean it feels 'mostly' right?" Georgette asked.

"Just that," Sarah said. "I can't explain it. I mean, it *looks* right, but I think something is . . . a little off with it . . ."

Georgette cocked her head, as if to view the tower from a different perspective.

"I've been dreaming of this, you know," Sarah said. "Only in my dream, I come here at night. There are a lot of other people, too, all standing around and looking up at something in the sky. I didn't realize it was the water tower we were all looking at until just now. I mean, it doesn't look like a water tower in my dream. It looks more like . . . I guess . . ."

"A beehive," Georgette said, completing Sarah's thought.

Sarah looked at the woman. She was pretty, but tired looking, the way Sarah's mom had sometimes looked after a long week of work and taking care of her family. "Yes. Exactly. How do you . . . ?"

"We've all been having the same dream."

"But *how*?" she asked. "Do you understand any of it?"

"I think it's because we're all connected somehow," Georgette said, and gently tapped her temple with an index finger; Sarah very nearly felt that finger tapping her *own* temple as she did so.

"So, what does this all mean?"

Georgette's eyebrows knitted together the tiniest bit. "We're still trying to figure that out," she said, and Sarah sensed that perhaps Georgette wanted to say more but was for some reason reluctant. "Do you know what your coat hangers are for?"

"I didn't think I did," she said, "until just now." She pointed all the way up to the water tank where those symbols stood out in ugly brown paint. "That triangle shape with the little hook at the top represents my hangers," she explained. "Those straight lines? Those are my hangers, too, only undone and straightened out into long wires." She kept thinking of the hangers she had straightened while hidden away in her bedroom (with the door locked), sweating and desperate to make them as straight as possible, which was a difficult task with unfolded wire coat hangers. Lining them up in perfect rows and columns, just like the links in the fencing wrapped around the base of the water tower. She felt the urge to go over to the chain-link now and pull it apart, widening the links, just as she'd done to the wire grid she had laid out on her bedroom floor. She had no idea why, yet the feeling was suddenly all-encompassing. She felt she wanted to explain this to Georgette, too, but lost her train of thought when she heard the sound of someone approaching through the woods.

A figure shambled out from between the trees. It was a man, his age indeterminable because his face was covered in what looked like small, knobby welts. He was wearing a Ravens cap so low on his head that it cast a heavy shadow over his eyes. As he approached, the lower portion of his face broke out into a wide and rather unsettling grin. Sarah's first instinct was to recoil in disgust—something about the man felt *off*, triggering the fight-or-flight response in her limbic system—but when she realized neither Georgette nor Alex seemed troubled by the man's presence, Sarah forced herself to relax.

"Well," said the man, pausing beside the wooden split-rail fence. He propped one grime-caked jackboot on one of the crossbars. "I see we've got a couple of new friends. How nice."

"You painted those symbols up there," Alex said. It was not a question.

"You know it," said the man. He removed the Ravens cap, and a tumble of blondish hair swung down over his forehead. With the shadow of the hat gone, Sarah could see that he was much younger than she had originally thought, maybe even in his twenties, though his face was so bruised, sunburnt, and . . . well, lumpy with those strange welts . . . that it was still difficult to pinpoint an age. Up in his hairline was a piece of silver tape, the outer edges of it stained the rusty brown of dried blood.

To Sarah, the man looked like a walking nightmare . . . yet she heard another bolt slide into place upon scrutinizing him, just as it had when she'd first laid eyes on the tower and then on the Braswells as they stood on the curb staring off toward Gladstone Park.

This was the man who'd come into Hollywood BBQ that day and fired a message directly into her brain—

*(I would fuck your brains out)*

—and this was *also* the man who had accosted her in the dream she'd had that night in the abandoned Trenton house: the man who'd crawled insect-like along the shell of the great floating hive and had shown her the symbols there, along with that one weighty but nebulous word—ENDGAME. She knew she should be afraid, but instead, the sensation of absolute *correctness* flooded through her, dulling any apprehension and fear she might otherwise be harboring.

"I tell ya, it was a bitch, though," the man continued, gazing up at his handiwork painted along the water tank. "Took me fucking *hours*." Then, as if an afterthought, he added, "I think."

"Do you really think it'll work?" Alex asked. His voice sounded throaty and nervous, like someone about to lose a lot of money at a poker table. "Do you really think people will come?"

The man with the lumpy, sunburned face looked first at Eric then at Sarah. The steel pins of his eyes settled on her—settled *into* her—but she felt no fear of him this time. He said, quite matter of fact, "These two came, didn't they? What's your name, honey?"

"Sarah Miller."

He closed the distance and extended a hand to her. She shook it automatically. His palm was rough and dry.

"I'm Stinger. Welcome to the Hive."

## 3

Nearby, there was a tree stump that rose approximately three feet from the ground, and that someone at some point had taken a chainsaw to it, so that its surface was flat and smooth, and about twenty-four inches in diameter. It made for a good drafting table, Alex thought. It felt good to think in measurements—in feet and inches and diameters—again. It was part of his old self, Alex Braswell the engineer, peeking through the eyeholes of whatever his body had so recently become. He had the others gather around him as he took a plain white envelope from the rear pocket of his jeans. Before he opened it, he announced to everyone, "Grab some small rocks, some stones. Anything with a little weight to it so these things don't blow away." They all hunted around and returned with handfuls of golf ball–sized stones, which pleased Alex, despite the fact that he hadn't felt as much as a slight breeze all afternoon.

"Georgette and I spent all of last night piecing this thing together," he said. He opened the envelope and took out the paper cutouts of the symbols, placing them delicately, in fact lovingly, one by one, on the flat surface of the stump. "Put a rock on each one," he instructed, and each time he laid down a cutout, someone quickly covered it with a stone so that it wouldn't blow away in the non-breeze. "Okay, see, they're not supposed to be flat. We've been thinking about them in two dimensions. It was an understandable but myopic way of thinking about things." He picked up the cutout of an X with a horizontal line across the top. "What's this look like?"

"And upside-down triangle with the bottom lines extended," Sarah said.

"A bowtie on its side, but with a line missing," Georgette said.

"An *hourglass* with the bottom line missing," Eric added.

"No," said Stinger. "That's the symbol for 'safe camp.' It's what hobos used to mark locations where other travelers would find safety for the night."

Alex was surprised. "How do you know that?"

"From books," said Stinger, curtly.

"I'm not so sure 'hobo' is the politically correct term," Eric suggested. "I think they're called 'unhoused' or 'someone experiencing homelessness.'"

Stinger frowned at him. "Are you fucking serious right now?"

"For me," Alex interjected, "I first thought of the symbol in mathematical terms. The horizontal bar at the top of the X looked to me like a macron. A line over an X stands for an arithmetical mean or average, which refers to the sum of a set of numbers divided by the count of those numbers—"

"Okay," Georgette said, touching his arm.

"Right." He cleared his throat. "Point is, we're all wrong. We need to stop thinking of these images in two dimensions. Do you follow me? Here, watch."

He took out a strip of plain white paper from the envelope. It looked like a narrow piece of tickertape maybe six inches long. He folded it until it approximate the shape of the symbol, then set it down on the tree stump.

"Now what does it look like?" he asked.

In unison, everyone said, "A chair."

"Exactly. Like a stool, or maybe one of those camping chairs that fold up, right?"

"Right!" Eric said, suddenly excited. "That's exactly what it looks like!"

Next, Alex pointed to the drawing that depicted that same "safe camp" symbol on the bottom half of what looked like a child's simple drawing of a door. Still thinking in three dimensions, he picked up this cutout and stood it up vertically, leaning it against the three-dimensional paper "chair."

"Door becomes chair," Alex said.

"Door becomes chair," Stinger intoned.

Alex grinned. "You see? Three-dimensional. It all goes together."

Sarah pointed to the image of the circle with all the lines radiating out from it, the thing that looked to both Alex and Georgette like a sun flecked with chickenpox. "What's this?"

"My colander," Georgette answered.

"And these lines coming off it?" Sarah asked.

Georgette shrugged. "We're not sure. We haven't figured *everything* out yet."

"I know what they are," Sarah said. "It's in the symbols, remember? The triangle with the hook on the top represents my coat hangers . . . but so do the straight lines. Can I see it?" She was looking at Georgette's colander, which Georgette cradled like a child against her breast.

Alex watched a gleam of mistrust flicker behind his wife's eyes. But then she looked back down at the cutouts on the tree stump and the little three-dimensional diorama Alex had made, and ultimately handed the girl her colander.

They all watched as Sarah set her backpack on the ground, took out a single wire hanger, and proceeded to twist the hooked end apart so that the whole thing unwound with a nearly audible *thwang*. She bent the wire into a somewhat straight line—Alex thought of all the times he'd done this with a coat hanger in the past to snake a clogged toilet—then she propped Georgette's colander under one arm, cradling it like a football, and less tenderly than Georgette had been holding it. As they watched, Sarah poked the end of the wire into one of the small strainer holes of the colander. She twisted it a bit to get it seated. It was a perfect fit.

"Holy fucking shit!" Stinger shouted, bolting off the ground and to his feet. He clapped his hands once, sharp as the report of a pistol.

"Yes!" Georgette said. It came out as a delighted squeal. She climbed to her feet as well and hurried over to Sarah, staring at the colander with the long, bowing wire poking from it beneath Sarah's arm. "My God, yes. That's it. Sarah Miller, I could kiss you right on the mouth."

Alex and Eric chuckled, Sarah blushed, and Stinger said, "Do it."

Sarah held the colander at arm's length, so that it was equidistant between her and Georgette. "Yeah, sure, I figured it out," she said, "but I'm not sure what this actually *means*. All I know now is that we're supposed to fill all these holes with these straightened hangers. But I don't know *why*."

"It's a start," Alex said. "We're all learning as we go. We don't know everything."

"Not yet," Stinger said.

"Well," Sarah said, looking back toward the base of the water tower. "There's one more thing I know."

"What's that?" Stinger asked.

She pointed to the base of the tower, and at the fencing that corralled the tower's legs, caging the tower inside. "There should be a doorway or an opening or something somewhere along that fence."

"Why's that?" Alex asked.

"Because whatever we're supposed to build," Sarah said, "we're supposed to do it on the *inside* of the fence."

Alex looked toward the chain-link fence wrapped around the legs of the water tower. "How do you know that?"

She shrugged. "It's just something I feel."

Then Alex saw her do a curious thing: she removed one hand from the colander and placed it against her abdomen. Tenderly.

"I'll get some bolt cutters from the maintenance shed," Stinger said.

Sarah nodded then looked down at the backpack at her feet. Wire hangers bulged from its canvas flaps like intestines from an unzippered belly. "And I think we're going to need a lot more coat hangers than what I've got in my backpack."

"Do you have any more?" Georgette asked.

Sarah Miller just laughed.

## 4

Stinger came out through the trees at the far end of Gladstone Park and unlocked the padlock on the maintenance shed. Another blistering day had kept all the kids either indoors or swimming down at any of the local beaches, for the park was deserted at this hour; yet another part of Stinger began to wonder if there was *something else* keeping them away from the park. Just like he and the Braswells had been drawn here, maybe that same force was having the opposite effect on the residents of Mariner's Cove who weren't lucky enough to be receiving transmissions. People who were not part of the colony.

Inside the maintenance shed, the air smelled of turpentine and astringents. The meager shaft of daylight that cut in through the elongated mesh window at the rear of the shed did little to brighten the atmosphere, which was stagnant, hot, oppressive. Stinger wasted no time snatching a pair of industrial bolt cutters from a pegboard on the wall. He was aware of things humming and buzzing and droning in the shadows. He thought of the carpenter bee he'd seen in here earlier, that awkward, lumbering denizen of the Apidae family, and the mindless way it had thumped repeatedly against the exposed bulb in the shed's ceiling. He'd been just like that carpenter bee for a long time, gracelessly drilling holes to nowhere and bouncing his head off the same stolid, immovable structure—his mother—for as long as he could remember. With the formation of this new colony, Stinger realized he had graduated to the regal honeybee. He and the other drones—Alex Braswell, that Eric kid—would start putting their heads and minds together to see this thing through, while the workers—Georgette Braswell, and that cute little Sarah whatshername—would continue to do what workers do best: work.

*People will all start to see what I've done to the Tower—people who aren't necessarily invited. It'll only be a matter of time before Doug Winslow starts on my ass again, and maybe some of those uninvited people might get curious and start coming around, too. We'll have to do something about that when the time comes. Before things get too ugly.*

Clutching the bolt cutters, he stepped back out into the bright sunshine, closed the shed's door, and clipped the padlock back into place. When he looked up, he saw someone walking across the back field and heading in his direction.

It was a woman. And Stinger didn't need for the woman to get any closer, for he recognized the semi-sultry wag of the hips, the drape of the hair down one shoulder, the pastel blue hue of the waitress uniform.

Marybeth Maysall.

He stood without moving, without breathing, until she arrived before him. She carried with her a large purse which she clasped to her chest and hugged with both arms. The look on her face was a none-too-subtle concoction of confusion, trepidation, and resignation. And maybe a little exhilaration, too, Stinger thought. Her face was freshly made up and her waitress uniform told him she had been planning to leave for work until she no doubt spotted the message he had left for her—for all of them—at the top of the Tower.

*Endgame*, he thought, and felt the nerve-endings in his back teeth tingle.

"Did you paint those things on the water tower?" she asked simply enough. Her eyes were locked on him. He couldn't look away, either.

"Y-yes," he stuttered.

"One of them is meant for me," she said.

"I thought so."

"Do you know which one?"

"I do," he said.

"Because you've seen it," she said. She left him no room to deny it. "You were looking in my window, weren't you, Jeremy?"

"I didn't mean to. I just happened to look out my bedroom window and you were standing there. You normally keep your blinds drawn."

"It was a rotten thing to do."

"I didn't mean it. I just looked and there you were."

"We talked, didn't we? Using only our minds? That wasn't a dream I had, was it?"

Stinger shook his head. It felt like his whole body was threatening to tremble apart, and that his skin was on fire. "It wasn't a dream," he agreed.

She took something out of the front pocket of her waitress uniform. A small piece of paper. She unfolded it, and Stinger could see it was the drawing of the tricycle wheel that he had torn from Alex's notepad and slipped through her mail slot. Then she opened her purse and took out the wheel, showed it to him.

He dug the key to the shed's padlock out of his pocket again, slipped it into the lock, and heard the satisfying *clink!* of the lock disengaging. He toed open the door of the shed.

"Come in here with me," he said.

She went, and Stinger closed the door behind them.

## 5

Once he had finished inside her, then felt himself evicted from her, Marybeth pulled up her panties then tugged down the hem of her waitress uniform. The back of her uniform was spotted with droplets of sweat that had rolled off Stinger's forehead while he'd fucked her from behind, and there were two damp handprints, one on each side of her waist, distinct as modern art. When she turned around, he saw that the top few buttons of her uniform were undone, and he recalled that in his haste and enthusiasm he hadn't managed to get them all the way open; only the tan cup of a bra and the slightest, pinkest hint of an areola was glimpseable before Marybeth closed up her top.

Stinger tucked himself back inside his pants. He felt relaxed and satiated. He wiped what felt like a gallon of sweat from his brow with the back of one bee-stung hand, the single bulb above his head distorting his shadow along the cinderblock wall of the shed. Hanging on that wall from a series of hooks were a few construction vests with reflective tape running down the sides. He'd worn one of those vests himself during clean-up days after park events and when he'd helped direct traffic during the annual Oyster Princess parade. He made a mental note of those vests and filed it away for later.

"The gas fumes in here are making me dizzy," Marybeth said, running her fingers through her sweat-damp hair.

Stinger shouldered the door open. The daylight that broke into the shed seemed brighter than it had just moments ago, and nearly assaultive in nature.

Marybeth grabbed her large purse containing the tricycle wheel and followed him out into the daylight.

"There are others, you know," he told her as he snapped the padlock back into place, then dropped the key into his pocket.

"At the tower?" she asked. Her lipstick was smeared and her mascara was smudged.

"Well, yeah, at the Tower," he said, but then pointed over her shoulder. "But there, too."

Two more people were slowly advancing toward them from across Gladstone Park. They were both men, and Stinger didn't recognize either one of them. One was carrying a duffel bag at his side while another dragged something covered in a sheet of green tarpaulin.

To Stinger, it seemed things were finally coming together.

# CHAPTER THIRTY-FOUR
# BRIGHTENING STAR

There was a subtle choreography to the evening, an unspoken understanding that the topic they were inevitably going to broach required a delicate touch. Brian and Ellen did not need the assistance of special magic to share in this unspoken understanding; they possessed the telepathy of lifelong siblings, and that was all they needed between them in that moment.

Cory had spent the afternoon and early part of the evening indulging in Brian's company, showing his uncle drawings that he'd made, school projects he was proud of, and playing boardgame after boardgame until Brian had to tap out. The two were seated now at the dining room table engrossed in a game of war, slamming cards down with zeal and laughter. It did Ellen's heart good to hear it.

At one point she took down the bottle of red wine from the cupboard over the fridge and poured herself a glass, but then paused, chewing on her cuticle. *Well shit.* She replaced the bottle in the cupboard and poured the wine from the glass down the kitchen sink. Hell, there was diet soda in the fridge. She'd survive.

"Cheater!" Brian yelled from the dining room, and Cory broke out into a peal of laughter. "This kid's a lousy cheater!"

Ellen smiled as she flipped the burgers on the stove.

After dinner, Cory and Brian cleared the table together while Ellen watched from the dining room, feet propped up on a chair, a mug of hot tea in her hands. They rinsed the dishes beneath a steaming stream of water then slatted them into the dishwasher. Cory played Chuck

Berry music on the Alexa, which prompted Brian to shred some air guitar. When they were finished and the music was turned off, Cory asked if Brian wanted to play Battleship, but Brian said, "Why don't we sit down and talk for a bit instead."

Cory took a breath. He nodded once, then said, "Right."

"Should I leave you two alone?" Ellen asked, swinging her feet to the floor.

"Stay, Mom," Cory said. He looked at her, and she could see Patrick in his eyes—fleetingly, but there, nonetheless. "It's okay."

"Okay, baby," she said.

Brian leaned back in his chair. "I guess you know why I'm here, Chicken Little," he said. He was smiling at Cory, and Ellen realized it had been a long time since she'd seen her brother's eyes so lucid. So genuine.

Cory nodded. He said, "Yes. I called out to you."

"That's right. And I heard you. Right *here* . . ." Brian pressed an index finger to the center of his forehead. His smile did not waver; in fact, his eyes seemed to brighten. "Right smack in the center of the old brain box."

Cory grinned a little, but he turned his eyes down and stared at his hands, which were fidgeting atop the table.

"How'd you do it?" Brian asked.

Cory's eyes shifted toward Ellen. She thought maybe he was looking for permission to speak about it, or maybe just some support.

"Is it the same as when you said you would peek inside people's heads? How you said you could see Mr. Zachs's thoughts that one time?" Ellen asked. Then, for Brian's edification, added, "Bert Zachs is our next-door neighbor."

"Not exactly like that," Cory said. "I didn't even know if I could call out and have someone hear me at all. I didn't even know if it would work. I tried it over and over again with you, Uncle Brian, whenever I would wake up from a nightmare in the middle of the night. I didn't know if you could hear me or not. And then I thought maybe you *could*, but since it was at nighttime, maybe you thought—"

"It was a dream," Brian finished. "Jesus, Cory. Yes. Yes, I kept hearing you. I just didn't *know* . . ."

"So then I thought I'd call to you during the day. When maybe you'd be awake and could hear me. So you'd know it's real and not a dream."

Brian shook his head in awe. "First time I heard your voice, kid, I was all the way out in Texas. And the first bad dream I had . . . Christ, I was still back in California, over three thousand miles away. I don't get it."

"I don't get it, either," Ellen said.

"Tell me how, kid. How did you do it?"

"Well, I guess, there's this little thing inside my head," Cory began. "I don't know really what it is or where it came from, but it was just there one day. I think of it as a garden gnome, like the little statues we have in the back yard."

Brian nodded. "Garden gnome. Okay. I like that."

"When I want to . . . to do something . . . I wake the gnome up and it just knows how to do it."

"So, you just think about this gnome calling out my name and it just happens?"

Cory's brow furrowed in thought. "No, not like that. Not really. I don't *think* about it. I *tell* it. I *tell* it what to do."

"So, you say, 'Hey, Mr. Garden Gnome, drop a long-distance dime to my uncle, wherever he may be'?"

Cory giggled, and Ellen felt something lighten in her chest. It was a surreal conversation, but she'd been so concerned about her son lately that this felt like progress, even if just a little bit. He seemed to have an easier time opening up to his uncle than he had with her.

"But is that it? Is that how you do it?" Brian asked.

"Yeah. Pretty much."

"Because that's pretty freaking amazing, kiddo. I mean, like I said, I was clear across the country. It's just . . . it's just incredible." Brian tapped a finger to his forehead once more. "Can you do it again? Right now? Maybe not shout it and blow my eardrums out . . . or whatever passes for eardrums when you're talking inside someone's head . . . but maybe just, I don't know . . ."

"A little whisper?" Cory suggested.

"Yeah, man. A little whisper. Can you do it?"

Ellen stared at her son, but his expression did not change. She didn't know what she expected—for his eyes to close, his brow to furrow even further, his hands to stop fidgeting and come together in a parody of prayer. But he just sat there staring at his uncle from across the table. Nothing more.

*That's because he can't really do it,* she told herself. It was saner to believe this. *He wasn't really looking around inside my head and reading my thoughts, just like he wasn't really looking around inside Bert Zachs's head and reading his thoughts, either. Cory's an empath, has been since he was a baby. A sensitive and clearly special kid who was only tapping into the emotions of the people around him. And whatever Brian thought he'd heard inside his own head, whatever that sounded like to him, maybe that's just a residual effect of years of—*

Brian bucked in his chair. That smile dropped away from his lips, but he was quick and thoughtful enough to reapply it before Cory might think he'd hurt or frightened him. He brought his hands up and ran his fingers through his hair, but paused halfway, as if to hold his scalp intact. Breathlessly, he said, "Holy shit, kid. I heard you. Cory, I heard you in my head." He looked at Ellen. His eyes were dancing. "I heard him, El. Clear as if he'd come up right beside me and whispered in my ear."

Ellen shook her head. She suddenly felt like *she* was dreaming. Or like *she* was the one losing her mind.

"He said 'hello,' El. I heard him say 'hello.'"

She looked at her son, who turned to face her at the same time. His face remained expressionless, except that she felt he was studying her with a sense of uncertainty now. She recalled how many times he'd asked her if she was scared.

"I just thought . . ." And then she paused and looked back at Brian. "Are you sure? In your *head*? I mean, you're not just . . . this isn't just some . . ." She didn't know what to say.

Brian laughed. "It's incredible," he said. "Go on, Cory. Do it to your mom. Show her, too. Show her what it's like."

"No, I don't want—"

"You need to experience it, El. It's incredible."

"No," Cory said. He was staring at her but talking to Brian. "I don't want to do it if she doesn't want me to."

"It doesn't hurt," Brian said. "There's nothing to be—"

Ellen said, "Okay, Cory. Let me see. Do it to me."

Her son made what could only be described as a sour face.

"Why not?" she said. "Uncle Brian is right. I want to see how incredible it is, too. Let me see." The words came out a bit too eager—she knew it the moment they left her lips—but she'd been so on edge lately, so concerned about him, that it felt like her release valve had been soldered shut for the past couple weeks. She didn't realize just how stressed she'd been until this very moment, as her bloodied, gnawed-to-the-quick fingernails dug crescent moons into the tabletop and hot tears threatened her eyes. "Come on, Cory. Show me. I want to hear it, too. Why can't you just show—"

*(STOP MOM STOP I DON'T WANT TO SCARE YOU I DON'T WANT TO MAKE YOU UPSET I DON'T WANT TO HURT YOU I LOVE YOU STOP MOM STOP STOP STOP STOP STOP)*

"Oh!" She bolted up out of her seat, knocking the chair to the floor. Her entire body tingled. It felt like there was a butterfly fluttering around inside her skull. "Oh, oh, oh . . ."

"I'm sorry!" Cory cried. "Was it too loud? Did it hurt? Mom?"

"No, baby, it didn't hurt. It didn't hurt at all. It's just . . . I didn't . . . I didn't expect . . ." She didn't know what the hell to say. It sounded just as Brian had described it, a voice speaking right beside her, only less a whisper and more a plangent cry.

"Isn't it incredible, El?" Brian said. He had a dumb, awestruck look on his face, eyes wide, something akin to a grin playing at the corners of his mouth. "Isn't it just fantastic?"

"I don't know . . ."

"You don't *know*? Ellen!"

"You were never able to do that, were you?" she asked him.

"No way. Nothing like that. Not a chance."

"But you *can* do things," Cory said. "Right, Uncle Brian?"

Brian ran his fingers through his long, greasy hair again. "When I was younger, yeah," he said. "It started when I was around your age. Lights would sometimes flicker when I came into a room, and I remember one time the blender just started whirring on the counter all by itself. Scared the bejesus out of your grandma."

"I remember that," said Ellen. She was still standing, watching as her hands shook. "Scared the bejesus out of all of us."

Cory looked up at her, concern for her still etched across his face. She managed to force a smile for his benefit, then went to him and rubbed the back of his head. "You didn't hurt me or scare me, and I love you, too," she said softly into his ear. Then she righted the fallen chair and sat back down.

"But those things would happen spontaneously, you know?" Brian continued. "Like, I mean, I wasn't in control of them at first, and I didn't even realize it was me who was causing those things to happen. But after a time, I found that I could make things move just by thinking about them. Small things, you know? A leaf fluttering on a houseplant or making the pullcord on window blinds sway back and forth like a swing. Stuff like that. Like maybe it was me doing it or maybe it was just a strong breeze from somewhere. Then, as I got a little older, and if I concentrated very hard, I could control it a little more—could make a glass slide along a table about an inch or so, or make a spoon jump."

"Did it scare you to do those things?" Cory asked him.

*He's so worried about scaring us*, she thought.

"Are you kidding? I thought it was the coolest thing ever."

"What about you, Mom? Did it scare *you*?"

"No, baby. Uncle Brian was my older brother, and all of a sudden, he could do all these amazing things. I was jealous. I wished I could do them, too. But if it's a gene, something in our bloodline, then it had passed me by."

"What about Grandma? Was she scared of it?"

"No," Ellen said quickly, before Brian could respond. She caught his eye and saw that he understood. "No, Grandma wasn't scared at all."

"That's right," Brian said, his gaze still lingering on hers. "And it wasn't just moving stuff, either, Chicken Little." He reached across the table and grabbed the deck of cards that they'd used earlier to play war while Ellen had been cooking dinner. He set the deck of playing cards in the center of the table, equidistant between him and Cory. "Used to be I could guess every single card before turning it over."

"Wait, no," Ellen said. "You never did that."

"I did," Brian said. He smiled at her, and there was something instantly sad in his eyes that made her sad, too. "It was short-lived, but yeah, I could do it."

She just kept shaking her head. She didn't believe him. "You never—"

Brian shrugged, as if this was no big deal, but that look of sadness persisted in his eyes. "It was when I was older. I'd already moved out of the house."

"So you could guess the cards just like Aunt Patty could guess songs on the radio," Cory said.

"Ah, your mom told you about old Aunt Patty-Wagon, huh? Yeah, well, sure—it was just like that."

Cory stared at the deck of cards on the table between them. "Can you do it now? Let me see."

Ellen leaned forward, both palms flat on the table. Her heart was suddenly thundering in her chest.

Brian turned his sad smile toward Cory. Something twinkled in his lucid gray eyes. "Ace of spades," he said.

Ellen watched as Cory's eyebrows drew together the slightest bit.

Brian reached for the deck. His hand trembled. Slowly, he turned over the top card and set it face down on the table.

Six of diamonds.

"You got it wrong," Cory said.

"Yeah, Chicken Little. I can't do it anymore. But," he said, and leveled a finger at him, "I saw your face just then when I said ace of spades. You knew I was wrong, didn't you? You knew it was the six of diamonds."

Cory leaned back in his chair. He was staring intently at the deck of cards. "I guess I did. I never tried to have the gnome do something like that before."

"Try now," Brian said. He tapped the next card on the top of the deck. "What is it?"

Pause.

"King of clubs."

Brian turned it over.

King of clubs.

"Oh, I don't believe it," Ellen muttered, then pressed a hand to her mouth. Both Cory and Brian chuckled.

"Again," said Brian.

"Eight of diamonds."

Eight of diamonds.

"Again."

"Seven of hearts."

Seven of hearts.

"Again."

"Uh, it's a joker."

"No way, bro. There are no jokers in this deck."

"It's a joker! Look and see!"

Brian flipped over the card.

Joker.

"This is unreal," Ellen said, her voice low. All of a sudden, she felt flushed, like she was having a hot flash.

"Yeah," Brian agreed. "It's unreal, all right. We gotta take this kid to Vegas."

"Do you want to see me do the thing with the fork?" Cory asked.

"Hell, kid, I didn't come all this way to *not* see you do the thing with the fork." He turned and looked at Ellen. "What's the thing with the fork?"

Ellen smiled and Cory laughed. She appreciated the levity.

Cory hopped up from his chair, hurried into the kitchen, and rummaged around in one of the kitchen drawers. He returned holding the fork in the way a king might hold a scepter. He set it on the table in front of him, then sat back down in his chair.

"Go on, kiddo," Brian said. "Show me what you can—"

The fork jumped, like someone had just pinged it with a BB gun. Ellen watched as Brian jerked backward in his seat, chair legs scraping along the floor. He laughed nervously as he dragged his fingers down the sides of his face.

"Make it spin, Cor," Ellen said. She twirled one finger in the air to illustrate. "Round and round. Just like last time."

"Yeah?"

"Yeah, baby."

Slowly, the fork began to rotate on the table. It made a dull whirring sound against the polished wood as it gradually picked up speed.

"Wow," Brian said.

Faster, faster. Leaving scuffmarks on the wood.

"Jesus, kid, you've got some control," Brian said. "I don't—"

The bulbs in the chandelier above the table dimmed, made a crackling sound, then grew bright, brighter, brighter. Ellen could hear their filaments crackling, could smell the electrical discharge frying in the air.

*Zzzzzzt.*

*Whir whir whir.*

The top card on the deck of playing cards pinwheeled into the air before fluttering down to the floor. A second card jumped up from the deck and rotated like a throwing star until it vanished behind the curio cabinet. A third card, a fourth, a fifth—then soon there were playing cards raining down all around them while, in the center of the table, the fork continued to spin, spin, spin.

"Woo-hoo!" Brian crooned, clapping his hands. "Goddamn, boy!"

In the kitchen, a trio of tin canisters jimmied across the countertop, causing Ellen's head to whip around at the sound of them. She watched as kitchen drawers and cabinet doors flung themselves open. The basement door shook in its frame. In the living room, she heard the TV switch on, filling the house with the canned laughter of some sitcom. A moment after that, the Alexa speaker on the kitchen counter began blasting music while the microwave turned itself on.

All the lights in the house began flashing.

The ceramic heirloom figurines in the curio cabinet trembled.

*Rattle rattle rattle.*

*Zzzzzzt.*

There was a crisp popping sound, like someone tearing a piece of brittle cloth down the middle. Ellen looked up at the ceiling in time to see bits of plaster rain down onto the dining room table.

"Enough!" she shouted. "Cory, enough! Oh my God!"

The fork stopped spinning.

The lights stopped flashing.

The microwave and the TV and the Alexa all went dead as the last few playing cards fluttered lazily to the floor.

And the silence that followed was as loud as a thunderclap.

Ellen's heart was in her throat; she had scooted away from the table in her chair and had her hands over her ears, her knees pulled up nearly to her chest. Shaking, she lowered her hands and set her feet back on the floor. There was a four of diamonds in her lap.

"Jesus Christ, Chicken Little," Brian said. He was gazing all around—at the playing cards scattered about the room, at the drawers and cabinets that hung open in the kitchen like broken appendages, at the lightning bolt crack in the dining room ceiling. "Like, Jesus *Christ*. I can't even *think* straight. Just give me a second to catch my breath."

Ellen, too, found it difficult to breathe. Found it difficult to *think*, in fact. Looking down at her hands, she saw that she'd bitten one of her fingernails so badly at some point that she'd caused it to bleed, leaving little red contrails of blood on her jeans.

"That was un-freaking-believable," Brian said. He stood partially from his chair and waved a hand back and forth in the air above the table. "Can you feel it? It's like an electrical charge crackling in the atmosphere. Look—it's making the hairs on my arms stand up." He sniffed at the air, then added, "Man, you can *smell* it. Like a burnt fuse."

"That," Ellen said, once she'd caught both her breath and her composure, "was not what happened the first time."

"No?" Brian said.

"No," Ellen responded. "Not at all."

"It's getting much stronger," Cory stated, matter of fact.

"Stronger, huh? Is that right?" Brian gave the kid a crooked grin as he lowered himself back down into his chair. If he was trying to keep his cool, Ellen thought he was doing a commendable job—except for the telltale beads of sweat that had popped out along his forehead, of course.

"Why did you stop being able to do things?" Cory asked him.

"Uh, well," Brian said, and for the first time, Ellen thought he looked ashamed. "Who's to say, really? Never knew where it came from, don't know where it went. Easy come, easy go, right?"

"Could that happen to me, too? Could I just stop doing all these things one day?"

Brian shrugged. "Suppose anything's possible."

"Did you have a gnome in your head, too?"

Brian flossed an index finger across his chin. The beads of sweat speckling his forehead were beginning to trickle down his temples. "I didn't think of it as a garden gnome, although I like that. For me, it was more like a small pinpoint of light, a distant star out in space. And when I would concentrate on moving small objects or when I would try to guess the suits and the numbers of the playing cards, that star would brighten. I remember I could actually feel the heat of it inside my head whenever it would happen."

"And then one day it just stopped?" Cory asked.

Brian smiled wanly at the boy. "Then one day it just stopped," he said.

Cory nodded. "I'm happy it worked."

"Happy what worked?" Brian asked.

"I'm happy you heard me calling out to you. I'm happy you're here."

Brian smiled, and Ellen could see that the twinkle in his eye returned. "Me too, Chicken Little. Me too."

Cory got down from his chair and proceeded to gather up the playing cards that were scattered across the floor. After a moment, and without speaking a word, Brian and Ellen got down on their hands and knees to help him.

## CHAPTER THIRTY-FIVE

# (WE ARE ALL ONE)

### 1

By seven o'clock that evening, the colony had increased to a total of ten people. Having seen Stinger's call to arms painted across the water tank, they had all congregated at the base of the tower, eager to contribute to the project that Stinger had begun referring to as the Hive. Each person brought their own item, and Georgette got the giddy sensation that, in a way, this was not unlike grade school show-and-tell. There was a woman in her mid-twenties dressed in a cornflower blue waitress uniform named Marybeth Maysall who carried in her purse the amputated front wheel of a child's tricycle, which she said she discovered stuck in a hedge on her front lawn the morning after that terrible storm. There was a man named Jack Gordon, who looked about as common and nondescript as his name, who'd hauled the frame of a dirt bike—sans wheels—out of the river behind his house after that same storm, wrapped it in a sheet of tarpaulin, and dragged it through the woods to the tower "like some Biblical figure on a quest," he'd added with a din of nervous laughter. And then there was another man who called himself Sergio, whom Georgette recognized as one of the kitchen staff at the Mexican restaurant where she and Tina Jarrett drank margaritas once a week while their daughters were in dance class, who brought with him the metal rim of a basketball hoop which he'd secreted in an old duffel bag, petrified that someone might want to steal it. Lastly, there was a woman of perhaps fifty years of age who, in her housedress and fuzzy purple slippers, had come through the woods behind Gladstone Park dragging something large and unwieldy wrapped up in a series of black garbage bags; when the woman joined them at the base of the tower, she tore away the plastic bags to reveal an old television antenna, the kind Georgette used to see on the roofs of all the tract houses where she grew up, in a time before TV signals went digital.

The items were all vastly different, though Georgette perceived two commonalities instantly: all the items were made of some type of metal, and each person had been compelled to conceal their item, hiding these possessions in purses or duffel bags or trash bags or wrapped up in a sheet of tarp, until they'd reached the safety of the tower. Only then did they reveal their treasures for the rest of them to see. As strange as it might seem, Georgette felt as if she was suddenly part of some secret society, one that she'd unwittingly stumbled upon and been granted membership before she fully understood what such membership might mean.

*And still, what are we doing here? We all agree that it is to build something—to put all the pieces of the puzzle together—but for what purpose? To what end? What exactly are we constructing?* That solitary word Stinger had painted across the face of the water tank—ENDGAME—blazed through her brain. She never stopped to contemplate whether they *should* put the puzzle together. In fairness, none of them did. And if Stinger understood more than he was letting on—and it sometimes seemed to Georgette that he did—then he wasn't telling the rest of them, for whatever reason.

The newcomers introduced themselves, and although they were strangers to Georgette and the others, Georgette couldn't help but feel a comfortable familiarity—no: a kinship—with each of them. That sense of *rightness* was still there even though it now carried with it a palpable sense of apprehension. Things were moving forward, whatever that actually meant, and these newcomers were proof of it; the gravity of what they were doing here together seemed to radiate off them in waves. They all kept peering up at the water tank above their heads as if to divine some significance—to harness some cosmic message—

from it. When they each looked back at Georgette and the rest of them in turn, she wished she could provide them with some answers. But she had no answers. In the end, all she could say was: "I think we're all supposed to be here. This is good. There's rightness here."

"There's rightness here," Alex repeated as he stood by her side. That made Georgette feel a little bit better.

She watched as Alex showed the newcomers the cutout drawings, which were still displayed on the tree stump and weighted down by the stones. It didn't take long for each person to locate their specific symbol—the symbol that matched the item they had brought with them—and upon doing so, Georgette couldn't deny that there was some gleam, some sparkle of . . . well, not *understanding*, because no one understood any of this, but of some simulacrum of *faith* in what they were here to do.

*We are a whole new religion,* she thought at one point, and when Alex looked up at her from where he knelt before the tree stump, she knew he had heard her think it.

"I've dreamed of you," said the woman in the housedress and fuzzy slippers as she sidled up next to Georgette. The woman startled her by gripping her upper arm. "I've dreamed of all of you." Then she glanced over her shoulder and at the water tower which had begun to turn a dingy gray in the quickly fading daylight. "I've dreamed of that thing, too, although I didn't know it until just now."

"We all have," Georgette assured her, then delicately pried the woman's fingers from her arm.

Just as the daylight completely drained from the sky, Stinger appeared at the base of the tower. The wall of chain-link stood at his back, a massive spider's web in the encroaching darkness. They had gone and cut the fencing down from the electrical substation on the other side of the trees, and these newcomers had spent the latter part of the afternoon assembling it above the sections that were already fixed to the base of the tower. The whole thing looked like a giant cylindrical cage. Stinger was holding a pair of bolt cutters in his hand, his lumpy face glistening with sweat. To Georgette, he looked like every tractor-pulling, mullet-wearing redneck she'd ever laid eyes on, but she supposed Jesus Christ hadn't looked much like the Son of God as he washed the feet of his disciples.

When he knelt and proceeded to clip a vertical line up the center of the fence, the sound of it alerted everyone else. They all looked around at each other. Georgette looked over at Alex, who remained kneeling beside the tree stump littered with his paper cutouts, and she registered a slack expression on her husband's face. He looked almost medicated. There was too much of a distance between the two of them for her to whisper to him, so she transmitted a mental message instead:

*(IS THIS RIGHT IS WHAT HE'S DOING RIGHT SHOULD HE CUT IT LIKE THAT?)*

Everyone turned in Georgette's direction. Beneath the tower, Stinger stopped clipping the metal wires. He rose slowly to his feet and turned to face her. "You have something to say to the class, Georgette? We're all ears."

She glanced quickly at Alex again but found no solace there; he seemed in some sort of semitrance, his vision unfocused, his face slack.

Stinger lifted a hand and extended the bolt cutter to her. "Come on over, Georgette. You're such an integral part of this already. Let's you and me do this part together."

She felt drawn to Stinger, sucked into his orbit as if by some gravitational pull. She set down the colander then felt herself ghost toward him, one arm similarly extended. When she reached him, she accepted the bolt cutters, then knelt in the same spot where Stinger had been kneeling just a moment before. She fed a piece of chain-link between the blades and squeezed the handle. She felt the wire pop, heard it like the snap of fingers, and thought for the millionth time: *Yes, this is right, this is what we're supposed to be doing.*

The idea to cut a door into the fence had been Sarah's, not Stinger's. As Georgette clipped more wires, opening up a doorway in the fence, she could see Sarah Miller advancing toward her from the periphery of her eye. Georgette paused, and watched as the teenage girl with the black nail polish slowly approached the fence at the base of the tower, ultimately bringing her hands up and curling her fingers into the diamond-shaped links of the fence.

"Do you feel something?" Georgette asked the girl.

Sarah turned and looked at her. She was still clutching the fence, and the expression on her face was similar to the one Alex wore—vacuous, empty. Georgette didn't think she was going to respond. But then she placed a hand to her abdomen and said, "No. It's too early to feel anything yet, I think."

"Come," Georgette said, and held out the bolt cutters to her.

Sarah's hands dropped away from the fence. She approached Georgette, took the bolt cutters, then looked up at the wall of fencing that was wrapped around the legs of the tower.

"How'd you know this was what we had to do?" Georgette asked, her voice so quiet so that no one else might hear.

Even quieter, Sarah replied, "The baby told me."

And then Sarah began to cut.

*Chink chink chink.*

Making a doorway.

Georgette backed away. She saw Stinger make eye contact with her, thought she caught some tacit approval there, but she wasn't interested in keeping her gaze on him long enough to find out. Instead, she retreated toward the colander which she'd set on the ground, and picked it up. Cradled it like she had both Callie and Denise when they were infants.

Still kneeling beside the tree stump, Alex blinked and caught her eye. She saw something jittery and unanchored in his stare and wondered if she might look the same way to him.

What was going on?

"Let me finish this up," Stinger said, and took the bolt cutters from Sarah. The girl retreated back among the throng of onlookers while Stinger clipped the last few remaining links to form a doorway in the fence.

The man named Sergio came over to her, still clutching the basketball rim in one hand, loathe to let it go. With his free hand, he pointed to the colander cradled in her arms. “Can I see that?” he asked. He possessed the soft, unintimidating voice of a librarian. Nonetheless, Georgette’s first instinct was to whirl away from him and protect the colander. But then something seemed to snap into place inside her head—it did so with a nearly audible *clack!*—and she handed the colander over to him.

Sergio lifted it up above his head, examining it. A crease appeared above the bridge of his nose. It was as if he were *concentrating* on it, Georgette thought. Then, quite simply, he seated Georgette’s colander inside the rusted orange basketball hoop. The colander sat snugly, perfectly, inside the hoop.

“Yes,” the man named Sergio said. “You see that? That’s right, isn’t it?”

Georgette just stared at what the man had done. Indeed, it seemed right—seemed *more* than right. A rush of excitement trilled through her.

When a piece of fence wire sprung loose and gouged a chunk out of Stinger’s hand, Stinger dropped the bolt cutters and quickly clasped his injured hand to his chest. He jerked away from the fence just as the loose section he’d been cutting slapped against the secured part of the fence, creating a discordant jangle.

Georgette felt it in her hand, too. She looked down at the palm of her left hand, expecting to find an abrasion in the flesh seeping blood. But, despite the pain, her hand was perfectly fine.

Alex sprung up and rushed over to Stinger. He pried Stinger’s hand away from his chest and examined his sliced palm. Even in the dark, Georgette didn’t need to get any closer to see that it was bleeding freely. “Take a knee,” Alex told him, and actually patted Stinger on one shoulder. “I’ll finish the job.”

“When you get to the top, you’ll have to cut horizon—”

“I know what to do,” Alex said calmly enough.

*We all do*, Georgette thought. *We are sharing a—*

*(COLLECTIVE CONSCIOUSNESS)*

*(THOUGHTS IDEAS UNDERSTANDING)*

*(HIVE MIND)*

The transmissions rushed through her brain, confusing and clouding her own thoughts. There was no pain, just a white-hot spark in the center of her mind, and a vague vibration in her molars. She turned her head and stared hard at Sergio, who in turn was watching Alex clip the remaining links in the fence with the bolt cutters while Stinger attempted to staunch the bleeding of his palm with a handkerchief provided to him by the middle-aged woman in the housedress and fuzzy slippers, who'd introduced herself earlier as Sheila Donaldson.

*(WE ARE ALL HEARING EACH OTHER)*

*(WE ARE ALL ONE)*

*(WE ARE ALL ONE WE ARE ALL ONE)*

*(WE ARE ALL WE ARE ALL WE ARE ALL WE ARE ALL WE ARE)*

When Alex finished, the cut in the fence resembled the letter T. The flaps could be pulled away to allow access to the inside of that cylindrical cage, directly beneath the tower.

*(WHATEVER WE ARE HERE TO BUILD IT NEEDS TO BE BUILT IN THERE DOESN'T IT?)*

Georgette thought it was Sheila Donaldson who'd transmitted this query, and so she sought out the woman among the small crowd, ultimately meeting her eyes. Georgette thought back, *Yes.*

The man named Jack Gordon, who stood beside Sheila, began nodding his head slowly. "Yeah," he intoned. "I mean, I don't know how I know that, but I do. Yes, whatever we're here to build, it's supposed to be *inside* that fence. It's true."

"It's true," repeated Sergio in his librarian's voice.

"It's true," said Georgette, as well as the rest of the brood, and she wasn't unnerved in the least by the nature of their words which, said in unison, took on the quality of prayer.

## 2

They eventually stopped for the evening once it got too dark for them to see what they were doing. Stinger, his hand bandaged with Sheila Donaldson's handkerchief, retrieved a few flashlights from the park's maintenance shed, but it was decided that they did not want to attract attention from outsiders by turning them on. They lingered there, not wanting to abandon their individual objects or the project at hand, but not knowing what else to do.

Stinger ambled up beside the doorway they'd cut into the fence. He cleared his throat and said, "I'm not much for speeches, and anyway, I don't think there's much I need to say. The fact that you're all standing here tells me we're on the right path. What we're doing here is important. What it *is* will reveal itself to us in time, I'm sure. We just need to be steadfast and have faith." He glanced up at the water tank high above his head then looked back at all of them. "Others will see the message, and they'll wonder what it means. They'll come here, too, trying to find out. We need to keep those people who don't belong away from here."

"How do we do that?" Jack Gordon asked. He was standing beside the frame of the bicycle he'd dragged out here, looking like he might want to strap it on his back and carry it home before leaving it here overnight.

"A few of us should stay here tonight to keep watch," Stinger said. "I'll volunteer for tonight. I'll need at least two more."

"I'm in," said Jack Gordon.

"I'll stay," said Marybeth Maysall. She had yet to relinquish the tricycle wheel; she'd been clutching it to her chest all evening.

The others began gathering their things: Alex scooping up the paper cutouts and placing them back into the envelope, Sarah Miller collecting all her metal rods and coat hangers, and all the others sort of milling about, unsure if they felt comfortable or not leaving for the night.

Georgette spied Eric Rhodes standing between the shaggy boughs of a loblolly pine. She drifted over to him, and as she drew closer, she felt a red-hot heat radiating off him—not against her flesh but inside her head.

"Hey, Mrs. Braswell."

"What's the matter with you?"

He was hugging himself and looking cold despite the mild temperature. His eyes kept jittering around the clearing, taking in everyone and everything. "Nothing," he said.

"Don't lie to me, kid."

He looked at her. "I don't have a thing," he said.

"What do you mean?"

"Everyone brought something. You've got that spaghetti strainer, Sarah's got all those coat hangers. I've got nothing."

"But you've been having the dreams, haven't you?"

Again: a pulsating red heat radiating from his mind to hers. Not so much a warning, she realized, as a natural—or *unnatural*—defense mechanism. He was actively trying to keep her out of his mind, not that she was trying to get in there in the first place.

"Yeah," he said. "I've had some dreams." His lips thinned. He kept his eyes off her. "I just don't think I'm supposed to be here."

"Well, Eric, I think we're all just feeling our way in the dark."

"Yeah, I guess you're probably right, Mrs. Braswell."

"Call me Georgette."

He shook his head. "No, that sounds weird."

Georgette smiled. "I guess I'm still just your old piano teacher, huh?"

"Sure."

He'd said it so dismissively that she wondered if it was something greater than that, like the way Alex no longer called her G. Like there was something in their heads that couldn't comprehend the informality and intimacy of nicknames.

She nodded toward Sarah, who was zipping up her backpack. "Maybe talk to her about it?"

He shrugged his shoulders. Said, "It's fine. It's nothing. Forget I said anything."

"Eric, hon—"

"Seriously, Mrs. Braswell, it's no big deal."

She thought, *Maybe I'll just peek for a sec—*

That red wave pushed her back. She figured she might be able to break through it without much difficulty—Eric Rhodes did not strike her as psychokinetically strong—but she also did not want to violate any sacred ground inside this boy's head. Hell, this was all new to her, too.

"I think that there's a place for all of us," she said after a time. She even put a comforting hand on the boy's shoulder. In that moment, she remembered he used to chew gum during piano lessons as a kid, and would sometimes stick it underneath the fingerboard of her piano when she wasn't looking. Then a second later, she wondered if that was one of Eric's memories, not hers. She found that she couldn't tell the difference.

Alex materialized before her in the dark. His eyes were wide and bright and there was a crooked and admittedly handsome smile on his face. "What do you think?"

"What?" she said. "About all this?"

"It's pretty incredible, isn't it? What we're doing here?"

*What* are *we doing here?* she wondered, but simply nodded her head in agreement. "Do you think I can take the colander home?"

Alex's smile faltered. "Jeez, I don't know, Georgette. I think Stinger wants everything to stay here, all in one place now."

The idea of leaving the colander behind made her uncomfortable. Anxious. She was reminded of the conversation she'd had with Denise on the phone, and how she'd been biting and bitter and angry because she'd wanted Georgette's colander. Like a junkie desperate for a fix.

"It'll be safe," Alex assured her. "Stinger and those other two are staying here all night, standing guard. You don't have to worry. Everything is coming together. Right, kid?"

This last part was directed at Eric, who still lingered somewhere off to Georgette's left, mostly hidden in the darkness between the trees. "Yeah, sure, Mr. Braswell."

Georgette watched as Alex's smile faded altogether.

"Let's get home," he said.

# 3

Despite Alex having driven them out to Gladstone Park, Sarah and Eric opted to walk home. They said their goodnights then Georgette and Alex walked hand-in-hand back through the woods and to the place where Alex had parked the Camry among the trees. Halfway to the car, Georgette stopped and pulled Alex to a stop. When he said, "What is it?" she just told him to shush. They stood there in the middle of the woods, the two of them practically holding their breath staring at each other.

"Georgette . . ."

"Can you hear?"

"Hear what?"

"Nothing," she said. "Absolute silence. No teenagers shouting, no dogs barking, no cars driving up and down Slope Hill heading toward the beaches."

"So?"

"And not just that," she went on. "No birds. No crickets or cicadas. I've never heard the woods so silent. Everything's gone."

Although *gone* wasn't the word she'd intended to use. She'd wanted to say *fled*.

He squeezed her hand and said, "Come on. I'm tired."

They got in the car and drove home in silence. Absently, Georgette wondered once more how long it had been since they'd dropped the girls off with Alex's mom. It had only been a few days, right? Three at the most now? She found her head too fuzzy to calculate.

She was already feeling desperate and unanchored without the colander. She didn't like to think of it left behind, back at the tower.

Sometime later, as they reclined side-by-side in their bed, exhausted from yet another bout of furious lovemaking, Alex turned to her, his profile limned in moonlight coming through the bedroom windows, and Georgette could instantly sense something was wrong. She placed a gentle hand against the side of his warm, flushed face, and whisper-asked, "What is it?"

"That kid," he said. "The one you taught to play piano."

"Eric?"

"He's in the wrong place."

"What does that mean?"

"I don't know. Just something I feel. It's like the pieces are trying to fit but they're still not perfect. Those dreams we've been having?"

"What about them?"

"You and I are there. Stinger is there. That girl Sarah, she's there, too. Those other people that showed up at the park today? They're all there in our dream. Except for that kid. Eric." Alex's eyes narrowed and his lips went thin. He reached up and looped fingers around her wrist—gingerly—and removed her hand from the side of his face. Again, he said, "He's in the wrong place."

"How do you know that?"

"Because I'm starting to feel that way, too."

And the sound of his voice frightened her.

# CHAPTER THIRTY-SIX

# ON THE PORCH AND IN THE BEDROOM (AND IN THE BATHROOM)

## 1

Brian sat alone on the back porch of his sister's house in the dark, a cool summer breeze rustling the trees. He held a deck of playing cards in one hand. On the back of the cards was a Conestoga wagon trundling over a prairie.

He thought, *Nine of spades.*

Turned the card over.

Ten of hearts.

"Fuck," he muttered, and reshuffled the deck.

When he heard the slider open and close behind him, he got up and dragged a second Adirondak chair next to the one he'd been sitting in. Ellen came over carrying two glasses of lemonade. She handed one to him as she sat beside him.

"Hopefully he sleeps through the night," she said. "He's been having a tough time lately, waking up with nightmares. As you know." Then she nodded at the deck of cards in his hand. "Did he inspire you to practice?"

"I guessed two out of fifty-two correctly. Fifty-four, if you count the jokers. Hardly prescient. You could do better just by sheer luck."

"Were you really able to guess the cards once?"

"For a brief time."

"You didn't go to Vegas and become a multimillionaire? That sounds unlike you."

"Hey, who's to say I didn't give it a try?"

"Oh? Did you?"

"Thing is, it wasn't always so reliable, and I lost as much as I made. There was this incident in Reno where I'd won a lot of money but the casino thought I was counting cards. Things got . . . dicey. But the truth is, I'd gamble and I'd win and I'd *drink* and then I'd lose the ability to see the cards, and then everything just went to shit."

"That's probably for the best," she said. "Imagine you with unlimited wealth."

"Tell me about it." He craned his head back and looked at the sky. "It's impossible to look up at all those stars and not see some great plan in action, huh? It's impossible to discount the idea of destiny when you see it all laid out before you like that. That nothing is ever just left up to chance, and that there's a blueprint in place for everyone and everything."

"You sound like you've found religion."

"I've found a lot of things."

"I want you to tell me about getting clean," she said.

So, he told her. By the time he'd arrived in California, he recognized that his grief and his guilt had reached uncontainable proportions, and that if he chose to want to live, then his life required a drastic overhaul. His mistake was thinking he could do it on his own, which resulted in a relapse. After that, he admitted himself to a month-long, in-patient rehabilitation facility, followed by two additional months of outpatient service. He told her about his withdrawal, the brutal night sweats, the delirium tremens, the merciless nightmares where the outcome of the car accident with Cory had been even worse than what had happened in real life, which had already been bad enough. He told her about the monsters he believed were after him, and not in a figurative sense, but very real demons that he believed crawled out from beneath his bed at night to torture and torment him and rake their blackened, talon-like nails across his quivering, goose-pimpled chest. He had lost track of time for a while, when the days and nights seemed to bleed effortlessly into one another until he no longer believed there was any difference between the two. He told her about his daily AA meetings and desperate, late-night consultations with his sponsor, Gideon, who was also a recovering drug addict and alcoholic who'd lost his wife and kids because of his disease. He admitted he had a problem, and that his life had become unmanageable. He had come to believe in a power greater than himself, which wasn't necessarily God or Jesus or Buddha or any of the notable big wigs, but in a singularly supreme consciousness of no precise denomination. He took inventory of himself and saw that he despised the person he had become. He began meditating. He made a list of all the people he had harmed because of his addictions, and he kept that list folded up in his wallet on a sheet of loose-leaf paper, and he wasn't afraid to admit to Ellen that he took it out and looked at it every now and again.

"You and Cory are at the top of that list," he told her.

She gave him a thin-lipped smile. He couldn't tell what she thought of all he'd just said. Then they were quiet for a stretch, content to sip their lemonade and gaze longingly at the vastness of the universe above without speaking.

"I lied to him tonight, you know," she confessed after a time. "I *am* scared. I *am* worried."

Brian nodded. "Just like Mom."

"No, not like Mom. Mom thought what you could do was against God. She went all religious fanatic after Dad died and so she looked at you like you were some sort of . . . I don't know . . ."

"Freak," Brian concluded.

"I was going to say 'anomaly.' But maybe your word is closer to how she truly felt. She was afraid of what you could do."

"Trust me, El. I remember."

"It got so bad for you that you had to pretend you couldn't do it anymore because you didn't want to keep dealing with her lunacy."

"It wasn't lunacy. It was fear. Fear of the unknown. She didn't know what to make of it. Heck, neither did I."

"But you were just a kid. Mom should have protected you."

"She thought she was."

"It was selfish and shortsighted of her."

Brian shrugged. Ellen wasn't wrong, but he also could see it in a different way, too, mainly because he'd had so much time to sit and think back on it. He'd mostly blocked out those early years, the near daily treks to the confessional at the Catholic church, the way their mother had wailed to one of the deacons in the church parking lot because she thought her son might be possessed. Brian, too afraid to show any of these men of the cloth what he could do, had played dumb. He confessed to shoplifting from the local grocery store and cheating on tests at school—things he hadn't actually done, but he'd had to confess to *something*—which made the clergymen think their mother was crazy. At one point, Social Services had been called, which prompted Brian to lie and say he'd been playing pranks on his poor mother. Brian knew it hadn't been fair to the woman, but he'd also known it wasn't fair to him, either. He wasn't some demon-possessed boy in need of an exorcism. And so, he'd eventually pretended to be "cured," and he'd stopped doing his little magic tricks around the house where their mother might see.

"I don't want to be like Mom," Ellen said.

"You're not, El. You're nothing like Mom."

"You know, the one thing she never did was to take you to a doctor."

"I'm not sure a doctor would have been any better than those priests. Might've even made things worse, to be honest."

"I don't mean for medical answers or solutions or whatever else," she said. "I mean a doctor to maybe help you cope. A doctor to help *Cory* cope. Help him deal with everything that's coming at him. You know?"

"You're talking about a therapist?"

She leaned back in her chair and stared out at the yard. The intermittent pulses of fireflies were out there in the dark, drifting among the trees. "I guess I'm less worried about this . . . this ability of his . . . than I am about his mental wellbeing now that he's discovered it. Does that make sense?"

"Listen, El, I want you to understand something, okay?"

"Okay."

"That analogy I gave him earlier tonight? How he's got the gnome and I had that star?"

"Yeah." The ice cubes in her glass clanked as she leaned closer to him.

"I think it all comes down to the same thing. He perceives it as a gnome, which, you know, is—"

"Unsettling," she said.

"I was going to say charming, but sure, you're his mom. It's unsettling, too. But it's the same as my star. It's just the way we interpret what it is that we have—or had—inside us. Hell, for all we know, old Aunt Patty-Wagon might have had an eight-foot pink gorilla in her head who was good at guessing Top Forty songs on the radio. I don't know. But I want to make something clear to you, okay?"

She nodded. "I'm listening."

He said, "I didn't become an addict because of my ability. I didn't seek out drugs and alcohol and everything else as a way of silencing voices in my head or dulling my senses or whatever trite cliché people might think. I wasn't hauling around proverbial demons because I could make a drinking glass slide a couple of inches across a countertop with my mind. I became an addict because that, too, is in my blood, and I was just too weak and too stupid to recognize what it was until it was too late."

"Aunt Patty was an alcoholic," Ellen said.

"That's right. And so was Dad. Dead before he was fifty from liver disease. And he possessed no special abilities, except for a short fuse, far as I remember. Mom's addiction became religion. Judging by our family's track record, I'd say the addiction gene is stronger than whatever gene gave me and Patty and Cory our abilities. Rarer still is whatever gene Cory's got, because what he can do is sure as hell more powerful than anything *I* was ever able to do."

"It's still all connected," she said. "It's still all coming from the same place."

"That star in my head was still there when I started down that bad path. It dimmed over time—*I* dimmed it, although I didn't realize I was doing it at the time—from all the booze and all the drugs. It was like dripping water on a tiny flame. After a while, it just went out. And now there's nothing but darkness in my head where it used to be."

"Well, that's sad."

"Not as sad as what my addiction has done to my life."

"Oh, Brian . . ."

"The point I'm trying to make here, El, is that they're *separate*. My ability did not necessitate my addiction. Just because Cory can do what he can do doesn't mean he's going to turn out like me."

Ellen turned away from him, but not before he caught sight of a tear sliding down one cheek.

"What he did tonight was incredible," he told her. "I keep comparing what I could do when I was younger to what *he* can do, but really, it's not even in the same ballpark. Can I tell you something without you thinking I'm crazy?"

"Christ, Brian, I think *I'm* the one who's crazy."

"On one of the nights I heard him call out to me, I'd been driving through Texas and blew a flat. A couple picked me up and promised to drive me to a motel for the night. There was a woman in the car, and from out of nowhere, I suddenly knew all these private things about her life. I said them aloud and scared the shit out of her and the guy she was with. Scared the shit out of myself, too, to be honest. I'd never in my life been able to do something like that and I didn't know where it had come from at first. But then later I thought about it, and now that I'm here and I've seen what Cory can do, I'm *certain* about it."

"Certain about what?"

"Cory's voice shooting through my head was like hooking up a couple of car batteries with jumper cables. I think he gave me a jumpstart, you know? Like, a bit of Cory's power was still pumping through me when I met those people, which was how I was able to know things about that woman. Like I had a little of Cory's charge left over from hearing his voice shouting in my head. Like he'd amplified himself through me."

"Oh, Brian." She turned away from him. "This is all too much."

"Nothing is too much. Everything is manageable. You just have to take small bites, El."

She went quiet again for a time. Brian set his lemonade on a small table between their two chairs then looked back down at the Conestoga wagon on the top of the deck of cards in his hand.

Thought, *Queen of clubs.*

Turned it over.

Five of diamonds.

There was no dim light far off at the center of his brain anymore, no distant star radiating with some preternatural energy. That star had been guttered years ago, and no jumpstart from his nephew would bring it back on a permanent basis. Why was he even wasting his time? Not to mention his head still felt funny, just as it had earlier that day when he'd pulled onto the shoulder of the road at the entrance to Mariner's Cove. A pressure, a dizziness, and a lizard brain declaration that *something was wrong.* He'd felt this way soon after detoxing back in California: that unanchored, jittery dislocation.

"He's become paranoid," Ellen said, snapping him back to the here and now. "For one thing, he thinks there's something wrong with Mr. Zachs, our neighbor next door. He shuts all the blinds and the drapes in the house whenever I go out, like he's afraid someone might be trying to look in the house. He's also become . . . obsessed, I guess you'd say . . . with some graffiti that's been popping up around the neighborhood."

"Graffiti?"

"I've seen it, too. Some childish drawings spray-painted in the street. I don't know why they bother him so much, they're not particularly unsettling, and he can't explain it to me when I ask. I'd think nothing of it, except . . ." She trailed off, her gaze locked on the web of darkness that spanned the length of the back yard.

"Except what, El?"

"Well, now you're going to think *I'm* being paranoid."

"Except what?" he repeated.

"Except I saw a man spraying-painting some words on our driveway the other night. When I went out to confront him, he ran off."

"It was a man? Not some teenager?"

"A grown man. I didn't recognize him, but it was also dark out and I didn't get a good look. But he had, like, tattoos on his face. He wasn't wearing a shirt, and I could see he had tattoos across his chest, too."

"What were the words he spray-painted on the driveway?"

"It just said 'the boy, the boy' over and over again. I've been parking my car over it so that Cory wouldn't see, but I'm sure he has. He isn't stupid, and I can't leave the car there every minute of the day."

Brian didn't know what to make of that.

"I guess it's not paranoia if there's something really going on, right?" she said.

"What could be going on, El?"

She looked down at the glass of lemonade clutched in both her hands. Her knees were drawn together as if she was cold, despite the mild temperature of the evening. "I have no idea." She looked at him. "I don't know what to do, Brian."

"Maybe this is all just coming at you fast," he suggested. "Like, maybe after you witnessed what Cory can do and how he's been behaving, some of Cory's fears and worries have become your own. I get it, El. You're concerned about him. It's stressing you out, messing with your head. Maybe just find some time to take a deep breath and recalibrate. Things may start to make more sense."

"Is that how you got through everything? By taking a deep breath and recalibrating?"

"Something like that. I won't lie, Ellen: it's a struggle every day to stay clean. Less of a struggle with the drugs—I don't really think about the drugs much anymore—but it's harder with the alcohol. That desire is always there. If I have a bad day, I think, hey, I can just waltz right into a package goods store and walk out with a bottle of Jack. Call it a day. But I know now that that's only a temporary solution. And not really a solution at all. It's like putting a Band-Aid on a gunshot wound. I know I'll eventually bleed out."

"How do you keep from doing it? How do you stop yourself from drinking?"

"By living life in one-minute increments," he said. "I don't think beyond the moment. I don't think in terms of longevity, but only in the here and now. My whole life has become a composite of a finite number of sixty-second moments in time."

"And that's all it takes?"

He couldn't help it: he laughed.

"No, El. It takes a lot. I struggle to hold onto some peace pretty much every day. It's why I took up meditation. It helps me realign my spiritual center. I've come to believe that there's a higher power out there that has plans for me. Like, I'm part of some great cosmic instruction manual. As we all are."

"You're talking about God again."

He could sense the trepidation in her voice.

"No, not necessarily God," he said. "More like a collective idea. A galactic consciousness. My old co-host on the radio show used to proselytize about how *we* were gods, because our voices were transmitted as radio signals into the vast reaches of space. I thought he was crazy at the time, but lately I've been wondering if maybe I was too quick to judge. Like, maybe we're all our own higher powers. There's a part of me—my voice, my ideas—still pinballing around the universe and beyond to this very day. What's more godlike than immortality?"

She reached over and briefly squeezed his wrist. "Whatever happened to that woman you once wanted to marry?"

"Donna Holmes," he said, and was dismayed that the name, which had once meant everything to him, now sounded so foreign on his lips. He hadn't thought about her in some time. Hadn't spoken her name in even longer. "I don't know. We never spoke after she kicked me out. And that was just before I showed up on your doorstep back then."

Ellen's hand slipped away from his. She was still staring out at the blanket of night that hung before them, so black and dense now that it could have been made of sackcloth. Even the fireflies had disappeared.

"I've hurt a lot of people," he admitted, and he could tell that his voice was beginning to shake. "That's what keeps me clean, too. All the things that have happened. All the things that I've done. Especially to you and Cory. Not a day goes by that I'm not regretful about that."

"It's easier to forgive other people than it is yourself," Ellen said.

He nodded, then stared down at the deck of cards cradled in one palm. "I hope that's true," he said. Then he cleared his throat and stood. "I'm going to get some sleep."

"I made up the pullout for you in the guest room."

"Thank you. And tomorrow?"

"What about it?"

"You should take Cory out for a while, spend some time with him away from this place. Enjoy each other for a while. In the meantime, I'll see if I can clean up that spray paint in the driveway before you guys get back."

She smiled at him. Sadly, he thought.

"That sounds like a wonderful idea," she said. Then, before he could leave, she said, "You came back here even though I told you never to do so because you thought my son was in trouble. That was brave."

Brian smiled. He had nothing to say to that. But in his head, he could hear Donna Holmes telling him, *Love is bravery.*

## 2

After he washed up and brushed his teeth, he crept down the hall toward the guest room. Cory's bedroom door was partway open, so he poked his head in.

"Hey," Cory said.

"You're still up?"

"I'm afraid to go to sleep."

"Worried about more bad dreams?"

"They're not dreams."

"No? Then what are they?"

"Something is happening. I think it's something bad."

"Happening where?"

"Here."

"In this house?"

"In this neighborhood. Did you see all the symbols when you drove here today?"

He hadn't, but he recalled what Ellen had told him out on the back porch. "It's just some graffiti, kid. You should've seen where I used to live in Baltimore."

"No," Cory said. His voice was sharp, direct. "It's something else. It just *looks* like graffiti, but it's not."

"Then what is it?"

"I think they're instructions."

"Instructions?"

"Like, directions. To build something. You know how you get a toy and they have the paper directions in the box on how to put it together? I got a science kit for my birthday last year and there were pages and pages of instructions on how to do different experiments."

"Why do you think they're instructions?"

"Because they fit together."

"You sound like you're half dreaming right now, Chicken Little."

"Here, I'll show you."

Cory rolled out of bed and went to his desk in the dark. He switched on the gooseneck lamp just as Brian came into the room. On the desk was an assortment of drawings on tracing paper. Brian peered over Cory's shoulder as he shuffled the papers around, then he glanced up and saw a photo of Cory on his shoulders pinned to a corkboard. The same photo Brian had clipped to the visor in the van. Above the photo was a shelf cluttered with books, but there was also the remnants of a plaster cast with some names printed on it, and Brian felt his throat tighten with guilt at the sight of it.

"You know, your mom is gonna kill us if she finds out you're still awake, kiddo."

Cory ignored the comment. "Look," he said. He showed Brian the various drawings on the sheets of tracing paper—odd symbols that, to Brian, looked almost like Germanic runes. And just like the letters in a foreign alphabet, these symbols looked both alien yet vaguely familiar.

Cory stacked two pages together then held them up against the light of the gooseneck lamp. What separately had looked like a rectangle and an X with a line across the top now sat layered together.

"These two symbols come together to make this *one* symbol," Cory said, and he nodded to a third drawing on his desk—a single drawing of the rectangle with the strange X on it. Cory looked up at him. "See? What do you think?"

"I think you need to get to bed," Brian said, plucking the pieces of paper from him and setting them back down on the desk. He reached over and switched off the lamp as Cory climbed back into bed. The ceiling was aglow with stars, a multitude of them, matching the one that hung around Brian's neck.

"The gnome can look inside people's heads," Cory said.

Brian ambled over to the bed and pulled the sheet over Cory's body. "Don't go looking inside *my* head, kid. You'll get a rude awakening."

"I looked inside Mr. Zachs's head, and it was like a tornado in there. It sounded like a million bees buzzing around. And it was like there was . . . I guess . . . I don't know how to say it . . ."

"Just say it."

"Like there was something else in there with him."

"In where? His head?"

"Yes."

"Maybe you shouldn't be peeking around inside people's heads to begin with."

"Do you want to know what I think?"

"Lay it on me."

"I think whatever was inside Mr. Zachs's head was also down at the park."

"What park?"

"Gladstone Park. Remember? Where the baseball field is? We used to fly kites there."

"You remember that? The kites?"

"This is *serious*," Cory said.

"Right. So, what do you mean the same thing inside your neighbor's head was also at the park?"

"I felt it there one day when I rode my bike. I was following the symbols on the ground and they led me there. I could . . . I guess, sense something in the park. The gnome reached out and tried to poke it, to peek inside its head, whatever it was, but it wouldn't let the gnome in. And then it knocked me off my bike just by thinking about it."

He could see how Ellen had become so concerned. Was this paranoia? Was Cory actually afraid of his gift and was manifesting that fear as a distrust of the world around him? That would be easier to swallow than distrust of oneself, Brian knew.

"What do you think it was?" Brian asked. He wasn't humoring the boy; he truly wanted to know what he thought.

"I thought it was a giant metal spider at first, but it's not. That's just where it hides, I think. A part of it, anyway, because it's also . . . I guess . . . all around us, too. All at the same time."

"Then what is it really?"

Cory lowered his voice and said, "It's really a dragon."

In Brian's head, he heard Lily Ming say, *Perhaps you dreamed of the Mizuchi.*

"Listen, kid, if it makes you feel better, I'll check out the park tomorrow, see what's going on."

"I don't want you to. It could be dangerous."

"Hey, I can be a bad dude when necessary."

"Besides," Cory said, "I don't think you'd be able to feel it."

"Well, I think I'd be able to see a dragon hanging out in the park, don't you?"

"It's not funny. This isn't a joke."

"I'm sorry." He brushed the kid's hair off his forehead. He was perspiring. "You want me to crack the window for you, get some fresh air circulating in here?"

"No," he said, a tinge of panic in his voice.

"Okay." Brian backed away toward the door. "You sleep tight. We'll talk more about this tomorrow, okay?"

"How long are you staying?"

"I don't know."

"I'm glad you came back."

Brian smiled in the dark. "So am I."

"Goodnight, Uncle Brian."

"Goodnight, Chicken Little."

He crept back out into the hallway thinking about dragons.

## 3

Brian awoke some hours later, disoriented and gasping for air in the dark. Another nightmare, the details of which lingered just long enough for him to recall Cory screaming for him while something large and indistinct spiraled like a cyclone into a night sky spangled with stars. He sat up, forgetting for a moment that he was in the guest room of his sister's house.

The demons from the rehab facility had come back for him. They had tracked him across the county and were ratcheting themselves up from the shadows, as if the shadows were doorways or portals to their hellish dimension. They collected around him, reeking of brimstone and filling his lungs with smog.

Something was wrong with him. He began to tremble. There was a sickness radiating out from the epicenter of his body and jangling through all his nerves. *It's the fucking DTs,* he thought frantically, pulling himself off the mattress. His bare feet struck the floor in a soundless thump.

He staggered out into the hallway and made it to the bathroom in the dark. He closed the door behind him, flipped on the light, then threw up the lid of the toilet before bracing himself above it. His stomach fisted into a ball. He closed his eyes, but that didn't help, because those mad devils from the rehab facility capered maniacally behind his eyelids. Their eyes blazed with a soul-searching yellow light and their mouths were crowded with teeth as sharp and narrow as needles. When they crept closer toward him in the darkness beneath his eyelids, Brian could hear their terrible black claws clacking along the linoleum tiles.

He vomited a string of pale fluid into the toilet. It tasted like battery acid and stung his sinuses. When he was finished, he swiped a hand across his mouth, then sat there with his back against the wall, his body clammy and foul-smelling. *Is this me?* he thought. It was what every single caller would say the minute the call-screener put them on their air for broadcast—*Is this me?*

*Here's a thought,* suggested the Air Man—or, rather, an imaginary version of old Gary Manheim who suddenly spoke up inside his head. *What if you're still in the rehab facility right now? What if you never left, and the past eighteen months has been nothing but a lucid dream brought on while you detox? What if you're not here in your sister's house getting sick in her bathroom at all, but in actuality you're puking on yourself while curled up in a fetal position on a damp, reeking mattress in some desolate clinic somewhere in the bowels of Los Angeles? What if the past eighteen months have really only been one week or one day or one hour, and you've only been living this time inside your own head? Let's rewind! Walk backward through the house, get back inside your van, drive in reverse through the neighborhood streets to the highway, then head on back to El Segundo. You'll scare the shit out of a girl named—*

(Jennifer)

(Merritt)

*—Horla while hitchhiking across the panhandle of Texas, then you'll blow a flat tire, then you'll be sitting in Mr. Ming's Chinese restaurant chatting with Lily in strange backward speak, and then you'll zip in reverse all the way back to your last day in the rehab facility, you son of a bitch, because you're still there, aren't you? Maybe your last day is really your first day and maybe the whole world now runs in reverse. You've been time-warped, my good friend. You're still there and you've been living a convenient daydream in your head the entire fucking time.*

"Fuck you," he groaned, knowing it wasn't—it couldn't be—true.

Yet when he looked down at his hands, he saw they were holding a bottle of Listerine, and he was in the process of screwing off the cap. The door to the medicine cabinet stood open, toothbrushes and hydrocortisone cream and nail clippers and a box of Ellen's tampons staring out at him. His hands continued to shake, and it took some effort to get the Listerine cap off. The pungent aroma of the mouthwash stung his eyes. He had never had to drink mouthwash before—he had always had alcohol on hand and never needed to stoop to such debasement—though he had certainly searched for it those first few nights back in rehab. But the staff had seen fit to take all mouthwash away. There had been one guy who'd been sent there under court order who had deliberately opened up a section of his forearm with a screw he'd unbolted from his cot, hoping the staff would apply rubbing alcohol to the wound, which he could then suck out when they weren't looking. Although Brian, even in his most troubled state, had found this to be more than just a little extreme, he had nonetheless followed the events as they unfolded just in case he might learn where they kept such things as rubbing alcohol. (In the end, they had simply transferred the injured patient to a different part of the facility, and Brian never saw him again.)

Those memories shuttled through his brain as he stood staring into the circular opening of the Listerine bottle. It was the goddamn DTs he was suffering; it was the *draw*, the *craving*. It was his acknowledgement that, yes, those goddamn demons with the blazing Christmas lights for eyes were right on his heels, and that there *was* some solace left for him inside the bottle, there *was* some wellspring of wonderment and peace down in the bowels of hell, and all he had to do was follow them down into that black mouth. It didn't matter if they never let him back out. Son of a bitch, he wanted a *drink*.

When he looked back at his reflection in the bathroom mirror, he wasn't completely surprised to find a ribbon of blood trickling out of his right nostril. This seemed to snap him back to reality. He screwed the cap back on the mouthwash and replaced the bottle back in the medicine cabinet. Then he snatched a Kleenex from the dispenser atop the toilet tank and blotted the blood away. His hands still shook, but at least he was able to use them. He felt best when he was able to put all the parts of himself to work.

By the time he crawled back into bed, he was shaking and sweating and trying desperately not to think about that bottle of mouthwash just down the hall. Instead, he forced his eyes closed and willed sleep upon him. If he suffered another nightmare, so be it: that just meant that he was still alive.

# CHAPTER THIRTY-SEVEN

# "THERE'S PLENTY WE CAN'T EXPLAIN"

## 1

Eric and Sarah walked together that night from Gladstone Park back to Sarah's house. It was a cool, bugless summer night, and ordinarily, Eric would have enjoyed the company of the girl for whom he'd been carrying a torch ever since he'd started working at Hollywood BBQ. However, things had changed over the past several days—changed between them, yes, but also changed within Eric himself—and while he still felt an attraction to her, even a need to protect her, there was something else thumping like a heartbeat in the forefront of his mind that had since taken priority.

"That guy Stinger," Sarah said as they walked. "He's the man I told you about. The man who came into the restaurant the other day whose voice I heard in my head."

Eric didn't like discussing telepathy. While he'd lingered all evening with the others at the water tower, his sentiment to Mrs. Braswell had been truthful: something about being there had made him feel out of place. The collision of telepathic voices in his head hadn't helped. It felt like randomly spinning a radio dial and catching snippets of conversation not necessarily meant for him.

"I don't think he knew I could hear him at the time," Sarah went on. "Or maybe he *did* sense something about me, and he sent that little message to see if I could hear him." She looked at him. "What do you think?"

"I don't know."

"Do you know a woman named Ellen McBride?"

He did not, although there was something jarring to him about the name—*McBride.* Had he heard it somewhere before?

"I don't think so," he said. "Why?"

"She came into the restaurant the other day to pick up a couple of dinners to go."

"Did she talk to you with her mind, too?"

Sarah smiled. Just seeing it, he felt that old desire for her swim murkily to the surface of his mind again. Despite his apprehension.

"No. But something about her set me off."

"Set you off?"

"I don't know. Maybe I'm not saying it right. I thought *maybe* I should know her. I wound up googling her and she lives here in the Cove, right on Cloister Road. She's a real estate agent."

"You've probably just seen her around the neighborhood."

"Probably."

"What was it about her that . . . what'd you say? Set you off?"

"I don't know. It was nothing that she did. I can't explain it." She laughed dryly, startling him. Somewhere in the distance a dog was barking. "I guess there's plenty we can't explain these days."

"Tell me about it."

Her hand brushed up against his while they walked.

He wanted to ask her if she knew there was a baby growing inside her. He supposed she must since it was her thoughts from which he'd gleaned that information, although he also wondered if it was possible he'd gleaned it from the baby itself. Did a fetus have thoughts? How could it without any experience? He also wanted to know who had put the fetus there but found he didn't like to linger on such things.

"What will you do about your car?" he asked instead.

"Shit." She was likely just remembering that it was broken down on the road near the entrance to the neighborhood. "I guess I'll have my dad help me with it tomorrow."

"I can come by," he said. "I'm off tomorrow."

"I'm sure you've got better things to do."

A million responses shuttled through his head, but each one would make him sound either pathetic, desperate, too eager, or all three at once.

As they came upon Sarah's street, she turned to him again. "Are you doing okay? You looked a little out of it tonight."

He didn't want to go into it, so he said, "It's just all a bit much. Like you said—there's plenty we can't explain."

"But it feels *right*, doesn't it? What we were doing tonight? All those people showing up like that?"

He smiled at her, though he felt cold inside. Her face was bright, her excitement palpable, but he found this only made him more aware of his lack of belonging.

"Sure does," he said.

## 2

His truck was still parked outside Sarah's place, right where he'd left it earlier that day. There were some lights on in the house and an old-fashioned car about the size of a tugboat in the Millers' driveway, so he assumed her father was home. He wondered how late it was but didn't want to check his phone.

"Thanks for the walk," she said when they reached the foot of the driveway.

He hoisted a shoulder and said, "I'll walk you to the door."

"Mighty chivalrous of you, sir."

On the front stoop, Sarah dug around in her backpack for her housekeys while Eric stood there with his hands in his pockets.

"I've got a bunch more hangers in my bedroom. I'm going to bring them down to the tower tomorrow, after I deal with my car. Did you want to go together or just meet up there?"

"I guess just give me a call," he said.

"Will do."

She produced her housekey but did not slip it into the lock.

*Kiss her,* he thought. It might change everything. It might eradicate that pulsing heartbeat at the forefront of his brain. *Kiss her, kiss her, kiss her.*

Before he could act, she leaned in and kissed him gently on the mouth.

"See you tomorrow," she said, and then she was unlocking the front door and slipping inside the house.

Eric stood there for a while longer—long enough to know that it was beginning to feel creepy. He slinked down the steps and got into his truck. It was late, and he winced at the sound of the truck's engine growling to life along this otherwise quiet street.

*Do you know a woman named Ellen McBride? She lives here in the Cove, right on Cloister Road.*

He pulled out onto the street and drove at a slow clip back through the neighborhood. Mariner's Cove was huge, and its residents were from all walks of life—from the uber rich to the blue-collar families and everyone in between. Eric's own parents were perhaps of the middle-class variety, both of them holding down unglamorous middle-management careers with the county. Their house was nothing like the waterfront mansions along Bay Road, but it wasn't like those crowded little duplexes at the far end of Macadam Street, either.

Which road was Cloister Road? He recalled seeing the street name in the past, but had never really paid attention to it. He could have taken out his cell phone and fired up the GPS, but it was a nice night and Eric was too wired to go straight home, so he decided to drive slowly up and down the dark, quiet streets of Mariner's Cove with his eyes peeled instead.

## 3

Twenty minutes later, just moments before he was about to give up and go home for the night, he came upon the intersection of Cloister Road and Capshaw Street. He turned the truck down Cloister Road and drove slowly. Most of the houses here were single-story ranchers, a good number of them dark at this late hour. Much like the name *McBride*, there was something familiar about this street, too, although he could swear that he'd never been down this way before.

And then he saw it: a small ranch house tucked discretely between two nearly identical homes, so average and unassuming that it was a wonder he didn't drive on by, none the wiser. But instead, something about that house called out to him—or, rather, *had* called out to him in the latest iterations of his crazy dreams. In those dreams, he sat crouched within a darkened cluster of trees, watching.

Watching this very house.

There was a car in the driveway and a clunky-looking Chevrolet van parked out front. The van had a mural of wolves airbrushed on the side. There'd been no van in any of Eric's dreams, but that didn't matter to him right now, because there was no denying the house. The drapes were drawn and he couldn't see any lights on inside, so he assumed that whoever lived there—

*(Ellen McBride)*

—was likely asleep.

He parked about a block past the house where the lights of two lampposts were spread too far apart to illuminate him. When he shut the truck's engine down, the silence that followed sounded as loud as an explosion.

*There's plenty we can't explain*, he recalled Sarah saying to him on the walk back from Gladstone Park, and right now, in that moment, Eric Rhodes couldn't think of a more apropos mantra. *There's plenty we can't explain. There's plenty we can't explain.*

Yet he wasn't driven by explanation.

He was driven by obsession.

A *need.*

Outside the house he stood on the front lawn in the dark. Stared at it, as if to harness some further instruction from it. The house from his dreams. *This* was where he was meant to be, not some fucking water tower at the ass end of a neighborhood park. *This.*

He stood there for an unknowable amount of time. If any conscious thoughts passed through his head, he was unaware once he finally came back to himself and realized that, Christ, he would look like a fucking lunatic standing here at this hour if anyone happened to drive by and see him. What would his excuse be? He didn't *have* an excuse; he had no idea why he was standing here in the first place.

*Maybe none of this is real. Maybe I'm going crazy and imagining it all.*

Perhaps he could have ultimately convinced himself of that had he not noticed something peculiar at the foot of the driveway—a single word in neon spray paint poking out from beneath the parked car:

He felt his heart stutter in his chest.

That word.

That fucking *word.*

He hurried over to the car that was parked there and dropped down on his hands and knees. Hard to see under there, so he dug out his phone and clicked on the flashlight. Pointed the beam underneath the chassis.

A fucking sign from the universe. Confirmation that *this* was where he belonged, that *this* was the fucking—

*(endgame)*

—puzzle piece that had been missing. The exact same thing that had prattled incessantly in his brain while his dream-self kept watch over this very house.

What it actually *meant*, he did not know. After all, Sarah Miller was right—there was plenty they couldn't explain. Plenty in this world, and plenty in any world beyond. But Eric Rhodes felt now that he was on the right track.

Practically giddy, he ran back to his truck.

*Blows shaky through causeways, tunneling between houses, through yards and concrete culverts, down drain spouts, rattling the chains of a swing, a seesaw creak, a swoop borne on a hiss of wind,* is *the hiss of wind, the skirl of dead-leaf tornados scraping against pebbled sidewalks, hovering momentarily, thought-blossoms like contrails streaking from jetliners, shuddery mailbox door flaps jolt open, little reg flags go* wicka wicka wicka, *up and down, while bamboo windchimes play their bone music, and the hanging baskets of red geraniums sway peacefully from a front porch awning as the sun rises, rises, rises, brightening the land and transforming the glistening dew on the flower petals to steam.*

*Presses up against the window screen of a particular house, then seeps through the mesh, coming to simmer in a bedroom caught in the confused and constipated midst of transition: a former child's bedroom turned teenager's bedroom desperate to evolve into a young adult's bedroom, that of a girl, having shared this space overnight with two other girls—friends—who have gathered in sleepover formation to commiserate upon their collective woes while also sharing details, some true, some exaggerated, some outright lies, about a boy,* the *boy, their friend—their schoolmate and neighbor and acquaintance, but also maybe "friend"—who disappeared that night at the vacant house, the Trenton house, on Poplar Station Road, found sometime later still in that same house by police, "found" if one might appropriately define the "finding" of a person as the discovery, the recovery, of a shell of that person, of a thing degloved, debrided, and left like discarded snakeskin behind.*

*One girl says, "He's blind."*

*The other says, "I heard he's practically braindead. He can't speak and he can't eat and he pees and shits his pants and he'll likely never leave the hospital."*

*The first girl responds, "Well, I've heard he screams every time someone tries to touch him."*

*The third girl, whose bedroom—that transitional, liminal space—they are currently in, sits atop her bed with her legs folded, hands wrestling in her lap. The boy, Mike Bliss, has some of his circulatory system on the outside of his body, she has heard. This girl, who herself is in transition, who herself is a liminal space, who is Tatum Klass, once desirous to lose her virginity to the boy with the circulatory system now on the outside of his body (whatever that actually means), finds her mind returning to that night. Following him up those stairs to the second floor of the vacant house. Hearing the tinny strains of Van Halen coming from the foam heads of his headphones draped casually, dismissively, roguishly around his neck. How she kissed him in that upstairs hallway and felt his excitement grow. How she felt hers, too. How she followed him into that bedroom at the end of the hall only to find the room empty, impossibly so, once she crossed the threshold.*

*Fine white hairs along the rim of an ear tingle, causing Tatum Klass to turn her head in the direction of the open window, where the hiss, barely perceptible, practically not even there, causes minute vibrations against the window screen. She knows nothing of the cracks, this girl (not just yet), but possesses a heightened sensibility of all things, so that she understands something, something, even if she doesn't understand that she understands.*

*"I heard his eyes turned white."*

*"I heard his toes are fused together into clumps."*

*"I heard all his fingernails fell off."*

*"I heard his* penis *fell off."*

*Nervous laughter.*

*Tatum does not think these girls know she is the one who confessed about breaking into the Trenton house. The others all lied when Mike Bliss's dad came around asking about his son, and they lied again when the cops came calling, too. Tatum Klass, liminal girl, did not lie: she told her parents what happened at the house and then spoke to the police while her father sat on one side of her, mother on the other side. Bookended by the deific fortification of parents. She told the cops about Mike Bliss disappearing, and how she and her friends searched for him around the house, thinking it was a prank, a joke, maybe even at her expense (she did not tell her parents of her desire to lose her virginity to the boy), searching everywhere (except the basement, because no one knew the house even had a basement until they learned Mike Bliss, or what remained of Mike Bliss, was found there), and when they couldn't find him, they all went home, because what else was there to do? It wasn't until Mike Bliss's dad made the rounds that things became serious, and she knew it wasn't a prank.*

*"He bleeds from his ears now, is what I heard," says the first girl.*

*"His shit is pure white and the consistency of cake icing," says the second girl.*

*Tatum Klass says nothing.*

*She sits crisscross-applesauce on her bed while her friends exchange half-truths about the boy whose circulatory system now resides on the outside of his body (whatever that means) and whose irises have turned white, and every once in a while, keeps turning her head, a slight turn, toward the window, as those fine hairs that parade along the satellite dish of her ear pick up a sensation, a vibration, a flutter, a knowledge—*

*—that there may be more than just the three of them in this room.*

# CHAPTER THIRTY-EIGHT

# "IF YOU GO TO THE PARK, BE CAREFUL"

## 1

Brian awoke to the smell of frying bacon, and while that scent would ordinarily incite his hunger, he found himself feeling a little bit . . . off . . . this morning.

He recalled waking in the night and staggering to the bathroom in the dark. He recalled a nosebleed and his own gaunt reflection staring back at him in the bathroom mirror. He recalled, too, how he'd stood there holding a bottle of mouthwash he'd scavenged from the medicine cabinet, operating like someone under a voodoo spell, desperate to drink it down in an effort to quell the shakes. And while the desire to drink was always with him, every second, lurking just behind him and clinging to his back like a shadow, Brian Russo hadn't felt such desperation and powerlessness in nearly a year.

*What's wrong with me?*

He'd felt funny since returning to Maryland.

*No, not Maryland.*

To Mariner's Cove.

*Get a grip. The kid needs you. Ellen, too. Quit being such a piddling bastard.*

Ellen and Cory were in the kitchen preparing breakfast, laughing and boot scooting to a Garth Brooks song streaming on the Alexa speaker. Brian paused in the doorway, smiling despite the sudden pounding inside his head and the minor tremors he could already feel threatening to rattle his bones. At one point, Ellen turned and saw him standing there.

She smiled, but her smile quickly dissipated when she no doubt took in the sight of him. Again, he recalled that gaunt wraith who'd stared back at him from the bathroom mirror the night before and wondered if that desperate cretin was standing here right now, staring back at her.

She tore a section of paper towel from the roll on the counter then carried a steaming plate of scrambled eggs over to the dining room table. She tucked the paper towel into one of his hands as she went by. He barely heard her speak since her whisper was so low: "Your nose is bleeding."

He pressed the paper towel to his nose as he retreated back down the hall before his nephew could catch a glimpse of him. Sure enough, that gaunt skeleton was back there behind the mirrored glass, eyes runny as egg yolks, dark, patchy saddlebags beneath both eyes. He looked like he had aged ten years overnight. He had also likely suffered a nosebleed in his sleep because there was not only a fresh rivulet dribbling from his left nostril, but a brownish crimson smear in the shape of a bat's wing along the whole left side of his face. No wonder Ellen had looked at him the way she had.

He cleaned up then headed back to the dining room to find Ellen and Cory already seated and awaiting his return.

"Look at this," he said, grinning despite the steady pounding in his head. He sat down, aware that Ellen's eyes hung on him for a bit too long. The food smelled good, the coffee was hot, and Brian Russo's hands shook conspicuously as he gathered the utensils off his plate.

"Are you feeling okay?" Ellen asked, still studying him from across the table.

"Haven't been sleeping. Still not used to the time zone changes," he said by way of an excuse.

"Cory and I are going to take your recommendation and get out of the house for the afternoon. Maybe catch a movie and some lunch. Is that still okay with you?"

"I think that's a great idea."

"Me too," said Cory, his mouth full of scrambled eggs.

When they were done eating, Brian cleared the table while Cory ran to his room to get dressed. Ellen came up beside him while he rinsed the plates off at the sink. "Seriously, is everything okay? You look like hell, Brian."

"I wasn't feeling too good last night. Woke up in the middle of the night feeling sick."

"And that nosebleed?"

"I don't know, El. Maybe I strained my brain too much trying to guess those playing cards last night." When her expression did not change, he added, "I'm not doing anything, if that's what you're worried about. I promise."

She nodded, and ran a hand along his arm as she crossed back into the dining room, not saying anything further. He saw the tips of several fingers were wrapped in Band-Aids. He watched her from the sink as she wiped down the dining room table with a damp paper towel. Then, once she finished, she did a curious thing: she went to the bay window and pulled the drapes closed. Then just stood there, gnawing at one of her fingers, and staring off at nothing in particular for several seconds.

He finished the dishes, then tossed the dishtowel onto the counter. There was a water glass there, empty, shining in a spotlight of sun coming through the window over the sink. Something about the sight of it enticed him. Slowly, he lowered himself to a crouch until he was at eye-level with it. Imagined that cold blue star bursting to life at the center of his skull. Imagined the rays of light extending from that star growing longer, longer, longer . . . until one sharp javelin of light reached out and pressed itself against the side of the glass.

*Move, goddamn you.*

Nothing happened, except that his headache grew incrementally worse.

Frustrated, he slunk down the hall to scrounge for some Advil or Excedrin in the bathroom's medicine cabinet—his brain felt like a car crash—but paused by Cory's open bedroom door. The kid sat on the edge of his bed staring at his cell phone. There was a distinct look of consternation on the boy's face. Maybe more than that—a look of concern, maybe.

"You get some bad news about the stock market?" Brian asked.

Cory jumped and quickly set his phone down on the mattress, screen facing down.

"Hey. What's the matter, Chicken Little?"

"I don't know," he said. "Nothing, I guess. I don't want to worry Mom."

"Worry me instead."

Cory seemed to consider this. "Listen," he said. "I'm going to keep Mom away for as long as I can today. I think she needs to get out of here for a while."

"Out of the house?"

"Out of the neighborhood." Cory stood off the bed and slipped his cell phone in his pocket—quickly, like he was hiding some secret. "Even if she doesn't want to go."

"Why wouldn't she want to go?"

"I don't know. Something's . . . different now. I don't know what it is." He looked at his desk, across the room. "Remember what I told you last night? The drawings I showed you?"

Brian glanced at Cory's desk, too, where those strange symbols had been painstakingly drawn on sheets of tracing paper. He could still see them, all laid out there. He could still see the plaster cast on the bookshelf, too. "Yeah, I remember," he said.

"If you go to the park, be careful."

Before Brian could ask anything more, Cory came over and wrapped his arms around his waist. Brian tugged him closer, squeezed him, and for that brief moment he felt the pressure inside his head let up the tiniest bit.

"I think you're worrying about nothing, Chicken Little. I think you're just overthinking things. And maybe that's starting to make your mom worried, too. Maybe that's all this is."

"I hope you're right," Cory said, and hugged him tighter.

## 2

There was a power washer in the shed behind the house. After Ellen and Cory had left for the day, Brian prepped it and spent a good twenty minutes blasting the graffiti from his sister's driveway. The spray paint was stubborn but still fresh enough not to have soaked too deeply into the blacktop, so when he was done, only the ghostly outlines of those strange, cryptic words—*the boy, the boy*—remained.

It wasn't lost on him that Ellen's neighbor, the portly Mr. Zachs, watched him the entire time from a beach chair on his front lawn. He sat there in a bathrobe and sunglasses, bald pate gleaming beneath the summer sun, his thick, hairless calves as white as ricotta cheese—a preposterous sight, to be sure. Yet Brian didn't find much humor in it; he kept thinking about what Cory had said to him about Mr. Zachs the night before: *I looked inside Mr. Zachs's head and it was like a tornado in there. It sounded like a million bees buzzing around. And it was like there was . . . I guess . . . I don't know how to say it . . .*

*Like there was something else in there with him.*

Brian raised a friendly hand in the man's direction. Mr. Zachs clearly turned his head to look at Brian but he did not raise a hand in return, nor acknowledge him in any way.

Brian wasn't sure what to believe. Yes, clearly his nephew was able to do miraculous things, and he'd certainly transmitted a thought directly into Brian's own head at will on more than one occasion. But Cory's worry over some neighborhood graffiti? His insistence that there was something like a buzzing tornado inside his neighbor's head? Maybe the answer was simply that Cory just didn't fully understand his newfound abilities and was misinterpreting things. Maybe his heightened senses were alerting him to consider things that were not even there.

That pounding was gathering momentum inside his own head now. He brought his hand up to his nose, certain that his fingers would come away wet with blood again, but they did not. Down off the curb, backing up into the street, and there were drawings spray-painted right there on the blacktop, no different than the symbols Cory had sketched on the sheets of tracing paper. They looked fresh, too, like someone had come along just hours ago and sprayed them there. Brian backed up further, moving across the street until he stepped up onto the opposite sidewalk. More of them.

Feeling eyes on him—eyes other than Mr. Zachs's—Brian turned and saw a man standing on the lawn at his back. He was middle-aged, dressed in a striped polo shirt and pleated khaki shorts. He was staring down at a cell phone, but when Brian turned to look at him, the man looked up, as if he could similarly sense Brian's eyes on him now, too.

The man's smile was sudden and off-putting. "Hello!"

Brian raised a hand. "Hey," he said.

"You look familiar," said the man.

"I'm Ellen's brother. I lived here for a while, couple years ago."

"Right. Right. I think I remember. I'm Tom Orem. Hello!"

The man—Tom Orem—crossed the lawn down to the curb, and thrust out his hand for Brian to shake. Brian shook it quickly, glad to be rid of it.

"Are they home?" Tom Orem asked.

"Who?"

"The boy. Ellen and the boy. Cory."

"They're out for the afternoon."

The man had a clean-shaven, rectangular face, with dark eyes and a banner of dense black eyebrows. As Brian watched him, those dense eyebrows drew together and the man's dark eyes narrowed. "Well," he said, drawing out the word, *wellllll*, "that's too bad."

"Yeah? How come?"

The man shrugged. He glanced down at his cell phone again—quickly, like he didn't want Brian to notice. "They're just . . . good people. And I know my son, Davey, was looking to play with Cory this afternoon."

"I'll let him know."

"What were you up to with that power washer?"

"Someone vandalized their driveway."

"Really? No! That's terrible. That's too bad. Who would do that? So awful."

"I'm wondering if it's the same person who made these doodles." He nodded toward the grid of strange symbols spray-painted on the sidewalk that was laid out in the space between them.

"Well," Tom Orem said, as if seeing the symbols for the first time. "Look at that."

Across the street, Mr. Zachs was watching this unfold from his beach chair. Suddenly, Brian felt like something floating around in an aquarium, observed by many eyes.

"Maybe you shouldn't have cleaned the driveway," said Tom Orem.

"Yeah? Why's that?"

Tom Orem's mouth tightened into a knot. His gaze shifted back to the phone in his hand, then across the street to where Mr. Zachs sat slouched in his beach chair. "If it's something nefarious, maybe you should have kept it there and involved the police."

"Has there been a lot of that going on around here?"

"A lot of what?"

"Nefarious things that should involve the police?"

Tom Orem tossed his head back and laughed—so enthusiastically, Brian could count the fillings in his teeth. "No, no. This is a nice, quiet neighborhood. What was your name again? I forget."

"Brian."

"Welcome to the Cove, Brian."

Brian smiled and nodded. The pounding in his head had reached untenable proportions, and, for some reason, he felt uncomfortable—felt exposed—standing here talking to this man.

"Have a good day," Brian told him, and wedged his hands in his pockets as he walked up the block.

It was a bright and sunny day, and he should have been feeling good, but there was something tumbling around inside his skull that kept him on edge. His stomach didn't feel so great, either. When he reached the intersection of Cloister and Capshaw, he noticed a bright red van parked along the curb, the words KOTARA WINDOWS & DOORS etched on the side in swooping blue letters. There was a man reclining in the driver's seat. For some reason, Brian felt an inexplicable tingling race up his arms at the sight of him.

After a time, he found himself walking down Poplar Station Road, which was the main drag that ran through the center of the neighborhood. He paused in midstride when he saw the symbol of a semicircle, or possibly a dome-shape, spray-painted in bright orange neon on the trunk of an oak tree:

Then a few blocks farther, on the trunk of another tree, was what looked like an X with a bar across the top:

Beside that tree and spray-painted along the outside of someone's mailbox was a third symbol, this one a triangle with a hook at the top—

—that looked to Brian like a child's drawing of a coat hanger.

These were the same symbols, among several others, that had been on the sidewalk outside Ellen and Cory's house. They were also the same symbols Cory had shown him the night before, drawn on sheets of tracing paper. Would Brian have noticed them had Cory not brought them to the forefront of his mind? No. Which suggested that it was

Cory stirring up all this paranoia in him now. Yet he found that he couldn't *not* see them, and in truth, there *did* seem to be something . . . well, something provocative about them, whether Cory had planted that seed or not.

He looked across the street, toward the entrance of Gladstone Park, where the park's wooden sign sat cocked at an angle welcoming all of Mariner's Cove through the park's gates. It was a beautiful summer day, but Brian noted that there wasn't a single soul in the park—no kids running bases on the baseball diamond, no couples chucking frisbees at each other on the lawn, no one walking their dog or having a picnic lunch or flying a kite. In that moment, he could hear Cory's warning echoing in his head—*If you go to the park, be careful.*

He crossed the road and stepped up onto the gravel path that wound up to the entrance of the park. The gate was drawn across the entranceway and a handwritten sign posted beside it said the park was temporarily closed. This gave him pause, though it would explain why there was no one else here. His head was still throbbing and his stomach wasn't doing so great now, either, but he'd told Cory he'd come check out the park, so that was what he planned to do. He'd find nothing here, of course, which would quell Cory's concerns, and then he'd hoof it back to the house and take a long nap until both his headache and stomachache dissipated.

He was halfway across the park grounds when a man in a construction vest came through the wall of trees at the far end of the park.

"Hey, hey, hey," the man said, holding up a hand. "Park's closed until further notice."

"How come?"

"Gas leak." The man jerked a thumb over his shoulder in the vague direction of the woods at his back.

"Oh. Well, I can't just hang around out here?"

"We need to keep the whole area clear. You know, to be safe."

"For how long?"

"For however long it takes for us to get things under control."

Brian nodded slowly. "Okay."

"Hey," the man said, taking a few steps back toward the woods. "You have a nice day." But then he just stood there with his arms folded across his chest, as if he didn't trust that Brian would leave.

Brian nodded at the man again, then turned and headed back toward the road. Was that the danger Cory had sensed coming from the park? A gas leak? Dangerous, he supposed, but hardly supernatural.

When he reached the road, he cast one final glance over his shoulder to see if the man in the reflective construction vest was still standing there watching him. He was. He'd also been joined by another man, this one not wearing a reflective vest, but only a saggy pair of workpants and a flannel shirt with the sleeves cuffed all the way to his biceps. Both men were watching him and, despite the distance, Brian could feel the intensity of their collective stare.

Brian's eyes scaled upward, past the tops of the trees, to where the top of a water tank was visible against the bright, cloudless, late-morning sky.

Someone had defaced the water tank. It now read:

And there were those strange symbols painted on it as well.

Brian felt a pulse of unease travel through his body—more potent than both the headache and stomachache which he'd already been dealing with. The world seemed to shift to one side, and he had to lean against the hood of a parked car just to keep himself upright.

*Endgame.*

*Endgame?*

Something was wrong with him. Something was broken inside his head. It felt like invisible fingers were moving about in there, rewiring his brain. And yet . . .

. . . for one brief moment, he thought he could see the dim, distant light of the brightening star at the center of his head. He glanced down and saw two distinct droplets of blood on his shirt. He touched his nose and the pads of his fingers came away slick with blood.

*Endgame.*

*End—*

## 3

Somehow, he made it back to the house. His head was still pounding, but there was some relief in his gut. Sweating and trembling, he went around and made sure all the windows were shut, all the doors were locked, and all the drapes and blinds were securely closed and shielding him from the world outside. From the window over the kitchen sink, he could still see Mr. Zachs perched on his beach chair, staring at the house through his wraparound sunglasses. That red van with the words KOTARA WINDOWS & DOORS had still been parked at the intersection, too . . . hadn't it?

At one moment, he found himself standing in Cory's bedroom, gazing up at the ceiling covered in stars. Then he looked down and saw all the drawings on those sheets of tracing paper. Assembled, the symbols came together to form a complete—

At another moment, he found himself standing before the bathroom mirror. The terrible thing that peered back at him possessed the hungry, haunted eyes of a ghoul, and the complexion of the walking dead.

His throat was dry.

His *soul* was dry.

He recalled in that moment the final conversation he'd had with Donna Holmes, the woman he'd once loved, though it had been less a conversation and more of a plea as he'd accosted her outside her apartment one rainy afternoon, and how she'd said—

Please move out of the way.
I don't want to see you again.

—and then he thought of Cory saying, *If you go to the park, be careful,* and he knew now that he *hadn't* been careful, that something was very, very wrong because he hadn't been careful, and in that instant of realization, something at the very core of Brian Russo snapped like a rubber band, *thwick,* and he felt his body drop weightlessly into what could only be described as a coal-black abyss.

# CHAPTER THIRTY-NINE
# BAD ELEMENTS

## 1

At 12:41 that Sunday afternoon, a police car was dispatched to the Bay Road section of Mariner's Cove following the report of a missing person filed by an airline pilot named Ken Harrison. The missing person in question was Ken's wife, Olivia Harrison, who had been missing since sometime yesterday afternoon, according to the Harrisons' teenage daughter. Ken, who'd only just returned earlier that morning from an American Airlines redeye, telephoned the police a bit shaken and confused after speaking with his daughter. Olivia's cell phone was still in the house, as were her purse and her housekeys. Her car was still in the garage. There were no notes left behind.

Had she been acting funny prior to her disappearance? Ken Harrison had to chuckle morosely at that one. Yes, she'd been acting *very* funny. It was concerning, really. Unusual behavior. What exactly was the nature of this unusual behavior? Ken Harrison didn't know how to answer that one. Was it the summer flu? Seasonal allergies? Migraines? Depression? Ken Harrison didn't know; all he knew was that she'd been spending nearly all her time cooped up in the house, not showering, wearing the same baggy T-shirt and sweatpants for days. She stopped preparing meals, stopped doing housework, stopped going to book club and other social events, and had even ignored all their guests the night of their luau. Ken knew his wife was prone to terrible migraines, but when those hit, Olivia typically stayed in bed for the day, the blinds drawn, the lights off, an icepack on her forehead.

He *did* find her on occasion in the parlor at the far end of the house—a room they rarely if ever used—seated in the dark on a peculiar foldable camping chair, just staring off into space.

Michael Danver learned all of this when two uniformed police officers canvassing the block knocked on his front door. They were two women, exceedingly young, and Danver thought they looked like children playing dress-up in their police uniforms. No, he hadn't seen Olivia Harrison since the party at their house. No, they couldn't speak to his wife at the moment because Miranda was not at home. No, he hadn't witnessed anything out of the ordinary in the neighborhood lately. Why was his right hand bandaged? He'd injured it doing some woodworking in the garage.

He thought one of the police officers looked like she might be coming down with something: she kept wiping sweat from her brow and smacking her lips together like someone about to be sick. Her skin looked pale and clammy. Green, almost. She seemed anxious to get off the porch and to move on, and Danver hoped that she would. He worried she might ask to come inside to use his bathroom. But she didn't.

"What about gunshots?" asked the other officer.

Danver blinked. "Gunshots?"

"Some of your neighbors said they heard what sounded like gunshots yesterday afternoon. Were you home yesterday?"

"Yes."

"Do you recall hearing gunshots?"

"I don't . . . I mean, no. No, I didn't. I heard nothing. But, you know, there's someone across the river that shoots off a potato gun from time to time. Maybe that's what people were hearing."

"Maybe," said the ill-looking officer.

"Well," said the other officer, cheerily enough, "if you happen to see or hear anything regarding Mrs. Harrison, please let us know."

"I sure will. I just hope we're all overreacting, you know?" He laughed nervously, then wondered if he sounded like he was overcompensating. "I mean, she's probably out shopping."

"On foot overnight?" suggested the queasy-looking officer, pointing out the ridiculousness of Danver's suggestion.

"Well," Danver said, "I hope everything turns out all right. I'm sure it will. Thanks for stopping by."

It was then, just as the police officers were about to leave, that Danver heard the familiar *clack clack clack* sound of Clementine's toenails tapdancing on the hardwood floor. He thought nothing of it at first, since he'd been hearing that specific clacking for years, relegated to the common background noise of living in this house, but then the cheery-looking officer peered over his shoulder and, with a sudden look of consternation on her face, said, "What kind of dog is that?"

Danver turned in time to glimpse a fleeting shape vanish into the living room at the opposite end of the hallway.

*Clack clack clack.*

"Uh, he's, uh, a Pekingese," Danver stammered. "My wife's dog. Clementine"

"Any idea when your wife will be home?" the other officer asked. Sweat rolled down her pallid face. "We'd like to speak with her, too."

"I really don't know. I'm sorry. Miranda's very busy. She's the publisher of a regional magazine and she's always taking meetings." He reached down and lifted one of the issues of *Look There!* off the stack that still lay splayed like a deck of cards in the hallway, thankfully out of the view of the officers. He extended the magazine through the narrow gap in the door.

"Oh, we get that at the house," said the cheery officer. "I live in the neighborhood, Dr. Danver."

"Ah," said Danver, and he could hear the quaver in his voice.

"Well," said the sickly-looking officer, already stepping down from the porch. She was looking greener by the minute. "You have a good afternoon, sir."

Danver watched them mosey down the walkway and head over to the Bridgeports' next door. Danver's head was a muddled mess, and he couldn't keep his days straight, but he recalled Donnie snooping around his back yard the same day Olivia Harrison had come over clutching that camping chair to her chest. Had that been yesterday? Had Donnie witnessed Olivia Harrison come around to the rear of the house, where Danver had let her in through the slider? She'd caused quite a commotion at the front door, too, when Danver had insisted that she leave. Jesus, had Donnie heard the gunshots, too? Apparently, some of the other neighbors had. Christ, his ears were still cottony from the sound.

What, exactly, *was* Donnie Bridgeport aware of? He'd come here looking to borrow a saw, but that was bullshit, because Danver had gone to an upstairs window and peered out into the Bridgeports' yard soon afterwards. There were no fallen tree limbs anywhere that he could see.

*Lies.*

Danver closed the front door and turned the deadbolt.

*Clack clack clack.*

Claws on hardwood.

"Clem? Clementine? Here, boy." He crossed down the hall just as the clacking of those claws ceased. As if the dog had suddenly frozen at the sound of Danver's voice. "Clementine?" He whistled.

The house remained silent.

When he reached the entrance to the living room, everything looked normal at first blush. But then he saw that the cushions on the sofa had been shredded to ribbons, with fat cubes of yellowish foam bursting through the rents in the fabric. He came further into the room and saw a puddle of what must have been piss on the hardwood floor beside the coffee table.

"Where are you, boy? Where'd you go? Come on out and let me have a look at you."

The damn dog didn't make a peep. Had it not been for the shredded sofa cushions and the puddle of piss on the floor—not to mention the comment from the police officer on the front porch who'd happened to catch a glimpse of the dog—Danver could have easily convinced himself that he'd imagined the clacking of those claws.

He crossed behind the sofa and saw that several copies of *Look There!* had been torn into strips, the pages tamped down like bedding.

How the hell did that goddamn dog come back from . . . wherever he had gone?

Danver went across the room to the door, which still lay horizontally across the seats of the two kitchen chairs. That shadow beneath it looked as dark and nefarious as a tar pit. While it seemed impossible that *anything* might claw its way out of there, he could see that that was exactly what Clementine had done: there were shallow scuffmarks on the floor from where the dog had likely clawed its way up and over the ledge of the shadow. Like crawling out of a hole in the ground.

*That world is not for you.*

"You still here in the house, Clem?"

Or had the goddamned thing crawled back inside the shadow beneath the door?

Danver wandered around the lower level of the house, whistling for the dog, patting his bandaged hand against his thigh. He poked his head into rooms, checked under furniture, looked beneath the desk in Miranda's office (which was where Clementine would sometimes curl up at Miranda's feet when she was in here working), but he couldn't find the damn thing anywhere.

And the house remained silent.

*I'm losing my fucking mind*, he thought.

Despite the sudden ache at the small of his back, he climbed the stairs to the second floor. All the doors in the hall stood open except the one to the master bedroom, so Danver poked his head into each of those rooms, peering under beds, behind shower curtains, in closets, but Clementine was nowhere.

Finally, Danver arrived at the closed bedroom door. No chance the dog could have gotten in there, since Danver had shut the door himself . . . but then again, there were a lot of things happening lately that Michael Danver would have previously thought impossible.

He opened the bedroom door.

The room was dark, the shades drawn. The shape of Miranda's body resolved itself in the gloom, a vague lump atop the bed swaddled in sheets from head to toe. He felt a pang of grief at the thought of her, but his grief was quickly usurped by that repeated, incessant ostinato:

*PROTECT THE DOOR*
*PROTECT THE DOOR*
*PROTECT THE DOOR*

A small shape rose up on the bed. It was Clementine, although it was too dark in the room to see the dog with any clarity, except for the imprecise outline of the creature. Danver stood there in the doorway, skin growing hot and prickly, back teeth faintly buzzing. He could hear the dog's respiration—a sound like air wheezing through a faulty bellows—and his phlegmy panting was almost comforting in its familiarity. The dog was sitting up on the bed beside Miranda's body, watching Danver from across the room.

Something was wrong with it. Before Clementine had gone beneath the door, he had been a bright orange furball, his bushy tail like the decorative boa on a fancy evening gown. Now, whatever sat on the bed next to Miranda's sheet-swaddled corpse, looked hairless and lumpy and *not right* in the half-light.

Danver's hand reached up to the light switch on the wall.

Clementine barked—a shrill, croaking bark—and then jumped off the bed. Just as Danver flipped the light on, the dog bolted past him, out into the hall, and then down the winding wooden staircase to the ground floor in a blur—*clack clack clack clack clack!*

Danver stood there, heart galloping. His hand slid from the light switch and hung limply at his side. For one wild moment, confusion caused him to wonder if any of this had just happened—any of it, to include finding the door in the cove behind his house, the accident with Miranda in the garage, and the seemingly systematic placement of symbols throughout the neighborhood that were feverishly burning through his brain.

After a time, he headed back downstairs. The dog had gone silent once again—no clacking of nails, no labored, phlegmy breathing. When Danver reached the ground floor, he called out, "Clementine! Here, boy!" His unsteady voice echoed throughout the otherwise empty house.

A snippet of the song that Miranda used to sometimes sing to Clementine when Clem was just a pup came back to Danver now:

*Oh my darling, oh my darling*
*Oh my darling, Clementine*
*You are lost and gone forever*
*Dreadful sorry, Clementine*

Only *this* Clementine was not lost and gone forever.

From the garage, he retrieved a container of antifreeze.

In the kitchen, he filled Clem's bowl with dogfood, poured some antifreeze on top, then picked up the dog's favorite squeaky toy. It was a featherless rubber chicken, and when Danver squeezed the thing, it unleashed a shrill, throaty squawk. Ordinarily, this would be followed by the sound of the dog's claws scrabbling along the floor as Clem bolted into the kitchen, every bit as efficient as ringing a dinner bell. Danver figured he had a fifty-fifty chance of that happening now . . . yet as the seconds ticked by with no sound of those nails scrabbling on the hardwood floor, those odds began to rapidly dwindle.

Yet—

Silent as a ghost, Clementine appeared in the entryway to the kitchen. There was enough daylight coming through the wall of windows to allow Danver to get a good look at him, and the revulsion that followed was as thick and tangible as a stone lodged in Danver's throat. As he stared at the dog, he absently brought his own bandaged hand up to his chest and cradled it there with his one good hand, thinking momentarily about the way the radial artery was now on the outside of his flesh, like a tree root breaching whalelike through soil.

It looked like the dog had been turned inside-out.

There was no bright orange fur. Instead, the whole of Clementine's body was made up of a moist, pink, membranous tissue, striated with a network of pulsing red circulatory. The dog's ears were missing, leaving behind two cavernous divots at the sides of its head. The face was the color and consistency of raw hamburger through which a set of wet, oil-spot eyes seemed to dribble down the sides of its jowls. As those eyes took Danver in, the dog—or whatever it was now—propped itself up on its hind legs. Danver saw the trachea running in a tract down the center of its pink, fleshy throat. Its beating heart was exposed, ectopia cordis, sheathed in a translucent layer of skin, the color of calf liver and about the size of a walnut. The thing's lungs were similarly visible, two kidney-shaped sacks that respired in conjunction with the dog's mucus-filled respiration.

As Danver stared at the abomination, Clementine dropped back down to all fours and trotted over to his food bowl. If Danver closed his eyes, the sound of the dog eating was no different than it had always been, but he had also caught sight of the creature's exposed stomach protruding just beneath the lungs, and imagining the digestive undulations of that glistening sac caused his throat to tighten.

He went into the living room and sat on the sofa while the dog finished his meal.

Sometime later, when he realized the house had been quiet for a while, Danver got up and went into the kitchen. Clementine lay beside his food dish on his side, legs stiff, mouth agape and fringed in white foam. Something about the thing's inside-out flesh reminded Danver of raw chicken breast. The dog's exposed heart was no longer beating.

He went to the pantry and retrieved a broom. In the living room, the door was still as he'd left it, propped horizontally across the seats of two chairs, that gaping black rectangle directly beneath it. He noticed, strangely, that a few bees were crawling on the living room wall behind the door, while one or two zigged lazily in the air.

That shadow looked like a hungry mouth.

*You are lost and gone forever*
*Dreadful sorry, Clementine*

He swept the dog beneath the door and watched as the pinkish, fleshy body with its outward-facing organs vanished into that dark and dreadful space.

## 2

He returned to the kitchen to retrieve some paper towels to clean up the urine on the living room floor but found nothing but a cardboard tube on the dispenser beside the sink. He looked beneath the sink for more, but they weren't there. And it occurred to him that he did not know where *most* things were kept in the house. Miranda took care of those things. At least, she used to.

He ambled back down to the vestibule and gathered up a handful of copies of *Look There!* He carried them to the living room, eased himself onto his knees, and proceeded to tear out pages from the magazine which he used to wipe up the urine. A page of advertisements here, an article on the grand opening of a children's theater in Annapolis there. Toward the end of the issue, there was one photograph above all others that snared his attention. Upon seeing it, he brought the magazine closer to his face so that his nose came to rest mere inches from the page. This was a full color shot that spanned two pages, taken by someone who stood at the cusp of Gladstone Park—the lush summer lawns, the baseball diamond, the rank of trees that made up the far end of the park. Yet it was the one thing in the distance that he focused in on—or, rather, the distance *itself*, for the blackened and bruised sky, swirling with thick, substantial clouds, was an exact duplicate from his nightmares: the tumultuous sky that was repeatedly revealed to him once his dead father swept away the curtain from the window of his study. And just as in those dreams, the same structure loomed in the background of the photograph, only now, unlike in his dreams, he recognized it exactly for what it was: the Gladstone Park water tower. It rose above the line of black, storm-ravaged trees like a beacon.

*Door becomes chair.*

*Take it there.*

Something cold and hard slowly descended Michael Danver's throat and settled in the pit of his stomach, solid and obtrusive, like a cancer.

He closed the magazine and tossed it on the floor. Bracing one hand against the wall for support, he levered himself off his knees, wincing at the twinge of pain that was beginning to turn into a persistent ache at the small of his back. At the hall closet, he slipped on a pair of sandals before snatching the jumble of car keys from the wire basket mounted on the interior wall of the closet.

He thought Miranda's Escalade was still parked in the driveway, so he slipped out the front door of the house, wincing at the sharpness of the sun in his eyes. He felt overexposed, like a snail extracted from its shell. The Escalade was not there, however, and for a moment he thought maybe someone had stolen it. *Bad elements*, he recalled Ken Harrison saying the night of the luau. *Next thing you know, we're infested. They slip in through the cracks.* Just like Clementine: a bad element that had somehow slipped in through a crack. But then he remembered he'd parked the Escalade in the garage following that . . . well, that unfortunate incident with Miranda.

Just thinking about that caused him to freeze right then and there in the middle of the driveway. His muddy eyes were drawn to the symbol spray-painted at the foot of his driveway, the details of it growing blurry as his eyes grew moist.

—*No time for this now,* Danver's father spoke up. *You're onto something, so follow your instinct and see it through. Door becomes chair. Take it there.*

He went back in the house where he wrangled the heavy wooden door—

*(becomes chair)*

—up off the kitchen chairs and set it down with an audible grunt onto the living room floor. The damn thing was heavy, and Danver's backache wasn't making the task any easier, but somehow he managed to drag the thing into the garage and load it into the back of the Escalade. Once he'd finished, he looked up and saw a cluster of insects crawling along the exposed bulb in the center of the ceiling.

Bees.

Just like in the house.

They'd been coming through the shadow beneath the door, Danver knew. He'd even witnessed one fly right out the other day, just as easy as you'd please. They were passing through the very cracks his father had told him about, passing from some other place, some other plane of existence. Some other—

*(that world is not for you)*

—world.

—*Things are moving quickly now*, said his father. The dead man's voice was so crystal-clear that Danver glanced around the gloomy, shadow-pocketed garage, expecting to find him standing in a corner beside a clutch of gardening tools, or perhaps beside the old car-covered Mercury Cougar. Just like the bees, Hal Danver had similarly come through the crack. But if the old man was physically in here with him, Danver could see no sight of him.

—*Can you feel it, Michael? Endgame is almost upon us, son. Door becomes chair.*

"Take it there."

—*That's right.*

And he could *hear* the smile spread across Hal Danver's face.

—*Just don't forget to*—

"Protect the door," Danver finished.

He went back inside the house, retrieved the gun from where he'd left it on the bar beside a mostly empty bottle of Chivas, then returned to the garage where he opened the garage door onto a sheet of scalding daylight.

The slender silhouette of a man stood at the center of Danver's driveway. Tucking the hand holding the gun behind his back, Danver shuffled forward, shielding his eyes from the glare with one arm. The man drifted closer, the silhouette resolving into Donnie Bridgeport.

"Hey, doc. Was just about to knock on your door."

"What is it?"

"I was just wondering if you or Miranda have seen Mia. I haven't seen her since I got up this morning and she's left no forwarding address." He offered up a smile, but it did little to displace the concern on his face. "All the cars are accounted for so I thought she might be over here."

"She isn't," Danver said. "I haven't seen her."

"You know, I didn't think to even worry until those cops came around asking about Olivia Harrison. And then I started thinking, well jeez, I haven't seen *my* wife all morning. Starting wondering if maybe this was some *Twilight Zone* episode, where all the wives have been taken aboard the mothership in the night, leaving us knuckle draggers to fend for ourselves. Is Miranda home? Maybe she's seen—"

"Miranda's not home and we haven't seen your wife," Danver said.

"Oh." Donnie blinked at him. "Okay." His gaze readjusted to Danver's bandaged left hand, which was still up shielding the daylight from his eyes. "What happened there?"

"Woodworking accident." Danver slipped the bandaged hand into his pocket while his other hand—the one holding the gun—remained behind his back. "Donnie, I'm very busy. If you don't mind—"

—*Shoot him,* said Hal Danver. *He knows too much. He's a problem. He'll make everything fall apart.*

"Right. Sorry, doc. Didn't mean to be a bother. I'll let you get on with it."

But Donnie Bridgeport did not immediately turn and leave: he lingered, the sun causing the left side of his body to glow. Danver imagined the space between them sparkling with electricity.

—*Kill him. Kill him. Kill him.*

"Anyway, I'm glad to see you're feeling better," Donnie said. His eyes narrowed almost imperceptibly.

—*killhimkillhimkillhim*—

Donnie raised a hand, then turned and ambled across the driveway, through the break in the hedgerow that separated their two properties.

A pent-up breath wheezed from between Danver's lips. He leaned against the side of the Escalade, his heart thundering, his body suddenly amphibious with sweat. He noticed in that moment an unusual weightiness to the breast pocket of his shirt, so he reached inside it and found that the four iron digits that had once been attached to the door now resided there.

# CHAPTER FORTY
# WATCHER

"Mom?"

"Yeah, baby?"

"Don't be scared, okay?"

"Cory, I told you, I'm not scared. You don't frighten me. I'm your—"

"There's someone watching us."

They were seated at an outdoor table on the patio of the Pink Penguin, a half-eaten greasy cheese pizza and two Cokes in plastic cups between them. Ellen met her son's eyes, then watched as his gaze drifted from hers to just over her right shoulder, toward the parking lot. Ellen turned her head, saw a few people seated at the next table eating ice cream, saw a teenage couple holding hands as they strolled across the walkway that wound around the building.

"The police car," Cory said.

She saw it: a police cruiser parked among a file of other vehicles in the Pink Penguin's parking lot. Unlike all the other cars, the cruiser had backed into its spot so that it was facing them. There was a cop behind the wheel, though the glare from the sun across the vehicle's windshield made discerning any details impossible.

"That cop?" she asked him.

"He's one of the police officers who came to the house to get you."

"How do you know that? Can you see him?"

"I can feel it."

She looked back at him. "Maybe he's just here for lunch."

Slowly, Cory shook his head.

"Cops have to eat, too, you know."

"Mom," Cory said, his voice dropping to a near whisper. He leaned conspiratorially toward her from across the table. "It's the same man. He's been watching us the whole time we've been here. He was watching us at mini golf, too."

She recollected the officer who had driven her home after they'd discovered the Bliss kid in the basement of the Trenton house. What had his name been? She couldn't remember, but did recall that he lived in the neighborhood.

*Grayson*, she thought suddenly. *His name was Officer Eddie Grayson.*

"You saw him at mini golf?" she asked.

"He was parked at the back of the lot, but he got out of his car at one point and just stood down by the trees, watching us. He's been watching us all day."

"Cory, that sounds . . ." Her voice trailed off. It sounded paranoid, yes, but she found she couldn't simply dismiss it anymore, either.

"I've been trying to peek inside his head, just like with Mr. Zachs," Cory continued, his voice still low, "but he won't let me."

"What do you mean he won't let you?"

"It's like he knows I'm trying and he's able to stop me. It was the same way with that man who came to the house that day to fix the kitchen window."

"Larry Kotara?"

"When I tried to look inside his head, he blocked me, too."

She wanted to say, *Stop looking inside people's heads without their permission,* but realized how trite that would sound. Besides, was that really the important thing here? *Don't be scared, okay?* Well, she *was* scared, or starting to be. Office Grayson had made her uncomfortable on the drive home from the Trenton house, she remembered, although she couldn't explicitly say why. There had just been something . . . *off* . . . about him. And now he was watching them from the parking lot of the Pink Penguin.

*He's been watching us all day . . .*

"You said he's blocking you. Does that mean he can feel you trying to—"

"He knows. He knows I was trying to look inside his head. He knows that I know he's here."

"Why is following us? What does he want?"

Cory seemed to consider this for a moment before shaking his head. "I don't know. But I don't feel good about it."

"Hey," she said, balling up her napkin and tossing it in her plate. "You about done?"

"I am."

"Let's get out of here."

"Yes."

They got up from the table and Ellen took Cory by the hand—something he would generally balk at in public, but he didn't say anything about it now. She realized she was clutching her keys the way she did when she had to walk alone through a particularly suspect neighborhood in Baltimore: the big key poking from between her forefinger and middle finger, ready to strike if it came down to it. Her heart was suddenly beating very fast.

They were parked six or seven cars down from the police cruiser, and Ellen dragged Cory along at a quick clip, her head down.

"Don't stare at him."

Cory looked down at his sneakers.

They got quickly into the car and Ellen jabbed the key into the ignition. The engine rattled then sprung to life, the radio bursting on in mid-Adele. Ellen switched it off, then sat for a second catching her breath. She peered past Cory and out the passenger window, through a rank of car windows, and could see the silhouette of officer behind the wheel of the cruiser staring through those windows right back at her.

She reached over and ran a hand through her son's hair. "It's just a coincidence," she said.

"Then how come you told me not to stare at him?"

She pulled out of the lot and dutifully paused the stop sign before rolling out onto the street. Once the Pink Penguin was no longer in her rearview mirror, she pressed her foot down on the accelerator a bit more.

She heard a buzzing sound, then glanced over and saw Cory digging his cell phone from his pocket. She didn't like the stricken look on his face.

"What?" she said. "What is it?"

"Davey. He keeps texting. Only it doesn't sound like him."

"What's he texting?"

Cory held up the phone so she could see the screen, scrolling so she could see the entirety of it:

come out

come out

come out

come out

come out

come out

come out

come out

come out

come out

come out

come out

come out

come out

come out

come out

come out

come out

come out

come out

come out

come out

come out

come out

come out

come out

come out

come out

come out

come out

come out

come out

come out

come out

come out

come out

come out

As she stared at the screen, another messaged buzzed in:

come out

"Why's he doing that?"

Cory shook his head. "I don't know. I don't think it's him. I don't think it's Davey."

"Put the phone away."

She glanced up at the rearview mirror to find herself chewing the Band-Aid off the middle finger of her right hand. Disgusting childhood habit that she'd subconsciously resurrected, seeded in her now like an obsession, a compulsion. She lowered her hand but kept her eyes glued to the rearview mirror. For a moment, she thought she saw a police car following them a few cars back, still on the other side of the last intersection. But when the traffic cleared and she took a sharp left, she realized it was only her paranoia.

# CHAPTER FORTY-ONE
# DOOR-BECOMES-CHAIR

## 1

Sarah called Eric's cell phone several times that morning, but he never answered. By noon, she had become antsy and nervous, and her FOMO was in full effect. Her father drove her in the Tank to where her car was still out of commission on the shoulder of the road. David Miller was no mechanic, but apparently possessed some divine touch, because when he cranked the key in the ignition, the vehicle sputtered to life. She thanked him, climbed behind the wheel, then watched as the Tank trundled out of the neighborhood toward the highway. She felt a pang of envy as she watched him leave, as though unlike him she had somehow become a prisoner of the Cove itself. Not a suburban neighborhood, but a cage. Maybe her car was in on the plot, conking out on her when it appeared as if she might make an escape.

There would *be* no escape, she knew. Not anymore. And right now, she didn't want one: there was important work to be done *right here* in Mariner's Cove.

She dialed Eric's number one last time, but he still did not answer. Then she drove back home where she spent the next forty minutes loading her collection of coat hangers into trash bags then stuffing the trash bags into the Festiva.

Something told her that instead of approaching Gladstone Park from the main entrance on Poplar Station Road, she should instead take Slope Hill to the nameless stretch of roadway that ran parallel to the woods at the back end of the park. It felt like sneaking up on something from behind, but it also felt like she could come and go unobserved more easily, since hardly anyone ever came down these nameless, unpaved roads.

When she arrived, however, she was surprised to find about a dozen vehicles parked along the side of the road and several more rolled up into the grass where they were partially hidden by the trees. As she pulled behind a blue Camry with a busted taillight, she saw a man climb out of a pickup truck a few vehicles ahead of her. He held a bundle of metal pipes under his arm and was glancing furtively around like someone about to commit a felony. As she watched, the man paused just before disappearing into the trees to gaze up at the top of the water tower, which Sarah herself could not see from her vantage. Sarah couldn't make out the expression on the man's face, either, but his body suggested a mixture of trepidation and eagerness. She felt it, too—it strummed through her like an electrical charge.

The bags of coat hangers weren't exactly heavy, but they were large and unwieldy (not to mention the wires were already poking holes in the bags), so she could only manage to carry one at a time, slung over her shoulder in Santa Claus fashion. *Ho, ho, ho,* she thought as she followed the unknown man with the metal pipes under one arm into the woods.

As she came into the water tower's clearing, her mouth dropped open. In a rush, everything they had done the night before came back to her, but that was nothing compared to what had been done overnight in her absence. What she was looking at now was not just some random bits of junk crudely assembled to suggest something of greater value beneath the water tower; what stood there now was a thing of *purpose*. In fact, she was so in awe of it that she didn't even register the people who were there working on it—about thirty people now, scuttling and bustling and busily buzzing about—that she simply dropped her trash bag to the ground while taking a few long strides toward the tower.

She felt drawn to it.

Powerless to resist.

Not *wanting* to resist.

*Stinger was right*, she thought. *It* is *a hive. But it's something else, too. A temple, maybe. I can't really tell. But it's certainly beautiful and wonderful and unbelievable.*

Two-thirds of the tower's center post had been wrapped in sheet metal. A rusted orange basketball hoop had been fixed to the sheet metal and Georgette Braswell's colander had been placed in the hoop, upside down, and held in place with metal brackets. Some of Sarah's straightened coat hangers still protruded from the colander's holes, with additional ones linked to those, creating a bowing daisy chain of wire that stretched all the way to the chain-link fence surrounding the tower's legs. Something that looked like a metal folding table had been set up off-center beneath the colander-in-a-basketball-hoop and there were countless items lining the inside perimeter of the chain-link fence—metal wheels, aluminum mailboxes, what looked like someone's clothes carousel, and many other less identifiable items.

There were people scaling the ladder that climbed the side of the tower. Others were carrying long copper-colored wires along the walkway that circumnavigated the tank, where more items were on display. Two people were leaning over the walkway railing, hoisting Sheila Donaldson's TV aerial off the ground by a long towrope. The people at the top of the tower all wore bright orange work vests with reflective tape down the sides, making them look like county employees operating in some official capacity.

She realized, too, that she was inadvertently catching snippets of thoughts that were caroming through the air, much like countless bees infiltrating the hive of her mind—

*(SHOULD BE ABLE TO HARNESS AND CONNECT)*

*(RIG THIS TO THE TOP OF THE)*

*(SOMETHING SOMETHING STILL NOT RIGHT STILL OFF WITH)*

*(SOLDERED METAL RODS KEEP BREAKING)*

*(HOT TODAY)*

*(AM I HUNGRY?)*

*(STILL NOT RIGHT WITH THE BASKETBALL HOOP AND THE COLANDER STILL NOT RIGHT NEEDS ADJUSTING SOMETHING NOT RIGHT SOMETHING STILL NOT)*

*(THIRSTY)*

*(TEETH BACK TEETH CAN HEAR IT IN MY)*

"People kept showing up all night," Stinger said, coming up beside her. The sound of his voice didn't startle her; in fact, for a moment, she couldn't be certain she'd heard him speak aloud as opposed to inside her head. "They brought their own parts and we just couldn't help ourselves. We kept putting it together in the dark and it didn't matter. In fact, it's easier at night. Safer. People can't see us up there. If we have to go up there in daylight, like now, we wear the vests. People who see us from the street will think we're with the county. But my guess is no one who's not a part of this already is paying much attention. Notice how most people have been staying away from the park? It's like there's a smell to it, or just a bad vibe, that's keeping everyone away. Except us."

She looked at him, this peculiar, single-minded man hitching up his pants and with a piece of metal wire—part of a coat hanger?—poking out from one corner of his mouth the way a farmer might chew on a stalk of wheat. He wasn't looking at her, but up at the tower, appraising it, and at the work being done. There was something akin to pride in his eyes.

"It just kept coming together. We haven't stopped. We never slept. I went all through the night. I never went home." She watched something darken in his face as he said this last part, but then he quickly regained composure. He flicked sweat from his bee-stung neck and said, "Look at 'em working up there. Like bugs."

"What exactly are we doing here?" she asked him.

Stinger looked at her. His eyes were yellow and moist, his skin sunburned and bumpy. There was a spot along his neck where he'd scratched those swollen, red welts to bloody streaks. (Sometimes, just looking at him made her itchy, and a part of her wondered if that wasn't all just in her head or if they were beginning to share more than just telepathy and obsession.) She watched as his eyes slipped lower down her body, and it took her a moment to realize that she had one of her hands pressed gently against the fabric of her Misfits T-shirt. Against her belly.

"Don't tell me you're worried this whole thing will have . . ." He paused, seeming to consider the words. "Lasting consequences."

*He knows I'm pregnant. He can sense it. Georgette was the only person I told, and I doubt she would have said something to Stinger. We're all in the same head together, all sharing the same mind.*

For some reason, this made her think of Eric again.

She looked back at the Tower, and at all those straightened wire hangers linked together, spreading out from the colander, and hooked into the surrounding chain-link fence like so many spokes in a wheel. "I feel it," she said. "I feel the importance of it all. I feel . . . the *need* for it . . ." She turned back to him. "I just don't know why. What is this thing? What are we building? Why are we doing any of this?"

Again, Stinger seemed to consider this. He craned his head back on his neck to stare up at the water tank again. The thrust of his Adam's apple was severe.

"Does the honeybee know why it's driven to pollinate?" he responded. "Does it understand why it secretes wax from its glands in order to construct a hive?" He shrugged. "It's just instinct. The obsession to *do*."

"We aren't bees."

"Oh, yeah?" Stinger cocked one eyebrow. Then his expression softened. "Listen, kid, I could tell you, but I think maybe I'll show you instead."

"Show me how?"

"Later. I need to work a few things out first."

Feeling like she'd just been unceremoniously dismissed, Sarah glanced around the clearing. "Where's Georgette?"

"Who? Oh, yeah—the chick who brought the bowl with all the holes in it."

"It's a colander," Sarah corrected.

"Whatever," said Stinger. He pointed to a group of people who were kneeling on the ground a few yards away, examining something. "Last I saw her, she was over there." He turned and looked at her again with those leaky yellow eyes. "What'd you bring in your bag? More hangers, I hope."

"Yes. And there's a whole lot more in my car back through the woods. I could use some help carrying them."

"Perfect," Stinger said, his yolk-runny eyes still on her. His face was in no better shape, and every bit the lumpy, bee-stung horror as it had been the day she'd first glimpsed him—and heard his thoughts—at Hollywood BBQ. "We could use as many hangers as you got. I'll get some guys to give you a hand." He surveyed the crowd of workers—and that was how Sarah thought of them, as *workers*, as if they were, in fact, bees—and then he yelled, "Nick! Barrett! Get over here, will you?"

Two men who were involved in decapitating the head of a shovel from its body both turned and looked at Stinger in unison. Then they looked at each other—almost comically so, Sarah noted—before dropping the shovel to the ground with a muted thud. They double-timed it over to Stinger, who jerked a thumb at Sarah and said, "Help her get some shit from her car."

"Sure," said one of the men. He looked in his thirties and had curly brown hair down to his shoulders. He was a stranger to Sarah, one of the people who must have shown up last night after she'd gone home.

"My name's not Nick," said the other guy, who looked a bit younger than his companion but whose face was a battlefield of acne scars so that it was tough to accurately estimate his age. Sarah didn't recognize him, either.

"Whatever, Not-Nick," Stinger said, not interested. "Just get on it."

The two men followed Sarah back through the woods, and although they weren't specifically thought-speaking to her, she managed to catch some of it—

*(SHE'S HOT YOU THINK SHE'S HERE ALONE?)*

*(I DIDN'T SEE HER COME WITH ANYONE)*

*(DO YOU THINK WE COULD)*

—in the way you'd catch a butterfly in a net.

She hugged herself as if suddenly cold. By the time they reached the road—

*(MAYBE SHE WOULD LIKE IT)*

*(MAYBE SHE WOULD)*

*(MAYBE SHE WOULD LIKE US BOTH)*

—she felt a soupy disquiet sloshing around inside her belly. Digging her car keys from her pocket, she said, "I *wouldn't* like it." Then, on the heels of that, added, "You boys think too loudly. Either you're both new at this, or you're both just stupid."

Again, the two guys exchanged a half-comical look, their faces turning instantly crimson. Wanting to quickly dispel the discomfort, Sarah asked the guy whose name was not Nick what item he had contributed.

"The draw band connector that goes around ductwork," he said. "I do HVAC so I knew what it was right away."

"Where did you find it?"

"Hanging from a tree limb in my backyard," he said. "Morning after the storm. Must've blown out the back of my truck."

"Do you know what we're building back there with all this stuff?" she asked.

Not-Nick nodded. His expression was resolute. "Sure do," he said, but offered up no more.

"You do?" she asked him, somewhat hopeful. "What is it?"

"Something really fucking important," he said.

A gleaming black SUV had just pulled up behind Sarah's car as she and the two men approached. She eyed it suspiciously, fearing that the person inside might try to overpower the three of them and abscond with her coat hangers. One of the guys behind her whistled and said, "Nice fucking ride."

An older, broad-chested man with a shock of white hair climbed out of the SUV and stood staring at them in bewilderment. As Sarah watched him, the man's mouth opened and closed several times, like a fish gulping for air on the deck of a boat. She saw that he held something in his hand, but it wasn't until Not-Nick's thought zinged through her head—

*(GUN HE'S GOT A GUN)*

—that she realized what it was.

"What do you want, fella?" Not-Nick said.

The old man's lower lip quivered. The hand holding the gun shook. "I want . . . I'm here to . . ." His eyes jittered between them all but then he looked beyond them and at the water tank with its cryptic symbols and declamatory words in dark paint rising above the tree line. His lips moved silently as he read one of the words painted across the tank, and she didn't need to hear him or even think his thoughts to know what he was saying: *Endgame.*

"I have a door," he said.

"A *door*?" said Barrett, as if he'd misheard.

The old man appeared to reconsider this. "I guess it *used* to be a door," he said, "but now I think it's a chair. Door becomes chair." He looked back up at the water tank and said, "Take it there."

"You got a gun, too, old man," said Not-Nick. "What's the deal with that?"

Once more, Sarah caught the two men's thoughts blaze through her brain, this time in a twisted knot so that they arrived simultaneously, and it was difficult to discern one from the other, although they both came to the same thing:

*(CAN JUMP HIM AND OVERPOWER) (DISTRACT HIM AND GO FOR IT)*

She could tell that the old man heard them, too, in his head. It was in the way his eyes narrowed and volleyed between the two men who were not-so-bravely standing behind Sarah. The old man glanced down at the gun in his hand, as if only just now realizing he was holding it. He said, "I just . . . I didn't know . . . who or what I'd find out here. I need to . . . it's very important that I . . ."

*(PROTECT THE DOOR)*

She'd heard that: loud and fucking clear.

"Jesus, fella," said Not-Nick, wincing while poking a finger in one ear.

The old man placed the gun on the driver's seat of his SUV, then lifted both arms at the elbows in a sign of surrender, or at least to show he meant no harm. His hands trembled, and Sarah could see that one of them—his left—was bandaged in gauze.

"It's in the back," he said. "It's heavy. I got it in by myself, but I can't carry it anymore. It's too much."

"Carry it where?" Barrett asked.

"To the Tower," Sarah answered for the old man. Barrett and Not-Nick, she decided, weren't the two brightest bulbs. *Or the cunningest bees.*

The old man's eyes lit up. "Yes," he said, his arms slowly coming down. He began to nod with the simplicity of someone being told the answer to a basic question. "Yes, that's right. The Tower. Door becomes chair. Take it there."

"Shit," Barrett said, moving around Sarah and advancing toward the old man. "We can do it. Stinger should probably have a look at it."

"And a look at *you*," added Not-Nick, still apparently jumpy from the gun.

The old man's silver eyebrows drew together. "Who's Stinger?"

"The Hivemaster," said Barrett. "He's puttin' this whole goddamn thing together."

"But what *is* it?" asked the old man.

Sarah watched as Barrett and Not-Nick exchanged another hapless glance. Yes, she now felt a familiar buzzing in her back teeth, but also another queasy pulse in her belly. She looked down to find her hands pressed there, as if to quell the queasiness . . . or as if to protect whatever was inside her. Just as she had when Stinger had been staring at her, and no doubt sensing the life that was growing inside her.

"Gonna take this gun, guy," Barrett said, plucking the gun off the driver's seat and tucking it into the rear waistband of his jeans.

Not-Nick went around to the rear of the SUV and opened the hatchback. As if it hadn't already been explained to him, he uttered, clearly confused, "It *is* a door. A *wooden* door."

"Just bring it," Sarah told him.

The old man joined Not-Nick at the rear of the vehicle just as Barrett swaggered over, too, the butt of the gun protruding above his waistband. "Listen," said the old man. "You boys must be careful with it. It's a door, and there are things on the other side of it, just like any door. An opening where you can fall in, but also an opening where things might come out."

Sarah didn't like hearing that. Even if the old man was crazy, something about that comment—about things falling in, things coming out—bothered her more than it likely should have.

She joined the men at the rear of the vehicle and peered at the thing inside.

Yes, an old wooden door, no different than the door on the front of her own home. Only this one had what looked like a camping chair nailed to it.

"Gimme a hand," Barrett said to Not-Nick as he leaned into the rear of the vehicle. He gripped the door and proceeded to drag it out.

The old man said something that, to Sarah, sounded like, "Careful, now, and mind the shadow."

Sarah walked back to her car, leaving the heavy lifting to Barrett and Not-Nick. Her stomach still felt funny, and that strange buzzing sensation was pulsing through her molars again.

*I could tell you*, Stinger had said, *but I think maybe I'll show you instead.*

Show her?

Show her *what*?

There was a muted thump as Not-Nick dropped his end of the

door to the ground. It didn't fall over completely—Barrett still had a good grip on his end—but a bottom corner of the thing wedged in the dirt, causing the old man to gasp as if he'd just witnessed some terrible accident. In that moment—

## 2

—Stinger, still gazing up at the work being done at the top of the Tower, a satisfied little grin slowly insinuating itself across the lower half of his bee-stung face, felt his phone vibrate in his pocket. He plucked it out and saw that it was one of several missed phone calls and text messages from Doug Winslow. If anyone in Mariner's Cove had noticed they'd closed the park down and had defaced the Tower, it would be that son of a bitch Doug Winslow, president of the Mariner's Cove Community Association.

"Stinger."

Stinger turned and saw Jack Gordon standing there. Like the people assembling items at the top of the Tower, Jack wore one of the reflective construction vests Stinger had found in the maintenance shed, only for a different purpose: Jack Gordon and a handful of others had been stationed around the perimeter of Gladstone Park to ensure that no wayward travelers decided to ignore the closed gate and the PARK TEMPORARILY CLOSED sign at the entrance to the park. For the most part, no one had been coming around—something was keeping people who weren't part of the Hive away, Stinger knew—but there had also been that damn fool who Jack Gordon had intercepted earlier that afternoon. Jack was quick on his feet—"Gas leak," he'd told the fool—and that seemed to do the trick. As the fool wandered back toward the road, Jack had transmitted a single missive directly into Stinger's head—

*(CURIOUS LOOKY-LOO JUST POPPED AROUND BUT I'VE SENT HIM ON HIS WAY NO WORRIES IT'S TAKEN CARE OF STINGER)*

—yet Stinger, who hadn't been too far from the cusp of the woods, had wandered out to stand beside Jack and catch a look at the fellow for himself. Jack Gordon wasn't a dummy and he wasn't someone who'd back down from a physical confrontation, but he didn't know all the things that Stinger did, so Stinger had wanted to see who this fellow was for himself. Just some guy in ratty jeans and a rattier T-shirt it turned out, although the sight of him as he wandered back across the street set Stinger's back teeth abuzz.

"What is it?" Stinger asked now, slipping his cell phone with all those unanswered messages from that prick Doug Winslow back into his pocket. "Another dummy wandering through the park?"

"No. But I think you should come have a look at this."

"What?"

"Something we found."

"Tell me."

Jack looked abruptly uncomfortable. "I wouldn't even know how to begin to tell it. Let me show you."

"Fine. Lead the way."

Stinger followed Jack around to the rear of the Tower, where the chain-link fencing brushed up against the tree line. There was an older woman in a housedress standing here among the trees, her face stricken, her painted-on eyebrows knitted together. Stinger couldn't remember her name, but the Hive Mind filled him in: Pamela Guerin. Her item had been the caster from an old shopping cart. Pamela, sensing the union of their minds, drew back from him a step. Her eyebrows knitted together further.

"Okay, I'm here," Stinger said. "What is it you wanna show me?"

"This." Jack pointed at the line of trees. When Stinger looked in that direction, Jack said, "No, Stinger, right here. *Here.*" He pointed again to . . .

. . . well, to nothing.

Stinger frowned. "What is this, some kind of—"

A honeybee suddenly appeared at the tip of Jack Gordon's finger. Jack retracted his finger just as the bee cut a zigzag pattern through the air. Stinger followed it with his eyes, trailing it until it came to rest on the chain-link fence.

"A bee," Stinger said, confused.

"So many bees," Pamela Guerin said. "I've been watching them come out for the past minute or so. And they're not just regular bees. Look closely at them, Mr. Stinger. Do you see? They're *clear.*"

Stinger brought his face close to the bee crawling on the chain-link fence. It *was* clear. Perfectly translucent. Damn thing looked like it was made from blown glass. "Well, shit, look at that," he marveled. Then he turned back to Pamela Guerin. "Come out of where?"

"Right there," she said, bringing up a finger to the place where Jack had been pointing just a moment ago.

Jack said, "It's like some rip. They just keep coming through."

As Stinger stared at the tip of Pamela's finger, another one of those translucent bees appeared, followed by another. Then another. They seemed to materialize out of thin air then drift off like ash on the breeze. A magic trick.

"That's not a rip," Stinger said. He reached out and lowered Pamela's hand just as another bee appeared and wove a jagged path through the air.

"What is it?" both Jack and Pamela asked at the same time.

"A crack."

Jack frowned. "A crack in *what*? Thin air?"

"A crack between worlds." Stinger brought up his own hand and extended his index finger to the place Pamela had just been pointing to—about four feet off the ground, right there in midair. Nothing visually different about that little sliver of air, except that—

Stinger slipped his fingers into the crack.

His hand vanished to around mid-palm. It looked like an optical illusion, something a magician might perform with mirrors. But there were no mirrors, and Stinger was no magician.

"Oh!" Pamela cried.

He could feel a cool, anesthetizing sensation begin at his fingertips, tingle along his hand, and slowly begin to travel up the stalk of his arm toward the shoulder.

"Jesus," Jack said. "You sure that's safe?"

"Beats me," said Stinger. He withdrew his hand and the three of them leaned in to examine it. Nothing out of the ordinary.

"Did it hurt?" Pamela asked.

"No. Just numb. Cold, almost, like dry ice."

"What'd you mean when you said it's a crack between worlds?" Jack asked again.

Stinger took a step back. He glanced up at the tower. The sky beyond the tank was either beginning to churn toward dusk or there was a storm brewing. The visual struck him as something from some barely remembered dream, and it made him both uncomfortable and excited at the same time. Distantly, he felt the phone in his pocket vibrate again.

"There are cracks starting to form everywhere," Stinger explained. "That's because we're almost done building this thing. The more we build, the more cracks form between our world and the other."

"What other?" asked Jack.

Stinger considered this, just as he'd considered how to respond to Sarah Miller when she'd asked *why* they were doing all this. He thought about that day when his mind, his consciousness, had been sucked into the beehive in the back lot, and how the voice of the Dragon had spoken to him through the buzzing of the bees' wings, explaining the need for Stinger to build this Hive, to protect it, and how the strength of the Dragon's voice had caused the world to shake and cracks to form in various places throughout Mariner's Cove. The only thing the Dragon hadn't told him was what purpose the new Hive served. But he couldn't say that now, could he? These people would think he was crazy.

Stinger said, "It's hard to explain . . ."

Jack shook his head. "None of this makes any fucking sense."

"It will," Stinger promised him, placing a hand—the hand that had passed through the crack—on Jack's shoulder. "It'll make sense to everyone very shortly, I promise. I'll show you everything I know, starting tonight. But I'm going to need your help, Jack."

"What about me?" Pamela asked. "Will you need my help, too?"

Stinger gave her a quick once over. "No."

Pamela opened her mouth to respond, but a commotion back toward the clearing silenced her.

Stinger hustled back there, with Jack Gordon close at his heels, in time to see Nick (or whatever his name was) and Barrett coming back through the woods carrying what looked like a large plank of wood between them. Following close behind them was a tall, pale-skinned man who looked to be in his late sixties or early seventies, although Stinger had never been very good at guessing someone's age. Sarah Miller brought up the rear, lugging another trash bag full of coat hangers over one shoulder, her face blistery with sweat.

Stinger ambled over to them. His heart had picked up speed at the sight of whatever it was Barrett and Not-Nick were carrying.

It was a door with a camping chair nailed to it.

And the sight of it caused a trill of excitement to barrel through Stinger's body.

Stinger placed a hand on Barrett's shoulder, causing the man to stop walking. Barrett and Not-Nick carried the door horizontally between them, breathing heavily with exertion. As they stood there, Stinger ran the palm of one hand across the door's surface, along the aluminum legs of the chair affixed to the door. Tested the tautness of the chair's canvas seat with a set of stiff fingers. Then he swung his gaze toward the old man. "Is this your item?"

The old man appeared to be sweating profusely and there was color in the cheeks of his otherwise pallid face. To Stinger, he looked more than just a bit out of sorts, like someone hastily roused from a hypnotic trance. When the old man didn't answer, Stinger went over to him and thrust out his hand. "Hey, fella. I'm Stinger."

The old man's hand inched up toward Stinger's hesitantly. Stinger snatched it and squeezed, pumping it once before letting it go. He noticed that the man's left hand was wrapped in a gauze bandage.

"My name is Michael Danver," said the old fellow. "I'm a retired heart surgeon. I . . . I'm not sure what I'm doing here . . ."

*(HE HAD A GUN ON HIM STINGER)*

This thought, courtesy of Barrett, was likely meant for Stinger's mind alone, but everyone within the vicinity turned and looked at Barrett in unison, including the old man.

"I need to protect the door," Danver said. "It's very important."

"Yes, it is," Stinger agreed.

The old man's eyes ticked in the direction of the door, which was still held suspended between the two men. "It's more than just a door, you know," Danver said quietly.

"Yeah," Stinger said, bobbing his head in agreement. "I bet you're right about that, too, old man."

"It . . . it does things . . ."

"That's what I'm hoping."

"Wait. Watch. Let me show you."

Danver grunted as he bent at the knees and scooped up a stone roughly the size of a golf ball. Curious, Stinger watched as Danver rolled the stone from his good hand to his bandaged one, as if trying to guess its weight. Then he tossed the stone directly beneath the door, where it bounced on the grass.

"Was something supposed to happen?" Stinger asked.

Instead of answering, the old man just rubbed a hand along the right side of his face. His teeth, Stinger surmised, were probably hurting him, because Stinger could feel his own teeth hurting now, too. In fact, they *all* could: the Hive Mind told him so, and projected it throughout each of them as a singular, shared pulse of pain.

Stinger patted the canvas seat of the camping chair that was screwed into the wood of the door. "Old man, it seems you've brought us not one but two of the three remaining items. Did you put them together like this?"

The old man's moist, yellowed eyes slid down toward the camping chair that was attached to the door. Stinger watched as his lower lip quivered. "I did," he said, his voice low.

"Strange. Everyone else only brought one item."

"Are you kidding?" Sarah Miller said. She'd set her bag of hangers on the ground and was standing just behind the old man. "I brought you like a thousand hangers, man."

"Still one *item*," Stinger told her. He looked back at Danver. "We've all been waiting on you, you know? Yours might be the most important piece. You're like a goddamn celebrity around here, old man."

"Am I?" Danver said. Like Stinger, he reached out and caressed the door. "What's the last one?"

"Last one what?" Stinger asked.

"You said these were two of the three remaining pieces. What's the last piece?"

"You know," Stinger began—

—but the Hive's collective voice crashed through the wall of his own thoughts—

*(WHAT'S THE LAST WHAT'S THE LAST WHAT'S THE LAST WHAT'S THE LAST WHAT'S THE LAST WHAT'S THE LAST WHAT'S THE LAST WHAT'S THE LAST WHAT'S THE LAST WHAT'S THE LAST WHAT'S THE LAST WHAT'S THE LAST WHAT'S THE LAST WHAT'S THE LAST WHAT'S THE LAST WHAT'S THE LAST WHAT'S THE LAST WHAT'S THE LAST WHAT'S THE LAST WHAT'S THE LAST WHAT'S THE LAST WHAT'S THE LAST WHAT'S THE LAST WHAT'S THE LAST WHAT'S THE LAST WHAT'S THE LAST WHAT'S THE LAST WHAT'S THE LAST?)*

—rendering him temporarily speechless.

They all wanted desperately to know.

"Hey," said Barrett, his face turning red. "This fucking door's heavy."

Stinger snapped back down to reality. "Put it at Hive Center."

Barrett and Not-Nick hauled the door across the clearing and carried it through an opening in the chain-link fence, where the chain-link flaps had been cinched open by a combination of padlocks and chains.

"Hive Center?" Danver said. He was staring at the structure.

Stinger raised an inviting hand in the direction of the Tower. "Go on, old fella. Have yourself a look. You're part of this, too."

The old man's wet, jaundiced eyes swiveled from Stinger to the base of the Tower. That bandaged left hand twitched at his side. For a moment, it looked like the old guy wouldn't move, but then Danver—

# 3

—crossed the clearing in his aching, sandaled feet, his back sore, the molars in his lower jaw feeling like they were being pulverized in a vise. There was a high-pitched buzzing in his skull. His mind was awhirl with mournful thoughts of Miranda, her body shrouded in sheets back in their bedroom in the house on Bay Road, and of the thing that had once been Clementine, only with the poor thing's organs on the reverse side of its body, flesh like raw chicken.

He passed through the opening in the chain-link fence that surrounded the base of the water tower, then immediately ducked so that he wouldn't collide with the network of thin metal rods that were crisscrossing directly above his head. There were countless metallic items attached to the chain-link fence so that the fence itself looked as if it was decorated for some unusual holiday. Danver surveyed each item, running the fingertips of his bandaged left hand across a dangling keychain, the dented red flag from a mailbox, a greasy bicycle chain that pulled taut from one of the diamond-shaped links in the fence, what looked like an old shopping cart caster slotted into it.

On the other side of the fence, Mia Bridgeport stood staring at him. Her head was slightly cocked at an angle, and she wore a vacuous expression on her face. If she was surprised to find him here, there was no sign of it. Nor was Danver surprised to see her, either. He recalled *thinking* they had engaged in some sort of conversation as he lowered his garage door, but only now realized that he'd been hearing her speak to him inside his head—asking him if he had *seen the instructions.*

"Watch your head," Stinger said, coming up beside him. Together, they stood beneath a crisscross of metal wires that extended from what looked like a spaghetti strainer attached to a basketball hoop which, in turn, was bolted to the center post of the water tower. "It's all honeycombed in here."

"It's like the circulatory system," Danver said.

"Huh?"

"Inside the body. Blood pumping. Lifeblood." Then, more to himself than to Stinger, he mused, "But where's the heart . . . ?"

"Listen, I know at first glance it all looks random and haphazard," Stinger said, coming up beside him. His tone was almost apologetic. "But really, everything has its place, and every place has required a particular item. Some people brought many of the same items, like Sarah and her hangers, while others just brought one. Yet every piece is just as valuable as the next . . . with one exception, of course."

"My door," Danver said.

"That's right. Your—"

"Door—"

*(BECOMES CHAIR)*

—they finished together.

Danver turned his head and looked at Stinger. "Chair for what?"

"I think," Stinger said, "that things will become a little bit clearer for everyone starting tonight. I've got an idea. A plan. It'll be the final thing I need to do before the endgame."

"Endgame," Danver repeated, and he could feel the chill that rippled through his body. For a moment, he wondered if it had been Stinger who'd just said that or Danver's dead father, standing beside him, whispering once more into his ear.

*Endgame . . .*

Danver looked past Stinger and watched as the two men he had met out by the road entered Hive Center and propped his door-becomes-chair against the center post of the tower's base. Then they looked down at the palms of their hands, as if the door had left some permanent mark there.

"You put all this together from the instructions?" Danver asked.

"Instructions?"

Danver opened his mouth to explain, but instead, wound up transmitting a visual of the chalk and spray-painted symbols directly into Stinger's head.

"Oh," Stinger said, eyes suddenly wide. "The symbols. Yeah. That's right."

"Where does my door go?"

"In the middle there somewhere. I'm not exactly sure about that. I'll have to ask Alex. He's the brains behind piecing this machine together."

"That's what this is? A machine?"

"That's as good a guess as any."

"A machine to do what?"

The man who called himself Stinger chewed for a moment on his lower lip. "That's one thing I still don't know. But like I said, I think it'll start making more sense tonight. Okay?"

Danver nodded. "Okay." Then he reached out and gripped Stinger by the wrist. His voice cracking and his vision beginning to blur, he heard the words rush out of him, a confession, before he even knew what he was doing: "My wife is dead. It's my fault. Oh my God, it's my fault."

The smeary visage of Stinger nodded its head.

"It's breaking my heart," Danver said, voice shaking.

Again: a smudgy nod of the head.

"There were bound to be prices to pay," Stinger said, then yanked his wrist free from Danver's grasp.

Just then, a chorus of shrieks rose up. Stinger—

## 4

—whirled around just as a group of people on the other side of the fence stared up at the tank high above their heads. Ducking beneath the wires, Stinger raced for the opening in the fence and joined them on the other side. When he looked up, he saw a man on the walkway that wrapped around the tank leaning over the railing, holding onto Sheila Donaldson's TV antenna with one hand. The rope he'd been using to haul it up had snapped and he was struggling to hold onto it, leaning way too far over the railing. As Stinger watched, another man on the walkway rushed over to lend a hand . . . but he was too late: the antenna slipped from the man's grasp and plummeted to the ground.

The crowd around Stinger dispersed, a number of people crying out and shielding their faces with their arms. Only Stinger remained standing there, watching the antenna barrel toward him, a thing that looked strangely like a ribcage made of thin metal posts. He thought he could hear a faint whistling as it fell faster and faster toward him. When it finally struck the ground and broke apart, it did so a mere three feet from where Stinger stood. A cloud of white dust rose up and swirled about him in the air.

"Well, fuck," Stinger muttered. Then he looked back up at the men on the walkway who, in turn, stared down at him. They were too high up for Stinger to discern the expressions on their faces, but he didn't need to because he could hear their collective thoughts—

*(FUCK SHIT FUCK)*

*(GODDAMN IT'S BROKEN WE FUCKING BROKE IT FUCK)*

—buzzing in his own brain.

Sheila Donaldson rushed over and dropped weightily to her knees beside the busted antenna. She seemed afraid to touch it, as if to do so might injure it further, and instead began to wail. Pamela Guerin appeared beside her, face pale and stricken. After a moment, Sheila gathered up one of the antenna's busted ribs and cradled it against her breast while she sobbed.

"We'll get it fixed," Stinger assured her.

Someone had the foresight to bring a cooler of water and some paper cups down to the site, and Stinger ambled over to it now. The cooler sat on the tree stump where Alex Braswell had once laid out all the paper cutouts of the blueprint. Alex was there right now; he had his arms folded while he leaned against the wooden split-rail fence, his gaze unfocused. He looked like he was daydreaming.

"Did you see that old guy come in with Barrett and that other fella?" Stinger asked him after he'd chugged a cup of cool water.

Alex blinked then looked around, as if he'd heard Stinger's voice but didn't know where it had come from. When he finally turned and stared at Stinger, there was a look of disassociation in his eyes. "What'd you say?" he asked.

"The old guy," repeated Stinger, nodding toward where Danver still stood at Hive Center. "Did you see him come in?"

"Old guy?"

"The fuck's wrong with you?" Stinger pointed to where Barrett and Not-Nick had leaned Danver's door against the center post of the tower. "You see it? The fucking door?"

Clarity filtered into Alex's eyes. "Is that . . . ?"

"It's two of the three final pieces. Door becomes chair. Just like your little paper cutouts."

"Door becomes chair," Alex repeated.

"You're the guy putting these pieces together. Where does it go?"

Alex dug the paper cutouts from the breast pocket of his shirt, riffling through them. He began to place them on the tree stump beside the water cooler—symbols for the colander, the basketball hoop, the straightened coat hangers, the door, the chair. Then he glanced back up and studied the base of the tower. "We fucked up."

"Don't tell me that."

"It's not bad, but—"

"How?"

"We screwed the basketball hoop with the colander to the center post of the Tower, onto that piece of sheet metal. They should be screwed onto the *door* and then the *door* should be bolted to the center post."

"You sure?"

Alex was looking at the cutouts he'd spread out on the tree stump.

As Stinger watched, Alex stacked them, layered, one atop the next. A three-dimensional puzzle. "Yeah," he said, nodding in confirmation. "I'm sure."

Stinger nodded, satisfied, then looked back at Barrett and Not-Nick, who were still standing beside the door within the deepening shadow of the water tower. He transmitted to them a mental image of what Alex had just suggested, and across the clearing, both Barrett and Not-Nick glanced up and met Stinger's gaze. Apparently, the message was received: they picked up the door and carried it around to where the basketball hoop hung from the center post. Barrett proceeded to unbolt the hoop while Not-Nick braced Danver's door against the post. The old man watched them as they worked.

"That leaves one symbol left," Alex said. He plucked one particular cutout from the stack and held it up so Stinger could see it, even though he already knew what it was: the hasty sketch of a person, as simplistic and lacking in detail as the emblem on the door of a public restroom. The only difference was that Alex had drawn a star on the figure's forehead.

"I mean, it's a person," Alex told him. "Not sure how that fits in with what we've got going on here. Not sure what the star's supposed to mean, either."

Unlike Alex, Stinger thought he had a pretty good fucking idea what the stick figure meant, an assumption that only increased toward certainty when he looked back at Hive Center and saw that Michael Danver's door-turned-chair was now upright against the central post of the tower with the upside-down colander in the basketball hoop affixed to its top.

*Door becomes chair*, he thought, and an instant later he heard the mental call-and-answer from the colony:

*(DOOR BECOMES CHAIR) (DOOR BECOMES CHAIR) (DOOR BECOMES CHAIR) (DOOR BECOMES CHAIR) (DOOR BECOMES CHAIR (DOOR BECOMES CHAIR) (DOOR BECOMES CHAIR) (DOOR BECOMES CHAIR) (DOOR BECOMES CHAIR)*

*(DOOR BECOMES CHAIR)* *(DOOR BECOMES CHAIR)*
*(DOOR BECOMES CHAIR)* *(DOOR BECOMES CHAIR)*
*(DOOR BECOMES CHAIR)*
*(DOOR BECOMES CHAIR)*

"What's that look like to you?" Stinger asked, nodding at the door, although he already knew the answer for himself.

Alex Braswell—

# 5

—looked up at the door that was now fixed at the center post and wasted no time in responding: "An electric chair."

Stinger nodded. "Which means the last remaining item is one of us. That's what your little symbol of a person means. One of us has to sit in that electric chair."

"And do what?"

"I have no fucking idea."

Alex heard a buzzing, thought it might be his teeth again, but then Stinger fished his cell phone from his pocket. He muttered something under his breath, then, to Alex, said, "I'm gonna run off with some people to take care of something later tonight. Just for a short while. But I'd like to put you in charge around here while I'm gone."

Alex thought about his kids, wondering just how long they'd been at his mother's house, and that he and Georgette should probably go pick them up. He suddenly wanted to do that very much. But when he opened his mouth, he heard himself say, "Sure."

"Good man," Stinger said, then ambled away while scrolling through his phone.

Less than a minute later, Georgette appeared by his side. In the heat of the afternoon, she had stripped down to a ribbed gray tank top and khaki shorts, though she wore tube socks and hiking boots on her feet—a near comical incongruity. Her hair was a frizzy mess from the humidity and her skin was slick with sweat. Her eyes, though, were bright and alive. She looked years younger.

"It's incredible, isn't it?" she said, her temples shimmering with jewels of sweat. "I don't even know how we're doing it, but we *are*, Alex. We *are*."

Alex smiled at her as she raked her fingernails gently down the center of his back, but he knew she could see through the façade.

"What is it?" she asked, her own smile slipping from her lips.

Not wanting to ruin the moment for her, he shook his head. "It's nothing."

"Don't lie. What is it? Tell me."

He looked at his wife. "Hey, shouldn't we call the girls?"

"I spoke to them earlier today."

"You did?"

"Alex, they're fine." She took his hand in hers. Squeezed. "Tell me. What is it?"

Once her stare became something he could no longer ignore, he said, "Something's missing."

"Missing from what?"

"This, I guess. All of it." He took the last remaining cutout from the breast pocket of his shirt. Stick figure with a star on its head. Could Stinger be right about what that meant? "Ever wonder who drew all these things, anyway? All those chalk drawings all over the neighborhood? The spray paint? How this whole crazy thing got started?"

"Alex, it got started with *you*."

No, that wasn't exactly true, he knew. Maybe he'd been the first to arrive at the water tower, but everyone else had been a part of it since then, too, even if he hadn't known it yet. Even Georgette with her spaghetti strainer that now sat upside down in that basketball hoop, screwed to a wooden door, with a camping chair beneath it.

*Yes. It looks just like an electric chair.*

Georgette turned her head and followed his gaze toward the Tower, and Alex could sense the heightened perception of her mind in the way she looked at the structure. People clung to the fencing, the Tower's spidery legs, and high above the treetops there were people scuttling along the tank's walkway like bugs. At Hive Center, the old man still stood staring at the door, his pale, wrinkled face an expressionless mask.

Georgette said, "What do you think it is? This thing that you feel is missing."

He shook his head. "I really don't know."

"You designed it. Don't you have an idea?"

"I didn't design it. Someone else did. Whoever drew these symbols in the first place, probably. I just copied down the diagrams and put them together." He added, "We *all* put them together."

"Stinger calls it the Hive. Sheila Donaldson and Jack Gordon think it's more like a temple, a place of worship."

"To worship what?"

She looked at him, and he thought he could see the faintest, fleeting flash of fear in her eyes. For the first time, Alex wondered why none of them were more frightened—why *he* wasn't more frightened. Why he wasn't driving the beltway to pick up his kids and take them home. Why all of this was so fucking important and unshakable. His grip on this whole obsession felt like it was slipping—Stinger had sensed it, too, Alex knew—and he wasn't sure if that was a good thing or not.

"I haven't a clue," she said, shaking her head. "And I can't tell if that excites or frightens me."

*That's how I feel, too,* he thought, and when she looked at him, he knew she'd heard him. It was in that moment that Sarah Miller came over. She looked distraught as she glanced at Alex, then went up to Georgette and said—

## 6

—"Hey, have you seen Eric today?"

Georgette shook her head. "No, I haven't."

Sarah frowned. "I've been trying to reach him on his phone all morning. No answer. I'm starting to get worried."

"I think if something happened, we'd feel it," Georgette said.

For some reason, that didn't make Sarah feel any better. She slipped away, taking her cell phone from the rear pocket of her jeans. There was a path that wound through the woods, and she crossed over to it now while her phone dialed Eric's number. She'd kissed him the night before, after he'd walked her to her porch. Had that scared him off? Had she been too forward? Could he sense she was pregnant, in the same way Stinger had?

Eric's phone went straight to voicemail. Again. Nor had he responded to any of the text messages she'd sent him.

She knew he didn't like it, but she *did* have one last option to contact him, although she was uncertain if she could do it without being close to him, and without knowing where he was. She'd never tried it that way before. Nonetheless, she closed her eyes and transmitted the thought directly to him: *Eric, where—*

## 7

*—ARE YOU ARE YOU OKAY?)*

It struck him as an intrusion, an unexpected assault that caused him to actively shudder.

Eric was where he'd been all morning: secluded within a patch of trees across the street from the McBride house on Cloister Road. He'd been watching the house all morning, having arrived (on foot; there'd been no reason to drive the truck) before sunrise this morning. He'd observed the McBrides' neighbor—

*(BERTRAND ZACHS)*

—creep from his front door just as the sun came up, dressed in nothing but a bathrobe, and plonk himself in a beach chair at the edge of his property. He, too, was watching the McBride house, and had been for some time; Eric understood this the moment their minds intertwined and Zachs turned his head in Eric's direction, despite the fact that Eric was very much concealed within that dense wedge of trees. Nonetheless, he could tell the old fellow was looking directly at him even though he wore dark sunglasses.

The same with the middle-aged neighbor directly across the street from the McBrides' house—

*(THOMAS OREM)*

—as well as the guy parked in the red van at the end of the block—

*(LAWRENCE KOTARA)*

—both of whom had also entwined their minds with Eric's, so that their thoughts bled together as if they were all sharing one brain.

From his hiding place among the trees, Eric had watched the McBride woman and her son drive off earlier that morning. Then, sometime later, a man had come out of the house. Eric guessed he was the owner of the conversion van that sat parked in the street, an ugly thing with wolves airbrushed on the side. He'd watched as this man power-washed Ellen McBride's driveway, then had a quick conversation with Thomas Orem, who'd come out of his own house to investigate. Orem transmitted the man's identity to the rest of them—

*(BRIAN THE BROTHER)*

—and then Eric watched as Brian the brother walked up the block and vanished out of sight, only to return sometime later stumbling like a drunk.

Eric sat back in the soft dirt now, the skeletal fingers of tree branches poking and prodding against the small of his back. He could feel Sarah's thought-voice attempting to infiltrate his mind again, so he quickly constructed a mental wall to keep her out. He didn't want her gaining access to his thoughts anymore. He was ashamed of them, confused by them.

Because he had finally located his special item.

It was THE BOY

He wanted to go to THE BOY or to have THE BOY come to him. He didn't know why; only that his obsession with THE BOY was no different than Sarah's obsession with those metal coat hangers, or Georgette Braswell's obsession with that spaghetti strainer. Yet he would be damned if he let Sarah Miller into his head to share those thoughts.

He observed Zachs turn his head and glance again in Eric's direction from across the street, probably because he'd caught a whisper of Sarah's message in his own head. Probably he could sense Eric building a wall against her, too. Eric was unsure how to fine-tune the destinations of these mental transmissions, or if such a thing was even possible. Was it like calling someone on their own personal line, or was it more like shouting to a crowd through a megaphone? Eric didn't know.

What he *did* know was that these men shared his obsession. THE BOY was their item collectively. And if they were ashamed by this, they did not build a wall to keep Eric out, but instead allowed their collective minds to entwine more tightly, like a cluster of tapeworms, until they became one solitary thinking brain.

*(THEY'RE COMING BACK)*

This from Kotara, who'd been keeping an eye on things from the red van at the end of the block.

Sure enough, a moment later, Eric watched as Ellen McBride's car pulled into the driveway of the house on Cloister Road. He watched as she jumped out quickly, and as the boy, her son, THE BOY, hurried up alongside her. She seemed frazzled, given her quick, furtive movements and the speed with which she and her son hurried up the walkway toward the front door of the house. Before going inside, she even cast a glance down the block in the direction she had come, as if expecting to see someone following her.

Zachs: *(SHE SEEMS JUMPY SHE MUST HAVE SPOTTED GRAYSON)*

Kotara: *(SOME COP THAT GUY IS)*

Grayson was one of them, too.

All of them, working together.

Watching.

Waiting.

Obsessing inexplicably over a ten-year-old boy.

*Waiting for what, exactly?* he wondered, and not for the first time. Why was he driven to be here, obsessed with watching this house, this McBride woman, THE BOY? To what end?

He must have been careless with his thought, shouting through that mental megaphone again, because Zachs once more turned his head in Eric's approximate direction and transmitted a response.

*(WE WILL KNOW SOON ENOUGH)*

Eric supposed that was as good as he was going to get for now.

And then: another muted thump against the wall of Eric's mind.

Sarah Miller.

He kept her out.

# CHAPTER FORTY-TWO
# "GO. NOW."

They came into the house to find it ransacked: chairs knocked over, cabinet doors hanging open, the fridge ajar, couch cushions and throw pillows strewn about on the floor. Cory felt the hairs along his arms rise, the way they had when he and Davey rubbed balloons on their arms at Winona's birthday party last year. His mother, who had come rushing into the house from the car just a moment before, slowed to a near standstill as she took in the condition of their surroundings.

He felt a wave of fear pulse off her like sonar.

She called out for Uncle Brian, the loudness and urgency of her voice echoing off the walls, sounding hollower than it should.

No answer.

She reached down and grabbed Cory's hand.

"Stay with me."

Together, they went into the kitchen where they found some broken dishes on the floor. The cabinet doors all stood open, and there was an empty bottle of his mother's wine in the sink, the cork bobbing around in a waterfilled bowl like a tiny buoy. His mother stared at that bottle for a long time, her grip on Cory's hand tightening. That sonar-like pulse of fear radiating from her changed to something else—anger. He roused the gnome and had it poke through the hazy membrane of his mother's thoughts, only to arrive at a single, compulsive declaration that repeated over and over in the center of his mother's head like the chorus to a pop song:

PROTECT MY SON
PROTECT MY SON
PROTECT MY SON

"Mom? What's going on?"

She said nothing but still gripped his hand tightly as she moved them down the hallway. Cory noted a picture frame askew on the wall. What had happened here? Had they been burglarized? Where was—

Uncle Brian lay unconscious on the bathroom floor. The medicine cabinet over the sink was open and there were bottles of pills and other items scattered in and around the sink. There was an empty bottle of mouthwash beside him on the floor, and a smudge of blood, impossibly red beneath the stark lights of the bathroom, leaking from his uncle's nose. He looked dead, and for a split second, Cory felt his heart rise in his throat . . . but then he heard the shuddery rasp of his breathing and saw his uncle's chest gradually rise and fall, rise and fall, with each unsteady breath.

His mother's grip tightened around his hand.

"You son of a bitch." The words hissed out of her in a way Cory had never heard before. It frightened him. That sonar-like anger was radiating out from her and Cory could feel it against his skin like sunburn. "You lousy, lying son of a bitch."

He watched as she kicked his uncle's thigh. Hard.

On the floor, Uncle Brian twitched. He'd been on his side, curled in a fetal position, but he rolled now onto his back. His eyelids unstuck and he blinked blearily up at them, clearly disoriented. The gnome peeked behind the curtain of his uncle's thoughts, but they were too jumbled and erratic for Cory to make heads or tails. Just that fact alone frightened him all the more and the gnome quickly retreated, troubled by that dark place.

"Go sit inside," his mother said, releasing his hand. Cory didn't move—didn't realize she had been speaking to him, in fact, until she said, "Cory. Go. Now."

He backed up from the bathroom door until his back struck the wall, but didn't move from there.

"Get up, you bastard," she said to Uncle Brian.

He groaned. Clutched his head. Struggled as he sat up, then looked around, seemingly desperate to piece together the events that had led him here and in this state. He saw the empty mouthwash bottle on the floor beside him, then looked up at Cory's mom.

She was trembling. And although Cory couldn't see her face from where he stood against the wall, he could tell there were tears in her eyes just by the sound of her voice. "You *promised* me. You *promised* me, Brian. Goddamn you."

"I . . . I didn't . . ." he stammered. His eyes were glossy and red, and they kept jittering around the room yet always seeming to return to that empty bottle of mouthwash. "I don't even know what hap—"

"I want you out of here."

"Ellen, wait, I—"

"Go. Now."

Cory watched as his uncle struggled to his feet. One foot sent the empty mouthwash bottle into revolutions on the bathroom floor. The sight of it spinning like that upset Cory for some reason he couldn't quite comprehend, as if he himself were strapped to that bottle, endlessly spinning.

*Circles, circles, circles.*

"Ellen, please," his uncle pled, dragging himself to his feet, one hand gripping the rim of the bathroom sink. "Something happened to me today, and I think I—"

"No!" she yelled at him. "No. I am not going to have this conversation with you."

"Please, Ellen, you have to listen to me—"

"I don't! I don't have to! I want you out—"

"—have to listen—"

"I want you to get your stuff and get out of the house!"

"El . . ."

"Stop it! Stop it!"

Uncle Brian's hands came up, shielding most of his face. They trembled. It looked like he was afraid she might strike him.

"And if you don't, I'm calling the goddamn police."

"Please, Ellen—"

"No!"

"—you've got to—"

She slammed the bathroom door on him, the sound as loud as a firework. Cory jumped. He was still staring at his mother's back, could see her bring her hands up to her face, could see the way her shoulders hitched the slightest bit. Then she whirled around and stared at him. She looked like she might scream at him. But instead, she just reached out and put her cool hand against the sweaty nape of his neck. Drew him toward her.

"Come with me," she said.

She led him down the hall and to the back of the house. She tugged open the slider to the back deck and told him to sit out there and to not come into the house until she came and got him. He didn't want to, but he wanted to argue with his mother even less, so he went. As he sat in one of the deck chairs, the sliding door whooshed closed at his back. Compared to all the shouting his mother had done in the house, the outside world sounded as quiet and remote as a distant planet now.

Cory pulled his knees against his chest and hugged himself in the big chair. He told himself he wouldn't cry, wouldn't cry, wouldn't cry. He dug his fingernails into his shins and stared at the changing colors of the sky beyond the nearby rooftops. Storm clouds loomed like cargo ships in the distance.

After a time, he heard angry voices speaking from inside the house. Too low and muffled to make out anything. The gnome stirred, but Cory was too upset to allow it to do any further poking around. Besides, he didn't really want to know what the gnome might find.

# CHAPTER FORTY-THREE

# INTERLOPER

## 1

By early evening, most of the items were in place. Stinger was pleased. He and his drones had done well. And although he knew he was little more than a pawn in all this, just like the rest of them, he couldn't help but feel a sense of pride, of stewardship, when he looked at what they had created together. Even his bee stings had ceased itching. They no longer pained him. It was as if his induction into this new order had shot him full of immunity. This was bigger than bees. This was the most important thing that had ever happened, *and it was all because of him.*

*I've done it, all right. I called them, I've assembled them, and they've constructed this at my behest. Those workers, those drones—they set one block atop the next, slowly building the Hive in the sky: the Dragon's revelation come reality.*

Now, he stood in the hollow chamber inside the Tower, darkness all around him. He could sense the vertiginous height of the chute high above his head, and a vague, pulsing sentience in there with him. When he let his mind go to it, tried to picture it, what came back was sometimes the twisting musculature of a snake, other times the undulating, segmented phalanx of a tapeworm. Yet he knew neither of those things were exactly right.

*Dragon,* he thought.

"They want to know why we're building this," he said. His voice was low, but it carried up the throat of the chute as if filled with helium. "*I* want to know why, too. I want to know what to tell them."

His words were greeted by silence.

*What are you?*

*Where have you come from?*

The image of the snake and the tapeworm were replaced by a more relatable one: the Langstroth hive in the back lot behind the carriage house on Macadam Street. He could see it as clear as if he was standing before it, the air swarming with bees, a fading slant of daylight spilling down through the breaks in the trees. As Stinger stared at it, the Langstroth hive began to slowly rotate.

*Circles, circles, circles.*

Or maybe *he* was the one rotating.

When he finally stepped back outside, he wasn't sure how much time had passed. The air had cooled and the sun was drifting low beyond the trees. At one point, he found himself watching Marybeth Maysall weave a length of wire through the links in the fence. There were others who might have been considered more classically attractive—the Bridgeport woman with the fake, perky tits was a particularly fine specimen—but it had been Marybeth who had captivated him for all these years, and who had been the star of his daydreams and fantasies. Beneath the blaze of the fading sun, Marybeth had unbuttoned the crossover panel of her waitress uniform so that it hung open at the neckline, revealing the dark, deep line of her cleavage. The upper part of her chest was dappled with sweat and tanned from the summer sun, though it was the whitish flesh of the lower part of her breasts that, when glimpsed, caused a trill of excitement to course through him. He had taken her that day in the shed, but even now, that seemed like some distant memory, or maybe even a daydream. Something that might not have actually happened. Time was something that no longer seemed to make sense to Stinger, and things other than the Tower itself seemed to be a façade, or a false reality. Like a painted wooden set on a theater stage.

Once Marybeth had finished with the wire she was working with, Stinger approached her. He said nothing; he simply took her high up on the forearm and led her across the clearing, out past the wooden split-rail fence, and into the trees. Marybeth offered no resistance. In fact, she said nothing at all. There, hidden among the trees, he turned her around so that she faced him. She was almost a full foot shorter than he was, so she had to look up at him to meet his eyes. He liked that. He grinned, already feeling an achy yet not unpleasant throb at the front of his pants. This close, he could smell her breath, the sour-sweet odor of someone who'd been working all day in the hot sun. Her upper lip sparkled with sweat. Her eyes darted back and forth, back and forth, as she looked first at his left eye then his right and then his left again. Stinger liked that, too. It was like she couldn't get enough of him. Like she was drinking him up.

When he kissed her, he felt something loosen at the back of his head and trail in a warm gush down his spine where it ultimately erupted like a nuclear explosion at his crotch. It took him a moment to realize he'd orgasmed, and when he *did* realize it, he shoved Marybeth away, ashamed.

"What's wrong with you?" she asked in a low voice. She could have meant anything, but Stinger took it to mean the most hurtful and embarrassing of all options.

"It just . . . happened," he muttered, dropping to his knees in the dirt while covering his swollen crotch with both hands. "I'm sorry."

"What?" she said.

He looked up at her—a reversal of roles. He felt his entire body shake. For a moment, he no longer felt like Stinger, but like Jeremy Stuckey again. "Why'd you let me kiss you just now?"

"Because that's what I do," she stated simply enough.

He shook his head. "What do you mean?"

"It's what I do," she repeated. "I feel it and I go for it. I've never been a prude."

"But I . . . I love you," he croaked, miserable.

"That doesn't matter. It's all impulse, Jeremy. It's all obsession and addiction. Don't you know? I'd take anyone right now. Anyone at all. It doesn't matter. It's a heat burning inside me."

*Queen bee*, he thought.

When she took a step closer to him, he lifted one hand toward her, palm out, and said, "No. Stop. Leave me alone."

She stopped.

"Go away," he told her.

"I thought you loved me, Jeremy. I'll be with you right here, if that's what you want. I'll let you do whatever you want to me."

He lowered his head. His heart was slamming so hard against his ribs it felt as if it might burst from his chest. Shaking his head, he said, "I want you to *want* to be with me."

"I do," she said. There was no emotion in her voice.

"Not in the way I mean."

"What does it matter? Look around, Jeremy. Look at that thing we've built. Look at what *you've* built. *You* did this. You're responsible. You've lived your entire life taking care of your sick, helpless, ungrateful mother, and cleaning up around this miserable neighborhood where people just look down on you, yet you've had it in you to be a leader all along."

For some reason, this infuriated him. He looked up at her and, when her image became smeary, realized there were tears in his eyes. When she smiled at him—smiled at his misery and bad fortune—he unleashed a scream that seemed to silence the world.

"Let it out," she told him. "It's okay. We all need to from time to time."

He struggled to his feet and staggered over to her. She did not move, did not flinch. In fact, the expression on her face suggested that she *wanted* him to come to her, and that she would let him do anything to her—anything at all—that he pleased.

So he did.

## 2

His head was still messy from what he'd done to her when he came back out from the woods and found most of the workers staring at a single individual who stood before them, speaking in a tone laced with incredulity. It took Stinger a few seconds to realize this person was Doug Winslow . . . and upon realizing this, he felt a strange disassociation overtake him. In that moment, he felt like he'd been living two separate lives on two distinctly different planes of reality, and now they had both converged. Chaos would undoubtedly ensure.

Doug Winslow turned and spotted him advancing through the crowd. His eyes went wide and he pointed a stubby finger at him. "You! You son of a bitch, get the fuck over here! What the hell do you think you're doing?" That look of incredulity still tattooed on his face, Winslow looked around at the rest of them. "Are you all fucking *nuts*? This is *county property*! This goddamn water tower is *federal* property! This is—"

"Hello," Stinger said, coming right up to within inches of Winslow's face.

Winslow flinched. He was out of breath, his respiration sounding like an accordion that someone had driven full of holes, and Stinger could clearly see the roadmap of bright red blood vessels that traversed the bulbous outcropping of Doug Winslow's nose.

"What . . . the *fuck* . . . is going on here, Stuckey?"

"A little project," Stinger said. "What do you think?"

"I think tampering with this equipment"—Winslow flapped a meaty hand at the Tower—"is a felony."

Stinger shrugged.

"You arrogant prick. I've been texting and calling you, and you've just been ignoring me like some . . . some . . ." His face was beet-red, his jowls quivering. His flared nostrils looked like subway tunnels. "I want your key to the maintenance shed. You're fired."

"You have the k—"

"You think I'm an asshole? You think I didn't see that you put a new lock on the door? What's the matter with you, Stuckey? In fact, what do you got hidden in that shed that you don't want me to see?"

"Nothing."

"Oh, yeah? Then show me. Show me."

Again, Stinger shrugged. "Sure."

Winslow looked out upon the sea of faces that was still staring at him in collective silence. "The rest of you people clear out. Go home. And don't think I don't recognize some of you."

Stinger wound around the perimeter of the split-rail fence, shoulders gently colliding with the shoulders of others, then headed in the direction of the narrow path that cut through the woods. When he didn't sense Winslow following him, he turned and saw the haughty bastard still standing there staring at him. Absently scratching his belly, Stinger said, "You coming?"

Winslow's nostrils flared. He moved forward like a bull, all shoulder and upper torso, head slung low on his neck, the ridiculous golfing visor askew on his head.

Stinger led him through the trees, the waning daylight poking through the green summer leaves in golden bayonets. Winslow came up quickly behind him, wheezing like an asthmatic. "You must think I'm a goddamn joke," Winslow said. His voice was low, almost conversational now.

Stinger said nothing.

"I'm talking to you." He reached out to grab Stinger high on the arm—

—but Stinger knocked his hand aside. "Don't you touch me, you fat fuck."

Winslow hesitated, but then that stout finger was back pointing at Stinger's face. "Mark my words, you hillbilly son of a bitch. I'll make sure you're prosecuted for theft, vandalism, assault, and whatever else I can throw at you. And don't think I'm gonna stop there. I'm going to make sure you and your mother—your fat, crippled, animal, disgusting *whore* of a mother—are bounced out of this neighborhood so fast it'll make your head spin. You hear me?"

"Just don't fucking touch me," Stinger said in a quiet voice. He was only half-seeing Doug Winslow now. But no, that wasn't completely accurate: he was actually seeing Doug Winslow from two different angles at once. It was as if Stinger had two heads and two sets of eyes, and that those two sets of eyes were viewing Winslow from conflicting perspectives. For a moment, the visages came together, and it was almost like Winslow was overlapping himself, like a double exposure.

"What *is* that?" Winslow said, looking at something on the knuckles of Stinger's right hand. "Blood?"

Stinger turned and continued moving through the woods. He didn't stop until he stepped out into the clearing where the maintenance shed stood. The sky had darkened as they'd walked, and there were now chalky gray clouds crowding around the perimeter of the park. Without a word—in fact, starting to whistle—Stinger pulled the ball of keys from the loop on his belt, right where a second smudge of Marybeth Maysall's blood had yet to dry. He selected the appropriate key, and slid it into the padlock latched to the door of the shed. The tune he was happily whistling was, for some strange reason, "Oh My Darling, Clementine."

"I want the truck key, too," Winslow said.

"Sure," Stinger said, opening the clubhouse door. Sheer darkness was laid out before him, the only suggestion of light coming from the narrow window at the opposite end of the shed, dull and opaque and crisscrossed in wire mesh.

Winslow shoved Stinger aside and barreled into the shed. Stinger watched as the fat bastard swiped a hand along the wall for a light switch. Casually, Stinger said, "Switch doesn't work. There's a pull-cord hanging from the bulb. In the center of the room."

Winslow glanced over his shoulder and shot Stinger an agitated look. He took his phone from his pocket as he crept deeper into the shed. The glow of the screen made his face look cadaverous.

Stinger slipped in after him. A row of gardening tools leaned against the nearest wall. Stinger grabbed the tool closest to him, which happened to be a long-handled cultivator with a trio of stainless-steel teeth at the head. To Stinger, it looked like some mad scientist had crossed a rake with a pitchfork. He gripped the cultivator's wooden handle in both hands just as Winslow began pawing blindly in the dark for a pull-cord that was no longer there.

"This place is a mess, Stuckey, you jerk. You've got some god—"

He was cut off as Stinger swung the cultivator and drove that trio of stainless-steel teeth into the right side of Doug Winslow's plump, red face. The man's cell phone fell away, its glowing rectangular screen quickly swallowed up by the darkness.

Winslow felt surprisingly solid; the cultivator's wooden handle vibrated in Stinger's hands for a second or two after the strike. With some effort, Stinger wrenched the tines free of Winslow's skull. It made a wet, squelching sound, like someone extracting rubber galoshes from a mud puddle. Winslow staggered around to face him. The man's mouth was unhinged in abject shock, and one of the cultivator's teeth had apparently buried itself in the right eye socket, because the eye there had burst and was leaking in a grayish, tallow dribble down the bloodied, dented side of his face. Below the leaky eye socket, Stinger could see a pair of divots left behind by the cultivator's other two teeth that, at first, looked about as harmless as impressions left behind after taking a nap on a particularly uncomfortable surface. But then a split second later, they swelled with rich, dark blood which spurted and spilled down the left side of Doug Winslow's face in a gushing torrent.

The president of the Mariner's Cove Community Association made a wet, gurgling sound way back in his throat.

Stinger cocked the cultivator back over his shoulder then took another swing. This time there was less resistance, and Stinger was awarded with a satisfied crunch as the tines sheared off the golf visor along with a section of Winslow's scalp. Winslow staggered backward and fell over a jumble of empty paint cans and wooden crates. The loose flap of skin at his scalp flopped forward over his forehead and remaining good eye, the underside red and raw-looking, its bloody triangular shape looking grotesquely like a slice of cheese pizza. The holes along the left side of Winslow's face continued to gush.

"I guess you don't have too much to say anymore, huh?" Stinger asked.

Winslow's body slid off the crates and onto the cement floor, scattering empty paint cans like bowling pins. One of Winslow's hands stuttered up blindly into the air. The wetness at the back of his throat congealed to form a word, a name, which was undoubtedly *Stuckey*, but given the lack of clarity in the man's voice, not to mention the amount of blood likely pooling at the back of his throat, it sounded like he'd said *Stinger.*

Stinger grinned.

"The endgame is almost here, Mr. Winslow," Stinger said. "Did you think I would let you ruin everything that we've done?"

Winslow made a strangled *gahhhh* sound. He brought one hand up to protect what was left of his face, but that did little good for when Stinger swung the cultivator again.

And again.

And again.

## 3

It was twilight by the time Stinger stepped out of the maintenance shed. He was breathing heavily and the muscles in his arms and back hurt from swinging the cultivator over and over. There was blood splashed across the front of his shirt, his pants, and patterned like freckles up and down his arms. What remained of Doug Winslow inside the maintenance shed was unrecognizable.

As he stood there, looking down at himself, figures emerged from the trees. They came like ghosts through a graveyard. Jack Gordon, Barrett Nesmith, Not-Nick. Two others whose names Stinger could not immediately recall. Bringing up the rear was what remained of Marybeth Maysall after Stinger had had his way with her back in the woods. Her face was bruised and swollen, her lip split and dribbling blood down the open front of her waitress uniform. There was also a visible bite-mark along the left side of her neck. She wore a vacuous, medicated expression as she maneuvered up the path, but when Stinger met her eyes, something in them sharpened. She grinned, and he could see that he'd broken one of her front teeth. She suddenly appeared eager to please, and Stinger liked that.

Stinger approached Jack Gordon. Jerked a thumb over his shoulder at the shed. "He's in there. Take care of it. Here." He pressed Doug Winslow's cell phone and car keys into Jack's beefy hand. "He drives a two-seater convertible, probably parked on Poplar Station Road. Go find it, leave the phone in it, and drive it out to one of the beach roads. He's divorced, got no kids. No one will be looking for him for a while."

"You got it," Jack said, and started to turn away.

"Wait."

Jack turned back. "What?"

"Don't tell the others about what happened here. Some of them aren't as . . . *invested* . . . as the rest of us." He was thinking of Sarah Miller, and how she'd questioned what they were doing here while pressing a hand to her (pregnant) belly, and of the detached and distant look he saw in the eyes of Alex Braswell lately. A few of the others, too.

"Obviously," Jack said.

"Let's get this shed cleaned out, too."

"Cleaned out?"

"Yeah. Take all the stuff out and just dump it in the woods or in the river or wherever. I don't care, just get it out of there. I need the shed cleaned out. Meantime, I'm gonna need a few helping hands. Let's just wait until it's fully dark." He was thinking of the vision he'd had back in the throat of the Tower.

"Whatever you need, Stinger," said Jack.

"Whatever you need, Stinger," said Marybeth.

"Whatever you need, Stinger," said the others.

Followed by a rumbling echo in his head:

*(WHATEVER YOU NEED STINGER)*

He felt good.

He felt pious.

He felt like everything was back on track and where it should be.

# CHAPTER FORTY-FOUR

# "SOMETHING BAD IS ABOUT TO HAPPEN"

## 1

His head pounding and his stomach full of lead, Brian gathered what he could, hastily filling his duffel bag, then staggered from the spare room and down the hallway. It felt like walking through a funhouse, where the floors were all slightly canted, and where the walls were pitched at weird angles. He was still disoriented and confused, although bits and pieces of that afternoon were filtering back to him in a highlight reel of hazy recollection. He recalled walking down to the park and the man in the work vest telling him that the park was closed due to a gas leak. He had headed back to the house after that . . . but something had come over him before he'd even reached Cloister Road, hadn't it? Not just a pounding headache and not just a touch of vertigo, but a delirium reminiscent of his darkest, most hellish days. He'd felt drunk without being drunk. He'd felt like he was going through withdrawal without having used any drugs. He'd felt, quite frankly, *fucked up*. Then: snapshots of rummaging through Ellen's house, yanking open cupboard doors and kitchen drawers, the refrigerator, drunkenly knocking over chairs, feeling at once like the walls of the house were closing in on him yet expanding toward some horizonless plane at the same time. Whenever he tried to get a mental grip on himself, he found those strange symbols crowding his thoughts, confusing him, beating him down, forcing him to—

What?

*Drink*, he realized now. *Forcing me to drink. Forcing me to give in to my addiction, my obsession.*

Ellen stood in the space between the dining room and kitchen, arms folded across her chest, back against the wall. She was staring at him with tears in her eyes and fury on her face. He opened his mouth to say something—

"Don't even bother," she said, cutting him off. She nodded toward an empty wine bottle that stood on the kitchen counter.

There was nothing he could say to that. He recalled ransacking the house, driven to a frenzy in his desire to *drink*, and finding the bottle of wine in the cabinet above the refrigerator. Yet after that, everything had gone dark.

She turned away from him, grabbing the neck of the empty wine bottle off the counter and dumping it into a trash pail. He just stood there, quaking in his skin.

"Get out and don't come back," she said, her back still toward him.

He waited a beat, likely for his heart to catch up with the rest of him, and then he went out the front door.

As he walked down the lawn toward the van, Cory came bursting around the side of the house. Brian froze, locking eyes with the boy. He suddenly felt ill, and knew that it had nothing to do with drinking.

Cory broke into a sprint, and before Brian could say or do anything, the kid had his arms wrapped around his waist. Brian hugged him tight, then pushed him away just as Ellen appeared in the open front doorway. He felt shameful, having her eyes on him as he hugged her son.

"We need you here," Cory said, his voice trembling. "Something bad is about to happen. I can feel it."

He just smiled sadly as he rubbed the back of his nephew's head.

"Go to your mom," he said, aware now that his own face was burning, his vision blurring. He forced himself away from the boy, then moved in a quick clip around to the driver's side of the van. He climbed behind the wheel just as Ellen came down the lawn, grabbed Cory around the wrist, and dragged him back toward the house.

Brian started the engine then executed a wide U-turn in the middle of the street. He saw Mr. Zachs still seated in that beach chair on his front lawn, observing. He saw, too, as he drove to the end of the block, the guy still reclining in the driver's seat of the red van that said KOTARA WINDOWS & DOORS on the side in electric blue font. Both men made something tremble inside him, and for the briefest moment, he thought he could see the light of his long-defunct star beginning to pierce through the darkness of his consciousness, as if that last hug from Cory had once again recharged his battery. But in the end, he attributed it to his drink-addled brain.

*What a fucking piece of garbage I am . . .*

As he drove toward the intersection, a police car passed him driving in the opposite direction, but Brian Russo thought nothing of it.

## 2

There was a motel off the highway that had a VACANCY sign in the front window. Brian rolled the van into the parking lot, shut down the engine, then sat there behind the wheel for nearly a full ten minutes while he let the world catch up to him.

*Keep it together, kid*, the Air Man spoke up in Brian's head. In fact, the voice was so clear and irrefutable in that moment, Brian glanced over at the passenger seat, half expecting to see Gary Manheim sitting there in his leather jacket, one jackboot propped up on the dashboard, cigarette poking from his lips.

Brian Russo felt like a house built precariously out of playing cards.

His head still spinning, he checked himself into a shabby, beige-colored room that smelled faintly of cigarettes. There was a narrow bed in the center of the room that looked vacuum-sealed in an argyle comforter, as well as a bland set of dresser drawers and a TV with visible handprints stamped across the screen. Brian set his duffel bag on the floor, stripped out of his clothes, then passed out on the bed.

## CHAPTER FORTY-FIVE

# IN DEATH, SHE IS A DOORWAY

They waited until the sun had fully set.

The GMC pickup's headlights cut through the back streets of the Cove, with Stinger propped behind the wheel. Crammed alongside him in the cab were Jack Gordon and Barrett Nesmith, while Not-Nick jounced along in the open bed of the truck. When Stinger saw the lights of the stone carriage house through the trees, he slowed the truck, then eased it up onto the smooth, paved surface of the driveway. He coasted up to the garage, whose doors were bracketed by electric lights that resembled old-fashioned, gas-powered sconces. The Stuckey house was recessed farther from the road than the others on Macadam Street and corralled by trees, so Stinger wasn't too concerned that anyone would see them and what they were about to do. Particularly now, under the cover of night.

Stinger shut down the engine and they all climbed out of the truck.

"This is some house," Not-Nick said, whistling at the sight of it. "Always wondered who lived in this big, ugly thing."

Stinger dug a set of keys from his pants. He unlocked the padlock on the double garage doors, then pulled them open. There was minimal clutter in here—Stinger had always been meticulous about the garage—so the three men followed him inside. Stinger flipped a switch, and a row of LED lights came on across the ceiling. There was some of Queenie's medical equipment in here, stuff that was mostly obsolete now: a couple of walkers, a wheelchair, gear for the shower that he'd once installed back when she was still able to amble her way down the hall. He nodded toward the beekeeping outfits hanging from pegs on the far wall.

"I've only got two," Stinger said, "so one of you will just have to weave and bob if things get hairy."

Not-Nick frowned. "Weave and bob? Seriously?"

"Christ," Jack Gordon said, staring at the suits. "Just how many bees are we talking about, Stinger?"

"They're mostly dormant at night," Stinger told him, which he knew wasn't really an answer. "Besides, I don't think they'll bother any of you. I think they know you're coming."

"That's nuts," muttered Barrett.

"What about you?" Not-Nick asked. "You're not gonna help us?"

Stinger sucked on his lower lip. His eyes suddenly felt itchy in their sockets. He couldn't remember the last time he'd slept. "I've got something in the house I need to contend with."

"Lucky you," Not-Nick murmured, stepping over to examine the beekeeping suits on the wall. He didn't look too pleased with what Stinger had tasked the three of them with. In fact, when Stinger had explained it to them back at the park, he could tell Not-Nick thought he was joking at first.

"Once you're done, wait for me back by the truck," Stinger said. "Under no circumstances do I want any of you to come inside the house. Do you understand?"

They all acknowledged that they understood.

Stinger shouldered past Not-Nick and snatched the two beekeeping outfits from the hooks. He tossed one to Jack and the other to Barrett.

Not-Nick cursed under his breath.

Stinger went to a shelving unit, rummaged around in a box, and located a number of ratchet straps. He handed them to Not-Nick, who stared down at them as if they were live snakes.

"It probably weighs about a hundred pounds, give or take," Stinger said. "Shouldn't be too difficult to carry. Use these straps so the drawers stay together."

Not-Nick looked up at him. "Drawers? I thought you said this thing was a beehive."

"It's a Langstroth hive. It's built as a chest of drawers. You'll see." He dug a flashlight from the box, tested to see that it worked, then handed that to Not-Nick, too.

"Explain to me why we're doing this again," Not-Nick intoned. He sounded like a sullen teenager.

"Just shut up and do it," Stinger responded.

While Jack and Barrett suited up, Stinger slipped back out into the night, went up the front walk, then slithered in through the front door of the house.

There was a smell in here that wrung water from Stinger's eyes. Honeybees crawled along the walls, and once Stinger turned on a few lights, he could discern the otherworldliness of them. Some were clear, like the ones that had flown out of the crack behind the Tower at Gladstone Park. Others possessed two heads, like the one he'd kept in a jar before he'd swallowed it. And then there were others whose digestive tracts, brains, and salivary glands were visible on the outsides of their bodies. They looked like socks that had been turned inside-out. There was a crack inside the Langstroth hive—or, more accurately, the Langstroth hive *itself* was a crack—and Stinger's bees, having inadvertently traversed through that crack to another plane only to return to this world again, did so in this abnormal fashion. Why going through a crack would turn some of them clear, some of them inside-out, and give some of them two heads, Stinger didn't know. What he *did* know was that the Dragon had spoken to him through that very same crack, and he was going to let it speak to the rest of the colony now, too. This way, they would all know what it was they were doing down at the park—or would at least be reinvigorated by the sound of the Dragon's godlike voice—and vow their unwavering allegiance.

*Like you, Alex Braswell,* he thought as he wended down the hall toward the rear of the house. *I'm sensing something off with you, my friend, like some Doubting Thomas. How can that be when you're the engineer who put this whole thing together in the first place? I wish I could tell what was on your mind.*

He'd attempted to plumb the depths of Alex Braswell's thoughts with his own mind, but Braswell had put up walls each time Stinger had tried. Stinger had considered saying something to him directly, but had ultimately decided against it. Without knowing exactly what the man was thinking, Stinger didn't want to tip his hand.

*Sarah Miller, too,* he thought. *Yes, you've obsessed over those wire hangers, collected them and cared for them like children. But now you've got a child of your own blooming in that womb of yours—I could tell it with just a passing glimpse into your mind—and you're beginning to question what this is all about. And I can't have that. So now you'll hear what the voice told me, and all will be right again.*

Once he had their full compliance again, he would begin addressing the last and final piece of the puzzle—that symbol of a person with a star on their forehead. Was it one of them? Did someone need to sit in that chair?

He didn't know, and he wanted the Dragon to tell him.

That foul odor grew stronger as Stinger crept down the darkened hallway that led to Queenie's bedroom. He tried to calculate just how long he'd been away from the house but found that he couldn't; days and nights blended together, and his sense of time lately was malleable to say the least. At the end of the hall, Queenie's bedroom door stood partway open. He could tell the TV was on due to the flickering blue light on the other side of the door—Queenie's TV was *always* on—but there was no sound, so it was likely muted. As he approached, a solitary honeybee materialized from out of the room, zipped by his right ear, then shuttled off down the hallway.

Stinger eased the bedroom door open a bit more. The stink that barreled out was obscene and assaultive, drawing more tears from Stinger's eyes and burning the interior walls of his nose. He covered his mouth and nose with one hand as he crept into the room.

"Ma?"

The giant shape of her, tinted blue from the light of the television, did not stir on the mattress. The room was silent—too silent. He stood there, holding his breath, and did not hear the *sssst* of Queenie's oxygen tank.

Stinger slid over to the bedside lamp and turned it on.

"Oh," he said, the word clicking dryly at the back of his throat.

She was dead, of course. For how long, Stinger had no clue. Her face was a colorless rubber mask, mouth agape, yellow pegs of her teeth thrusting from a receded gumline. The pale, pupilless orbs of her eyeballs had recessed in their sockets, giving a pushed-in look to the upper portion of her face, and there were streaks of strange urine-colored fluid that had dried in the creases at the corners of her eyes and left stains on her pillow. The fine red threads that, in life, had blossomed from the sides of her nose in delicate crimson bouquets were now a dark, sludgy black, making it look like someone had pumped her corpse's veins full of old motor oil. One of Queenie's hands lay exposed, palm up, on the mattress, the fingertips a moldy gray green, the mottled discoloration in the palm akin to a swirling, angry storm that has yet to settle.

As had happened when he'd led Doug Winslow through the woods toward the maintenance shed earlier that evening, Stinger was once again overcome by that strange sense of *doubling*. It was as though his consciousness had just been split down the middle and separated, and both versions of himself now stood staring down at his mother from conflicting perspectives.

One perspective saw the unsettling ripple of Queenie's enormous white nightshirt as something—or many somethings—squirmed beneath it. The opposite perspective noted the way something twisted and writhed about in a patch of Queenie's unwashed, salt-and-pepper hair. Both perspectives reached out simultaneously. The nightshirt was peeled away from the swollen, bloated belly of the corpse, to reveal that there was nothing necessarily squirming under the *shirt*, but under the *skin*, while the brittle, clumpy hair along the left side of Queenie's head was smoothed over with a palm that felt the strum of bees buried not in the *hair* but beneath the dermal layer of Queenie's *scalp*.

*There's a crack inside her, too,* Stinger realized—or, rather, *both* Stingers realized. *Just like in the Langstroth beehive, there's a crack inside her, too. A passageway to a whole other world. In death, she is a doorway.*

There was a steak knife on a greasy plate beside the bed, its blade gummy with congealed tallow and flecks of black gristle. His eyes kept returning to the sight of it, the rivets in the wooden handle shining like devil eyes beneath the glow of the bedside lamp.

Both of Stinger's perspectives unified into one again. His vision returned to normal. He took a breath and found that, beneath the stink of decay, there was an undercurrent of something . . . well, *sweet.* Something pleasant. Something like . . .

Like . . .

He reached out and grazed the urine-colored streaks that had leaked from his mother's eyes and lay in shiny gold ribbons down the sides of her face. The stuff was sticky, and it stretched into tacky threads as he peeled his finger away from his dead mother's cold, unyielding flesh. Brought the finger to his nose and sniffed. Brought the finger to his lips and let his tongue flick against the shimmery golden droplet there.

Honey.

He reached down and picked up the steak knife. The looming rotunda of his mother's bare belly glowed with a faint blue hue in the light of the television. Stinger pressed the point of the steak knife against the creased pocket of flesh just below Queenie's yawning black hole of a bellybutton. The flesh dimpled as he pressed down, and for a moment, he thought he might not be able to pierce the skin. Instead, he could imagine plunging that knife all the way into that pocket of flesh and those rolls of belly fat straight up to the handle, and all that mileage of flesh would just simply stretch and dimple and accommodate the blade, and never become taut enough to split open.

But that was not what happened.

With a bit of additional pressure, he felt the tip of the knife puncture the abdominal cavity. He heard it—a sound like stepping on a peanut shell, followed by the hissing expulsion of fetid air. He expected blood to spurt out from the hole, but that did not happen, either. Maybe she'd been dead too long and the blood inside her had congealed or evaporated or whatever happened to blood when a body has been dead for too long. Nonetheless, he drove the knife in deeper, and could smell that nauseating and incongruous olfactory combo of rotting decay and raw honey grow stronger, infiltrating his nostrils and making him lightheaded.

He sawed the knife through the flabby, deflated bladder of Queenie's belly, moving upward across the mound of gut and past the navel. The flesh parted, and while the blood still refused to flow, he could see tears of golden honey spilling out, dribbling down the sides of her pale and marbled abdomen. He dragged the blade even higher, still sawing, pressing down to puncture through countless layers of dermis and epidermis, through swollen coils of spongy yellow fat that, to him, looked like cake or pastry, through the delicate tendrils of a circulatory system gunked up with used motor oil.

*No, not motor oil,* he corrected himself. *That's honey.*

When the blade of the steak knife hit the bones of Queenie's sternum, Stinger backed away and watched as the incision continued to weep golden tears. He dropped the knife back onto the dinner plate and just stared at her corpse, transfixed.

*She is a doorway.*

*She is a doorway.*

*She is a—*

The first bee exited the incision and spiraled lazily into the air. It looked as if it were made of glass, and its entire body glowed with the light from the TV as it drifted in front of the screen. A second bee followed. Then a third. Then a fourth. Soon, they vacated the split husk of Stinger's mother in small, buzzing knots, then in greater numbers, climbing toward the ceiling, dozens of them, their collective hum a motorized cacophony that resonated in Stinger's back teeth. They crawled upon the ceiling and scuttled up and down the walls. They took flight and orbited Stinger's head, so preposterous a sight that Stinger couldn't help but lower the hand covering his mouth and nose and laugh.

He felt them go inside him, rattling down the stovepipe of his throat, dozens of prickling, buzzing balls of agitation. He also remembered how they had once come out of *him*, making him wonder if he, too, had a crack, a doorway, deep inside him.

Cracks, it seemed, were forming everything.

*It's because we're so close to the endgame now. So close. I just need to know what to do with that last piece of the puzzle . . .*

He stood there for an unknowable amount of time, victim once again to that eerie sense of doubling—a mitosis of the mind and soul, a splitting and dividing of cells following a hasty quickening. Two minds in one body . . . or two bodies sharing one Hive Mind? He didn't know.

Once the air cleared and most of the bees had dispersed for other parts of the house, Stinger blinked gummy tears from his eyes. He looked down at what remained of his mother's body—the flayed rolls of lumpy, pallid flesh striated with the fat, spongy bulges of cellulite, as well as the trench that Stinger himself had dug through the center of her torso. In death, Queenie Stuckey looked inconsequential. Deflated. Hard to believe, staring down at what was left of her now, that she'd taken up so much of his life.

He leaned over her body and ran a hand up one cold and punctured flank, his palm gliding along on a flume of fresh honey. It felt warm, like blood. He peeled away a section of the cut he'd made and looked inside.

She'd been hollowed out, the interior of her body shored up by a scaffold of hexagonal, honeycombed grids, through which a shining, syrupy nectar dripped and dribbled and pooled at the base of that Stinger-made crevasse like a river of molten gold shining at the bottom of a canyon. He slid his hand up and over the crude incision he'd made with the steak knife, and down into the open belly of his mother. His hand passed between the honeycombed walls of the canyon; his fingertips touched that warm, honeyed river. Further still . . . and he felt a numbness overtake his hand, no different than when he'd pushed his fingers through the crack hanging in midair behind the Tower in Gladstone Park. Deeper still, and his arm vanished inside the crack that ran the length of Queenie's eviscerated torso, the numbness traveling up his arm straight past the elbow. For a moment, he wondered what it would be like if he just *crawled in there*, a reverse birth, sliding through the crack in Queenie's womb, but before he could consider this further—

*(STINGER WHERE ARE YOU WE ARE READY TO GO)*

This yanked him from his reverie. He withdrew his hand, the feeling returning to him instantly, and wiped the residual honey on his shirt. He looked down at his mother's sunken face.

"Sorry, Ma. But we both knew there'd be sacrifices." He smiled grimly, tears welling in his eyes again. "Hey. I love you."

He bent down and kissed her on her forehead.

And his lips came away sticky and gold.

# CHAPTER FORTY-SIX
# SHAKEN

Brian had left her shaken.

She cleaned up the broken glass and straightened the furniture while Cory, upset, hid in his room. She let him be, choosing instead to marinate in her fury. It had seemed so *right* when he'd shown up yesterday. Had she been that desperate to believe such a thing? Had she been so helpless and therefore so blindly hopeful? What had he done, anyway? Gone on some berserk rampage around the house in search of booze and drugs?

*Son of a bitch.*

She dumped shards of broken glass into the trashcan beneath the sink, then realized the index finger of her right hand was bleeding. Not from the broken glass, but from her subconscious gnawing at her own flesh. Without realizing it, she'd chewed through the Band-Aid and gnawed her fingernail down to the quick.

*I'm losing my mind.*

She felt unanchored. Unsettled. Not just the thing with Brian, but the police officer who'd been watching them earlier that day at the Pink Penguin. Had she let Cory's paranoia get to her? Because surely there'd be no reason for some neighborhood cop to follow a single mom and her son around town.

*He's been watching us all day*, Cory had said. *I've been trying to peek inside his head, but he won't let me.*

She went into the dining room and to the drapes that were pulled closed over the bay window. She'd pulled them closed herself this time, another piece of Cory's paranoid contagion. They were slowly becoming two people sharing the same mind.

*Well, if I'm going to act paranoid, then I might as well go all the way.*

She turned off the dining room light then peeled back a section of the drapes. Beyond the bay window, Cloister Road appeared dark and silent. The moon was hidden behind a bank of clouds, so the only light came from the lampposts staggered at intervals down the block.

She thought she saw a police car parked in front of Mr. Zachs's house.

*No, that's silly, it's not a police car.*

But she could make out the silhouette of the rack lights on the roof, backlit by one of those lampposts.

*No.*

She found herself drifting down the hall toward the front door. Yes, she'd also bolted the door, but she unlocked it now and crept out onto the front porch. The night was silent—even the crickets had vanished for distant lands—except for a repeated wheezing sound. It took her a moment to realize it was the sound of her own nervous respiration.

Yes, it was a police car. She could see it clearly now. Was there someone sitting inside? Maybe even watching her house?

*Why would he do that?*

She crossed the lawn, went down the driveway, and stood on the sidewalk, herself suddenly exposed beneath the glow of one of those lampposts. She could not tell if someone was in that police car or not, but she could see a light on in one of the upstairs windows of Mr. Zachs's house. Mr. Zachs's portly silhouette was framed perfectly in that window, watching her.

*I'm really losing it. I'm letting Cory's fears get to me.*

She went back inside the house, where she shut and bolted the door. Down the hall toward Cory's bedroom, she pushed his bedroom door open, expecting to find him at his desk, or maybe on his phone, but instead found him curled in a fetal position atop his bed, sleeping.

She stared at him for a while, feeling ashamed in the realization that she'd come in here to glean some comfort from him. Her son. Instead, seeing him asleep on that bed made her feel all the more alone.

His cell phone was on his nightstand. She picked it up, opened the text app. There were even more strange texts from Davey Orem than there had been when Cory had showed it to her earlier that day:

come out

come out

come out

come out

come out

come out

Unsettled by them, she set the phone back down on the nightstand.

She went to his desk and saw a bunch of drawings laid out on tracing paper. Cory was a good artist, but these pictures were nothing more than hasty line drawings: something that resembled a spider, something that looked like half a sun, a spiral that reminded Ellen of the design on a snail's shell. At the center of these was one drawing in particular that, for whatever reason, made her uncomfortable. It was a stick figure with a star on its forehead.

She looked up at Cory's bedroom ceiling, where all those glow-in-the-dark stars were spread out there. An entire galaxy of them.

*Stop it. You're making things worse. Take a pill and go to sleep. Things will be better in the morning.*

She hoped that might be true, but as she retreated out of Cory's room and back down the hallway, she felt something nag-nag-nagging at her. Like a hangnail, which she realized she was currently chewing on, it irritated her.

*What? What?*

She went around the house, doublechecking that all the doors and windows were locked. The shades and drapes drawn, too. In the kitchen, peering out the window over the sink before lowering the blind, she could still see Mr. Zachs's silhouette facing her house in the lighted upstairs window.

*What? What?*

Turning off all the lights in the house.

*What?*

That stick figure with the star on its head.

That phrase, *the boy, the boy,* spray-painted on their driveway.

It felt like there was something *right there* on the cusp of revelation that was just out of her reach.

In the end, she decided to forgo the sleeping pill, and instead took up residence on the couch. Despite her exhaustion, she'd stave off sleep tonight. She had her cell phone clutched in one hand, and although it seemed ridiculous to call the cops *about* a cop, that was exactly what she planned to do if that police officer—

*(Grayson)*

—decided to come knocking at their door.

## CHAPTER FORTY-SEVEN

# THE ALTAR

### 1

Jack and Barrett were waiting for him in the driveway when Stinger came out of the house. They were still dressed in the beekeeping outfits, and there was an agitated snarl of honeybees hovering around them like a bad smell. Not-Nick, who didn't have the luxury of a beekeeping suit, stood farther away, at the foot of the driveway, where he kept swatting indiscriminately at the air.

The Langstroth hive stood in the bed of the pickup truck, those ratchet straps wrapped around the draws so that they wouldn't come apart.

"I got stung like six times, Stinger!" Not-Nick shouted from the foot of the driveway. He was examining some lump on his arm. "I thought you said these fuckers were dormant at night?"

*Shut the fuck up*, Stinger thought, and that seemed to quiet Not-Nick.

"Keep the suits on," Stinger said to Jack and Barrett. "Ride in the back of the truck and make sure this thing doesn't topple over." He glanced over at Not-Nick, who was frantically fanning the air again. "You ride in the cab with me."

Jack and Barrett climbed in the back, and Not-Nick ran in a serpentine fashion through a labyrinth of bees toward the passenger door of the truck. He hopped in and slammed the door so quickly and with such force, the truck rocked on its shocks.

Stinger cast one final glance at the house where he'd grown up, then slid behind the steering wheel and turned over the engine.

"I don't see what this has to do with what we're building down at the park," Not-Nick groused as Stinger pulled out of the driveway and onto Macadam Street. It was still early evening, but Macadam Street was generally a quiet one, and theirs was the only vehicle on the road.

*That's because you're just a dumb automaton*, Stinger thought, not caring if Not-Nick snatched that thought from the air or not. *You're just a worker bee, doing what you're told. The Langstroth hive isn't for you. Some others, however, may need reinforcing. They may need to be shown why this is so important.*

Stinger wanted to be shown, too. He wanted the Dragon to speak to him again, to tell him what the endgame was, and how they would achieve it.

He wanted to fulfill his destiny.

"Fuuuuck, man, there are bees in *here*!" Not-Nick howled. He rolled down his window and flapped his hands at the bees swirling about the cab, desperate to shoo them out into the night. A few were dragged out on a slipstream of wind; others crawled along the dashboard, and Not-Nick leaned forward to get a better look at them, his fear temporarily ameliorated by curiosity. "These things don't look right."

Stinger felt one bee land squarely on the knob of his Adam's apple. He felt it move in a tickling, circular motion, round and round and round, like a dog about to bed down for the night. Then it went still, and Stinger was careful not to exhale too vehemently. In fact, he held his breath.

The bee planted its stinger into his Adam's apple.

Just a quick, hot pinch. Nothing more.

As he took the turn onto Poplar Station Road, Stinger transmitted a thought directly to Marybeth Maysall, whom he'd tasked with overseeing the purge of the maintenance shed:

*We are on our way back.*
*Make sure the entire shed has been cleared out.*
*Make sure the symbol is on the floor.*
*We need to get this started tonight.*
*People are getting restless.*

Not-Nick jumped in his seat like someone zapped with a cattle prod. He kept swatting at the air. "Fuck's sake, they're *everywhere*! Get 'em off me! Get 'em off me."

*Shut. The. Fuck. Up*, Stinger thought.

And Not-Nick suddenly went still.

## 2

When the top of the Tower came into view, rising above the treetops at the far end of Gladstone Park and dripping with moonlight, that single word, ENDGAME, painted starkly across its hull by Stinger's own hand, Stinger considered driving the long way around on the nameless road and coming up through the woods on the Slope Hill side of the park. It was safer to do it that way—fewer houses, fewer people, less chance of a problem—but it also meant a lengthy, uneven trek through the woods, across the Tower's clearing, and then down the path toward the maintenance shed on foot. He didn't care if Jack or Barrett blew their biceps out while carrying the thing, but he was worried they might become fatigued and drop it. So, instead, he decided to drive straight across the park itself, then down the gravel service road that would take them straight to the maintenance shed, unimpeded.

When they arrived, the GMC's headlights washed over a small cadre of people hauling the last remaining bits of junk from the shed and dumping them into the surrounding woods. Marybeth stood there in the glow of the headlights; like someone on the tarmac of a runway, she waved him in.

Stinger brought the pickup to a halt. The vehicle rocked, and he heard both in his head and aloud as Jack Gordon, struggling with Barrett to balance the hive strapped down in the bed of the truck, cursed. The hive skewed to one side, and those straps went taut. A curtain of bees clung to the rear window of the truck.

Stinger jumped out just as Marybeth approached him. "The shed's empty, Stinger. What are we doing now?"

Stinger transmitted not a word nor a phrase but an image directly into Mia Bridgeport's pretty, blonde head. He watched her eyes widen as she received it. Then he turned to Jack and Barrett, who were still in the bed of the truck, bracing the hive to keep it steady. Their beekeeping outfits were crawling with bees, and even from this distance and in the dark, Stinger could see that some were malformed while others sparkled like translucent crystals in the moonlight.

"Show me," Stinger said, and gripped Marybeth high and tight on her forearm. She gasped a little at the strength of his grip, but said nothing as she led him over to the maintenance shed, whose door stood open on a threshold that looked black as roofing tar. He followed her inside and saw how the interior of the shed seemed to positively *yawn wide* now that all the community equipment and junk had been cleared out. He moved toward the center of the shed, the only light coming in a meager chute through the wire mesh window toward the back. Above his head, he heard a dull thumping. He looked up to see the carpenter bee bumping against the dead bulb in the ceiling fixture.

*Still hanging around, old friend?*

Just as Stinger had instructed, Marybeth had painted a spiral in the center of the cement floor in dark, russet-colored paint:

"That beehive is an altar," Marybeth said. It wasn't a question. She was staring at him with an intensity that caused his molars to vibrate painfully in their sockets. He thought maybe she was reading his mind, but he decided to respond verbally nonetheless.

"Yes. That's exactly what this is. It's also a conduit for hearing the voice of the Dragon."

"The Dragon?"

He didn't bother to explain; she would know soon enough.

"Once we get the beehive—the altar—in here," he said, "we are going to round everyone up, make a line at the door. They will each take turns coming inside to commune with the hive. I want them each to hear what the hive will have to say."

"How long will that take?"

"I have no idea."

"Can I go first?"

He shrugged. "I think maybe there's someone else I'd prefer go first." He was thinking of Alex Braswell, and how he'd been feeling Braswell's mind becoming distracted and slowly slipping away. He needed to lock Braswell back in. Braswell was important.

"Things are moving very fast now, aren't they?" she said, her breath sweetly sour against his face. She was staring at him with wide, soulful eyes, although one of them was swollen from Stinger's knuckles, the skin beginning to purple.

"Oh, yes," Stinger agreed, grinning at her in the dark. "Very fast, indeed."

## 3

Stinger and Marybeth came out of the shed to find Barrett and Jack, still in their beekeeper suits, hoisting the Langstroth hive from the bed of the truck. It wobbled like a too-tall wedding cake, and Stinger heard himself shout, "Careful!"

The men righted it and regained control. Not-Nick, still wary of the bees, hung a distance from them, but looked ready to jump in and help if things went to shit, despite the lack of beekeeper gear.

"In here," Stinger said, holding the door of the maintenance shed open as Barrett and Jack approached. They carried the hive inside, and a contrail of honeybees followed them. "Place it on the spiral," Stinger told them.

They looked like two men in radiation suits carefully placing a case of plutonium on the floor. When they were done, they exited the shed, brushing bees off their arms and away from the screens of their hoods. Barrett stomped his feet and bees fell away like blackened clumps of snow.

"It's in there," Jack said, pulling off his protective headgear. Sweat rolled down his face and his hair was damp and matted to his head. "Good to go, Stinger."

Stinger looked at Marybeth—at her ruinous face, split lip, and the streaks of dried, russet blood down the front of her waitress uniform. A part of his mind buried deep beneath the fog of obsession felt a pang of pity and guilt. "Okay, go ahead," he told her. "You can go first."

Marybeth kissed the side of his face, then moved around him and drifted toward the open doorway. Bees filled the air, so plentiful they looked like the shadow of some malformed creature drifting across the outside of the shed. She paused briefly at the threshold, turning her head and looking at him. "Will I get stung?"

"Probably," Stinger said.

Undaunted, Marybeth crossed the threshold and stepped into the humming darkness of the maintenance shed. When she was no longer visible, Stinger casually reached over to the door and pulled it closed.

## 4

Stinger had no idea what time it was when Marybeth Maysall finally exited the maintenance shed. He'd been lying in the grass, hands laced behind his head, half dreaming of a giant mechanical beehive in the sky. When he sensed her—when the Hive Mind alerted him to her—he flipped open his eyes and saw her bruised and battered face staring down at him, backlit by a full moon.

Stinger sat up abruptly. He could see Not-Nick sleeping in the bed of the pickup truck, and both Jack Gordon and Barrett Nesmith snoring as they sat on the ground, backs propped up against one wall of the shed.

"What was it like?" he asked her. "What did you see? What did you hear?"

"The Dragon," she said. She glanced around, perhaps at the others who were asleep nearby. Stinger could see fresh bee stings along her arms and even one, like a Frankenstein bolt, on the side of her neck. They'd stung her good and proper, which Stinger thought might be the only way for the Dragon to impart its wisdom. "You were right all along."

"Of course I was," he said. "Did it tell you what we're building this thing for? What the endgame is?"

She shook her head.

"Did it tell you which one of us is the final piece?"

Again: a shake of her head.

"Then what did it tell you? What did it show you?"

"A great flash of light," she said. "It made me feel . . . feel like I was a part of something. That we were *all* part of something. And that made me feel *good*."

"But nothing about the endgame? What we're supposed to do?"

"No."

"It showed you nothing else?"

"Well, for a minute, I thought of the guy who's helping us build this thing. The guy with all the paper cutouts."

"Braswell?"

She shrugged, disinterested, then bent at the waist and peeled her panties off from beneath the hem of her waitress uniform. Tossed them away in the darkness behind her. A moment later, she was straddling him beneath a section of moon that kept drifting behind dark clouds. Stinger let her buck her hips against him for a while, but then he grew impatient and rolled her off him and onto the grass. If her feelings were hurt or her orgasm interrupted, she did not let it show, and merely kept staring at him with dark, ravenous eyes.

He stood, swiping dew from his clothing. He began buttoning his pants. "I have to go see him."

"Who?"

"Braswell."

"Now?"

"Wake everyone up."

She asked something else, but Stinger was no longer paying attention. He slipped into the trees and maneuvered back down the path toward the Tower just as thunder rumbled overhead. The rest of the colony was there, many still securing sections of the Tower, while others dozed briefly in the grass. It struck Stinger as odd that he could not hear the sound of even a single cricket.

Alex was sitting on the ground, his back against the tree stump. He was shuffling those paper cutouts while observing the work still being done to the Tower. Georgette was asleep beside him, her head on his shoulder. She didn't stir when Stinger approached.

"I want you to go sit in the chair," Stinger said.

Alex looked up at him, as if startled by his sudden appearance. "What?"

"You're the only one without an item. Got me thinking—maybe *you're* the item." He nodded toward the Tower. "Go sit in the chair. Let's see what happens."

Alex peered over at Georgette, whose head was propped against the side of his neck, still asleep. Stinger gave her a little mental zap, and Georgette's eyes snapped open. She sat up, groggy, and looked around. "What? What is it? What's going on?"

"I'll be right back," Alex said, rising to his feet.

"Where are you going?" She looked from Alex to Stinger, and Stinger didn't necessarily approve of the vibe he got from her stare, either. It was starting to feel like the whole system was breaking down. There was such a thing as Colony Collapse Disorder, or CCD, Stinger knew, which was when all the worker bees abruptly disappear from a hive, leaving the queen and her brood to fend for themselves, and the colony itself to ultimately die. Stinger got that sense now, and he wasn't happy about it. They were too close to the endgame to fail. "I'm coming, too," Georgette said, climbing quickly to her feet.

Stinger shrugged.

He led them both to the base of the Tower, feeling everyone's eyes on them now. Work stopped, conversations halted. People peered down at them from the walkway surrounding the tank. He could feel the entire colony collectively holding its breath.

Alex passed through the opening in the fence. Stinger followed, and Georgette brought up the rear. A few others came right up to the fence to watch. The thing they'd constructed at the base of the Tower still looked very much like an electric chair, and perhaps that was why Alex paused before sitting down on it. There was no electricity running to this thing—it was just a heap of junk strung together out of sheer sweat, perseverance, and obsession—yet Stinger held his breath as Alex sat on the camping chair and eased his back against the wooden door. His head slotted perfectly into the upside-down colander.

"Now what?" Alex asked, looking up at Stinger.

Stinger didn't know. He'd been hoping something might happen the moment Alex sat in the contraption—perhaps the flash of light Marybeth had spoken of after her visit to the altar—but there was nothing. Stinger could feel everyone's eyes pressing against his shoulder blades. His face was turning hot.

"Maybe we jumped the gun here," he said ultimately. He even offered Alex a sheepish little grin that stretched the tight, bee-stung topography of his face. "But I have another idea." He waved Alex up from the chair. "Follow me."

"Where?"

"To the shed."

Alex's eyes narrowed. Stinger felt the Hive Mind ripple, and Alex's consciousness attempt to slip inside his head, but Stinger put up a wall and blocked him from poking around in there, much as Alex had been doing to him all day, if for no other reason than to reestablish just who was in control around here.

"Altar," Alex said, having gleaned that much from Stinger's head before the wall went up. But there was still confusion on his face, so he hadn't glimpsed what it actually was.

"I think you'll get your answer there," Stinger told him.

"Answer for what?"

"Don't be so cagey with me, Braswell. The answer for the question you've been asking yourself for too long now."

"And what question is that?" Alex asked. He was toying with Stinger and Stinger didn't appreciate that.

"What your final role is in all this," he said.

Alex climbed out of the chair. He exchanged a look with Georgette, and then the two of them followed Stinger back through the opening in the fence and into the clearing. A sea of people parted as they came through.

Stinger led them back down the path in the direction of the maintenance shed. Once they cleared the trees and the shed came into view, Stinger could see everyone had been roused from their slumber and had taken up positions, like guards, around the shed. The only person who was no longer there was Marybeth, but that didn't matter; she'd been his guinea pig and had come out enlightened.

Stinger felt Alex's hesitation, so he reached down and casually pressed a hand against the small of his back, propelling him forward. Jack Gordon repositioned himself by the entrance to the shed, like a bouncer beside the door of a nightclub.

"What is this?" Alex asked. "What's in there?"

"You said it yourself," Stinger responded. "The altar."

"But what *is* it?"

"The voice of the Dragon," said Stinger. "You need to hear it, Braswell. It's important we get things back on track."

Jack Gordon opened the door to the shed. Strangely, and for just a moment, Stinger expected some golden, godly light to spill out, even though that hadn't happened when Marybeth had gone in there, but there was only the dark maw beyond the open doorway leading into the shed.

Stinger looked down and saw that Georgette had grabbed her husband's hand, and Alex—

# 5

—looked down and saw her hand, too, then looked over and saw his wife, the face of her, Georgette, smiling at him. He knew in that moment and without having to search her mind that she'd lied to him earlier about calling the kids. She was being torn in one direction while he went in another. What had started out as his own personal obsession had transferred to her, like a disease, while he was left feeling dislocated and alone.

"Go on, Alex," she said.

"Georgette," he said back . . . although what he'd meant to say was G, just G, her initial, which was how he'd always said her name, even back before they'd been married. Just G. But something alien had seeded in his brain, one consciousness pressed right alongside another, *occluding* the other, and it wouldn't let him do it.

Stinger's hand at the small of his back urged him forward. Georgette's grip tightened on his hand then let go completely—one final squeeze of confidence before sending him to the wolves. Alex felt himself drift toward the open doorway, and now it seemed that Jack Gordon's gaze was brightly illuminated, much as Stinger's suddenly seemed to be, and even Georgette's as well. He arrived at the threshold and could smell the interior of the shed—a mixture of gasoline, mown grass, turpentine—wafting out at him. Other things, too, wafting out at him.

Bees.

He hopped backward, covering his face with his arms.

He heard Georgette cry out, "Oh!"

He jumped a few more steps away from the shed, still covering his face until he was far enough away from the shed to lower his arms. His gaze fell instantly upon Stinger, who remained staring at him with a mixture of confusion and disappointment on his face.

"Bees," Alex said.

Stinger shook his head, not comprehending.

"He's allergic," Georgette said.

Stinger shrugged. “So?”

“Deathly allergic,” she added. “One sting would kill him.”

“How quickly?”

“Fuck you,” Alex said.

“I don’t know,” Georgette responded. “It could be quick or it could take a couple of minutes.”

“What if he wore one of these bee suits?” Jack Gordon suggested. He was wearing one right now himself, except for the headpiece.

Stinger shook his head. “No. I don’t think that will work. I think you need to get stung to hear it.”

“Hear *what*?” Alex said.

Stinger’s eyes swung in his direction.

“If he can’t go in there, then what do we do?” Georgette asked . . .

. . . and just hearing her ask it, Alex felt a traitorous knife in his back. He thought about getting in the car and driving to his daughters, thought about—

*(NO ALEX NO THIS IS IMPORTANT THIS IS ENDGAME)*

He looked at her through a hazy zigzag of bees.

A shape appeared beside him along the path. It was Sarah Miller, and she stepped forward without hesitation into those bees. Both her hands pressed against her abdomen, she said, “I’ll go.”

Stinger frowned. “It’s gotta be Braswell. He’s holding the key to this whole thing. The last piece of the puzzle.”

“No,” Alex said, shaking his head. “You don’t know that.”

But Alex could feel it, and Stinger had been right: he was the only one who hadn’t brought an item to the tower. Whatever was in that shed, Stinger believed it would enlighten him and snap that final piece of the puzzle into place. And Alex couldn’t deny that he was probably right.

“I’m not afraid of bees,” Sarah said. “Let me go in. I want to . . . to *know*.” She was staring at Stinger. “What harm would it do?”

Alex watched as Stinger appeared to consider this. After a time, he simply nodded his head, then waved a hand toward the door of the maintenance shed.

A fair distance from the shed now, Alex watched as Sarah Miller approached the door. Jack Gordon tugged it open, and that black, depthless, rectangular space revealed itself once more. Georgette came up beside him, rubbed his back gently. When she brought her face close to his ear, he turned, anticipating a kiss. But instead, she whispered, "I'm going to go in there next. I want to see what's in there. I want to hear what it has to say."

"That shed is full of bees."

"It doesn't matter. This is important."

*I don't know what I'm supposed to do*, he thought, and fired that thought into his wife's head.

She returned one just as quickly, and with unwavering certainty:

*(YOU WILL)*

For some reason, that didn't make him feel any better.

*(YOU WILL ALEX YOU WILL YOU HAVE TO WE HAVE ALL WORKED SO HARD THIS IS IMPORTANT THIS IS ENDGAME)*

And then there was the Hive Mind rumbling just beneath the transmittal of Georgette's thought, a mantra repeated over and over, coming at him from the rest of them still back at the water tower, all of them, unified against him.

*(ALL HAIL THE DRAGON)*

*(ALL HAIL THE TOWER)*

*(ALL HAIL THE DRAGON)*

*(ALL HAIL THE TOWER)*

*(ALL HAIL THE DRAGON)*

*(ALL HAIL THE TOWER)*

Across the clearing, Alex watched as Sarah Miller entered the shed, and Jack Gordon closed the door behind her.

## 6

There in the darkness of the maintenance shed, Sarah Miller knelt down before the altar, which she could see, once her eyes grew accustomed to the gloom, was nothing more than a whitewashed chest of drawers glistening with honey and filled with bees. Even in the darkness, she could feel the air around her alive with bees, the humming and strumming of them matching the buzzing in her bottom molars. It was like a language she couldn't quite understand, but maybe had known in another lifetime. The only light came in through a horizontal panel of glass covered in wire mesh at the far end of the shed, but the longer she knelt there before the hive, the more that sliver of moonlight appeared to focus itself on the hive itself—on that whitewashed collection of drawers set up like an altar in the center of the room.

She felt a tingling up and down her arms. When she looked, she could see the honeybees crawling along the pale tracts of her skin. Some looked like tiny glass figurines, or maybe living teardrops. Others were two-headed monstrosities whose wings made a mechanical zipping sound when they fluttered. Suddenly, she could feel them everywhere—crawling along her neck, her jawline, the sides of her face, squirming in her hair. She felt one become snared in the eyelashes of her right eye, and she furiously blinked it away. She felt, too, them moving around *inside* her, or at least imagined she did, their bristling, segmented legs scaling the soft internal tissue of her body, their furious wings fluttering in every hidden cavity inside her.

*Show me, show me, show me, show me, show me,* she thought, and—

*—breath comes breath-whispery through the slaloms and corridors and channel-chutes of this girl's inner workings, the mechanics of her, the machine that is what she is, and as she breathes in, so does the wispy wisp breathe out, a commingled breath, a sharing, a sense of life-air exchanged, of communing, a conveyance, and there in that forever slipstream—*

—she saw the chambers of the hive, was *inside* the hive, within those hexagonal, honeycombed walls that glistened with golden light, and an image, undeniable, of her wires, of her coat hangers yet also the wires *inside her*, the soft machine of her body, unraveled to create a tapestry of circulation here within the hive, a union of the two, while a thing beat like a heart at the center of it, and her mind recalled, once again, the memory of the Chinatown parade with her father all those years ago, and that festive, sparkling dragon weaving in jaunty dance steps down H Street in downtown D.C., crepe streamers fluttering, hinged jaw jabbering, eyes sparkling like golden coins, a crown of multicolored horns—

*(ALL HAIL THE)*

—only it wasn't a dragon, not really, not completely, but a thing so close to the *idea* of a dragon—

—or serpent—

—or snake—

—that *dragon* was the closest thing her mind could relate it to, was how she could define it for herself, and as she realized this, she thought—

*—of traversing these bodily corridors, snaking through an impossible network of veins and arteries, and up, up, up through the column of the spine and into the gray matter of the brain, sizzling, then down into the trench of the stomach, carving wide berths, spreading invisible fingers through each chamber of the heart, wearing the heart like a glove, occupying every red and white blood cell, every atom, every nucleus, filling them, only to arrive in the control center of the womb, a fireworks explosion, and a sight, an image, a twist of fibril tissue and a thing that exists as the possessor of its own heartbeat,* whump whump whump whump, *a small, living galaxy harnessed by connective tissue to a rich and nutrient wall, heartbeat strong, heartbeat strident, heartbeat* whump whump whump*ing, as a consciousness comes alive—*

—so, too, did Sarah see it all for what it was, and the understanding that the Dragon was not malicious nor benevolent—that those concepts did not even mean anything to the Dragon, did not *exist* for the Dragon—but merely a thing that simply *was*, and that it was stuck, and it needed to get home, and that she, Sarah Miller, and her unborn baby, too, were all workers summoned and possessed in order to facilitate this transference.

A heartbeat that went *whump whump whump.*

A thing bigger than herself.

Two things, really.

And when she came out of it, she understood that the world was really something else entirely.

## CHAPTER FORTY-EIGHT

# TRANSMISSION

*(COME NOW TO THE ALTAR HEAR THE VOICE OF THE DRAGON THE DRAGON WILL TELL ALL THE DRAGON WILL IMPART ITS WISDOM THE DRAGON WILL FILL IN THE HOLES THE GAPS THE TROUBLED PLACES THE CRACKS THAT REMAIN DARK AND QUESTIONABLE TO YOU COME NOW TO HEAR THE VOICE OF THE DRAGON SPEAK TO YOU THROUGH THE ALTAR CRACK COME NOW TO HEAR THE VOICE OF THE DRAGON WHO WILL IMPART WISDOM COME NOW COME NOW COME NOW ALL HAIL THE DRAGON ALL HAIL THE TOWER)*

## PART FOUR

# ENDGAME

A man said to the universe:
"Sir, I exist!"
"However," replied the universe,
"The fact has not created in me
 A sense of obligation."

STEPHEN CRANE
"A Man Said to the Universe"

*Waits for first light, this liminal girl, this Tatum Klass, piloted by her own breed of obsession, mind awhirl, girl awhirl, a flurry of fear and anguish and culpability, a tornado of it, returns alone to the location where it began, the locally-known Trenton house, a fever pumping in her veins, her mind a zoetrope of images flitting by, flit flit flit, each one more grotesque than the next, of Mike Bliss, of course, and of the stories she's heard from friends and neighbors alike, real or exaggerated, factual or fabricated, whatever they are, this girl-in-transition cannot shake—*

*—cannot shake—*

*—cannot shake—*

*—cannot shake—*

*—those terrible flitting images from her mind.*

*Something happened in that house that night. She knows she should let it go, and leave some things unexplained, because maybe some things* cannot *be explained,* refuse *to be explained, but she also knows she cannot—*

*—cannot—*

*—cannot—*

*—cannot—*

*—as it will drive her mad not to know. It will drive her to the brink of some existential precipice where she will teeter indefinitely, always wondering, always somehow complicit and forever in limbo, and never truly knowing what is real and what is not. Because what happened to Mike Bliss in that house that night is . . .*

*Impossible.*

*Shhhh.*

*Goes in through a back window,* the *back window, same as on that night, sneaky-quiet, but desperate and urgent in her movements, too, breath a high whistle in her throat, temples sweaty, muscle jumping in her left eyelid. The house feels the same, but also somehow different. A draftiness where it had been previously sealed shut, is the only way her mind can think of it. As if—*

(cracks)

*—walls have shifted, leaving imperceptible spaces between them, except that they* are *perceived, if only subconsciously, and only in the heated, fleeting moments when her panic is at its most heightened and aggrieved.*

*Where does she go? Whisper-ways through the house to the staircase near the front, just as she did that night when the boy, the friend, the schoolmate, the neighbor, Mike Bliss, had led the way, thinking now in a rhyme, as a poem, like a song:*

One step, two step, three step, four
All the way to the very top floor

*The air is alive with buzzing wings. She thinks they are houseflies, or maybe even very large fruit flies attracted to some unseen rot buried somewhere in this house. But then one pistons its stinger in the tender meat of her left upper arm. It's a hot pinch, and she swats at it, feeling the—*

(bee bee bee BEE BEE!)

*—bee's body crushed beneath the palm of her hand.*

*She can go back now. Right back out that window,* the *window, at the rear of the house. It isn't too late. She can live with the mystery if only she will allow herself.*

*She cannot allow herself.*

*Up the stairs, where the early morning light pools on carpet and frames itself on bleak and empty walls. Something hopeless about this place now. Something frozen in space and time. Is it the burgeoning daylight that makes it feel this way? Probably safer to come at night, to break in at a time when no one will see her, but that is too frightening a prospect, so here she is in the stark light of dawn, in a house of gloom and shadow and panels of bright pink laid out like squares on a checkerboard. Right there to the end of the hall where the bedroom door stands open, she goes. The bedroom into which Mike Bliss vanished. The bedroom she followed him into on that night, only to find the room empty as she crossed the threshold. How does a teenage boy vanish from a second-floor bedroom only to reappear later in a basement? What magic trick exists in this world that allows someone to slip through a—*

(crack)

*—hole in the known universe like that? To start in one place and end up in another?*

*She is sweating and scared. She is anxious and queasy in her belly. She is remembering the things her friends have said, all the things, whether they be truth or lies, about the boy, the friend, the schoolmate, poor Mike Bliss—that his eyes have turned clear and he's now permanently blind, among other terrible and impossible things. She tries to imagine what "clear eyes" might look like—little fluid-filled orbs? spherical lenses that magnify the bone structure of the eye sockets in which they sit?—but then she stops because, let's face it, she is already frightened enough to be here in this house, moving toward this open bedroom door, and does not need to heighten her fear any further.*

*She enters the room.*

*It is bright at the windows, dark in the corners that bend away from them. Dark, too, in the closet, which stands just minimally open, like a mouth about to breathe her in.*

*She breathes . . .*

*. . . and, yes, it is like something in there breathes back.*

*She goes to the barely open closet door, where the darkness inside is greater than the darkness of the room around her on the night she was here with Mike Bliss. She remembers thinking that Mike Bliss was hiding in there, ready to jump out and give her a scare. She stands before this closet now, and feels—*

*—thinks she feels—*

*—a cool, aestheticizing breeze. Just enough to stir the delicate hairs on her arms. Just enough to make her stomach feel like it has begun to move slowly on a wheel.*

*She pulls the door open all the way. Some of the sunlight from the windows on the opposite wall breach that dark place, but some of the light does not. In fact, a vertical strip of shadow only appears to intensify, to coalesce. As if growing stronger, bolder, in the face of daylight.*

*That cool, numbing breeze comes from there.*

*The shadow.*

*The other side of the shadow.*

*Tatum Klass closes her eyes.*

*Thinks,* Keep them closed, keep them closed, keep them closed.

*Thinking of Mike Bliss and his clear, see-through eyes. Or so they say.*

Keep them closed, keep them closed, keep them closed.

*Steps into the closet.*

*Passes into it.*

*Passes—*

*—into an airless vacuum of numbness. She feels herself drift. She feels, too, her stomach still strapped to that slow moving wheel, going round and round and—*

*—round and round and—*

*—round, never ending. Nothing, it seems, here in this liminal space for this liminal girl, shall ever end. Nothing shall ever end. Nothing shall ever end. Nothing shall ever end—*

*Until it does.*

*And she is no longer in that vacuum, and she can feel the real world pressing down on her again, the actual, physical weight of the air. She can hear, too, the buzzing of many bees all around her. She has slipped through a crack, and when she dares open her eyes, she finds herself in a small basement with a drippy sink. The air is positively humming with bees. They collect in her hair, upon her clothes, in her eyelashes. There is a stairwell that goes up, dark because there is no light on down here, just a slender window above the drip-drip-drippy sink through which the meagerest shaft of daylight projects, but in her panic, she resorts to retreating backward, back into the crack, back through it, and into that transitional place, that airless, breathless vacuum once again, eyes closed—*

(keep them closed keep them closed keep them closed)

*—breath held, the buzzing of the bees following her down,*

*down,*

*down,*

*down,*

*down,*

*down—*

*—and there is a sense that she may exist here, now, in perpetuity, indefinitely flailing and lost, a fate worse than that of the boy Mike Bliss, for hers possesses no ending, just an unraveling tapestry of eternity with no termination in sight, and she runs but her legs do not move, and she screams but her throat makes no sound, and she hunts desperate for another crack, any crack, any opening, any portal to the world she perceives as her own, as long as it is an escape pod from this place which, in truth, is no place at all, panic-stricken, desperate, can't breathe, can't breathe, can't BREATHE—*

*—until every particle of her is thrust back out into the real world, or at least as "real" a world as perceived by someone such as a girl in transition. Only not in an empty bedroom on the second floor of the space known as the Trenton house—in fact, no longer in the Trenton house at all—but in the center of an unfamiliar residence, decrepit, abandoned, remote. A house, yes, but one that she has never visited. Still, the air is tumultuous with bees, and they still crawl in her hair, on her clothes, cling to her exposed and sweat-slickened skin. Her eyes are open and she is no longer in THAT PLACE, wherever THAT PLACE had been, but she also does not know where she is RIGHT NOW. Panic tightens around her throat.*

*She turns and sees daylight framed in a perfect yawning rectangle some distance ahead of her. If this is indeed a house, then that is the front door, standing open, allowing her—beckoning her—to exit. She runs for it, a scream building in her throat. The bees scuttle over her and tears stream from the corners of her eyes. She can still* see *because she kept her eyes* closed, *or maybe none of this is real and she is still trapped in that airless void, her mind unhinging as she runs, or thinks she runs, that rectangle of early morning daylight growing larger, larger, larger.*

*Until she is free.*

*The scream breaks loose, the tears run down her face, and this girl awhirl, this transitory creature who has traversed the cracks and returned, runs straight from an abandoned house at the tail end of the bayside neighborhood of Mariner's Cove, a house that has no front door, right down through the overgrown yard, still screaming, disoriented, not knowing that she will ultimately realize she is back in the neighborhood, only in a different place, because all the world is a neighborhood—*

(ALL THE WORLD IS A NEIGHBORHOOD)

*—and not knowing that her skin will look sunburned the following day while stippled with bee stings, not knowing there exists a solitary tooth near the back of her mouth that has gone clear and shiny as glass, not knowing those things now and in this moment, only running from the house and down the overgrown lawn beneath the bright cowl of day toward the street, hopping over a curb where the numbers, the address, 1183, is painted in a bleak and fading white, and where this girl, for just a moment, feels the presence of a separate consciousness graze up against her, bumping, like something snaking its way between your legs while you swim in the blackest of subterranean pools.*

# CHAPTER FORTY-NINE
# PLIERS

At some unknowable hour of some unknowable date, Raj Subador, his nude, emaciated body covered head to toe in hieroglyphics, opened his mouth and studied his teeth before the bathroom mirror of his Plainview Street bungalow. The shower was on, filling the bathroom with steam, and clouding up the mirror except for the small circle Raj's hand had cleared away so he could examine those teeth. The obsession with these symbols was being transmitted to him through the molars of his lower jaw. There was an incessant buzzing back there, painful most of the time, strangely pleasant at other times. He became convinced that these back teeth were the source of his sudden and inexplicable madness. Even now, his finger was describing those strange symbols in the condensation on the glass; when he realized what he was doing, he lowered his hand and forced himself to stop. The buzzing ache in his molars intensified.

He did not know what day this was because time had become a tangled ball of twine in his mind. He did not know what time it was because the madness had stopped letting him see numbers and letters. Everything had turned into a symbol. He couldn't recall the last time he'd eaten, the last time he'd gone to sleep, and the thing hidden behind the foggy places of that mirror was nothing more than a walking corpse with haunted, empty eyes. This obsessive behavior was all-encompassing, and something had to give.

Raj picked up a pair of pliers off the bathroom sink, which he'd brought in from the work shed out back just moments before. There was also an old bottle of Percocet on the sink, now empty, though it hadn't been just moments before. Mouth still open wide, he worked the pliers past his lips and fumbled around a bit until he was able to catch his lower right molar between the jaws of the pliers. Raj squeezed the rubber-gripped handle.

There was a popping sound, like stepping on an acorn. Bright red blood cascaded from his open mouth and spilled into the sink. Powdery bits of tooth came with it.

The pain came next, hitting him with all the force of a fall from some great height: exquisite, blinding, unmerciful. It wrung tears from his eyes, smearing his reflection in the cloudy mirror. He could feel his heartbeat throbbing in the fresh cavity at the back of his jaw, insistent as some mechanical device. Before he lost his nerve, he transitioned the pliers to the left side of his mouth, the metal head of the tool knocking against his upper teeth, and filling his bloody mouth with more bitter powder. His hand was shaking now, but he was finally able to grasp the molar on the bottom left side of his jaw.

The pop of the tooth echoed inside the walls of his skull. Unlike the first tooth, which had mostly been crushed to powder, this one came apart in two jagged kernels. They rolled around sharply in his mouth upon a pool of blood-powdered enamel before he spat them both out into the sink, *tink tink*.

He only prayed this would silence the madness. Would end the obsession. Would give him his true sight back.

His hand shaking, he set the pliers on the sink then picked up the bottle of Percocet. With his other hand, he pawed away the tears from his eyes. When his vision cleared, he attempted to read the label on the bottle of Percocet—

—but found, with sudden horror, that he couldn't. The text was nothing but jumbled, indecipherable nonsense.

*No no no no no no . . .*

He dropped the bottle, which bounced once off the edge of the sink before clattering hollowly to the bathroom floor. He watched it roll across the tiles until it struck the base of the toilet.

And when Raj Subador looked back up, he saw the trembling finger of his right hand once again tracing one of those odd and menacing symbols into the condensation on the glass.

# CHAPTER FIFTY
# FORGIVENESS

## 1

Brian Russo awoke on the bathroom floor of his motel room, naked and cold, and with a pennant of bright red blood snaking from his left nostril in a lazy river across the tiles. He sat up, disoriented, his neck and lower back painfully kinked. Bits and pieces from the night before washed over him like a cool tide, concluding with him checking into this motel out by the highway. How he'd wound up on the bathroom floor with a nosebleed, however, was beyond him.

He saw his deck of playing cards splayed out on the floor before him, and the shot glass that said GIDDY UP sat on the edge of the tub. The faucet was on, the sound of running water burbling down the drain—a sound Brian typically found soothing, but that now caused a measure of anxiety to buoy up from the core of his body. He leaned forward and shut the water. When he eventually stood, there were playing cards stuck to his bare thighs.

The thing in the mirror was mostly him.

He cleaned up the blood, then gathered up the cards and the shot glass. Strangely, he did not feel hungover, yet there were pieces missing from his memory of the night before, which typically went hand-in-hand with an evening of excessive drinking. He leaned toward the mirror and opened his mouth wide. His tongue wasn't purple, yet he could still remember yanking that bottle of red wine down from above Ellen's fridge.

*Can't remember drinking it, though, can you, cowboy?* It was the Air

Man, interjecting with his particular brand of wisdom.

No, he couldn't. He could remember flinging open cupboard doors, but he had no memory of drinking that bottle of wine, just like he had no memory of downing that mouthwash. Didn't mean he hadn't done it—God knew he forgot more than he remembered after a night of drinking—but it also made him feel a bit . . . suspicious . . . about the past twelve or so hours.

He dressed then opened the door to his motel room onto a gravel parking lot that overlooked the highway. He was surprised to see the sun directly overhead, and he winced at it like some terrible, subterranean thing that had crawled out of the sewer. His body was stiff from having slept on that bathroom floor—what the hell had he been doing in there, anyway?—and his head pounded with a faint but steady drumbeat. Despite this, his stomach growled with hunger, but he could see no place to grab a bite on this side of the highway, so he hopped in the van and pulled out into traffic.

As he drove, he tried to piece together the events from yesterday that had led him here. He recalled his walk to the park, and how it had been closed due to a nearby gas leak. He'd gone back to Ellen's house then, only to find himself in the throes of some . . . well, mental and physiological collapse was the only way he could think of it. He remembered rummaging through Ellen's cupboards and medicine cabinet, accidentally breaking some dishes and knocking over furniture like some drunk stumbling around the house. He had a memory of discovering the bottle of wine in the cupboard above the refrigerator, of course . . . but now, in the bright light of a new day, also a memory of emptying it down the sink before he succumbed to the weakness of it. Same thing with the bottle of mouthwash he'd found in the bathroom: glug, glug, glug, straight down the toilet.

Was that what he'd done? Or was his mind recalibrating his memories to suit his need?

The next thing he remembered was being jostled awake on the bathroom floor by Ellen. This part was still a bit swimmy in his head, but he also had no difficulty recalling how irate she had been. And how frightened Cory had looked staring at him from behind her in the hallway.

What exactly had *happened* to him?

Fast food restaurants and 24-hour diners whipped by along the shoulder of the highway, but Brian didn't stop at any of them. He just kept driving.

When he'd left last night, Cory had hugged him and said . . . what?

*We need you here. Something bad is about to happen. I can feel it.*

Yes. It was coming back to him now. Ellen had been furious, Cory had been afraid. He remembered feeling a similar fear as he'd left the house, his mind woozy and worked up over what had happened to him after returning from the park, not to mention waking up disoriented and feeling hungover on the bathroom floor. But now, in the light of a new day, he began to examine things from a different perspective. He hadn't been to an AA meeting since that impromptu one in Indiana, and he hadn't spoken to Gideon, his sponsor, in weeks. Perhaps what had happened to him yesterday afternoon was nothing more than a physiological relapse without the actual imbibing of alcohol. He'd heard stories of people who'd quit drugs and booze only to find themselves falling apart months or even years later. Sometimes, too, they died.

Brian dug his phone from his pocket, fired up the GPS, and hammered out a search for AA meetings nearby. A handful of red dots appeared on the map, scattered as buckshot.

*We need you here. Something bad is about to happen. I can feel it.*

Maybe the *something bad* was Brian himself.

## 2

After sitting through an AA meeting, he checked into a Sheraton. He felt clear-headed and desirous to get a piece of himself back.

It occurred to him in that moment that *getting it back* was exactly what he'd been trying to do last night, with the playing cards and shot glass in the bathroom of the motel. Even if he couldn't remember doing it.

*That's because there had still been a veil over my eyes last night. I was still suffering under the influence of whatever has been happening in Mariner's Cove.*

And what, exactly, *was* happening?

He didn't think it was as mundane as a gas leak.

Standing in the middle of his rather nondescript hotel room, Brian looked down at his hands. They'd stopped shaking. Moreover, he felt a familiar calmness coming back to him, the same sense of peace he'd found during his best weeks and months in El Segundo, when both his mind and his body were clear and clean and strong. There was still the old weakness within him, of course: that beckoning coil of a blackened, snakelike finger nudging and tempting him to take a drink. But that sensation had *always* been there, and he had learned how to cope with it and, sometimes, sing it quietly into hibernation. That wasn't anything unusual. What *had* been unusual were the chills, the shakes, the motherfucking merciless DTs, and the pervading and unrelenting notion that those black, toothy demons were once again crawling out from under his bed and perching atop his chest. He hadn't felt like that since his earliest days in treatment . . . yet he had started to feel like that back at Ellen's house. However, now that he was out of the house . . .

*Not out of the house, but out of the neighborhood*, the Air Man clarified.

Whatever it was, it didn't make sense.

He did then what he clearly had done last night while in some sort of fugue state: he stripped out of his clothes, then took the deck of playing cards and the GIDDY UP shot glass from his duffel bag. He carried them into the bathroom, setting the cards on the sink and the shot glass on the edge of the tub. There was a small tower of plastic cups on a metal shelf above the toilet, each cup individually wrapped in cellophane. He opened each one, tearing at the cellophane wrappers with his teeth. There were five cups in all, a good set of numbers, *one two three four five*. He filled each one with water at the sink then placed them in a huddle atop the closed lid of the toilet.

The cups of water was an old trick, something he had found useful in his earliest days of sobriety whenever the desire for alcohol had become overwhelming. He would fill up cups with water, set them in a conga line, and stare at them until his hands shook and his mouth salivated. When he couldn't take it any longer, he would permit himself just one cup, and he would chug it down with such ferocity that he usually wound up spilling half of the water down his chest. It was just water, but the physical act of drinking, of *imbibing*, helped satiate that coiled belly-snake and even managed to keep the demons at bay, if just for a little while—if just for seconds, sometimes.

The craving wasn't strangling him now, as it had been back at Ellen's, but just the sight of those five water cups sitting on the closed lid of the toilet was like a security blanket.

At the tub, he turned on the faucet but did not stop up the drain. The sound of the running water soothed him, but it also helped narrow his focus and attention, like a wall of white noise. There were two towels folded over a metal rod on the wall. Brian grabbed one of the towels and laid it down on the cold bathroom tiles, just as someone might do with a picnic blanket.

He sat naked and cross-legged on the towel and grabbed the deck of cards from the edge of the sink. This time, he didn't bother setting each card face-down in front of him. Instead, he shuffled the deck then cut it. Then he gathered the deck in one hand and touched the top card with the index finger of his other hand.

*That nephew of yours gave you a little charge*, the Air Man whispered into Brian's ear. *Don't let that flame gutter completely, if you'll mind the mixed metaphors, cowboy. Stoke it. Bring it back to life. Raise it from the dead. Maybe it's just like a muscle that needs some exercise.*

Could he do it?

*Give yourself some grace, kid. Give yourself some forgiveness. You're not all bad. No one is.*

Closing his eyes, concentrating, he thought, *Eight of diamonds.*

Turned the card over.

Queen of hearts.

# CHAPTER FIFTY-ONE
# PROTECT MY SON

Cory opened his eyes. No nightmares last night—none that he could remember, anyway—but there was a foreboding sense of doom tightening around his throat. He thought of that field trip he'd taken to the petting zoo and how he'd seen the older boy perched up in the hayloft lighting pieces of straw on fire, and how he'd just *known* something terrible was about to happen, all of which was confirmed later on a TV broadcast. That same sense was upon him now. Tenfold.

He got out of bed and crept into the hall. The door to his mother's bedroom stood open, but when he poked his head in, he saw that her bed hadn't been slept in. That sense of dread squeezed his throat even tighter, and he felt no relief until he saw her asleep on the couch in the living room.

The gnome was restless.

Something was wrong.

He went to the kitchen and raised the blind over the sink. Through the window he could see that Mr. Zachs was once again in his accustomed position sitting there on the lawn in his beach chair, bathrobe, and sunglasses. Mr. Zachs's bald head was a blistery red from the sun and even from such a distance Cory could see great teardrops of sweat cascading down the sides of the man's round, fleshy face.

There was a police car parked in front of Mr. Zachs's house now, too, and Cory could discern the shape of the officer crouched there behind the wheel. It was the same policeman who'd been watching them yesterday while he and his mother had played mini golf, and later while they'd eaten pizza at the Pink Penguin. Cory unleashed the gnome, let it spread its impossible fingers to all the thinking minds along this stretch of Cloister Road. But the gnome was roadblocked in every direction, slamming into a wall the moment it tried to access Mr. Zachs's thoughts.

*There are others out there, too,* he realized . . . or, rather, the gnome informed him. Each one fortified against the gnome's poking, prying finger, their communal power greater than the gnome's alone.

This frightened him.

He moved quietly into the living room, realizing that his mother had pulled all the drapes on all the windows in the house. She was still asleep on the couch, curled in a fetal position, cell phone tucked between her knees. There was only one light on in here, a lamp beside the couch that shone on her bare feet. She was feeling strange things, too, he knew. Yet unlike with Mr. Zachs, the policeman, and the window repairman (and whoever else was out there), the gnome could still breach *her* mind.

The Band-Aids on each of her fingers had come unraveled, and he could see the shorn and bloodied skin around each of his mother's fingernails. She'd been chewing on them a lot lately, something she did whenever she was stressed or upset. But after the fight with Uncle Brian last night, she had bitten them so much they'd begun to bleed.

He crept over to her now, silent as a church mouse, and stared down at her slumbering face. Watched as her eyelids kept tightening, as her forehead kept creasing. *A nightmare,* Cory thought. He got down on his knees beside her and slowly pressed his forehead against hers, so gentle that she did not stir.

Closing his own eyes, he had the gnome peer into his mother's thoughts, his mother's mind, feeling ashamed and intrusive and downright awful for doing it, the phrase *THIS IS NOT FOR YOU* blazing beneath his eyelids as the gnome tunneled deeper into his mother's mind.

He knew that Uncle Brian hadn't done the thing his mother had accused him of. Something *other* had been manipulating his uncle, puppeteering him and screwing around with his head. *Exploiting his weaknesses* was not a term with which Cory, at ten years old, was familiar, but he felt the crux of it nonetheless, weighty as gravity. Now, he worried that same force was imposing itself on his mother. Changing her, manipulating her. Weakening her, somehow. And this frightened him even more.

He felt the gnome slip inside, no more intrusive than the ghost of a whisper. A moment later, the gnome returned to him nothing more except the obsessive, compulsory desire to PROTECT MY SON at all costs, because the only thing that mattered was to PROTECT MY SON. If she didn't PROTECT MY SON then she would vanish into nothingness. Her love for him, he saw, was all-encompassing . . . but it was also the source of great fear for her, as well.

PROTECT MY SON
PROTECT MY SON
PROTECT MY SON

Before the gnome withdrew from his mother's mind, Cory imparted a single message unto her, fired like a flare in the night sky: *Uncle Brian didn't do what you think he did, Mom. Something bad made him act that way.* It felt important for him to tell her that, even if she was asleep and wouldn't have any knowledge of it upon waking.

Cory withdrew his forehead from his mother's. The house was silent, but he could suddenly hear a dull ringing sound coming from somewhere. It took him a moment to realize it was his cell phone ringing from his bedroom.

He hurried into his room and saw Davey Orem's name on the phone's display. The sight of it caused an additional finger of panic to tighten around Cory's throat. *Come out, come out, come out, come out, come out.* However, unlike those unsettling text messages, Cory—or, rather, the gnome—did not feel a sense of trepidation this time. He hesitated, but then he picked up the phone and answered the call.

"Hey, I gotta say this quick." It was Davey's voice on the other end of the line. Nearly breathless, too, as if he'd just come running from some long distance. "My dad took my phone away and he's not letting me use it, so I had to sneak the call. He's had my phone for days, Cory, and I saw that he kept texting you all this weird stuff. I asked him why but he just told me to go to my room and took my phone away. It's *weird*, Cory. Like, he's been acting so *strange* all of a sudden."

Cory swallowed a lump of spit that felt like a walnut.

"Hey," Davey said. "You there? Cory? Hello?"

"I'm here." He realized he was whispering. "It's not just your dad. And not just Mr. Zachs anymore, either. Are you home?"

"I'm in Winnie's bedroom."

"Look out the window. Do you see that police car?"

A pause. Then: "The one in front of Mr. Zachs's house?"

"Yes. Something is wrong with that cop, too. Also, there's some guy parked in a van up by the stop sign. I saw him when Mom and I came back from dinner yesterday. I can't see him from my house, but maybe you can. Do you see a red van parked down by the stop sign?"

"Hold on."

Cory drifted back out into the hall and through the kitchen. Mr. Zachs was still there, staring at the side of Cory's house.

"Yeah," Davey said, back on the line. "There's a red van parked there, all right."

"That guy's name is Larry and he's the guy who fixed our broken window. Only . . ."

"What?"

"Davey, something is not right with him, either. Something is not *right* with all of them."

"That's why I'm calling you. Hey, hold on," Davey said. "Winona wants to tell you something."

Cory listened as Davey handed the phone over to his sister. Cory could hear the Beatles playing in the background, which was Winona Orem's most favorite music in the world. It sounded like "Yellow Submarine."

Winona came on the line, equally as breathless as her brother. "Hello, Cory!"

"Hey, Winona." His eyes were still glued to Mr. Zachs out there on that beach chair, and that police car sidled up against the curb in front of Mr. Zachs's house.

"Do you remember the drawings in chalk, Cory? The ones put there by the strange man I saw with messages on his face?"

"Y-yes." He heard himself stutter.

"Those drawings are in my dad's head now, just like they're in Mr. Zachs's head. Just like they're in other heads now."

"How many heads?"

"Lots."

"How do you know that?"

"I just do. I feel them *bad* just like I felt those chalk drawings *bad*."

Cory exhaled a shaky breath into the receiver.

"Cory? Am I fancy?"

Voice shaking, he gave her the standard reply: "You're always the fanciest, Winona."

"Good." And he could hear the smile on her face. "And Cory?"

"Yeah?"

"Don't go outside. No matter what you do, don't go outside."

"I don't—"

A figure appeared on the other side of the kitchen window. The suddenness of the figure's appearance caused Cory to jump back, and a small, barely audible squeal escaped his throat.

It wasn't Mr. Zachs, but Tom Orem, Davey and Winona's dad. Unshaven jawline, eyes narrowed fixedly in their sockets, he placed one palm against the windowpane over the sink just as a terrible, toothy grimace overtook one corner of his mouth.

"Hey," Mr. Orem said, voice muffled by the pane of glass between them. "Hey there, Cory. Davey's been asking about you. Why don't you come out?"

Cory took a step back. His heart was suddenly pounding in his throat.

"Cory? Cory?" It was Davey, back on the phone. "You okay?"

Mr. Orem's palm kept clapping against the windowpane. That wolfish grin grew even wider.

"Cory?"

"It's your dad," Cory breathed into the phone.

Davey said, "What?"

"He's here. He's right here."

Soundlessly, Davey's father mouthed *come out come out come out come out come out.*

Another hand-slap against the glass.

"He's scaring me, Davey."

"He's my *dad*, what am I supposed to *do*?"

Mr. Orem's palm dragged audibly down the windowpane. That shark's grin was glued to his face.

*Come out come out come out come out come out.*

Over the phone, he heard Davey shout, "Wait, Winnie—"

—and then he heard Winona shout for her father, not over the phone but distantly out in the street.

Tom Orem turned his head, his eyes swinging in the direction of his house across the street. He cast a final glance at Cory through the window, then disappeared.

Cory hurried into the dining room where he poked his head between the part in the drapes. Across the street, Winona came bolting out of the open doorway of her house, waving and shouting for her father. She ran down the lawn toward the street just as Mr. Orem's shambling form filled up the front window, mere inches from Cory. The sight of him caused Cory to jump back, his breath snared in his throat.

Mr. Orem glanced at his daughter as he moved swiftly across Cory's front lawn with a long-legged, arm-swinging gait that reminded Cory of that grainy filmstrip of Bigfoot trudging through some forest. Winona slung her arms around her father's waist, causing Mr. Orem to stiffen and freeze in mid-stride. A moment later, Davey came bursting out of the house, down the lawn, and across the street. He jumped on his father's back—

—and administered a swift kiss to the side of Mr. Orem's face.

Tom Orem stood there like a mannequin. His face suddenly expressionless, he looked abruptly like someone lost in the woods, uncertain about where he'd been or where he was going. Davey slid off his back and grabbed one of his father's hands; Winona scooped up the other hand, and began tugging him back toward the street. Unmovable at first, Mr. Orem just stood there, his arms pulled like ribbons on a maypole. He kept looking back over his shoulder at Cory's house, muddled confusion on his face. Cory watched as Davey and Winona walked with him back across the street and up the slope of their lawn toward their house. More than once, Mr. Orem turned and looked back over his shoulder, and once, Cory thought the man was capable of seeing him perfectly through the slender part in the drapes.

Cory held his breath until his friends ushered their father back inside their house and closed the door.

Cory exhaled his pent-up breath. He felt like a car tire that someone had suddenly punctured.

*Okay,* he thought, desperate to calm himself down. *Okay, okay, okay.*

In the living room, his mother screamed.

# CHAPTER FIFTY-TWO
# ENDGAME IS NIGH

## 1

All through the night and well into the following afternoon, members of the colony began to disappear. Some stayed away for long stretches of time, while others returned after only having been gone a little while. Alex noticed this with a kind of morbid fascination, much as a man might observe the peculiar habits of a school of fish in an aquarium. He knew where they were going, of course: one by one, they were each summoned to the maintenance shed and to the altar—whatever it was—that resided within. They went as if triggered by some mental alarm, sometimes dropping whatever it was they were in the middle of doing only to zombie-walk down the wooded path that led to the shed. Alex attempted to access the Hive Mind and to glimpse what it was Stinger had placed inside that shed, but he found it had grown more difficult to do so. In fact, he was hearing fewer and fewer thought transmissions as the day went on.

This, he assumed, was Stinger's doing: mentally blocking him because he was no doubt bitter about Alex's refusal to enter the shed. *If you'd like to make a call, please hang up and dial again.* Stinger had also relegated him to security detail for the day, which obligated him to wear an orange construction vest with reflective tape down the sides as he strode around the perimeter of Gladstone Park, making sure to keep any wayward travelers a good distance away. He did this in a repetitive loop, walking the entire boundary of the park, then cutting back to the clearing to observe what was going on at the tower before heading back out to the outskirts of the park again. For the first time in what felt like days, his stomach growled with hunger, and he found that he couldn't recall the last time he'd eaten anything substantial. Moreover, he felt himself flooded with an increasing sense of despondence and despair. He longed to be with his children, missed them terribly, and missed Georgette, too; his wife had never felt more distant from him than she did now.

He began to notice that some of the people who had returned from the maintenance shed were back to work at Hive Center, a renewed desire in their eyes as they tinkered with and fine-tuned the mechanics of the machine. At one point, he saw Sarah Miller meticulously unhooking the straightened coat hangers from the chain-link fence, one at a time, only to reconnect them a moment later a few rungs lower. Alex wandered over to her, watching her work in silence for a while from the opposite side of the fence. These were the wires that ran from the fence all the way to Georgette's colander which sat upside-down in a basketball hoop that was now nailed to a wooden door. He wanted to ask Sarah what she'd witnessed inside the shed, but he couldn't summon the courage. Besides, he had the strong impression that she wouldn't tell him, anyway. He was becoming more and more of an outsider among them, he realized.

The whole thing was beginning to feel preposterous.

Finally, he couldn't help himself. He had to know, and he felt that the future of his family depended on knowing.

"What are you doing?" he asked her.

"Adjusting." Sarah did not look up at him, did not take her eyes from her task.

"How do you know they need to be adjusted?"

"I just know now."

"Is that what you were told in that shed?"

Now, she *did* look at him—a dark and cunning look that, for some inexplicable reason, made Alex feel foolish. "I was told a lot of things," she said, and he watched as one of her hands let go of the wire and slipped down to her stomach. She did not seem to be aware she was doing it.

"Can you tell me?"

She shook her head. "I can't do that. Besides, it wouldn't mean anything to you. It was specific to me."

"Do you know what I'm supposed to do?"

"No. I only know what *I'm* supposed to do. I need to lower these wires."

He backed away from her then, unsettled.

High above the tower, dark clouds continued to collect in the sky. It had seemed as though a storm might come through the night before, but it hadn't. It had held off. Those clouds hadn't moved, however. It was like a thing building momentum, gathering strength for some nefarious purpose. If impending doom had a look.

He backed up into someone. Apologizing, he turned and saw the old man, the owner of the door-turned-chair, standing in a similar fashion, gazing up at the water tank high above the trees. He kept mumbling something over and over beneath his breath. *Endgame*, it sounded like.

Alex quickly sidestepped around him.

*I think it's time I get Georgette and we get the hell out of here. We need to get the girls then get away from this place. From Mariner's Cove.*

Because something, he knew, was about to happen.

Soon.

## 2

He found Georgette standing at the end of a short line that wound from the closed door of the maintenance shed and across the clearing. The sight of her standing there—the sight of *all of them* standing there, not to mention Stinger with his arms folded beside Jack Gordon, appraising the scene like some wartime general—gave Alex a sick, curdling feeling in the pit of his stomach. There were bees in the air, floating around like embers from a bonfire, and Alex was careful to avoid them as he hurried over to his wife.

"Hey," he said, his voice low. "Can I talk to you?"

"Of course."

"Somewhere else, I mean."

She frowned. "I'm in line, Alex."

"It's important."

*(I'M IN LINE ALEX)*

Those thought-words were like a wrecking ball through the center of his skull. He winced, and felt a shock of nerve pain race through his back teeth.

"What's the matter with you?" Georgette asked.

He pressed his lips to her ear and said, "I think we should leave. Please."

She looked at him. For one beautiful moment, she was a college student again, their eyes meeting from across the floor of a rustic Georgetown bar, Alex's heart snagging in his throat at the sight of her, then willing her to come to him, as if he'd possessed some supernatural power over her, *come here come here come here*, and astounding himself when, in fact, she *came*.

But then she blinked and the memory vanished. She was looking at him with a cold, hard stare—a look that couldn't be any more alien on his wife's face.

"This is *important*, Alex. What we're doing here is so *important*. You of all people should know that."

She'd raised her voice, which had attracted the attention of the people in front of her line. Attracted the attention, too, of the two men in the beekeeping suits—Jack Gordon and Barrett Nesmith. They had their mesh helmets under their arms, their faces purple and sweaty from the summer heat. He suddenly realized that he'd been here at the tower for several days with Jack, but only now recognized him as a construction foreman from a project Alex himself had worked on last year over in Pasadena. He lived alone in a small house on Tamarack Way. How had he not recognized the man until now?

"What about the girls?" he said.

Georgette just blinked at him, confused. "Alex, the girls are fine. We haven't left them fending for themselves. They're with your mother. In fact, I just spoke with them on the phone. Everything is—"

"No, you didn't! You didn't speak with them. *Nothing* is fine. *Nothing*."

Jack appeared on his right, Barrett on his left. Someone's hand—strong, immovable—gripped him painfully on one shoulder. Blunt fingers dug into the muscle.

"You're disturbing the peace, Braswell," Jack Gordon said.

"G, please," he said, and reached for her.

She did not reach back.

## 3

They led him back down the path, but when they reached a fork in the path, instead of cutting in the direction of the water tower, Jack and Barrett guided him toward the outskirts of the park, where their cars and trucks were hidden in the wooded areas along Slope Hill. Before they reached the street, Jack pawed at him, peeling the construction vest from him, and slinging it over one beefy shoulder.

"Hold up, bud," Barrett said, arresting Alex's forward momentum with a hand against his solar plexus. He set the beekeeper helmet on the ground. The suit he wore was lined with a confusion of zippers, but Barrett seemed to know how to undo them all without thinking twice. The suit sloughed to the ground like some reptile shedding old skin and Barrett stepped out of it. He reached behind the waistband of his jeans and produced a pistol.

"Jesus," Alex said, and flinched.

"You should have just gone in the shed," Barrett said to him.

"I'm allergic to bees."

"So fucking what? It's important, what we're doing here. You used to understand that, Braswell. Your fucking *wife* does. Maybe you not going in that shed is fucking things up for the rest of us. Ever think of that?"

"I don't think anyone around here has been doing much of their own thinking lately."

"You fucking turncoat coward," Barrett said, then he pointed the gun at Alex's head.

Jack said, "Hold up."

Alex felt a buzzing in his molars. He may have been excommunicated from the Hive Mind—blocked by Stinger like an operator dropping a call—but he could still sense when someone was on the line.

"Put the gun away," Jack said. "Stinger says we're not done with him yet."

Barrett looked disappointed, but he tucked the gun back into the rear waistband of his jeans without protest. Then he gathered up the beekeeping suit and helmet off the ground. "So, what do we do with him in the meantime?"

"Let's bring him back to Hive Center. Final adjustments are being made to the Tower. Stinger says he thinks it's tonight."

"What is?" Barrett asked.

"Endgame."

"Endgame," Barrett repeated, a look of ecstasy passing swiftly across his face.

Jack swung his steely gaze in Alex's direction. "Stinger also said that if you think about sneaking off, going to the cops or whatever, we'll know. And we'll kill your wife."

*This can't be happening. This can't be real.*

"Okay," Barrett said, giving him a shove. "Let's get to moseying, turncoat."

Somewhere in the distance, thunder rang out.

# CHAPTER FIFTY-THREE
# "WE ARE NOT SAFE"

Ellen screamed herself awake, the tendrils of some heinous yet disremembered nightmare still clinging to her. Trailing at the heels of that nightmare, a solitary phrase that seemed disjointed and out of place, like someone else's thought inside her head: *Uncle Brian didn't do what you think he did, Mom. Something bad made him act that way.*

Hearing her scream, Cory rushed into the living room with a stricken look on his face. Not wanting to upset him further, she made a show of smiling and brushing her sweaty hair from her face as she sat up on the couch.

"It's okay, baby. Just a bad dream."

Her son looked terrified.

"What is it, Cory? What's wrong?"

Cory said, "Everything."

She got up and went to him. He felt feverish, his body clammy with sweat. "Tell me," she said, brushing his damp, curly hair out of his eyes.

He took her by the hand and led her into the dining room. The drapes were still drawn and the lights were off, so the room was dark, gloomy. Cory swept aside a section of the drapes and said, "That cop is parked right outside, Mom."

She looked out the window. Yes, there was a police car parked in front of Mr. Zachs's house. The moment she saw this she remembered her dream—of having seen that exact police car from this exact window the night before, and even going outside to get a better look at it. But then she realized that hadn't been a dream at all, that it had actually happened, and that the police car had been parked out there overnight.

"It's the same policeman from yesterday," Cory said.

She believed him.

"Mr. Zachs is still out there, too," he added. "And Mr. Orem across the street."

"Mr. Orem, too?"

"They're all watching us. Also, the man who fixed our window."

"Larry Kotara."

"Yes. He's in a red van parked at the end of the street." Cory, still holding her hand, led her out of the dining room, down the hall, and into his bedroom. He climbed onto his bed and swept aside the curtain. He pressed a finger to the glass. "And there's someone hiding in those trees across the street over there, too. I don't know who it is, but I can sense that he's there."

"What are they all doing?"

"Waiting."

"Waiting for what?"

"For something to happen. For something to . . . to *start.*"

"What, Cory? Waiting for *what* to start?"

Cory turned and looked at her. "I don't know, Mom. But it's something bad. I can feel it." His eyes grew glassy. "We are not safe."

She steeled herself, tried not to let what he'd just said rattle her any more than she already was.

"Listen," she told him. "We're going to be tough, you and me, okay? I won't let anything bad happen to you, Cory. I promise."

"Okay, Mom."

"Come with me."

He followed her into the front hall, where she gathered her purse, car keys, and slipped her feet into a pair of sneakers. Then she searched around the house for her cell phone, ultimately finding it wedged between the cushion of the couch.

"Get your shoes on. We're going to leave here for a while."

"No."

"What?"

"We can't leave. Winona called me and said that whatever we do, we shouldn't leave the house."

"*Who* said this?"

"Winona from across the street."

"Cory, that's ridiculous. Get your shoes on. Please."

He went to the hall closet and tugged on his shoes as Ellen checked her phone. Yes, she could call the police, but what would she tell them? Her neighbor was watching them from a lawn chair on his property? That a *cop* was parked down the block and had been spying on them for the past two days? The police would think she was crazy. She slipped her phone into her purse then headed to the front door.

"Mom, *please*," Cory begged.

She turned to him. "If you think we're in danger here, then I believe you. But that means we should leave, doesn't it?"

"Maybe it's more dangerous out there."

From the foyer, she could see into the dining room and through the part in the drapes over the bay window. She could outrun Mr. Zachs, if it came to that, but that cop car was still there, the shape of a man propped behind the wheel. She doubted she could outrun *him*. Then, on the heels of that: *What the hell am I thinking? Mr. Zachs isn't going to chase us down the block. Some random police officer isn't going to kidnap us. I've got to stop this.*

Maybe she should just step outside and prove to her son that nothing bad would happen to her.

"Listen, Cory. Let's just get into the car and drive away for a while. I think being stuck in this house is doing more harm than good."

His eyes looked fearful . . . but he ultimately nodded his head. A tear slipped down his cheek.

"Don't, baby," she said, hugging him. "Don't get upset. You'll make *me* upset."

But wasn't she *already* upset?

Her mind was a whirlwind: stormy, unsettled.

She unlocked the front door then together they stepped out onto the porch. The midday sun was blazing hot—just how long had she slept on that couch, anyway?—but there were dark, brooding storm clouds collecting along the horizon. Over Gladstone Park.

Together, they moved at a quick clip to the car. Ellen opened the driver's side door and Cory jumped in ahead of her then scooted across to the passenger seat. She saw Mr. Zachs watching them from his beach chair, those ridiculous wraparound sunglasses seeming to squeeze the swollen red tomato of his face. Countless summer days spent in that chair on his lawn had burned him to a crisp.

She got in behind the wheel, slammed the door shut. She heard Cory's seatbelt buckle as she slid the key into the ignition and gave it a crank.

Nothing.

The car would not start.

"Mom?"

"It's okay, babe."

She kept cranking it, but nothing happened. She turned a switch, but the dashboard lights did not come on. The interior dome light above her head was dead, too.

*Dead battery.*

"Mom," Cory said, an elevated sense of urgency in his voice now. She saw he was looking out the passenger window at Mr. Zachs, who had risen off his beach chair. The man stood on the bowed stalks of his pale legs poking from the bottom of his terrycloth bathrobe. She could see the sweat peeling down his crimson face as the sun reflected along his bald pate.

A tingling sensation along the nape of her neck caused her to turn around in her seat. Through the rear windshield, she saw the front door of the Orems' house open across the street. Tom Orem's large, athletic frame suddenly filled the doorway.

"You know what, let's get back in the house," she said, yanking the keys from the ignition.

They hopped out of the car just as Tom Orem began shouting "Hello! Hello!" from across the street. She snatched Cory's hand, rushed up the front walk, and into the house. She felt lightheaded and foolish, because surely their *neighbors* meant them no harm.

*Hello! Hello!*

Cory bolted past her and into the dining room, where he peered out the front window through a part in the drapes. Ellen locked the front door—

*(this is crazy)*

—then came up behind him more slowly. The hair at the top of Cory's head tickled her chin as she peered over him and out the window.

Tom Orem stood in the middle of the street, not moving. There was a bewildered expression on his face. *That's because I ignored his hello and ran into the house like a paranoid lunatic.* Mr. Zachs stood at their property line, his portly body packaged in that too-bright terrycloth robe a ridiculous if not unsettling sight. Maybe, like her, Mr. Zachs was having a mental breakdown.

But it was the cop she couldn't reconcile. At some point, he had gotten out of his police car, and he stood there now, one arm casually on the hood of the car. Like Mr. Zachs, he wore mirrored sunglasses, but she could tell without question that he was staring directly at their house.

*I am losing my mind.*

*This isn't happening.*

"I can't tell what they're thinking," Cory said, his breath fogging up the glass. "They're blocking me."

"Come away from the window."

But he didn't: he leaned so close that his nose nearly touched the glass.

A red van with the words KOTARA WINDOWS & DOORS printed on the side rolled slowly down the street.

Ellen pulled her son away from the window and closed the part down the center of the drapes.

All around them, the lights in the house blinked repeatedly then went dark. She looked at her son. "Was that you?"

Cory shook his head.

# CHAPTER FIFTY-FOUR
# SPOUSE

They had Alex seated on the tree stump, where he'd laid out his paper cutouts once more, each one held in place by a stone, and studied them, or at least pretended to. Georgette watched him from the base of the Tower, as she helped some of the others adjust their items. She was giddy and ebullient, had been since she'd stepped out of the maintenance shed, yet every time she looked over at Alex, she felt something hard and heavy roll over in the center of her chest. He looked like he was studying those cutouts, but she knew Barrett Nesmith, who stood beside him, had a gun in the waistband of his jeans and had no compunction about using it, if Stinger were to give the word. Georgette wouldn't let that happen, of course, but she also did not think things would come to that. The gun and the threat were just parts of an insurance policy. They couldn't have Alex take off, contact the police, contact *whomever*, and have this whole thing shut down. Not now. They were so close.

Anyway, Stinger liked to puff his chest out and show he was in charge. If this made him feel better, then so be it. Still, she wouldn't let anything bad happen to Alex. Of course she wouldn't.

She glanced down at her bare arms and upper chest, the sweat-shiny skin there rippling with bee stings. She hadn't been inside that shed for more than five minutes, but she'd been stung nearly a dozen times. The poison had left her woozy and a little euphoric . . . although maybe that was just the aftereffect of having been shown what she had been shown, having heard what she had heard.

*All hail the Dragon.*

*All hail the Tower.*

It still gave her chills.

Across the clearing, Alex's eyes flashed up in her direction. He wore a pitiable expression, one that appeared so alien on his otherwise compassionate, stoic face. She fired off a thought to him before he had time to look away: *Can you hear me?*

She watched him wince painfully and clamp a hand to his jaw.

*Nod your head if you can—*

He squeezed his eyes shut and plugged one finger into his ear. Beside him, Barrett glanced down and frowned at him.

He couldn't hear her.

Couldn't hear her *words*, anyway.

*(MEET ME ON THE PATH COME ALONE COME NOW I NEED TO TALK TO YOU)*

It was Stinger's thought-message, a sound no different than the thunder that had been rumbling directly above the Tower all afternoon. She slipped out from the bustling confusion that was Hive Center and stalked with her head down across the clearing. She felt Alex's eyes light upon her again—she didn't need special powers to feel it, only wifely powers—but she made sure to keep her head down and not return his stare.

She slipped into the trees and headed down the path in the direction of the maintenance shed. She made it only halfway before Stinger stepped out from the trees just a few feet in front of her, startling her.

"There you are," he said. He was grinning, and what daylight that managed to penetrate the tree branches this deep in the woods fell upon his face in a pattern of shine and shadow. Aside from the knobby red bulges of bee stings along the ridge of his jaw, his face looked nearly skeletal.

He reached out and caressed her bare shoulder. She drew back from him, then watched that grin transform into something more suggestive of a bitter, ugly grimace. He let his hand drop and dangle loosely at his side and didn't try to touch her again.

"Listen, I've been thinking about something," Stinger said. "A guy like your husband, so deathly allergic to bee stings, he must have a few of those . . . whatchamacallits . . . back at the house?" He made a vague jabbing motion that also looked like he was miming masturbation.

She understood, regardless. "EpiPen."

"That's right!" Stinger's eyes lit up. "So why don't you go home, grab a bunch of them, bring 'em on back here. This way, when he goes into the shed and gets stung, you can just . . . you know . . ." Again, with that jerking off motion.

"Maybe if he's stung once or twice that would work. But I got stung about a dozen times. And look at you. You look like fucking braille."

"So then give him more than one 'Pen."

"It's epinephrine. He'd have a heart attack."

"Well, shit. Just so happens we've got a fucking *heart surgeon* on staff. The old guy who brought the door."

"You know, I don't like what you're doing. How you're treating him."

"The old guy?"

"No, Stinger. Alex. He started this whole thing, in case you've forgotten, and you've got Barrett standing guard beside him with a fucking gun like he's some prisoner of war."

Stinger's mouth tightened into a firm, lipless slash. "First of all, *we all* started this. Together. But to be more specific, let's not forget that your husband was out here wrapping the legs of that Tower in fucking *twine* until I showed up and fixed the problem for him. Second of all, your husband is the only one here who has not brought a fucking item. Do you know what that means?"

"Tell me."

"It means that *he* is the missing item."

"The stick figure with a star on its head," she mused.

"Goddamn right," Stinger said.

"That's why you had him sit in that chair beneath the Tower. You thought he might . . . trigger something to happen."

Stinger rolled his shoulders. "Was worth a shot."

"Maybe it's not him. Maybe it's another one of us who's supposed to sit in that chair."

"No." His voice was flat, immovable. "It has something to do with Alex. I know you know that, too. The voice told you, didn't it?"

She couldn't deny that the voice she'd heard coming from the beehive altar had forced the vague suggestion of Alex upon her (among other things), but she hadn't clearly understood what it meant. She came away with the impression that whatever was speaking to them all from inside that beehive wasn't all-powerful and couldn't just impart whatever wisdom it wanted upon just anyone. It had to be the right person. And Stinger believed her husband was that person.

"Let me go back in the shed," she said. "Or, better still, *you* go back in the shed. We might learn what it is without having to involve Alex. Maybe it will come to—"

But Stinger was shaking his head fervently. "No, no, no. It doesn't work that way. You know that, Georgette. We hear only what we're *supposed* to hear. It's all very specific, for whatever strange, cosmic reason. Our . . . our channels . . . aren't opened up enough to hear what's meant for someone else, anyone else. *Just us.*"

She sighed. And when she felt Stinger's eyes running up and down her body, she folded her arms over her chest. "Maybe you should quit ostracizing him, at least."

"What do you mean?"

She pointed to her head. "Blocking him. Cutting him out of the Hive Mind and leaving him on the sidelines."

Stinger frowned. "I'm not doing anything."

"Bullshit. I just tried sending him a message and he couldn't understand me. In fact, it looked like it hurt his head."

"Hey, lady," Stinger said, holding up both hands. He took a step back for exaggerated effect. "That's not me. I'm not blocking anyone."

"Then why can't he hear my thoughts anymore?"

"Because he's a vanishing worker bee," Stinger said. "He's got his mind clouded with other things—his wife, his place in all this, his fucking kids. He's lost the drive, which means he's a threat to the entire colony. That's how colonies collapse. And the only way for him to *get it back*, Georgette, is to get his ass *in the fucking shed*."

The problem was, she knew Stinger was right.

"What happens if he doesn't go in?" she asked. "What happens if we don't get an answer for who's supposed to sit in that chair?"

Stinger appeared to consider this. Scratching the back of his head, he said, "You see the cracks that have been forming? The one behind the Tower? Some others here and there?"

She was aware of the one behind the Tower, as well as a crack that Sarah Miller had found in the bole of a tree: a depthless shadow that she'd watched Sarah toss a rock into, and the rock had just disappeared. As Georgette and Sarah had stared at it, a giant bee that looked like it had been made of pure crystal scuttled out. Its stinger looked like a barbed scimitar and its wings fluttered in a blur.

"Yeah," she said.

"Well, I imagine they'll just become wider and wider. And more will form, all over the place, until this whole neighborhood—hell, maybe this whole planet—becomes one giant crack. Not sure what happens after that, but I imagine it won't be too good."

"You're just trying to scare me."

"This shit *should* scare you. Besides, don't you want to finish this? Don't you want to see it to the end?"

She did.

So fucking badly.

"Endgame," she said.

That elongated grin stretched across Stinger's face again. "Endgame," he said. "So . . . maybe go have a chat with your husband. With, uh, words. Not your mind."

She watched as his hand came up, and she thought maybe he'd stroke her shoulder again, but he didn't. He just scratched his head once more, then pivoted on his heels and marched back down the path in the direction of the maintenance shed.

*Well, I imagine they'll just become wider and wider. And more will form, all over the place, until this whole neighborhood—hell, maybe this whole planet—becomes one giant crack.*

She thought maybe he had been exaggerating in order to convince her to do what he wanted. In fact, she'd stepped out of the maintenance shed with the sense that whatever had spoken to her from within that beehive was weak and scared and possibly on the verge of dying. While Stinger may have been right, and those cracks might very well continue to spread throughout the neighborhood and even the world—

*(the world is a neighborhood)*

—she thought it was just as likely that everything might just return to normal if whatever was in that beehive died.

But she didn't want that to happen.

Was *terrified* of letting that happen.

She turned and headed back toward the Tower. Alex was still perched on the stump, Barrett Nesmith still standing beside him, arms folded like some bouncer at a nightclub. Overhead, the sky had darkened considerably. A storm was coming.

"Hey," she said, coming over to Barrett. "Take a hike for a couple minutes, will ya?"

"Stinger said to hang here."

"Stinger told me to tell you to get lost. Few minutes, tops."

Barrett's eyes narrowed. He wasn't the sharpest tool in the shed, but she could tell that he knew she was telling the truth. Or at least she wasn't here to cause trouble. He rubbed a finger beneath his nose, hitched up his pants, and said, "Five minutes." Then he strolled across the clearing to where Sarah Miller was still adjusting her wires inside the mesh cage at the base of the Tower.

Alex looked up at her morosely. He patted the flattened top of the stump beside him. "Have a seat."

She sat. Slipped a hand into his. Then she dug out her cell phone and held it out toward him. "You wanna call the girls?"

"How many days has it been since we've seen them?"

"Two. Three, tops."

"You don't find it strange that we can't remember?" He was looking at the phone, knowing he could scroll through the logged calls and check the dates, but he made no effort to take it from her. "I think it's been much longer than two or three days."

"So then give them a call. It'll make you feel better to hear their voices."

"I think right now it would make me feel worse."

She hesitated, then tucked the phone back in her pocket. "Listen," she said. "I want to tell you what happened to me in the shed."

He nodded. He was staring intently into her eyes. For a moment, she thought of the day they'd come out here, to Mariner's Cove, looking for a home. Her belly had been swollen with their eldest, Callie, and she recalled how entranced she'd been with the quaint little house in the middle of the neighborhood, with its perfect yard and picket fence and neighbors who smiled and introduced themselves before they'd even bought the place. How she'd gotten spooked by a snake in their front yard on that first day of moving in, and Alex had laughed, hugged her, and told her it was good luck. How after their first week in that house, after neighbors had come on a rotating basis to drop off food and introduce themselves, Alex had leaned over to her in bed and whispered into her ear, *The neighborhood is the world and the world is a neighborhood,* and she had wrapped her arms around him and—

*All hail the Dragon.*

*All hail the Tower.*

She blinked her eyes and said, "I heard a voice come out of a beehive, Alex. The voice of God, maybe. The voice of the Dragon, as Stinger calls it. Maybe it's the same thing, maybe it's not. It showed me how I needed to readjust my colander, to set it lower on the door than we'd originally put it, but it also explained itself to me, or as much as something like . . . something like that . . . can explain itself."

"Something like what?" Alex asked. "What is it?"

She shook her head. "I really don't know. It's nothing you can *see*, just something you *feel*. Stinger calls it a dragon, but that's not really it. I think maybe that's close, but that's not truly what it is. Do you know what I saw when I went in there?"

"What?"

She squeezed his hand in hers and said, "You ever see that movie *Stand by Me*? Where the kids go looking for a dead body that got hit by a train?"

"Sure."

"That scene where they all go swimming and come out of the water covered in leeches?"

"Yeah, I remember."

"That happened to me when I was a little girl. No, not a whole body full of leeches, but one, sucking on my blood right here." She released his hand and pointed to the soft underbelly of her left arm. "I was maybe five or six, Denise's—"

"Denise's age," they said together.

"—and I was so scared when I saw that thing sticking to me that I couldn't scream. Couldn't even move, as I remember it. Just stared at it, terrified, until my father came over, saw it, and pulled it off me. And I remember how it left a little ribbon of blood on my arm."

Alex nodded, and reached for her hand again.

"That's how I pictured it in my head when I was in there," she said. "In the shed. In the . . . in the beehive. It's hard to explain. Kind of like a leech. But I know that's not right, either, just like Stinger calling it a dragon isn't right. It's just what my mind reverted to, because it's the closest thing to what it is that my mind could come up with based on what I've known."

"What does it want from us?"

"For us to send it home."

"Home where?"

"I don't know. A different world. A separate plane of existence. We need to open a doorway for it to pass through. It isn't strong enough to do it on its own."

"But it's strong enough to get us to do all this," he said, and he didn't phrase it as a question. He looked up at the Tower. "And that's what this thing is supposed to do? Open a doorway? Send it back to wherever it came from?"

"If we can finish building it before tonight, yes."

"What's tonight?"

"Endgame."

"But what if the tower isn't ready by then?"

"It has to be." *Because it will die otherwise,* she thought, but did not say.

He looked at her. "If it's here, then where is it now? In that shed?"

"It's everywhere," she said. "All around. It's not a physical thing like you and me. It's not something you can see or touch. But also . . . I mean, I think at the same time it *might* be, too. It's not what we think of when we think of something alive. It's more like a . . ."

"Consciousness," Alex finished.

"Yes. Exactly."

He turned away from her. Looked back at the Tower.

"It's wonderful in there, you know," she said. "In the shed? It makes you feel great. It makes you feel like you're . . . I don't know . . . in between places. Does that make sense? Those bees sort of . . . pull you in . . . and they fill your mind. Stinger keeps going back inside and getting recharged. It's like a drug." She gave his hand another little squeeze. "Things just might be all right for you if you went in there, you know. Whatever that thing is, it needs your help and wouldn't hurt you."

She watched as his face went still. Expressionless. Even his eyes became lackluster. Had she said something wrong? She suddenly worried that she had. "I love you, Alex," she amended quickly, "but this is very important. We need to see this through. We need to finish this tonight so we can get our lives back."

"Why does it matter, G? Why does any of this matter one iota to us?"

She felt that hard and heavy *thing* roll over in her chest again, followed by a wave of disgust that seemed to radiate throughout the entirety of her body. She let go of Alex's hand and stood from the tree stump. She'd said those things—those things about the girls, about getting their family back together—because she knew that was what he'd wanted to hear. But he was looking at her like some . . . some traitor now . . . and she found herself distrustful of what he was even doing here. Yes, he'd located the Tower, had strung that string up around the base, but Stinger had been right: *Stinger* was the one who'd replaced the string with chain-link fencing, *Stinger* was the one who'd brought them all together to the place to facilitate the endgame. And now Alex wanted to ruin it all?

*All hail the Dragon.*

*All hail the Tower.*

And the Hive Mind returned:

*(ALL HAIL THE DRAGON)*
*(ALL HAIL THE TOWER)*

Barrett sauntered over, eating an apple. He looked bored.

"I have things to do," she said to Alex.

"Wait—"

But she didn't wait.

Her mind was racing.

She had things to do.

## CHAPTER FIFTY-FIVE

# CONCENTRATION

It was the Air Man breathing down his neck, whispering in his ear, hot breath like vehicular exhaust:

*I am your brightening star, cowboy.*
*Ten of spades.*
*Eight of clubs.*
*Eight of spades.*
*Five of clubs.*
*Queen of diamonds.*
*Ace of hearts.*

The backs of his hands were smeared in blood from his nose, the cards themselves tacky with bright red fingerprints. The tiled floor of the hotel bathroom, too, was speckled in bright crimson splotches.

*Jack of diamonds.*
*King of clubs.*
*Five of hearts.*
*Nine of spades.*
*Seven of clubs.*

He felt like he wasn't where he was supposed to be.

He felt like the human version of a missed call.

*Six of spades.*
*Two of clubs.*
*King of diamonds.*

He looked up from the cards splayed out before him on the bathroom floor and at the shot glass on the edge of the tub. Inside the tub, the water pounded and gushed down the drain: liquid white noise.

He heard it before he saw it.

The GIDDY UP shot glass rattled against the enameled surface of the tub.

A dull, pulsing light appeared in the center of his brain, the rays of that light growing in intensity, lengthening, lengthening, lengthening . . .

*Rattle rattle rattle.*

A ray of light swept the shot glass along the edge of the tub.

He watched it slide.

*Heard* it slide: *shhhhhhttt.*

*Two of hearts.*
*Three of spades.*
*Jack of spades.*

He redirected his gaze toward the water running from the spigot in the tub.

Liquid white noise.

Stared at it.

Stared . . .

. . . and the whole bathroom seemed to tilt to one side.

No, not the whole bathroom: just that column of running water.

His mind bent it at a forty-five-degree angle, like an elbow.

*King of hearts.*
*Joker.*
*Joker.*

The world went black.

## CHAPTER FIFTY-SIX

# THE ARCHITECT

Despite the cooling temperatures of the early evening, Alex felt a heat prickling along the nape of his neck. He was still seated on the stump, a paper cup of water in one hand, Barrett Nesmith beside him trying not to look bored. He watched as Stinger appraised the tower, hands on his hips like some basketball coach. Most of the adjustments being made were at the base, in Hive Center, but others had climbed the ladder, scaled the chain-link fence, and crowded upon the walkway around the tank, too. It was reminiscent of the dream Alex had been having back when this all had started—being drawn to this place in the night, surrounded by others, and of a multitude of people clinging to the sides of some great—

*(hive)*

—object in the sky. He hadn't had that dream lately—couldn't remember the last time he'd slept, to be honest—but it rushed back to him now with perfect unshakable clarity.

Hands still on his hips, Stinger turned and looked once more in Alex's direction. He began ambling over to him, and as the distance closed between them, Alex saw that there was blood—or something that looked very much like blood—splashed in russet patches across the front of Stinger's shirt and pants. Worse than that, though, were Stinger's eyes: they were ablaze like the headlamps of a car, and nearly glowed in the dark.

*Stinger keeps going back inside and getting recharged,* he recalled Georgette saying. *It's like a drug.*

"Hey, Barrett," Stinger said as he approached. "Why don't you get something to eat? We've got sandwiches up by the shed."

Barrett's eyes ticked toward Alex. "What about . . . ?"

"Alex is one of us. No need for this ridiculousness. Besides, Jack misinterpreted the transmission I sent him. We're not here to hurt anyone. We're family."

"Family." Barrett seemed to chew on the word. Then he shrugged and strode off toward the footpath that led through the woods to the maintenance shed.

"Sorry about all that," Stinger said. He tapped a finger to his temple. "Misunderstanding. Or, I guess, miscommunication. We're all still getting used to it."

Alex smiled weakly. He didn't believe a word of it.

"It's tonight, you know," Stinger said. "It'll happen soon, in fact."

Alex stood from the stump. "Endgame."

Stinger grinned. There were fresh bee stings on the right side of his face, one of which was oozing a glister of pus. "That's right."

"What about the missing piece? Which one of us is supposed to sit in that chair?"

Stinger sighed. He glanced again at the tower from over one shoulder. "Maybe the machine will work without it. Or maybe it'll blow us all to hell. Who really knows? I just know that things have been set in motion and we're all powerless to stop it at this point."

Alex couldn't tell if Stinger was bullshitting him or not. There was no "on" switch to whatever it was they'd built beneath the tower, no power source. How could Stinger be so confident that anything was going to happen tonight?

Georgette appeared out of nowhere and sidled up beside Alex. He felt the faint grazing of her hand at the small of his back, and was instantly troubled by the notion that there was nothing comforting about it anymore.

"I feel it, too," Georgette said. "It's like the air's thickening all around us."

"Tightening," Stinger corrected. He interlaced the fingers of his hands, and Alex could see there was dried blood in the creases of his knuckles, too.

"Yes," said Georgette.

As if cued by this statement, thunder rolled directly overhead—a low, sonorous grinding that, to Alex, sounded like the ancient motors of the universe coming to life. Everyone who was still in the clearing glanced skyward, and those on the catwalk at the top of the tower were briefly silhouetted against a flash of lightning. For a moment, the silvery orb of the moon was occluded by dark, scudding thunderheads that seemed to coalesce directly above the water tower.

"They should get down from there," Alex said, nodding up at the people gathered along the tank's walkway. They were done working, and Sheila Donaldson's television aerial had been repaired and was now firmly fixed to the top of the tank, but they had remained up there, some seated on the walkway, legs dangling over the side.

Once more, he recalled the dreams, early on, where he'd arrived in this very clearing only to have himself and others clinging to the sides of a giant—

*(hive)*

—structure hovering high above the ground.

Stinger followed Alex's gaze, but didn't seem too concerned. Alex didn't trust the feverish look in his eyes. Beneath the moonlight, his welt-lumpy face looked inhuman.

Toward the west, another pulse of lightning creased the sky, a tremendous, forked ribbon of bluish white light. Alex watched as the lightning flashed across Stinger's and Georgette's faces, and was reflected like an electrical fire in their eyes. He could suddenly smell ozone.

There was a man standing several yards behind Stinger. He'd been cloaked in darkness and was only visible now in the lightning flash—there and then gone, in the blink of an eye. With everyone else's eyes turned toward the sky, Alex was the only one who saw him.

Alex stepped around Stinger and approached the man. Stinger called after him, as did Georgette, but he ignored them both. His heart was sounding a steady drumbeat in his ears. He meant to ask the stranger who he was and what he was doing here, because there was something *poignant* that he sensed about the man, yet as he approached and when he opened his mouth, he said, "My name is Alex Braswell. I'm the engineer."

The man nodded, as if he'd expected as much. He was wearing bright red spandex running shorts and a white tank top, and what appeared to be a pained and disoriented expression on his face. The man's face was too thin, except his cheeks looked swollen, making it look like the proportions of him were all out of whack. As Alex stared at him, the man opened his mouth and reached inside, his fingers digging around in there. After a moment, and like a magician pulling a cascade of multicolored silk scarves from his sleeve, this man pulled out a streamer of snarled and bloodied gauze. He released the gauze, which fluttered to the ground at Alex's feet, and then he extracted a second bloody banner of the stuff. When he was done, the man made a dry, sucking sound way back in his throat. Ultimately, and with some apparent discomfort, the man introduced himself.

"My name is Raj Subador. I am the architect."

It was then, during another flash of lightning, that Alex saw that the man's bare arms and legs, his upper chest and neck, his face, were all covered in those strange symbols. He couldn't tell if they were tattoos or if they'd simply been drawn there by marker—some of them *did* appear to be smeared—but regardless, he knew right away what they were. Which meant he knew who this man was, too.

"You're the one who's been drawing these symbols in the streets," Alex said.

"I'm sorry," said Raj Subador. It wasn't the response Alex had been anticipating. "I couldn't help myself. I still can't." The man's voice was mushy, as if talking caused him great pain. His hands shook, too, and when Alex looked down at them, he saw the palms were streaked with bright orange spray paint. There was a spiral drawn in black marker in the center of his left palm, a stick figure with a star on its head on the right.

Alex reached out and gripped the man by the right wrist. "What does this symbol mean?"

"I don't know. I don't know what any of them mean. I just see them in my head and am compelled to reproduce them."

"I need to know what it means. I need to know who it's supposed to be. Which one of us?"

"I tried to silence the . . . the voice in my . . . my teeth . . . telling me to do these things. I'm just so sorry for any confusion it's caused." The man's mushy voice sounded close to cracking.

Alex released the man's wrist. "Where did you first see them?"

"In my head. And then, after that, everywhere I look. Everything is a symbol to me now. Everything is a sign. No words, just symbols. Except for this. This one looks familiar. This one suggests *words* to me."

He turned his left arm over. Written on the flesh of his inner arm in that same black printing, it said:

the Boy

"I don't even know what it says," said Raj. "Only that it's like a memory from before, when I could read and write properly. Before whatever it is that came and crawled inside my head like a parasite . . ." There were tears standing in the man's eyes and a sad little smile on his lips. He appeared to look down at the phrase written on his arm with a mixture of melancholy and longing.

"It says 'the boy,'" Alex told him. And something about it . . . something about that phrase, *the boy* . . . provoked something indistinct inside him. His back teeth began to buzz. "What does it mean? Who's 'the boy'?"

"I don't know. I don't know what it means. They just come to me and I'm helpless not to write them down." Raj Subador looked up at him, those dark eyes glistening. A tear spilled down one swollen cheek. "I became obsessed. They got inside my head, these symbols, and held me prisoner. Prisoner from the inside-out. They're still doing it, even though I took my teeth out and tried to stop them. I can feel some separate living, *thinking* thing inside my head. Its mind has roots like a plant and its thoughts are intertwined with my own. I can't stop them, and *I* can't stop. It won't let me be. It won't . . . it won't leave me alone . . ."

He looked down at his paint-splattered palms, which shook all the more now. The man looked like he wanted to drop to his knees and weep, and Alex Braswell felt pity for him.

"If it's any consolation," Alex said, "I think it ends tonight. One way or another."

A weak smile cracked the man's features. It was then that Alex realized just how terribly *thin* he was—nothing but skin and bones packaged in a tank top and spandex running shorts—and the corners of that hideous smile seemed to extend beyond the boundaries of his face. "That," said Raj Subador, "would be nice." Then the man's eyes grew foggy and distant. "I'm so . . . goddamn . . . *tired*," the man gasped . . . then collapsed into Alex's arms.

Georgette and Stinger rushed over. They watched as Alex eased Raj onto the ground. Raj was shivering, although when Alex touched a hand to his forehead, he found the man's flesh to be burning hot and sticky with sweat. Some of the inked symbols came off on his palm as he drew his hand away. A number of others came ambling over to watch the spectacle.

Someone said, "I'm a doctor."

Alex looked up and saw the old man who had come with the door standing above him. There was a look of paternal concern in his somber, gray eyes. As Alex stared up at the man, the Hive Mind abruptly spoke up and told him the man's name:

*(MICHAEL DANVER)*

The sound of the Hive Mind was like a jolt to his system, and Alex felt himself recoil. A moment after that, he thought to himself, *Guess I'm back online.*

Danver leveraged to his knees to examine Raj Subador. Raj wasn't unconscious—his eyes were wide and staring, darting from side to side in their sockets—but he didn't look altogether there, either. Danver leaned close to Raj's face, examined his pupils, then pressed an ear to the man's frail and heaving chest. As he did so, Raj released a desperate wheeze of air that concluded in a disquieting rattle.

"This man is having a heart attack," Danver said. He looked up at Alex and the others, his expression impossibly calm. "He needs an ambulance to get him to a hospital if he's going to survive."

"Who is he?" Stinger asked.

*The architect*, Alex thought. And then he looked up and saw them all standing there, including himself, reflected in the faces of all the others. He saw the old doctor and thought, *The heart.* He saw Sarah Miller and thought, *The lifeblood.* He saw Georgette and thought, *The soul*, and when he looked at her more closely and saw himself staring back, he thought, *The engineer.* They all played a part; they were all exactly what they had brought to the table. They had become their own puzzle pieces.

Stinger repeated, "Who is he? Where'd he come from?"

"He's the architect," Alex said. Looking up at Stinger, and feeling somewhat ill as he did so, he thought, *Stinger is the drive. He's the determination. He's the juggernaut who will see this thing through to the end, no matter what the cost. He's the brain.*

Stinger lowered himself to his knees beside Alex. He ran a hand along the symbols printed across Raj's exposed flesh. "Jesus, look at 'em all," he muttered.

Raj's eyes rolled back in his head. His body bucked, then he went still. It looked oddly peaceful.

Danver leaned over the man and began administering chest compressions.

"Let him die," Stinger said.

"Oh, no," Sarah Miller said. She was standing beside Georgette, hands clasped together against her abdomen. "Please, no."

Stinger waved a dismissive hand. "His job is done. There are more important things to attend to. We need to prepare for the endgame." His gaze swiveled toward Alex, who felt his stare against his skin like hot embers.

Danver leaned over Raj's face. He tipped his head back on his neck with one hand, pinched his nose with the other, and exhaled into his mouth.

"Let him *die*," Stinger repeated.

Danver's eyes flicked briefly in Stinger's direction, then Alex's, but he did not stop. It wasn't so much a thought that the old doctor transmitted into Alex's head, but a tumult of conflicting emotions that resonated with Alex like mental nausea. Danver administered another breath, then returned to giving chest compressions. His forehead was shiny with sweat.

Alex stood and backed away from the scene. He could hear the rumbling of the Hive Mind again, a low but raucous din of multilayered thoughts swirling beneath the surface of his own.

Stinger stood as well. His gaze was still locked on Alex. Behind him, Jack and Barrett appeared like two henchmen. Barrett held the gun in one hand and wasn't too concerned about hiding it.

"Like I said," Stinger announced, his voice loud yet his eyes still locked intimately on Alex. "It ends tonight."

Barrett lifted the gun and pressed the barrel against Georgette's temple.

*"No!"*

He lunged for Barrett, but Jack Gordon suddenly filled up his field of vision, right hook swinging and slamming Alex along the left side of his face. Fireworks exploded before his eyes and his knees turned to jelly, though he managed to keep himself upright as the world spun around him. The sudden pain in his jaw momentarily rivaled the buzzing in his teeth.

Before he could clear his head, Jack was spinning him around and bending one arm behind his back, painfully thrusting his wrist toward the center of his shoulder blades.

"Don't break the fucker's arm," Stinger commented offhandedly.

Alex's vision cleared. He saw Georgette still standing there, the barrel of the gun still pressed to her temple, an empty expression on her face. No, not quite empty—she looked *compliant.* Like she would allow this man to shoot her in the head if her husband continued to resist.

"Let's go to the shed," Stinger said.

## CHAPTER FIFTY-SEVEN

# THE WIDENING GYRE

When he closed his eyes, Cory could sense the widening of some great and impossible gyre, a crater in the face of the planet that had not been caused by some mighty celestial impact but as the ghost of something that had yet to occur. He attempted to move items around the house with his mind—simple things, like spoons or pencils—but he found that the gnome was unable to do so. It felt like something from the *outside* was restraining it.

His mother appeared in the hallway holding her cell phone. When she sensed his eyes on her, she looked up. The fear on her face frightened him. He attempted to search her thoughts but found that he couldn't—that the gnome, restrained by those men watching the house, had been rendered powerless. This realization frightened Cory all the more.

"My phone has no signal," she said. "Let me see yours."

"Mine doesn't, either."

She ran a hand through her hair. "Okay, okay, okay . . ." She went to a window, peered out through the blinds. It would be fully dark out there soon, and that did not make Cory feel much better. That encroaching sense of doom—that widening gyre—was growing stronger by the minute. He could tell that his mother felt it, too; her emotions radiated off her like an odor, her fear that outside was *danger,* outside was *unsafe,* and she needed to PROTECT MY SON at all costs. He didn't need the gnome to tell him these things.

Those men outside were blocking the gnome from accessing their minds, yes, and also restraining it from accessing his mother's thoughts as well. But could he go *beyond* them, like shooting a flare over the wall of a castle? The same way he'd fired off that mental S.O.S. to Uncle Brian when he was halfway across the country?

The gnome inside his head was frightened, too. It hid now in the farthest recess of Cory's mind, cloaked in darkness, not moving. Cory closed his eyes, and for one brief moment, he could actually *see* the gnome, which wasn't truly a gnome at all, and he told it to fire off that shot to wherever Uncle Brian was—

—but the gnome couldn't do it. Those men outside had trapped it in the cage of Cory's mind. He could feel their collective mental energy pressing down on the gnome like a physical weight, restraining it and its power.

*Why?*

Those men out there didn't want him using the gnome's power. For whatever reason, they wanted to keep Cory powerless.

He glanced over at the TV remote that sat on the coffee table. He told the gnome to move it, but the gnome did not respond. He focused harder, but it felt as though the gnome was retreating deeper and deeper into his mind. No, not retreating: something was dragging it off into the darkness. Holding it prisoner.

*Those men outside.*

He felt something tickling his nose, and when he touched his fingers to it, they came away wet with blood.

"Oh," his mother said, looking at him. "Oh, Cory."

She rushed to him, wrapped him in a strong embrace. When he pulled away, he could see the blood he'd left behind on her shirt.

Once again, the lights fluttered.

"Please, Cory, tell me—*are you doing this*?"

"No."

"Are you making me crazy like this? Are you the one who's doing it?"

"I'm not doing anything, Mom."

She gripped the sides of her head with both hands. "This isn't *happening*."

*I can't move things anymore, Mom,* he wanted to say, even opened his mouth to say it, but only a hiss of air came out. *I can't move things anymore and something is about to happen and I'm so scared, Mom. I'm so scared.*

"I'm going to make sure the windows are locked," she said, rushing out of the room.

Cory went into the kitchen, pulled open the junk drawer, and rummaged around in there until he found an old deck of playing cards. He brought them into the living room and sat on the couch, setting the deck of cards on the coffee table in front of him.

*Queen of clubs.*

He turned the first card over.

Six of spades.

*Wake up!* he shouted at the gnome. *We need your help!*

But the gnome did not respond.

# CHAPTER FIFTY-EIGHT

# 1183

A ferocious growl caused Danver to look up at the night sky. Storm clouds had collected directly above the water tower, occluding the moon, and dousing both the clearing and Michael Danver himself into absolute darkness. This was the exact image his father had shown him over and over again in his dreams, when Hal Danver, a section of his head blown apart, would lean forward in his wingback chair and draw back the curtain on the window to reveal a storm-riddled landscape with something huge and momentous hovering above the earth in the distance. A dream come to reality.

Danver looked down at the man who lay dead on the ground before him. Throughout his career, Danver had lost a number of patients on the operating table—it was par for the course, something that couldn't be helped—but looking down at this man now, he found himself shaken by such a profound sense of failure and grief that he felt his face grow hot and his hands, those lifelong steady instruments of his, begin to tremble. He was thinking of Miranda, her body swaddled in sheets atop their marital bed back at the house on Bay Road. How had she died again? A fall, an accident, or maybe something to do with her dog, Clementine?

*What am I doing here?*

The clearing surrounding the water tower was now empty. Everyone else had followed Stinger and Alex Braswell to the maintenance shed, leaving a cold emptiness in their wake. Leaving Danver leaning over a dead man whose life he'd been powerless to save.

Movement in the periphery of his vision, then: a woman in a waitress uniform ghosting toward him up the gravel path that wound through the trees.

*Where am I? What am I doing here?*

The woman in the waitress uniform came right up to the body of Raj Subador, then she slowly lowered herself to her knees. Her face was bruised, her left eye swollen, her lower lip split, and there was some dried blood on the front of her outfit. But when she smiled at him, Danver felt a heat radiate off her, as if she'd been touched by the Finger of God, and something about that smile brought to him a modicum of serenity.

"You're crying," she said.

He was, although he hadn't realized it until she said something. He pawed the tears from his eyes and the thought of Miranda quickly fled from his mind, replaced by the incessant drumming of a thousand bees. "I've been dreaming of this," he said. He stared up at the water tower, and at the storm clouds roiling directly above it. As if to underscore this, lightning leapt within those clouds, followed by the guttural grumble of thunder.

"We all have," said the woman.

"I don't know what's happening here," he confessed to her. "I don't know what any of this is about. I don't know why I'm here or why I'm doing any of this. Yet I can't stop. I can't help myself."

"Yes, I know." She extended a hand to him, but the distance was too great for her to reach him. And he didn't extend a hand to her in return. "You should have visited the altar."

"They took that man Alex to the altar."

"Yes. Maybe that will fix everything. I feel that maybe it might. Still, you should have gone. It would have renewed your sense of purpose here among us."

Danver looked down at the man who lay motionless before him, as if this was some excuse. "Have you visited it?"

"I have."

"What did it tell you?"

"It told me what my role is in all this. And it made a crack inside me."

"A crack," he repeated, his voice a low growl. "I've been inside one, you know." He held up his bandaged hand.

"I think it's time we start up the machine," she said, and then she brushed back her hair and tilted her head to one side, exposing a pale, slender, moonlit panel of neck. Danver didn't understand what she was showing him until a solitary honeybee flew out of an invisible gap just below her left ear. As he stared, more bees spiraled out, until there was a dizzying black swarm of them orbiting around the woman's head. Danver sucked in a breath and felt a number of those bees go down into his throat—felt them squirm and twist and wriggle as he gulped them down. He felt their bristling bodies crawl into his nostrils and gather in his ears. He inhaled, taking a whole clot of them into his lungs. He brought both hands up to his throat, feeling like he was choking. But then the feeling passed, and when it did, and he found himself still kneeling there in the soft loam of the clearing, staring at a young woman in a waitress uniform with a dead body splayed out on the ground between them.

The woman tilted her head forward, eyes leveling on him, hair falling back over the invisible crack in the side of her neck.

"All hail the Dragon," she said.

"All hail the Tower," Danver responded. He stood and turned around. In his sandaled feet, he shuffled across the clearing toward the Tower. When he stepped through the opening in the chain-link fence, it was like stepping into a sensory deprivation chamber. The world went silent. The air became motionless. Something felt funny with his hand beneath that gauze bandage. A tingling, almost.

*The door.*

He went to it now. It was bolted to the center post of the Tower, a metal spaghetti strainer in a basketball hoop nailed to it. But below the strainer, he could see the holes in the wood where the numbers had once been.

He dug them out of his breast pocket now, those four metal digits. They felt weighty and important in his hand.

There was a hammer and some nails in a toolbox at his feet. He gathered them up and, one at a time, gently hammered each digit back on to the—

*(door-becomes-chair)*

—door.

When he was done, he stepped back to review his handiwork.

## 1183

He frowned, took a step forward. Reached out and repositioned those numbers so that they laid now on their side:

11 8 3

A pale bluish light radiated down from the colander, forming a spotlight on the canvas seat of the camping chair that was attached to the lower half of the door. Slivers of light poked through the holes in the colander and radiated along the wires that were sticking out of them.

A single bee flew out from beneath the colander, spiraled lazily in the air, then disappeared into the night.

*Cracks*, Danver thought . . . or maybe it was his dead father, muttering inside his head. *Cracks all over the place.*

He was suddenly aware of the woman in the waitress uniform standing directly behind him.

She slipped a hand into his.

# CHAPTER FIFTY-NINE
# IN THE HIVE

Darkness.

Alex sat cross-legged on the floor of the shed in front of a chest of drawers that hummed as if with an electrical current. The only illumination was in the form of a bland shaft of moonlight issuing through a narrow window toward the back of the shed. The air around him was alive with bees; he could feel the stirring of their multitudinous wings as they bulleted past his sweaty flesh and coasted along the fine hairs on his arms. There was a humming inside his head, too, radiating from his bottom molars, branching out until it vibrated throughout the marrow of his bones.

*Spiral.*

The word came to him without meaning. He recalled one of the symbols as a never-ending spiral, a vortex that might serve as a portal that might serve as a wormhole that might serve as a—

The room began to rotate all around him.

Or maybe *he* was in rotation.

*Zzzzz . . . zzzzz . . .*

Little by little, he began to feel the bees light upon his flesh. He closed his eyes and braced himself for the inevitable burning pinch of their stings, those tiny, poison-filled rapiers that would bring about his death, but that did not happen; the bees merely crept along his arms, his neck, across the curved plane of his forehead, the backs of his trembling hands. They were in his hair and whispering in his ears. In his mind, as the room spun, he was imagining the links in the chain-link fence at the base of the Tower, and how it had all started out with a simple ball of twine and an inexplicable obsession, wrapped around and around, much like the shed itself rotated around and around, interlaced over and over, a repeated—

*(zzzzz zzzzz)*

—hashtag pattern—

*(zzzzz)*

—that looked like—

*—honeycomb.*

A hexagonal channel at the center of a hive. Walls strumming with the sounds of countless bees. Things here *breathed*. And there, at the end of that deep channel: a tiny pinpoint of light.

He pursued the light, somehow knowing there was salvation in it, that there was *enlightenment* in it, an altogether different type of illumination, and as that pinpoint of light grew incrementally larger, so did the strumming of the bees within the honeycombed walls of the hive. Their sound grew louder and louder. The bees were furious. The bees needed to extract THE THING that was stuck in here with them. Also, the bees *were* THE THING. Conjoined. As one. This symbiotic coexistence. This unsteady, unnatural totem. This could not last much longer. The bees were desperate to go about their mindless, obsessive business. Desperate to get THE THING back home.

That widening sphere of light . . .

. . . opened . . .

. . . upon a bright, sunny day.

And Alex opened, too.

He—

*—stands here beside his wife in the front yard of their new home, a sense of pride filling his chest, his wife, G, always G, cradling the bump of her belly, and he thinks,* Family, *thinks,* This is how you start a life together,

*thinks,* This neighborhood is our world now and our world is this neighborhood, *and she says, "Oh, babe, feel," and she takes his hand and presses it to the swell of her abdomen, and he can feel the baby in there, the child they will name Callie, a start of a family that is bigger than just the two of them together, grander, because it is a new life they have created together from nothing, from a wispy-wisp, and then G, she says, excitedly, "Look! Look, Alex!" and she is pointing excitedly and yet with evident trepidation to the bright green lawn at their feet, at the grass, at something* in *the grass, and Alex does not see it at first, or maybe he does, only in a flash, a wisp, a spousal transmission from his wife's head into his own before he* actually *sees it, and there it is, a thing moving in a winding series of S-shapes through the grass, sleek black body, maybe three feet long, the miniature plates of its reptilian hide shimmering like an oil slick beneath the summer sun, and Alex says, "It's just a snake, hon," and G says, "I don't like snakes," and Alex says, "They have them in the suburbs," and G says, "I'm afraid of snakes," and he laughs, and says, "You don't have to touch it," and adds, "It won't hurt you, G," and G says, "But they bite," and Alex says, "It's good luck," and then he hugs her, and G says, "I want to tell you something," and he says, "What?" and G says . . .*

*. . . G says . . .*

*. . . says . . .*

There once was a snake that came upon a beehive. The snake had never seen a beehive before, and it was curious, so it wound its long body around the hive, making circles, circles, circles, until it found an opening. Curious, the snake went inside.

Just as the snake had never seen a beehive, the bees inside the hive had never seen a snake. This was because they were from two different worlds. The strangeness and alienness of the snake prevented the bees from seeing it, which allowed the snake to slither its way through the multitude of chambers that comprised the interior of the hive, unobserved by the bees.

The snake, being from a different world, was equally as unfamiliar with bees, and so there was much for it to see and learn as it watched and listened and tasted the air. It kept winding itself through the chambers of the hive, deeper and deeper, circles upon circles, hungry for more things to see, more things to learn. It did this for a very long time, until one day the snake grew so tired that it fell asleep.

When the snake finally awoke, it found itself stuck inside one of the narrower chambers of the hive. It tried to slither out but couldn't. It tried to break the hive apart with its strong, muscular body, but all that did was create cracks in the hive through which the snake could glimpse pieces of its world but could not reach it. You see, all its travels had made the snake weak, and now it feared that it might die in the hive.

With its last bit of strength, the snake gave a twirl of its tail, which created a storm inside the beehive. Things were cast about in disarray. Droplets of honey and beeswax were dislodged from their cells and scattered about the various chambers of the hive. And while the bees could still not see the snake, they could no longer deny its presence among them.

Together, the bees used these dislodged bits of honey and wax to construct a doorway through which the snake could escape and return home. It was a grand doorway, and the bees were very proud of it. The only problem was that the snake was still so very weak and could not flee from the hive on its own accord. The snake needed *power.* The snake needed—

the
boy

—and with this newfound power, the snake burst through the doorway, whipping its tail one last time as it fled for home, destroying much of the hive and many of the bees who had helped rescue it in the process.

Alex opened his eyes. He was no longer standing in the bright sunshine of his front lawn with Georgette, nor was he sitting cross-legged on the floor of the maintenance shed in Gladstone Park. Instead, he was standing in the center of Poplar Station Road, sweat boiling into steam off his body, his heart speed-bagging against the desperate, heaving wall of his chest. Moonlight illuminated a series of cryptic symbols spray-painted in the center of the road, and he started out in a jog, following them, his breath rasping up the ragged channel of his throat. His body felt thick and swampy. Something wasn't right, but he kept running, running, running.

By the time he reached Cloister Road, the streetlamps were blinking and the sound of distant thunder was a steady, unrelenting tumult. He ran through what felt like a web of jumbled thoughts—not his own—and a man in a red panel van jumped out of the driver's seat and jogged alongside him. Alex glanced at the man, not slowing his pace. They did not need to exchange words for Alex to know this man was *with him*, had been *waiting for him*, had been biding his time for this very moment. It wasn't until he was within a block of his destination that he saw two more people gathered in the middle of the street, their slack-jawed faces staring at a single-story house with all the blinds and curtains drawn. Despite the hollow pounding of his footfalls on the pavement, they did not turn to look at him.

The night was humid but windy. The air was redolent with static. As he and the man from the van slowed to a walk, he saw the door to a police car which was parked along the curb pop open. A cop climbed out, glanced briefly at Alex, then joined the other two men already in the middle of the street. In silence, everyone turned and stared at the boy's house. Alex heard additional footfalls; he looked over his shoulder and saw a younger man hurriedly crossing the street. It was Eric Rhodes, Alex realized, though he wasn't surprised. The kid had felt out of place back at the Tower; here, among these other men, watching this house and tamping down the boy's powers was where he'd been meant to be.

Alex thought of the stick figure with the star on its forehead, transmitting that image to the other five men who had gathered around him. He could feel their steamy, commingled breath on his sweaty skin as they crowded closer. They were a pack of wild animals.

*Bring the boy.*

They all served a purpose—the architect, the engineer, the heart, the lifeblood, the soul, and so on. The boy served a purpose as well, and it was the boy that was truly the most important piece.

The boy was the *engine.*

"He's in there," said a man in a blinding white bathrobe and wraparound sunglasses. "He's got some . . . some power . . . but I've been blocking it and holding it down." The man seemed to just now realize he hadn't been doing this alone, and added, "We all have."

"What do we do now?" asked Eric.

Alex said, "We go in and get him."

## CHAPTER SIXTY

# THE BOY

### 1

They came.

It started with the sound of the doorknob on the front door jiggling. Cory heard it and looked up. He could see it from across the living room, where he sat on the couch before the small coffee table, a deck of playing cards splayed out before him. He'd gone through the deck three times, hadn't guessed a single card correctly, and he could no longer see or feel the gnome anywhere inside his head. He'd been abandoned.

The doorknob jostled again. It was almost imperceptible, a mere wiggle, as if the person on the other side was simply testing to see if it was locked. Cory stared at it, his eyes widening. When the doorknob rattled more forcefully, he opened his mouth to scream for his mother, but his throat had tightened, and only a reedy, pained whistle came out.

He heard glass break in the kitchen—it shattered and tinkled to the floor. The window over the sink.

His vocal paralysis broke. He screamed for his mother then bolted off the couch just as he heard footsteps tromping the boards of the deck at the rear of the house. As he backed into the hall, he saw first one window shatter, then another, behind the couch. A pale hand streaked with blood and clutching a large stone pushed through the broken window and got tangled in the blinds. It was like watching something crawl from a grave.

When he felt someone rush up behind him and snatch him up in a bear hug, he screamed again. The person shouted his name over and over against the side of his face, but he wasn't listening. He kicked his legs but that only caused the person holding him to tighten their grasp.

"Cory, *stop*!"

It was his mother.

She released him, but he spun around and clung to her again. Running her fingers through his hair, she said, "We need to—" when more glass was busted from the window frames and shattered across the floor. When his mom screamed, he squeezed his eyes shut, buried his face into her chest, and wished the gnome could make them both disappear.

"Get in your room!" his mother shouted. When he didn't budge, she screamed, "Go!" and gave him a shove down the hallway.

Through tear-blurry vision, he saw someone climbing through the busted window behind the couch. A hairy forearm poked through the slats in the blinds and pawed blindly at the air. There were deep, bleeding gashes carved in the skin from the broken, jagged teeth of glass protruding from the windowsill, but that didn't seem to slow him down. With mounting horror, Cory saw it was Mr. Zachs from next door. Yet there was nothing of the former Mr. Zachs in the scowling, lacerated face that poked sneering through the blinds, both hands clawing their way over the couch while leaving bloody streaks on the cushions. Mr. Zachs grunted as he wormed through the window, the blinds crashing down around him, his bathrobe peeling from his back, and ultimately collapsed on the floor beside the couch in a heap.

"Cory!" his mother shouted again, and he could hear her voice rupture. But then she shrieked again as Mr. Zachs rose from the floor beside the couch.

Cory turned and was about to bolt down the hall toward his bedroom when a second figure ambled into sight at the opposite end of the hallway. The man took a step toward him, hands splayed out in front of him the way someone might approach a dangerous dog—wary, but with authority.

"Get out of my house!" Cory shouted at the man.

Implausibly, the man placed an index finger against his lips and said, "Shhhh," then took another cautious step in Cory's direction. It was the man who'd come to replace the kitchen window, Cory realized, his hair in tangles, his mouth a sour grimace, as if it pained him to take each step. He was still wearing the work shirt with his name, LARRY, stitched upon the breast.

Somewhere behind him, he heard his mother scream again. Cory turned and ran in the direction of that scream just as Mr. Zachs struggled to climb to his feet. His bathrobe swung open, revealing a startling white, hairless paunch and a pair of Bermuda shorts. His meaty thighs were bleeding, too, and he staggered forward in a determined daze. His sunglasses gone, Mr. Zachs's eyes were moist and squinty, and as Cory stared at him, he could see the man's mouth begin to work, an intonation rumbling up and out of his throat: "*Relax... relax... relax...*"

The policeman came into the living room through the kitchen. He held a club in one hand, which he'd likely used to break the kitchen window. Bits of broken glass glimmered like raindrops on his uniform. He was followed by a boy perhaps in his early twenties, face smudgy with dirt. Another man appeared in the foyer and began advancing toward Cory and his mom with the slow, measured gait of a jungle cat.

"We're not here to hurt you," said the man in the foyer.

Larry the window repairman filtered into the room, too. He swiped a ribbon of blood from his forehead, examined his scarlet fingers, then frowned. When he looked back up at Cory and his mother, the man looked about as confused as someone who'd just been sucker-punched in the face.

"We just want the boy," said the man advancing toward them from the foyer.

When the policeman crept further into the room, Cory's mother gave Cory another shove, propelling him forward. "Basement!" she shouted at him. "Now!"

He ran and she ran after him. They skirted around the cop, then cut through the kitchen just as someone crashed into the side door of the house. The whole frame shook then splintered. When the door swung open, Cory saw Davey's father, Tom Orem, standing there. Cory leapt over a scatter of broken glass and gripped the basement doorknob with both hands. He yanked it open just as his mother slammed against his back, nearly sending him cartwheeling down the stairwell. But she looped an arm around his waist at the last minute and prevented the fall.

"Go! Go!" she shouted, swatting him on the backside.

Cory raced down the stairs. Above, it sounded like someone sliding a heavy piece of furniture across the floor.

His mom rushed down after him, but not before slamming the door behind her. When they reached the bottom, he found himself vibrating like a knife that had been flung blade-first into a plank of wood. If asked, he would have said that their basement contained no weapons . . . but he soon realized this was wrong when his mother dumped a metal toolchest over onto the floor, spilling out its contents. *Anything*, he realized, could be a weapon. Screwdrivers, a hammer, a hacksaw: perhaps unconventional, but they could certainly inflict some damage. His mother snatched up the hammer and one of the larger screwdrivers and thrust them both toward him. He only stared at them, frozen in place.

"Take them!" she shouted at him, hair swinging in damp rattails across her face.

He took them, one in each hand. Each item felt like it weighed two hundred pounds.

*Wake up, wake up, wake up!* he screamed at the gnome.

There was a small axe beneath the stairwell—a hatchet, really—which his mother yanked from its wall brackets. When the sound of something heavy scraping across the floor above came again, they both glanced up at the low ceiling rafters. Dust wafted down into Cory's eyes. The pull-chain that served the exposed bulb at the center of the ceiling swung lazily, as if stirred by a soft breeze.

*Why aren't they coming down after us?*

Then all the noise stopped.

His mom clutched the handle of the hatchet in both hands, her teeth gritted. She took two steps toward the bottom of the stairs then peered up at the closed basement door. Cory could hear her violent respiration, the aching pulse of her heartbeat. Or was that heartbeat his own?

Then: footsteps. Slow and deliberate. Cory felt the weapons in his hands shrink. The footsteps moved across the floor above—the kitchen floor now—until they stopped directly behind the closed basement door.

"They won't get you," his mother rasped in a near whisper. It was a mantra she began to repeat: "They won't get you . . . they won't get you . . ."

Above his mother's whispering, Cory thought he could hear other voices, too—voices from upstairs. They were talking in low, muttering, unintelligible tones. The only other sound he could hear was the blood rushing through his ears, a sound as loud and as furious as a waterfall.

The basement doorknob slowly turned. Cory held his breath. His mother took a step in front of him, the hatchet held out before her like a religious artifact. The rich odor of fear filled his nostrils.

*Wake up, wake up, wake up!*

The basement door creaked open. Slowly. Cory's mom sucked in an audible breath. A man's silhouette revealed itself at the top of the stairs. The other men crowded around behind him, and Cory glimpsed briefly the peeling, sunburned crown of Mr. Zachs.

"We're not here to hurt anyone," said the man at the top of the stairs. "We've only come for the boy. We need his help. That's all. We don't mean to frighten you. We just need to bring the boy. If you would just give—"

*"Who the fuck are you people?"* his mother screamed up the stairwell.

"We're neighbors," said the silhouette. "The world is a neighborhood, and the neighborhood is the world."

*"Get the hell out of my house!"*

"Not without the boy."

The silhouette descended a step.

*Wake up, wake up, wake up!*

But these men were using their minds to keep the gnome from doing its tricks. How they were able to do this, Cory didn't know, but he could feel their probing, tentacular thoughts suspended like cables in his head, holding the gnome down. Restraining it.

"Don't you move!" his mom shouted. "I've got a gun!"

"No, you don't," said the man as he descended another step. "Officer Grayson here does, but we'd prefer not to use it. We really don't want to hurt anyone, lady. Not you or your son. And I'm sure you've got something down there that you could use to inflict some serious damage, but that's not what we want, either. It's not what any of us want, is it?"

The man descended another step.

Then another.

Then another.

And then there he was: a regular-looking guy whom Cory had seen around the neighborhood before. In fact, he knew the man had two daughters and a wife who'd once taught him piano lessons and he thought their last name was Braswell.

The man's hands were up, either in a defensive posture or to show that, despite breaking into their home, he meant them no harm.

His mother took a step toward him, chopping feebly at the air between them with the hatchet. A sob ratcheted from her throat, filled with more terror and hopelessness than Cory had ever heard.

"Cory," said the man—Braswell. He was looking past Cory's mother and right at him. The man's eyes were calm yet purposeful. Intelligent. Cory was almost lulled by them. "That's your name, isn't it? Cory McBride."

Cory just stared at him. He couldn't answer.

*"Get out, get out, get out,"* his mother sobbed, still chopping listlessly at the empty air.

"You've known about this for some time," said the man. It wasn't a question. "You've felt it even if you weren't sure what it was."

"Stop talking to my son!" his mother screamed. She swiped at the air one more time with the hatchet, nearly grazing one of the man's outstretched, pacifying hands. "Get out of my house . . ." But it sounded like much of the strength had fled her voice.

"We can't do that, ma'am. We need to bring the boy. It's very important that he comes. We're all playing a part in this, but your son, he's the most important piece."

"Just *grab* him!" someone called from the top of the stairs.

The man—Braswell—closed his eyes and exhaled audibly through his nose. When he reopened his eyes, that same sense of lulling serenity was back in them. For one terrifying moment, Cory felt himself desperate to go to him.

Braswell came down one more step, but Cory's mother sprung on him: she rushed forward and swung the hatchet with enough force to wedge the blade into the wooden banister at the bottom of the stairwell. She made an *umf!* sound as she tried to pry the head of the hatchet free, but before she could, Braswell reached out and casually wrapped a set of fingers around the handle.

"Enough," he said calmly.

At the top of the stairs, another set of legs appeared.

## 2

Ellen's vision went blurry. Still struggling to free the hatchet from the banister, she hardly registered the man as he came all the way down and stood calmly beside her. He took his free hand and gently pried her fingers from the handle of the axe until her hands trembled uselessly at her sides.

"No," she whimpered, raising her hands at pounding futilely at the man's chest with her fists. "No, no, no, no, no . . ."

The man jerked the hatchet free of the wood just as two more men descended the basement steps. Ellen couldn't bring herself to look at them. Instead, she raced over to her son and collected him in her arms. She maneuvered them into one corner and had already made up her mind that she would claw and bite and fight and kick if any of them came any closer. She might not be able to successfully fend them all off, but she would wound as many as she could . . .

The man now holding the hatchet extended a hand toward them—toward *Cory.*

From within his mother's embrace, Cory dropped the hammer and the screwdriver and extended a hand of his own.

*"Noooo!"* she screamed, and tugged her son's arm down. She clutched him more tightly, bringing her mouth to the side of his face, his warm, heat-flushed ear, where she begged him in a torrent of words, "Do your thing use your special gift hurt them make them go away make them leave I won't be mad I won't be scared do whatever you have to do to make them leave us alone hurt them hurt them *hurt them*—"

## 3

But he couldn't. The gnome would not respond. And something about this man's outstretched hand was—

Cory blinked. It felt as though the world was swimming in and out of focus, much in the way it did on occasion when he stood up too quickly from the couch after watching TV. He thought he might pass out—welcomed it, in fact—but the feeling quickly transitioned into a less familiar one: the strong and sudden urge to *go*, to follow this man and all the other men back up the stairs, through the house, and out into the night. To go wherever it was—

*(Martian war machine)*

*(mechanical spider)*

*(the water tower)*

—that they wanted him to go.

*No,* countered a small voice in the back of his head. Not the gnome, but some innate sense of self-preservation. A consciousness inside his consciousness. *It's a trick! Don't give into it! That's what they want you to do! Make it hard for them! Make it impossible! They can't hold the gnome down forever.*

He allowed the basement and everything in it to fall out of focus—everything except the hatchet gripped in Braswell's hand. He imagined the floor dropping away so that the hatchet hovered in midair . . . and then he swung the world—

*(is a neighborhood)*

—around in a somersault. The hatchet should have obliged, first jerking up and pulling free from the man's hand, and then spinning in an arc toward the man himself.

But none of that happened.

Those mind-cables were still there in his head, restraining the gnome. Cory did not possess the strength to overpower them and cut them loose.

But Braswell had felt it—a subtle tug in the atmosphere between them. A look of uncertainty washed across his face, but then he quickly recalibrated. "If you don't come with us, Cory, I'm afraid we're going to have to hurt your mother. It's not something that we want to do, but the truth is, she isn't important. She means nothing to us, and nothing to the endgame. The only thing that matters is you. You're the engine."

"Just *take* him!" Mr. Zachs shouted. He was halfway down the stairs and leaning over the railing, his face nearly the color of an eggplant. His robe was still hanging open and there was a line of spittle descending from his lower lip, extending five, six inches, before it detached and plopped wetly onto the pasty white swell of Mr. Zachs's belly. Blood was dribbling in rivulets down his hairless shins.

"Go back upstairs," Braswell said to Mr. Zachs. His voice was as placid and unthreatening as his eyes, which were still locked on Cory.

"We're wasting *time*," Mr. Zachs growled back. "It's already begun. *Endgame.*"

"I know what it is," Braswell replied, still perfectly calm. "Now go back upstairs."

Mr. Zachs's nostrils flared like those of a bull about to charge. The bands of his heavy, sunburned forehead sloped down so that his bright, piggish eyes were nearly obscured completely by the folds and creases of his face. But then, in an exasperated huff, he turned and clumped miserably back up the stairs.

"You, too," Braswell said to the young man who had come down the stairwell with Mr. Zachs—a young man no more than a teenager, with an athletic build, and hayseed-blond hair. Cory had never seen him before, but suddenly understood that this was the consciousness that he had sensed hiding in the trees across the street, watching the house. Without a word, this young man turned and followed Mr. Zachs back up the stairs. "Now," Braswell continued, extending a hand to Cory once again. "Will you come?"

Before he could react, his mother's embrace fell away. She leapt at Braswell, shrieking. Startled, Braswell staggered backward, slamming his back against the cinderblock wall. But he didn't drop the hatchet. His mother did not relent: she barreled toward him, clawing and screaming like a madwoman. Cory watched as a set of his mother's fingernails—those blunt and gnawed fingernails—dug themselves into the side of Braswell's face with enough force to leave a trio of ragged, bloody lacerations in the flesh. Braswell sucked in air through his teeth, then swung the hatchet, striking her, just as—

## 4

—a sharp and sudden pain radiated from Ellen's left flank, just below the curve of her ribs. The wind was knocked from her and she felt her legs, those traitors, surrender beneath her. She collapsed like an old folding chair to the basement floor, the pain in her side spreading in a hot gush throughout the entirety of her abdomen.

As the man made his way past her, she reached out and snagged his ankle with one hand. She dug the nubs of her fingernails into the soft flesh there while her mind spun wildly, thinking crazily, *they made me bite my nails so I couldn't claw them apart*, and when she rolled her head to one side and looked up at him, her vision less than perfect in that moment, the pain in her side like a spreading wildfire, she saw his dark shape raising the hatchet above his head, intent on bringing it down on hers. But before he could, Ellen heard Cory cry out, *"No! Stop! Leave my mommy alone!"*

The man slid out of her line of sight. She could no longer turn her head to see where he went. She heard commotion, heard Cory cry out, heard something sharp and heavy and metallic clatter to the basement floor. It was then that she realized she wasn't breathing—hadn't been breathing since she'd been struck—and when she gasped for air, all she could accomplish was the opening of her mouth and nothing more. Her lungs felt as if they'd been filled with cement. A reedy whine escaped the chimneystack of her throat. Fresh tears sprung from her eyes.

"Mommy! Mommy!"

A blur of movement flitted across her field of vision.

*"Mommy—ahhhh!"*

She tried to scream, as if her scream might be able to catch Cory's in midair and tether them together, but she still could not make a sound. There was no air to breathe; she was sinking deeper and deeper toward the ocean floor, and could feel the thickening weight of arctic waves as they piled on top of her.

And then the great weight was lifted from her chest, and she drew in her breath, feeling some tremendous and impossible chasm open up in her mind, as she—

## 5

—transmitted a thought that ricocheted through Brian's mind with all the force of a gunshot:

*PROTECT MY SON!*

All around him, a butterfly swarm of playing cards moved about him in the air, like dead leaves on a breeze, and the water from the running faucet in the tub was pulled into threads and beads and tinsel streamers that hung, too, suspended in the air, and Brian's eyes, wide at the sound of that voice suddenly infiltrating his consciousness, his *sister's* voice, barreling through the center of his head, expanded in focus like the wide and yawning arms of a blue and distant star, while the cards came fluttering down and the sudden jolt of gravity sent the threads and beads and tinsel streamers of water splashing all around him, his concentration broken, while—

## 6

—she screamed, *"Cory!"*

The man was carrying her son up the stairs—she watched his footsteps as if in slow motion plodding with great effort up each riser—and she felt herself roll over onto her stomach and crawl toward the stairs, then *up* the stairs, in pursuit of them. She did not stop to think about the wound at her side and the guts she must be spilling and trailing behind her on the cold concrete floor of the basement.

She thought only of her son.

# CHAPTER SIXTY-ONE
# ENGINE TO THE TOWER

## 1

The moment Alex reached the top of the stairs, the boy was wrenched from his arms. It felt like losing a part of his soul, and he instinctively cried out, as if mortally wounded. The boy was carried away upon a tidal wave of pawing, grasping hands and strong arms, kicking and shrieking and crying out for his mother. For a moment, Alex almost regretted what he had done and what he was about to do . . . but then he remembered the final remaining paper cutout—the figure with the star on its forehead—and how when he'd taken his first really good look at the boy down in the basement cowering behind his mother, Alex had perceived a vision of a small, glowing star at the center of the boy's forehead—and he had no doubt that this was *right*.

Before leaving the house, he glanced back down into the basement and saw the boy's mother slumped halfway up the stairs. She moved with great effort and pain, he could tell, but she was not giving up. When she had attacked him, he'd swung the hatchet purely out of reflex. He hadn't meant to injure her, and thankfully, he'd only managed to strike her with the blunt side of the hatchet, not the blade. He'd hit her hard enough to knock the wind from her and he thought he'd felt a few ribs break, too, but unless one of those ribs had managed to puncture her lungs, he didn't think he'd mortally wounded her.

"I'm sorry," he said to her, and she looked up at him, her eyes messy with tears, strands of hair stuck to the sweat on her face. There was a pleading expression in her eyes.

He shut the door and locked it.

## 2

She heard the door lock and screamed her son's name. An instant later, it was like she was being buried beneath an avalanche. Gathering up what strength she still had, she continued to climb to the top, step by painful step.

## 3

They carried him swiftly from the house, Mr. Zachs squeezing his arms together as he carried him horizontally around the chest, while Tom Orem had both of Cory's legs held steady within one tight grip. The younger man had a hand clamped to Cory's mouth. When Cory opened his eyes, he found himself staring up not at the faces of these men, but at the vast blackness pinpricked with stars high above him. For a moment, it almost brought him peace, but then they were stuffing him in the back of the police car, and he could smell the sweat radiating off them in waves, the desperate, animal stink of them, and once more, he began to scream.

## 4

"I'm driving," Alex said, moving around Grayson. He slid behind the wheel of the police car while, in the back, Bert Zachs and Eric Rhodes pinned the boy to the seat and struggled to keep him from flailing. When the kid screamed, Eric clamped his hand back over his mouth. Alex felt the scream shudder down the length of his spine. Grayson dumped himself into the passenger seat just as Alex cranked over the engine. Larry Kotara and Tom Orem ran past them and in the direction of Larry's van.

The boy's feet kicked at the seats, and he kept twisting his head and freeing his mouth so that he could scream for his mother. Alex turned around in his seat and said, with as much serenity as he could muster in the moment, "Please keep him quiet and still."

"He's a ten-year-old boy," Grayson said from the passenger seat, sounding much more agitated than Alex had. "You'd think the two of you would be able to keep him from kicking the fucking seats?"

"He's squirming around!" Zachs shouted back.

Grayson groaned. He sat forward and pulled his handcuffs from his belt, then passed them to the backseat. "Cuff him up."

Alex glanced at him. "Is that necessary?"

Grayson scowled at him. "Are you fucking serious right now? Just drive the fucking car."

Zachs fumbled with the boy's wrist, trying to loop one of the cuffs around him while Eric attempted to hold him steady. This made Cory shriek louder . . . and Jesus Christ, Alex could feel those screams resonating straight down to the marrow of his bones. He heard the ratcheting of the handcuffs' teeth, saw the boy in the rearview mirror attempt to struggle with his hands now bound behind his back. There was a look of abject terror on his face. Zachs drew a meaty thigh across the boy's lap, and the weight of him forced the child to go still.

Alex spun the wheel, whipped around in the street practically on two tires, and then sped off toward the intersection.

"It's okay, kid, it's okay," Eric Rhodes said. His tone was practically pleading.

And then just like that, the boy's cries were silenced. Startled, Alex glanced up at the rearview mirror again, not sure what he was expecting to find, and was surprised to see the boy sitting calmly now between Bert Zachs and Eric Rhodes, staring straight at Alex's reflection in the glass. His face was red and tear-streaked, but his eyes were sober. Guilt as strong as an electrical current cut up through the core of him, and Alex found himself suddenly thinking of Callie and Denise, and what he would do if someone ever tried to hurt them or take them away from him. He felt his resolve begin to weaken. But then that thought was obscured by another—

*(ALL HAIL THE DRAGON ALL HAIL THE TOWER)*

—and he blinked his eyes and redirected his gaze out the windshield again.

"You hurt my mom." The boy's throat was clogged with mucus, but he spoke with a surprising serenity now, particularly for a boy his age who'd just gone through such an ordeal.

"I'm sorry," Alex said, and he felt Grayson glance at him disapprovingly from the passenger seat. "I didn't mean to."

"Don't talk to him," said Grayson. "We shouldn't talk to him." To Zachs and Eric in the backseat, he said, "Make sure you're keeping that thing inside his head restrained. Don't loosen things up now."

Headlights appeared in the police car's rearview mirror: Larry Kotara's van.

"Everything will be fine, kid," Eric Rhodes kept saying.

Alex did not know if everything was going to be fine. Was he really here, speeding through Mariner's Cove in a police car, a kidnapped kid held hostage and handcuffed in the back seat? Was he—

*(ALL HAIL THE)*

*It's all part of the plan*, he reminded himself. *Don't lose sight of that now. As Stinger has been saying, there were bound to be sacrifices.*

"Little fucker keeps trying to get inside my head." This was Bert Zachs, leaning forward so that Alex could feel the man's warm, sour breath against his ear. "I can feel him."

"Keep the bomb suppressed for just a little bit longer," Grayson responded.

The bomb, of course, was Cory McBride. The engine to the machine—that was his purpose, as explained to Alex back at the altar hive by a . . . well, some parable of a snake stuck in a beehive. That was how his mind had interpreted, at least. *Not a snake*, he knew, *not really*, but that didn't matter right now. What mattered was that they transported this kid to the Tower in Gladstone Park so they could bring about the endgame. If the boy's abilities weren't dampened—and it was taking the collective work of them all now, mentally holding down the vein of magic that pulsed deep in the center of the boy's mind—then the engine could easily become a bomb that would blow them all sky high. This made Alex think of his initial dreams, the ones he'd first had back when he'd been spending every day alone wrapping twine around the base of the water tower—coming through the woods in the dark, himself and faceless others clinging to the outer walls of the Tower, and then the Tower itself ultimately coming apart, spilling pieces of itself to the earth, along with Alex and all of the others.

Endgame.

"I didn't mean to hurt your mom," he said again, not sure why he felt the need to repeat this. Grayson was right—he should just drive and not talk to the boy. "She'll be okay," he heard himself continue nonetheless. "I promise."

"What about me?" asked the boy. "Will *I* be okay?"

Alex didn't know.

The snake in the beehive hadn't showed him that part.

The boy said, "I know one of your daughters, Mr. Braswell. Callie. She's a little older than me, but we used to go to the same elementary school and I still sometimes see her playing down at the park."

A bead of sweat coasted down the left side of Alex's face.

"One time she fell and cut her knee at Gladstone Park," the boy went on. "Me and Kip Ransom and Davey Orem walked her back home because she was crying and upset. The cut on her knee wasn't that bad, but I think she was just afraid and maybe a little embarrassed."

Alex felt something sting his left eye. He swiped at it and tightened his grip on the steering wheel.

"You answered the door that day, Mr. Braswell. You thanked us for walking her home and invited us in for lemonade. And your wife was there, and she remembered me from piano lessons. Do *you* remember? Do you remember that day, Mr. Braswell?"

"Shut up, kid," growled Grayson.

As much as he didn't want to, Alex kept glancing up at the boy's eyes reflecting in the rearview mirror. He was doing it now, unable to look away, his mind filling in the details of that forgotten memory, seeing Cory McBride and those other boys standing on the porch with Callie, who was nearly inconsolable about the abrasion on her knee. But even now, that memory was being pulled apart by the strident, unshakable obsession to *keep going with this*—

*(ALL HAIL THE DRAGON ALL HAIL THE TOWER)*

—and he couldn't stop himself.

"I know it's not you," said the boy. His voice had a hypnotic, singsong quality that, under different circumstances, might have lulled Alex to sleep. "I know this isn't *any* of you. You're not doing this. It's something else *making* you do it. Controlling your minds."

The boy's eyes floating there in the rearview mirror. Alex unable to look away.

In the passenger seat, Grayson shouted, "For Christ's sake—*look out*!"

Eyes darting back toward the road, Alex swerved just inches from hopping a curb and driving straight into a lamppost. Everyone was jostled first to one side and then to the other as Alex overcorrected. Tires squealed. "Jesus *Christ*, man!" shouted Bert Zachs from the back seat.

Once he'd regained control of the vehicle, Alex glanced back up at the boy's reflection in the rearview mirror. The boy was still staring at him, his expression stony, his eyes incrementally narrowing.

*Bomb*, thought Alex.

## 5

"I've never seen lightning like that before," Georgette said, coming up beside Sarah Miller. Along with the rest of the worker bees, they had taken apart the wooden split-rail fence, widening the clearing at the base of the Tower. They all were now gazing up at the sky. Directly above the Tower, thick black clouds had coalesced and were slowly beginning to rotate in a counterclockwise direction. Whenever lightning would flash, which was becoming more and more frequent, it did so in a brilliant white garland of light that leapfrogged horizontally from one cloud to the next to the next.

"Me, either," Sarah admitted. Strong wind whistled through the surrounding trees and whipped the hair back from her face. "It looks bad, doesn't it?"

"I think . . . I think it's supposed to happen this way," Georgette said, although she had no idea why she believed this.

"Looks like another bad storm!" the man called Sergio shouted over the rising wind.

*Not a storm*, Georgette thought. *The Dragon is waking up. It's getting ready for its journey home.*

She felt Sarah turn and look at her.

As if she'd just heard her thoughts.

## 6

At the top of the stairs, Ellen used the railing to bring herself unsteadily to her feet, then threw her weight against the basement door. It hardly budged. Sobbing, she tried to turn the knob despite it being locked, but her sweaty hands kept slipping off the brass. She pounded on the door, feeling it quake in its frame. It was a sturdy door, something she had been grateful of the night of the bad storm, but which now felt like a death sentence.

The pain in her side was still intense, but when she summoned the courage to look down, she was surprised to find that she was not bleeding. There was no ragged gash vomiting up glistening, purple coils of her intestines. Yet when she pressed a hand to her ribs, where the pain was most intense, a jolt of pure agony blossomed into a nearly audible cacophony inside her head.

As she waited for the pain to subside, she turned around and sat down on the top step, her back against the locked basement door. Her first instinct was to sob miserably into her hands . . . but then she saw the hatchet down below on the floor, right where the man had discarded it before snatching up her son, and something within her sharpened to a point. Temporarily forgetting about the pain, Ellen hobbled back down the stairs toward the hatchet.

## 7

The brakes squealed as Alex jerked the police car to a halt along the nameless road that ran parallel to Slope Hill. As they all climbed from the vehicle, heat lightning briefly lit up the sky directly above their heads.

Grayson went around to the rear of the car and assisted Bert Zachs and Eric in pulling the kid from the back seat. Judging by the resignation on the boy's face, however, Alex didn't think such a show of force was necessary, but he didn't say anything. Cory McBride's eyes were still boring through him, making Alex uncomfortable. He looked away.

Headlights appeared behind them. Alex sensed rather than saw Grayson unholster his firearm and point it at the oncoming vehicle, but when they realized it was Larry Kotara's van, Grayson seated the gun back in the holster and buttoned the snap. The van growled to a stop, the headlights went dead, and Larry and Tom Orem jumped out.

More heat lightning lashed across the sky, reflecting across all their faces.

"We need to hurry," Alex said.

As they led the boy closer to the cusp of the woods, Alex saw Cory look up towards the top of the giant water tank rising above the tree line. A mass of dark clouds swirled directly over the Tower. Alex watched as the boy's legs quit cooperating.

"Come *on*," urged Grayson, reaching out and gripping the kid high on the forearm. He gave him a yank that could have dislocated the kid's arm from its socket, particularly with his hands still cuffed behind his back.

"The kid will come," Alex assured Grayson. "Just go easy with him, will you?" Then he went over and hunkered down in front of the boy. It was no different than he'd done a hundred, or maybe a thousand, times with one of his own daughters—taking a knee before them in order to impart something important on their own level, or to perhaps chase their fears away—but it did him no good to make such a comparison now.

*You answered the door that day, Mr. Braswell. You thanked us and invited us in for lemonade. Don't you remember?*

Alex shook the thought from his head. There was too much going on in there as it was. Then he reached out and took the boy by his shoulders—gently—and said, rather quietly, "You're quite an important young man, Cory. I think you know that."

The boy's face remained expressionless. They were all still collectively dampening the power in Cory's head, but Cory was stronger than he looked, and they were all growing mentally fatigued. It was like making your arms like airplane wings while holding buckets of water, only with your mind. The boy would overpower them very soon if they didn't hurry.

"This thing, it's bigger than all of us. I know you can feel it, Cory. I just think it would be easier if we all just cooperated. Because at the end of the day, none of us really have a choice. You were right about what you said in the car: there's something else making us do this, making all of this happen."

"What if it was Callie they wanted instead of me?" Cory asked him.

At that, something seemed to short circuit in the back of Alex Braswell's brain—he actually heard a *pop-fizz,* followed by a temporary distorting of his vision. For one moment, he felt like he'd been split down the middle, and was watching this whole thing unfold from two entirely disparate perspectives.

He shook his head, tried to clear it. Said, "It wouldn't work that way, kid." He squeezed the boy's shoulder just the slightest bit, in what he hoped was a comforting way.

"Enough of this bullshit already," Grayson said. He had his right hand back on the hilt of his gun, his other hand massaging his temple as if to dispel a migraine.

"Yeah," seconded Larry Kotara. "What's all the gum flapping? My head's about to explode. Let's get moving all ready."

Alex's hand still on the boy's shoulder, they walked into the woods together.

## 8

Stinger swiped the heel of one hand across his wet eyes the moment he saw the boy emerge with his entourage through the woods. The kid's arms were behind his back and Alex Braswell's hand was on the kid's shoulder, yet Stinger was surprised—and pleased—to see that the boy seemed to be coming of his own accord. Within him was a great welling of emotion, more powerful than anything he had ever felt before in his sad and miserable life. The crowd of worker bees parted for the boy as Alex led him straight through to the center of the clearing. Stinger could not wait; he moved forward on a wave of nervous energy and met Alex and the boy halfway. When he reached them, he dropped down on one knee in front of the boy, in quite the same way (unbeknownst to him) Alex had done just moments ago. He smiled his sad, lumpy smile at the boy.

"My name is Stinger. I'm the Hivemaster." Stinger's eyes jittered up and down the boy. He wanted desperately to touch him, to confirm the kid was actually *real*. "We've been waiting for you. You're the final piece. The most *important* piece. We're so glad . . . so *honored* . . . to have you. *Cory McBride*."

*(CORY MCBRIDE)*        *(CORY MCBRIDE)*

*(CORY MCBRIDE)*        *(CORY MCBRIDE) (CORY MCBRIDE)*

*(CORY MCBRIDE)*

*(CORY MCBRIDE)* *(CORY MCBRIDE)* *(CORY MCBRIDE)*
*(CORY MCBRIDE)*

*(CORY MCBRIDE)*

*(CORY MCBRIDE)*

*(CORY MCBRIDE)*

Then he *did* reach out and touch him—a hand, gently, on the upper arm, pivoting the boy's body so that he could see his wrists handcuffed behind his back like some criminal. A pulse of anger radiated through him. He looked up and found a police officer among the newcomers. Before Stinger could open his mouth, the cop seemed to sense his disapproval. He fumbled a handcuff key from a Velcro pouch on his vest and unhooked the boy. Free—sort of—Cory brought his arms up across his chest.

Stinger rose to his feet and stepped aside. Indeed, all the worker bees who had gathered in the moonlit clearing parted before the boy like the Red Sea before Moses. They revealed to him, for the first time, what they had built—built for *him*!—at the base of the Tower.

Anxious, and knowing time was of the essence, Stinger beckoned the boy to follow him as he closed the distance to the Tower. When he reached the wall of chain-link surrounding the base of the Tower, Stinger turned to the boy, who stood just a few feet away, Alex Braswell's hand still on his shoulder. "In there is what we call Hive Center. That means you're the queen bee, bucko."

Overhead, thunder growled. Lightning flashed, looping from cloud to cloud, and as Stinger glanced up at the night sky, it was all too easy to see the eerie, soupy swirl of the clouds as they slowly rotated—

*(circles circles circles)*

—gathering speed.

"I want my mom. I want my mom and I want to go home."

And he began to cry.

# 9

Because he did not believe in coincidence, Brian Russo would not have considered it luck that he arrived at the McBride house less than fifteen minutes after his nephew's abduction, but as yet another active mechanism in the great clockwork contraption that was the known universe. He had been in a panic on his drive out here from the hotel, but it wasn't until he'd approached the entrance of Mariner's Cove that he was assaulted by the irrational notion that he would be prevented from entering. He'd even slowed the van as he drove past the community sign, in the unlikely event that some invisible barrier had been erected and that the van might actually smash into it. Of course, that hadn't happened . . . although what *had* happened was that he'd nearly buckled over seconds after crossing into the neighborhood by a crippling desire to *drink*. That black belly-snake was back, breathing fire and pissing venom, and it wanted Brian *under.*

*Fuck you*, he told the demons, for they were very real and all around him once more, crawling across the upholstery of the conversion van, banging against the quarter panels from inside the framework of the vehicle, even under the hood clawing at the engine block like gremlins. *Fuck you, fuck you, fuck you!*

Now, as the van's headlights washed along the front of his sister's house, the first thing Brian noticed was that both the front and side doors were standing open. The next thing he saw was that the windows had been broken and that the drapes billowed out from the sill and into the night.

*Christ, please, no . . .*

He jumped from the van and raced up the walkway to the house, screaming, "Cory! Ellen!" as he burst into the front hall.

Furniture lay on its side and there were busted shards of glass everywhere. His eyes fell upon the living room couch, and at the terrible crimson streaks across the couch cushions. A bloody handprint had been stamped distinctly onto one wall.

And then—*chunk!*

It was the sound of a loud, splintering crash. A second one followed, and Brian pursued that sound down the hall and into the kitchen. The kitchen itself was empty, the window above the sink busted, leaving triangular teeth of glass scattered about the floor and countertop. He opened his mouth to shout his sister's name again when the sound—*chunk!*—not only came again, but barked so close to his ear that he whirled around, expecting half of the kitchen wall to come tumbling down on him.

It wasn't the wall, but the basement door. The door itself was striated with splintered cracks, and as he stared at it, trying to reconcile what he was seeing, a sliver of metal that had been protruding through one of the cracks in the door vanished, leaving behind a narrow, black gap.

He reached out, jiggled the knob, found it locked. He thumbed the lock free, then yanked open the door.

The wretched creature that stood on the other side was a stranger to him. A stranger, he duly noted, about to bury a hatchet in his skull. But as the woman leaned forward and collapsed into his arms, hatchet striking the floor and cartwheeling down the basement steps, he realized it was Ellen, and that she had been through some version of hell he could only imagine.

Her fingers dug into his back as she cried into the side of his face: "They took him! Brian, they *took* him!"

He grabbed her around the wrist and pulled her toward the side door of the house, which hung open upon a rectangular panel of night.

"I don't know where they went!" she sobbed as he dragged her out into the night. "It was Mr. Zachs and some others, *and Cory had been right*, and Brian, they *took* him! They took my baby!"

At the street, he shoved her in the passenger seat of the van, then ran around and jumped in behind the wheel.

"I don't know where they took him!" she screamed, pounding her fists on the dashboard.

Brian popped the van into reverse and said, "I do."

He left tire marks on the pavement.

# 10

The man who called himself Stinger peeled back a jangly section of fence that had been cut to suggest a doorway, and pointed toward the place beneath the water tower that he had referred to as Hive Center. Countless items had been erected here beneath the tower, and as Cory took them all in, he could see that they each glowed with a faint bluish light, which he supposed could have been just the light of the moon, even though the moon itself was buried beneath that strange, swirling tornado of clouds. As Cory's eyes acclimated to the dark, he began to see even *more* items, including a whole system of stiff metal wires branching in every direction above his head.

"Do you see that chair?" the man called Stinger said, nodding toward the heart of the contraption at Hive Center.

Cory saw a door with a spaghetti strainer nailed to it. There was what looked like a camping chair screwed into the lower section of the door, and the whole thing was propped behind a metal folding table. And while it looked far from what Cory would call a *chair*, he knew in looking at it that a *chair*—

*(door-becomes-chair)*

—was exactly what it was.

He nodded but said nothing.

"That," Stinger said, "is your chair. It was built specifically for you."

Cory looked at him. The man's face was bumpy with welts and peeling with sunburn. He looked like a horror show. "Did you build it?" Cory asked.

"Not exactly, although I guess you could say I'm responsible for it all coming together. Do you want to go sit in it?"

Again, Cory looked at the chair. The spaghetti strainer now looked to him like a helmet, and it had a number of those long metal wires extending from it, each one running suspended in the air to the chain-link fence surrounding the base.

The last thing Cory wanted to do was sit in that chair.

"No," he said.

"But it's *yours*," Stinger said. He was trying to grin and look amiable, Cory could tell, but he was nervous and sweating and humming with a palpable anxiety that made him seem desperate and reckless. Also, his lumpy face was frightening. "It's for *you*."

"You can't trick me," Cory said.

"It isn't a trick, kid. It's just . . . it is what it is."

"Then what is it?"

Stinger's eyelids fluttered. The grin on his face faded, the corners of his mouth drooping down to angular points. Cory saw a nerve twitch beneath Stinger's right eye. "Why don't you sit and we'll find out together."

Cory took a step back from him. Alex Braswell's hand was no longer on his shoulder, but the man hadn't gone far, and Cory sensed him coming up behind him now. In case Cory decided to run. "I . . . I don't want to," he stammered.

Grinning that jack-o'-lantern grin, Stinger closed the distance between them then crouched down so that he was at eye-level with him. This close, Cory could see with perfect moonlit clarity the distorted bumps along Stinger's face, and how they wept clear fluid that glistened beneath the starlight. Hairline fissures ran down Stinger's cheeks and were grouped around the corners of his twisted, peeling mouth; as Stinger's grin widened, the fissures cracked and split. There was blood on his teeth.

*Wake up, wake up, wake up!* he shouted at the gnome.

Stinger's eyes went wide. His tongue poked out from between his lips and licked one of his bloody incisors. "That's a useless endeavor," he said. "We won't let up until you're secured in that chair. Then we'll turn your power back on so you can start up the machine. You're the goddamn engine. That's what your power is *for*."

# CHAPTER SIXTY-TWO
# POWER

## 1

Brian jerked the van to a stop halfway down the nameless road on the far end of Gladstone Park. There were a handful of other vehicles parked here, and the lights from a few sparse houses buried deep in the woods in the distance, but otherwise it was like being on some remote jungle planet. Both he and Ellen were out of the van before it stopped rocking.

"Where are we going? Why are we here?" Ellen asked, frantically looking around.

Brian backed up to the opposite side of the road, where Slope Hill gradually descended in a serpentine fashion down to the water. As he looked up beyond the line of trees at the back end of Gladstone Park, lightning ignited the sky. The Mariner's Cove water tower came into stark relief. He could see the strange symbols painted there, the words MARINER'S HIVE replacing MARINER'S COVE. He could see, too, the furious word emblazoned beneath those words and surrounded by those symbols, like something held in a snug embrace:

ENDGAME

*Yes,* he thought. *Yes, it is.*

And that thought gave him chills.

He ran toward the woods, just as Ellen shouted after him. He shouted back, telling her to come, to hurry, that things were happening very, very fast now, and when he reached the line of trees, he practically dived into it.

Immutable darkness swallowed him up. He swatted at errant boughs and prickly pine branches while pinecones and dry, brittle twigs snapped underfoot. He sensed Ellen struggling to keep up behind him, so he reached back for her, blindly, and grabbed a fistful of her shirt as he yanked her toward him. She shrieked but galloped right alongside him now.

Ahead, he could see a clearing beyond the trees where the moonlight painted the landscape in a bright, staticky white. No, not precisely moonlight, but some miasma of light twisting about in the sky, slowly rotating like the eye of a hurricane. That coiled black snake in his belly reared up and sank its fangs into the soft, tender flesh of his stomach lining. Brian cried out and buckled over onto the ground.

"Brian!" Ellen cried, coming down beside him. "Brian! What is it?"

"It's in my head," he said through clenched teeth, wincing through the pain. The snake sprung up into his skull and began thrashing about. He could see the brightening star in there along with it, a radiant pulse of light whose hue was no different than the eerie, staticky light he'd glimpsed spilling down from the sky overtop the water tower. "It isn't real . . . but I *feel* it . . ."

"Brian, you need to get up! What's happening to you?" Her hands were working across his back, up and down his arms, prodding him to rise up and keep running. Finally, she gripped him about the chin and twisted his head in her direction. Her image was pixelated. "You need to get up! I don't know what's going on and I *need my son*!"

*It doesn't want me here. It doesn't want anyone here who isn't a part of this madness. It's keeping everyone else away, making them sick, making them think they're losing their minds . . .*

He reached up and grabbed hold of a nearby tree limb. The serpent was slithering back down now, coiling around and constricting his spine. Gritting his teeth, tears springing from his eyes, he managed to hoist himself off the ground. His legs quivered.

"Brian—"

He stood straighter and locked his knees. The serpent's constriction vanished. His head felt instantly hollowed—he could almost hear an audible *whoosh!* as the snake vanished in a cartoonish puff of smoke—and there was no more pain in his guts. "Okay," he gasped, breathing against the bole of a tree while his fingernails dug at the bark. "Okay, okay, okay . . ."

Ellen touched him tentatively on the shoulder. Crying freely now, she whispered his name.

He nodded. "Yeah, I'm okay, El." He released his hold on the tree and found he could stand on his own again. "Let's go get your son."

He grabbed her hand and together they ran through the trees toward the clearing. He sensed rather than saw movement on the other side of the trees, but it wasn't until he had cleared the woods that he saw just how far-reaching this whole thing was.

Somewhere around thirty people stood surrounding the base of the water tower, their bodies rigid and seeming to shine beneath that eerie, preternatural light spilling down from the sky. At the base of the tower was something that struck Brian as both perverse and divine at the same time—an arrangement of random items behind a chain-link fence. At the very center stood what looked like a chair made of a wooden door with a metal helmet hanging down, looking to Brian like an old-fashioned electric chair. Before the crowd slowly closed in around the base of the tower, impeding his view, Brian could see the dark shape of a boy climbing into the chair with the assistance of a tall, lanky man.

"No!" Brian screamed, and all their heads turned to him at once. They all seemed stunned into motionlessness by his shout. But then some of the onlookers dispersed toward the cover of the trees while others began taking steps in his direction. Ellen squeezed his hand more tightly. "What are you people doing?"

His query was met with nothing but blank stares.

"Cory!" he yelled at the small shape on the other side of the chain-link fence. "Cory, come out here!"

The boy froze beneath the tower.

*"Cory!"* Ellen wailed, and she began running toward him. She was stopped when a number of the onlookers reached out and grabbed her, holding her back. She screamed and thrashed but they wouldn't let her go.

Brian approached the tower. The crowd of people around him stepped aside, as if fearful of him, or maybe just curious. He wondered if maybe they could sense that pulsing blue star gathering strength in the center of his skull. He thought maybe they could.

"It's okay, Ellen," he said as he walked past her. She was struggling within the grasps of a handful of people, crying out for her son. "Cory? Can you hear me, bud? It's Uncle Brian. Come on out. It's okay."

A small, reedy voice laced with uncertainty: "Uncle Brian?"

Brian stopped short in front of the chain-link fence. A section of it had been cut into flaps, which had been peeled away like metal curtains held in place by heavy chains. This close, he could see the assortment of seemingly unrelated items on the other side of the fence, and the realization of what had been going on out here for however long—that these people had united to *build* this monstrosity—was horrifying.

"Yeah, Chicken Little. It's me. Come on out of there."

"I don't . . . I don't think I'm s'posed to," his nephew stammered.

"You don't have to listen to these people. Come on out."

"Come here, Cory!" Ellen yelled somewhere behind him in the dark. Her voice sounded throaty and strained, full of anguish, and ready to break apart.

Again, Cory's small, uncertain voice: "Mom! Are you okay? Are you hurt?"

"Come to me, Cory! Please!"

"I don't think . . ."

"You're interfering here," said the tall, lanky man who stood beside Cory on the other side of the fence. He was staring directly at Brian. "You don't belong here. You're not part of this."

"Who are you?" Brian asked.

The man approached the fence. As he cleared the shadow of the water tank, Brian could see that his face was a map of welts and weals, of bloodied ridges and scabby, swollen flesh that shined like scar tissue beneath the strange light issuing from the sky. The man curled his fingers around the links in the fence, and Brian could suddenly *smell* him: a stench like sewage and sweat and the coppery, eye-watering sting of blood.

"I'm the Hivemaster."

Brian was about to cross through the fence when hands grabbed him around the forearms and shoulders. A pair of arms encircled his chest, clutching him in a bear hug. Someone else's arm was attempting to snake around his neck to cut off his air supply.

Distantly, he heard Ellen scream.

"Get him out of here," said the man with the ruined face.

The crowd began to pull him away from the fence; Brian reached out and clutched at the chain-link, grabbing hold with both hands. He cried out as they wrenched the fingers of his left hand free. Still, he hung on with the other, fingers burning and straining and aching. Along the periphery of his vision, he caught a glimpse of someone approaching. An instant later, he howled as the man karate chopped at the muscle of his inner arm.

Brian's fingers unlatched and his entire arm was rendered momentarily useless. As they dragged him farther from the tower, Brian shouted, "Run, Cory! Get out of there and *run*!"

Blessedly, he saw the boy come darting out from between the curtained opening in the fence and make a beeline for the trees . . . but he didn't get more than a handful of yards before two men snatched him up and hoisted him off the ground. Cory screamed, his legs continuing to pedal futilely in the air.

*"Leave him alone, you bastards!"* Brian shouted. Somewhere in the darkness, Ellen cried out again, but her cry was quickly stifled. Brian was dragged down to the ground. There were hands all over him, elbows pressing into his body, knees digging into the muscles of his thighs. "Please," he begged them. Hands kept trying to clamp over his mouth but he kept twisting his head on his neck to stop them. "Whatever you people want—whoever the hell you are—please don't

hurt him. Let me take him home. Please." He reached out through the mob of limbs that were struggling with him, a hand thrust upward, groping blindly at the air, at the stars above. A man in a police uniform filled his line of sight. He watched as the cop leveled a gun at his face. "Plea—"

He felt a hand wrap around his.

It was like grabbing hold of a live wire. Brian's head jerked back. The hands and elbows and knees that had been pressing into him and pinning him to the ground retreated. Brian's eyes opened wide, but for a moment all he could see was that strange swirling of light and color high above the water tower. He felt something akin to a numbness radiate from his gripped hand and travel down the stalk of his arm. That numbness exploded throughout his chest, and he suddenly found himself staring into a gaping chasm that loomed impossibly huge and bottomless, and it was into that chasm that Brian Russo tumbled.

And saw—

## 2

*—a thing that has come from beyond this world, a vast and altogether separate plane of existence, a sentient consciousness that was neither benevolent nor malicious, a thing that simply* is, *and that despite all that has transpired, it has not meant to inflict fear or harm or strife—that it does not care, in fact, because the creatures of this plane are so inconsequential to it, they serve only as a means to an endgame—and that it does not extend compassion or empathy or understanding, that it is a thing that merely* exists, *and that all it does is a function of what it needs and what serves its Purpose. The thing has merely, simply, quite effectively exploited our greatest weaknesses and compels us through our addictions, our obsessions, our basic human compulsions, to do its bidding when necessary. These are the things that make us weak, make us vulnerable. This is how it has been since the beginning of time, when interactions such as these have inadvertently transpired, and that the endgame is nothing so grand or monumental as epiphany or revelation*

*or divinity, but something as simple as Function: we are its way home, for it has been here, slothful and trapped, its own power draining, waiting until THE BOY was mature and developed in his abilities in order to send it home. We have built the machine, but THE BOY is the most important part. THE BOY is the motor. THE BOY is the engine. THE BOY is the battery that starts it up. His powers, exaggerated by the Purpose's own ancient, dwindling abilities, are the source that will finally open a large enough crack and send it back to where it comes from . . .*

# 3

A man's visage appeared within Brian's field of vision. This man stood above him now, his hand in Brian's. What thoughts or notions or *feelings* that had been transmitted from that man into Brian now fled, along with the numbness that had radiated up Brian's arm and spread like a fever throughout the entirety of his body.

*Stinger*, Brian thought, the thought coming from nowhere. *The man holding my hand calls himself Stinger.* He knew this and a million other things with sudden, unwavering certainty.

Stinger let go of his hand. Beyond, Brian could see those colorful lights rotating faster and faster in the night sky. Something close to thunder rumbled, but it didn't sound like any thunder Brian had ever heard.

"If you need a battery to start this fucking thing," Brian said, "then use me."

The man—Stinger—only stared down at him as Brian remained there, splayed out on the ground. After a time, a number of others filtered into Brian's line of sight, crowding around him, each one of them staring down at him in unmeasured silence.

"Well, look at that," Stinger said, and there was a quantity of undeniable awe in his voice.

## 4

As Stinger and the rest of them stared down at the man on the ground, they all crowded together to see the thing that had caused such awe to rise up in Stinger's voice.

The man wore a necklace upon which a glowing yellow star hung as a charm. In the jostling and wrestling this man to the ground, the necklace had flipped up, and the star, glowing as if with some sentient, otherworldly light, lay squarely at the center of the man's forehead.

## 5

The man called Stinger beckoned him to rise. Brian did so with considerable difficulty; his entire body felt hollowed out, and he did not fully trust his bones to hold him upright. He looked around the clearing and could see Ellen's arms still held by some of the onlookers, but Cory had been set back down on the ground; he stood between the two men who had initially grabbed him, his eyes momentarily locked with Brian's. The sound of someone's voice—Stinger's?—rumbled through Brian's head, causing his back teeth to ache.

*(GO ON GO ON GO ON)*

Cory moved slowly in Brian's direction, gathering speed as he went, until he was in a full-fledged run by the time he reached Brian and wrapped his arms around his uncle's waist.

*(GO ON GO ON GO ON)*

Ellen was released and she staggered in his direction before breaking into a sprint, too. She collided with him, hugged him, and he hugged her back.

"I love you both," he said to them . . .

. . . and then Ellen and Cory were removed from him by another series of groping, restraining hands. They retreated toward the semicircle of onlookers, each one seeming to glow beneath the swirling lights from that rotating gyre in the sky.

Once again, Stinger extended a hand to him. His face was impassive. Brian took his hand, which was cold as a hunk of stone. Stinger led him through the opening in the fence. They both had to duck their heads as they walked, for there were stiff metal wires crisscrossing everything at eye-level. Stinger led him to the peculiar—

*(door-becomes-chair)*

—chair that was fixed to the center post directly beneath the tower. Two others appeared: a teenage girl and a middle-aged woman. Brian felt their names rumble through his head as their eyes briefly met his.

*(SARAH MILLER)*

*(GEORGETTE BRASWELL)*

There was a metal colander clamped to a basketball hoop that was, in turn, screwed into the wood of the door. The woman named Georgette unscrewed the hoop then raised it several inches while studying Brian. She ultimately bolted it back into place, a few inches higher than it had previously been. Similarly, the teenage girl—

*(SARAH MILLER)*

—repositioned a series of long metal wires that were attached to the holes of the colander and connected to the chain-link fence surrounding the base of the tower. Once they were done, they retreated back to the other side of the fence. Stinger released his hand, then motioned to the chair.

Brian lowered himself into it. When he sat up straight, he found that his head fit perfectly into that upside-down colander hanging above him, like a helmet. The thin metal wires—

*Coat hangers, those are coat hangers, only straightened out*, he suddenly thought, with no real reason for knowing this—

—protruding from the holes in the colander and extending to the chain-link fence jangled almost musically.

Ellen called his name. Having broken free of her captors, she made it as far as the fence before she was grabbed again. She was crying and saying his name over and over again. Cory stood beside her, clutching Ellen's hand. Brian saw nothing but love for him in the boy's eyes.

"It's okay, El," he told her, smiling as best he could muster. "It'll all be okay."

Ellen dropped to her knees, one set of fingers curled around the links in the fence, as Cory reached over and hugged her around the shoulders. She buried her face against her son's chest.

Stinger reached down and placed both of Brian's arms upon the metal table in front of him, palms down. Then another woman appeared, and Brian was similarly able to snag her name from the ether, too:

*(MARYBETH MAYSALL)*

This woman set what looked like the front wheel of a tricycle on the table in front of him. There was no tire, just the metal rim and spokes, and the arm bars for the pedals, one bar on either side of the wheel. The arm bars had been fitted into a piece of bent metal that served as a stand. This way, the wheel could spin freely when suspended off the table.

The woman pointed at the wheel then described a slow circle in the air with one finger. A spiral.

Brian nodded his head and said, "I understand."

She then pointed around the perimeter, where so many items either hung from the chain-link fence or had been placed up against it, each one interconnected to form a daisy chain of random items. She continued making the slow rotations in the air with her finger as she pointed out all the items to him, one by one.

"Okay," he said. "And what happens to me?"

The woman stared at him for a heartbeat. Then she shifted her gaze to Stinger, who looked back at him. After a moment of silence, Stinger said, "I guess we don't really know that part."

The woman slipped out through the opening in the fence. Stinger, too, retreated toward the opening, moving backwards so he could keep his eyes locked on Brian's. Once he, too, passed through the opening in the fence, some men came and unchained those metal flaps, sealing him inside.

Cory approached the fence. His face was slack, pale, but his eyes were glassy with tears. In a surprisingly strong voice, he called out, "Uncle Brian . . ."

"I love you, Chicken Little," he said, then turned his attention to the wheel.

# 6

He did just as Cory had taught him—just as he had managed to do back in the hotel room—and after a time, the wheel on the table began to spin without Brian having to touch it. With his palms still flat on the metal table, Brian could feel a distant strumming, a vibration, rise up through the legs of the metal table. He dared not look, maintaining all his focus on the wheel, the wheel, the wheel. As he did so, the wheel began to spin faster and faster. He thought of Cory spinning that spoon on the table where it drilled a perfect tiny hole in the wood; he thought of Cory saying, *When I want to do something, I wake the gnome up and it just knows how to do it.* Brian did not possess a gnome, but he *did* have that distant star radiating in the center of his mind, growing stronger, stronger, the beams of its light extended to the wheel, spinning the wheel, spinning the—

*(circles circles circles)*

—world.

The wheel spun. And although he was only peripherally aware of anything beyond the wheel, Brian could still sense the vibrations emanating up through the table. The legs of the table rattled against the sheet metal at his feet. Moreover, he was conscious of a build-up of energy within him, energy that was rising to a certain point before attempting to break out of him. He was a kettle near to whistling. When he felt that it had reached its zenith, he let that star radiate brighter, and felt the power of it not so much *drain* out of him as *launch* out of him, *burst* out of him, as if fired from a gun. At the same moment, a pulse of bluish light strobed down the length of the metal wires coming out of the colander seated snugly on his head. When the light-strobe reached the chain-link fence, the entire perimeter lit up momentarily with that dazzling, spectral light.

The wheel continued to spin.

He heard the Air Man in his head, saying, *We crank a few knobs, radiate a few dials, tweak and praise the tower. All hail the holy fuckin' tower, am I right? And then you know what you've got? Probably the biggest goddamn megaphone in the history of the modern world . . .*

A second build-up of energy, this one reaching its zenith more quickly than the first, trembled through him. He felt the star pulse once more, shooting that eerie bluish light down the length of those wires and once again briefly irradiate the fence. This time, after the fence lost its illumination, Brian saw—or sensed—that the items that had been fastened to the fence or leaning up against it retained their charge. They glowed like radium.

Faster, faster—the wheel spun until the spokes blurred.

A third pulse blasted out of him, and he was only just barely aware of it this time. The items along the fence continued to glow, some of them kicking up sparks of blue light on their own, each holding its own guttering charge, like lighters struggling to birth a flame. He was faintly aware that all the onlookers on the other side of the fence had backed away, though they were still watching him, a sea of wide, hypnotic eyes out there in the darkness. Ellen and Cory had retreated with the rest of them, and he could no longer make them out among the crowd. The only figure he saw with any clarity was Stinger, and each time that pulse of light fired through him and along those stiff metal wires to the fence, he could see the light reflecting in Stinger's eyes, too.

He thought of Ellen, sweet El, who'd always loved him and done her best by him despite all his flaws and weaknesses. He heard her voice soften and speak through the burning solar flare in the center of his head, three simple words that set him free, set him free, set him free:

*I forgive you.*

Spinning, spinning, spinning.

The look on Cory's face as he rushed into his uncle's arms, hugging him, squeezing him . . .

Another pulse of light. Then another. The wires above his head kept their charge now, as did the items around the fence. The fence itself continued to flicker with that same light, but now Brian could see—could sense—a single diode of light traveling quickly in a counterclockwise fashion along the fence. With each pulse that Brian fired from his mind and down the circulatory system of those metal wires, that diode expanded and became brighter, brighter. A pulse of light kept whipping around the fence like a centrifuge, rotating in circles, circles, circles, until it went so fast the light became a streak, a blur, an inferno.

He caught a whiff of something burning.

*(capable of throwing up to three motherfucking kilohertz into the stratosphere while reclining in cushioned office chairs, sipping Irish cappuccinos, doin' some blow during commercial breaks, and patting down our shirt pockets for our last pack of—)*

*(pack of—)*

*(of—)*

He was blinded by a great white light. There was no heat; instead, he was engulfed in an absolute numbing iciness. His eyes were open but he could see nothing but that blinding white light. The world had lit up around him, on fire—brilliant, ice-cold fire.

The words that rattled through his brain next were those of the Air Man, but they were spoken in the soft and loving voice of his nephew:

*You and me, kid.*
*We'll sail between the stars.*

It was his last conscious thought before he did just that.

*Comes fire in light through a channel of thought, up a conduit of spectral glimmer, comes whisper-ways in a spiraling spiral, up and up and up, swirling, twirling, and resounds the deafening crack of two existences colliding briefly into one, a unity of worlds, a sharing of cosmic consciousness, flash and smash and crash, rising up, rising up, rising UP—*

—and in the darkened bedroom of a Baltimore City apartment, a woman named Donna Holmes bolted upright in bed, the vestiges of some half-remembered dream of a man she once knew clinging to her, while knowing deep in her heart that something—*someone*—once knitted into the fabric of the known universe (and into the fabric of her soul) had been hopelessly and irrevocably removed.

# CHAPTER SIXTY-THREE
# ENDGAME

## 1

There was a flash of white light that caused them all to scream. A streak of blazing electrical current sizzled up the full height of the tower where it burst from a TV antenna that had been hooked to the top of the water tank. The bolt of light leapt into the sky and appeared to be sucked into that swirling miasma of light rotating in the air above the tower. Its afterimage lingered in the darkness for several seconds before fading, although anyone who closed their eyes in that moment could still see it resonating on the underside of their eyelids for much longer.

In that flash: an image of something intangible and fleeting, massive in shape and consciousness, ephemeral as smoke, swirling in an unending spiral as it floated up, up, up, and the eyes of those still conscious watching it, seeing only what their minds were capable of letting them see.

## 2

Cory McBride, who had retreated with his mother and the rest of the onlookers the moment fiery sparks of bluish light began to pulse along the network of wires and rotate along the chain-link fence, was blown off his feet by what felt like the shockwave of an explosion. His head struck something hard, and for a second, he thought he might pass out.

But then the feeling passed and he was able to sit up in time to see what looked like a great snakelike phantom, its body a translucent column of swirling, twisting smoke, rise up from the water tank. Its body was comprised of iridescent hashmarks of colors Cory had never seen, and so to him, they did not even register as colors, but as a menagerie of sensations that filled his head with a raucous, buzzing cacophony.

## 3

Sarah Miller was also blown off her heels. She went reeling across the clearing, coming to rest against a cushion of underbrush along the cusp of the tree line. Hands pressed protectively against her belly, she blinked her eyes and watched as the Chinese dragon she'd seen as a child with her father at that parade in downtown D.C. erupted from the water tank and spiraled into the air. No, not a Chinese dragon, but something, *something* reminiscent of it, a thing of gossamer and flame, of taut threads of cobweb dressed in the shimmering jewels of morning dew, the closest thing her nineteen-year-old human mind could reconcile . . .

## 4

Georgette Braswell sat up in the wet grass, her head pounding, her back teeth alive with a white-hot pain. What she saw rise up out of the water tank and pull itself into the sky was, at first, the sleek, black garter snake she had glimpsed sliding through a patch of sun-bleached grass on the front lawn of their house the day she and Alex had moved into the place, their first home together, her belly swollen with Callie, a snake, a snake, only *not*, only *now* it was a fat greenish brown leech fixed to the underside of her arm, yanked away by her father, leaving behind a startlingly bright red streamer of blood that dribbled down toward her wrist . . .

## 5

Where the thing Alex Braswell saw was the ruptured tube stripped from the tire of an old bicycle, deflated and snakelike, and how, as a child, he'd come across one on a playground and *thought* it was a snake, and felt his whole body stiffen at the sight of it, the idea of it . . .

## 6

Where Pamela Guerin saw a blood-red, serpentine creature undulating across the top of a takeout menu and along the border of a freebie calendar hanging on her wall back home . . .

## 7

Where Eric Rhodes was suddenly imagining a water moccasin with its telescopic head rising above the murky surface of the bay, eyes like shiny drops of oil, the utter soundlessness of the thing equally as terrifying as the sight of it . . .

## 8

Where Michael Danver was reminded of the bulging, thumping valve of a human heart . . .

## 9

And where Jeremy Stuckey saw not the Dragon, but a sentient, serpentine cloud of honeybees, weaving through the air as a single consciousness, a hive mind alive with a collective, obsessive need, a cosmic Purpose, and as his body was blown back from the explosion, it shook and rattled and split apart once again, two halves of the same whole, a consciousness torn down the middle, followed by the sensation that he was struck in the chest by some great, unbending force, over and over, pierced hotly through the body by countless bee stings, rendering him motionless, powerless, his consciousness threatening to crumble apart at the sheer agony of it . . .

## 10

The shockwave blew apart Hive Center. Sections of the chain-link fence went soaring into the air, while all the items that had been so lovingly placed in their appropriate places beneath the tower were fired like missiles into the night. The TV antenna at the top of the tank plummeted to the ground, driving itself halfway into the earth where it vibrated with an audible *thung-ung-ung.* The metal colander sheared leaves from branches as it went sailing through a cluster of trees, ultimately gonging against the trunk of a massive oak with such force, that it was sent back in the direction it had come, boomerang-like. The straightened metal javelins of wire coat hangers were launched in all directions, driving themselves spear-like into the earth several dozen yards from the base of the tower. The night sky rained with metal debris, bits and pieces of the machine slamming into the earth like mortar rounds. In fact, the only item that wasn't expelled from beneath the water tower was the large wooden door, since it was reduced to nothing but a pile of ash.

And then there was a weighty thunderclap, and everything went silent and dark.

# 11

Cory struggled to his feet. The shockwave from the explosion beneath the tower had sent everyone flying; they lay now in heaps all around the clearing, groaning, disoriented, and writhing in the grass. Somewhat dazed himself, Cory meandered around them, his eyes locked on what remained at the base of the water tower, which was essentially nothing. There was the smell of electricity sizzling in the air as well as the acrid and more specific odor of something burning. The bright lights and the loud, crashing thunderclaps had vanished, leaving in their wake a simmering darkness and a silence so profound that it took on a heartbeat of its own.

"Mom? Mommy?"

She was nowhere.

He wandered closer to the tower, his skin feeling sunburned despite the utter darkness of the night. His mind was on fire. The sections of fence had been blown away by the force of the explosion, or whatever that powerful burst of light had been. Stiff metal wires jutted from the earth, unmoored from the sections of fence, and the spaghetti strainer that had fitted to his uncle's head like a helmet lay on the ground now beside a cluster of trees, charred black with carbon. Other items had fallen over or been tossed about, half-buried in the earth by the force of the shockwave. What these people had built beneath the water tower had looked fierce and dangerously purposeful when Cory had initially laid eyes on it; now, however, what remained seemed no grander than a heap of junk at the local dump, or perhaps discarded bits of randomness tossed about by the winds of a great storm.

The wooden door that his uncle had been propped against was gone. The only thing that remained of it was a smoldering pile of ash and single javelin of wood that burned at one end like a guttering torch.

"Hey, kid."

The voice startled him.

He turned and saw no one at first . . . but then his eyes fell upon the man who called himself Stinger. He was lying against the shorn stump of a tree, his head cocked at an unnatural angle, blood leaking from the corners of his mouth. There were a number of those long metal wires protruding from his chest, looking to Cory like enormous porcupine quills. The man's shirt was soaked with blood and his respiration had a punctured, wheezing quality to it.

"I guess we pulled it off, huh, kid?" Stinger said wetly. He twisted his head on his neck to survey the collection of metal wires that had been driven into his chest by the force of the explosion beneath the tower, some so deep that only two or three inches were visible. To Cory's surprise, the man chuckled, and a fresh runnel of blood spilled out of his mouth and down his chin. He glanced back up at Cory, and he could see there was blood in the man's eyes, too.

Cory shuddered.

"Here." Stinger extended one arm, his hand balled into a fist. When he opened his fingers, Cory saw the glowing star from his uncle's necklace in the center of his palm. "Damn thing came flying right at me in that blast of light."

Cory reached out and plucked it from Stinger's hand. There was a smudge of blood on it, which Cory wiped away with his thumb. Then he looped the shoestring necklace over his head, the glowing yellow star hanging at the center of his chest.

"No hard feelings, huh?" Stinger said, grinning a bloody grin at him. Then he eased his head back against the tree trunk and stared up at the sky. Those wires poking out of his chest seemed to sag each time he took a labored, ragged breath.

"Cory! Cory!"

He whirled around to see his mother running toward him across the clearing. Behind her, others were climbing to their feet, unsteady, and staring around with a dazed look on their faces. She wrapped him up in a fierce hug, then cried out in pain. She grabbed her left side and winced, but still clung to him with one arm, refusing to let him go.

"I'm okay, Mom. I'm okay."

He looked up at her. His mother's clothes smelled sooty, like she'd been pulled from a fire. The whole world, he realized, smelled like an electrical charge. She looked down at him, eyes soaking him up, hands pressed to his cheeks. It was as if she couldn't quite believe he was standing right here with her. His mother's face was gritty with dirt and looked reddened by the flash of light that had erupted beneath the tower before arcing up into the sky. Had she seen the thing that had come swirling out of the water tank? Had they all?

*It was a dragon*, he thought. *Just like in a fairytale, it was a dragon hiding in the water tower, trapped here and desperate to get home. Uncle Brian opened a door for it and the dragon fled through a crack in the world.*

His mother was looking at the remaining debris beneath the tower. He could feel a wretched sob rising up through the core of her body. The gnome could feel it, too, albeit in an entirely different fashion now. She released him and staggered over to the collapsed section of the chain-link fence. One hand still pressed to the left side of her abdomen, she stepped over and onto the fence, then down into the place where all those items lay scattered and strewn about. As Cory watched, she began rummaging through the debris, calling out Uncle Brian's name over and over again. Cory let her do this for a while, his eyes momentarily drifting to the tricycle wheel still hooked in its stand, still slowly spinning on a patch of grass. Then, after a time, he approached her, hugged her gently (cautious of her injured left side), and said, in a quiet but steady voice, "He's gone, Mom. He's gone."

She sobbed, and he just squeezed her more tightly.

A deep, sonorous moan unfurled across the clearing. It rose in pitch and volume until it became a roar. Both Cory and his mother looked up, for that was where the sound was coming from. Others were looking up, too—toward the tank at the top of the tower. As Cory stared upward, he felt something whoosh by his face. He flinched, just in time to hear the *tink tink tink* of something metallic rebounding off the concrete beneath his feet. It was a metal bolt, about the size of a thumb, and it was sheared in half. As he stared at it, a second bolt struck the ground then bounced away in the shadows of the night.

His mother gripped his arm and dragged him away from the base of the tower. She was staring up at the tank—everyone was staring up at the tank—and he followed her gaze.

The lights around the water tank were dark, but there was enough moonlight now that the sky had cleared for Cory to see the railing coming undone from the walkway. It bent outward like a broken bone and sagged in midair. That grinding, roaring sound grew loader.

"Goddamn thing's gonna fall!" someone shouted from the crowd.

Tiny bits of debris rained down on Cory's face, stinging his eyes. He dragged a set of fingers across one cheek and saw that his fingertips were powered with brown flakes of rust. He glanced at his mother, who was still staring up at the tower and she pulled him slowly backward, eyes widening.

The railing fell and crashed to the ground.

"Get away!" that same voice shouted to the crowd. "The whole tower is going to collapse!"

"Let's go," his mother said, grip tightening around his upper arm. She was in too much pain to run—she kept clutching her side—but she dragged him across the clearing nonetheless, the breath whistling up her throat shallow and weak.

He saw it then: the entire tower gently tipping to one side, so enormous against the night that it looked like some Hollywood special effect. The roar grew louder, industrial bolts and screws raining from the sky. People were shrieking and running for the woods now. His mother was wincing in pain but desperate to drag him away.

The roar of bending, twisting metal filled the night. The tower continued to tip, tip, ever so slowly as to almost be polite. In a flash, Cory saw the outcome, knowing it would crush the thirty-odd people who were too slow to get out of the way.

*Rrrrrrrriiiiiii—*

"Cory!" his mother—

*Pop! Zing!*

One of the tower's eight legs gave out, the sound like a plane crash, and then it was coming down faster, faster, too fast—

*—iiiiiiiiiiikkkk—*

"Cory!"

"Mom!"

The people—

She pulled him toward the woods, his heels carving trenches in the dirt as he resisted, as the tower came down—

The gnome's eyes blazed awake.

Cory threw his hands out and felt the gnome reach out, too. The roar of the falling tower grinded to a high-pitched, metallic shriek, until it went altogether silent. It hung suspended at an angle above the rushing crowd, everyone dispersing, screaming, some of them stunned into gape-mouthed motionlessness beneath the shadow of the tower. Cory could physically *feel* the tower in his hands, its smooth metal hide, its water tank like an enormous manmade beehive, the tank itself split by a crack in its hull the jagged shape of a lightning bolt, a glittering, jewel-like froth of water arcing out, suspended in animation, motionless as the few remaining people who stared dumbstruck at the tower high above them. Cory tried to tip the tower in the opposite direction, to spare those people, but the gnome was too weak. It was hard enough to just hold it suspended in the air, which might at least—

The people beneath the tower broke their stupor and began to scatter. Cory's mom kept dragging him toward the woods, but his eyes never left the tower, his hands still outstretched to prop it up if just for a little longer . . .

Then: *rrrrriiiiiiiii*—

A motionless cloud of reddish rust began to swirl around it. Beads of water separated from the frozen wave arcing from the crack in the tank and drifted in slow motion toward the ground. The people had fled, everyone having run off through the woods, yet Cory still tried to keep the tower upright, tried—

Tried—

*—iiiiiikkkk—*

That monstrous roar wound to a shriek as the tower came down and his mother, screaming into the night, dragged him off into the trees.

# 12

With the shrill keening of a missile, the Gladstone Park water tower came crashing to earth. Dust and debris erupted in a cloud that momentarily blocked out the moon, while the tank itself, dumping over a million gallons of water through its lightning bolt crack, collided with the electrical substation at the far end of the woods. There sounded an explosion as loud as the Voice of God, followed by a column of bluish white fire that could be seen from Poplar Station Road. As the sound of the crash gradually dissipated toward weighty silence, the woods surrounding Gladstone Park began to burn.

# CHAPTER SIXTY-FOUR

# ESCAPE

## 1

The force of the tower striking the ground was felt in Cory's chest. He thought he might never forget the feel of it.

Uncle Brian's van was parked on the other side of the trees. Cory's mom yanked open the driver's side door and shoved him inside, where he scrambled over to the passenger seat just as the windshield lit up in a blaze of white light. Cory looked in awe as a blast of fire shot up into the night sky. His bones were still reverberating from the force of the tower falling, but he could now feel the ground rumble with the sharp growl of an explosion.

The keys were still in the ignition, the engine still running. His mother punched the van into gear then launched them across the wooded roadway, narrowly avoiding a stream of people pouring out of the woods like startled and frightened animals. The column of fire was gone, but there were bright flashes of electrical light on the other side of those trees, and the air was already beginning to fill up with smoke. People were scattering in every direction.

The rain didn't start until they were on the highway. She slowed the van a bit then looked at him hugging his knees to his chest in the passenger seat, her face a mask of pain and worry and terror. She ran a hand through his rust-flaked hair.

"Are you okay, baby?"

"I think so." Seeing that she was clutching her side with one hand, he asked, "Are *you*?"

"I am now."

He watched as she swerved around slower moving vehicles.

"Where are we going?"

"Not back home. Not tonight."

They drove on.

## 2

Eric held her hand for their entire escape through the woods. When the tower fell, Sarah's back teeth clacked together from the force of it. When the electrical substation exploded a second later, she felt it like a wrecking ball to her chest.

When they reached the nameless street beyond the woods, there were others crowded around, watching the flashes of light through the trees. Panic tightened around her throat, but Eric gave her hand a comforting squeeze, and that helped.

"Come on," he said, tugging her across the road toward the cusp of Slope Hill. There were no houses here, no vehicles or commotion—only a bluff that overlooked the moonlight waters of the bay. At the top, Eric paused so they could catch their breath. From this vantage, they could see straight out to Poplar Station Road. All the houses and streetlamps were dark, the explosion of the substation having cut off all power to the neighborhood. "Jesus, look at that," Eric marveled.

The woods at the far end of Gladstone Park were on fire.

She turned to him, watched the fire reflected in his eyes. He looked confused and terrified—all the things that Sarah also felt—but when he focused on her, he gave her a grim smile.

"I don't know what just happened," she said, breathlessly. "It's like a part of my mind was sucked up into that storm cloud that was hovering above the tower."

"I feel it, too."

"I'm trying to remember, but it's like trying to access someone else's memories."

"Maybe it's best we forget," he said.

She turned back around and watched as the fire devoured the dark swath of woods. Eric came up behind her, wrapped his arms around her. One hand briefly—tenderly—pressed against her abdomen before pulling her against him in a hug. When the rain started, they didn't make any effort to find shelter. They were content to just be in each other's presence while they watched the world burn.

## 3

Somehow, at some point, Michael Danver returned home to a large and darkened house. He crept slowly up the stairs to the second floor, and arrived at the threshold of the master bedroom. He could see a mound of sheets lying on the bed, which caused him to drop to his knees and weep.

The pain started in his left arm. An electrical jolt, sudden and biting. He felt it work its way up to his chest, where it spread like the tendrils and fronds of some undersea vegetation. Soon, the fingers of his left hand went numb. A moment after that, steel bands tightened around his chest. Casting one final glance at the shape beneath the bedsheets, Danver thought, resignedly, *Myocardial infarction*. And because it seemed like a fitting way to go, he let it take him.

## 4

Somehow, too, Jeremy Stuckey found himself returned to the old stone carriage house on Macadam Street. He couldn't remember his escape from the park, couldn't remember how he'd gotten here, but here he was: bleeding in the front hall of the house he'd grown up in.

He glanced down and saw a series of bronze metal wires poking through his blood-soaked shirt. He tried to grapple with exactly what had happened down at the park and how he'd come to be in such a terrible way, but found his mind cloudy with confused and jumbled thoughts, and he wasn't so sure that they were all his.

He tried to pull one of the wires from his chest, but that caused his breath to catch—not in his throat, but deep in his left lung—and a geyser of blood spilled out of his open mouth.

Out of some vague sense of duty, he proceeded down the hall toward Queenie's bedroom. He couldn't remember the last time he'd been in the house and worried that she might be hungry, thirsty, or just lonely.

But he only made it halfway down the hall before he collapsed.

He rolled onto his side, hearing the scrape of those metal wires against the floor and walls, and feeling them twisting about inside him. Feeling the bees' venom moving about inside him, too. He gasped for air, his lungs rattling, his body on fire. So many bees. So many bee stings. You didn't have to be allergic to die from so—

## 5

By the time they fled the park and arrived back home, Alex was gasping for air. Georgette placed both her hands against the sides of his sweaty face, pulled him close to her. Stared at his frightened, jittery eyes. Someone had raked a set of fingernails down one cheek, leaving behind a trio of bloody lacerations. She pulled him closer, examining him more intently in the moonlight coming through the front windows. One of her fingers grazed a hard nodule on the left side of his neck. A bee sting, the damn stinger still poking from the reddened, tender center. As she brushed her fingers along it again, it fell away.

*Oh no oh Jesus oh please no—*

She ran down the hall to the bathroom, tore through the medicine cabinet in the dark until she located one of Alex's EpiPens. When she returned to him, he was curled in a fetal position in the front hall, gasping for breath and clawing at his chest with stiff, talon-like fingers.

Georgette popped off the blue safety cap then jammed the business end of the EpiPen into her husband's outer thigh. She held it there, counting aloud, *"One Mississippi . . . two Mississippi . . . three Mississippi . . ."* while her entire body trembled.

She felt Alex's body relax beneath her. Heard his breathing begin to regulate. Those stiff, talon-like fingers fell away from his chest as he let his body go limp on the floor.

Georgette curled up beside him. She could hear sirens blaring through the neighborhood.

They'd done . . . *something* . . . down at Gladstone Park tonight. The memory of exactly what it had been, however, was quickly fading. Something about the water tower, a group of people. A little boy.

This made her think of her own children.

Twenty minutes later, once Alex had regained some semblance of normalcy, she wrapped her arms around him as they remained lying there on the floor. Into his ear, she whispered, "Let's go get the girls."

"Right now?" he said.

"Right now. I miss them."

"I miss them, too."

"What exactly happened tonight?"

"I don't know, G. It feels like someone dug out a portion of my mind with an ice cream scoop."

"I feel that way, too."

"Maybe it's best we don't remember."

"Maybe it is," she agreed.

They kissed, and then got on the road.

## 6

Eventually, Ellen and Cory pulled into the parking lot of a motel off U.S. Route 50. Ellen shut down the engine, leaving the two of them wrapped in a silence so profound it wrung tears from her eyes.

*Brian.*

When she looked back at her son, she found him turned around in his seat, staring into the yawning black space that made up the back of the van. He was staring at something, a look of awe on his face. She turned, wiping the tears from her eyes, and followed his gaze.

The dark space behind them was spangled with countless glow-in-the-dark stars. They were stuck to the walls, the ceiling, and there were even a few on the floor. For a moment, it was enough to convince her—convince them both, she was certain—that they were no longer on this planet, if just for a moment, but instead floating through the vastness of the cosmos, where the essence of who we are and the ones we've loved exist in perpetuity.

"Shhh, baby. Shhh."

She pulled Cory into an embrace and he wept against her shoulder.

*And the Dragon closes its eyes . . .*

# EPILOGUE

# THE WORLD IS A NEIGHBORHOOD

Hours later, lying together in the king-size bed in their motel room off the highway, Cory remained awake and staring at the ceiling. Beside him, his mother slept fitfully, be it from nightmares or the pain in her side. He told the gnome to access her mind one last time, but found the gnome's power, while still there, was greatly diminished. He wondered if whatever thing he'd witnessed rise out of the water tower—the thing that had poisoned the minds of his neighbors—had also been granting the gnome extra power, in anticipation of firing up its great machine. Or maybe, like Uncle Brian had suggested, it was only a matter of time before the ability would leave him completely.

Despite the pain in her side, his mother had helped him peel all the glow-in-the-dark stars from the interior of Uncle Brian's van. They glowed now upon the ceiling of their motel room. Cory stared at them until his eyes grew moist and his vision grew bleary. At one point, he reached up and fingered the star at his chest. Uncle Brian's necklace.

*I love you, son.*

Wearing it as he drifted off to sleep, he found that it brought him some comfort. It was a small but important constellation.

# ACKNOWLEDGEMENTS

The first draft of this novel was written over a decade ago. It was a big, ambitious novel back then, and I'm not too proud to admit that it got away from me even as I pushed through to complete it. My agent agreed; never one to mince words, she read it then suggested I set this one aside and work on something else. (I followed her advice and wound up writing a novel called *The Night Parade* instead, a much more intimate tale about a father and a daughter and a disease that makes people lose their minds.) Yet this tale—back then, titled *The Cove*—never fully left my mind. I would occasionally find myself thinking about the characters that populated that old manuscript, one that was nearly a thousand pages long—Uncle Brian with his special gift squandered into dormancy by his addictions; Dr. Michael Danver, the retired heart surgeon, who would seemingly do anything to protect his precious hunk of driftwood; that strange fellow who kept a beehive in his backyard; and Georgette Braswell, who wanted nothing more than to keep her family together until the power of obsession ultimately took hold of her, too. Whenever I was driving and I'd see the tank of a water tower cresting above a distant tree line, my mind would be shuttled back to the jumble of fictional streets and economical little homes that made up my make-believe neighborhood of Mariner's Cove. The story lingered, and I wondered if I would ever return to it again.

My undying gratitude to the folks who, in some form or fashion, helped me make this book happen: George Sandison, Fenton

Coulthurst, Julia Lloyd, Rich Mason, Bahar Kutluk, Katharine Carroll, Paul Simpson, Andy Dawes, Katie Shea Boutillier, Matt Snow, and Cameron McClure for her sage suggestion that I set this thousand-page manuscript in a desk drawer until it was ready to see the light of day. Lastly, thanks to Daniel Carpenter, who trudged up the steep side of a proverbial mountain with this novel strapped to his back and never once dropped it, and to Rebecca Rowland, who ensured I carried it across the finish line: much love and gratitude. And of course, thanks to my family for putting up with me, as aways, during the writing of this novel.

So, what was the impetus for this story finally seeing the light of day? Soon after that first draft was written, two close friends of mine—filmmaker Kevin Kangas and roustabout Ty Lewis—each read it. Despite my agent's (astute) conclusion that the novel just *wasn't working*, these two guys championed it from the beginning. Every time I was about to embark on a new project, they would both ask the same question: *Are you going to rewrite* The Cove? No, I would tell them, I was not going to rewrite *The Cove. The Cove* was a trunk novel, something best left forgotten…

Until it wasn't.

Thanks for never letting me forget this one, fellas.

Happy reading.

RONALD MALFI
December 16, 2025
Annapolis, Maryland

# ABOUT THE AUTHOR

Ronald Malfi is the *New York Times* and *USA Today* bestselling author of several horror novels, mysteries, and thrillers. He is the recipient of two Independent Publisher Book Awards, the Beverly Hills Book Award, the Vincent Preis Horror Award, the Benjamin Frankling Award for Popular fiction, and his novel *Floating Staircase* was a finalist for the Bram Stoker Award®. In 2024, the Maryland Library Association presented Malfi with the William G. Wilson Award for Adult Fiction. When he's not writing, he's fronting the rock band VEER.